THE ABOMINATION

THE
ABOMINATION

PAUL GOLDING

ALFRED A. KNOPF   NEW YORK   2000

THIS IS A BORZOI BOOK
PUBLISHED BY ALFRED A. KNOPF

Copyright © 2000 by Paul Golding

All rights reserved under International and Pan-American
Copyright Conventions. Published in the United States by
Alfred A. Knopf, a division of Random House, Inc., New York.
Distributed by Random House, Inc., New York.
www.aaknopf.com

Originally published in Great Britain by Picador,
an imprint of Macmillan Publishers, Ltd., London.

Knopf, Borzoi Books and the colophon are registered
trademarks of Random House, Inc.

ISBN 0-375-41055-4

Manufactured in the United States of America
First American Edition

This book is dedicated to Richard Fowler.

ACKNOWLEDGEMENTS

The author would like to thank Cara Denman,
Nigella Lawson, Susan Moncur, Jane Reid, Sarah Spankie
and, especially, Meredith Daneman.

THE ABOMINATION

PART ONE

HIGH SUMMER in a sweltering London club, and I'm getting into my drunken stride after midnight, rubbing sweat with the shoulders that pass by, and thinking vaguely about another drink, or about cruising the pissoirs, or about peeling off my vest and closing my eyes and drifting through the dry ice into the dancing multitude, which is a great safe wave to me, when suddenly the lights blast on, white, as on a stage, and the music goes dead, a bang of silence, and it seems that the air-conditioning's packed up and they can't get anyone to fix it this late at night, and the management regrets that for reasons of safety our club has to close, so could we finish our drinks up and remember to collect our coats on the way out, and no dawdling on the street, lads, and don't make a racket out there; and get yourselves safely home; hurry up please, it's time.

I wander away, disconcerted by this sudden sense of having been cut short, frozen in mid-flow. Timing is crucial in this business and you have to pace yourself to a tee if you want a decent score. Have you trapped?, they used to ask in the old days, before the troubles, and mostly you had. But tonight, well, who could have known? And besides, who cares in the end? Perhaps I do, a bit, and so, perhaps, does he: a young boy in an old suit, still clutching his pint-glass to his chest, weaving like a maniac through the traffic, flirting with death to reach me and he is smiling as if at a memory. And his hair is drenched, and he has a face that could shatter your calm, and he just follows me back to my flat, five paces behind, past the garden gate, up the entrance steps, through the front door, which I've left slightly ajar, and into the lift, which is the beginning of every one of my many nameless one night stands.

He wants a drink. He wants a smoke. Do I have a joint? He wants to go to Australia to work with handicapped kids. Drops his jacket, and the dregs of his beer, around the corridor. Lurches into the bedroom, staggers towards the bed. Sits down, then slumps. Tries to pull off his trousers; can't. Kicks away his shoes, which bang against the wall. Falls back against the pillows and stares up at the ceiling-light, which is dimmed and shaped like the moon. Half-opens his mouth; seems to give up. But now he looks down, as if puzzled, and pulls from his heart-patterned boxer shorts a half-hearted hard-on. Tugs absently at the foreskin, forgets to air his balls, fiddles about briefly, calmly, humming to himself as if already he were in Australia; and before I can prove a thing to him, or please myself, he has blessed the patch of sheet between his thighs with a glutinous emission, like a weak stream of snot, devoid of colour or fervour or sense. And then he tells me to get him a towel. And he tells me to fetch him his clothes. And he tells me that he hates my fucking guts, you fucking bender. Which is enough; and I am suddenly enraged and awake and strong; and I yank him by the knot of his tie and hoist him back onto the floor and pull him staggering behind me; and I pick up his shoes as I go along, and I drag him all the way to the hall and grab hold of his jacket and push him like a bag of filthy garbage onto the communal landing and I hurl his junk out with him, telling him, as secretly I tell myself, to get some fucking dignity. And all that I'm left with is the small sight of him assembling himself through my spyhole, then skulking off. And as I turn back into my life, shaking slightly, I let out a sigh of the sort that you don't, not unless you really are alone.

I begin to turn off the lights; but as I approach the bedroom, I notice, on the floor, fallen from that poor pathetic boy's dark coat, a lurid, flimsy, men's contact magazine, hardly even pornography. But I take it to my bed. And backwards I open it. And desultorily I scan the personal ads. And then I come to the escorts, the models, the whores. And my eye flickers about, jumping over words such as young, and new, and anytime. And then my eye drops like a stone into a lonely printed pool, which reads, like a message from the depths: Big Uncut Man. Handsome, lean, muscular, mature, trustworthy. 0370 566 909. And I dial. But the voice of some unpromising female tells me that the mobile which I have called may be switched off, please try later—

which I don't. Instead, I extinguish the lamp by my bed and think of that drunken boy and tell myself a different, better story about us as I masturbate myself to sleep, over his patch, still in my clothes. Good night, sweet ladies, good night.

LATE IN THE MORNING, near noon, I dial again—only to hear the woman once more. He'll be at it already, I suppose, servicing some punter, or some female, come to that, or out shopping with his wife, or posing in a porno flick, or recovering from an arduous night, or worse, worse still, and probably there, right next to the disconnected telephone, asleep in his lover's arms. I replace my ivory receiver, affronted, offended, red. His penis, I hear myself think, may well be uncut, but I bet and I hope that his heart has been cut a thousand times. My reaction takes me aback; why should I feel even the hint of a rising jealousy over some printed fragment, over a mere string of syllables at the end of an absurd mag, a figment who fails even as a character, who lacks face and voice and name, and is probably dull, and whose face and voice and name and very dullness I could have at a whim, done, for less than the price of a decent dinner or an elementary leather mask? I'm getting angry. And yet I cut him gently out of his page and tuck him into my wallet, and I place the wallet inside the jacket on my chair, the chair where one day he will sit; and the wallet slides with treacherous ease into the very place where he should not be, which is close to my breast, poised to bang into my heart.

I rise and stretch and shower and shave and pace about, and smoke about him once or twice. And God knows what I do all day but, at dusk, I dial again—for the third and surely final time. Click. (A pause.) Hullo, he goes, so low and loud it's almost risible. And then, again but softer, he goes: hullo. I am breathtaken, thumping inwards, lost in my own time, at my great leisure, in my own home. My mouth is dry; I am unvoiced; but I persevere and, somehow, manage to admit about the ad, the mag. That, I say, is pretty well it. How can he help me, he asks with the seductive innuendo of a shrink or priest. First, I reply, he can help me by explaining whether, were I to, erm, engage his services (what can I sound like, like my father?), we'd be dealing with a big man who happens not to be circumcised, or with someone possessed of a large uncircumcised penis, or what exactly. He chortles profoundly. I loathe him already. And he savours his retort for a few smug moments before conceding that yes, people do often ask him that. Well?, I snap. Well, he explains, his entry is (momentous silence) deliberately ambiguous. Deliberately Ambiguous. Catch that mouthful? Hope it promises good head. Anything else I'd like to ask? Yes: what he looks like. And now the (metric) statistics begin to roll, like credits one can never quite catch, and the meaningless self-description ends with the news that Mr. Big Uncut Man elects to sport his hair close-cropped—Number Two, to be precise—because he's thirty-nine. Articulate perhaps, but no slave to logic, this guy. Any other questions? Well, inevitably, I suppose, his fee. Sixty, in cash, he says. And to come out, I ask, to come to my flat? Seventy. (My silence now.) Pricey, I meanly remark. He's worth it, he assures me. But I cannot resist assuring him that he'll have to allow me to be the judge of that. Still, the bargain is effectively struck. So, when can we meet? He's afraid he only works nights (the vampirical harlot—how's that for a mouthful?), and I'm afraid I have no nights to spare this week, but I should like, if I may, to ring again when I'm less tied up, as it were, so to speak, and, when I do, so as to spare us both a reprise of this introductory chat, he may as well know, and I tell him, my name. His name is Steve. Yes, well, goodbye Steve, and thanks. No problem, he replies: he looks forward. As do I. And I hang up, first. And then I go out for supper, sickened but starved.

IN THE MORNING, early, after a choppy night of unrecordable dreams, I drive south, too fast, to Hampshire, to my friends R and E and their doll-sized daughters, D and W and J, who make me melt and make me laugh and at times make me envy the lot of that other, greater half. Bowl of soup, glass of wine, and, with E, the mother, the young wife, a stroll along the beach beyond the pines, sidelit today by a hesitant sun that teeters on the brink of the Isle of Wight; then back to the house. She treats me timidly, retreatingly, as if I were a prince with woes, in need of rest, and she suggests a siesta in the room with the best view. As I draw the ivy curtains closed, I see R, the father, the poet, mowing the high grass out there, and the girls, further out still, white bobs flying in their faces, taking turns on the swing which hangs from the tree that shields and secludes them from the world, and I turn and collapse on the bed and am gone.

I awake, exhausted, after sundown. The girls, in old linen night-
gowns of Chekhovian white, have already been fed and bathed, and are
running about barefoot, clambering into cots of wrought iron in the
small room where, a summer ago, their mother painted the walls with
flowers. On my way down I meet their father, my old friend, older now
of course, but glowing in a way that he never did as he climbs the
wooden steps to double-check nappies and read a tale to his girls,
whom he calls ladies, his Ladies, before kissing them good night and
laying them to sleep, which they do by candlelight, and this is the sort
of scene I mean when I speak of envy.

Supper is such an easy affair, with heaps of plain food, and plentiful
drink, and candles all about, and home-made medleys of recorded
songs from remembered (and imagined) times, and teasing, and laughter, and waves of silent calm, broken occasionally by pensive smiles, or
unconscious hums, and, as always in this house, flowing, flowing
effortlessness. I leave the table earlier than I politely should; earlier
than I should have liked, but I feel washed-out and these are my friends
and nobody minds, and on my way to bed I think of them intimately,
the perfect pair in their perfect life and, although I know that nothing
ever can be perfectly perfect, I think: If this is imperfection, I wouldn't
mind a slice. And as I go under the blankets in the dark, I turn to my
side and press a pillow to my gut and then I hear, piping up from the
ground, the sound of one of the Waterboys singing out, asking himself
how long he will love, and want, and hold a beloved whom I don't
know but dream I could become. And then comes his answer, his theory, his own dream, which is the eternal beautiful lie, as he claims and
believes and belts out in his innocent Irish voice that he will love as
long as the seasons need to follow their plan and as long as the sea is
bound to wash up on the sands. And I'm left with no hope of sleep. Yet
I don't hear my friends retire, nor chatter into the night, much less
make love, which I'm certain they do the whole time. And the next
thing that I know is a hardened sun pushing through the curtains, and
my watch pointing to the fact that the dawn is still unthinkably young.
Yet I know that I must rise and not rest, and go, and hope to be forgiven, which by such friends I always am. And I brush my teeth and wet
my face and comb my hair and, like a disappointed thief, I light a cigarette and creep out into the frost, past a congregation of moronic

partridge—probably on their unsuspected last day out—and I get into my car. And then I race back to town with the thrill of a sinner returning to hell.

I walk into my flat with the guilty pleasure of one who has taken an extended holiday at the cost of neglecting the things that he loves. I shower and dress afresh, in colours of stone, and make myself a fiddly, spinstery breakfast; and while I pick at it, I also pick through the bones of the newspaper delivered to my mat. Nothing strikes me, nothing save a shoddy piece in a Saturday magazine about escaped criminals living in the community, a piece redeemed and lent life by a good hard shot in black and white of a man's hands with grimy nails, held behind a hairy arse, and manacled by a pair of gleaming chromium cuffs. And when I fold away the paper and slide it along the table to open the mail with a kitchen knife, I find, malingering near the telephone, that small, excised, oblong, hooker's ad. And I scrunch it into a tight ball and flick it into the dustbin and forget entirely about him. And on my way out, I ring the house in the country—not to explain, since I don't myself quite understand, but to try to apologize. And I am told by my friend's adorable wife, who has become equally my friend and doesn't even listen to my discomfited mumbles, that I must return soon, at no notice at all, whenever I want.

DAYS PASS. The worst part of a week, in fact. The middle part. Dull, drizzling, pewter days in an autumn without charm. And the following Friday, it must be—yes, Friday—I go for supper to the flat of a girl whom I like, whose good-looking boyfriend is away for the night, and who says she can do with a laugh, which I attempt to provide, along with two bottles of wine, one red, one white, both drunk. Then, a couple of Armagnacs and we go on to dance at my vapid local club, where I presume that the air-conditioning vents, if not the odds of success, have been fixed by now, and on our way we swallow some drug, Ecstasy probably, the drug of the times, and after a long, sweaty spin with the people who grin and touch and contort beneath the strobing ultraviolet stars and lipsynch to hits about making it to the top and putting your loving arms around me in the full knowledge that none of it means a thing and never did, we stagger out, my friend and I, back into the vaporous street, grinning and touching and unable to care very much. And I deliver her to her door, safe and dishevelled and seem-ingly sated, in a dodgy man's battered minicab with a fluorescent rosary and a keyring of miniature boxing-gloves dangling under his eastern eyes on the rear-view mirror at the front.

Then something happens to me, snaps inside, because, instead of telling him the obvious—my clear-cut home address—my voice seems to switch slightly, to deepen, darken, and I tell him to take me to a sub-terranean club I've heard of, in a distant and more dissolute part of town. Name?, he asks. You mean of the club? Yeah, he replies. Fist, or Shit, something like that, for queers and stuff, stays open till six, ring a bell? Jumping a red light on a tame Chelsea street, he swerves acutely to the right and speeds like a poisoned arrow, poisoned by the horror of his snap commission, which is to ferry filth to further filth, in the direc-tion of a rough borough on the south side, over the river, which looks perfect for suicides at this hour, so calm, and he turns and cuts and hurtles through flickering backstreets towards my foul, underlit desti-nation, which lurks beneath a disused railway bridge and, like so many of my adventures, starts with a lift, but not like the lift to my flat. This one is vast, industrial, wooden, empty, doorless, piss-drenched, and only going down.

I alight at a neon lobby which pumps music that I cannot recognize but only guess at, and at the ticket booth, a fat, half-naked dole-queen, pierced through the dugs, loaded with delusions of importance and munching a soggy cigar, takes my jacket with disdain, and informs me—in no uncertain and, in retrospect, quite funny, finger-jabbing terms—that if I want to pass the portals of this place, which is special-ist, Specialist in case you didn't understand, not for naff bloody Sloanes, I can start by taking off my shirt, mate, and the body'd better be worth it, and lucky I'm wearing jeans, otherwise: Forget It. And next time, he adds, wear leather or rubber or combat or (give us a tenner) you're Out. And don't flick your filthy ash all over my tip-plate-like. And take that smirk off your fucking face, girl. Thanks so much, I reply (and thank God I'm still stoned).

I VENTURE WITHIN. Beyond the metal swing-door, which opens onto a scene less like a nightclub than a busy screen inside a hard-core cin-ema, I have no recollection of steps or ramps or other forces of physical descent; yet my impression, instant and cold, is of being lowered morally, and medically, into a threatening pool, made pestilent by the seepage of sexual incontinency, fetid with the fumes of decomposing amyl nitrite, heavy with fungal sweat, rank and virile and truffled and glandular and muddled and strong with emanations of putrescent cheese and rotten eggs and cabbage and trenches and plagues. And though my impulse is to flee, my compulsion is to stay—to taste and imbibe and partake of these rites. So I wade, half-blind and half-stunned, through the miasma, towards a distant light which I take to be a bar; and there I order a bottle of mineral water, which I drink in a frenzy and chase down with a tumbler of vodka, no rocks. And then I start to look around.

The place is heaving, but no one utters: the music, the noise, is too loud, like bombs coming down. Heads droop and loll inanely. Everyone seems to be drugged and, as far as I can tell, more efficiently, more resolutely drugged than I. I can see a spectral teenager wilting in a corner, sobbing, claimed by some mournful trance, gazing away, possessed of a strange sombre beauty. For I don't deny that a strange loveliness lurks in this place at this late hour, a doleful slowness, a stateliness almost, a certain elegance—among those who are resting, among dancers beginning to flag, even among the hardened cruisers, the scavengers.

When a man passes by you, which, on account of the crowd, is closely, he generally moves unaccompanied, and is courtly of demeanour, and he lowers his eyes even as he sizes you up from the ground on which you stand to your crotch and back down, and he only raises an eyebrow (appreciative or otherwise) if he's a fool, or if he's very sure—and that type of man, to my mind, tends to be both; but a serious man, one worth his salt, say this one, him now, will move on past you, smoothly beyond you, and only turn to look when he thinks that you think that he's gone, is lost to you. And then he scans the next stage of you, the stage that you cannot see: your arse, your back, your nape, your ears, whatever he wants; or the parts of you which of course you can see but might at this moment have forgotten: your tattoo, if you have one, or your brand, if you've gone that far, or your smoking hand, if you still smoke, or a vein down your arm, or the line of your shoulder, or the texture of your skin, or its colour, or some godforsaken spot. But he is polite about it, this man, discreet, regardless of his impression, whatever his predilection. That is my point. After all, as he well knows (and he looks to me like he's been round enough blocks to do so) the boot of appraisal may yet find itself on the other foot—yours—in which case he'll be grateful if it turns out not to kick or stamp or crush.

Now let us imagine that he wishes to take matters one step further, that he wants, having sized you up and liked the size, to give you a try, to try to spark a story which, even if it turns out not to need a formal ending, even if it dwindles halfway, which sometimes can be way enough, nonetheless warrants, in his opinion, the benefit of the doubt, the chance of a start. Well, then, he's going to have to catch your eye—however falsely bright the lens may be upon your iris, however dilated the pupil at its crux, however retracted, however shot your deadened white may be with blood—he's going to have to catch it; he must. For it is with the eyeball that all stories of this order, since forever in our history, have started, and, despite all the setbacks, continue to start.

Whatever scrutiny may have led up to this moment has been but preparation, research, vague hypothetical wanky musings akin to scanning the contact mag that I described. Incidental; largely irrelevant. Because here, not over there where he stands and peers, is where he needs to be. He can't hope to engage you from afar. We're not at the spacious Savoy Grill now, nor at the empty crush bar during boring acts at the Opera House, much less flying to Sydney, First Class, for Mardi Gras, with time and space and lots of champagne to hand. No. We're in the very underworld, and the place is packed. So he's going to have to come out for the thrill, in for the kill, and he'd be wise not to hang about.

I know that no one likes to sin of over-eagerness, but nor should he, the man, prolong his game too much: for if he takes what seems like undue time to you, and makes you begin to fear that you're being messed about, or not wanted enough, and it all begins to rattle you, you might feel forced to pull yourself together and start to epitomize the only useful word in the French language; and you'll perform that word to perfection, like a star-among-stars, which you are, because you, after all, and after all the hard practice, can act it up and act it out and act it all the way to bloody oblivion. And the word, the word is this: *In-sou-ciance*. And such is yours, so subtle and chilled and acquired, like an oyster, that by the time that he, the miracle of miracles, deigns to materialize, he may find himself forced, retching very slightly, to swallow his pride. For by then, which is sorry-too-late, he may find that your eye, your vital historical eye, is otherwise occupied, or pretending so to be, or closed (which is just about allowed), or so close to the eye of some other man that it can no longer focus, never mind bequeath upon the former Mr. Sexual Salt the favour of a sideward glance. Because you, my dear, are not cross-eyed but cross. And he, less fucked than fucked right over. But let's not be petulant at this late hour, three-thirty, four, can't make it out; and who cares anyhow: you know it backwards—the hour when you must score even if it kills you, when you would trade for the germ of triumph, which is greedier and deadlier than the germ of lust, every racing corpuscle in your power. Admit: who wants to go on and on and on and on, living endless, unsuspected, undetected, unrequited, single-handed love affairs alone, night after night after night? Not you, you swear, no longer, no more. In which case, look at the whole thing another way, more dreamily, more bravely now, and put your precious untouchable dignity on the line for once. Reel back, rewind to the point where the target of your desire deserves, even as he stands apart from you, to know where he stands; for he has seen you and, as you have seen, passed by you and then observed you from a distance and liked you—yes, liked you—and he's decided, for richer, for poorer, for better, for worse, in sickness and in health, to come to you, and he has not a thing to lose and whole firmaments to gain and he's going to catch your eye, which darts like a comet, and he's going to entrap it and hold on to it, and devote to it the total, undivided best of all his stuff, till death or daylight do you part. And as far as he's concerned, which concerns you utterly, the rest of the club can die. And this is the point at which you have to banish all defensive foreign tongues and concentrate upon another word—trickily English this time, and murderous to enact—a word which yields and tugs and yields and tugs like the very valve that drives you, and the word is: Compromise. So do it. Now. And smile. And don't look sarcastic. And remember that just possibly, remotely, maybe, if you could see yourself from where, and as, you are now, you too might want to love you. And relax.

Which, of course, you don't. You can't. It may be late and you may be drunk and you may still, marginally, be drugged, but as for smiling, well, you'd rather swill down a long glass of saliva. Yet you do manage, and without edge for once, to look at him as he advances: hotly, directly you look, and long enough to verify that although he doesn't smile either, he hugely stares back, as if ravenous. And you think to yourself that this is a man who could stand on a cliff and place his open palm beneath the small of your back and raise you like the feather of a gull and send you flying. And you see, as he draws away his can of beer and his Adam's apple gulps, you see the outline of the shadow of the orb of the back of his head, which in your mind's eye you have already sculpted a thousand times, tilt back, as if in agony. But you cannot help or redeem him. You have expired. And then, as you begin to turn your neck minutely away, by two degrees, in sheer black terrified panic, he does that thing which strong, modern, hopeful lovers do with their mouth, and he does it pointedly, unmistakably and without question at you, aiming at the outer ridge of your right, bared, clavicle. He blows. Like a god bringing you to life, he blows. And then he blows again. And that's when you know that you've won. Which is the very instant of your loss. Again and again.

THIS IS HOW IT LOOKS to you: as if you were standing impassive on the hillock of a battle where, though you had not greatly advanced, you had at least managed to hold your ground. And this is how it feels: as if you were staring over a fog of gunshot and puncturing lights into the theatre of a war which, unbeknown to you, had already been declared lost; and it feels, too, as if, too late for apology or a gesture of surren-der, you had, bewilderingly, been bayoneted below the neck by one of your own men; and as if, in the split seconds before your fall, you couldn't recall a final prayer or summon the sign of a cross. For this, for you, is how it always is: your triumph as defeat; your victory as death, time after time. And this, it seems, is how it must always be: an image, a false memory of yourself as some other, as a frightened, witless sol-dierboy, picking yourself a bunch of valedictory excuses on your way home, like thistles—fresh, but actually old, and randomly chosen, and messily gathered, and dated long before their prime. And you desert the battleground of your own making without the head of the enemy that you lost, without the heart for which you hungered, telling yourself Oh Christ, who cares: that was no leading man, and this, this morbid bloody set, no production to write home about. A mere nocturnal obsession exhumed within the safe confines of a catacomb. That's all.

So forget it, and spare yourself a gutful of regrets. View the man properly, with clarity: sure, you like the quick allure of his tricked-up musculature, but go beneath the sheen of his skin, and, in your bones, you will know that when he turns to you and opens his mouth, which is the true horn of his plenty, bound to have sucked on every cock in Christendom and spat into every arsehole in the pagan world, you will be struck not by some sacred introduction to a lifetime of romance, but by the collective stench of all the men who pump up and stuff themselves with tuna fish and steak tartare before venturing into clubs in the dark, men whose pores and pits and groins, though coated with the musk of soap *pour homme,* cannot suppress the festering reek of carrion, like the belches of street dogs fed on the droppings of passing garbage trucks. And remind yourself, while you can, that his voice, when it comes, is likely to be high and crass and pitched in a minor key, and could never in a million years engulf you in the moaning groaning rumbling waves of abandon, only irk you with its piercing coital squeaks, like the spirited yelps of some skipping majorette. And think beyond the veneer of his front teeth, think of the rasping surface of his reptilian tongue, and of the abscesses hidden along his gums, and of the tang of his suppurating dental blood, like a slow warm sea, flowing down his gullet, carrying in its stream gobs of soft mucus and the undigested fishy remnants of his supper. Come on, get out. You've had enough.

Yet far from getting out, you find that with the inadvertent ease which sometimes is ascribed to fate, you've gone right in, and that far from having followed any guiding light to any bar, you've in fact crossed an imperceptible black arch and drifted through the final boundary-line and gone beyond the pale. And what you have entered is the pulsing heart, the very sanctum of this club: the flower of its evil, which is the back room, the dark room, the dungeon, the tabernacle, the underbelly of the mire. And you are blinded for a while. But you can smell rising fumes of flatulence and spent rivers of urine and wafts of rotting poppers and the bitter discharge of loss. And you can hear gasps and sighs and slurps and gobs and the creak of heavy chains being adjusted, and thudded blows being delivered, hard, by gauntlets onto rumps, and you can hear cries being sent up from a valley of rapture and pain and proof and surprise and wonder and hunger and terror which is the valley of this haunting, unspeakable variant of love; and now you begin to believe your eyes, which seem to sting; and through a foggy cloud of dope, the first thing that you discern, in the unfathomable distance, is a fat joint, or a cigar, its tip aglow, circling the shadows like a red halo—quickly described; then, sunk behind a horizon of amorphous mounds.

You decide to lurch towards a wall, avoiding as best you can a couple of pairs of interlocked army boots and, above them, kissing leather masks. And you reach out for the backdrop, and you touch it at last, and it is a sheet of black rubber, weeping but cold, and you turn your back to it and stand there, not quite leaning. And as you linger thus, not even thinking, an unknown hand from nowhere strokes you, with disarming gentleness, where it presumes that you wish to be stroked; and you find, to your surprise, to your slight relief, that already you are hardening, approaching hardness. And the hand which by now has earned itself a wan, emaciated arm, begins to fiddle, a little frantically, as if it were pilfering from a cash-till, with the buttons of your flies. And you try, calmly, to remove the hand, to move it away, but it latches onto your own sweaty unsteady one, your right—no watch to worry about—and it grabs you, bites at your wrist, as if for comfort, as if for more; but you think to yourself Fuck-off-you-bore-why-don't-you; and now you push the hand away more harshly down, making it drop. And this is the sort of moment when, whether you like it or not, whether it's openly admitted or not, you must move on: because you might get hurt, punched in the dark. And so you wade away, vaguely in search of an exit but uncertain of your route; and what you thought was a way out turns out to be a secret grove within a grove, a hidden arbour, wrought of scaffolding and oily ropes and sagging nets of camouflage and, like dead birds, leaves of grimy cloth. And as you turn to quit this corner that is forever Sodom, you find yourself entangled: you find that you are caught, caught by the wrist once more. And as you try to pull away, you look down to the source of your trouble and discover that this time the trouble does lie with your watch, which has become entrapped in the glinting nipple-ring of a downturned, genuflecting, shaven-headed, all but naked, leather-harnessed clone, whose weakling face has, against all the rules of his role, swung up to meet yours, eyes wide, mouth closed. And as you release him from his torture and his shock, you catch yourself, absurdly, and in equal contravention of the rules, apologizing, for God's sake, blurting out how you're So Sorry, and forgetting, in the process, even to deepen your voice. Just like the naff bloody Sloane for which you were taken, unable to pass muster even as a voyeur. Like some pitiful bumpkin, staring at guests at a Vatican ball.

You must move, preferably towards a different arch—that one, for instance, which, viewed from within this darkened maze, glows with the outside promise of an amber sky, and a storm of flashing tropical lights, and the hope of escape onto some bank near the dance-floor. And so you decide to head for it, keeping your eyes firmly upon it, like a captive nearing his goal. But first, before you reach it, you must, as if by way of final forfeit, steer your course round a many-headed heaving beast, a core of vultures set about a carcass, a team of attendant midwives at a critical birth—though in the place of muslin draped from the beak of some unseen stork, what you see (for your vision has swerved towards the action, admit it) is a black leather sling, suspended by chains from a blackened vault. And slumped on the sling, bare as a monstrous baby except for his studded collar, which is fit for a mastiff, lies the self-appointed, self-evident victim, the sacrificial beast, his wrists manacled behind him to chains which act as head-columns on his fourposter cot. And he is moaning from a place of high pleasure, his own mid-heaven. And leaning into him, between his parted knees, between his splayed legs, which dangle lifelessly, stands the master of the ceremony, the expert, the surgeon, the high priest—inserting, slowly, and slowly sliding into the protagonist's distended anus, which is a cathedral of mysteries, a considerate, considerately lubricated (but ungloved) fist. And in, *in* it all goes, the whole worshipful offering: the wrist, the base of the forearm, its widest part, masterfully flexed all; and just as the fist-fucker seems on the point of introducing his elbow, which is when matters are stretched to their optimum without risk of what medics call trauma, the arm begins, almost ruefully, its retreat, like a great slug, slowly releasing itself, and releasing along with it an unearthly stench of sewage which men who say that they know, men who claim that they have lived, however ignorantly, swear is no stench at all, no, but the ultimate perfect exchange of elemental manly everything, a sort of life-force, communion. And out, and down, comes the arm, which the assemblage admires and exalts in tones of reverence, yessing and hissing with envious wonderment. Down all the way to the knuckles it slips, and round a bit, an extra twist, then back, back in once more, but easy, easy man, that's it, and further, and up, and over and further still and, eventually, sadly, down again; then up, all the way, and once more out, and in, and on and on it goes. And you, of course, of course you can believe what you're witnessing. In your time, after all, you've seen this ceremony performed not just with saving hands, but with penitential feet. And also in your time, which is the old days really, before the troubles, such scenes, such spectacles, were routine, even mandatory, at least among those who liked to be considered worldly. But to watch it now, in the aftermath, well, it practically gives you goose pimples. Because it feels nostalgic. Like fan-dancing in discos.

So, what do you do next? It's so predictable: you topple, you fall from your voyeuristic podium and throw your hand in, literally, placing it on the hairy breast of the victim, over his heart, which has been touched from within but seems to beat slower than you have ever known a heart to beat. And you slide your hand down that soft hairy belly, which is strewn with other hands, and a whole assortment, you suppose, of amalgamated substances; and you proceed to move your fingers over the man's shaven pubic mound and onto his penis, which is withered, half-asleep; and then, as you remove your hand to leave, you bring the fingers that you have driven down his person up, up to your face, and you press them into yourself, inhaling for traces of faecal grease or semen or spittle or piss. But the cream which you smear onto yourself smells, puzzlingly, of nothing. Nought. And then you drift away from the feast, and out, into the brightness once more.

As you emerge, you find yourself frozen by the glare of a hard beam, which bleaches your jeans to a whorish pallid hue, a sleazy half-white. And your torso, drenched with the sweat of the back room, is turning cold. And your nipples, chilled by some draft, have stiffened suddenly. And your eyes, though shielded by your hand, the hand that smelt of nothing, tell you that out here, beneath the brilliant lights, is where the true victors can be found, the sinister beauties of tonight. Strange and distracted and almost too well-angled sometimes. Heavily shadowed and sinuous and raw. Impossibly lovely. Impossible ever to love. And you can tell me to grow up, to realize, Christ Almighty, that they're only spotlit, oily, anabolic, ordinary boys; but I am here to tell you that in their way they're gods, gods parading in pouches of chainmail, pouches worn under black leather chaps that proffer ideal naked buttocks up, as if to dare you, as if for grabs; gods strutting in black Lycra jockstraps, visibly engorged, and proud: catch their bodies in profile, in motion, and you will see their swollen bollocks straining to get out; gods glinting with metal studs: studded belts and studded cuffs and studded armbands gripping muscles into which you would sink your teeth, for which you would become a cannibal; gods with perfect gleaming flesh—shaven, front and back and scalp and all around, this very night. Even their mouths, for the present, are perfect: slim-lipped but wide of cast, and glossy, and fractionally opened, as if set for a photograph, yet free of vanity, devoid of curl, and soundless. And sometimes these mouths are all that you can see below the visor of a leather cap. And at other times they are accented by a close-cropped beard, or by the circumflex of a moustache. But always, these beautiful mouths, whatever their raging inner thirst, seem to be warning: No: Back Off. Because the trouble for these rare, preternatural creatures, you see, is that their very electedness is a sort of bane, heavy to endure. Can you not understand? They have more to protect; must take greater care. How can they hope to make headway when burdened with the contraband of their present incredible bloom? They must be patient; must save themselves; ride out the storm; wait until the clouds of youth have passed and simplified the sky. And they dance while they wait. And they dance like a dream. Like dreamers. Eyes closed. Souls shuttered off. But where, tell me, where, for any of them, for any of us, is the victory in that?

Nor is fate kinder to their admirers, to those who, faithfully as they harbour secret hopes of miracles, and gladly as they would have, oh, any one of these unbelievable young men, and gratefully as they might take from them, and give to them, and trade with them, and hold them and hold onto them, and perhaps, who knows, even teach them the distinction between saving and salvation, are, for their very believable

pains, repeatedly, more repeatedly than can be good for any man, punished, thwarted, denied the chance of a chance of a chance. Because all
that they, these hopers without a hope, are ever granted by way of consolation is a jumble of false images, snatches, like the trailer of a film
too sublime and risky ever seriously to have been meant to be coming
to a cinema near them soon. And as a consequence, all that these pitiful
crestfallen idolaters ever do, ever can do—and you can spot them a
mile off, trudging away, slightly stooped, before the final lights of the
club come on, before the merciless truth can dawn—is make their solitary way back to their flatlets, to steal into their moistening beds and
roll about the seas of their synthetic quilts and float on their flabby
backs and frott themselves to kingdom come about some golden
argosy that could, but would hardly, have set sail for such an unpromising shore. Inventing, as best they can, as they go along, a groaning dialogue that never was.

I must get out, go home; for though the music thunders on, the
scene looks quieter, emptier now, grown morbid. I catch quick sight of
an unsung hero, a tall youth, wandering like a star without a sky, unat-
tached, his eyes scintillating with exasperation. And not far from him, I
see a pair of ageing skinny men in rubber, lizards of liquorice, clinging
yet entwined without harmony: one stands pinned to a metal pole, bent
at the hip like some travesty of St. Sebastian; his partner slithers about
in an attempt to engage, to immerse himself, almost slipping at one
point, but then he lunges forward, only to miss the other one's mouth.
They smile like débutantes. I walk morosely down a passageway which
has a shiny black floor and glistens like a stream through a darkened
cavern; and halfway through this stream, which widens, I have to veer
round some lone rock of a man whose chest is bare as an undiscovered
coast, but whose firmly crossed great arms seem to proclaim: Into
These Waters You Will Not Go. His leathered legs, thick as a hench-
man's, are wide of stance and, frankly, too rigidly parted either for his
comfort or my conviction. His very ruggedly handsome face—more
handsome now than in its youth, I would suppose—is so determinedly
fixed on the opposite wall that he must be stoned, or hell bent on not
seeing me. Trying to fend me off. But as I, less a golden argosy than a
cautious dinghy, steer round his promontory, I catch him breathing in,

sucking from the belly, which strikes a chord in me, of two clashing notes: high admiration for his indefatigable self-absorption, underscored by a pity that borders on scorn.

And at last I make it to the coat-check, where the freak with the perforated tits, still munching a cheroot and still enthroned, is busy, by the look of things, extracting grot from the underside of an elongated fingernail with the assistance of a car-key. The platter for the tips seems to be gone. I place my numbered ticket, 19, or 61—who gives a toss—on the beer-slopped counter, and I watch it gradually turn to a liver shade of pink as I wait a reverential, needless length of time for his bovine holiness to arise from his great arse and fetch my contentious jacket, which, when restored to me, is held out at arm's length, extended with the sneering sort of spite that some people affect when dealing with furs. I quickly snatch it back, and turn, as if to escape. But a few steps on, I hear a reprimanding, under-parlour-maidy whine pursue me: 'Ere gel, 'ere, don't forget yer T-shirt now; ooh dear, someone seems've trod on it. Sorray—followed by a stage guffaw. So back I go, and while I'm at it, grab another, and another of those useless pick-up magazines from piles placed on two stools beside a counter where choice regulars of this discerning venue (Specialist; beg your pardon) like to perch, earlier in the evening, cross-leggèd and all neat. And I lurk, getting dressed, by the grill to the lift, until I twig, of all the final straws, that the lift doesn't go up. And actually, I think, why the fuck not? But I'm just too tired to find a reply. And I trail behind a few dilapidated queens, the last of whom, like some dumbfounding angel of redemption, holds open the fire-door for me; and I climb the concrete stairs, only just avoiding a strategic gob of bloodied phlegm on the first landing, and I go round the second, and the third, until, after a couple more, I'm returned to the real world without end. And eventually I get back to my flat. Don't ask me how. Feeling like shit.

(I suppose that, if only for the sake of accuracy, I should here include a recollection snatched from the interval between swallowing thirty milligrams of soporific and succumbing to its eventual drowse; a recollection of lighting candles all about the sitting room—on the gilt sconces and along the mantelshelf and on the marble console—and of playing, inconsiderately loudly for my neighbours, who've just had a baby, one of those ancient gorgeous stupid sentimental pop songs that form a part of everybody's secret repertoire, its title both too precious and too crass to be divulged. Yet what I can divulge is that in this recollection I'm shown kicking off my shoes and ripping off my clothes and flinging the whole bundle in the direction of the door; and then, dancing, dancing can you believe, naked, and alone—or almost. And I say almost because, in this shaming, swaying recollection, I can hear myself, despite the noise, and oblivious to the lyrics of the song, mumbling as if into the ear of no one in particular, no one that I know: Oh my great love it's been so long. And, more shaming still, I fail to pay this camp vignette the usual tribute of a good sob. Because, as you know, I'm bad at going the whole hog.)

I CANNOT TELL YOU to what sort of day I come around, but I seem to be walking about the flat a little too jauntily to be, as yet, properly sober; and as I go to boil water for strong coffee, I notice my distended image spreading itself on the kettle's mirror; and then I gaze vaguely down and, as the water gathers steam, my gaze seems to drift over the Mandalay tiles of the kitchen floor, which are all a different shade of tawny slate, like unlikely relatives, and prone, even on clear-headed days, to distract: you keep wanting to bend down and pore over them singly, over each one's individual mottles and contours and tones, as if every one of these tiles were a map of some elusive place to which you might, at some point, wish to go. And when the kettle clicks off, I open the cupboard for a cup, and I look, above it, at the clock, and discover that already it's past half-past-four in the afternoon. I plonk the cup down on its saucer, unload some coffee into the small cafetière for two, for one, then chase the grounds with boiling water and, before pushing down the plunger, I cross the hall and go to the front door for the paper, which I scoop up, along with the post: a few buff envelopes, which can wait; a computer catalogue for the flat's previous owner, now deceased, I'm told; a promising, festively stamped letter from an American friend in Paris, which I stash, for suspense, in the drawer of the table at which I now sit, staring at a postcard from a trick who recently tried, hunched over my lavatory bowl, to impress me by vomiting and ejaculating in unison—some unrepeatable mistake of a man to whom I recall having given a fictitious, or maybe just erroneous, telephone number, but who, on taking leave of me, has obviously also taken stock of my address. Because his postcard, which was funny fifteen years ago, bears an overvivid colour portrait of a dog, with its back turned to the viewer, defecating by a picturesque canal. And the caption, which oozes below the beast in fuchsia toothpaste script, laments, or asserts: "Amsterdam . . . Shit City," a sentiment with which I could not agree more. But to what I cannot quite as easily agree is the message from its sender, who, plainly unwise to my telephonic ruse and to the disenchantment which, if learnt, such a ruse would teach, barks, imperatively, as if in an attempt to dominate his own submissiveness: Next time <u>Beat</u> me for this!! And, underneath, he inscribes the more revealing and pathetic symbol of a puppy's paw, tiny claws and all, and, beside it, in cobalt blue, the initial T (Trevor? Terry? Tony?), toppling backwards—the entire tacky missive addressed, simply, wrongly, and naturally without a surname, to Jim. When I never lie about my name.

I slide the postcard under the telephone, pour myself some coffee, light a cigarette and, pushing my sleeves up try to figure out how I come to be wearing a nightshirt after a night like the last; but my attention shifts to the newspaper, or rather, to its magazine, for my feet seem to have become embroiled in some rustling supplement which must have fallen to the floor and which I rescue without looking. But picking it up, I realize that what I'm holding, far from being some Business section, or Sport (the sort of rubbish whose prompt disposal makes the chore of keeping up with the world so much less onerous), is, in fact, the head of a cover-boy on one of the contact pamphlets that I dragged home—his lubricious, touched-up face smirking out defiantly at me. Or at you. Or at his mum. Or even, I suppose, at the woman within him.

I push aside the weekend papers, which have lost any hope of a hold on my curiosity, and instead, I move on to the trashy contact mag, backwards of course. And next, guess what? Bull's eye: you've got it: here, and gracing, I note, a different publication, he appears once more. Big Uncut Man, swelling beyond the print. And so? Go on, give him a ring, why not. Enough time has passed, after all. For what? For your interval to seem decent. Are you completely insane? Controlled then, controlled. And if, after this interval, he's forgotten our original talk, well, so what? Big deal. Call it an omen; take it as a sign—to abstain, leave off, dump the whole nonsense. Dear God, it's so simple:

you dial, you speak, you see; and if you catch him at a loss, or pretending so to be, you just hang up, quietly. Done it before. Come on. Look: just go and have a bath, and a good think.

I have never found it easy to obey myself, so instead I take a shower. And as I stand beneath the scalding torrent, scrubbing my back with a long-handled brush, and trying to find a word that describes the indolent play of sunlight against the pale mosaic tiles, a strange inkling crosses me, and stops my senses, will not pass. And what I see, though I have closed my eyes and am lathering shampoo onto my scalp, is a vision from last night, a brightened memory of the surly behemoth in the dark corridor, the lone rock-of-a-man, still staring vacantly over his rebuffing arms, chest still pushed out, head still borne high. But his lingering presence seems—with the incredible certainty at which bearable fiction scoffs, but which flashing intuition insists its bearer must not ignore—to connect in some way with the words at the back of the contact mag. And out of nowhere, everything seems to fall, neatly, sinisterly, into place. And, for an instant, I bet myself anything that my premonition will be proved right, and an instant later I tell myself to pull myself together and drop the whole absurdity. And I turn off the shower, and towel myself dry; but in the steamed shaving-mirror I catch sight of my face, blotchy with anticipation, flushed, and curious beyond care now.

I dial. His phone rings once and twice and again and then a fourth time and, on the fifth ring, his unmistakable voice, fractionally more sullen perhaps, replies. I start to talk. My words echo round a hollow. I reach the end of my opening circular line, and wait, and, at last, Yeah, he replies, he thinks he remembers me, how's it going? Fine. (Silence.) I thought we might meet up. Sure, he brightens up; if I like. How's he fixed? Actually, pretty quiet, can fit me in, well, sort of more or less whenever. Like? Like, howsabout tonight? Tonight why not what time? Eightish suit you? Eight'll be fine. So I surrender my address, and spell out my street, which he reads back, mispronounced. My whereabouts sound dreamy in his mouth. Anything special I'd like him to wear?, he wonders. My mind groans at the thought of the word Specialist, the prospect of combat gear and gas mask, or rubber vest and waders, or wellingtons and fireman's helmet, or brown acrylic three-piece suit with cowboy hat, or overgrown boy-scout uniform, or zip-mouthed balaclava, or muzzle and collar, or diapers and outsize bonnet, or riding boots and jodhpurs plus equestrian crop; and I hear myself reply, though less decisively than I should have liked, that he should wear whatever feels comfortable. He wonders whether he should give me another buzz before he sets off. I think, Whatever for?, but I say: Why? And this time it is he who spells it out: In case you've changed your mind. Which is when I grasp that this is a game with fluctuating rules, where the hottest man is allowed to get cold feet and still pass Go— wallet intact. But I say: No, just come at eight. And he says: Anyway, if you need to, you can always access me on my mobile. And talking of Access I reiterate the holy sum of seventy pounds. And he reiterates the words In Cash. And I conclude with Sure, of course. And then he hangs up with a stroking See You. And God knows why, but I'm smiling inside, profusely.

HE ARRIVES BANG ON TIME. I know because as the voice of the telephone-clock gets to Precisely, I hear my front door buzzer go. But on the entry screen, all I can discern is a blurred ear, uttering my name with the close conspiratorial charm of an old friend who has not visited me for years, or perhaps hasn't been here before. I direct my caller, too dryly for comfort, up to the third floor, on the right. I hear his ear say Thanks. And during the suspense of his ascent, I torment myself with all the dimmers in the flat, turning down each switch a further minuscule notch. I close the bedroom door for no reason at all. My sweating palm slithers round the knob. I suddenly find myself fearing the impending scene with the same fear as, in the past, used to grip me during examinations, round the throat. Morning, boys. Welcome to the world of impossible multiple choice. Subject: Global Economics— General Knowledge Paper One. You will be given thirty seconds to formulate your answers. No dictionaries; no calculators; no slide-rules; no help of any description. Understood? On your marks, get set, ding.

I hide my notes, three twenties and two fivers, inside a silver cigarette-case which, like a mocking relic of my past, lies, these days, on the table in the hall, but which, in its prime, sat snugly in the linen pocket of the waistcoat of an ancestor of mine who boasted the finest hands around, and a nose like a knife, and the narrowest trews in town, and philandered his way through the coastal estates of his much younger wife, but ended his days slumped like a cur on a boat bound for nowhere, biting at the spikes of his lavender-waxed moustache and railing at the shameful ravages of syphilis and God, and growling, on occasion, at the pet names of low women whom no one had ever heard of. And I snap closed the sapphire clasp and replace the silver case, and gaze around, and try to wonder whatever next, and turn, of a sudden, pale with the shock of two knocks at the door, strong knuckle-raps, delivered high, nearer to the spyhole than the letter-box. Odd that I shouldn't have heard the lift creak ajar and clatter closed. My guest must have come up the stairs. And I find myself retreating, tip-toeing back from the entrance, as if the event ahead were a high-jump which, for success, required preparation, needed gathered momentum. Yet when I do set off to open, it is too slowly, too loudly, over-deliberately; it is with the saunter of a gentleman whom I could never be; it is at the leisured pace of that disgraced forefather before he fell from grace; it is a ghost of a spatted walk from another story. Nothing to do with me. And yet—oh for Christ's sake, he's only a bloody whore, not some mighty conqueror demanding an audience. Open up, and have done with it. And since, ladies and gentlemen, my hand is on the key, and my fingers are now turning it, and the door is already starting to swing open, allow me to present to you: Steve, the lean, the handsome, the muscular, mature and trustworthy: Big Uncut Man, aka BUM.

No feet on the mat. They stand, army-booted and at ease, far back against the remotest wall of the landing, which has never seemed so wide or bright before. He wears the same gladiatorial stance as last night at the club, but his head is now tilted down. And as I flick a look at him, I see his thighs flinch with surprise, then soften out; and from his gut I hear the sound of my name rumbling to the ground and rolling incredulously towards me. I swing the door wide open, as if I had nothing to hide and he were welcome to verify as much, but only once my back has been safely turned to him do I tell him to come in, Steve. He closes the door with noiseless calm, as if he'd been to this place a thousand times, almost as if he were home at last; and he follows me to the kitchen. But he prefers to stand outside in the corridor, out of the lights, posturing very slightly, just enough to convey that even though he's a nice uncomplicated regular kinda guy, he can also play the host and the hero and the heart of any elaborate creepy fantasy that I might happen to espouse. Good at his job, remember. Worth it.

I pour myself some whisky, attack the freezer for ice, stroke my soggy palm on my thigh, return the cap to its glassy spiral. Would he like a drink?, I ask. In a soft husky whisper he replies that water would be nice. I don't bother asking whether fizzy or still, because a man who doesn't use a lift is bound to want it straight from the tap. But for the nervous hell of it, just to be certain, I repeat to myself, low as I can: Water. And he nods and goes—not Yeah, not Yup, but—Yuss, before claiming that he's afraid he's driving. I think: Oldest trick in the book, and I try to restrain my eyebrow as I pour his libation into the most delicate, fanciful, feminine, devotedly cut glass that I can find, while the rocks of my drink rattle round a beaker crafted from a horn of buffalo. But when I hand him his water, which glints for a shaky instant between us, he proves to be possessed of agile, competent hands, for, despite their hairy enormity, and the girlish fragility of the glass, and the whole horrible embarrassing exchange, he manages to make his knuckles gently stroke mine. What a tosser, I tell myself; hookers shouldn't pretend to be in the business of romance. And by the time I've clicked off the kitchen light, he's walked ahead, away from me without a word, into the room where, not so long ago, I was dancing alone in a blaze of candlelight, and it now feels, oddly, as if I'd abdicated all charge of the proceedings and it were he who was in charge, as if I'd been summoned by this stranger to this flat. He moves along on the balls of his feet, like a child that's been pushed to walk before time; but before I can tell him that he can sit down, he already has, widely and squarely at the centre of the dark velvet sofa, knees far apart, toe-caps turned out. And he puts down his glass and shrugs off his leather jacket and lays it on the floor; and then he waits on the edge of his seat, hesitating at last. But I'm still drifting about, observing him through the mirror as I light a cigarette and inhale, keeping my head down. Would he like one, does he smoke? No thanks, not tobacco. Mind if I do? Your life, he replies. Most people's are, I retaliate, like an idiot. But cigarettes can kill you, he pipes up. And I smile, and say that so can lots of things, including love. And he smiles too, but hardly back; no, he smiles past the curtains of bronze taffeta, out of the window and abroad, as if trying to picture the features of some other man. I settle in the end for the wings of a chair across the room, diagonally distant, diametrically opposed, in a quarter of my own making. I do not recall ever before having sat with such awkwardness, with such gaucheness or discomfort—for all of the fine feathers that upholster my flanks. I find myself having to fight every fibre of my being not to cross my legs, as if I were my mother, but I can't bear the tension, so once more I stand up, pretend to stomp around. I think: the fact of the matter is this: if a third and neutral party were to see us now; to witness us thus—he, Steve, with his pale unhappy handsome face, dressed in a loose brown T-shirt and baggy, blue-black 501s, and looking, for all the world, content, even smug, and I, by contrast, glossily tanned and carefully toned and trashily vested and trussed into strategically frayed and fitted jeans and utterly lacking in composure or class, like a soubrette who's fluffing all her lines, well—the conclusion would be foregone, wouldn't it: Steve, inevitably, would be cast as the lucky punter, while the rôle of the whore would be perfectly mine. None of this fits any bill. And another thing: I look younger than he does by far too far. Because Steve here, let me tell you, is Big all right; Uncut, I have little doubt; most of the other things that he claims to be, perhaps; but as for the business of age, about his being thirty-nine, well, even in the soft embrace of my charitable light, and I happen to be feeling polite, I'm dealing with a liar who was probably already twenty-five and most likely getting Coca-Cola bottles shoved up his arse during the Stonewall riots of '69. This man could be my sire. And the ludicrous irony, though he will never know the cost of his lie, the sheer waste of it, is that, had he only volunteered the truth of his years from the start, and not presumed that I was hoping for some imbecilic Tom of Finland cut-out, I would gladly have tripled his price. But he shocks me back to my senses with one dreary word: Relax. I want to say Fuck off, get out. But I say, revoltingly: I am; just a bit shy. And then I sit down.

I stare at him with the lengthy impudence of a newly rich collector mulling over the actual worth of an inflated piece of art, and while I'm trying to formulate the proper words for this-shit-is-a-rip-off-man-come-on-you-must-be-mad, he asks whether I had a good time last night. I answer back: Last night? Yes, he persists, You know, at that club. (Christ.) No more than usual, I reply; why, was he there? Mm, he grins, wincing around the eyes. Oh, I lie, I didn't see him. And I put on some distracting music, crap that I think he might like, banalities from adolescent chartland that I habitually play for the sake of pick-ups. Nothing like the songs which, secretly, I might have elected to support us, chosen as our perfect background. And then I start to fire my questions at him, like a vengeful examiner at a viva, determined to wear him down, resolved to see him out.

I refer to myself as the Punter. He prefers the term Client. And what, I continue (not imagining Big Uncut Man really to be admissible), does he reckon that we should call him? Steve will be fine. Oh will it? I take it that Steve is a pseudonym. I'm correct, he says (not right). He also has Another Name. And might we know what that other name happens to be, or would such a disclosure seem sort of unprofessional? He's afraid that it would, seem sort of. Well, I must say—and I do— that he strikes me as a likely Keith. He ignores my snotty quip and moves on to The Point, which is that he needs to protect his identity because he has a job, a proper job, you see. Only does This for the money, short-term-basis type of thing, in the evenings; needs to supplement his income for a bit. I see. His life during the day is, he says, altogether different. Oh-my-God-don't-tell-me-Steve: you're a writer, right? Not exactly; but writing does, he concedes, have something to do with it. Journalist, maybe? Look, he asks, could we just leave this? Please not quite yet, Steve; it was just starting to get interesting, honestly. All right, he yields, but only for another couple of minutes, then we drop it, agreed? Agreed it is. And then, Yes, he admits, his job does have something to do with the written word; and yes, it is creative to a degree; and yes (yet again), writing does happen to be something which, though he says so himself, he can in fact do pretty—er competently. And then, as if to round off the clues, he explains that this accounts for the surprising success of his advert. Because it's designed to intrigue the consumer, you see, to attract a wide spectrum of interest. How, specifically? By being deliberately ambiguous, of course. Of course: Deliberately Ambiguous. I'd almost forgotten. But so it is, so it was. And so, back to square one.

Stalemate. Tell you what (I'm suddenly finding it tricky to say Steve, his other, other name): let's start again. If I like, he goes. Good: we're going to play this game another way, would he mind? He claims that he wouldn't (not yet, at any rate). Given which, I begin: Right, let's say that you're the Punter, and I, the Whore. No, no, he blurts, he must stop me right there; he insists that I be the Client; and he, his name, as I know, is Steve. I give up, give in. First round to him. We proceed.

Round Two, question one: Is the stopwatch still busy ticking? He half-smiles and removes some overflashy contraption from his diver's wrist and deposits it rather preciously in an inner pocket of the bomber-jacket at his feet. No need to worry about the time, he assures me. Whereupon he starts to look around as if hoping to discover a clock.

Question two: What, realistically, should be the extent of a punter's—sorry—client's expectations? Silence. He's thinking. He imbibes his first, and only, sip. Gulp. Wipes his mouth with the side of a finger. I elaborate: For instance, is a client justified in expecting a full erection from the hooker—escort I mean? Steve feels, a little sniffily, that yes, a client is in principle entitled to a hard-on from a guy who's Working. What principle? Well, come On, he says, everything is relative. Relative to what, exactly, Steve: to the efficacy of one's genital jewellery, the tightness of one's energy-ring? Or to a drug-induced upswing in the pervading mood? Steve laughs at this point, but not altogether freely. I'm becoming flushed. No, he explains, with great slow labour: It doesn't work that way. Oh really? Well how then would he, in his wisdom and experience and incredible desirability, propose that It, whatever It may be, did work? His face grows sombre suddenly; his knees spread absolutely, shamelessly; his arms reach forward and flex as if to welcome me; and then, baring a set of American teeth, and purring profoundly, as if he were some naughty-naughty daddy-oh, and I, a sensationally dumb blonde, suggests: Hey, c'mover here. He doesn't, I regret to say, add the endearment Baby; but after a pregnant pause, he does propose: Let me show you.

I do not think so, Steve-whatever-your-real-name-is, but thanks for the offer anyway. Try to relax, he suggests again; you're very hyped-up, he diagnoses, and prescribes, this self-appointed doctor-prostitute, that I help myself to another whisky. D'you know, I say, I think I will; top-up for you? If he replies to this inanity—and I wouldn't have put it past him—I'm no longer around to hear him. Already I'm in the kitchen, downing a great swig from the bottle-neck and guzzling it quickly, like a mutinous servant-girl, then pouring myself a liberal, trembling, triple. When I return to him, he is standing by the window, presumably still vainly searching for a clock, but platitudinizing now, if only for expediency, about the favourable nocturnal panoramic out yonder, and the surprising quiet within, and the miracle of decent—by which he means expensive—insulation, and the admirable reduction of the disturbance rising from the bustling—by which he means sordid—street below blar blar blar. I turn the tape over, and sneak a look at my watch (wrong watch to've worn—too chi-chi, too small) and I see, unbelievably, that we're only half an hour into this misery. I swing round, and resume: Won't he sit down? He'd rather not. Please, he's making me anxious. Why? Well, I mean, he's just so Big. All right, he weakens; if I insist. Oh I do, Steve; I really do.

We progress, or rather descend, to Round Three, which is our Special Subject section. My treat. A single question of many parts, otherwise known as the thousand-dollar mother-fucker and devised, since Steve is the sole candidate entered for this heat, especially and all for him. And I do cross my legs now; it seems almost befitting: because I have become, not just literally and figuratively, but also self-gratifyingly, Chairperson of the Evening. And though I may be growing a little agitated from within, I'm still managing to smile at him—a trifle coquettishly, I will admit; because, shame of low-down secret shames, I'm hardening slightly, I do believe.

He looks as ready as he will ever look, legs stuck out defiantly at me; but one of his knees is beginning to twitch. So enough suspense, I privately decree. The question, let's just sock it to him. Here goes: Given that Steve (he nods encouragingly) saw me at that club last night, which patently he did (nods again), and given that he elected not to make any contact with me then—am I not right to deduce a fundamental lack of interest from him in me, to infer that I failed to attract him? Already he looks eager to interject, but I can't allow it. Instead, I repeat what I've said, word for bumptious word, with the precise recall and fluid articulacy that a sharp intake of alcohol can sometimes bequeath. After which, I proceed: And given his indifference, can I now seriously be expected to imagine that he could suddenly, as if miraculously, find me to be pleasing? (Poor man's frantic to butt in, so I soften.) Look, he splutters, he doesn't know where any of this is leading, quite, but last night, if I really must know (my turn to nod vigorously), he had a really-really busy time and, after his appointments, just went to that club because it's near where he lives—Battersea actually—and because it stays open till late, and he needed to chill out for a bit. Get it? Just happened to be there. Just as I happened to be. He wasn't on the look-out for anyone or anything, though I may've been. And anyway, where's this all leading? He thinks I'm getting heavy.

Hear that? Catch it? Steve thinks I'm getting heavy—which comes as a surprise to me, because, my dear, *I* feel as if I could be waltzing around the place in a crinoline, or bombing about on pink-diamond amphetamines. I mean to say, it's hardly as if we're talking the third-degree here, Steve. Be realistic. Heavy? This? What, for a great Big Uncut Man like you? (Needless to say, I don't risk voicing any such thing, much less what I mean, which is: Heavy, Stevie Babe, is the shit I'm about to sock to you. And if you're half the hulk you proclaim to be, you'll manage to shift it. Because I, don't forget, can bring you good business; and you, if you're to be believed, have quite a name to keep.) Instead of which, my eyes glaze over a painting of a naked woman above him as I try to gather back the threads of where I was headed, before the Heavy bit, and then I continue: Let me tell you where I fear that this is leading, Steve: to nowhere that I can think of. Because it all went wrong almost as soon as you walked in. No fault of yours, of course, unless we choose to regard your revelation about having spot-ted me at that club last night as foolhardy, which perhaps we ought to do, since that one snippet alone has, in my opinion, exposed you more than any amount of nudity or disclosed pseudonyms or flights of heartfelt writing. In normal circumstances, or should I say general, I suspect that parties involved in exchanges such as ours, transactions such as this, would not have clapped eyes on one another before the initial tryst, which we might call exploratory. And in the extraordinary instance that their paths *had* crossed previously, I suppose that both would feel at liberty, and have the sense, to just say Hot Potato, let's call the whole thing off. Because my belief, but do correct me—once I've said my piece—is that so long as both sides come together as strangers, which is half the point, and in a climate of secrecy, which probably constitutes the other, the whole question of satisfactory congress remains open; there still exists a world of possibilities, not least since

it's in everybody's interest to make the bloody thing (Calm Down) succeed. Repeat jobs, of course, are another matter entirely, dependent,
ultimately, on whether the punter has found the whore to have been,
how can I put this, worth it, and worth further bookings. The whore's
opinion, I have to be candid, scarcely impinges, since the objective for
an accomplished prostitute, as for any gifted professional, is not so
much to notch up an infinity of one-off commissions as to secure a
steady commercial stream, to earn a flow of dependable regulars: in
short, to win a following. And a whore will countenance most things,
will brave almost any indignity, in the hope that a performance be
judged a bravura, and that he, or she, be rewarded with a string of con-
tractual encores. But it remains, in the final analysis, the punter who
decides whether a rendition has, or has not, been pleasing. Which,
strangely enough, brings us back to us, to here and now, doesn't it?

STEVE STANDS UP ABRUPTLY, and stares, and does at this moment
look enormous. His face glowers down at me, and sags as if he were
fucking me from the front. His mouth begins to open, but it's just too
bad: I have to go on. He has come to me, I claim, from nowhere, from
a tatty page torn out of some tatty publication. I have never clapped
eyes on him before. (I can hardly believe my gall. It inflames my loins.)
Yet it would appear that he, by contrast, has most certainly seen *me*—
clocked me, so to speak—and, for all that I know, already scrutinized
me. He cannot, I go on, have volunteered the snippet about the club
out of stupidity, for even I know that in these competitive times, the
epithet Rent Boy is not synonymous with the words pretty moron. A
great many prostitutes, I understand, are as bright as they are person-
able, tip-top post-graduates in some instances, champions not just of
the bed chamber but also of the boardroom. And Steve, who's clearly
been around rather longer than such boys, and doubtless, in his time,
learnt more than they could possibly yet know, must have been
prompted to divulge his information for some reason subtler than
mere shortage of conversation. Could the reason have been a desire in
him to impose, with the bombshell of his foreknowledge, some sort of
control; or could it even have been a suspicion that what I seek is a figure of authority? Because the facts, as I see them, are that Steve (out
there on the open market, in the great dark open) was prepared to

throw me, and whatever I may have had to offer, overboard. And did. And I'm sorry, Steve, because, strange as it might seem, I do not fuck with men who would not fuck with me. Just isn't stuff I get off on. Correction: stuff on which I get off.

He huffs around, then stops; and hammering a fist against the marble, protests that he just happened to see me, that's all—adding, for inexplicable measure, that when he saw me he remembers thinking: Dishy (which dates him). Yes, he continues, he's not too proud to admit it; why should he be? Reckons I might fare quite well on the game myself if I chose to—assuming, and don't get him wrong, that I'm not already on it. Steve has often paid for sex, he says. An interesting scene, he explains. Hotter, very often. Hotter than what? You know what I mean, he replies; don't try to get clever with me; and as for this stuff about reasons and control, well, it's way out of hand man. Kind of neurotic. Neurotic, says Steve, who feels that I have some weird agenda simmering, as if I bore the world some sinister grudge, as if I needed to settle some bizarre earlier score, nothing to do with him. All of my shit, he concludes, lies way outside the realm of his (considered pause) obligations—no, responsibilities. And he wonders whether I've ever thought of getting help, like therapy. I ignore him. So he rounds off his monologue with the revelation that although it takes two to Get It On (the man is sickening), I seem determined not to give him the opportunity. I suddenly feel lonely, as if I needed a friend to partake of my ridicule.

I say OK, wait there. And now he does do as he's told. And I go back to the hall and pick up the cigarette case, and slip the wages into one of my back pockets; and I return, and I address him, and I ask whether a chance is really what he needs. And he replies that it rather looks like it, doesn't it? So I tell him that I'll offer him two. First: here's his money: he's free to leave. And I pause enquiringly. He looks, to my confusion, shattered, as if he'd been delivered a sudden, hefty blow; seems to be deflating on the spot; I wouldn't be surprised if he began to sob. Because I do understand, with just a tinge of guilt now, that the part of Major Reject doesn't figure in his work description; it lies out of his bounds. Let's face it: this is someone who's accustomed to flirtation, adulation, salivation, masturbation, fornication, gratification—things that can be played with seasoned panache—handsome remuneration even. But to be relegated to the shadows thus, thus unceremoniously? Must be a first for him. *My* first. *Cum Laude.* Ding. And yet the man will not be moved, will not be shown the door, not quite so easily, oh no. So instead, I show him the Roman face of my prissy watch, and offer him Chance Two, telling him that as he can see there still remain thirteen minutes, or just under, left to go. And I challenge him with my proposal that, if I'm to be persuaded that he amounts to anything more than a disappointing piece of print, he'll manage the seemingly impossible, which is to fix the damage of his conversational blunder by getting into top gear, fast, and redirecting this whole trip—skewed, I fear, so regrettably off-course. And I add, to taunt us both, that should he prove able to find a way to do so, to turn this awkward corner, I would like to think that we might even continue, the exchange of money becoming incidental, the sum of his prowess and my pleasure becoming all.

I'm standing with my back against the wall next to the corridor. He approaches me with astounding new calm and stops one step away from me. He spreads his legs, and lowers his hips, and stretches out his arms and brings them round to place the palms of his hands on the wall behind me, in line with my jaw. I can feel the heat of him. My back is frozen. I want to close my eyes. But he starts to twist his face into a contortion which, though it looks deranged, I recognize as meant to seem turned-on, and he puffs out his chest and tells me to go on, to relax, that I can touch him, not to be inhibited, that we should have done all this last night, at the club, when he first saw me. But suddenly I push away his arm, and stagger beyond his resistance, and I can hear myself cackling in response and, through the convulsions of my sickening laughter, my voice says: Forget It, Steve, really don't worry, thanks, but I think that it's better if you go.

Next thing is incredible: like some spurned and mortified great love of mine he murmurs that he'll only go if I'm quite sure it's what I want. And I confirm, seriously now, though smiling with aborted hope, that I'm certain that it is. Yet still he stalls, and wonders now, if you don't mind, whether he could borrow, Borrow he says, my john. My john; like some laid-back old New Yorker. The idiot. And in he goes, and closes the door; and while he's in there in the dark (I know because the switch is on the outside wall), I hear absolutely no noise. And a pang of loneliness chimes inside me as I try to envisage him. No rising lid, no gurgling flush, no gushing tap being turned off. He might be counting the lucre, I suppose; but I conclude, more realistically, more resignedly, that he must have gone To The John to remove some winching-contraption from his big, uncut, and unrequited cock. And when he emerges, which he does almost stealthily, as if expecting to be told off, he gathers his bomber-jacket from the floor and resurrects his sinister charm in order to touch me once more, somewhere vaguely around my shoulder. And I confess that as I lead him out I do feel slightly victori-ous, as if I'd vanquished temptation, beaten down some common dog. And at the door he leans towards me strangely, and strangely we kiss; but it is with the formal, chilled hypocrisy of concelebrating priests. And then he pats me on the buttock, routinely. And then I draw back. And once he is out of my darkened sphere, and safely on the bright landing to the world, he looks round, sees no one, and remarks, for the third and final time, that I should learn to relax. And just to finish me off, he adds, sneering rather than smiling, that he thinks I think too much.

I LOCK THE DOOR so silently that you might have thought that I'd left it open, but my head which thinks too much is yelling so hard inside that you could drown in the noise. And I go to the bog, where there is no sign of him, not one, and I apply a winching-strap of my own. And in the bedroom I open the wardrobe and fling myself into a black leather jacket which makes me feel squashed but has, in the past, proved a reliable draw. And on my way out, I ignore the great Venetian mirror in the hall, and the framed photographs of friends whom I love, or whom I've loved (for some of them I have lost), and I just walk out, out of the flat, ignoring the reasons, but ashamed to find myself alone. I creep down the stairs very slowly, to be sure that he has properly gone; and he has; and I step into a stinking urban night of the most dispiriting sort, full of belching louts and their clattering molls, and hooligans chanting retarded football songs and munching fish-'n-chips, or puking up, or pissing against the trees on the road; and I set off in the direction of my nearest faggot pub, which is famous for being rough—though it's decades since I've found it to be so—and famous, too, for being the oldest of its type in town, which I can well believe, because it is so historically sad.

And walking along, disengaged from the world, as if jet-lagged, or lost in some foreign town, I realize, from the liveliness of the traffic and the eagerness on the faces that pass by and the glow of the street-lights and the vigour of the wind in my eyes, that—for all of my detachment—I'm slap in the middle of the rush to a new night out. And as I approach a zebra crossing, I hear, through the open window of a car that I cannot make out, a recording of some unknown adolescent's voice, singing a laughable song of the sort which, you know, dissolves me. Because this unknown voice, which is the voice of a starry-eyed loner like the frightened witless soldierboy of whom I spoke, is chanting in a wild, hypnotic monotone that his corny quest, his, is to fight the unbeatable foe, and to bear the unbearable sorrow, and to run where the brave dare not go, and to right the unrightable wrong. And then, the lights go red. And I begin to cross. And I seem to be engulfed by a rowdy, rolling crowd which prevents me from hearing any more; which, in fact, is just as well, because my idiot face is coursing with filthy tears that I have to wipe with a black leather cuff. But later, what seems like ages later, and from a growing distance, as the car speeds away behind me, I hear the boy's voice once more, telling me, warning me to be willing to march into hell for a heavenly cause. And I think, fleetingly, of Steve, who by now will be racing back home; and I wish, absurdly, that the voice of that boy had been streaming like a banner out of Steve's own car-window; and more absurdly still I wish, in my waking, walking dream, that the voice had not been the anonymous issue of some recording, but that it could have been mine, my own voice, and that I were still myself as hopeful, as willing, as young as that boy, and travelling away with Steve, being carried along. And then somebody bashes into me, which is what always happens at such moments, and a voice says Sorry Mate, and I go back to thinking of Steve, though in a more credible realm now, in a more realistic mental film where he can be pictured approaching his home and drawing up to the kerb, probably parking at this very moment, then grabbing his keys, and fumbling about for his mobile to check whether anyone's tried to get hold of him, and deciding that, if not, he'll just go indoors and make himself a cupper, right out of beer but too knackered to go to the shops; and he'll take off his boots and put up his feet and roll himself a joint with the last of the grass that he keeps on a tray in the airing-cupboard; and he'll switch on the Box, in case there's a chat-show or some old sitcom to take his mind off things; and if not, he can always watch a dirty video, get him horny. But first he's going to put away the dosh from this really fucked-up guy he's just been to, totally, up on the shelf which is stacked with mags he used to pose for, plus some paperbacks that he's enjoyed, thrillers and what have you. And at the very top—you can just see the lid—there's a box labelled Hollidays, which come-to-think-of-it reminds him that he'd better give a bell to this bisexual mate of his called Nige who's also on the game (potty about his kids, mind you), used to be on the rigs, still has a brilliant bod, goes to the gym four times a week—when he's not on a bender, that is—and all-being-well-touch-wood, plans to go with Steve to the States to visit friends of his—of Steve's, he means—friends from the old days, who they can stay with, but probably for the last time: not too good, apparently, the pair of them. Oh well, no good moping and OK, so San Francisco's not what it was in the Seventies, but Christ bloody knows they could do with a break and the weather's always great out there, and you can get these really cheap return flights now-days; and anyway, word is the scene in the U.S. of A.'s starting to look up again with loads of hunky boys and brilliant bars and nobody gives a toss whether you're a hustler or whatever and, hey, Steve reckons he might decide to just say Sod It, and stay on for a while, rent a nice place, nothing too flash, put himself about, meet some new blokes, ring his mum in Grimsby once a fortnight, keep things ticking, turn a few tricks, pays for the blow, can't be bad.

I push against the door of the pub and walk into a hot, tenebrous fog. I should be able to describe the place to you, on this of all nights, but I can't, because, two steps in, two breaths on, I practically collide, of all pathetic jokes, with Steve, Big Uncut Man. Standing alone. Looking, to grant him his due, not unembarrassed; and I, though I might well be shocked, seeming merely surprised, I hope; ironically struck. Yet I feel, for reasons which I cannot fathom, secretly pleased, half-comforted, as if I'd run into someone I liked in a place where generally I don't. Does he offer me a drink? Does he buggery. Do I offer him one? Of course, like an automatic Sloane—which, speedily, he de-clines, frowning and smiling at the same time, as if my gesture were preposterous. And I, using the din and the dark and the crush as my alibis, lean up to him, into him, and I mouth to his ear, which is cold, that after this evening I should like, if we should meet by accident, to think that he might afford me the passing courtesy, however slight, of an acknowledgement. And he has the front to suggest, this sombre sullen god of a man, that he would never not, that blanking isn't his style. And I look at him with flat neutrality, and make no excuses as I push my way to the bar and order myself a drink and dawdle about for the change. And only once a golden coin has plopped like a discarded talisman into my quaking, outstretched hand, do I dare turn my head—to see the back of the head of this stranger who corrodes me walking away, out of the pub. I swallow my double in one, grimacing as if it were linctus; and then I, too, get out.

Next stop is ten yards down the road: the club where the air-conditioning broke down what seems like yesterday, but must, in fact, be the best part of a month ago. Doesn't time fly? Isn't it fun? This is the place which gave me the boy who left me the mag which carried the ad that led me all the way to Big Uncut Man. I don't know who to thank. I walk in, past a leather-gloved bouncer who calls me Love, but this time I come warned—as well I might—and no sooner have I dumped my jacket at the coat-check and disappeared through the haze to yet another bar for yet another ineffectual vodka than I catch sight of him, Steve, over there, looking out from the wings, as if in wait for someone. Only a beam of lilac light catches his thighs. The rest of him is dark—holding, I think, a can of mineral water. And I begin to reel with strange pique, to move beside myself, to fly toward my shadow as I turn into my own best enemy, my own worst shining example.

I work the bogs quite fast. I flash my cock around, manipulate it, and bare the top-slice of my buttocks for the benefit of the queue behind. I certainly don't piss, but I wear my blossoming sleaziness like a prize, and I belt up noisily and walk out before I'm ready, like a slattern, flies still half-undone. I stagger onto the couple-stricken dance-floor and move around for a while, trying to make sense of the nonsensical phonetics that issue from some vocalizing robot, and I try to have a quick one-man romance, a romance with no body. Then I grow bored; walk off, mid-song; trip on a step, and get offered a drink by some dickhead from the urinals. Another vodka. My suitor orders me a large one, in sign language. He already possesses a beer, untouched. Attacks the froth. Grins straight at me. Starts to talk: German; married; wife understands; children grown up and gone; lives in Cologne; here on a convention. London, he assures me, is *goot* for him. And I, for him (what shall I be?)—a croupier, that's it. Club in Mayfair; members only. Do I enjoy this? Quite, I reply discouragingly. And Tonight? Night Off. *Quelle chance,* he exclaims, bewilderingly. And so, as if this were the logical course of action, I invite him home. To spite Steve, who doesn't warrant the spiting; Steve, who, on my way out, throws me a look that is hard to define, a look less of acknowledgement than of enlightenment, yet tinged with complicity—as if he were the Deus, and I, the mere machina, as if, at last, he understood me to be some prowling domestic feline who had dragged a mangled rodent to the feet of its master and, for its pains, expected, if not actual recompense, at least some attention, or a good slap.

Of the incidental German, needless to say, I recall not very much: that he fumbled down the back of my jeans for a while; that, using both his hands to conceal a soft-on, he tossed himself off; that he came, desultorily, over the kitchen floor; that he went to the bathroom for a posthumous leak, which splashed onto the seat and also hit the floor; and that following a quick wash of hands (no soap) he consigned himself, with dull ease, to history. Every queen has had one of those.

I wipe up the spunk in the kitchen, which is too clear and runny to be flattering; and, with private embarrassment, I go to the bathroom and crouch to wipe the drops of piss around the lavatory bowl. And then, though now with no shame at all, I find myself, against all wisdom or sense or best interest, ringing Steve's number once more. And the recorded message clicks on, then drones along, finally halting for me to talk, and I just say, without thought, like the machine that I've become, that I'm sorry if the evening went wrong, could he call me at midday. Which he does—at ten minutes past.

THE 'PHONE AWAKES ME. I can hear the rasp of my voice; I cough; I try to clear my throat. I summon what meagre spittle I can, phlegmy gunk. Hang on, I croak, and put down the receiver while I fumble for the bedside lamp. I grab a bottle of water from the floor, and swill down the dregs, straight from the neck. That's better. But I can hear Steve's diminished voice, still drifting unawares towards me from the handset, which lies abandoned on a pillow, asking whether this is double seven double six, and whether I'm all right, or is this a bad time. I pick up the 'phone. No, it's fine. Did he wake me?, he wonders. Yes, but I ought to be getting up anyhow: going out for lunch. Ah, he goes. Makes no mention of last night, thus banishing all awkwardness, and adds without the slightest tremor that perhaps we should consider giving this whole Thing another go. Makes me fetch my diary. I light a cigarette during my search for it, and then I sneak into the bathroom for a piss, and I squeeze a gob of toothpaste into my mouth, which is ridiculous. I lick it around as I climb back into bed. I shake the blankets about. Right, I tell him, and we discuss our respective availabilities for the coming week, sparing ourselves undue details about other commitments. In the end we settle for Wednesday, eight-thirty, here. But no, on second thoughts (of his), could we make that eight o'clock? Sure, if he wants. He'd prefer, he says; would make life easier. Doesn't elaborate. And so: eight o'clock it is. And I ask him whether perhaps, this time round, he might dispense with his car: he can always use my cab account. Good idea, he replies, though his tone sounds unpersuaded. Fine, I begin to end, See you then; yet before I can repeat our financial reality, or thank him for having rung, he has again engulfed me in one of those great, sonorous goodbyes. Instantly I replace the receiver, sweating. Almost as fast, I grab it back and dial Directory Enquiries. I ring the restaurant where I'm supposed to be lunching, to check whether the friend I'm meant to be meeting has booked, expects me; and he has, he does, dependable to the last. Two people; table nine; reservation for one-forty-five. Thanks very much.

I get up. Strange chorus of birds in my heart. I unbutton my nightshirt. I open the wings of the wardrobe. I glance inside. This time next year, one year from now, I promise myself, I shall be redefined, shot of all this stuff. I shall wear myself like a man, and like a gentleman at that: in single-breasted suits of faultless cut; in pure white shirts of various weights but one plain style. No rings; no links; no pins. No giddy breast-pocket handkerchieves. No dapper braces. Sober socks only, devoid of pattern. Trousers and cuffs without turn-ups. Shoes without accent: lace-ups. And briefly I picture myself on the crest of this forth-coming prime, grown faintly grey at the temple, dressed in Prince-of-Wales at springtime, or blue-black linen on summer nights, walking, walking without a conscience down some corso or rambla or boulevard towards a waterfront full of departing boats and flags and lights and—

God give me new horizons.

PART TWO

No BEGINNING: just an ingrained sense of embarrassment, of ancient, premature sadness, of displacement, of too much knowledge too early on, of wishing that all were otherwise, that I were adult, elsewhere, of having missed some crucial joke; yet no formal beginning. Press me (as you do) to recall it, and watch me redden, stumped by my inability to reward your interest with a single, clear, determining first truth. But yes, there was a general flavour to my infancy: rich and slightly sickly and tending to warm, like *marrons glacés* eaten in the sun.

When sounds from that first era return to me, faint and diffuse, they seem to filter through the summer curtains of my earliest siestas— starched white poplin, polka-dotted—from an unknown middle distance. I hear the plopping of tennis balls, an occasional clap, idle laughter . . . but then these sounds become muddled in my turning head (No pillows, darling, not for little boys) with the echo and the fall of a fairy-tale picturebook closing, sliding, dropping to the waffled bedside rug, which is laundered daily.

In my dreams of childhood I still hear, while my parents lunch on the terrace, splashes like cymbals from neighbouring swimming pools, and the hush of tropical afternoon breezes soothing the hot red feathers of a dozen flamboyants, planted in a great circle, like a botanical bandstand, at the front of our house when I was born. Sometimes I hear the slow creaking of giraffe-bamboos, tall and tougher than drought, scratching their necks against my shutters. Their leaves seem, from the harbour, to fringe our high wall from the world but, within my world, they shed a cool, lime light on the blank wall behind me— blank but for a wrought old Spanish crucifix of silver, a relic from my christening which, though hammered into the brick with a large black nail, appears suspended in mid-air by a flawlessly arranged, arrow-tailed, aquamarine satin bow.

Ahead of me, when I lie sideways, folded into that state of woozy dormancy which continental children remember as enforced repose, I glimpse, at the outermost edge of my domain, like a blur beyond the hillock of my knees, those long white poplin curtains of my first few summers: full enough to evoke presences, silhouettes, postures, yet short enough to prevent any unseemly tumbling to the ground, the curtains rise, then withdraw like spectral, absurdly balletic messengers from the nearby sea—now filling out like intrepid twin sails set for unimaginable realms, or slimming down, brushing, overlapping, soft and oblivious as the skirts of novice missionary nuns, then stretching out once more, and tautening into the flanks of deserted tents from the Old Testament, but finally fluttering, and lingering in space for a moment, rueful, reluctant, lost in a landscape which, from the inclination of my sombre young eyes, already suggests flags of surrender, leaving forever, waving goodbye. Life has changed since the day when my Mam'zelle packed her bag, was quiet, went away.

THE NANNY WHO REPLACED her comes into my room with such slyness that I do not hear the turn of the green-glass four-leaf clover which acts as doorknob. But her appearance heralds the second half of my day and follows directly upon her lunch, taken in solitary silent splendour in the breakfast room, that socially indeterminate region which, tucked between the kitchen and the dining room, is papered in blue china teacups and whiffs, on account of its closeness to the swimming pool, faintly of chlorine. My parents will be drifting calmly through their own lunch still, the tempo of which, in summer, on the terrace as I said, is orchestrated by my mother with the assistance of a small, jewelled bell, a wedding present I seem to recall, whose frivolous tinkle, in my memory, is invariably accompanied by the jingle of her charm-bracelet, which glints with keepsakes and talismans and whose most recent addition is my first, gold-mounted milk tooth.

From autumn until spring, however, the tempo, which runs more legato, is conducted by means of an electrical contraption concealed beneath the carpet in the dining room, which, when my mother elects to extend her slim foot and press, manages, by some act of inexplicable wizardry, to buzz in the pantry in a variety of coded signals, thus alerting the servants as to what precisely is required: more iced water, more white wine, more red, more bread, second helpings, or the next course, or the next.

Nanny now rushes in to me, filling the air with her personal rendition of whatever hit happens, this week, to have taken her fancy—Winchester Cathedral (You're Bringing Me Down), I'm tempted to imagine—as she trots over the mottled granite tiles towards me. She sports—though of course I can't yet see them, for I'm still pretending to be asleep—her freshly painted, white leather lace-ups, and her signature stockings of seamed white lisle. All of a chirrup she heads for the room's centrepiece, a circular rug of thick-cut moquette, festooned along its sandy border with a miscellany of prancing circus beasts, at the heart of which there presides a bewildering mutant—turned, at my insistence, to face away from me—whose lower half may suggest a clown with pointy pumps and pom-poms, astride a penny-farthing, but whose upper body unquestionably belongs to some muscular ringleader with a handlebar moustache and a flying whip. Over the rug Nanny proceeds, in the determined direction of the curtains which, once reached, she always attacks with simultaneous outward arm-swings, like a conductor launching into a symphony, and then ties back—invariably, and with blithe indifference, parting them at the summit with a carelessness that both offends my precocious sense of order and elicits a deafening ring-against-pole squeal.

Within seconds, she is cantering back to my white iron bed with such gusto that her presence can no longer be ignored, not politely. I open one eye. Her straining thighs, striped in blue and white, are the first sight to confront me, swiftly followed, as she bends down, by the top of her pin-stabbed head. She stoops and reaches down for my favourite sandals, which are cherry-red and have been standing on the floor, waiting at the foot of the bed, patiently and slightly pigeon-toed, like friends. She carries them away, across the room, to the rocking chair where my clothes sit folded, and she lets them drop, like dead weights, to the ground. Then she returns to where I am and, tearing my top sheet away from me, exhorts me, far too loudly, as if trying to earn the attention of an adjoining room, Wakey Wakey Now. As if anyone could possibly not have done.

So down I clamber in my underpants, which are all that I'm allowed to wear during my siesta, and I tip-toe over the chilly tiles to the furthest edge of the rug, from where, avoiding the floor and stretching across, I manage, just, to grab my piqué shorts, the ones with cross-over straps; yet no sooner have I found the balance to insert a foot into them than I am told, No No, to start again, Properly, which means in Nanny's particular order. Off with the shorts, on with my shirt—short-sleeved, tiny-holed, abrasive—and at last into my sandals, though even this part is spoiled, for socks aren't allowed in summer, despite the grate of toes against the petal cut-outs on the leather. I crouch down, resigned, and, in a posture of sulky genuflection, deal with the buckles, but as I finish tucking away the second strap, I feel myself being lifted by the elbow and directed, with a vigour that practically levitates me, towards the dressing-table, which has recently been glossed, like the bed, with a coat of white.

With the possible exception of the wardrobe, under which I'm the only person small enough to crawl, the dressing-table is my favourite piece of furniture here, with its collection of small, intricate drawers, and its vast, swivelling mirror, which lends a mysterious underwater floatiness to the ceiling and its hanging lamp—this, fashioned as a dovecote and complete with feathered doves along the parapet. But much as I might favour it, I have often been reminded that the dressing-table, which saw my mother through her fragrant youth, is mine on temporary loan only, which means until such time as we're blessed with a Sister, in whose honour pink tassels will swing from the dainty keys, and the drawers be lined with hand-printed seraphim, and the contents be laced with pomanders and sachets and frills. And the girl's array of silver brushes and frames and porcelain figurines, and her pearl and coral beads and half-eternity rings, and candy-striped enamel eggs on jade and amber stands, and tortoiseshell haircombs and hairbands of grosgrain, and goblets of powder with ivory-handled puffs, and crystalline phials from the great perfumerers, and velvet ranunculi, and daily-delivered posies, and fans of billets-doux, stashed with flirty insouciance beneath the faceted edge of the table's sheet of glass, which, by then, will surely have been tinted to the perfect shade of oyster-pink, will, at long last, restore the poor dejected dressing-table to its former glory. Which my mummy calls much more Appropriate.

Before the mirror we now stand, Nanny and I, a ludicrous coupling: she, panting and decapitated by the frame; I, stuck in front of her, and, although up on tip-toe, deprived of a visible body, like a head-and-shoulders putto by Murillo fluttering about the aura of some obscure Virgin. But with greater spirit than grace, Nanny now sets to work on the final phase of my grooming: taking a small white brush in her left hand and, in her other, a bee-embossed bottle of eau de cologne, which she nearly drops, she pours a torrent of lemony liquid onto my scalp, narrowly missing my eyes; then, noisily, she puts the bottle back down, and stoppers it. Gripping the brush while ruffling my dark hair with her unencumbered hand, she suddenly takes off, still Winchester Cathedralling, but much faster now: down, down, down and across, she brushes, then over, hard; and she delivers one last stroke to the back of my head, which, after biting into my nape, stumbles onto my collar. Which means that I'm ready. The time has come.

As on every afternoon except Sunday, when the servants are given their day off and I must go to Church and stay awake, Nanny and I rush out of my room and scurry along a landing which, in my memory, will forever be suffused with the immoderate scent of the tuberose. We run past my parents' rooms and, once beyond, Nanny hurries me down the top flight of stairs, which I tackle by grabbing the banisters one at a time—climbing them is easier, for some reason, and I can manage without props. And assuming, which generally we can, that I haven't skidded, or tumbled onto a polished board, or tripped on the end of a brass rod, soon we arrive at the landing below, on the first floor, which (unless there are luncheon guests—in which case, this is where we halt, outside the double doors to the drawing room) we go round, and down to the level of the ground, to the lily-pond courtyard and quickly past the front door, which is often left ajar to encourage a breeze, and along the shaded edge of the entrance, under the palm tree where once a blood-red macaw which had escaped from the municipal gardens trailing the chain of its captivity to the skies became entangled and was shot, until we reach the musty room which my father calls his study, where he likes to smoke his (medium-sized) cigars. This, too, is where he and my mother choose to sit after lunch, to drink the tiniest cup of coffee—Black for me, my dear; no, no sugar, thank you, is what he says, always; or, if she is tired, camomile tea for my mother—a preferred, if less proper, prelude to her siesta, which is later and longer than mine. And at the study we stop. Nanny has suddenly vanished, and I, gripped to the post and blinded by the light that comes crashing through the french windows, am grimacing rather than smiling, and alone. There he is, my parents proclaim in weary unison.

But when I recall this tableau, it seems at once to reel me back to an earlier occasion. I must be in my second year and fresh to the trauma of walking. Same room, same cast, same time, same time of year. As if jolted from some nocturnal terror, I find myself struggling from my father's flannel knee, scrambling as if for my life, appalled by his smooth, veined hand, which holds me round the ribcage as he laughs, a little nervously. I see his great fingernails curled monstrously about me and I'm fighting with all the passion I can summon to divorce myself from his grasp, from his ghastly contact, until, finally, after a suicidal leap, I'm down on the rug and, though paralysed in mid-intake of breath, raising myself to my bare feet; and after a suffocating eternity, as if I'd been held below water for perilously long but in the end let go, my long-awaited howl breaks out, a howl of such outrage as, since, I have only heard rise from the hearts of our beautiful expiring men; and I am rocking, bent double, swaying on the spot with such rhythmic violence as, since, I have only seen madmen sway; and I'm holding my arms up, though they rise no higher than the suede arm of my father's chair; and then I fall; and no amount of sugar-crystals will appease me; and then, through the tears that course from my nose, I see my mother rise with a long regretful sigh from her brocaded chaise, and I watch her pale slippers move gracefully to the door, and as I turn my neck towards her heartbreaking head, I see her lacquered nail press the bell by the lightswitch once, twice, and a third time; and, in no time at all, my nurse, the nurse that I lost, my Mam'zelle, appears; and after a quick exchange of busy mumbles I am raised like a runt saved from drowning, and taken in those strong womanly arms out of the room, back upstairs, disgraced but released.

To the nursery. Mam'zelle doesn't talk: she holds me on the nursing chair, hot and close to her large, low breast; and when I look up, I see her looking out into an impossible distance, and then, from the far corner of her upturned eye, like a sacred answer to a despairing prayer, one slow, heavy tear bursts forth and demurs, then slides down and down her beloved face to my mouth. And then I fall asleep.

I AWAKE TO THE EARLY evening light, swaying, floating in space. Mam'zelle, still silent, is smiling down. She kisses my brow and rises, like a goddess from the seas, my limp body ever in her arms, and paces proudly about the nursery, which is shaped like a horseshoe, with barred gable windows at the extremities, and suffused with shafts of dust; and she parades me about as if I were a princeling, bears me aloft before my vassals, my entertainers, my playthings; and I, restored, revived, as if after a mutinous battle, survey the exotic wasteland of toys in this barren kingdom of mine.

Now that it no longer exists, and that I've grown to appreciate the distinction between fantasy and falsehood, I view the nursery which my mother conceived as a victory of good taste over good will: consciously arranged in that Anglophilic, puritanical fashion which we associate with English suburban life between the wars (a punishing decorative manner which corresponds more precisely to the period of my mother's own infancy than to mine), this arid paradise, which demanded the use of electric light at all times, must, then, have struck the innocent observer as a reflection of the domestic propriety which underpinned my parents' style of life. I do not recall ever having seen this room in the state of jagged disarray which customarily denotes a child at play: I recollect it as a place of stasis. My memory even tricks me to picture it in sepia, as a meticulously appointed, sparse but discerningly styled variation on a softly focused photograph, carefully excised from some half-forgotten *Country Life,* already dated yet emblematic of young discipline *chez les hauts-bourgeois.* I happen not to be left-handed (let's leave left-footery for later) but I was born to that last high wave of well-intentioned people who considered it their duty to knock this sinistral aberrance, along with thumb-sucking and bed-wetting, out of the systems of their testing, if adorable, progeny.

All around me then, and round the corners of the horseshoe, lie poised, as one might expect exhibits in a museum of toys to lie, such specimens as my begetters, and legion other begetters of their generation and class, felt best fomented the wholesome (gender) development of their suggestible—dare one suggest malleable—offspring.

Thus, at the entrance to the nursery and to the left, on the floor, we see a miniature railway, already antique and embellished with tiny telegraph poles and sponges of shrubbery and station-masters and diminutive flags, which, on account of the monotonous circularity of the track and the engine's irritating chug, I don't think that I ever once, of my own volition, cared to activate. But I daresay that, on occasion, I may have been instructed so to do, probably as a courtesy to whichever of my parents' (male) minions happened to amuse himself some overcast autumnal afternoon assembling the contraption, or possibly for the sake of guests. For I do distinctly envisage myself, at various intervals in this early phase of my life, sitting sullen and cross-legged at the centre of the action, feigning rapt fascination for the benefit of those adults—cooing, upstanding ladies, ruby talons on short-skirted knees; and closer still, their crouching husbands, knees swung apart—but fancying myself, the while, some Arabian mountain, or Apache chieftain, or lumpen great Buddha, mildly riled by the hypnotic locomotion of this mechanized, wingless, overgrown fly.

Further along the flank of whitewashed wall, and neatly fitted into the first corner of the room, directly beneath a large framed engraving of a pond under a prison that is called my father's Alma Martyr, sits, again on the floor, a downscaled model of a garage, some two feet wide by three feet long by, let us say, twelve inches high—crafted of balsa wood, with a vaulted roof, and painted charcoal. In front of this building, someone has parked a whole gleaming fleet of primary-coloured Dinky toys, along with a mystifying contraption, a Noddy car, and a bulbous black one, a Cab; then there's a Red Cross ambulance, and an army lorry in camouflage, and, oddest of all, a crimson double-decker bus. I've had it explained to me, though I cannot think whom by—the family chauffeur? some clever-dick cousin who's occasionally foisted on me? I certainly don't think of my father as a visitor to my recreational quarters; still—it has been explained to me that the object of this garage-versus-vehicle exercise is to drive all four-wheelers into the depot and park them, not prang them, then drive them all out again and reposition them, perhaps in a new line.

Well, I can't speak for grown-ups or cousins or anyone very much, but nor can I see the point in crawling around on splintery planks of floor, so the game which I've devised for myself is this: leave all the cars exactly where they are (perhaps move the ambulance as a mitigating formality); then, with extreme care, crawl into the garage and curl up, like a snail into its shell, as tightly as you possibly can, knees hitched to your chin because the space can hardly accommodate you but feet sticking out is cheating; and remember to keep your head twisted to the right, turned into the room, so that once you're installed in your new habitat, you can gaze through the midget windows and imagine the world as a snail might, or an ant. In reality, however, with my overscaled face squashed and steaming against the panes of celluloid, I must more closely resemble the monstrous tabby in the *Tailor of Gloucester* at that ghastly moment when he glares into the workshop to menace the embroidering mice; for, on the occasions when, to my mortification, I've been caught in the throes of this covert ritual, the expression which has instantly attached itself to Nanny's face has been one of sudden frozen gaping horror, revulsion almost, which, following the arching of an eyebrow, has gradually settled into a look of relieved perplexity.

AGAINST THE FIRST of the two nursery windows, too low for me to be able to install myself and simultaneously watch the shaking, angry heads of the tallest trees outside, though I can sometimes hear them, languishes a dark, old desk for a child, which, to judge by the deep compass-graffito on the side nearest to my elasticated belt with a snake-clasp, was once the property of my maternal grandfather, who died in the year of my birth and everyone says I look like. This is incredible to me, for I have seen his picture peering down from the top of the tall-boy in my mother's dressing room, where she wears her petticoat, and he is old with shiny hair and a wonky bow with spots, none of which I've ever been or had, and very dark eyes, which I do, I suppose. But anyway: Juan Zamora Gonzaga, the inscription on the desk goes (I'm told), and then continues: Santa Cruz 1906, which is long ago and how I know that this desk belonged to him one time.

But the whole artefact seems a mystery to me, for the seat is attached to the writing part by means of parallel metal bars, rather like train tracks, which run along the uneven wooden floor and make the whole thing wobble. Where you sit is too far back from the writing part for you ever to get comfortable, and, even if you slouch forward (the way that you're not supposed to at lunch), the lid slopes so hard that you must hold your book, or block, or the leaves which you might want to press with blotting paper, down, or rather up, otherwise everything will slide and slip and tumble to the ground. And the white porcelain ink-well is all very fine, as is the rusty dip-pen, which you're not allowed to touch, not ever, because it's sharp and you could spike yourself blind; but as I'm only just beginning now to write my first name, which is long, in pencil not in pen, I can only surmise that this strange departed grandfather of mine, when he was young, must have been very clever, very fat, and very bored.

Deeper down the nursery hangs a pair of ornamental shelves, white as the dressing-table, and set too high for me. But I can see that the upstairs level carries a collection of lead soldiers in fancy Waterloo dress belonging to my father, who is confident that I shall learn to enjoy them once I'm sent to England to his school or Alma Martyr where he was once Head Boy, although it seems to me that, well, by then, if I am bigger, surely these small soldiers will have grown too small; I do not know. But the lower of the shelves holds a pageant of pieces in wood of black and red for a game that is slow and Mam'zelle calls *échecs* and my father calls chess but my mummy, who knows best, says that here, which is Spain, it is called *ajedrez*. And she promises to teach me very soon how it goes, as already I can almost play a thing called draughts, which is a start, and I keep the board, which is also Appropriate for this chess, in the desk of my grandfather who died.

In the middle of the horseshoe attic, behind the nursing chair and facing a sprawling sofa of loose-covered cretonne, ablossom with verdigris hydrangeas, stands the bookcase: tall as a temple, important, its lower half perpetually locked, the section above encased by doors of harlequin glass. Reaching the contents is a perilous enterprise, for it entails dragging a chair up to the bookcase and kneeling on its seat, and then, drawing myself, despite its rickety legs, up to my full height, in order to open the outer of the two doors, taking care not to let anything fly back and topple me before I can pluck out a book, maximum two, which I tuck under one arm while, with the other, I slowly close the case, until at last, like a one-armed mountaineer, I climb down, backwards, to the swaying floor and, once returned to terra firma, I run over to the sofa, hurl myself onto the hydrangeas and position myself to start. And inserting the chilly spine of some chosen book between my thighs, I part the covers and explore the pictures and the colours, not the words.

WHEN I RETURN to that earliest indigestible reading matter, I am filled with a sense of no wonder. Savour the cream of my first library: a small accordion of Beatrix Potter books with pastel yarns of dolled-up persecution; upper-case tales from the Holy Bible, with muted pictures of a basketed baby posted downstream in a nappy, and of a denuded old man being hurled to the lions, and of a bearded head swimming in a lagoon of aubergine blood on a silver platter; the illustrated lives of the Saints, blinded but smiling, or ravaged by leprosy, or aflame with stigmata, or bucked to the ground in the night, or traversed by quivering arrows of gold, or immobilized into eternity by rusty ropes and rusty chains, or simply stoned to death; a synopsis of *A Midsummer Night's Dream,* in Spanish, with its appurtenant visual freak-show; enough crusty volumes of Dickens to fill the whole toy garage, one monochrome sketch to every fistful of unreadable pages; the adventures of William, Just William—or was it Poile de Carotte?—whose freckled face resembles a saffron-spattered tambourine; a Tintin book—extraordinarily, for cartoons were normally taboo, and in French (so presumably a smuggled present from Mam'zelle)—in which our intrepid young Belgian, bizarrely attired in a kilt, is accosted by a grunting great gorilla, object of my first remembered erection at five years of age; an *ABC of Names* (X is for Xavier); an *ABC of Musical Instruments* (X is for Xylophone); an *ABC of Ancient Cities* (X is for Xanthus, or sometimes Xanadú); an *ABC of Rivers* (X is for Xingú); an *ABC of Anatomy* (X is for Xiphisternum); an *ABC of Minerals* (X is for Xenocryst); an *ABC of Plants* (X is for Xerophyte); mercifully summarized biographies of Thérèse of Lisieux and Teresa of Avila and Joan of Lorraine and Bernadette of Lourdes and Francis of Assisi and John of the Cross and Jesus of Nazareth. Spoilt for choice.

But my real choice propels me away from the books and the saints and the cars and the train and, rather, round to the far, forbidden end of the horseshoe nursery, which lies virtually concealed from view and briefly basks in the dusty, roseate warmth of the late-afternoon light—that remotest region of my kingdom which I shall never legitimately conquer, that most delicate wing of the toy museum which, as if set apart by an invisible cordon, I can never honourably visit, only trespass upon. My mother's former province. My future sister's province. Not mine.

It seems strange to me now that the fondest fragments of my earliest remembrance should simultaneously suggest themselves as the stillest, stealthiest, saddest you could say. For on the rare occasions when I do, despite the risks of rebuke and ridicule, dare to venture over that unseen but hotly felt boundary line into the outlawed section of the nursery, which draws me like a shaming fetish to its bosom, my spirits lurk at half mast, the tide of my restraint has dropped treacherously low. I seem always to be wearing my tartan velvet slippers, and a creamy Viyella dressing-gown which skirts to the ground, and I'm generally convalescing from some demoralizing ailment: measles, or mumps, or chicken pox, or croup, or newly excised tonsils, or (rare this) infant haemorrhoids, or (rarer still) the myxomatotic bloating of an eye, occasioned by a well-aimed hornet's sting.

I find myself confined, as for days past, to the nursery, consigned to my own devices. And almost involuntarily, as if directed by a trance, I seem suddenly to have turned that beckoning corner and entered the sanctum, to have disappeared from the world, and I am moving with consummate care about the tabernacle of my mother's childhood treasures, avoiding certain critical floorboards yet scarcely raising my feet from the hallowed ground, as if floating, or walking on waves. I come to rest before a colossal rocking-unicorn, a former incumbent, I imagine, of some fairground carousel, for I can see the tonsure at its neck through which a lance of brass would once have been driven, and I look at its painted lashes and astonished eyes, and then I hitch up a knee and insert my slipper in a gilded stirrup and strain to lift myself, and swivel slightly as I mount, and at last I lower myself, softly, sideways, onto the animal's buttoned-velvet saddle, which is profoundly pink—upholstered, as it once was, for my young mother's pleasure. Poised like a Highness set for uncharted lands, my excellent robe tumbling over the muscular flank of my valiant borrowed stallion, I stroke its flaming, windswept, wooden mane, and its spiralling silver horn, and the braid of its bridle, and its inhaling cheek and neck and gently pulsing shoulder and I've begun to sway forward, am moving, moving with elegant gathering speed, galloping toward the high realm through the window, beyond the bars, heading for the distant palms, and the mossy roofs, and the violet hills and, further still, the glittering colour-less sea, and the descending sky-without-a-cloud, and on and on until evening begins to fall and the first halo of a moon smokes into view, but my horse must not grow weary; he must rest; we must wait; so I slide off and drift over to a low platform like an altar, on which stands my mother's doll's-house, built for her in honour of her First Holy Communion, with visible, lasting devotion, by a former family carpen-ter, Cook's father, in fact.

THE DOLL'S-HOUSE: behold it, marvel: three paces wide and three storeys high, white-white and august it stands, with a pink-gravelled entrance and crescent-shaped benches like the ones that we have in the garden outside, and a front colonnade with a diadem pediment, shaped like a Russian crown whose central wreath of ivy-leaves looks out, like the eye of God, from the face of my mother's first house. And look, there are marbled lateral terraces, and a tradesman's entrance discreetly to the back, and a miniature topiary, and a kitchen garden with a per-gola of tiny lilies-of-the-valley, like dots; and still, a generation on, that old carpenter's surviving gift of love presides intact, grand as an embassy, bright as a bride. And if you walk your fingers round the cir-cular drive and step them up, one at a time, as if they had alighted from a long, long-touring motorcar, smartly but exhausted, up the steps to the front, and if you help them to push the front door ajar, it will not creak, and you will see, though you should not climb, the principal staircase, which is shaped like a lyre, and if you listen hard, you may just hear the forgotten tinkles of the ear-ring chandelier, and all but inhale the smoke of the birthday candles that lit it once, and you will know, without a doubt, that magic has happened in this great, miniature house.

And next to it, in the ottoman of calico, is where my mother's dolls lie, have lain for twenty years: a wool-plaited Poupée which she made at her convent, with a circular mouth and appliquéd cheeks and limp long legs and plaits; and then there is Celia, who sometimes smiles and opens her eyes if you lift her head of china, and never worries if you hold her, and is patient. And she has many dresses, Celia does have, made for her, an age ago, by my mummy's mummy in the days when everyone was young. Of course, the red gingham one with matching bloomers and white smocking is the one that she prefers, and is my favourite also, and my mummy when she was a girl who liked to play with Celia had a dress the same exact, and my father keeps a picture on his desk and, though the photograph is dark, you can see Celia being cradled by my small mummy, and they're identically dressed, the two of them, smiling out from the past. And Celia's other clothes, which are also hidden in the ottoman, are many: see: a tartan Viyella one; an organdie party dress with a sash; a velvet coat with a matching winter bonnet; her First Holy Communion gown, with gloves and veil and tiny missal; and every time that Celia had a dress, my mummy, who was little then (but not so little as Celia) did also have one.

When I'm in the nursery for a length of time, I sometimes go to visit the ottoman which is a best place to play. I lift the lid and take Celia by the arms and pick her up and hold her while I close the lid back down, and I sit upon the ottoman and talk to her, and I change her clothes if she asks. But always I must not forget to put her back in the red gingham dress with matching bloomers because no one is allowed to know that Celia is my friend, apart, that is, from Mam'zelle, who went away, for once upon a time while I was giving Celia one pretendy-bath on the hydrangeas, Nanny, who came after my Mam'zelle, crept up without making her noise and saw us both and laughed, and how she did laugh, and then, in a sudden whispering fury that made her face go white, No No she said, and then there was a noise that burnt the back of her hand across my face and made me cry, and she threw Celia harshly to the ottoman and Celia also cried. I remember. But it was never so with Mam'zelle, who did like Celia, and said that she could be my friend, but friend in secret, don't forget, for grown-ups do not always understand these things of friendship, which I do not think they always do—understand.

AND ALSO MAM'ZELLE did say that she would help me soon to send a note to Papá Noel, which she, my Secritty, would write but I shall be in charge and I'm allowed to sign with my own thumb in purple; and what I wish to say is this to him: that this year, when he comes, what I would like, and Please, is not more books or cars or engine-trains with which the nursery is replete, but: a turquoise trampoline to help me leap and summersault like a blue dolphin from the Cape of Good Hope to some very farawayness; and a retinue of sea-green seahorses, and terrapins with flaming cheeks, to escort me through the night on my voyage to the honey-coloured coastline of Hawaii, perhaps; and an iridescent sherbet-lemon hoolahoop to dance around my waist as I circulate along the lilac beach when I arrive; and a garland of hibiscuses to blossom round my neck for when I meet the wide-eyed faces of the ladies of that land; and a rainbow-speckled ray-fish with wings wider than a carpet, on which to sit like an Aladdin and escape if the ladies are not friendly, or the men; but if they are, which my Mam'zelle is sure they very are, then I shall need a dressing-up box with a shirt of tiger-lilies to protect me from the sun which in Hawaii is Huge; and a loincloth of Sicilian leopard with a tail down to the sand, and a waist-length wig of mermaid-hair for my Mam'zelle, who says you never know, she may yet come, and a skirt of finest grass, which I believe she will be needing if she does; and I would like a picnic-hamper with a checkered cloth in black and white to lay politely upon the ground and teach them, using gold and silver coins of chocolate, which nobody is allowed to eat, how to play draughts, and I hope that in exchange the ladies of Hawaii might teach me how to pluck and strum their caramel guitar, and teach Mam'zelle to do their dance; and in the hamper I do think that we should have a never-ending set of saucers and of cups, and a pot, shaped like a dragon, to spout refreshing tea (they should have sugar in Hawaii), and teaspoons, don't forget; and a coffer full of treasures from the bottom of the sea (pearl and coral beads and half-eternity rings and candy-striped enamel eggs on jade and amber stands and tortoiseshell, like the treasures for my sister) with which to buy, and bring, when Mam'zelle and I come back eventually to our island, a young orang-u-tang to play with me when I get bored at home, and a magician's cape and a top hat, and glasses for the sun, and one cigarette (a trick one), and a ball of bubbly gum—but Mam'zelle says that she's afraid that, even in Hawaii, bubbly gum is not allowed and anyway, she thinks that I've already asked for far too much, it's high time for my bath.

WHEN I THINK of my first nurse, even now, all this time later, a strange soft weakness wells within me, a stillness, a pang which almost comforts me. I think of her rescuing me from my father's study, and parading me about the old nursery; I think of her awaking me in the morning, fresh and strong and ready to do battle all day long on my behalf; I think of her dear face, astonished each and every time that I pick lowly flowers from the kitchen garden for her delight; but above all, even today, when I think of her, I think of her when I take a bath.

My Mam'zelle is full of grace, blessed among women as she leans at the edge of my eau-de-nile porcelain. I stand beside her on the sunny mosaic floor, my ankles kissing, purely naked, while she ties the ribbons of her apron. And once the waves have been stilled, she takes me into her warm wet hands and raises me reverently and with love towards the heavens, as if I were an innocent being returned to celestial flight; and she holds me above her open, upturned face for an instant, frozen in time, like a host, like a chalice, then lowers me in slowest gentlest motion through the mystical steam, through my personal cloud, down into the uterine waters of my scented bath. My Mam'zelle.

While she soaps my ribs and panting chest with a sponge of softest ocean-plant, she holds my nape, which tends to loll, in the cradle of her other arm. I raise a leg into the scented mist of evaporating bath-salts and gaze at the receding motions of the tropical fish that swim about her apron. The blossoming sponge dips between the cleavages of my toes, strokes the rigid arch of my foot, which slithers on the palm of her hand; and then, I feel the sponge lather my calf and slide to the back of my knee and roll onto my kneecap and float up, like a whisper, up my left thigh. I close my eyes. I breathe through my mouth. I arc my back. Through the song of the cicadas and the retiring tropical birds and the occasional sound of a passing gull, I hear Mam'zelle, as she assumes my other leg, suggest, then glide into our regular chant, last year's winner of the Eurovision, which, through the slow velvet monotone of her rendition, I have come to learn and learnt to love:

Un premier amour (she begins), *premier amour, premier amour,*
Ne s'oublie jamais, s'oublie jamais, s'oublie jamais,
Un premier amour, on le cherche toujours dans
D'autres amours; toute sa vie on court après.
Il nous a troublé, et fait rêver, et fait trembler,
Ce premier amour, premier amour, premier amour;

Mais, l'enfant qu'on est, l'enfant qu'on est resté,
Frémira toujours au souvenir de cet amour.

The sponge swims around my front, circles my navel like a wreath, then dies, sinking very slowly to the bloom between my thighs, separates my legs, navigates the gulf, charms the crevice of my buttocks up from the bed of the bath and reaches, as I straddle her forearm, the hollow of my back. And then she turns me. My chin now rests on the ledge of her elbow, as if I were a fish that couldn't swim, though my feet are beginning to paddle and froth about, and I feel the sponge on my back, on my neck, around the secrets of my underarms. And Mam'zelle, who has sailed to the brink of her verse, now pauses and waits for me to take over, and my reply flies out, cuts into the air like an injured swordfish, glittering and shrill and far too fast and stupid and doomed:

Et toi, et toi qui j'aimais, Qu'as-tu fait de toi? Qu'as-tu fait sans moi?
Et moi, moi qui t'ai perdu, Qu'as-tu fait de plus? Qu'ai-je fait de tant
   de bonheur?

I'm back on the fringed bath-mat and about to start to shiver, but Mam'zelle wraps me in an enormous peppermint towel, which cowls about my shoulders and trails about my feet, and she hugs me to her kneeling warmth and dries me with the vigour of her arms. She withdraws the towel, as if to inspect me one last time, and peppers my person with talcum, front and back; and then she enfolds me once more, pausing only to blow a few random specks of powder from my fat cheeks. Rising, she guides me into the sleeves of my nightshirt, white, and combs my hair, and helps me brush my teeth; but realizing that she's forgotten my slippers, she lifts me to dangle about her; and as we leave the bathroom and set off to the bedroom where she will kiss my brow and lay me down, I hear the heavy sound of soap falling into the frantic escaping water with a great splash.

THEN THERE ARE SMALLER SPLASHES, choppier, harsher, stuck in the faded Kodacolour album of my childhood scraps: I must be four, certainly no more, because I'm wearing the primrose towelling swimming-trunks that I wore on the day that Kennedy died and everyone went home looking glum—the trunks with that impossible metal clasp which I can never undo alone and is a source of agony to me if I need to go to the Lav; the belt-clasp which, a magnet to the sun, scorches my tummy every time that I bend down for seashells in the sand. But I'm not at the beach villa now; no, I can see myself from high above, as if from our town house at the top of the cliff, a seagull's view. My head is a dot like an aspirin far below, blinding-white in the noonday sun, white and almost wider than my shoulders, and crowned, I realize as I zoom down, with my sailor-hat—ghastly: the elastic cuts into my chin, and the brim just won't stay down. Endless tantrums.

I'm at the Nautical Club, where Nanny and I have been driven and, from eleven until one, deposited for my one-to-one beginner's swimming class, which lasts half an hour. This will be our weekday routine for the whole of the month. And what month might that be, dear? June is the month. June did you say, dear? Are we quite sure about that? Don't mumble now. (I'm Positive.) This Nanny thinks that she's so funny, always trying to catch you out, but my last Nanny, Mam'zelle, who was much more *gentille,* which means nicer in another country, and smelt of oranges not lavender, and did not wear white gloves and had no Exima, taught me all of the months, in English and in French as well as Spanish, which I have not forgotten, though I miss my Mam'zelle when the time comes for my bath. And do you know how *this* Nanny says Junio, which is June in Spanish? Like so, with her mouth all wrinkled up: Joo-Knee-Oh. *Joo-Knee-Oh! Imaginez-toi!* And just because I don't repeat the months out loud to her a lot, this English Nanny thinks that I'm a bit not very clever, which I am Not not. I shall show you: I shall tell you how I know that June, which is now, is June: because May comes before June and now cannot be May because my birth-*anniversaire* does always fall in May, near to its end, which was too long ago; and now is not July, which comes straight after June, because in July (but Nanny doesn't know because she hasn't been my Nanny long enough), in July is when our chauffeur Pepe throws his cap into the air, which Mummy says is naughty, and then goes off into his Hols, and so do we. We all jump into our motorcar, my mummy and daddy and nanny and me, or I; and our motorcar is long, long as a bus but black, and white on the inside but not in the boot which is dark and scary with a light that comes on when you open it up.

But in July the boot is not scary one bit, for it is chock-oh-block of suitcases and a big round box with stripes of pink and white, which is where my mummy hides her summer hats; and also in the boot is where we put my net for catching butterflies, and my kite of lilac, which on my own I cannot fly, but Daddy helped me once when the kite flew up and up and far-far away and too high from the beach because of the wind and the clouds, or so my daddy said, and then it dropped down, and still more down, and it fell to the waves and very nearly drowned; it did; and also in the boot we put another net, the one with smaller holes for fishes, which I do not like to catch as they are wet. And anyway in June, I mean July, the car that is our motorcar is also huge and high with trunks which get strapped to the roof: *two* huge trunks which Mummy hugely packs with the help of Mam'zelle (but this year it is Nanny) and Mummy says that I'm allowed to help as well if I do learn to swim before July without my yellow rubber ring or armbands at the club (but not to dive), which I very want to do because in July, in *July* is when we get into the car and drive past the cathedral and out of the city and up to the forest and over the mountains and stop for a minute so I can do weewees and put on a pully, then round the volcano which often is snowing and down to the town where we park to have lunch that is always in fiesta and then we go on past banana plantations with baby bananas and fields of tomatoes that belong to my aunts and, further along, we turn left onto a track that goes bumpitty bump and is not straight at all but now that I'm bigger I never get sick and we sing "Frère Jacques" until I go wrong which is sometimes quite early but we all have such . . . *fun;* then we cross a small bridge with plants that are cactuses over a ditch that floods in the winter and sends all the lizards all dead to the sea but not in July which is when we go down at the end of the day to the house in the south which is christened La Villa and my grandfather built for his wife my abuela before he was dead, but she died as well so it's Mummy's house now though Daddy's invited and I am allowed and it's white with round windows like moons, though there isn't a garden or trees or a pool which we do have in town, but the Villa which sits overlooking the ocean you reach from the door at the back of the house, which is really the front, because there are steps made of wood that is blue and go down to the sand, which is sandy, and the sea, which in summer is warm, and the sky, which does shine all day long, but of course not at night when you look at the stars from your bed and then sleep with the sound of the waves in your dreams with the sound of the waves in your dreams.

NO DREAM. I'm back at the Nautical Club, that sprawling Deco gem which, designed to mimic a great liner, dominates the city's splendid maritime avenue and welcomes strangers from the seas. I am four or five. The sun is near to noon. I'm wearing my uncomfortable sailor hat. I've already given Nanny my small, square Omega (whose time, in truth, I can't yet tell). Nanny has zipped the watch into the inner pocket of her soft, pink-lined basket, a hand-me-down from my mother, and extracted her wing-tipped sunglasses, which she now applies, along with a gob of lotion, to her long nose. Humming out to the horizon she hands me my beach towel, which is vast and in one corner bears the tangled monogram of my initials, floating in ornamental symmetry within a life-saver's ring:

She deposits herself with a book and a sigh on a bench and waves me away, past the awnings along the terrace and the tennis courts of clay and the poolside bar and the boat-huts and still further, beyond the sheds for water-skis and the stand that sells ice-cream, to which I hope to return, and along the edge of the Olympic pool, which has diving planks to the sun, and round the salt-water one, all the way to the glinting square beneath the cliff, which is the pool for beginners. I turn and wave to Nanny, who could not see me. I think that her specs are too dark.

I am sitting on my towel, perched like a question mark at the shallow end of the pool, the paddling end, where there are no steps and my coach, who's just finishing with some other boy, older than I, has exhorted me, with the vigorous use of his stiff forefinger, to wait, *esperar*. I can see my grey feet, distorted, dangling like jellyfish in the water, netted by my detestable transparent plastic sandals.

The other boy is being hoisted like a jubilant monkey, knees swinging in the air, onto the pool's far pumice shore. Beneath his dark glossy waist, where his wet trunks have fractionally dropped, a line of pallor flashes across his upper buttocks. His flat, unbladed back is turned to me as he wipes his eyes; and his thick dark hair now rises in spikes, like a black sun, or a sunflower by night. His mother (I presume—because she's not wearing a uniform) threads his head through the eyelet of a towelling poncho, flattens the rebel hair with her palm, kisses the wet crown of her small victor and leads him away, and both are smiling and thanking and gone.

The swimming coach now turns, his hand still waving, round towards me. He wades slowly in my direction, vastly, like Poseidon rising from the waves. His opalescent teeth emerge through his dark beard, flashing as he speaks to me; but I can hear nothing. I see his tongue dart across his lips. My innards are thumping at me. I drop my face into the shadow of my lap and remove my hat, and fumble about, and push the hat into the wrinkled folds of the towel beneath me; and then I look out. His shoulders are wider than the very pool now; his strides are monstrous. The water froths about his hairy thighs, teases at his indigo trunks as he comes towards me, hands outstretched, water falling like great wings from his colossal arms. I think of my mother momentarily; then his fingers are upon me, freezing the breath out of me; but he is kneeling at my feet.

We begin gently, like dear friends, or lovers. As he lowers me gradually into the font of my induction, I clamp my puny frame to his gleaming shield of a chest; I cling to his power like a blind orphan limpet. I panic. I dig my fingers into the muscles round his neck. He says that everything's all right and tells me to relax, to calm down, which I can't, and he orders me to let go, commands me, and again he commands, and then, it happens: he just wrenches me up and throws me like a sponge to the clouds, up and up and I am spinning and my legs are thrashing and my mouth, though agape and howling, is soundless; I must be dying; and then I come crashing down on the volcanic edge of the pool, splat, and my head is thrown back into the water, splash, and the sky is suddenly below me, then vanishes in an explosion of loud, deep bubbles; but my foot, I realize as I swallow and choke and splutter below the world, is still stuck, ripping, to the border of stone. I must be dead, or divided. And then he fishes me out, and he is laughing, laughing; but at last I find my voice and it is murderous and rages out, shouting: Don't push me! Don't push me! Don't! *Nanny!* Tell him to *stop*! *Nanny!* But she is nowhere about.

When, in the fullness of time, my nanny does materialize, it is with a mien of genteel weariness, as if she'd been caught in the sun carelessly long without a hat. She bundles me into my towel without a murmur, and raises her dark-spectacled visage to the heavens as if for sustenance. She wrinkles her desiccated features into a prettily puckered grimace of distaste and lugs me under one arm—my mother's old basket swinging about the other—through the bronzed, brow-raising multitude, up the reverberating white steps of iron to the cocktail terrace, past the archipelago of clubhouse stalwarts, through the hollow vestibule, and fast across the cloakroom as I bawl and bawl without further care or restraint. But discovering, as she reaches the high front portico of the club, that our driver has not yet arrived, she nods, commendably unflustered, to the doorman, who nods to a lingering taxi, whose driver opens a door for her to step inside as she issues instructions in atrocious Spanish and, simultaneously, dumps me on the sweaty beige leatherette beside her. And as I drop and slump against the open, full-to-bursting ashtray, my head collapses like the head of my mother's forgotten rag-doll, and I see the blood from my ankle leak and blossom through the paleness of my towel like a dark flower of foreboding.

(The event above, I was later to learn, did in fact occur during the month of June, and not July; for our family's summer vacation that year was, exceptionally, relegated to August on account of three factors: one, a miscarriage suffered by my mother in the sixth month of her second pregnancy; two, the quiet posthumous baptism of the baby girl, named Constancia after my mother's own dead mother; and three, ensuing gynaecological complications for the patient, who underwent an expedient, if, as it transpired, unnecessary hysterectomy in her thirty-third year—my age now.)

MY NAME IS Santiago Moore Zamora, but my mummy, who is Spanish, calls me Iago when she likes. My father is English. I am six years old. Today is my birthday. I was born on 28th May, the feast of Corpus Christi. And today, though not a holy holiday, is the last such day that I shall spend at the house of my birth: future ones will pass at boarding school abroad and, I suppose, beyond. But now I'm sitting in the breakfast room for the first time. My mummy has her breakfast later, poised high on her high bed, with a posy on her tray. My father has gone to his office long ago. Still, Nanny is here, and Cook's about, and the sun is shiny, and the sprinklers are chugging on the grass. Happy Birthday to me.

Ever since I was a little boy, my birthday chair has always been a special one, decked and adorned with flowers and leaves like a throne; and today, though I am sitting on a proper grown-up chair known as a carver, today is no exception: for this, my latest (final) birthday throne is of a beauty full: its legs and arms and back are planted with palm leaves like spears or high fans, arranged for me by Cook, I think, or her husband who's called Gardener. And the back of the chair, which when undressed is heavily carved in wood, is today laced and over-laced with tendrils of ivy in many waxy greens; and on the seat, one upon the other, sits a pair of cushions that I have never seen before in a colour called vermilion and a cloth of damask silk, plumpy cushions with tassels like golden grapes at the corners, and fringing, and, at the soft centre, a garland, shaped like the heart of a lady, with African violets embroidered, and miniature daisies, and ivory strawberries, and occasional tufts of moss. And spread about the palm leaves of my birthday throne, are, like a painting or a dream, real roses of red, and dahlias, which are flowers of jollity, and sweet-peas in pale blue and pinky white, which do not really smell or last but my mummy calls divine, and yellow carnations, like sponges, where I rest my arms; and behind me, looking startled above my head, twin purple-and-orange strelitzias, which means, for they do resemble, birds of paradise.

This my anniversary tablecloth, which smells of soap or summer fruits, of something imprecise but strong, falls to the floor like a vestment, and appears, at the corners, to be pushed out by ghostly linen knees, paler than vanilla milk. And this cloth, though starched to fresh rigidity, is older, richer in birthdays than I; for every faultless stitch along the border of its broad and oscillating hem was rendered hollow, one by one and perfectly, by my mother in the afternoons of the days of the months when she sat, not thinking, garnering her trousseau.

My parents were married on Christmas Eve, two years before my birth, at the chapel of the convent which my mother attended; but it was not a grand affair, their wedding, for her father, my abuelo, is said to have contracted such a virulent exception to the match that the event was restricted to what Spaniards of a certain swagger term *petit comité*. And yet, despite the pursed discretion of the occasion, insular folklore relates that my mother, the loveliest ice-organza bride of her day, wept disconsolately, and without maids in attendance, throughout the religious ceremony; and further, that no sooner returned from the honeymoon, which conveyed the newlyweds to Palermo by night, thence to Portofino and on to Venice, where she first became homesick in her waterlogged hotel, and via the Vatican to Fommentor and Barcelona, then back, at last, to the embrace of their hesperidian isle, my mother dragged her melted, wilted wedding dress up the servants' stairs to the sewing room, where she instructed the sempstress to unpick each seam and stow away the diaphanous great skirts of her miserable matrimony: skirts which were, in due course, to be released from their paper tissue pupa and chrysalized into the gossamer wings of my first crib.

SIX YEARS ON, I'm trying to smooth down the hardened breakfast cloth, which threatens to engulf my legs in its folds as I survey the festive promontory on the long table before me. Nanny secures the corner of a napkin to my neck with a safety pin of gold, which pierces, then emerges from the Peter Pan collar of my primary-school pinafore. The napkin reaches down to my knees. My feet, buttoned into sandals, swing about as if I were perched on a branch of hope. I think I'm smiling at the array which, like a great necklace of jewelled stones, or islands, or planets, grows outwards from my sides and sweeps in a lavish curve as far as the opalescent glass comport, a legacy of my mother's unhappy honeymoon, which, these days, bears honeycombs of butter and crystal jars of syrup and plum-tomato jam and, like a neutral principality, divides Nanny's dull end of the table from mine.

Some of the presents before me are large, some not, but all, with one diminutive exception near the centre, look covetable, wrapped in brilliant sheets of tissue, and cellophane like stained glass, and decked in dancing patterns of dice and air-balloons and dominoes, and candy stripes and tangerine tartan, and frigates and sailors and pirates, and embellished with watery bands of moiré and ribbons of wired taffeta. Yet I cannot reach half these birthday fruits alone. Nanny's going to have to help me. Nanny? Please? She looks across and—First, she announces, we breakfast like grown-ups, birthday or no, *then* we can open our (our?) prizes, which she calls Gifts. I cannot think that I'm still smiling.

Nanny is spooning up her cornflakes and sipping, slurping really—Mam'zelle would have died—her cup of special particular tea which is posted to her from a London street called Pecadillo or Piccaninny or some such thing; and Nanny says it is a special street and very special tea indeed and grey, though, from where I sit, it looks like a perfectly normal tea to me, the colour of sweet consommé. And my mummy told me in a whisper once that no lady, or gentleman come to that, should even think of drinking El Grey tea before the proper time for scented tea which is at four in the afternoon and not at breakfast; but never, she said, mind.

So, breakfast. Mine unfolds in careful stages, like a play, and opens with the juice of three carrots, freshly uprooted from the kitchen garden, and scrubbed and peeled and shredded and pulped and liquefied by Cook, who's just made her entrance in the breakfast room. She winks in my direction and, swinging her huge, hilarious hips to the rhythms of a soundless folk *Isa,* which, for fear of puncturing Nanny's seemly English air, she dare not hum, much less whistle, which is what she does while washing up, she slow-waltzes her espadrilled way to my throne. Bowing with comical reverence over my left side, she strokes my back with her free hand and now drums it with her great fingers, as if mine were the back of a battered, but unbroken, old guitar—which nearly makes me burst out laughing; but Nanny, engrossed in the final shovellings of her cereal, doesn't catch us. With a theatrical swing of her other arm, Cook now presents me with my juice, in its usual Russian tea-glass, with its matching frosted saucer, on which, to one side, to the left as always, lie two bright carrot-leaves and the crescent of a lime. And I take the crescent between my middle-finger and thumb and, without squinting, without flinching, squeeze it over the mouth of the tall glass into the carrot juice, which is more intensely orange than the juice of any orange, or any blossoming sun. I stir my drink with a spindly silver spoon, and I remember Mam'zelle who went away. And then I raise the liquid to my lips, and drink it in one smooth motion, silent, my gullet open as that of a mute, resentful bird which, starved of sound, can only swallow its imaginary song. And as the empty glass lands back on its saucer, Cook returns to the room.

She moves more purposefully this time, bearing aloft, as befits a proud feat or trophy, and on a silver salver with three lions' claws which, far from clawing, seem tamely to paddle in the rippling morning light, my egg, medium-boiled, which I prefer, and pinkly-pied, and poised, as if in an open carriage, on its ivory cup, ivory with a tinily-engraved band like a fine belt for a young girl—the egg-cup which my abuela won when she was young and a girl at a tennis championship before the Nautical Club existed, before even my mummy and her dolls existed, at the (I can't make out the spidery inscription) in the days when they say that this volcanic, mid-Atlantic isle of ours was, truly, paradisal.

Cook shadows over me, interrupting my shoulder to remove the emptied glass; and after a couple of slow seconds have elapsed behind me, introduces, with a slight rattle, the next installment of my break-fast, the egg. I take up a small knife that is almost a butter one, with a mother of pearl handle but a serrated blade, and, forgetting briefly that the egg is but an egg, supposing instead that it's the head of someone not exactly far away, I deal it one good blow. The crown gapes open, creaks almost, and then, to my very glee, it plonks pathetically onto the plate below—plain white, a boring plate, really.

I pick up a small spoon of gold that does not tarnish or taste tangy, and start to investigate the veinless yolk which, even if unveined, I dread to pierce. When I was less than six, and took my meals in the alcove beside the kitchen where Cook does sometimes sneak to make her pastry, I was allowed to dunk a toasty soldier in the crater of my egg and dunking always did the trick in those straightforward days; but now that I have moved into the breakfast room for grown-ups, Nanny says that soldiers will no longer do, and I suspect that she is looking at me now, in wait, so I must act, and lance the yolk without a toast or soldier, lance it with my spoon, like so, and done it is; and out, after a spurt, the yellow smoothly oozes, threatening to overflow. Quick-quickly I dig the spoon into the jelly-white and excavate the lump to allow the liquid of the egg to curl into the scoop and form a pool and stop a more disgusting mess, which I have done, but only just, and just in time, and I am starting not to like this everyday boiled egg; but if I eat and eat without a breath or thought, soon breakfast will be done and over with. Nanny turns a wing of her newspaper and pretends to be behind it. But do not think that I am fooled: she could still catch me.

COOK IS BACK, thank God, and though my head is down and I am putting down my spoon, I'm looking at her hard, and harder still I pray that, though I haven't finished by a long chalk, she will pick up my egg and take away its ugliness and straighten out my birthday morning—which, yes, is what she mercifully does. Next: a prickly pear of amber-green complexion, which Cook, with Gardener's gloves, in case, has from our spiralled cactus tree pulled down; and she has snapped away the painful spikes and scrubbed, under a tap of brass, the fruit; and she has lain it on a wooden slab and taken up a kitchen knife and brought the knife down sharply, thus, and thus again, truncating both the ends, which are like elbows of a bogeyman; and she has sent the severed elbows in a wide arc like a rainbow through a shaft of morning light into the furthest of the noisy metal bins, which is reserved for dumping pods and bones and rinds and skins and apple-cores for the wild boars which she keeps captured in a dry reservoir near her home on a hill called the country. And though I have not ever met these boars, Cook has made their scary noise for me and laughed out loud, predicting that her Gardener soon will slaughter one in honour of his brother's bride-to-be when she becomes a bride which means a wedding belle. For boars, Cook says, and Gardener agrees, can be, when roasted out of doors, beasts of special succulence. And the prickly pear, also a thing of succulence, though not a beast, is, once plucked, soft and warm and regularly bumped, like the peel of the belly of an ostrich. And the belly of the pear before me is neatly cut from side to side. And I'm allowed to use my hands.

I tease at the gash, struggle with it till the pinkish innards of the cactus slide out of their sweating yellowing husk, and plop, exhausted and stillborn, onto the porcelain. But slicing is easy: the knife works mechanically, like a toy saw, through the skinless body, which falls away in neat wheels, collapsing to the side. The bony pips squirm, like mag-

gots, as I push the posthumous flesh into my face, which begins to
bloat; I cannot swallow; can scarcely breathe; am about to retch, when
Nanny lowers a corner of her newspaper and declares across: Eat up
now, slice at a time, no need to be greedy. I am munching like a cow;
can hear myself. I look down, then lift the napkin fast, and hurriedly
void the contents of my foul mouth into it, pretending to be calm, but
I think of Mam'zelle again, and return the lumpy cloth, crumpled and
warming, to the shame of my thigh. On my birthday.

I sink back into the floral throne, defeated, deflated, to think. I don't
know where to look. I look to the shadows. Nanny comes into gradual
focus as she forces her napkin into its ring and consults her watch and
clicks her specs and vanishes her paper away; and then I hear her loudly
proclaim, as if triumphantly, to the kingdom of my prizes, which is
lost: Oh dear, we have taken far too long, have we not, yes indeed, and
look, not even properly finished our especially delicious breakfast
which Cook took trouble to prepare; hardly what one would expect of
grown-up boys of six who've been allowed into the breakfast room for
the first time, is it? More like the behaviour of a silly baby, very silly
indeed because as a result we haven't left ourselves sufficient time to
open all these glorious-looking gifts, not if our Birthday Boy's to get to
school in time. Driver Pepe must be waiting by the car, doubtless wilting in this heat, poor man.

Everything, says Nanny, must be left untouched for later, lunchtime
at the earliest, when Mummy and Daddy are here, and they can decide.
I am dumbfounded, blank; but Nanny, like some darkening great
queen, now turns to leave the room and, as she strides towards the hall,
booms back: And you can get down from that ridiculous throne. Now.
And then, she's gone.

I HAVE TO MOVE FAST: dump the sodden napkin on the table cloth,
scramble over the embroidered cushions, crouch onto the table, crawl
in a meanderline towards the centre, stretch out and grab the tiny, most
ordinary-looking prize, which no one will notice has gone, and I stuff it
into the pocket of my school pinafore. And now, over the arm of the
carver I go, and back down to the floor; and next I'm sprinting over the
dark Persian flowers of the carpet, and across the parquet, and past my

distorted reflection on the samovar between the windows, and through the pair of lacquer screens that lead back to the hall, which smells of lilies, and sounds of a clock. Nanny is opening the front door. I snatch my satchel from the console and, for the first time that I recall, I race out into the light, down those long steps of stone.

I stop to look. Beyond the visor of my hand, I see, stationed by the flamboyants, which this year are late to blossom, my father's gleaming black motor, waiting to take me to school. As Pepe turns towards me, a yawn of cigarette smoke spins out of his shaded face, spirals beside him briefly, then dissolves into the morning. I reach the passenger door ahead of him, but cannot open it. He does it for me. I step into the creamy interior and, before I've managed to position myself properly, the door, with a padded thud, has closed. We set off without a word. He sucks the final breath out of his cigarette, then flicks it reeling through his open window to the blistered tarmac of the drive. He switches on the wireless. A foreign song from England, or perhaps America. I rummage in my pocket and extract the little package lifted from the breakfast table. It is wrapped in brown paper, and tightly strung, and stamped from a land that begins with a B, with the face of a king, and my heart is everywhere. I bite at the knot and wrench the string round a hard corner, and pull away the paper, and am filled without warning with the scent of oranges from the past. Within the paper folds, there sits a small, domed, purple leather box, and, inside the box, which is lined with purple velvet, a thwarted dream, look, from my departed Mam'zelle who went away but never did forget the thing I wanted most in all the world for this my sixth anniversaire, which once I did to her confess, and here it is: a grown-up ring, with a setting like a crown, and, in the crown, a huge, cut-glassy oval stone known as an Esmerald, which is greener than a thousand 7-Ups lined on a wall against the setting sun.

When I take the ring with care out of its cushioned bed and put it on the palm of my hand, it does not feel too heavy, which is good. And though, when I come to try it on, it flips right over because the golden hoop must be too large, I need not worry. This ring is so well-thought that you can squeeze the hoop and make it quite more small. Which I do. But my fingers still seem loose and slidy, until, at last, the esmerald from my Mam'zelle who went away glides onto the fore of my fingers, which is your index and never for pointing, and the ring is perfect, fit for a pontiff.

Pepe rounds a corner and I'm suddenly aware of loud squawks from the school yard, the screeches of many children in flight, and I find myself secretly longing for the quietness of my nursery, and for days gone by, and for the scented stillness of my vanished Mam'zelle. There is pain around my throat. There is damp around my eyes. We have stopped. The passenger door opens. I get out. Pepe has no cap and does not speak to me. I tell him, as I step onto the pavement, that today is my *anniversaire*. And Pepe peers far down until his stare meets my right hand. And That, he says, pointing hard, is a Sissy Ring; now get to class. I do not even bother to look back, for Pepe does not know a thing and he is smelly.

MY SCHOOL LOOKS over a square with a floor of Andalusian tiles, and a central fountain of china swans spouting watery rhymes to the sky. My school looks like a castle in a book from olden times, with pointy turrets of fish-scales, and tall granitty stairs, and railings painted in silver, and an everlasting palm tree at the front. And children are everywhere, huge and wild and flapping and screaming about. The bell has rung. I must go up, three flights, to the infant class. I clench my fist. But at least I can feel the heat of the ring in my hand.

This is how my class goes: twenty low desks in a circle with a high desk at the front, which belongs to our teacher, Don Jesús, who has a face with cheeks that flush, and a dark moustache. His suit is always of a stripy grey, and the tips of his collar are pinned down under his tie. His shoes are large and black with little holes, and his hands are fat and puffed, with many great hairs from the knuckles to the cuffs. He is not a priest, which often teachers are, for he does not wear a skirt of any kind. But what he does wear, in the pocket of his jacket, is a hankie, bright with flowers.

The day begins with a prayer, standing up. Then we sit down. The lesson is a drawing one and we must draw a happy house to fill with colour. And while we draw, Don Jesús returns our homework to us, one by one. My mind is in blank. Is it Spelling that he's handing back? But anyway, my turn won't come till near the end, because although my

English surname, Moore, falls near the middle of the Spanish alphabet, there are lots of B and C boys in this class, not really friends of mine. Yet by the time I hear myself called out, I feel the butterflies. I do not think they show, although my pinafore gets caught on a corner of the desk as I get up. The class is in hush. I hear traffic outside as I walk over the tiles to the teacher. I stand by his side. He smiles and always breathes too loud somehow. And I see him see my ring. He sees every-thing. He winks, and whisperingly asks about it. So I explain, not loud and looking down, that today is my birthday, and the ring, a present from my Mam'zelle who went away and calls my birthday my *anniver-saire*. And the butterflies do start to rise but I must not, not cry. Which I do not, for I am six now. And as I watch his pencil-hand hover over my words, which were correctly spelt—for it says B for *Bien* in red at the bottom of the page—I feel his other, big, warm hand moving down the back of my thigh, then up, and upper to my shorts, and down. And I say nothing. And although there is a sort of shame, it does feel nice. And then he gives me back my spelling-book and I return to my place and the rest of the morning melts away until, somewhere in the midst of chanted multiplications, the bell rings out, and I wake up, and Pepe must be back with the car. But I wait for the stampede to pass before I go down.

AT HOME ALL IS CHANGED, gone dark, grown cool. Shutters drawn against the midday sun. Beeswax and flowers. Gleaming floors. But in the breakfast room, look: presents all gone. Table: covered in trays that are covered with tea-cloths, damp. Sandwiches in shadow. Row upon dewy row; serried ranks of cheese and cucumber, and watercressed egg, and mustardy ham. My throne: also vanished. I turn about, and walk. Dump satchel in the hall. Think of school and Don Jesús as I march towards the kitchen and push open the swing-door and am struck without warning by the heat and the disorder. A wild commo-tion. Cook is leaning over her sink, which is a battleship of pans, issu-ing instructions through the window, telling someone outside in the garden to hurry, hurry up, that's fine, yes, back a bit, fine, there, stop, for heaven's sake, just leave it there.

I ask if anybody's going to help me undo my pinafore. Cook tells me to come over here and promise to be good because we're busy getting

ready for the—there, take the pinafore—the party. Her word smacks
me across the forehead. What party? Yours, you silly boy, like last year,
remember, when you were given the swing and the slide and all those
other children came along and the magician did a . . . Cook is cut short,
because now Nanny strides into the steam and all goes quiet. She's
wearing her going-out uniform with starchy hat and cuffs and her
bright badge, but I have my ring on my hand. Where have all my presents gone?, I ask. Nanny takes my hand without answering, squeezing
the esmerald without meaning to, and leads me away into the still
rooms of the house.

No sooner out of earshot than her prattle starts: First, young man,
we're going to the hall to pick up the satchel which, as we very well
know, we've been told a thousand times, belongs not—and don't drag
that pinafore—anywhere that happens to take our fancy, but, quite so,
in the nur-se-ry, where we'll find a tray with a light lunch. The breakfast
room is full of preparations for the party. And your presents, which are
upstairs, you can open after lunch.

And my mummy, will she be there when I open my prizes?

Your parents are both busy at the minute, but you're to join them
over coffee in the study before you wash and change for the party. Now
come along and hurry. Of course you're not tired. Ridiculous notion.

LOOKING BACK, I seem to muddle the presents from that particular
birthday with presents of other early years—always stylishly wrapped,
yet their substance somehow disheartening, richly dull, which I presume is why, all this time on, as I struggle in search of a truth for you,
the general inappropriateness of those objects seems to eclipse more
specific details, harder facts. If, for clues, I attempt to rummage
through an imaginary catalogue of toys likely to have been given to a
child in Spain in the mid-Sixties, my visual memory blurs instantly, fails
me, and merges with another, more nebulous but more pervasive fac-
ulty: emotional recall. And what I recall is a sense of abasement akin to
receiving a trick chocolate and having to smile at the joke, of having to
pretend to appreciate a thing which fundamentally one does not. And
coupled with this discomfort comes an instant need for its conceal-
ment, in order not to cause offence, not at any cost, even if the cost be

dishonesty, and even if I am alone, for no amount of privacy can dispel disappointment, or diminish feelings that might seem out of joint.

What little I can tell you about this birthday party I owe, in fact, to a photograph which, over a decade later, while clearing out, I was to find lodged at the back of a bureau in my old bedroom. The date is written faintly in pencil on the back. The shot, taken in the garden, is aimed vaguely at a tree—an avocado, I think—much of which is missed: only the trunk and a segment of a branch can be seen. The bottom of the picture, which is the only section in true focus, is crowded with the backs of heads, swung up, of children whom I suspect I knew as scarcely then as, now, they are recognizable. But something about those soft napes, untouched as yet by barbers' clippers, and those gleaming ponytails, tied back with the pastel velvet ribbons which were then in fashion, feels, to me, typical of the period. Hovering over the image of those children, you can almost smell the cologne that would have been sprinkled onto their heads, almost feel the hot pudginess of those greedy little hands, wanting more sweets forever.

Around the blurred edges of the discoloured image are some nannies, variously uniformed, holding the odd small cardigan and smiling a little sardonically, almost competitively, past one another. But at the centre of the scene, which presumably explains why the shot ever came into my property, you can see me, aged six, knock-kneed, fat-arsed, caught turning awkwardly away from the camera, my mouth twisted into a tentative grin. I am stuffed into the classic party clothes of the era—white poplin shirt, with pleated front and short sleeves; pale shorts, of a yellowish cream, which seem to button at the sides; white ankle-socks, turned down, and, improbably, white lace-up shoes. My eyes are covered by some dark sort of blindfold, and I seem to be trying to hold up what looks like a broomstick. Above me, from the branch, hangs the *piñata,* a staple effigy at children's parties in those days; perhaps, for all I know, a staple still. Fashioned of *papier maché,* embellished with fringes of crêpe paper, and loaded with streamers and trumpets and treats, this particular one, which is almost bigger than I am, is intended, I suspect, to resemble Charlie Chaplin.

The point of the *piñata* game, which has always struck me as self-defeating, is that each child, in dreary turn, be blindfold and armed with a stick and given three tries at cracking open the effigy, so that eventually its colourful entrails spill forth and cascade onto the children. And I say it's self-defeating because, by the time the supposed victor, the child who has brought about this torrent of wonderful things, manages to remove the blindfold and to put down the stick, the rest of the company has grabbed all the goodies. And try telling the empty-handed winner to cheer up and not to be spoilt because the last shall be first in the kingdom of heaven.

Observing the photograph slightly more closely, I notice that on my white-knuckled fingers, which are gripping the broomstick, there's no sign of the treasured green ring which Mam'zelle had sent and I had with such pride put on to go to school that morning. And now, as if it were then, the whole incident floods back—not so much the memory of being shoved blind into the centre of the clearing under the tree; nor my three pathetic failed attempts at hitting the effigy (or was I just pretending to miss?); nor even the jeers of derision from older cousins and their nannies, whom I could tell had joined in, along with assorted other creeps, my beautiful treacherous mother included; no: what floods back still is the grief, for, inflated as it sounds, I do think grief is what sank me when I discovered the loss of that precious ring, which Nanny would doubtless have deemed a common, nasty, unsuitable thing, and spirited away while I was changing, that's when she would have done it. And next I recall standing by the garden gates at the start of the party, and being told to greet other strange infants, and being nagged, over and over, to thank them for the presents that they were carrying, probably their own repackaged rejects; and then, bang, I realize, and panicking, suddenly need to rush upstairs, desperately to look for my missing trophy, and I even ask permission to do so, which of course is denied me, until at last, like a fool, I grasp Nanny's trickery. To this day I can picture that visage of hers, arched with simulated ignorance as she offers me—Silly boy, what a fuss about nothing—her snide assurance that tomorrow she will help me find the ring, when in my bones I know with a terminal, adult certainty that my most prized possession is gone, and gone for good; and I can still see, as if they were being exchanged at this instant, covert winks being trafficked by grown-ups above me; and I can practically summon still the tears which my rage could ill contain but my pride could not permit to be seen. And yet, oddly—such is the resilience of memory, or its selective fickleness—I now seem, in mid-reminiscence, to break off, as if bored, and my party seems to lead into, merge with, indeed become, some further party, later that day perhaps, or perhaps on some other evening. For what now enters my head is a much larger, lusher affair, nothing to do with children.

UP IN MY BEDROOM, although my light has been turned out, I'm wide awake, not so much because of the lingering evening heat and the pink sun which splashes onto my shutters, as on account of the bustle downstairs, and the mysterious sound of adult laughter, and the noise of high shoes, clickety-clacking on the parquet, and the air of flirtatious excitement. I creep out of bed and, not daring to open the door to spy through the banisters, I go, instead, to the window and, from there, watch the activity unfolding in the garden. Much later, at boarding school in England, where I imagine that, as respite from the misery of cross-country runs during hailing winter afternoons, other boys perhaps sought comfort in fantasies of being at home, sitting cosily by a fire, toasting crumpets with long forks, or playing Monopoly with their siblings while the family spaniel lay snoring about, I would seek escape from the gloom and the splattering mud and the stench of pig manure which, for me, was to become integral to that whole landscape, by remembering snatches of scenes from the parties which my parents used to give for the beautiful people of their small island all those summers ago under the ocean stars.

Envisage the women of my childhood, alighting at our house from their highly polished, slightly old-fashioned motorcars and being led with studied casualness through the courtyard, round the high palm tree, by their husbands, who, for the most part, wore tuxedos during the hot months, and whose bronze heads, slicked back, would incline to meet and almost kiss the satin hands extended to them by other men's wives. Savour the rising American tobacco, and the Parisian fragrances which filtered through that house; and picture the smoke of chiffon stoles floating back from the necks of those powdered women and fluttering, as if whispering, behind them; listen to the swish of their shantung shifts as they head for oval silver platters, borne high, from which, expertly, scarcely glancing, they pluck a glass of something chilled and strong and tropical. And you can hear the clinking and the surprising, and greetings in various colonial languages and, once in an occasional while, a trill of delight as some young girl, recently married and new to the art of hosting parties, steps out onto the terrace and marvels at the set where, soon, dinner will be served on white-skirted tables round the swimming pool, which tonight, on my mother's instructions, has been covered with a glistening floor of parquet so that guests may, in due course, dance.

I'm peering down through the slats. The falling night is decked with paper lanterns—rust, green, amber, occasionally ivory—which glow suspended from the high bamboo trees lining the walls of the garden. As people begin to drift through the terrace into the cool stillness out-side, onto the darkening grass, they break off in small groups, or cou-ples, or, every so often, into pairs of young women walking arm in arm and laughing superbly, their pearlescent lips casually parted, their gigantic lashes blackened, their elaborate hairpieces tilted back. From up here, high, I see an elderly accordionist appear at the edge of the scene and start to wander about, weaving old Spanish melodies into the gathering, shrugging his shoulders this way and that, half-bowing as he advances. But the women, hearing themselves serenaded with old tangos and *fandangos,* tunes from way back, from the romances un-known of their own mothers, seem, after inadvertently striding in time for a few bars, to grow nostalgic and pause, and to turn to one another, trying to recall the words of some particular, particularly saccharine line, which now they chant out, half-embarrassed, half-convulsed, like the convent-girls that they were not so far into the past; and then they amble on, smiling separately, a little distractedly, slowly to return to their earlier subject—their own unflavoured marriages, per-haps—and as they stroll under the lanterns, which highlight them momentarily, ethereally, they seem to become ghosts of themselves, then pass. Starched servant-girls, with aprons that cross at the back, tied into stiff bows of excessive size, pursue such wayward guests, with the pretext of canapés, out of the shadows and back to the heart of the party, where my mother, whom I can distinguish only by the ostrich hem of her tunic of sand gazaar, is darting about with a zest unknown to me, at once kissing cheeks and holding out her high hand and trying to steer people towards their respective tables, which flicker with long candles planted into bowls of bloodshot camellias.

As guests begin to take their seats, gilt chairs with backs like fans, I hear, then see tuning up, a small band, discreetly lit on a low podium at a slight distance from the furthest diners. The accordionist is up there now, next to a guitarist, and behind them, a drummer; and seated cross-legged, some other character plucking a mandolin, while, at the front of the platform, standing by a microphone, a fifth performer, with a head of black gelatine and a shirt of frilly icing, wields a gaudy electric guitar. But the sound, when the group first strikes up, is so subdued that you're hardly aware of it, and to begin with rises only in gentle waves above the drone of the diners, deferring to the racket of cutlery and to shrill outbursts of laughter; yet, as the merriment grows, so, gradually, does the prominence of these performers, who, around coffee time, begin to play in earnest. And now the accordion, which is like a full heart, begins to swell and contract in that childish, enquiring way that it has; and the electric guitar properly to slide; and the plectrum of the mandolin to pluck; and the metal brush to stroke and tease at the snare-drum as the voices of the band mingle and chant, in the syrupy, high-pitched harmony that was then the style, hopeless lyrics about hopeless, shipwrecked love. But the effect, for all of the hopelessness, is so sublime that you could be in Hawaii tonight, I swear to you, hoola-hooping on its honey-coloured coastline with hibiscuses garlanded about you. And next, unable to resist the lure of the musicians, some couple unknown to me, not my parents, a younger pair, smiling, rise and, as if this were their own party, take to the floor and open the dance; and the people from their table start to cheer and to clap at the sheer enchanting audacity; and the growing applause spreads out to embrace the members of the band, who beam back delightedly. I can see that the dancing man has an arm wrapped around the woman's low-cut back, while his other holds her right hand up, to the moon; and as they turn and turn again and again, her glittering bracelet catches the light. But now she signals excitedly, and exhorts her dinner companions to join her—Come-on-you-lot-you-promised, she shouts, as if caught-out—and by the time that I've fetched a cushion to make myself comfortable, a whole crowd has leapt up to dance; and you should see the sudden burst of colour, like a float at carnival-time; and now the band is in full swing, no holds barred, and the beat is growing more frantic, and people are spinning and whirling, and some of them are even dancing apart, and changing partners over and over, and suddenly, at last, I see my mummy down there among them, arm in arm with some man whom I can't quite make out, my father most likely, and every time her head turns towards the house I hope that she will glance up to my shutters, and I hope it for a patient while. But she doesn't— which doesn't really matter, because as I climb, yawning, back into bed, I can still pretend to myself that I'm saying good night to her, and that I'm telling her that she's the most beautiful of all the mummies and that her party's been an absolute—what's that word which she likes?— triumph. And I remember, vividly, awaking the morning after, and finding, floating about the granite tiles, like kisses blown, like promises forgotten, wisps of feather, warm as sand.

My mother stands in ballerina slippers in the linen room upstairs, ironing an evening dress which makes you think of an enormous gaping flower. She says you cannot trust the servants with organza. Layer after layer of skirt she lifts and turns inside out, with gestures rhythmic as nocturnal waves unfolding onto a coastline. The dew of her spraystarch clings to the heavy air in tiny pearly bubbles which, when you peer at the window that frames her profile, you can see refusing to burst, struggling to survive, but in the end floating down the peachy light, to drown. I am sitting on a stool by the door; my back, warm against the wall of papered violets; my head, conscious of the ivory lightswitch next to it with its twin buzzer. Her slowered motions fascinate me—the way she steers her iron, the way it sails heavily along the scalloped shores of her ball-gown, the fizzing sound it makes as it navigates the frothy patches of starch, the clouds of scented vapour, like incense, which result, the mounting mounds of pale diaphanous stuff, like chalky cliffs, behind her arm, which, in a rolled-up shirtsleeve, now removes the iron and parks it on its rack. Her bracelet jingles with charms as the painted tips of her fingers raise a further layer of underskirt—the seventh that I've counted—delicately up and over, to make way for the next, paler than dust, which she now smoothes out along the calico-quilted board before starting to iron. Sometimes she sighs;

and yet, if you ask why, she seems not to notice you, hardly answers. Occasionally, if pressed, she might momentarily gaze at the wall in front of her and say, half-absently, that she doesn't really know (which is a lie), that having me watch her makes her uncomfortable (which is more like it); and then she will resume her ironing, even humming sometimes; and then I will pretend to swivel my attention, because, although she mesmerizes me, I feel embarrassed, impolite; and instead I peer into the open cupboard behind her, with its shelves of faded gingham boxes brimming with treasures from, I don't know, before she was married: creamy flowers of faille that may once have sprouted from her hip, or shoulder, or from beneath the brim of some picture-hat; glittering buttons that I vaguely recognize from photographs around the house; a sewing-basket that plays a waltz when its lid is lifted; secret bits of history and haberdashery and stifled passion. But I do not think that turning my attention to such objects can improve matters, because, sooner or later, she always seems to say: Aren't you getting a bit old to be dawdling about doing nothing, what on earth's become of Nanny? And with that final word, she lands the iron on its backside, walks to where I am, aims her hand somewhere close to my head and, exhaling resignedly, presses the buzzer three times, which— give or take the minute it takes Nanny to arrive—means, as it always did, Off you go now.

My mother kneels on the circus-rug at the foot of my bed, arched over an open wooden box with corners studded like a trunk, but smaller, into which you can tuck secrets if you want to, which is why it's called a Tuck-Box. One of her slippers is slipping off but I don't suppose that she can have noticed, because she's busy flustering over a roll of shiny, papery plastic with a sticky back that makes a squishing noise and is causing her aggravation. And collapsed about her lie her tape measure from the waltzing basket, and a pencil with a crimson tassel, and an India rubber, pink and blue, and huge scissors which must weigh a ton; and everywhere about are curls of shaven scraps in chaos. The paper that she's trying to cut has brightly coloured shapes with heavy outlines, called cartoons—a dog and a boat and a tree and a clown—and although she's too occupied to explain things to me, I think that she wants to stick the sticky paper in the box, inside, to line it.

In the afternoon we're going to the photographer's, my mummy and I, for me to have my picture taken for a book not meant for reading, called a passport. And I must wear, she says, a tie for the first time for this, which she knows how to do up because she used to wear one in her day, when she was younger and went riding at gymkhanas; and she tells me to keep still for just one second, would I, and to stand in front of her, and face the mirror on the dressing-table, and to stop, for once, bombarding her with questions over and over; I'm giving her a migraine. She says she's sure I'll learn to do my own tie soon enough, but her voice sounds wobbly to me, like when you know you're not to cry. This tie is Scots, which means a type of tartan—grey and blue and bottle-green with now-and-then a tiny yellow stripe—but it is not a happy one, which I think would be red as a ladybird with dots dancing the polka. My hair she combs to the side, and makes a parting—boys to the left, girls to the right. My coat is flannel, double-breasted, and the collar, which is green as the ring that was lost from me, is upholstered in velvet. But she says I may not wear, although it is my favourite, my velvet beret with the petersham rosette. Not for a passport photograph; please don't be tedious.

A MATTER OF DAYS LATER, we're all on our way to the airport and squashed up in the back, me in the middle and my mummy dressed in tweed and Pepe wearing his cap and driving with a pile of luggage stacked beside him, plus in the boot, plus on the roof-rack, plus he's talking to my father through the mirror about a problem known as Franco, with the car even more loaded than the car is when we go down to the beach house in July. I have kissed goodbye to Cook and Gardener, who say that I must write to them from England in my neatest fountain-hand but not in English, or they will not understand, and then they laugh and say that they will miss me double-much. This is a joke, because the truth is that although I have an English Nanny at our house, I do not yet speak English rightly, nor escribe its spelling which can trick you up, other than my name, which is Santiago; but in English you write James; and to learn my father's language is a reason why we're going to England now, my mummy says, and to make the Friends Who Last Your Lifetime. (I think that I may miss my Cook and Gardener.)

Today is the first time that I do climb upon a plane, which is exciting 'cos an aeroplane does fly as high as any kite and faster than a train, but you must promise not to be sea-sick in the sky, which sometimes people are, which is not brave nor, Nanny says, considerate. Nanny has to stay behind upon our island, but the sight of us, readied and packed and on our way out, gives her, she says she must confess, a nostalgia for Blighty, and you could easily call this feeling a homesickness, but not if you're Nanny who must be brave and considerate as she waves a hand and wishes us Bon Voyage, which means au revoir in the language of my Mam'zelle who went away—but none of this will make it easier for Nanny or her homesickness one jot, or even an iota small as an ant. Because I did not forget about the vanished esmerald.

In the plane I'm allowed to have a window seat, which has a view, and my mummy's going to sit beside me, and on her other side will sit my father, who calls a corridor an Isle—if ever, he says, he's given a chance. She straps my safety belt as tight as it will go but still it feels loose around me. She says to never mind. She hands her camel coat up to my father. She removes her gloves and her sunglasses and puts them in various pockets of her handbag. She undoes her silken headscarf, which ripples with reins and stirrups and bridles, and knots it round the handle of her crocodile bag. Now she closes her eyes, as if she had one of those headaches that she says are confounded; and when the plane at last kicks off with a great rumbling Vroom down in the deep of your tummy, she makes a sign of the cross, which means, she says, asking God to grant us safe passage. This does not mean an Isle.

We have landed now, but it is dark. Through the rain we're driven in a high black cab, like the one in the toy garage, and I'm going backwards on a seat that flips down, captivated by the sight of receding rows of identical houses, unpainted but beamed and bricked and stained-glassed, moving away round long distant bends and vanishing; and there's the constant intermittent glow of Catseyes on the carriageway, blinks in the night; and splashes like tiny fishes hitting the approaching headlights; and, inside the car, there's the exhausting lullaby of windscreen wipers, and I suppose I must have drifted off into some sleep, because, next thing, there is a jolt; and I can hear voices announcing that we've arrived; and now we're driving up to a white hotel with flags from many countries waving in the middle of a town that must be London, and the taxi-doors are opened from outside, and open hands in gloves assist us to the ground after our travels, and lead us up the front steps, as if we were smart but exhausted fingers going into my mother's doll's-house, into the hall inside, and we're swept into a lift that goes many floors up. My room is pallid green, like water when you get out of the bath, and the lamp-light by the bed is fuzzy-dull. The candlewick bedspread, like a garden scattered with ashes, is grey and embossed with grey flowers; and, if you stand very still in my room, you can't hear a sound, but you can smell the strong smell of ashtrays and of steamed suppers floating up from the dining room. And if you peer beyond the curtains, which are sticky to the touch, you will see a park even paler than ash, like sand after dusk, spread out before you and planted with a lake, and clouded with a mist that looks like the mist that you make when you suck a strong mint and breathe out.

I AM UP, and dressed already without Nanny, and with my parents I have been to breakfast in the dining room, which was fullish with ladies both elderly and smiling, and whispering waitresses, and a few sorts of grandfathers, and a very beardy man wearing a monocle, which doesn't mean my uncle, stuck to his eye. And also we have been to a shop with many floors like an hotel but with a staircase made of iron that rises as you climb and is an Eskilator, and you must keep your wits about you the whole time because if you mislay your wits about you for one second even and forget to jump at the last second Off, you could get swallowed by the metal teeth and gobbled up.

And we have carried many shopping bags downstairs and back away with us, of uniforms of clothes like jumpers with a stripe to wear for when I meet the friends who last your lifetime, and shorts that look too long for me, I think, and shirts both grey and white; no nightshirts: striped pyjamas; and ties to wear on weekdays, green and white, and one plain dark one, almost black, for Holy Days and Sundays, and a suit of worsted charcoal, and elastic garters to make sure your socks stay up, and, in one bulging bag, three burgundy rugger shirts and three pairs of football shorts, and different socks for games called sports I have not played, and plus, at the bottom of this biggest bag which my father carries, a cricketing blazer the colour of an esmerald which is a

colour that reminds you but you're not allowed to wear until the summer term comes round after the autumn and the winter which is not
yet now, for patience is a virtue.

Back in my parents' room at the hotel, I'm dazed by the sight of
their beds, which are heaped with folded stacks of my new clothes, regulation items that couldn't be purchased earlier, at home, abroad. My
mother is sitting in a quilted chair shaped like a shell, her legs crossed
tight and held together as if bound, angled in a prim posture sharply to
the right, her ankles rigid, her feet locked out in the manner of a deco-
rous stocking advert. I, meanwhile, am hovering over a desk with stationery racks, complimentary Biros and a folded street-map, which
lurks under the window at the far side. My father has just opened the
door—to go out to a nearby pub in Kensington to meet old friends of
his, who're called The Chaps and he claims not to've seen since he was
a bachelor. He looms on the threshold, puffed up. My mother, immobile, looks small to me by contrast, reduced in stature, as if vanquished
in this foreign land where, stripped of her native vassals and the riches
of her language, she seems to have lost the power to conjure. Possibly
she feels humiliated. Certainly she won't be humbled. I know my
mother. I flow with her blood. Rage has frozen her over, paralysed her
in her shell of quilted satin—but only momentarily. Suddenly she leaps
to her feet and flies to the adjoining bathroom. My father stops in his
tracks, closes the door, steps back inside. I hear the sound of her
enamel pill-box being rattled; then, prized ajar. I recognize the snap of
its clasp, which can be obstinate; there follows a respite of water,
gluggelling into a toothmug. She must be swallowing her pill down.
Silence. Keep quiet. And now she returns to the bedroom, a little slop-
pily, sulkily, dragging her body behind her like some exiled empress
who, without warning, has found herself embroiled in a conspiracy
that is beneath her. She makes for a cracked china vase that is propped
on the mantel, a vessel conceived along classical lines which, at some
stage, has been dropped and glued together in a hurry, so that arteries
of dark adhesive run down it, but which, since, as if to camouflage the
damage, has been bunged up with dried flowers, stiff and miserably
coloured, beige and peach and lilac. And this is where my pathetic
impoverished mother now runs, to fiddle with those tawdry stems, to
tease at their desiccated petals—her back, though hunched, resolutely

turned against my father. But from where I stand, a little anxious, I can observe her figure in profile: her breathing is consternated, her ribcage has grown frantic; her fine hands, so full of composure once, are apprehensive now; her lacquered fingers peck at the foliage erratically; the stars in her rings glint angrily; and although her bracelet jingles as it always does, its peal seems less carefree, more measured, somehow.

THERE ENSUES the first open quarrel that my parents ever held before my eyes; and even if my memory has admittedly repressed the most part, or perhaps because my shock at the time prevented me from absorbing the scene with any degree of accuracy, nevertheless there remains, ingrained in me, the image, the sight of them turned animal, like hounds baying at their shadows; he, aiming his growl at the door leading out; she, directing her howling diatribe toward the fire. I feel seized by a fear that she might shatter the vase, yet part of me wants her to do so, to prove to me her courage; and though I am shamed and disgusted by the revelation of my mother's latent violence, yet my sympathies somehow lie ensnared with her unhappiness. Neither she nor her husband is listening to the other, nor properly answering; rather, they are yelling simultaneously, though not in unison, and often in discordant languages. My mother is babbling in Spanish as she staggers over to her low cheap throne of quilted satin and dumps herself onto the sheen of its padding. Her legs do not cross now: they're stuck out, heels dug hard into the carpet. My father doesn't look at her, but keeps imploring, over and over, as if she were a fool, or in the clutches of hysteria: For goodness' sake my dear calm down—over and over. And she, the while, is shouting, over and over too, *Lo siento, lo siento muchísimo,* I'm sorry, I'm frightfully sorry—meaning not that she feels regret, but that she refuses, that she won't do whatever it is that he wants. And then, like the solution to some absurd enigma, comes, I remember, the fated mention of Nametapes, which I think is what must have ignited the flare-up. And although my mother's strength is beginning to flag, I surmise from my far corner that she's referring to all the things that need to be marked in time for my departure tomorrow: those mounds of dull clothes which lie heaped, like remnants gathered from some skirmish, upon the battlefield of their twin beds. And she's frightfully sorry, she says yet again, she can't be expected to manage without help, he should have thought of this whole problem earlier, she hasn't come to London to play the seamstress, the trip has all been of his making anyway, if he likes he can talk to the chamber-maids, they're bound to do the job if he pays, or he can ask the nuns at the Assumption if he prefers, not that she could care, not less, does she make herself plain? After which, switching tack minutely, she modulates from the problem of the clothes to the true heart of her problem, and she mumbles something about the boy being given a bit of attention and his last day with her, would a trip to Madame Tussaud's be too much to ask? And God, she exclaims, what a spectacle he's had to witness, it's a disgrace. Lamentable, she calls it, and suggests, in a burst of sanctimonious outrage, that her husband go to confession, and then, to my horror, she drops her beautiful head in her beautiful hands and wails as if this were her end. Which leaves me winded.

THE FIRST WORDS that he utters the next day, pacing about my room but facing out, as if addressing a crowd in the frosted park, are that we're running late thanks to my mother. Typical, he says. Never mind that there's a train to catch. Nothing to be done; woman simply will not hurry up, not for anything, nor anyone. (I like my mother's slow calm, her elegance.) Doesn't *know* the meaning of the words On Time—never did, matter of fact, practically drove your grandfather to drink, poor man. I explain, in case he doesn't understand, this frothing un-bridled father of mine, that my mother needs her length of time in order to become—and then I can't think of the word, and I say: Beautified. *Beautified?,* he splutters, What kind of pansy word is that? Be-a-ti-fied more like, which is what I deserve to be when I'm six foot under. I ask why. Why?, he shouts at the quaking window; Good God Man, for putting up with her ruddy nonsense every day of my life, hang it all. Beyond a joke. Drive one to drink. Wouldn't say no to a shot of brandy, matter of fact. I mean, it's not as if I mind how bally long she takes to get herself togged up; all I've ever asked is that we be Punctual. Punctual, that too much to ask? I tell you, he tells me, Though for heaven's sake don't tell your mother: number of Masses we've been to which, strictly speaking, haven't been valid because we've walked into church bang in the middle of the blasted Consecration (my father can be vulgar), well, it's beyond count. And is she ever embarrassed, one might be forgiven for wondering? Is she my arse (he really can). And has she ever, once in her life, so much as apologized? Oh no, not she. Woman couldn't care a damn, floats about with her head in the clouds like some blessed film star. Too blimming much. And, while we're on the subject, I'll have you know the same goes for dinner invitations, same exactly: never mind the fact that other guests might be famished, or that the soufflé might have gone phut, or that the hostess might be cursing us, swearing never to have us back. Why should any of that worry your mother? What's the big hurry? Oblivious, the woman; always was. You realize that even when we were courting I used to be made to wait outside in the car for at least half an hour? Well I was, m'boy, without fail, every confounded time. Almost put me off the wretched gal, truth be told. Miracle, quite frankly, she ever made it to her own wedding: 'parently your grandfather had to put a stop to her silly carry-on: great last-minute drama to do with the veil, too thick to see through, or too transparent, or was it the train, hardly matters: old man, end of his tether, just stormed into her room and dragged her out of the house. And then, few weeks later, what d'you think she does? Gets this barmy notion into her head, sneaks up to see the sewing-woman, has the whole bally thing cut up. Arm and a leg it had cost, I gather, silk or what-have-you from Brussels, orgranzy. Can you credit such a thing? Stark raving mad. For your crib, you say? Don't recall to be honest, wouldn't put it past her. Take my advice, m'lad: steer clear of women long as you can. Nothing but trouble. I'm not saying—don't misunderstand me: she does always look marvellous, your mother, prettiest woman on the island, no doubt about it—which is actually, actually, my point precisely: why must she fuss so, fuss-fuss-fuss, every single time we go out?

And now, as if enlightened, he threatens: Anyway, time gets too tight, I'll just have to take you to Euston m'self and see you onto the train without her, what? Simple as that. Only herself to blame, m'afraid. Oh do stop snivelling, for God's sake; try to act like a man. And then, what the hell, he knocks back a brandy.

I stand pinned to the wall, next to the tuck-box that my mother tucked, which is secured with a combination known only to the pair of us, a duffel coat with clumsy wooden toggles, folded roughly, a chestnut satchel with my new monogram, punched in black onto the flap—

all these piled like a pyramid onto my padlocked trunk, the key to which is buried in a pocket of my shorts. Wedged between these strange belongings and the door-frame to the bathroom, I'm beginning to squirm sideways because I need to go to the lavatory: I've been holding and holding as hard as I can, but I don't think I can last much longer. I'm going to have to ask him for permission. What?, he barks, Speak up, laddy. I confess the question a second time, but to me it sounds no louder, half-strangled. Well, *go* then, for God's sake. And as I escape, he mutters that the boy's got the bladder of a puppy-dog, which I take be a compliment. I sequester myself, but I do not dare to lock, and I sit to pee so that no one can hear me outside. I wash my hands and smell the soap. There's a face in the mirror that I hardly recognize. A foreign boy in foreign uniform. I ignore him and open the door.

MY BEDROOM has suddenly grown loud with a pair of bell-boys wheeling a trolley and lugging my luggage onto it; and a chambermaid being told to come back later, but would she thank the ladies who marked the boy's clothes—by my father of course. And when my mother enters, knocking hesitantly, she seems not so much late, as lost. To me, she looks like never before—disguised, remote, hounded almost. Her head does not swoon about the clouds that my father had thought, but is held together, bandaged, in a turban dark as ebony. Her unfed body, camouflaged in spotted fur which has been dragged out of cold storage, rattles in a swing-coat of ocelot. Her eyes convalesce behind black lenses. A dark foulard, tight as a snake, throttles her neck with a knot, flips over, then slithers inside her collar. Her hand grips a limp pair of gloves, suede the colour of mole, and flicks them about as if swatting flies in the servants' quarters. She wears no charms this morning. There is no jingle. As she moves towards me, I catch sight, instead, of a slim band of diamonds simmering on her wristbone, mute and cold. One ring upon her finger only, an eternity. She comes to rest directly in front of me, breathing shakily, and lowers herself slightly from the knees. She inspects, then adjusts my tie, but only cursorily, a formality. Her powdered earlobes quiver with small brilliants. Her lips are hard and bloodied. Her jaw pulses wildly. The scent of her gardenias devours me. I look down to her feet, in high brown lace-ups, like hooves for treading concrete, or stampeding. Not a murmur from her, but she pats my cheek in benediction. She rises, straightens up, and turns to survey the emptying room, retrieves her moribund handbag from a stool, and hooks it hard round the pelt of her sleeve. She exits. I follow suit. My father lingers on, probably to leave a tip. And this time, as my mother and I proceed ahead, as we start to begin to take our leave, she elects the stairs rather than the lift, and as we descend and descend soundlessly, almost floating, my hand feels the grip of her fingers, icy, twitching involuntarily.

Once our taxi has been loaded by a disgruntled cabbie and one of the hotel minions, and the partition glass inside been shut with due asperity, we are ferried across to Euston—in solid silence, its weight almost palpable. My parents, whose legs are crossed pointedly away from each other, direct their heads to opposite sides of the wide city roads, as if engrossed in disconnected, or conflicting, versions of heavy traffic. Despite the chasm of leathered upholstery throbbing between them, I, again, am travelling backwards: it has become our custom. From where I sit, I feel tempted to stare at them, to scrutinize their every action, for, faced at such proximity, they seem magnified, like characters towering in the foreground of some film that I were watching from the front row at our local cinema. And yet, just in case, not to provoke matters, I keep my sights low, allowing my eyes to wander no higher than the region around their feet, which wiggle sporadically. I notice now, above my line of vision, the silhouette of my mother's sleeve moving very slowly, like the sleeve of a dowager, to raise a tiny hanky from her tiny bag toward her cheek. She sniffs embarrassingly, then sighs extendedly; and just when I think that she's run out of breath, she states, in Spanish, with spirit, that she wants him to remember that she never wanted this whole boarding thing, which sounds like a secret between them. He clears his throat, pulls down the pane of his window, and proceeds, with some ceremony—cuffshooting, that sort of flourish—to ignite one of his medium-sized cigars, at which he puffs repeatedly. He inspects its glowing tip and seems to grant himself approval, and, wriggling about his patch of seat, stretches a trouser-leg of herringbone towards where I sit, diagonally; then, carefully avoiding my mother's acutely elbowed sleeve, he insinuates his glistering lighter into the entrails of his pocket and lets it drop, and down it goes, clinking against the loose pieces of his silver.

My mother wonders if I could possibly open her window, which is my privilege. The great noise of the street now invades our echoing interior and claims it, and I turn around in the cab to stare through the front windscreen, I can't resist, and I watch us being driven towards a vast building beginning with an E. And next thing, we are hurtling down into a tunnel, full of taxis, braking and screeching.

THE SLOPING PLATFORM swarms with boys identical to me—identical, that is, till we draw near: all of us are uniformly dressed, of course, but there are bigger boys, blonder boys, more animated, stronger boys shouting to others like them whom they've known since before the summer holidays and who shout back as if repeating some coded joke, meaningless to me. Their mothers, none of whom seems to be wearing a fur coat, much less a turban, are trotting about in A-line skirts, or kilts, and patterned cardigans, and dragging, at their stout heels, the odd fat Corgi. My mother reclaims my hand; her soft glove, now assumed, possesses me. I think that she and I must be walking too slowly, because my father seems suddenly to be surging ahead, forward beyond us, separately. He is waving at something in the distance, and laughing aloud for no reason that I can think of—as you might from the terrace at the Nautical Club wave and laugh at strangers on a passing liner. He turns abruptly to the porter beside him, tells him to deposit my trunk and tuck-box in the guards' van, along with that of other boys who've missed Luggage In Advance, jiggles in his pocket, pays the man off, and then hands me my satchel, and my mother my coat, which she unfolds and hangs over her arm with distaste, I can tell, as if it were the cloak of a vagrant. He tells my mother to go and find a seat for me, anywhere on coaches A, B, or C, and tries to explain to her, in urgent panting blurts, that he's just caught sight of Such-And-Such, some great old long-lost chum from school, Deputy Head when he was Head Boy, triffickly brave in the war, we'll forgive him if he dashes over, must just say Hullo, train won't be leaving for a few minutes, no need to worry, back in a jiffy-what. And rejuvenated by the sudden prospect of this reunion, he canters off—knees knocking, thighs rubbing, Old Boy tie flapping proudly over his shoulder.

My mother seems depleted, too sedated to be annoyed. She inclines her head towards me, and attempts, with her narrow painted mouth, to summon the ghost of a smile. I grin back forcedly, as if for a camera. She links my arm around hers, but it must feel wrong to her, not comfortable, because now she swaps us round, laces her arm through mine as befits a proper couple, weak woman leaning on stronger man, and I do try to support her, and I'm flattered by the compliment, even if it raises the level of my elbow to the level of my jaw. Yet in truth, as we advance down the ramp, I don't suppose that we could look more foreign, more preposterous, the two of us: she, garbed in the anachronism of her finery—her robes and furred gowns; and I, despite the banality of my uniform, tarred by the hot brush of our tropical sun. And I remember pacing down the concrete, which unrolls before us like a sombre sprawling great road to nowhere, and humming, without a scrap of irony, a few bars from a laconic old *milonga*—conceived, no doubt, in Buenos Aires, but inspired, I have since learnt, by the futile chants, centuries old, of slaves who, manacled in Africa, used, after a brief stop on our beauteous island, to be commended to the high seas and sold at the harbour of Havana—a song which my mother had hummed to me by way of lullaby, long before I knew it by heart and its dreadful lyrics could impress me with their mawkish loveliness:

No me llames extranjero porque baya nacido lejos,
O porque tenga otro nombre la tierra de donde vengo . . .
No me llames extranjero porque fue distinto el seno,
O porque acudió a mi infancia otro idioma de los cuentos . . .
No me llames extranjero, ni pienses de donde vengo,
Mejor saber donde vamos, adonde nos lleva el tiempo.
Y me llamas extranjero porque me trajo un camino,
Porque nací en otro pueblo, porque conozco otros mares
Y un día salté de otro puerto. Si siempre quedan iguales en el adiós
Los pañuelos y las pupilas borrosas de los que dejamos lejos.
No, no me llames Extranjero: traemos el mismo grito,
Y el mismo cansancio viejo que viene arrastrando el hombre
Desde el fondo de los tempos, cuando no exitían fronteras,
Antes de que vinieran ellos, los que dividen y matan,
Los que roban, los que mienten, los que venden nuestros sueños,
Ellos son, ellos son los que inventaron esta palabra: Extranjero.

Don't call me foreigner just because my birth was far away,
Or because the land whence I come goes by another name . . .
Don't call me foreigner just because I knew a different breast,
Or because my childhood tales were told with other words . . .
Don't call me foreigner, or wonder whence I hail:
Better to know whither we go, whither time takes us.
And yet you call me foreigner simply because a path conveyed
    me,
Because I began in another place, because I know other waves
And once from another port I sailed. Farewells do not
    discriminate
Between the handkerchieves or misted pupils of those left in
    our wake.
No, don't call me foreigner: for we carry the same wail
And the same ancient weariness that man has been dragging
Since the beginning of time, when there were no frontiers,
Before they came: those who divide and kill,
Who steal, who lie, who sell our dreams.
It is they, they who invented this word: foreigner.

OF THE THREE COACHES, C is the furthest from the gate. It requires the longest journey, but A and B were taken. My mother, imperious as a warring queen, leads our small procession down the passageway, and ignores, with the bristle of her coat, the insignificance of other parents and their braying offspring. Some sticky teenage daughter, someone's lumpy sister, is rushing back against the flow, is headed towards us, and pushes past with an unconvincing Sorry. My mother's neck turns round briefly, high above me, astonished. I seem to be shaky, churning for some reason—as if I were in trouble. I clutch my satchel to my stomach. My mother halts, having found, to her right, a carriage with an empty seat for me, next to the sliding door, which she now slides, her glove gripping the handle heavily and pulling open the partition. My seat is furthest from the window, next to the corridor. The boys already boarded are screaming—unintelligibly to me, in an unheard other idiom—and shoving and horsing-about and cheering. I catch occasional words only. All look several years older than me, apart from one, quietly opposite where I'm to be seated, who could conceivably be my contemporary. His mousy head, with ginger spectacles attached, and freckles, is buried in an action comic. I notice, in passing, soft flecks of dandruff around his dark collar. No one stops, or lowers the noise when we come in; but my mother, undeterred, inspects the luggage-rack directly above the empty seat—only to find it stuffed with other people's belongings. She tells me to sit down, ensconces me. And now she swings round to the boys in here, and tells them, in her execrable continental embarrassing English, to remove the offending articles—which one of them does, ashen with terror. And then she tells him to learn to stand up when a lady comes in, and would he be so good, since I cannot reach, as to put my duffel coat up on the rack for me. Flabbergasted, he obliges. Most kind, thank you. The compartment is deadly stilled. Yet my mother, to my utter horror, now begins to prattle at me in Spanish with a voice that is not hers—it's absolutely bewildering, squeaky and quick and almost silly—about being a good boy, and saying my prayers last thing, and writing to her very soon indeed and—she breaks off paralysed by the sound of a whistle. She must go and find my father, she says, fetch him back immediately. She is vanished in an instant.

I must be blushing: my face is scorching. Everyone is staring at me, and I can tell that it isn't just with interest. Theirs is a different sort of stare: at once slimy and superior. I try to fix my sights directly ahead of me, over the head of the boy with the comic, because I lack, for now, the courage to look out of the window. My mind is charging back to my origins, crashing down to my beginnings. I can't think what I'm thinking, but a voice in my innards finds itself suddenly rattling off bits of the Hail Holy Queen mother of mercy hail our life our sweetness and our hope to you do we cry poor banished children of Eve to you do we send up our sighs mourning and weeping in this vale of . . . And then, the sudden black moon of my mother's turban appears to me from the platform. Another whistle goes, lengthier. My father is not with her. He must be on his way, or perhaps she cannot find him. She peers, worried and frowning slightly towards the place where I must be, but I don't know whether she can see me through the resurrected antics within. My own view is obstructed by the bobbing heads of these wretched older people, as if, today of all days, it were I who were stuck at the back of our local cinema while they, from their front-row seats, were lapping up the best scene. As the train begins to pull away—and for once I'm moving forward, face to the future—the glass that freezes my mother from me seems to grow like a great screen. And to me, despite her face of absolute shock, which stares aghast at the inevitability, she looks every inch the famous film star now—glamorous, beautiful, stricken. And yet, as if condemned to the melodramatic mime of a silent picture, she can only mop her brow with her glove, and wave a little languidly. But at the desperate last, her mouth opens wide, in a cavernous rictus, and seems to groan like the mouth of a battered ocelot, going, very slowly, from a great Oh, to a deep Ah, and from that, back to an incredulous Oh, and, as she stands there, abandoned, unescorted, I can't properly tell whether her dying vowels are meant to mean Iago, or *Adiós*.

PART THREE

M<small>Y NEW NAME</small> is James Moore, and my number 293, which I
must not forget, but if my memory should fail me, my mother
says that I will find these details written on my handkerchief. After
hours of chugging drudgery through increasingly unpromising territo-
ries, relieved only by spells of simulated sleep and quick visits to the
lavatory, where I could not reach the mirror to check that my tie looked
decent, we have finally come to a juddering halt, and trooped off the
train with the others ahead of me; but when I had a panic on the platform about my suddenly remembered trunk and tuck-box, which I
fear may have gone missing, and which, if she finds out, will make my
mother not pleased, a man with a hat and a coat and a whiteness at the
collar hurry-hurried me *this* way, boy, pointing and shouting over the
confusion: To the bus. He slaps me on the back as I lag behind the rush
of pupils, struggling to get into my duffel coat, which is too large and
cumbersome and impossible to toggle closed. I feel frozen. I can't
seem to find one of my gloves. No time to search for it. Later. I pretend
to trot along, as if my body were in sympathy with the general urgency,
but my insides have ground to slow motion.

Our bus is double-decker like the one in my toy garage, and even
though the ride is bumpy here above and full of swerves, you can see a
good deal around you, or could, if it weren't already getting dark. I have
a window seat, which is a luck, and the boy by my side looks new like
me, which means that we don't have to talk, another luck. The roads
wind with the convoy of our many buses through the muddied countryside, and my bus, which is for Juniors, is the last in line, so it's not
much use trying to look out of the front.

It is night and quite dull. Nothing to call special that I can notice,
just ordinary houses and a village with a tavern called a Swan and some

cottages with gnomes smirking like gargoyles, and fields of something ploughed, and trees and hedges and roads, but not a single windmill in sight as round more roads, getting smaller, we go. There is much noisiness here inside, as well as on the floor below, which must mean that some of the boys have been on this bus before, and some of the new ones, I think, may have older brothers who do not want to know them any more because it's soft. But when we come to a cross in the middle of a minor roundabout, everything seems to stop. There is a general quietening, and now we go through a rusty gate along a shady, still more narrow road.

I sense that things are changing. I feel our final approach. The buses hurtle onwards, gathering speed perhaps. But the way is growing darker, seems to be bound for some distant forest. I don't know. Headlights cast mad circling beams across a sea of black fields beneath us, like introductory spots wanting to prove that the next act of the circus will take place without nets for protection. Fields seem neither to rise nor to fall, but gently to slope like an arena for miles around, until, ahead of me, as we grow closer, I catch sight of a vast great statue of stone, a frozen ghost of Our Lady, balanced on a crescent-shaped trapeze and presiding over a black uncharted globe. One arm she holds out, as if wishing to direct you to another school; but her head is coyly tilted away from view, and her other arm lingers about her breast in an attitude of beatific insouciance, so that the language of her posture is rendered unfathomable.

And almost quicker than I realize, the bus now veers with such violence to the right that the boy sitting next to me topples into the aisle, then gathers himself back up, blushing—to a sudden angry burst of public cackles. But rubbing the steam on my patch of window and staring out, I now witness the thing that is my father's Alma Mater. And it is an eternal concrete road, much longer than any station platform, flanked on both sides by enormous carpets of dirty grass and, further down, huge sheets of corrugated water, and there are fields all around, and trees so distant that they look tiny under the brown sky, and, at the end of where you look, there are small lights, to show you a building quite enormous which for centuries has lain in wait for you, like a massive tarantula. I do not flinch: I am not sunk. But my chest tightens so hard that I have to let myself breathe out. The bus rushes on regardless, without apparent caution, as if there really were no danger, as if the spider were held fast, or were stuffed; but as it draws closer, it seems to grow very much larger, which means it can't be stuffed because then it would stay the same size. And here all goes quieter and quieter, and the merriment is starting to die, and some of the buses ahead seem already to have parked in the drive, in the middle of the night, and to be disgorging onto the glistening tarmac bigger boys, who are shouting but no longer really laughing. And yet, just as our turn comes, my turn, the bus for Juniors sweeps in a great miracle to the left and ferries us away to an escape somewhere beyond, as yet out of sight—which, a few hundred metres down some curving lane, I discover leads to another building, not so fearful-looking now, more like a great block of boredom—in fact a former seminary, even if its glumness does suggest a sanatorium, or asylum—which is the place known as Preparatory.

I still don't know what has become of my trunk and tuck-box. Perhaps they were stolen by my father's porter, which I may have to report, as I have no pyjamas to put on. When I climb down, my nose instantly begins to run, like a tap, and I have to blow it at least twice with the handkerchief of which my mother spoke. My hands are numb. I still can't find that other glove. Perhaps it's in the satchel after all. But the pressure to my chest exerts such force upon my ribcage that my skin somehow seems loose for me now, too large, baggy, and my movements accordingly awkward, gormless as I lollop on the ground, stunned by the lamps on the school façade and the glare of headlights. I see some cases being pulled from the boot of the bus, then plonked down at random. I turn around disoriented, but can see no sign of a horizon, only hedges and fences and goalposts for some game or other. And now I see my tuck-box appear, like a mercy, like a prize; but the driver dumps it without care, without the care with which it was packed. I go and pick it up and put it by the entrance. By the time my trunk emerges, and it seems to be the only one about, most of the boys have already gone inside, but I can't lug this weight alone, and I'll never be helped by that driver; and then, at the final hour, a teacher comes, the teacher, my saviour, and he smiles into my eyes more warmly than any parent ever smiled; more warmly, too, than any friend who might ever last your lifetime. Because although I do not even know his name, and though you'll scoff because I'm childish, I know with absolute certitude that this redeemer, this most handsome smiler-among-smilers, who from this juncture onwards makes my life just about sufferable, will one day be mine.

OF THAT FIRST NIGHT at boarding school, which so many children, right through their lives, recall with an intensity that verges on the bridal, I remember nothing save collapsing into bed, shattered, and, just before falling over the cliff into sleep, being seized by a quaking, chilling inner rage, a rancour so profound and unforgetting that although I've managed to tame it, I don't think, puerile as it may seem, that I've ever quite managed to exorcize it.

But I do remember, with a searing lucidity, escaping after breakfast to the passage where tuck-boxes were kept at that place, stacked on slatted shelves which ascended according to seniority. And I remember kneeling reverentially on the painted concrete, the level for new boys, and my hand shaking for the secret combination, and I remember feeling that sacred click, and then, as if I were opening a tabernacle, gradually raising the humble wooden lid, and being assailed without warning by a wave of such sadness as nearly deranged me. I went dizzy. Nobody must see, I remember thinking, not for anything, because the contents of this box, the fruits of my mother's labour, which a matter of days earlier I'd observed with such spoilt indifference, were suddenly splashing with tears.

I wipe my face with my sleeve before proceeding. Then, momentarily robbed of courage, I close the lid once more and blow my nose for relief. When I resume my inspection, I see, first of all, the inside of the lid, papered with the clowns and the boats of my mother's vinyl, and this alone transports me to a time which, morosely as I spent it, now strikes me as idyllic. Lost children of Eve. But next, as I hunch on the floor and crane my neck in, just as she had done while I sat back at a distance, I'm assaulted by the mass effusion of her scent, which is communion to me. I inhale as you would inhale after being strangulated, bestially. And again. I can hardly control it. Then I decide to stop and be quick, to save it, to keep the genie of my mother's loveliness trapped within.

The contents of this box, which was to become like an altar to me, a place of worship which I would visit with dogged regularity, were, in fact, largely treasures of redundancy. At the top of the trove lay a small mohair travelling rug, of the sort which a lady might spread over her knees on a car ride up to the hills. This rug, of softest aquamarine, was to grow, for me, into a sort of security blanket, and I used, when nobody was looking, to rub it against my face as if the mohair were my mother's cheek. And though this ritual felt like a sin, and regressive, like a betrayal of all the prayers for progress which my parents had offered up for me, yet it felt irresistible. And I went on doing it, compulsively, for week after week, until the memory of my mother was all but extinguished.

Beneath the rug was a collection of beautiful obsolete things: my old silver crucifix, which nobody, so far as I could see, hung over beds in dormitories; a hot water bottle in quilted satin, which Matron, spying it on my pillow before I'd decided what to do with it, confiscated for safe-keeping and would, at the end of that first term, return to me—one corner blemished with the frotted remnants of some pinky lipstick. There was also a box of *turrón,* packed among these things because it would survive the journey without perishing, and because it was typical of my homeland, sweet and rich. Then there was an oval silver frame like a large pendant, with a hanging-loop through which my mother had laced a long sad ribbon of green petersham, like the ribbon which had rosetted the beret of my last spring of liberty; and into this locket she had inserted a formal, sensual, softly focused portrait of herself, draped in a shawl from Manila—an image which, like the silent-film star that she appeared, she had dated and dedicated to me. And so, although with the exception of the *turrón*—which I learnt to nibble meanly, calculating as I did so, as if it were an advent calendar, the remaining days of my imprisonment—all the contents of my tuck-box were useless, yet they were, paradoxically, life-saving. But then, in the little side compartment, which had a further lid, I found, tucked between a cartoon dog and a cartoon tree, the first letter which my mother ever wrote to me.

THIS, THOUGH UNSTAMPED, was the model on which all her subsequent letters would be based, its airmail envelope flowing with pen-strokes of deep turquoise—an apt reflection, you might say, of her mildly exotic femininity—and addressed (as if I were a teacher, I remember thinking at the beginning) to Master James Moore. But she, unable, after writing my surname, to resist the force of her own blood-line (just as she was to prove unable, throughout the years that we held a correspondence—though correspondence does seem too fine a word for the vapid bulletins which I, week after week, before Mass on Sundays, was compelled to invent and surrender, unsealed, for franking), she now attaches to my surname, as is customary among her people, her own, her maiden one, Zamora—its capital dealt a spectacular flourish. And though this very flourish would instantly mark me out as an object of peculiarity in the eyes of those who huddled, every lunchtime, over a table reserved for incoming mail and tightly rolled comics, I cannot claim that even then I minded this conspicuousness, for the lineage to which my mother drew such exaggerated emphasis is, for all of its heated arrogance, what has, I sometimes believe, saved me from drowning.

But she didn't merely write, my mother: to say that she Wrought comes closer to the fact, for hers, unlike that of her spouse, whose scribblings scuttled along his company stationery as if scratched by the Osmiroid of some pent-up secretary with aspirations to librarianship, hers was a patrician hand, bold and angular and elegantly inclined and identical in style, if not in colour, to that of all girls of her background during that era. And although her words were frequently illegible to me, and later merely uninteresting, for they told of a world which had relinquished me, or which I was myself relinquishing, the fine tissues of her pages, which used to be known as onion-skin, and which traversed the heavens headed with a cross of her own making, were always infused (even if she was later to deny such an absurdity) with the enduring scent of her white gardenias. And it was for that, for her scent, more than her news, that I then lived.

Queridísimo Iago, Dearest Iago, she begins, adopting the diminutive that she was to favour, oh, for terms and terms to come—until the chill set in, when she chose to dilute the intimacy to a more correct, more cool *Querido Hijo,* Dear Son. She addresses me in the slightly archaic Spanish which I would come to associate with her, and tells me, without further ado, that she misses me greatly—a thing which, in this first letter, I find tricky to believe, since her thoughts must have been concocted while I still hovered in her company. She tells me that the house feels empty without me, which again I find puzzling, since, at the time of her writing, I did little but dwell in her vicinity. She hopes that I approve of the items included in the tuck-box, and trusts that I won't eat all the *turrón* at one sitting. I must try to make it last, but I may share with other boys if this seems suitable. She's sure that I'm enjoying my new life and making friends aplenty. She reminds me to be courteous at all times, for in this way, I shall see, I shall make myself popular among my peers. She encourages me to pay attention in class, and not to be frightened to say when I don't understand things. She has no doubt that before I realize it, I shall have become a fluent Englishman, and how that will please my father. She thinks that she may have to accompany him on a cruise to Sicily, stopping off at Madeira on the homeward lap, but, if the plan goes ahead, she promises to write from her cabin, and to send me postcards numerous. Nanny, alas, has had to leave us, and has gone to look after a large family. Anyway, I'm a big boy now, aren't I? She reminds me to say my prayers without fail every night—¡even if it's in Spanish!—and then, after declaring that she is my mother who loves me, she signs off with great old-fashioned ceremony, her name trailing away like a plume claimed by the wind from a magnificent hat.

LOOKING BACK, I think of my earliest days at that establishment as a time not of anything so obvious as crisis, for, despite my outward manner, which was more sedate, more self-possessed than that of most of my contemporaries (and, for that matter, than that of some of the staff, who, soon enough, I began to overhear referring to me as supercilious—an observation which, rather like my father's bladder-of-a-puppy-dog, I took to be a plaudit), inwardly I felt too fraught with the business of keeping up with the changes which were flying at me, like pigeons in a bathroom, to register what beneath the smoothness of my surface was really happening. I would find myself walking down endless galleries, close, wherever possible, to the radiators and heating-pipes, and alone most of the time, as if where others went I knew not to venture, for my sense of difference from them could only aggravate my sense of loneliness in their company. I think that even the poor teachers regarded me with bewilderment at the beginning—later they would do so with a prurient disgust, for rumour, by then, would whisper that I held the key to some unspeakable vice, some monumental sin which both repelled and engorged them. But for now, they merely extended to me the semblances of smiles, sidelong and suspicious, sly as the smiles which my parents might have proffered to some deaf-mute servant, preferably a black one. But that these teachers should, by allowing me to wander unsupervised in my spare time, fancy that they were granting me a chance to dispel my foreign anxieties, to adapt to my new environment, to settle down, did not, even then, cut ice: to the young, such ruses are transparent. I entertained no doubt that these pedagogues-apparent were, in reality, summarily washing their hands of my irksome linguistic handicaps. Yet ironically, this very negligence was to prove vital to me, for it enabled me not so much to recover from the alteration in my external life, which couldn't have been drabber, but, more pressingly, to come to terms with my false reality. Because although I may have appeared to be a pretty child, and assured, and refined—not that such attributes are of advantage at places that peddle holy dogma—I knew that I'd become, and dramatically, something quite other, which is what I needed to learn to manage. And my air of confident precocity, which resulted, I suppose, from that congenital bravado filtered down to me through my mother's line, served to mask the fact that I was trying, much more than to adapt to my surroundings, to contain the rage that now belched like a beacon inside me, and which at times, such as during indoor games, or sports, or runs—none of whose rules or objectives I could fathom—surged to murderous fantasies incorporating my detestable father. So that whereas, in their absence of didactic nous, those foolish guardians of my welfare believed that by leaving me to my own devices they might at least seem to be granting me indulgence, showing me compassion, such a notion could not have been further from the mark. For the real transformation, the sudden conversion, had already happened, like a crack, on that first night. And the result had been a fissure in my being so pronounced that any possible further claim to the realm of childhood had been swept away; and I, at once neglected and indulged, found myself suddenly landed at that bleaker place, perilous and more dark than any satanic mill, which is the inarticulable province of the premature adult, of the lover before time. I had learnt, with a bolt, the meaning of corrosive anger, and it struck me with a force that was as good as biblical. Not once had I felt abandoned, for my emotions then were still entangled, like weeds, in the waters of my mother, but I did feel made over to danger, thrown to the lions. And my task, more crucial than any education, English or otherwise, became, from that first day, to discover a means of survival. Guile, manipulation, call it what you like. Art. Slime. But I needed an accomplice, and I wasn't going to find him in class.

I MUST WRITE in Quink of royal blue and not in black, which my mother says is the best colour for a man, though not with my own fountain pen which glows like lunar opal, but with a dip-one handed out from the cupboard. And exercise books no longer come with squared paper, to help you make your letters round, but lined with line after line after line. Orthography they call spelling; Calligraphy, writing. Even punctuation is different: colons are no longer to open the way like headlights: they're out of bounds. And semi-ones are no longer like long commas, to give you respite, but sloppy foreign excuses for a perfectly decent full-stop. And words may no longer be broken by means of a hyphen at the end of a line; no, you have to pace yourself, pause, then move on to the next level down. And if for some reason, the teacher said, you make a mistake, don't use that expensive rubber of yours and make a great mess, much less tear a page out, which isn't allowed: simply (and he explains this at a snail's pace, as if I were deaf) put-a-sin-gle-stroke-through-the-off-end-ing-sy-lla-bles—like so, denoting an error—and use your brain next time, that's what it's there for. And my Sevens can no longer be crossed, nor can my Zeds, nor the figure One be given a hat—continental habits, to be discouraged. When your parents have sent you all this way, boy, it isn't for nothing, it's for an Education—by which he means a Proper One. For which, the teacher says, I shall one day be grateful.

And in the margin at the top of your essay, you have to insert AMDG, an acronym for Latin words which I don't yet know, meaning To the Greater Glory of God. But in order to remember I just say to myself: *Alas Me Den Gloria,* let wings give me glory, which seems to do the trick. And then, at the end of your Prep, which stands for homework not done at home, you write the letters BVM, for Blessed Virgin Mary, though some boys, to be funny, squash their Vs at the bottom, so that it reads more like BUM.

No more pesetas, of course, but pennies which, when small, are hate-pennies, and, when bigger, grow into pences. They come in dozens, called shillings, not *decenas,* which are tens. And finished are litres and grammes: it's gallons and ounces now, and different pounds, though these aren't for spending, and anyway, spending a penny is another matter. And kilos have become stones, but not as in throwing. And insects of metres, like millis and centis, are inches—twelve of which make up a foot which is twice the length of your shoe on a ruler. And three such rulers equal a yard, which has nothing to do with patios. And miles is more than kilometres, and can also mean a lot, and afar, like your home and your homeland.

Of all the boys in my class this morning, I'm the only one who knew the meaning of a Diphthong, which I guessed from the *diptongos* taught by Don Jesús. But my guess did not, I do not think, impress this teacher here, because he looked put-out, as if I'd ruined his joke, as did the other boys, who call me a Dago, which is one sort of foreigner, but different from a Wop or a Frog, though any foreigner is, I think, known as a Wog.

I suspect that people in this language must be colour-blind, because so many shades turn out to be not what they seem: a lilac flower, for instance, they call a Bluebell; and a dog which is fawn, a yellow Labrador; and a red coat for the foxes is described as pink, when pink, deep and true, is what you get on the cape of a toreador. And when they say that a horse is grey, they don't mean like our horses in Vienna: they mean it's white as snow must, I suppose, be driven.

And there's a new page in the Atlas to be learnt, full of green and pleasant lands and mountains running up the middle like a spine. But when I was asked about this, I went into a confusion and heard myself reply Pyrenees, when I meant Pennines, which everyone did find Hilarious (new word). And after my mistake, the teacher, who has spearhead sideburns such as I have only seen on peasants in the mountains of our island, told me not to look so constipated, boy—which seemed to me like his mistake, because, in Spain, when you're *constipado,* it means you've caught a cold, a thing which I have not, as yet. But everyone laughed anyway.

I WALK INTO the communal lavatories, which are empty and tranquil with the sound of trickling waters. I head straight for the middle cubicle. As I go in, I notice, washing his hands behind the door, the school carpenter, who makes fences and teaches woodwork and is called Mr. Brown. Quite a fat man. Not young. He does not even say Good Morning. I go into the cubicle and lock the door, which needs a shove. You would think he might repair it—Carpenter would, in no time. As I barricade myself in, I hear the steps of older-sounding boys, with deeper voices, approaching, and now using the stand-ups—without partitions, which I think is Ancestral (another new word). I begin to pull down my shorts but, as I turn to face the lavatory, I suddenly see, sunk in the water, and surrounded by a yellow glow, like a revolting sea-monster in the depths of the bowl, a massive turd, so fat and solid that it has failed to flush and swim into the sewage. Logged. I am appalled. This has been done by him. I could never have produced such a monstrosity. I have never witnessed the like. I can hardly believe it. And now I have a problem: I can't walk straight back into some other cubicle because I'll be seen by those boys outside. I can't flush and then flush again because I'd be stuck here for hours, which would look peculiar, and even if I did, it might not go away, and then what? Yet I can't conceivably Go while this Thing lurks below me. And even if I went, just supposing that I did, over a whole lot of paper, how do I know that it won't make things worse? Someone could think I was responsible.

I pull up my shorts and close the lid. I flush in the hope that the monster will go, and I leave quickly—tricky because of the stiff door—and I pretend to wash my hands, flick them about, don't bother to dry, and go off, press ahead and escape to the yard behind the kitchens, near the shed for carpentry, and then, as I begin to relax, just then, I hear myself, half-sick with the tension, half-dead with the shock, having an Accident. Blessed is the fruit of Thy womb. I think of my mother. It feels like her fault. I walk, trying to be invisible, unsmellable, up to my dormitory, which is empty, thank God. I stand by the far side of the bed, facing out, and in a flash I have my shorts off, and with them, their repulsive contents, which I'd happily throw out of the window, except that they have my nametape on, and anyway, I don't have fresh undies. The rest of your uniform they lock in the linen room.

I roll the pants as carefully as my squeamishness allows, get into my shorts once more, and hide the soiled rag in my pocket. I go off, fleeing from my own stench, half-closing the door behind me in an attempt to stifle it, and I walk, much faster now, scampering along the top corridor; and when I come to the stairs, which are adorned with cases of stuffed pheasants and partridges and pelicans, I race down to the washroom, where I rush to a remote basin of cracked porcelain, without a doubt ancestral also. I run my filth under a scalding gush of water, and my sins flee down the plug-hole. I leave the mess for a second, and go to fetch my nail-brush and soap. I try to scrub in a manner that approximates the motions of the maids at home. I pound the pants against the side of the basin, trying to keep down the noise, and mercifully the stains do seem to lose their colour, gradually begin to look as if they might go. I squeeze with fury, rinsing over and over. And then I hang the pants, to dry, on the hook which bears my number, and I hide them under my towel, which is yellow and long, but I'm frightened that someone might come in and notice strange drops plopping to the floor. I take the risk. I have no option. And then I quickly unzip my shorts, and using my sponge, which was plucked from the bed of the ocean, I wipe myself between my thighs all the way to my bottom. And I feel the damp and fetid patch inside my shorts grow cold. And then I have to throw away the sponge. And, half-relieved, half-revolted, I spend the rest of the day worrying. But when later I return like a robber to the washroom, my pants, though stiff and wrinkled, have dried, alleluya, and look vaguely white once more. My heart recites the (Spanish) Gloria. And I creep upstairs to put the pants back on, and I pray that tomorrow may come soon, which means clean bundles of clothes.

A THING THAT IS PECULIAR: nobody here puts on clean clothes in the morning, only on the days known as Laundry. Nor do they have baths every evening. Not allowed. You have your bath in a room full of other baths, ranged like boats in a harbour, after games one afternoon a week; otherwise, communal showers, which I find difficult. And when you have a bath, using a tiny towel called a flannel which is fit for a dolly not a boy, you have it under the beady eye of Matron, whose other title is Miss Hogan, and I find that sometimes she smells a bit like the brandy to which my father wouldn't say no. And she twitters in a trilly voice at bathtime, and when she gets to where I am she always tells me not to wash sitting down, to stand up, which is embarrassing; and then she sings to me as she goes by: Calypso, Calypso, Calypso My Own— which of course I'm not her own, because I belong to my Mam'zelle who went away, and because none of these boys did ever have an esmerald, which once upon my finger I did sport. And while I'm sploshing about, thinking of the seagulls and the bathsalts of my past, and wondering whatever happened to the Eurovision, the others scream and laugh and throw nail-brushes behind Matron's back and sometimes they sing some hymn about a golden chalice or a cup, and a saint or hero by the name of Bobby Moore, though he can be no relative of mine. Time's up, she shouts; Everyone get dried. We step out. And to me she says, Buck Up Now, and clatters away like a lady-pig on trotters, still singing about her Calypso.

They often tell you to Buck Up here, which doesn't mean that your shoes need buckling. Except that mine, which are loafers from the Americas, turn out to be non-regulation, according to a teacher of older boys, not a Mister but a Kernel. My mother bought them for my uniform, I reply, somewhat affronted. Bully for you, he barks, your mother should learn to read instructions, doesn't she understand English? You're to report to the linen room and knock on the door and ask one of the ladies to order you a proper pair of slip-ons from the village cobbler, same as other boys. Tell her that I said so. (But I do not know his name, apart from Kernel, and the slip-ons that he means are *elasticated,* very hideous.) I nearly say *Muy Bien,* but luckily I remember to switch over, and reply: Very Well. *Very Well?,* he yells, infuriated. What you mean, boy, is Yes *Sir.* I pause to consider this, which sounds more like the answer you'd expect from a waiter . . . but in the end I just want to get away from all the staring, so I parrot back: Yes Sir. That's better, he reckons. Now go and do as you're told.

And this linen room which is warm and full of ladies' cigarette-smoke is at the other end of the school, upstairs but far from my dormitory, which is where I sleep without the sound of the waves in my dreams. And although I try to rest in peace, this is not always simple.

For I have a voice in my head that always wants to translate, and though I try to tell it to stop and let me learn the English which my mother, for my father's sake, does hope, it will not stop, not even after lights out. And sometimes in the night, the others wake me up, shouting Shut Up, which means Keep Quiet, because this voice of mine, they say, bursts out from my mouth and starts jabbering rubbish in Spanish. Which must be lies.

I REMEMBER, in the mornings, being awoken by the sound of a bell which, as if Rise-'n-Shine were not enough, the master on duty would clang from dormitory to dormitory. And as it drew nearer to yours, its gloomy knell would make you feel that you were being returned from the coma of purgatory to an insipid version of hell. That's how it felt. And then he would switch on a measly frosted bulb. It made me rabid. I would want to scream, not just groan, which is what the others did, good sports that they were; yet for all my stifled rage, my inherent petulance would incline me to ignore the bearer of these dreary matutinal tidings, to play dead. However, my show of indifference must, if anything, have proved too effective—to have spoken, rather than stifled, the silent volumes of my derision—for I recall, on several occasions, having had my sheets torn off me by a teacher—a Liverpudlian with a streaky page-boy cut and elongated nails on his right hand, who, aside from his penchant for the popular guitar, though his lack of aptitude would have inspired the ridicule even of schoolchildren in my country, was partial, I could sense, to natural blonds who were also natural athletes. And the impertinence of his assault provoked in me, such was my rising bile, a much keener resentment than ever I had felt when similarly accosted by my former Nanny after the siestas that I have recounted. Now, I would fantasize about leaping, as his hand dragged my bedclothes up, onto it and biting. Drawing blood. Licking the blood from my canines. And I did leap up whenever he thus affronted me, but predictably in a manner that was less mordacious than cowed, for although I may have been imaginative, I was also a coward. And so, shivering on my threadbare bedside-rug, I would strip off in prudent stages, to protect my pudor, and pull on my long socks and underclothes and shorts and, as I did so, I would catch the outlines of other boys standing about without shame and stretching like barn animals, which at my house would never have been countenanced, and I would hear them burping and farting and laughing, which, in my prissy former Eden, would have been *inaudito,* unheard of.

After breakfast, which first acquainted me with school porridge, I would return to my dormitory to fret about my bed, which nobody had ever taught me to make, and which, particularly when stripped to its foundations, to its stained mattress, I could never properly redress. And I would rue the beautiful crispness of my former beds, and the gentle care which my mother's maids had taken, and the pristine comfort of my daily laundered, waffled bedside rugs. But as often, I would rail in silence at my defective father, who—just as he had failed to inform me of the various rules pertaining to various games, or about the apparently proper way to eat at this place, which seemed to involve leaving one hand limply on your lap—so, similarly, he had never troubled, along with how to polish my shoes and knot my tie, to prepare me for this trivial task which others had already refined to the pitch of hospital-corners and apple-pies. And then, by extension, I would hate my mother for ever having married the man.

BUT THE FINAL STRAW of my disabusement came with my eau de cologne. This was the fracas that really caused the scales to fall from my smarting eyes. For, in my folly, in my blindness to the peril which, as predictably as day follows night, my actions would give rise, I would use a splash of toilet-water to flatten my hair in the morning, as I had done throughout my recollected life. This went unnoticed for a brief while, because people were still keeping their distance, sounding me out. But when the aroma of those few paltry limes was eventually retraced to me, and accusatory fingers duly pointed at my blushing outline, there rose from my peers, in the break between two periods, such an avalanche of (largely incomprehensible) spite that I grasped in a flash what is meant by wanting the earth to open up and swallow you. And next I recall plucking from the great babble, and hoping against hope for relief from the insults, which stung like stars, one word alone, and it was Woman. I thought of my mother. But then I understood that even those two short syllables were aimed derisively. And in that split second, the crowd, as one, realized that whereas the gamut of their other names had left me looking nonplussed, here at last was a something that I did understand, and wounded me. And Woman, You Woman, they would constantly chant, preferably when a teacher was about. And I swore to myself then that one day, even if it killed me, I'd get my own back. On each and every one of them.

The bell for the next lesson goes, but the disruption drags on regardless. The teacher walks in, and smiles routinely, then tells them to quieten down. I'm sitting, as I was to sit for the remainder of those early years, at the back of the class, next to a window, which, for now, is set too high to see out of, to fly through. The teacher wants, inevitably, to know what's been going on, what all the rumpus is about. And then one of them, Steel (a boy of skewering intelligence who will dog me in years to come), gets up, cool as a dozen cucumbers, and tells him. And I don't need to understand the details of the disclosure, for the accuser's tone is jubilant. All heads, uncontaminated by cologne, are turned to me. Open up earth. But now everything alters, backfires. I can tell that the teacher, the one who helped me with my trunk on that first night, is telling them off, and I hear from his lips words that delight me, like Stupid and Silly and Childish. And though his comments incite a steam of hissing and, by way of grudging compromise, an audible shift from Woman to Dago, basically the room has returned to order. But now I know where, in this order, he, Mr. Wolfe, stands, which is as if above, apart from the scum. And once the storm of the majority has been calmed, and as books are finally being opened up, he looks over to my corner, where the sun is suddenly shining, and smiles directly at me, and he embellishes the smile with a well-aimed wink, which shoots out. And it flies straight as an arrow. And it must have pierced my side. Because I think, looking back, that I may, at that instant, have fallen in love.

NONE OF THIS, naturally, does a thing to improve my standing in the class hierarchy, of which, in any case, I wasn't ever really a part—I was viewed, which indeed I felt, as a separate object, like a mule among cart-horses, or a blade of grass sprouted in spiked mud; but the incident did inspire in me the intuition that the closer I could bring myself to the man who had already saved my skin twice, the further I would be placed from danger. And though during Prep I would pore over my mother's letters, only to discover with what ease her Iago could, by means of a few treacherous curlicues, be embellished into a Dago, and although, when I defaced the backs of her envelopes with dagodago-dagodago and then, a second later, looked again and the line seemed to insist that there was agodagodagod, I knew that the only god who could help me now was not floating around vaguely up there, but cor-recting essays two doors down.

At lights out, when he was on duty, I felt able to endure anything, even the day to come, in the knowledge that this Mr. Wolfe would soon be coming along to say good night. And after reaching our door and telling us all to be quiet, and just before the light went out, he would wink at me, which no one ever seemed to notice; and although, to begin with, I would just smile at him lopsidedly, in time I gained the confidence to wink back. And this happened often: he was often on duty, for he was our supervisor. And when the winking grew dull, I noticed that he had added a further motion to his repertoire, and this gesture was a sort of sulking mouth which I think was meant to mimic mine, but which I now recognize as a pout—a thing that my mother had sometimes done and which I must have contracted through her blood. And so, as the weeks passed, and the lights went out, Mr. Wolfe and I, this foreign Moore, would exchange the briefest of winks and the slightest of pouts, like kisses in the making, and when the lights went out, I would sleep as if under the stars, praying for the sound of waves in my dreams.

WHEN HALF TERM STRUCK, a strange thing happened: it suddenly transpired that since my parents were still on their cruise, there was nowhere for me to be parked, and although I imagined that some cor-respondence on the subject would have passed between my father and the headmaster—a lip-smacking advocate of corporal punishment who worried his fingernails, sweltered profusely, and liked to tuck his tie inside his shirt during lunch—I was, until the last minute, kept in ignorance of my status as a Problem. In the event, some kindly couple offered to put me up, local publicans whose poor son, a day-boy two years my senior, and therefore a complete stranger, dragged me on foot, one dark afternoon, to the nearby village—even offering (I re-member because it left me flabbergasted) to carry my bag. I would have accepted, of course, for I then found such attentions to my liking, but the suspicion that his courtesy, which was delivered in the guise of a mumble, resulted less from spontaneous good manners than from his mother's instructions, made me think twice. If it were secretly to embarrass him, I judged, my acceptance could ultimately prove detrimental. At any rate, I know that I declined. And we spent our half term thus: he, wearing his mufti; I, trapped in my uniform, though it was decided that I might dispense with my tie; he, playing with trains and electric cars of unremitting dreariness; I, pretending to read bad children's books on a bad sofa. At night, the plan was that we would share a bed—which, despite my new fear of waking others up, I rather welcomed, for such a sophistication was new to me. Yet on the first night, just as I was getting into my pyjamas, it was suddenly sprung on me that the arrangement did not stop there: it came with a codicil, namely the accommodation of his magisterial tabby. This prospect paralysed me, and I recall that we argued about it—I may even have tried to bribe him—but he won out. This was his bed, his room, his house. And I did see his point, little as the point pacified me. To me, that creature was hair-raising, for, on my island, cats had been wild marauders of the mountains; and sometimes you would hear them scrapping and yowling and up to Lord-knew-what in the night. So that when this beast eventually ensconced itself between the two of us, emitting purrs which I found repugnant, I recited my prayers with a fresh degree of fervour, but took care to leave my parents out. And at the end of that break, I complained to them about the whole arrangement as strenuously as the limitation of unsealed envelopes allowed, but while it is true that never again was I farmed out to strangers, it is also true to say that the alternative did not exactly improve matters. Because, for years to come, I found myself foisted upon distant relatives of my father's, fusty people who, far from feeling like relatives of mine, habitually voiced their contempt for anyone who elected to live under that Generalissimo chap and, in their demeanour, differed scantly from the teachers who disliked me. I think that just as I dreaded being inflicted upon these assorted couples, most of whom were dotted about London, they too regretted my appearances on their doorsteps. All were far too tied up ever to meet me off any train, and besides, there was no need, I should just jump in a taxi, there's a good fellow, and when I arrived, or so they claimed, they would pay the cabbie. In the event, none of them ever did, not until I plucked up the nerve to ask for my taxi fare. But their repeated oversights had bitten hard into my funds, as if to aggravate the fact that my father (I would invariably discover at the Bureau de Change in London) made a habit of short-changing me on my pocket money. Without exception, those disparate relatives seemed to view me, particularly as I grew more contorted and rarefied, with an edgy discomfort, and were at certain stages to inform my parents, I later learnt, that I struck them not as other boys of my age, but as withdrawn, peculiar. They should keep close tabs.

THE SECOND HALF of that first term is less memorable for the ritual indignities which I brought upon myself on the playing field, where it seemed to be permissible for members of staff to flex the muscle of their tongues (You're meant to be a Full Back, Moore, not a bloody Goalie, you great Woman), nor for the minor ailments which I suffered—chapped hands, chilblains, colds, the usual trivia—nor even for my growing awareness of the nauseous smells which, as the weeks passed, seemed to filter with increasing pungency through the establishment—rotting fruit in the locker rooms, exudations of recycled lard in the refectory, manure from outside creeping into the galleries— as for the alterations which, without conscious planning, had begun to suggest themselves to my behaviour. It seems to me now that I grew, in her absence, more like my mother—by which I don't mean effeminate so much as romantic, sentimental, taciturn.

In the afternoons when I wasn't at games, I would make a habit of knocking on Mr. Wolfe's door, not even armed with a decent pretext half the time, and he would smile over his music and beckon me in, as if for my succour, to look after me. I would stand by his window, taking care to remain out of sight, brushing myself on the curtain and thanking my lucky stars that I wasn't stuck outside in all that filthy mud. Sometimes he would offer me an apple from a bright bowl which he kept on a shelf, and I would accept, charmed, despite the fact that I was nervous to chomp at it, to eat it without a knife. But I would never have admitted this reluctance: I just tried to keep the noise down, because the juice that sprang from the pulp of his crushed fruit was sharper, lovelier to me than nectar. As I grew bolder, I took to standing by the chair where he sat working at his desk, and sometimes he would stroke my thigh, as my former teacher at primary school had done, but my grateful pleasure now must have been apparent, for my knee would often be heard to crack. While one of his hands wrote on, the other was warm with protection. This gentle bond between us seemed to me to compensate for my general sense of exclusion, my loud unpopularity, and to reduce my fears, to grant me reassurance, if only for a brief while. It nourished me. And in time, I grew hungrier—and more guileful.

Despite my absolute lack of comprehension, my complete inability to figure out any plot in English, never mind the intricacies of some raffish wartime cine-drama (though I found myself perfectly able to understand *Lord of the Flies*), I would attend the films which were shown on Sunday evenings, and I would ensure that I sat right at the back, for I knew that as soon as the lights went out, Mr. Wolfe, who showed the films, would emerge from the projection room and sit beside me. Thus placed, we would both, as if by tacit agreement, cross our arms, and this combination enabled me to smuggle my hand into his cuff and stroke his palm, and his wrist, and even the stem of his forearm. Sometimes he would stroke me back, but despite the darkness, it was never with the same ease as in his room, which was marked Private. Without ever needing, at that time, to verbalize matters, I think that we both understood that although what we were doing was in some way extraordinary, almost beautiful, it also lay beyond the horizon of what was admissible. In chapel, during prayers, he would stand in a small loft to supervise the congregation; but no matter where I stood or knelt, and though I resisted the temptation to turn round, I knew that his eyes were burning into my back.

THEN CAME the Christmas holidays, marking my first of countless trips in the unenviable capacity of Unaccompanied Minor, which, in my experience, simply involved needing to be supervised for longer than necessary, having to ask permission even to go to the lavatory, being pestered to join some club for peripatetic pre-pubescents from all over the globe, and being smothered by the condescending sympathies of uniformed women who resembled my snappy former Nanny. Contrary to what one might have supposed, I do not think that when the moment came I was ever as exhilarated by the prospect of returning home as were other boys, for the complicated journey back filled me with trepidation. I would have to navigate my way through the stormy spirits of my peers, which would grow less bridled, more venomous, on the train as we approached London; next, I would have to pretend to be indebted to some uncle and aunt in Kensington, who were in due course to be appointed my official guardians; and after being dumped the next morning at an airline terminal in town (assuming that this was when the plane took off, which sometimes it was not, thus furthering the protraction), came a bus trip to the airport, a possible planestop halfway through the haul—sometimes at Madrid, Málaga more usually—and at last, at night, I would walk down those metal steps, back onto the tarmac of the island of my mother's ancestors.

My first return was odd, for though she came to meet me at the airport, and demonstrated every sign of effusion, and kissed me repeatedly, and still, to me, looked captivating, yet something about my mother wounded me. Even if her gardenias had not altered, her tone was unquestionably more animated, more frothy than I remembered, as if my absence, far from having depleted her, had rather served to effect a revival. And to me, even if I couldn't rationalize it, this felt, though venial, like a betrayal. She found me pale; my tan had waned. She found me skinny, but perhaps I had grown. She'd organized children's parties for me to attend. In addition, of course, though I could hardly even admit this to myself, there was a corner of my soul which now yearned for, missed, the uniqueness of that teacher's attention. The power of his protection seemed to me, in my confusion, of greater worth than that of my parents, for it was only towards him that I felt grateful. My bedroom at home—and this had been trumped up as a Surprise, so as to exonerate my mother from the need to consult me—had been redecorated in a manner that I disliked on sight and never thereafter ceased to dislike. And for the first time that I recall, I risked earning her disapproval by telling her what I thought; but she replied that I was young, that my taste was not yet formed. There was something autumnal about the paper—leaves, I suppose, or bracken, possibly; and the floor, in line with the new insular vogue, had, from wall to wall, been carpeted darkly as pounded olives, which must have been intended to convey manliness. My circus-rug was gone. I took to snoozing in the nursery, on the sofa with hydrangeas of cretonne, because, now that Nanny was no more, there was less general bossiness. And I used my bedroom as little as possible, for although the nursery was short on secret drawers, there was, in any case, nowhere for me to hide my secrets now other than in my chest, which was locked.

Nothing about that holiday was special, memorable. But a month later, to the day, just after the feast of the Epiphany, which at home was not observed because my father, being English, saw fit not to, I was returned to the airport and waved off. I did not feel that my mother liked me so much any more. She had such a multitude of other things to like now, you see, she who, disguised as an ocelot, had struck me as so desolate only a brief while back, whose sadness had half-slain me when I left her stranded on the platform at Euston; she who, since that time, had penned me at least a dozen epistles of turquoise longing. But she appeared to have grown frivolous, skittish, lightweight, and to be absorbed by flitting trends and forthcoming balls and glossy magazines and her couturier in Barcelona and, how can I forget, the heated argument of whether her lustrous chestnut mane should, or should not, be cropped. She seemed forever to be attached, laughing, to the telephone in her bedroom; and though, even outside it, she had become less reserved, yet she had become, somehow, less accessible. Her siestas were briefer now, she was less tired, but the issues which excited her were no longer of concern to boys.

THE WINTER TERM that they call spring cannot, by contrast, be forgotten, for it was punctured by a pair of shocks. The first concerned Mr. Wolfe. I had dared to wonder whether he had thought of me. I had thought of nothing but him on that long journey north. And when the bus dropped us off, I witnessed, to my stupefaction, that he was transformed. He still smiled. He was still handsome. But he had grown a beard, and I'd been given no warning. It was full, and dark, and belonged to that complex tone of brown which coppers in the sun. I found myself bristling with the same resentment as I had felt over the alteration to my bedroom. Why had my feelings been ignored, I to whom it mattered so crucially? But unlike the bedroom, to which I was never to warm, I did, despite my initial stabs at sarcasm, soon warm to his new mask, which at once seemed to conceal my passion from the public and to render me lustful, for the child is capable of lust. Gradually, and almost without realizing, I grew consumed. My visits to his room in the afternoons became more frequent; my conduct, less demure. Now, as he stroked my leg, I dared to stroke his beard, and as he smiled, I hardened in my shorts. It was, from then on, only a matter of time. The road was paved; I did not plan it; but it glittered before me.

I wake up in the middle of the night, and put on my slippers and my dressing-gown. I go to the lavatory, squinting. There's a soft votive light in the corridor, to guide me O thou great Redeemer. And on my return, like a sleep-walker, I choose to lose my way back to the dormitory and find myself, instead, at his door. I'm nine years old. Don't look so shocked. I knock. He says: Come in—as if he'd been expecting me all along. My eyes, now, are like orbs. I am in orbit. I say: I cannot sleep. He tells me to close the door. I lock it. And I walk, as always, to the window. His curtains are not drawn.

IN THE SEDUCTIVE GLOW, which, two storeys beneath the radiator where I stand, facing out, spreads across the purple grass beyond the school portico, I see, I saw, like a sombre revelation from the darkened English heavens, brown-paper leaves, fluttering down, long after autumn, fluttering in pairs from the birches beyond the window, swooning for a moment in the sky-without-stars, being sidetracked briefly by a misleading gust, and shifted, but ultimately abandoned and falling, falling first not so much furious, as disenchanted after the event, like spiralling butterflies resigned to die.

I TURN INTO THE ROOM, which seems pungent suddenly, acrid, and deathly quiet despite the soft whirr of his gramophone. I stare blind into the glare of his anglepoised light for what feels like a lifetime; and now, though I can neither breathe nor give credence, he brings me over to where he sits and I find myself within his crouching, trembling hold. His great knees, like quaking horses, are about my thighs. He levitates my heavy dressing-gown from my shoulders, and it rises to reveal my buttoned-up front, then drops, with the posthumous thud of a tassel, to the forgotten ground. And now he takes me up, and I, at last, am suspended in the heights, caught up but safe, and out of the spot, and in the embrace of his arms, which are thicker than my thighs, and held, like a swing, behind my rump. My slippered feet have flung out and crossed idly round his lower back. His glorious head, like the head of an unhappy conqueror, or an accursed emperor, now bows forward to meet mine; and his soft clean hair tumbles over his eyes and I can no longer see out, for his lips are sealed to my brow; and I am blessed at last. Do not be mistaken: this first gentle bearded kiss was perfectly, sacredly right.

My lover takes me up fully now, gathers me like a word of honour to his breast, which feels stronger and broader than the bed of my early siestas. I am cautiously calm, as if I'd come unharmed through some perilous crossing yet were not quite landed. His heart, which I can feel thumping against my side, must be anxious, fearful; and for a split second only, and only for him, I am filled with a sharp, inexplicable sorrow, like some lost mother wailing out from another country.

Together we seem to rise, he and I, into the clouds of this unknown land, to drift about like joined but uncertain spirits, to turn and turn like slow dancers about the edges of our floor, softly knocking into an occasional table, brushing past some unexpected frame and fumbling for safety—but together, held in unison. One of his arms has moved away from me, like the arm of God, and with a muffled click extinguished the light. We are awash in moon, flooded.

I tighten the grip of my thighs and kick off, one-two, my slippers. As they hit the wooden planks, he flinches with surprise, recoils a fraction; but now he relaxes from the mounds of his shoulders, down his veined arms, to his hands. And though I can hardly make him out, I can tell that his outline has smiled in the dark, for the creases round his eyes have cracked and burst like rays of silent laughter. The comfort of his lips is returned to my brow. And now my arms shoot out without thinking, enraptured, up to the skies, like parallel fireworks, bursting at my fingers, which stretch like starbursts. My sleeves are sliding back, gathering in warm wrinkles about my shoulders; and my hands now join and twist around, holding tight behind the neck of this new god of mine, then dropping like a lament over the vale of tears which is his muscular back.

Clasped head-to-head, as if inseparably, he steers us round the desk of our unspoken courtship, and past the shelf with the bowl of shining apples, to the far wall by the fireside. My head tilts back as he leans forward, over me, to replace with his uncommitted hand the needle which has been hovering at the end of a record—some Nocturne—back on the outer groove of its vinyl, on its soundless introduction. He closes the lid as if impatiently, a little roughly, and by the time that the music has once again struck up, we're moving toward his bed, which is single and open and white. He brings me down to his sheets, which smell of him, more delicately that I recall ever having been brought down, until I'm placed, most gently, on my back; and then I let go; and we separate for a brief while, are in limbo.

He exhales, or sighs, and stretches out before me, twisting up like the trunk of an ancient Roman tree, some great laurel. And next I witness the terrifying miracle, for which I have longed, for which I have lusted, which is the absolute fullness of his nakedness. But I feel diminished by it, as if reduced by some mysterious shame, probably my ignorance. I close my eyes. I suppress the urge to cover myself. I wish I knew how to pass out. The retch of a match strikes out from nowhere, and I hear the fizz of a wick bring alive a candle, vaguely behind the pillow, somewhere near a pile of exercise books above the bed, essays unmarked. One of mine festers among them. I blush in my shadow. The room must be catching fire. I cannot believe the heat. Only my feet are frozen.

He starts with my pyjama top, which he undoes almost desultorily, as if already I represented a let-down, some small (but irrevocable) error—button by button, sleeve at a time, nothing that I couldn't myself have done; and he discards the jacket in the murky direction of the radiator, where it drops. I hear, aghast, a button clank against the iron, and it sounds like a coin of little value clanking into a begging-bowl. And to me, the merciless echo of this brittle sound, as it races along the trembling labyrinth of school pipes, seems to announce to the slumbering world that although I'm not personally accountable for the mishap, yet I have transgressed, passed over. Treachery is in the air. I tell him to check that my nametaped handkerchief hasn't escaped from the breast-pocket. It had.

The unveiling of my pyjama trousers, their shedding, I cannot relate on account of the blinding embarrassment which invades me as he tugs at the bow of my cord, which seems to have squirmed down towards my hip-bone. I turn for respite onto my front and try to escape into thoughts of those indolent days spent, pretending to be dead, on the beaches of the summers of my past. My mouth is salty, dry; but as I swivel further round, to face the wall, to face the waves, I hear my breath rasping loud and too fast, like the breath of a lecherous mongrel. Yet he, as if to dispel any spectres that may be hovering about my head, as if to show to me that he can read me like a testament, slowly and with devotion now approaches the soles of my feet with his beard, like a faithful animal.

I am rigid. His eyelashes, like insects, teeter over the backs of my heels; the hair of his head brushes the hollows of my knees; and then I sense the mattress beginning to move, shifting heavily, like a sand dune. He is crawling like a predator over me, but he does me no harm. He merely breathes, pants vaguely above the line between my utterly clenched buttocks. With his tongue, which flicks, he licks at the globes behind me, one of which, I have a sudden memory, bears a small birthmark, like an island. Then he moves up, along the length of my back, pausing on every knuckle of my spine until he comes to rest at the clearing between my shoulder blades, my wings which give me glory, my AMDG.

But now he must have risen slightly, for his head is inclined, and his mouth rests, clasps, half-bites the back of my neck with a kiss of life, hot into it. He is upon me, yet he does not weigh me down. His elbows are like brackets beside me, scaffolding. All I can feel is the tremor of his fur, and the assumption of his beard. Hovering over me, over my ear, too closely in fact, and audibly demurring but ultimately finding the courage, he now whispers to me those words which have been whispered since time immemorial, the fatal line that this is, must be, cannot but be, and I must never, ever forget, our Special Secret. I do not flinch. I could not for the life of me. And then he goes and shows me, proves it all to me. Bequeaths me the very world. Undoes me. I have never cared less. Take this, all of you, and eat it: this is my body which will be given up for you.

He turns me round onto my back, to face him, to face the ceiling; but his enormity now covers my nudity entirely, conceals me from view. His head, collapsed, rests on the bed much higher than my own head does; his feet lie far beyond mine. Yet his chest and his thighs and his mound and all of the hair that is stifled between us, all of these things are precisely poised as he slides himself, slowly but not entirely surely, between my upturned thighs, which are reluctant, and under my horribly white parts, which have yet to ripen.

He withdraws unexpectedly and, in a faint huff, seems to kneel up; and though my eyes-without-scales are closed, I hear him spitting like a tramp; and though I cannot tell at what, nor why, my instinct feels insulted. But yet again, I must be mistaken; for now, with greater ease and a little less calm, and after coaxing the banks of my thighs slightly apart, he introduces himself like the wetted neck of a swan, or a serpent, or a dragon. And there begins a motion, a rhythm of such balminess as I have never before experienced; and gradually a progress is established, and my knees, of their own volition, seem to rise with his rising thighs, and to fall with them and rise and fall and rise, and our breathing is absolutely one—though his, of course, is much louder than mine, louder still and louder, and then I hear, after his latest fall and rise, a sudden gasp or grunt, and then another, and then I sense some vague diminished writhing, a cooling rallentando. And returned to life, I now grow conscious of a smell exuded by some warm creamy substance, like a disease of slime which, smeared along the insides of my thighs, is starting to slither backwards.

Ours is an understated unwinding, unremarkable even, and the curtain which comes down on this first act, a slightly abrasive stripy towel of many colours—introduced between my loins, inserted to allay my repulsion. And it is left there to rest a while, quietly. But there is loud applause in my heart.

As I put my clothes back on, I look out of the window once more, but now from the perspective of somebody other, older somehow. And the tiny lights that wink from afar, motorways or rail-tracks racing over some viaduct, and the hoots which I can hear in the distance, or perhaps can only imagine, all seem to point to a world of freedom beyond, into which I would like to run, to the circus, to the Russian ballet: I would learn to do the splits, to dance on wires, to tame great tigers, to swallow tongues of fire. I could do anything. And yet, as I gather myself up and unlock the door and creep back into the world of linoleum corridors and extinguished chapels, a part of me wishes to turn back, to rewind, that I were once again a child, and that just as he had lowered me to his sheets by candlelight, he would now raise me in his arms and carry me, like an ailing infant, back to the feathers of my eiderdown. But, of course, such thoughts are futile: the cage that entraps me allows for no such devoted licence. My job is to reach my bed undetected; and while the others snore and grunt about pitches where they score every run and every goal and every try, and where the roars of approval are theirs entirely, I sneak into bed and slide back into a coma.

ON THE MORNING after that first night, I remember stealing into Mr. Wolfe's room while everyone was on the way to breakfast and, whether out of shame, or jealousy, or perhaps out of straightforward love, approaching his sheets and removing a few pubic hairs which horrified me, for I did not possess such things, and proceeding, I who could hardly make my own, to make his bed, to cover our tracks. I felt as if propelled, however prematurely, into the role of lady-of-the-house, or perhaps I was just the valet. In any event, my days now became lengths of enforced patience, like stretches of unrelieved cloud, perpetually overcast: Being your slave, what should I do but tend upon the hours and times of your desire? I have no precious time at all to spend, nor services to do, till you require. And while I waited for the world-without-end hour, to which I would awake like clockwork, like some mechanical cuckoo, at eleven o'clock every night, I delivered myself to a life which I now see was upside down. I longed for nothing but the dark. It was like existing in reverse. Like dwelling inside a negative. But I was, in fact, never tired. That, I suppose, is what love does: it adds, not subtracts. And those hours of nocturnal rapture, which meant more to me than any number of runs or goals or tries, were my soaring score, my constant prize. I felt revived by them as my mother had been revived by my absence.

Towards the end of that term, leading up to Easter, I think that my patience must have snapped, or my sense of power suddenly risen, for I remember going to the wall outside the changing-rooms, which was covered with notice boards for all the various matches—elevens or fif-teens or whatever-it-was-a-sides. Anyway, these boards were cluttered with names on movable wooden pegs, each peg denoting a given player's position in a game, as allocated by whichever master happened to be the referee for that particular match. I viewed these boards, which were arranged on a daily basis, with abhorrence, for to me they spelt only one thing: humiliation: they reminded me of my father . . . until one day I realized how easy it would be simply to remove my peg, to disappear from sight. I'd been an idiot not to think of it earlier. So I stole my surname from its hole—goalie, full back, whatever—and threw it with some gusto into a dustbin, pushing it hard to the bottom. I told no one, nobody noticed, and for a while I just lurked, basking in the glow of my own ingenuity, behind the door of my dormitory. If anyone happened to step onto the corridor and threaten to approach, I would slide under a bed and hide. It was not difficult. But eventually, predictably, I was found out, and the teacher in question, the geographer with the sideburns, sentenced me to four strokes.

This needs explaining. Although the standard instrument for the infliction of pain at that school was a thick rubber object, known as a ferula, which was shaped like an ox-tongue, and which, depending on the culprit's status, was administered either to his buttocks, or later, when he was older, on his open palms, younger boys such as I were beaten across the bottom with a table-tennis bat, of all silly contrivances. (My father, needless to say, later boasted that in his virile day the birch had been the crowning glory of punishment, but by the time that softies such as I were sent along, the latter had been rendered obsolete.) I now recognize the custom of penalizing pupils' misconduct by means of a wallop less as barbaric, or retarded, than as laden with sado-masochistic undertones. I can only compare the punitive measures of those days with antics which, in the fullness of time, as you know, I was to witness at heavy orgies, or in night-club dungeons. For without exception, and whatever the weapon or number of strokes, which could, if necessary, escalate to a dozen (I think that this was the maximum, but I couldn't swear to it), the pupil was obliged, under penalty of a repeat dose, to thank the teacher for the pleasure. Thank you, Sir. Amazing, no? And although, until the peg fiasco, I had never myself been beaten, it was the concept of verbal acknowledgement, more than the agony, which made me baulk. My brain could not digest the idea of being coerced, within this context, into a semblance of gratitude. And, as if such a semblance were not sufficient, the custom regarding the bat for Juniors was that following its infliction the boy must sign his name along the instrument, both to prove his wordliness, and to symbolize that no grudges were harboured against the aggressor. It made my Spanish blood boil. And when the hour for my first beating loomed, I discovered (which was my next shock) that the master on duty, was, of course, Mr. Wolfe.

There is a jumpy queue outside his door. Just gone seven o'clock. I'm third in a line of four. First boy's already in there. Whack, whack, whack, the bat goes; then, brief pause, presumably for the autograph, and—hey presto, here comes the hero, hopping about, face flushed like a tomato. In goes the next transgressor, who, like me, is up for four. It passes surprisingly slowly. But when I walk in, to say that Mr. Wolfe is staggered would be to sell him short. He is panic-stricken, frozen; and I, by contrast, am suddenly struck with a wily notion. It doesn't need to be spelt out—it's better than eloquent—for I have narrowed my eyes and locked my jaw. I cannot now recall the details, but either I wouldn't bend over, or he couldn't bring himself to exact the punishment. Either way, a frantic wordless compromise is reached: he places a cushion over my rump and thrashes it dramatically. But he looks both shameful and furious. Not a whisker of a smile now: he's biting his own mouth. He loathes me. And then, with consummate smugness, I stuff my hands in my pockets and leave him no option but to inscribe his weapon with the daft irony of my surname, Moore—which he does in capitals. But when I walk out, I do, if only for the sake of fair play, manage to simulate a passable, agonized hop. God only knows how the fourth boy got on. Yet this was the start of my trouble, the real one, which was my sudden discovery that, in my grasp, I held a great pot of molten gold.

AT LIGHTS OUT HE BLANKS ME, and instead, can you believe, beams at the creep in the bed next door. And in the night, though as always I wake up with a jolt, I dare do nothing. I feel too nervous. This is my true penance. I fear that if go to him he might ignore my knock, or turn me away, or worse, take me to task for the whole fiasco. What happened, he will say, was all my fault. Only myself to blame. I mean, removing one's peg, how stupid can one be? And how dared I undermine his authority as I did? I've behaved disgracefully. He's ashamed of me. Never again, he'll claim. He means it, he'll say. Couldn't I just steer clear of trouble, for God's sake? And what if it happened again, what then? (Silence.) He wouldn't hesitate to beat me, he insists. Same as anyone else. And I tell myself that I'd answer back, counter him, refuse point blank. In which case, he'd reply, I'd come off the worse: he'd hand me over to some other member of staff. Oh really? And what would his reason for not beating me be? A meeting, something, mind my own business. Sure, sure thing. And as I lie awake in bed, with all this conjectured hogwash tumbling around my skull, I feel the force of my split: yes, of course I've won out, got off scot-free, and two fingers to the yob with the sideburns who calls me Woman; but, deep in my darkness, my conscience gnaws at me, for secretly I feel guilty, unworthy of the privilege of Mr. Wolfe, unfit for his intimacy, which is vital to me; and so, in a sense which is more real, I conclude that I'm defeated. And, though I skip my prayers after all this worry, I do resolve, before drifting off to sleep, not to give up. To bide my time, wait for a sign, be prudent, muster an apology if need be.

Yet in the morning, I rise feeling stronger, more invigorated, and I bypass his pubic bed, condemn it to its own making. Perhaps, after all, I can survive without his services. Who can tell? I go about my business as if there'd been no mishap. I don't clap eyes on him at breakfast, much less do I seek him out. Instead, I back my resolution to reform, to quash my sinful love, with an elaborate internal analysis of his basic wickedness. How can a man keep, just along from those apples, which are the fruit of Paradise, a figure of some devil called Beelzebub and not be at least a Heretic? Explain that to me. He pretends that his small ogre is the original Lord of the Flies, but I've heard that, actually, which sounds more likely, it's the prince of devils who presides in hell alongside Satan. And what's more, the little bronze idol is so especially treasured by its owner, who calls it his Mascot, that one boy who wouldn't listen, and carried on playing until he dropped it and it broke, was given three Detentions in a row, plus three thousand lines—which he had to do all over again because he couldn't spell Beelzebub. No question about it, Mr. Wolfe must be a Heretic, which, as sins go, I'm afraid is a whopper; and besides, the demon is horrible to look at, reminds me of the gnomes which I caught smirking at the bus when I was first sent to this dump.

I compound my inner diatribe with reminders about how, when you stop to consider, his room is stuffed with creepy things: the skin of a sheep, a blackish kaftan, joss-sticks; and what about that picture called the Tree of Misery and Death? Who, in their right mind, other than a Heretic or secret worshipper of Satan, would want such a thing near them, advertising Misery and Bad Habits and Torment and Derangement and Guilt and, biggest of all, running proudly up the trunk, which is coiled with the snake of Eden, Drunkenness? See what I mean?

And then I tell myself that anyway, his desert boots are hideous, and I hate their squeak, and his patchwork ties are ghastly, as is the fact that, though I detest it, he insists on liking rugger and dragging mud into his room and leaving dirty kit strewn about. And those films he shows are boring anyhow. I should just revert to being good while I can. So I try to summarize my predicament with the fact that whatever the perks of his company, which can't be that great because next time, he says, he'll beat me regardless, he's basically using me to do that thing, that secret, which, sooner or later, I might have to admit at confession, though at the moment I couldn't begin to describe it.

I make myself scarce. Today he doesn't teach my class, and I get through my other lessons without particular trouble. In the afternoon, which for those in my year is recreational, I don't bother going to basketwork or leatherwork or pottery or carpentry. I walk out into the wilds. This valley, like a shallow bowl which, abandoned in a damp courtyard, has begun to rust, is dotted with a few stone houses, like dead flies. It makes you yearn for the red flame of a brick cottage, which, if ever you spot one, always turns out to belong to some master, and brings you back to bleak reality. The wind around these parts blows not as the wind on my beach had done, whose sound was like the salty music of a shell brought to your ear by seas from sunny lands. This wind engulfs you, races through your head, renders you deaf to your own mind. It claims you. And though it brings water to your eyes—which, even if such tears are unfounded, you feel you should disguise—yet there is a peace despite the howl, for, with luck, you will cross the path of no one, pupil or master. And you can stop at the Post Office on your way back, and buy a bag of pear-drops and a bottle of pop with your pocket money. And when you walk into school, at least you can remove the weight of your duffel coat, which is heavier than a camel, and forget the problem of your missing glove, and, despite the smell of sprouts, the warmth of the school feels almost comforting.

I DECIDE TO GO to the library. I do not read the notice on the door, for I have read it once, which is enough. Because it threatens, in letters like those of an old Bible:

> **For him that stealeth a Book from this Library, let it change into a serpent in his hand and rend him. Let him be struck with Palsy, and all his Members blasted. Let him languish in Pain crying aloud for Mercy and let there be no surcease to his Agony till he sink in Dissolution. Let Bookworms gnaw his Entrails in token of the Worm that dieth not, and when at last he goeth to his final Punishment, let the flames of hell consume him for ever and aye.**

Talking is not allowed, though you can look at the *National Geographic*s if you want, and, if no one's got there before you, you can go to the shelf marked Records and play, say, the *Carnival of the Animals*. But never loud, boys.

This was not, however, always easy, owing to a pudgy mythomane by the name of Hardy, whose soft great head was attached to the rest of him by means of a much-vaunted spastic neck, which, whenever he pleased to raise it in the infirmary, exempted him from games. Hardy boasted an impressive line in faking teachers' signatures, and I now suspect that he may have been my (thwarted) rival in the affections of Mr. Wolfe. He further claimed to be in direct descent of the Marlboroughs, and did, to grant him his due, succeed in hoodwinking lots of us, including the more gullible domestics. But perhaps as a consequence of his high claim, he would, in much the same way as a certain class of tourist insists on monopolizing the best deck chair, insist on monopolizing the library gramophone, only ever to play the rousing strains of "Land of Hope and Glory," which projected him into visible raptures. It made you want to strangle not just the smitten devotee, but also both the Sirs whom, in their different ways, I held accountable: Winston Churchill and Edward Elgar.

This strange fantastical creature was older than I, and more eager of body, so that when his number was finally up—because someone with a conflicting passion for Purcell's Trumpet Voluntary clobbered and nearly properly crippled him—he resolved, instead, to become Grand in a manner which, to me, was far more intriguing. And his party trick became, for the benefit of anyone who cared to request a viewing (I don't think that he charged a fee), the leisurely retraction of his advanced foreskin. A specific facial attitude accompanied this action, but I'm sure that you can envisage it. And yet his grandeur did not stop there, for when he gained access to that realm which, to us, was far more fabulous than any Blenheim, namely the realm of the honest-to-goodness Ejaculator, he would, by way of confirmation, trap the jisms of his seed in the glassy confines of an old ink-bottle, which he carried about his person—you never knew who might require proof positive.

I suppose that in his keenness to earn the popularity of which my mother spoke so highly, he could conceivably have concocted his magical goo with a pinch of sherbet and splosh of milk, or by rummaging around in the chemistry laboratory, but such ruses then eluded me, for I wasn't so much devious as deviant. And later, when I learnt about the whole mystery of cavaliers, a clan of which, it turned out, I was a member, I did obliquely badger my mother for an explanation about the phenomenon that was roundheads—among whom, once I grew more inquisitive, I discovered Mr. Wolfe to figure—but she simply blanched with pure ignorance. And when, one day on the terrace at lunch, she was inspired to invoke my father's assistance, the latter replied that circumcision was a thing that happened to Jews. Which, since the school was so rampantly Catholic, somewhat baffled me.

MY RESOLVE TO AVOID Mr. Wolfe was to prove, needless to say, short-lived, not so much because I feared myself incapable of surviving without his favours—after all, insults and bullying didn't kill you, they just made your life a misery—but for other, more delicate reasons. What I found myself in, where I was steeped, little though I then realized it, was a place infinitely more risky, which is, I'm ashamed to admit, (or was), the pit of idolatry. To me he mattered more than a mountain of Beelzebubs. And aside from all his other attributes—his strength, his touching humour, his gentleness, his kindness—the man was just so beautiful. My mother had declared that men could not be such a thing; it was not possible: a man could only at best be handsome, and a handsome man (by which, I suspect, she automatically meant a gentle-man) should play his looks down, carry himself with modesty, not like some flashy word in italics. But Mr. Wolfe (for even in my recollection that is what he would always be—his Christian name having somehow felt inadmissible, unutterable) really was beautiful. Oh Mother he was, though you were never to see it. You were too busy seeing to your own exquisiteness.

His (how could it not have been?) was a shifty kind of beauty: large but twitchy, strong yet uneasy, almost criminal, or political, or wounded. Certainly there was, to me, a magnetic danger about it. His head may, I think, have been too small for his frame, or perhaps his body was too massive, or perhaps it's simply that I became accustomed to admiring him upwards. He was the tallest member of the staff, and, though hugely adult to my mind, among the youngest. I now surmise that he must have been in his mid-twenties, but the great age-gap between us felt more miraculous than mad, like a stormy sea that had been crossed against all wisdom, but crossed without (apparent) mishap. When I did observe him, and astonish myself at the sight, he was always fully clothed, for his nakedness, to me, was simply a fluores-cence in a dream, otherworldly, flickering and shadowed and amor-phous as a wilderness, to do with everything but my eyes, which, during our nights, preferred to be closed. No, it was in the day that I absorbed my good fortune. But after hours, it was he who feasted on me and my young prettiness, which, then, was the most that I can have provided. Yet our appreciation, if not simultaneous, was mutual. Of that, to this day, I remain certain.

There was something athletic about him. You could imagine him throwing a discus high over my father's Alma Mater, and then smiling at his triumph, but coyly. And it was really this mix of strength and unlikely demureness that I found so striking, of vastness and vulnera-bility. Perhaps others weren't aware of it—which suited me: I had no need of eagle-eyed creeps like Hardy (not yet, at any rate). My lover's trousers were always, in my opinion, a fraction tight. When he sat at his desk marking essays, the seams of his inside legs puckered like scars, and these emphasized his thighs, which, conflictingly, I never thought could be tight enough. I tried never to look at his crotch. He had no hips; he was built like a man. But when he stood in the refectory during grace, he sometimes fidgeted with his buckle, or with the metal tongue of his zip, which drove me to hunger. Because he was my sole appetite, you see, my only nourishment.

His eyes were Irish, or American, beyond England. They were grey and dappled and heavy-lidded, a little sinister, with very long straight lashes, immensely dark. His skin was, by contrast, most fair, and fine, and might even have veered towards a pale sort of freckledness. And then there was, of course, that savage beard, clipped but thick and coppered, both redder and coarser than the hair on his head, which was soft, and which often flopped, and which, in another life, he might have let grow like the hair of a Christ. But the beard, you just wanted to stroke it, to rub it, as if, by doing so, you might tame a wild animal, the one inside you. The thrill of it was audible.

He wasn't really a talker, as I recall, other than in class, but there, in any case, everything was the wrong way round. He taught me English for a while, but the language that he really taught me was far richer and sweeter and more complex than any language ever to issue from my father. Mr. Wolfe had a weakness for poetry; but when he read it out, he sometimes bit his lip between stanzas, as if he were harbouring a distraction. And those poems, well, you have to believe me, they were principally recited for my benefit. Who else in the room, other than the two, the two, the two of us could possibly know how the world, which seemed to lie before us like a land of dreams, so various, so beautiful, so new, hath really neither joy, nor love, nor light, nor certitude, nor peace, nor help for pain? As I say, there was something wounded about him—but beautifully so, heartbreakingly.

Once I began to nurse my own half-broken heart, the remembrance of gardenias seemed no longer to suffice. I had too much lonely blood inside me, too much of it to pump around, and I needed help to keep myself alive. Ultimately I believe that it was my emotional hunger, my craving for survival on this front, more than any precocious desire for control or wish for exemption from those activities which I considered unpalatable, that accounted for my susceptibility in the face of this new surrogate love. Its physical dimension felt, at the start, but incidental, part of the life-saving package, and I think that the satisfaction which I derived, the replenishment, lay closer to solace than to anything approaching sated lust: I was too prudish, too mental. Too childish. I sometimes suspect that my pleasure then was akin to the pleasure felt by many grown women, which flows without a need of climax. My ungrown body, smooth and fresh and tanned, may have provided him with incentive, provocation even, but in retrospect, from my perspective, I would say that it gave me away, betrayed me, for its awkward incompleteness manifested outwardly the unformed state of my character. Still, I was grateful to have been perceived by him, and adopted, and salvaged; and besides, there was more to our union than mere reciprocal charity.

AT EVENING PRAYERS, I sit carefully towards the rear of the chapel but, on my way out, I catch sudden sight of his bearded mouth beaming from the loft above, baring its teeth at me; and though I instantly avert my eyes, as if I'd noticed him before he'd clapped eyes on my back, my entrails are going mad, leaping and jolting and banging. Singing praises; giving thanks. And when he goes round the dormitories later that night, his composure is such that never in a million years would you have dreamt that any obstacle, least of all a Ping-Pong bat, had ever separated us. You would have assumed that I'd genuinely been thrashed. His smile, now, as if to verify this fact, is broader than ever, loaded with indulgence, persuading me that we must let bygones be precisely that. And it is followed, this shameless subtle smile, by the wink and the pout of better times, which makes me melt, and close my eyes, and start to choke up.

There follows the inevitable resumption of our romance, its first reunion having felt perhaps a fraction rough. I remember him biting me, quite hard, but I also remember feeling so exhilarated, so grateful that he should have chosen to rise above, to leave unmentioned the original subject of our discord, which stemmed less from any inherent fear of violence on my part than, ironically, from an abhorrence of sports involving contact, that frankly, I would have let him, had this been the price of his generous silence, take a chunk out of my calf. For just as one might recognize an old flame on a busy street even after decades have passed, I recognized, however briefly, however confusedly, what it was to be Back. And I was unwilling to go without my twilight happiness. My difficulty, if any, became less the business of offering myself up than the thought of tearing myself apart from the making of our inexplicable love; and returning to my bed is what began to feel like the real, cold lie. And thus we met, in this enchanted, repetitive ritual, which sometimes lasted until the sky diluted to violet, night after night. And my person was never once harmed. And as term grew to a close, what began to fill me with dread was not so much the return to the land of my forefathers as another severance from the source of my love.

DURING THE EASTER HOLIDAYS, because I was growing more obviously disagreeable about my (public) school life, and also, she had remarked, because I seemed "introverted" around the house, my mother gave me, to mollify me, a tiny battery-operated record player which was, then, the last word in technical gadgetry. This, when I returned to school, I locked among my other tuck-box secrets and, when I was free, I would (though always clandestinely) play my Spanish forty-fives. Those banal renderings, which unlike their English counterparts seemed always to tell stories rooted in regret and duplicity and rotten love, were like hymns to me, anthems, chants of disembodiment. I knew every lyric; I learnt every harmony. There was an imaginary nostalgia attached to the whole experience, as if truly, at that moment, I were the long-suffering secretary, or the neglected wife, or the Love of Man (Amor de Hombre), or the woman singing Eres Tú (You are), whose words, swollen into hysterical orchestrations, sobbed along with lengthy eulogies versed in abstracted similes—like a dagger when it cuts, or a cloud which raises me from the ground and nails me to the sky like a word, or like a game of chance which seeks neither to lose nor to triumph, or like a guitar in the night. And just as later I was to identify with the hero and the victim and the mongrel and the woman and the close-up in the pornographic pastimes which were to crowd the years of my maturing, so, here, I became every voice, every mood, every wretched figure in the songs, for they appealed to my sentimental hollows, and taught me, if not as yet to lie persuasively to others, to do so, and soundly, to my own innards. Yet there was to my activity, which felt risky as well as thrilling, a basic honesty, a pure suspension, such as is recommended when receiving the sacrament of Communion.

To begin with, I played my records covertly, in places where I knew that I wouldn't be seen: behind the gymnasium, or in the woods if it wasn't raining. The showers, too, when empty, provided me briefly with an indoor venue—at least until, one careless afternoon, I found myself being bawled asunder by the Kernel and his band of mountaineers. Drenched in the torrent of their collective ridicule, I was thereafter to find sanctuary in Mr. Wolfe's room, where our arrangement became that if he went out he would lock me in, and, on his return, after protractedly fiddling with his noisy keys, would kick the door as though it were jammed (like the door in the lavatories) three times before walking in. As the plot thickened, of course, we were to devise more sophisticated codes, to denote hide-in-the-cupboard-I've-got-people-with-me, or blow-out-the-joss-sticks, or stop-smoking-and-open-the-window, or get-off-the-phone, that sort of thing; I can't recall the exact details. But for now, this small trinity of kicks did me nicely.

IT WAS AROUND THAT PERIOD that a nebulously sacred show was set to hit the West End scene, the libretto of which, with canny commercial prescience, had already been scored, recorded, and widely distributed. The songs of this musical (which luckily remained, as yet, unseen, for it turned out to be a trifle racy) provided the archaic religious sector with the means to doff a biretta vaguely in the direction of modernity, which I suppose encompassed contemporary Christianity. This music became popular both among staff and pupils at my school, and although Mr. Wolfe had not exactly struck me on account of his spiritual leanings, nowhere was this double album more prized than in his room, for he was devoted to theatre-going generally and to musical theatre in particular. For my own part, I disliked the majority of those numbers, which, one after another, seemed to scream and shout towards the genre of rock-'n-roll—an anathema to me still—but there was one ballad in particular which did manage to bewitch me horribly, and I use that adverb advisedly: for, while I was magnetized by its melody and the visceral soprano of Mary Magdalene (who'd been no saint, that much I knew), her lyrics about not knowing how to love him, or what to do, or how to move him, and about being changed and seeing herself and seeming like someone else—all of these things discomfited me. And then she would ask the whole world whether she should bring him down, whether she should scream and shout, whether she should speak of love, let her feelings out. But the woman was a tease: much as I listened to her moaning and her fretting, she offered me no solutions, she came without answers. But anyway, Mr. Wolfe—and perhaps this was my doing—contracted an equal fascination with the song, so that the Nocturnes of our earlier congress now gave way to the first of those LPs. And though bizarre as an accompaniment, it felt almost mandatory. But because I was only really obsessed with that one minor hit, which was to become weirdly ours, and ours forever, long after it was all history, I would get up with greater frequency than the Land of Hope and Glory boy could, even in his most outlandish imaginings, have dreamed conceivable, ever to return the needle to its place of origin, which, as the nights grew longer, grew scratchy. And I remember how, in my idiocy, every time I crossed that candle-lit room to fulfil my self-inflicted duty, I would hide my corrupted but unfinished body in my dressing-gown, which itched.

Sometimes, though, I'd let the record run to its natural end, particularly if Mr. Wolfe had risen to a second apex, which, though heavier for me, and more arduous, somehow felt more flattering, more amorous: it must have been for my benefit, I imagined, that he was putting himself through this additional exertion. It was as if, unable to believe the experience, he were forcing himself to return to the top of a beautiful mountain to show me the view. And after his descent we would both, briefly, feel more tired, so that the needle of the record, left to go round and round, would suggest the dreamy sound of a small wave lapping against a harbour. And occasionally the candle would go out. And we might even snooze for a while, my body saved from the cold of the wall by the wall of his warm arms. But I would never allow myself to drift off entirely, for I sensed danger in that extravagance, and furthermore, the flexing floorboards in the corridor never properly let up.

TODAY, HOWEVER, the most natural thing happens. I awake in his bed to the initial clangs of the early-morning bell. Obviously Mr. Wolfe isn't on duty, which for him is just as well, but for me this feels like my certain funeral. I must, without detection, get myself back to the dormitory, and sharpish. I leap into my pyjamas. Mr. Wolfe, in his stupor, doesn't seem to grasp the catastrophe. I ignore him for now, and, paralyzed, stand inside the doorway. Then, once the duty master has gone by, and his bell died down, which means he's busy ripping someone else's blankets up, I unlock the door and creep out; but I feel so hot that it's far worse than blushing. More as if a raging fever had suddenly claimed me, as if I were starting to die. I'll have to pretend to the rest of the dorm that I was feeling sick and went to the night-lav.

But when I reach my dormitory, I know that I've had it. The master on duty, who, though he looks Indian, claims to be a Scot of Italianate extraction—Mr. Bonifacio was, I think, the name under which he travelled until dismissed for playing strip-poker *tête-à-tête* with some older pupil—is engrossed over my bed, and patting my bottom sheet, which must be incriminatingly frosty, with the palm of his dusky hand. For a man rarely without either a cigarette or jibe to mouth (and usually it is both), today seems like a miracle, a nightmare: he is absolutely silent . . . until at last, and rather quietly, he asks me to account for my absence. (I can't say the chapel because it's locked at night. I can't say the lavatory because you can't be there for hours. I can't say my classroom because the lights have been dark.) So in the end—and fast thinking is required—I produce a clever fabrication of what's really happened. I say that I've just been with Mr. Wolfe. Oh *really*? (He seems not quite to believe me, which feels unjust.) Yes, I reply, I went to see Sir because I couldn't sleep, but he said I wasn't allowed a sleeping pill, and told me to watch TV for a while, and then I must have gone to sleep, because he didn't wake me up until I woke up on his sofa. Mr. Bonifacio grins as if he's suddenly got the gist, and I think that I may have fooled him, because now he's walking very slowly out, looking pleased with himself, or with me, relieved that I haven't done anything really serious like stealing, or setting the place on fire. And then he starts to swing his bell again and, nodding to left and right, he resumes his early-morning round. And although all these oafs with gunky eyes stand about gawping at me, no one quite dares to mention the subject. Peace in our time.

After the drama with the missing rugger peg, and the unspoken difficulties to which it gave rise, I decide, sensibly enough, not to scuttle off like some sneak to tell Mr. Wolfe what has happened; instead, since Mr. Bonifacio fell hook-line-and-sinker for my version, I resolve to keep this new matter, which seems trivial by comparison, quiet. On second thoughts, I might just tell Mr. Wolfe tonight, for a laugh.

I AWAKE WITH THE GLARE of a torch pointed hard at my eyes. I turn to my side, try to identify the clever prankster. But it's Mr. Bonifacio, prodding my shoulder and whispering to me in his frantic Scottish voice to get up fast and not disturb the others. He tip-toes back to the corridor and dawdles on a creaky floorboard. I fumble around in the dark, belt my dressing-gown tightly, and follow him outside. In the gloom of the tunnel he shines the torch along the floor, like a stream of yellow brightness, like a river running away from India; and about his face I glimpse a smile that looks a bit nervy, sort of servile, as if he needed to request some favour from me, help with a translation or something. I feel quite flattered, grown-uppish. This might spell the start of my mother's keenly commended popularity. And I'm almost excited when he lets me accompany him down the principal staircase, which is thickly carpeted and reserved for the use of staff and prefects, although one of the latter once toppled over the banister and fell to the feet of Our Lady, crashing against the stone floor and fracturing his skull. This was before my time, but people still spoke, with expressions of recollected horror, of the tragedy. Because all the school's doctors and all the school's prayers couldn't put Prefect together again.

Mr. Bonifacio cedes me the way into his room, a courtesy which slightly surprises me, but still, I thank him, go in ahead, and wait in the middle of his shag-pile. He closes the door behind him—thereby suggesting to me that the matter under discussion is to be adult, confidential. He goes over to his desk, sits down with a cough, and offers me the opposite chair, which must be for parents because it feels high and rather comfortable. The room is dimmed. Only an anglepoise lamp stands, like a stork, on the oxblood leather of his desk, and now he directs the light straight into my eyes, like a spot in a circus. My sudden exposure blinds me. I can no longer even imagine his outline. I ask whether the beam could be shifted slightly. He says it's fine like that, which irks rather than frightens me, for his behaviour strikes me, particularly after the entrance ceremonial, less as menacing than as ill-mannered. I know that I could move my chair back a fraction, but something tells me not to push my luck. I put my hands in my lap. I look down. I resign. I hear him opening a drawer and plonking a paper pad in front of him. He plucks a Biro from his jacket and clicks it ready for action.

He begins: Now, I want you to tell me all about last night. What exactly were you up to, you and Mr. Wolfe? Goes without saying you can rest a hundred per cent assured nothing you say will go further than these four walls. Strictly private and confidential. (I was right.) He offers me his word of honour. His Biro now seems to be on its marks, and set . . . and yet it cannot go, for though my shrivelled heart is racing like the clappers, my mouth just will not start, is cramped at the gullet. We remain in our respective attitudes for what seems like an embarrassment, until he sighs and pretends to reassure me: Take your time; it's all right; I understand this can't be easy for you . . . —But the oils of his charm cannot assuage the turbulence of my muddy waters.

Next, he tries another tack: he's going to make things less difficult, he says, and provides a few simple questions. He asks whether I like Mr. Wolfe. Yes, Sir. Glad to hear it, he replies, and does Mr. Wolfe like you? I rein myself in and reply that I think so. Quite right too, you strike me as a nice chap, though we don't really know one another all that well, do we? I suppose not. Now tell me, why was it that you couldn't sleep? Don't know. Don't know *Sir.* Yessir. Does this happen to you often? Sometimes it does. And when it happens do you go to Mr. Wolfe? Not always. But sometimes you do, right? Yes, Sir. And then, what happens? Nothing, Sir. Are you sure? Positive. (Doubtful silence.) Listen, he smarms, you know you can trust me, don't you? I've given you my word of honour, haven't I? Yes, Sir, I know; you have. So tell me, what went on? (Eternal almost blissful nocturnal pause.) Nothing, I reply.

I can tell that I'm beginning to get up Mr. Bonifacio's nose. He extracts a packet of fags. Offers me one—his little joke. Would I like to light his cigarette for him? If he likes, Sir. He puts a shiny lighter on the desk, and slides it across to my side. I stand up and, at long last, am out of the beam, which has been scorching me like the white sun from the cliff above my childhood. He hoicks the bulge in his trousers, leans forward in his seat, and approaches me. As my flame trepidates toward the tip of his cigarette, his hand, like the hand of Judas, embraces mine; it kisses my fingers. My loyalties screech with sudden outrage, but I don't let on. Not a flinch; not a hint. For I begin to see more clearly now the place to which we're headed; yet though I glimpse the signpost of our dealings, it seems to point, like a two-headed eagle, in opposite directions. I decide that whichever road he hopes to take, whether it's to fetch me into his life or to slay Mr. Wolfe, both routes must be blocked. And I yearn very fleetingly for the softness of my lover's lips upon me. Mr. Bonifacio inhales superlatively, like an elderly maharani reliving her story, and when his smoke is in due course expelled, pearl-grey ringlets seem to hang about the shiny edges of his face. I want to go.

But this is not going to happen yet, I can tell you. Indeed, the interrogation drags on and on and on and on. He's trying to wear me down, to run me out, and he's not doing the job half badly. I stifle a yawn. I reply in monosyllables to what my mother would call his impertinences. He manages to ascertain, and to record, the facts that on That Night I couldn't sleep, that I went to Mr. Wolfe's room, that we sat on the sofa, that we watched TV, though I can't remember exactly what (*Colditz?*)—a lapse of memory which strikes him as unlikely, no? I do not admit whether Mr. Wolfe did or did not touch me during the proceedings. There are limits. Three times I refuse. The room is so still that you could have heard a cock crow.

Mr. Bonifacio is not too pleased with me. He thinks I'm not being co-operative. I think that he's being nosy. He says that I'm not to mention our little chat to anyone, understood? I allege that I won't. He tells me to go straight back to bed now; and as he pats my creeping back, he adds that he hopes there won't be a repetition of this unfortunate incident, by which I don't think he means our interview. Good night, Sir. Good night, Moore. And once he has closed his door, I make my leaden way all the way to the end of the corridor, lit only, and only at occasional intervals, by misty forms which, like oblongs of grey gauze, seem to steal in through the classroom windows. And I climb, exhausted, up the back stairs—for servants and common-or-garden boys. I do not, though I long for his embraces more fervently than ever before, dare to knock on Mr. Wolfe's door, and I drift like a diminished ghost back to my dormitory. And although, once in bed, I tell myself that I've acquitted myself passably, nor do I imagine that I'm yet out of the woods: for my intuition fears that I may yet find myself hurtling, like the rapids of a river, towards a forest without clear exit. And were it not for the fact that my stomach is still in spasms, you could have thought that I was already dead, dead meat, a corpse.

IN THE MORNING, my former caution now thrown to the rising winds of panic, I scour the place in search of Mr. Wolfe: dormitories, washrooms, dining room, chapel loft. I put my ear to the masters' lavatory: not a murmur. I even stick my head round the door of the staff common room: nothing. But, just before assembly, I find him at last, coming, drained of blood, out of the headmaster's study. He yanks me aside and orders me, with a lack of caution equal to mine, his eyes wilder than fury, to meet him in his room at once, to skip assembly, get up there fast.

He closes his door. Seems already to know what's gone on. Doesn't appear annoyed so much as fretful, and now begins to shake with sinister force, like a man in the late throes of Parkinson's. Even the legs of his dark trousers seem to be quivering, which I find alarming. Shouldn't he go to the infirmary? As he tries to talk to me, his mouth sounds drained of saliva. He clears his throat several times. He stays well away from me, as if he feared me suddenly, as if I were a Danger sign. Doesn't bother to berate me—no time—nor even to ask me why I didn't warn him I'd been caught by Bonifacio. Appreciates how, after the interview last night, I didn't dare to come to him. It's all right. He'd actually suspected something might be up.

It turns out that Mr. Bonifacio has recorded the entire interrogation, and taken the tape to the headmaster, who's already played it back to Mr. Wolfe, who says that they're determined to get to the bottom of the matter. Mr. Wolfe tells me, with sudden gravity, as if everything depended on my grasping this fact, that he is not, repeat not, a Homo-section, but Bi, which sounds confusingly mathematical. I nod moronically. He tells me that we're in serious trouble, both of us, but stresses that his plight is more critical than I may realize. His entire career, he says, hangs in the balance. They're out for his blood, even though yes, the whole thing's a set-up, it's obvious: Bonifacio just wants to stab him in the back and go for the job of supervisor. More responsibility; better money. For both our sakes I must call the headmaster's bluff, which sounds like he wants me to insult him. I must deny-deny-deny. Nothing went on, remember. Not a word on that tape that I need to retract. Mustn't give in to the pressure. Stick to my story, volunteer nothing. My age, my innocence, my lack of experience all count in my favour. But Mr. Wolfe says I have an old head on my young shoulders, and that he knows he can rely on me. He's proud of me. If I play my cards right, the whole thing might just blow over, storm in a teacup stuff. Head-master says he wants to see me straight after assembly, but is eager that the business be kept under wraps, so I'm not to stand outside his study: his orders are just to go in without knocking, and wait for him to arrive. Mr. Wolfe's trembles have abated marginally, but I, by contrast, now find myself steeped back in the waters of my turbulence, and being dragged alone downstream, flailing, as I had feared, towards the forest of disaster. I can go now, he says, sitting down. And good luck.

I FOLLOW MY INSTRUCTIONS. The headmaster's study, to which I have never before been granted access, is identical in shape to the room of my nocturnal travels, but more busily decorated, in shades of chest-nut and almond and raisin and walnut, like breakfast cereal, or feed for a hamster. The overall effect of his walls, which are flocked with papers of clashing pattern, as if slapped up with unrelated ends-of-lines, brings to mind a struggling provincial restaurant, too genteel to stoop to white, too poncy quite to fool the punter. The drapes, tied back with cords better suited to a dressing-gown, are Georgian-striped in treacle and milk-chocolate. The pelmet droops lopsidedly. Next to a foam-filled sofa, covered with a stretchy homage to autumnal foliage and cir-cular cushions of fake tapestry, is a three-legged side-table bearing an onyx ashtray with a dainty brass plaque, and a lamp in the shape of a Taiwanese pagoda, its ruched shade swooping in creases of caramel nylon, and festooned, in café-au-lait, with dolly tassels. I suspect that implicated in these arrangements has been the proud plebeian hand of the headmaster's wife, a pockmarked lump of a woman with puffy ankles, a frantic tic about her piggy eyes, and a propensity for perfume such as is to be found at funfairs, who ekes her own stipend by helping at Reception part-time—courtesy not of her husband but of Mr. Pit-man, she'll have you know, can touch-type good as the next one. Along from the desk stands a teak-effect filing cabinet, its top drawer, half-opened and labelled Juniors, set too high for me to peer inside. A vast, engraved and crested cup of silver plate, lid dented, worn to copper round the handles, and set upon a flaking pedestal of simulated ebony, presides over alphabetical folders of cardboard. On the radiator sits a soggy tea-towel with a harvest scene, shepherdesses on haystacks, stained with patches of unattributable gunge; and, propped next to the pipes, directly below where my pyjama-button once struck, a folded shooting stick with a seat of pigskin, in plastic. On the other side, a muddy bag of golf irons, no putt. A cracked-veneer bookcase, gleaming with leatherette volumes amassed by mail-order from Sunday supplements—some laid horizontally, for the style—displays, on a dusty Bible, a pale wooden crucifix with a basic stand, its resinous Christ glued into agony and designed to be luminous. Flung into the wastepaper basket there huddles a small mound of teabags, like a drowned litter of newborn mice. And on the desk itself, peeping from beneath a mess of timetables and files stacked over a virginal dictionary, I detect, for the first time, the black oxtongue of a ferula. I have no desire to touch it. I perch on one end of the sofa, avoiding its clammy arm, and let my eyes glaze over the fitted carpet which, needless to say, is richly patterned with lozenges and goldy medallions. But my body leaps to its feet as soon as I hear him arriving.

AS HE ENTERS in sharp profile, led by his paunch and followed by a tweedy hump, the headmaster resembles a pompous great hamster, like a puffy rodent from a children's book, but sweatier, and exudes the powdery stench of that class of man who, a stranger by birth to pomade and essence of vetiver and sandalwood and extract of lime, has lately broadened the coal-tar of his toilet to encompass, as well as unisex hair-lacquer and an electric dryer (handy for the reduction of moisture from unwashed underarms), musky products which, found at the local supermarket and designed to deodorize, he employs, less complicatedly, simply to mask. Fabergé, if I'm not mistaken, was the misleading brand.

He sees me, of course, but pretends to find himself in private. He goes to the window and looks out absently, in an unconscious approximation of my motions by candlelight one floor above; then, he turns abruptly to face me, his coat-pockets flapping. He smacks his lips. Beads on his upper lip jump. Long, gingery hairs creep up from the

slack collar of his paisley shirt, which he wears with a natty corresponding tie. I cannot, even for the sake of Mr. Wolfe, to whom I owe
my courage, muster the travesty of a smile. Sit down, Moore, says the
headmaster, and I return myself to the stretchy sofa, trying not to look
too disgusted, like a society woman at the lodgings of her wet nurse, as
if this were the kind of motion I underwent every day of my life.

A matter of some gravity has, he announces, been brought to his
attention; and although the circumstances, he adds, may not be my
responsibility entirely, he would, notwithstanding, like to be availed of
my version of the facts. (Deny-deny-deny: this is my mantra.) His
questions are dull, identical to those of Mr. Bonifacio, and I answer
them just as dully; but I pretend, for the sake of authenticity, for the
sake of my lover, to be more thrown than I am: I have a bash at melo-
drama: I fidget with my hands, jiggle my ankle, yank an earlobe once or
twice. And, when chance allows it, I sneak a look out of the window
and think of the viaduct, of the circus, of Russia.

The headmaster makes one error only—though, to me, it is of significant advantage: by failing to disclose Mr. Bonifacio's recording of
our séance, which is the sole source of his (somewhat restricted) information, and instead pretending that we're starting from scratch, he cannot even fast-forward me to a more detailed confession. His feigned
ignorance empowers me, feels like a second try at the same demeaning
part—and now, furthermore, performed in easy broad daylight and
before a less ambiguous auditioner. He encourages me to blab, not
least by sliding out, from beneath the mound of administrative paper-
work, his pet ferula, and by tapping it against his podgy hand. Wafts of
his onion-odour pass me. I disregard them, but long to wrinkle my
snout, and wish that I were upstanding, for my mother's haughty blood
is pricking at my snobbish arteries. I don't look down, I don't look up. I
look straight ahead, and from where I sit, all that I can see, as he struts
about like a fat fool in a pantomime, is his low-slung wobbly rear and,
when he paces back, the compression of his tautened little crotch—
which I keep dodging. To stare seems inadvisable.

Behind the sweaty blubber of my inquisitor hangs a large monochrome photograph, like an advert for invisible hearing aids, depicting
the side of a corvine head in a pose of burning concentration. The sitter, the 28th General of our Society, otherwise known as the Black

Pope, who, to my sudden shock, I now read to be a Spaniard, bestows, in a looping but disjointed hand, his holy blessing, to which the headmaster is welcome. And next to the crow, in gaudily contrasting colour, hangs the face of an ancient nurse or nun, with gums grinning out through a burnished landscape of wrinkles, and whose veil, though less pastoral than the article on the radiator, closely resembles a tea-towel.

We're not doing very well, the headmaster fears. I fear we could be going round forever, ring-a-roses. He keeps repeating, with dogged circularity, the impoverished repertoire of his enquiries—bed, Wolfe, sofa; TV, sleep, Bonifacio—as if in the hope of boring me into bleating some titillating new snippet, but of course he comes too late, poor man. For, overnight, I have become the sort of liar blessed with the gift genuinely to believe his own lies, to merge with his fiction. Yet there is no confusion about me: I could recite my replies in my dreams, or under oath, or back to front if needed be—at least in Spanish. Yet he does hold one, great, trump surprise up his sleeve; and, after a colourful bunch of what sound like clichés about chickens and eggs and rights and wrongs and sanctity and marriage and smoke and fire and rhyme and reason and method and madness—plus, obviously, about old heads upon young shoulders—he unearths a poisoned fork from within the fronds of his verbal shrubbery, to inform me that my father has been apprised of my activities, and is, even as we speak, winging his way over. Won't be long before we get to the bottom of this whole matter. And then, with one last triumphant smack of lips, he alludes to pipers and to tunes.

THE WEATHER, when my father came, could not have been more fair to him: I remember it as one of those rare idyllic days when the English countryside seems to be sanctified by radiance. Seas of green velvet, hills of magenta rhododendrons, cornflower skies unblemished by a single worrisome cloud. Sunshine fit for Alma Maters, worthy of fathers and sons.

I had been instructed, by means of a scrappy telephone message, to meet him at the front of the school tomorrow, Saturday, straight after class; and as I stood there on the entrance steps while the others trooped off to lunch, I remember that I didn't know quite how to be, whether apprehensive about his visit or relieved by it, but I had

dressed as sprucely as I could, not so much to present a neat picture—
a front of impregnability—as in the hope of pleasing him. He might
even tell my mother that I was looking smart. Meanwhile, I reviewed
the question of my innocence from every conceivable angle: my mind
was clear: nothing at all had happened: couldn't have done: I couldn't
let anyone down: deny-deny-deny. But I *was* frightened, I can't claim
otherwise. For my father, even if no shrewder a man than the teachers
to whom he had entrusted me, was a better placed examiner, had
stronger access to my insides—and not because he understood me
any better than the headmaster or Mr. Bonifacio, never mind my lover
(he certainly didn't), but because, unlike them, he did enjoy a claim
upon my history. And perhaps because I associated him with my beautiful fragile mother, or perhaps because I had not yet properly crossed
the border of the Commandments and learnt (though I did already
dishonour him) to despise him, I knew that my work with him would
be more arduous. And this knowledge seemed to accelerate my pulse,
for, now, as well as concealing my activities, I would have to preserve
the tenuous fabric of my emotions from unravelling. I think that I
wanted my father to love me. I don't think I knew that he didn't know
how to.

He rolls up at the wheel of a rented car, maroon of all colours. I try
to quash my embarrassment, and tell myself that it doesn't matter. I
notice, as he steps out, that he's wearing the same tweed suit as he wore
when he dropped me off at Euston, along with his Old Boy tie, and
something about the repetition of this costume briefly calms me. But
now, as if to symbolize the victory of his pride in the school over my
failure to do it justice, his gold-and-navy stripes defy the balmy wind-
lessness and flap over his shoulder, which is strong as any burden, I am
sure, resilient as the shoulder of St. Christopher.

When he climbs out of the car, he seems a kingdom away, closer to
my motherland, and the gravel that divides us feels like an ocean. As he
proceeds in my direction, although his steps never shorten, his pace
seems to diminish. His chestnut brogues grind into the gravel. His face
is briefly shaded, but as it emerges, I see, I fear, how badly he wishes
that the reason for his descent were otherwise, that he were come to
visit some other pupil, a properly English one, a promising sportsman,
a future prefect, a mathematician if you must. And now, as he looms

over me, he confirms my suspicion by withholding from my cheek the kiss of Latin custom and, instead, sticking out his right hand.

I shake it credibly, convincingly, as my mother might have shaken the hand of officialdom. He brings his tie back down, and strokes it nostalgically, which makes me oddly sad, almost sorry for him. Together we turn our backs to the building, but he leads the way, walking markedly faster now. I half-trot to keep up. Inside the motorcar, I notice the prong of a loose spring under my seat, but I tell myself that he can't have known this; it's not his fault; stop it. And then I'm struck by the smell of his cigars. I think about asking for permission, decide not to disturb him, and unwind my window—which is reluctant. I struggle. He switches on the radio . . . only to be rewarded by an irreparable wartime crackle. He flicks off the contraption and tuts, fed up. We drive along in silence, through the fields and lakes and past the insouciant Madonna, and I pray that no one will recognize me in this hideous car. But then I tell myself that I don't care: I'm travelling with my father, and what's good enough for him is good enough for both of us.

He stops at the next village, not far from my half-term pub, and we go into some kind of inn, where I suspect that he may be staying, though I don't attempt to enquire. None of my business. He goes straight past the bar, walks into an underpopulated dining room which smells of sprouts, and settles for a corner table by a window overlooking a meagre lawn with a hillock of mown grass. Our waitress would like to offer me choices, but he orders on both of our behalfs. Simpler.

Though I'm learning my father's English in leaps and bounds, I haven't opened my mouth—which is just as well, because it would appear that he, bafflingly, has all but forgotten my mother's Spanish. Still, I can understand him—perhaps because, to start with, he restricts his talk to the weather and the bore of driving on the left-hand side. He is being chatty, I can tell, as if I were a car enthusiast. Our food arrives: pure cuisine Alma Mater. Trouble with the vegetables. He says he hopes I'm not going to play up. (Biafra.) I pretend, as I munch, to find myself suddenly and inordinately captivated by the sight of that great lump of mown grass outside. His reflection in the glass tells me that his interest, conversely, is turned inwards, has fixed itself on other diners, on the heartening sight of ordinary English life in progress. He decides that we'll skip pudding if that's all right. He lights one of his smallish cigars, puff, puff. No coffee for the boy, thank you; just for him, yes, black; no sugar, thank you; and I say, he adds, might he have a brandy?

WE RETURN TO THE CAR and trundle back over humps of pocked asphalt in the unmistakable direction of the school, as if the place and the man should not be parted, as if their proximity lent him sustenance. Halfway down the length of the drive, he grips the troublesome gear-stick and forces it down, and down again, and then, as we pass a damaged, spindly railing which, despite its mangled metal, has recently been glossed in white, he brings us to a halt, shudderingly. He turns off the ignition, but allows the hired key to linger in its crevice, as if our stop were only a stop-gap. We could not be more prominently, or uncomfortably, parked. We are tilted into a ditch of grassy mud. Surveyed from the building thus, this fine Old Boy and his unequal son, we must look like a couple of soggy dolls abandoned in a rusted pram by some careless child. I think of my mother and her forgotten doll's-house.

He lights another cigar, which in church is not allowed, but he thinks that we should be joined, he says, in prayer. Luckily he suggests the Our Father, which I now know by heart, and perhaps that's why he's chosen it, to help me out, to make it easier. It can't be easy for him either, all this travelling. Full of grace, he begins, surprisingly loudly. He's a grown-up, that must be why. Then: hallowed be Thy name (I seem to be lagging behind a fraction; I can't hear myself quite; but he doesn't seem to mind, perhaps he isn't angry). And forgive us our trespasses . . . and lead us not into temptation. His Amen, which vibrates upwards, is of fervour, meant—even as it echoes and dwindles around the dank upholstery of the car. His cigar has gone out.

I stare out of the windscreen to free my eyes, and I let them gambol about a hill in front of us, which is bordered by a leafy lane favoured by local sweethearts. I can't think of anything intelligent to ask, or even funny, such as whether in his day wolves ever marauded about these parts, but just as I'm starting to rack my brain for the start of that thing which is the art of conversation, he begins on my behalf. He lets me off the hook, kindly. I listen hard, as if this were an oral exam, but so baroque and intricately strung are the pearls of his investigative wisdom that, by the end of his soliloquy, I'm afraid I've lost any hope of a grip on their unifying clasp. Befuddled silence. I think of my mother's letter last autumn: Don't be frightened to say when you don't understand. And I do just that. Could he please repeat the question? His brow shoots up to his hair-line, which is scraped back, and his eyeballs turn, I think, briefly to white. But I couldn't swear to it, because his head, like mine, seems to be glued to the countryside. Perhaps he was just invoking Our Father for patience, because he doesn't lash out. He understands. He is a clever man.

So he repeats his complicated words and, for my benefit, does so in slightly baby language. He tells me everything that he has heard from the headmaster, which the headmaster heard from Mr. Bonifacio, and of course there are words like Untoward and Irregular and Peculiar and Suspect, but then, as if he were swerving round some awkward question-mark, he adds that he knows how I can be imaginative (which I can), and how this is all very well, but not, you see, always wise, because sometimes stories can be construed (which I think means constructed) as fibs. What is fibs, I mean what are? Lies, boy, bloody lies. (I hope this swearing doesn't mean he's cross like when we went to Euston.) No, it's all right, I don't need to worry, because now he's talking slowly down, so that I can understand and see what he thinks, which is this: that I was probably nosing around, or up to some minor Mischief (which means naughty, not an important young lady) and that I just panicked when I thought I might be punished. But now, uh-uh, I'm starting to follow him without any difficulty at all, because although his pace is speeding up and his volume rising as in prayer, the sense, the sense of his words could not be clearer—my nonsense, he calls it.

My father is quite sure that nothing Untoward (again) can have happened, least of all with my supervisor—who's an Old Boy, he gathers, though I had no idea—nothing at all, not possibly, let's be realistic; so really he has no option but to dismiss the whole rumpus as some childish fabrication on my part (which means a sort of construction, as in building-blocks and castles in the sand and dreams and sounds and waves and sea). Making up. Inventing. Fibs, or lies, whatever. Sins even. But it doesn't feel fair, not really.

To my relief he says that it's all right. I can profit by this incident. I can treat it as a lesson for the future, to do with self-control or something, and now he talks about Truth. And next we're back to prayer. Because at difficult times prayer can help you, help you out, you see. Prayer can provide comfort (like a mohair blanket?). He recommends it, and he also recommends—though it sounds more like an order to me—that I do the decent thing, which, though he sees it won't be easy, will certainly be honourable (this sounds important). And the important thing is that after confessions tonight, I go and apologize for the embarrassment which I have caused to Mr. Wolfe and Mr. Bonifacio, not forgetting the headmaster. My father is confident that they'll be understanding (which means more than translating, it's more like forgiving our trespasses)—kind men all, as well as good Catholics. He reassures me, even though I cannot feel it, that in no time this whole fuss will die down and become a thing of the past. The sooner I get back to a normal school life, the better, he says, for everyone.

BUT SOMETHING HAPPENS NOW. It feels as if I'm stuck, unable to wind back the clock of love, yet unable, too, to go forward and do what he wants. I want to please my father, but I cannot tell more lies. They are too much, too heavy to carry, and I do not have the shoulder of St. Christopher. Stuck. I feel myself flushing. I sink in a pause. I must not blub. I think of my mother. And then I stop thinking and tell him that I've made up none of the things which he calls Inventions. What happened, I insist (feeling a little stronger because he's keeping quiet), happened. We remain dug in this silence for a small while, but then he starts to argue in a telly-offy sort of way, and he tells me not to Contradicked him, and I tell him that I'm not, that I'm just sticking up, not being a liar. Not-not-not (Deny-deny-deny).

He never knew, he says, that I could be so Tarsome. And now the question marks, despite his earlier avoidance of the first awkward one, do, like sudden gunfire, begin to fly. And you could understand them in any language, even in Biafran, because there is something enormous about them. What in God's name, he wants to know, is it that I propose be done about this whole preposterous matter? Do I think he's come all this way just to have me waste his bally time? Can I honestly suppose that he's prepared to go to the headmaster to corroborate my stupid lies? How can I conceivably imagine that anyone believes I spent the night on the supervisor's sofa? Isn't it more likely that I was up to—

does he have to spell it out—no good, so to speak, rifling about, pinching something for instance? (My face is scarlet now.) And why, he adds, am I blushing if he's so white-of-the-mark? Am I some kind of idiot? Do I think he never went to school himself, that he doesn't have a clue what he's talking about, that he's entirely devoid of experience, that he was born yesterday? And what, pray, *what* is he meant to tell my poor mother?

Which is when I crack. Like an hysteric and without warning I just begin to howl. He gazes back towards the school flag, relieved finally to have been blessed with a reaction. And I go on howling, as I once did at the Nautical Club, spluttering with anger and longing and misery and injustice. He tells me to cut out the blubbing and pull myself together. At once. Got a good mind to smack me. I stop as abruptly as I began. Right, he decides, that's more like it, perhaps now we can get down to business. Wiping my tears from my chin and my lap (using my nametaped handkerchief) I nod that we can. I've had enough.

But I still need to protect my lover, so I decide to leave out the bits that might get him into trouble. Yet I do tell the (tyrannous) father (who has dared to lash me with the memory of the lost mother) that I'm tired, that I'm not popular, that I can't understand half the time, that I'm no good at anything, that the other boys are ghastly, that nobody washes here, that you can't even use cologne, can you imagine, that the teachers despise me—yes, they despise me—that some of them call me Woman, that I sometimes despair, that I give up. I also tell him, warming to my defence, that Mr. Wolfe is the only kind person among all these Catholics, the only one who likes me, and gives me apples, and cares when I have nightmares, and sometimes, when I feel sad, gives me kisses and hugs because he says affection matters. And although I feel more trapped than any endangered David, I now find the courage to tell the truth to my Goliath, which is that I'm sorry to be such a letdown. But again my tears burst forth in a second rush.

HE FLIES, NAUSEATED, out of the car, plods about the grass, and punches the boot a few times. We're going for a Walk! he orders. (Oh no.) He heads up Lovers' Lane. I take my time. He reaches a stile, and hitches his knee to the first step, as if posing for a hearty snap. He shouts: For God's sake hurry up! And: For God's sake, I think to myself, he's dragging me into that swamp of cow-pat. I stop at the top of the stile before jumping down, not just because the leap worries me, but because now I can peer at him from above, as if I were a high-diver for a moment, and he, still floundering in the beginners' class. Predictably enough, the thought of a helping hand doesn't occur to him. What kind of a sissy am I? Jump.

He forges ahead towards the horizon, less as if he sought to face the future than as if he were in search of his schoolboy past, trying to relive that moment of all moments when he was crowned Victor Ludorum—which, to me, had always sounded like some matinée idol, related to Rodolfo Valentino perhaps, whom my father scarcely resembled, though my mother's own father had done. (I think that even a whole silver jubilee down the line, my father still kept, in one of the drawers of his study, a commemorative medal of the cruel honour—cruel to me, for, in time, that small tarnished coin would come to reflect the sheer magnitude of my failure in his eyes. But I'm sure that whenever he took a peep at that medal, his eyes would have grown sentimental, and the strings of his gold-and-navy heart would have struck up, as the strings of mine, which was livid, had done when I'd floated in my belovèd nurse's arms, or later, as I'd watched my beautiful mother dance, or more lately still, as I'd brought my lover over to the land of rapture.)

I saunter along beside him like a dim-witted beagle, and try to ease matters by kicking a solitary tuft of grass, but, so pitiful is my attempt to be more boyish than I am, I trip, stumble, and nearly go flying. He must have noticed, of course, but, presumably out of pity for me, he refrains from rubbing my nose in the bungle—or so I imagine, until I discover, to my shock and dismay, that now the floods of self-pity are pouring from *his* eyes, not mine, as if *he* were the little boy lost in the middle of nowhere. I pretend to tie my laces while he mops his sorrow with a starched handkerchief—no nametape; white monogram—but I realize, as soon as I reach the ground and genuflect, that my shoes are held together with elastic. Now, he says, with an air of regained composure, let's remain calm about all this, shall we.

Things have to be sorted out, and he's sure that they can; but nobody needs a scandal—wouldn't help anyone. Naturally, he adds, he will make no decision until he's sought guidance tomorrow at Mass. Nothing rash. My welfare is, it goes without saying, of concern to him, but we can't allow that single issue to cloud our judgement. My personal circumstances are—how can he put it?—let's just call them Specific; don't affect other pupils; he doesn't see why the rest should suffer. One can't hold a whole community to ransom, you know. So let him make one thing absolutely crystal clear: the standing of the school is what he considers Paramount (as in a film?). We can't allow the reputation of the place to suffer. I had better understand that. So whatever I'm insisting has gone on Must Not, he says, Get Out.

This last imperative makes my position sound like a cul-de-sac, and yet he forges ahead regardless. He's not saying what's my fault and what isn't; he's just saying that we can do without negative press from provincial hacks, never mind the national papers—field day, they'd have, the school's detractors, all those chippy Protestants; he can practically read the headlines. So—am I listening?—this whole thing Must Not Get Out (Deny-deny-deny). Anyhow, he concludes, he's sure I've had a tiring afternoon, so I'm to run along for tea or what have you now (what have I?) and he'll see me in the morning after Mass.

I SLEEP LIKE A LOG. Not a wave, not a sound, though by the time we convene outside the chapel, it transpires that a good deal of confabulation has gone on during my slumbers. But now that matters seem to be settled, my father is in a sudden hurry, would like to be off straight after lunch. He suggests a quick bite and a chat, and he'll be on his way, long trip back. He claims to have been satisfied by his three sets of drinks with the three relevant members of staff. Mr. Bonifacio my father found a most affable fellow, solely keen, you understand, to pre-empt unwanted trouble—you know how in small communities tongues can wag. And Mr. Wolfe also struck him as most pleasant, perhaps a trifle shy, but clearly a gent: turns out that my father was at school with one of the Wolfe uncles, isn't that a coincidence. Mr. Wolfe's principal concern, or so my father reckons, revolves around my problems adapting to English boarding-school life, and my apparent unhappiness; but my father has explained to my supervisor—as if the latter were ignorant of such platitudes—that it's only natural that boarding school should prove tricky at the start, tricky for anyone, particularly an only child, but next year everything will seem routine to me and my spirits are bound to improve dramatically, he's certain, especially after a summer in the sun. As for the headmaster, well, my father does agree that the man seems rather to err on the plebby side—a convert, he suspects— filthy booze and most peculiar newfangled views on education. (Later, when it was all beyond repair, I discovered that there'd been talk of sending me to a child psychiatrist, which must, as my father swilled his filthy booze, have contributed to his splutters.) Still, he tells me that I'm simply to stick to the rules, and that if things get tricky—say I'm being picked on or whatever—I can write home and tell him about it: he has a couple of chums who sit on the board of Governors. I remind my father that letters are censored on the way out. He reminds me not to be such a ninny: write in Spanish.

I reiterate that I'm miserable. Couldn't I just be moved to some other school, where at least they taught Spanish, so that I could be good at Some Thing? He nods and smiles at the same time. No, no, he explains: I don't seem to quite follow him; there's no need for drastic measures. All public schools are much on a par, none is more or less fun than any other, and furthermore, very few of them are Catholic. He's adamant that a sound religious education is vital, and from that vital point he won't be budged. But he does offer me two pairs of alternatives. First, either I stay where I am and lump it, or I go back to day school at home, thereby squandering any chance of a decent education. Well? he demands. Make up your mind. Which would you rather? It doesn't feel like a choice to me, but: To stay, I reply. Good, so that settles that. And second, he says, if I'm absolutely certain that my plight (and I should examine my conscience carefully on the matter) would be improved in the absence of Mr. Wolfe, he's prepared, just this once, to approach the Governors and moot the possibility of his removal. And something about my father's machination, its confidentiality, its cool corruption, alerts me to the sudden vastness of my power, to the fact that I could wreak havoc—should I bring him down, should I scream and shout, should I speak of love—but of course, it's futile: how could my existence be rendered anything but unendurable in the absence of my saviour? And so, with a look of mock-maturity, I wave this last option aside: No; no need, things aren't that bad. (But I shall never again play rugby.)

Last he reverts to the subject of my mother, with whom he can't possibly be expected to discuss the less savoury aspects of this regrettable saga: wouldn't be fair on her; she wouldn't understand; would just upset her; no point in that. So what he's resolved (again), to help me out, is that he'll pretend I was involved in a theft, some internal enquiry, nothing to worry about, schoolboy stuff, all sorted out. With which, he slaps down his napkin, stands up, tells me that I'll be home in a month, so to look forward to that, and then he suggests that it's probably best, while he settles his account, if I see myself back, he's got to get going. And remember, he adds: no more trouble, get on with your studies, write home when you're told to, and not a word about this to anyone, least of all your mother. He (too) counts on me. I stand back far enough to avoid his hand, and as I lead myself out, backwards, I ask him, in Spanish—which seems to disgruntle him—to give her my love. And I notice, as I scarper, a slight dent on the boot of the maroon car.

BUT MY FATHER's determination to spread a coat of whitewash over the mess of my misconduct did not succeed in halting the rot of the walls which have ears, for within a matter of days, they began oozing waxy tell-tale stains of my corruption. To begin with, I perceived an alteration in the attitude of teachers, whose formerly indifferent glances gave way to glances of (supercilious) aversion, and, soon there-after, in the attitude of other boys, now grown fearful as well as hostile. No one went so far as actually to confront me with the reports which, like a racing tumour, must have been spreading through the body of the school, but wherever I went, I sensed the unmistakable vacuum of a wide berth. In class, you could not but notice that the desks to either side of mine had been shifted away, shunned it; and even in the chapel people went to pains not to sit beside me. Those who happened to find themselves on my bench (and they varied every time) had to be told to move up, to close ranks; but as they did so, they positioned themselves at an emphatic outward skew, their neighbouring shoulder turned away from my pestilence. It was as if a great sea of repulsion had parted around me, and although I understood the meaning of this new long solitary road ahead, which, even if open-ended, was a sort of prison, and although I could hear the echoes of my hollow search for a way out, I found that I had nowhere to walk, nowhere to run, and no means of filling the chasm of this new life which I had, in my manner, but thanks to my father, chosen. A similar reserve is, I know, traditionally afforded to boys who've recently suffered a bereavement in the family, or who find themselves stricken with eczema, or to persistent bed-wetters, or to those who face expulsion, but this distance of mine somehow felt more marked, icier, more akin to the distance which, at his departure, I had kept from my father's hand; and though the width of the road before me was later to alter, and to surprise me with unforeseen turns of direction, and though its climate was to brighten with odd patches of sun, as a feature, as a state, it was to remain permanent.

THAT FIRST SUMMER back on the island, part of which was spent by the sea, marked, I now realize, a turning-point of sorts for me, for I became properly cut off, deaf to my surroundings. A variety of factors probably contributed to this, but the most obvious (though its cause was so deep a secret that I can scarcely, then, have considered it) was my need to uncrush, as if such a thing were possible, my spirit. I had no real quibble with my mother, who disported herself much in the manner that I had come to expect of her—stylish, languorous, comfortably superficial—but I felt that her obdurate refusal to allude to those events which, but a few weeks earlier, had summoned her husband to England, betrayed a new seed of mistrust between us. This seed had, of course, been sown and fomented by the man who, whatever his claims to my welfare, had plainly, I now see, not only reneged on me but further dared to insult his wife with the patronage of his protection. It amazes me to realize, now that he's dead and well-buried, with what terminal efficiency that despicable great Catholic, who was a disgrace to his religion, succeeded in stunting any future possibility of growth in his wife, whom he cultivated at a temperature of such beautiful static ignorance that, though she flowered by the fashion season, she was never to know maturity, and became, as a consequence of his artificial limits, severed from the development of my being—a being which, though certainly twisted, he, at least, was never quite able to cripple. But that small, deft, tactical switch of his, that invented theft which in truth was but the purchase-price of my survival, for which I was to pay dearly, turned out to be a stroke of vicious genius. For by thus dividing his wife from her son, he managed to create a mutual suspicion between my mother and myself which, like some venomous prehistoric cactus, grew and grew and was to prove, in emotional terms, catastrophic. I suspect that neither she nor I was ever fully to recover from the damage of his interference, and even if my mother suppressed the desire to dwell on such intimate deficiencies, I can safely speak for her now. It ruined her; it left her a midget. And next to that brittle, pristine, frozen, covetable figurine of a woman, I felt, as I grew more embittered and unruly, nearly desperate. I no longer knew what she knew, nor what she can have imagined, nor what she feared. Indeed, the mystery was never to be solved; the topic, not once discussed in all the time that I knew her. And though I also remained in ignorance of my father's activities, largely because I had no interest in those subjects which appeared to engross him, I did find that whereas once the man had merely bored me, now, after this ill-quashed scandal, he struck me as more than a mere occupational stranger, for he had already proved to me his mettle as an enemy—as, indeed, he would continue to do. I learnt to view his presence as hazardous: I feared him more than any overactive fantasy of the sort that he called fibs. And from the refuge of my distance, I grew to recognize in him the simpler traits of the bully: for when he lied, it was not, as was the case with me, out of a frantic need for safety, but simply in order to get his way, to impose his will, to be more spoilt than me. I had not yet made the connection between tediousness and tyranny, not yet realized with what pathetic ease one can be both a bore and a bully, but, despite my blindness, I could, even then, recognize one thing: that my father's was a strong sort of weakness.

I WAS RELIEVED, of course, no longer to be under the control of a governess, yet the freedom which her riddance afforded me felt more like a burden than anything approaching luxury. Luxury to me meant emeralds. Now, I had to drag myself about the hidden gloom which, despite all the apparent blessings of my gilded domestic privilege, was henceforth to blight all of my school holidays. I would read when my concentration allowed it; rise as late as I wished; choose my own daily breakfast; play my records at will; swim in the pool without supervision, sunbathe occasionally, feed my bones with heat.

I also tried to write to my old Mam'zelle, though taking care (in order not to upset her) to circumvent the shame that had befallen her birthday jewel. I strove, in a muddle of languages—but without

entirely omitting to hint at my condition, which, though more pronounced of late, remained what it had been from the moment of her
leaving, which was a state of isolation—to imbue my words with biographical embellishments, hoping to make her earlier devotions to me
appear rewarded by some semblance of fruition; but I realized, as I did
so, that the task which I had set myself lay beyond my infantile capabili-
ties. I could not please everybody. I could hardly please myself. For
while the chronology of my recent life was easy enough to relate, the
events comprising it, like the dark beads of my mother's rosary, which
she kept in a drawer by her bed, I found harder to tell. Yet even if I
hadn't, at that stage, mastered the skill of writing between the lines, and
though doubtless my letter glinted with transparent fantasies, my childish tales were never really designed to inspire wonderment: they merely
longed to earn your smile.

In the event, however, my efforts to reach my former nurse were to
be dashed, for, once I'd drafted a neat copy of my letter to her, and the
moment came to enquire after Mam'zelle's address, which I had never
known, my mother claimed to be no wiser on the subject than I, and
suggested that, if I must, I try my father—assuming, of course, that
the woman's details still held good after all this time—and assuming,
too, which she rather doubted, that his pigskin address book still concerned itself with such forgettable redundancies. *(Un premier amour ne
s'oublie jamais . . . Et toi qui j'aimais, qu'as-tu fait de toi? Qu'as-tu fait sans moi?
Et moi qui t'ai perdu, qu'ai-je fait de tant de bonheur?)* As one grew up, my
mother had added, one should look forwards, not backwards.
Mam'zelle's job was done; she had moved on; that was the way of the
universe. I had another life now. The world would soon be her Iago's
oyster. But the truth is that I, my father's James, lived in dread of the
future, and had already begun to think in retrospect—not so much
because I rued the calendar of my history, strewn though it was with
leaves of disenchantment, but because some frustrated part of me
would have liked for my story to have been granted a second chance,
the chance to start afresh, to rewrite itself in a new garden, to recover
lost ground. But as I hoped, so I lost hope. The letter was never posted.
And Mam'zelle, though she was never forgotten, was never, even with
lies, to be thanked for her devotion.

.   .   .

My mother, in an attempt to lend respectability to my passage from childhood into puberty, further complicated matters by orchestrating a subtle (and awkward) modulation in the manner which her servants were now meant to regard me, for, in advance of this first long holiday, they had been instructed no longer to call me what they'd called me ever since I'd been in nappies, which was Santiago, but instead, from now on—which, to be fair, was the ridiculous convention in all the households of my parents' acquaintance—to address me as Señorito. Later, in my late teens, this prissy courtesy would alter once more, to a more honourable, more authoritative Don, which, in the event, I didn't have to endure for long, since neither honour nor authority were to prove my strong points. But for now, this Señorito stuff killed me, and robbed me, in addition to the loss of Mam'zelle, of the affections of Cook and Gardener, both of whom, though I daresay they didn't blame me personally, must nevertheless have understood the meaning of the switch: I was being groomed away from their friendship and primed for a chilly superior distance. All very well, my mother had declared, to be familiar in infancy, but after a point you couldn't continue to fraternize with these people, not in the same way, there'd be hell to pay, they'd walk all over one, anarchy. For we're all, *all* of us (she would remind me gravely), slaves to someone.

At meal times, I noticed that with the pretext of encouraging my English, conversation was increasingly turned away from my mother-tongue toward my father's language, yet this occurred most noticeably between courses, so as to ensure—as if the demands of balancing all those pitchers and trays and tureens were not sufficiently demanding—that whoever was waiting at table couldn't enjoy the illicit added thrill of eavesdropping on my parents' spoutings. Never did this device prove more convenient than on the occasion when I, returning from some errand, pressed the entryphone at the front gate (for such measures had, of late, become security must-haves, like baubles from some desirable *bijoutier*) and the buzzer duly went off, as it was wired to do, in the kitchen; but finding myself alone on the street and forced publicly to volunteer my poncy, false identity to Cook, who had answered the ring, I side-stepped the mess of my mother's protocol and simply stated that it was Santiago, to let me in. Inevitably, the Lady of the House happened at that moment to find herself in the kitchen (peeling sticky price-tags from her delivered groceries, to spare the servants the shock of the cost of living), and managed, just as inevitably, to over-hear my voice blaring down the receiver. But she chose to make no mention to her staff of the liberty which I had taken, and which, I was soon enough to discover, she interpreted as impertinent, undermining of me, a barefaced betrayal of everything in which she and my father believed. Instead, she decided to wait until the three of us had sat down to lunch, so that her consort could support her in my verbal lynching—which, when delivered, after the soup, proved, though rife with his-panicisms, to be strategically versed in English.

EVEN AS I PACKED my trunk, a month in advance of the beginning of term, so that it could be shipped across the Atlantic, it hadn't occurred to me, such was my short-sightedness, that despite the changes which had taken place at home—the broken trust, the barriers of formality—I would nonetheless miss the peace, and I would miss the sun, and above all I would miss the spell of the sea. But by the time that my parents took me to the airport (and my father was driving, for some reason), I remember sitting alone on the back seat, queasy with fore-boding. For I had a habit, resulting perhaps from my mother's capri-cious influence, but, more likely, from plain insecurity, which my father found maddening; and although as a trait of ill-discipline it has dimin-ished, I do not think that, to this day, I've altogether conquered it. Because whenever I take a trip, and wherever this may be, however near, however briefly, I feel compelled to pack far more than I could ever need—the Just-In-Case syndrome, the What-If disease. So my father, determined to set an early precedent, had, in tones of heavy authority, cautioned me to pack into my trunk as much junk as I pleased, but to remember to restrict the weight of the suitcase which was to accompany me on the plane, to the regulation limit of twenty kilogrammes. And yet, regardless of the trunk, which had long since disappeared, my spiralling dread of the hell to which I was returning propelled me at the last minute to cram my case with all manner of things, to do with comfort and identity, which I would never be able to find in England—a giant bottle of avocado hair-conditioner, a great sausage of heavy chorizo, extra shoes to wear outside the bounds of school, wooden shoe-trees—all in the belief that such extras would render less daunting my progress through the minefield of the next twelve weeks. And although my father had been perfectly firm, perfectly fair about my need to observe the official weight restriction, I, as the porter lugged my case onto the scales by the desk where I was to be checked in, and as my mother rummaged in her handbag for a scented handkerchief, and as her husband tapped the spine of my passport against the counter, witnessed the gleaming silver arrow of my latest atrocity swing round, right past twenty, which was doomsday, to twenty-three, thereby formalizing the start of my association with Excess Baggage—which was to remain something of a love/hate relationship, for while baggage makes me groan, excess has never displeased me. But my father simply stood there and glowered down at me, not even needing to tell me that he had told me so, that I'd been given ample warning, and forced me, through the pressure of his silence, to pay for my indulgence with what meagre funds I'd managed to save during the holidays. I think that my mother must secretly have disputed the timing of such exemplary severity, for while her husband, in an interlude between two brandies, stalked off to use his urethra, she turned to me and slipped into the pocket at my breast a large fresh banknote, which smelt of gardenias. And just as my father had counted on me not to divulge to his wife my regrettable little incident at school, so she now counted on me not to divulge to him her kind act of treachery.

MY SECOND YEAR at prep school did not, despite my father's forecast, see any improvement, let alone a dramatic one, in the temperature of my spirits: mere scholastic drudgery had never been a factor in my difficulties. I remember noticing the occasional new boy, looking as demolished by the shock of this bleak environment as I had been at my start, but after the complications which had later arisen for me, and all the ensuing skulduggery, I still felt too wary and, frankly, too lacking in conviction to muster a tenor of reassurance for the sake of anybody. I recall, in particular, a diminutive Belgian boy, hair cut *en brosse,* eyes of a screaming electric green, forehead stricken with the furrows of a frown which seemed never to spare his forsaken countenance, and feeling for him a pang of sympathy—perhaps because he hailed from that same elusive place as had given me my Mam'zelle, my stolen emerald; but perhaps, more simply, because, like me, he was nationally alien, a proper exile. Du Castel was his surname; and I remember noticing that when he went to bed he wore over his pyjamas a *matelot* jumper of the type which buttoned at the shoulder and instantly spelt a Continental; and some part of me recognized that beyond the cold in the dormitories, which was considerable, his striped pullover was meant, like my mother's mohair blanket, to alleviate a greater coldness, which was inner. And I did briefly consider exchanging with him, in what meagre remnants of French might still be squatting about the corners of my cluttered memory, a few vague words of friendliness; but, almost as swiftly, I realized that any association between us, even one of those hilariously formal handshakes at which young Gauls seemed then to excel, could only have worsened his predicament, have spelt trouble for him: because the other pupils, despite whom, amazingly, I had managed to survive a year, seemed, rather than to have been civilized by a period spent among their families, merely to have returned fatter-faced and fortified, and this fortification had done nothing to diminish their enduring derision for me. Not only had they grown physically, but also in the breadth of their worldly wisdom, and they seemed, along the way, to have gleaned a clearer, more vivid and censorious picture of my supposed wantonness, my whispered iniquities; so that whereas earlier they had straightforwardly avoided me, now, since they publicly voiced their suspicions, I knew that they were properly on the look-out, spying, longing to catch and report me—if not actually to the authorities, which might have been construed as Sneaking, at least to their parents, which, from my point of view, amounted to the same thing. Yet as targets went, I, second time around, cannot have presented much of a challenge, or offered any great novelty, but better the devil you know, a bird in the hand, that kind of cliché. And, of course, I still exuded a certain blue-tinged mystique, which they, armed with their brave new knowledge, wanted further to investigate. The bottom of it.

BUM-CHUM, SUCKER-UPPER, arse-licker, such were the terms which now flavoured their references to me, for the conspiracy was, as I say, no longer tacit; and though I had, in all probability, sailed close to the foul rocks of which I stood accused, I couldn't yet fathom the literal meaning of those pejoratives. But one insult which I did understand— in part because, like the word Woman, it was so simple, but partly, too, because it fell so pathetically short of the truth—was the tag Daddy's Boy, a misnomer which was unmistakably intended to relate me to Mr. Wolfe, who, for all of his childlessness (then), had been dubbed Daddy by some previous wave of schoolboy geniuses. I must admit that, as nicknames went, Daddy's Boy didn't strike me as impressive, but then this was a place where impressiveness was not encouraged. Excellence was—and not, it goes without saying, when applied to the exertions of adults and minors in their shady privacy, but to the exertions displayed on the playing fields by strict contemporaries.

It is almost superfluous to relate how, once delivered back to the mire, I discovered what little solace was to be found in non-regulation shoes, or bottles of hair-conditioner, or the bloodied chunks of pig which, like a ravenous savage, I devoured, skin and all, from the arm of chorizo that lay entombed in my tuck-box, and which, once I was embarked upon the gorge, did not survive beyond the first measly novena. Its loss enraged me, for, even as I tore my way through the fiery flesh, I saw, clear as any writing on any wall, that no amount of school sausages, which tasted more of rancid dishcloths than ever they did of pork, never mind humbugs and gobstoppers, which were but suckers' fodder, would ever sate the mournful hunger that corroded my soul. It was like devouring the contents of some great love story, only to be punished for one's gluttony by the discovery that, whereas the unlikely protagonists had, after all their tribulations, ascended to the plane of happiness-ever-after, you, greedy reader, were left at a loss, dumped back in the very place of your starving lovelessness.

Throughout this time, Mr. Wolfe resembled a flag at half-mast, seemed out of sorts; but his discolour didn't only become manifest, like some sudden debilitating virus, when he happened to drift into my vicinity; for though, causally, I may have been contributory, the symptoms were there for all to witness. Now, when he smiled, stars no longer burst from his eyes, which bore crescents of gloom beneath them. Only seldom did you hear his laugh, and when you did, it sounded dry, closer to a cough provoked by nicotine. His walk no longer squealed with its former brio: it had grown spongy, stodgy, like the walk of the sickly—for the heart, I knew, had gone out my former lover; his flame, now, only flickered. He moved like a drab shadow of his earlier charisma, paler, drabber; and as we trudged over the linoleum and the rugs of our designated wastelands, he treated me not so much with distance as with polite neutrality, like an excellent footman, and even took care, I suspect, not to upset me, not to ignite my volcanic ill-humour, which, in this confined inferno, he must have feared to be simmering just beneath the cool sourness of my surface— because the repercussions of my father's visit had never been discussed between us: the meeting held by them while I was sleeping; the narrowness of our respective escapes; the burdens thrust upon me since the whole upheaval, and, of course, the heavy debt which, little though Mr. Wolfe could as yet suspect it, his imperilled career now owed to me. But any possible way forward, any possible stab at reparation, seemed, after the summer hiatus, blurry to me, open to question; and our former nocturnal congress, if not quite consigned to history, did become relegated to the back burner of our dealings. He still winked at me occasionally, and occasionally, at lights out, a nostalgic pout might return to my lips, but it all felt tepid, unconvincing—and with good reason, for he had resolved, I was subsequently to learn, that our safest course of action lay with the transfer, from him to me, of the burden of initiative. And once I'd run out of hot Spanish food to nurse my inner freeze, and my hair had drunk up all its conditioner and gone dry, and my tasselled loafers, stylish as they seemed to me, found themselves buried without apparent hope of an airing, I found my feet, slippered in sheepskin at eleven o'clock, set once again upon the long and winding road that led to his door.

I KNOCK. His reply sounds too vigorous, too sudden for him to be expecting a visitor, never mind this one. I go in: it is not difficult: it feels, in fact, like the most natural thing, like the rightest progression. He's already in bed. His lights are off. He says nothing. I close the door behind me, less out of discretion than because I don't want the dirty light of the corridor to filter in, to pollute me. He doesn't ask what's wrong, which previously, between us, had been the pretextual form. Instead, he now tells me not to lock the door, not to make a noise, just to slide the latch which he's installed—and which I treat as the sign that I've been waiting for. I do as I'm told. Plain sailing from now on. I go to the window and draw the curtains wide open, as if to reveal to the world the next episode, as if we'd run away to the circus and no longer cared a tinker's toss. I move to the gramophone and flick through a few records, skipping the Nocturnes, because to me this feels like a positive dawning, and skipping Mary Magdalene, since, now, I do know how to love him, and I settle for an album which provides us, at a gentle and low volume, with a bridge over our troubled waters. He lights, as if it had been reserved for this moment, a virgin candle, bigger than his earlier ones, and taller and, instead of churchy white, green as grapes, and veined like marble, and boasting, at its plateau, not one but two small wicks, like pilgrims on a darkling plain, carrying flambeaux in the wind.

If the first night after the rumpus of the vanished rugger peg had been rough, this one couldn't have proved more tranquil or, in its way, more poignant. I remember clambering into his bed in my pyjamas and, on this occasion only, keeping them on. And just as he'd trembled after the Bonifacio episode, so, now, he began to tremble once more. But there was nothing wrong, he claimed, no problem other than a rush of emotion, and instead of telling me that he was bisexual, he now held me close and told me how he had missed me, how sorry he was, and how relieved that I hadn't given up on him. He would make it up to me, he said; he would show me. We must, of course, be more cautious than ever, but we weren't going to let anyone or anything stand between us from this moment on, no more separations, it was a promise. Our time was precious, he explained: for all we had left (and he seemed to have counted, because when I said Two years, he replied Not even) was a mere eighteen months. Before we knew it, he said, I would be gone and it would all be over; but to me, regardless of his love, the thought of another eighteen months buried in this catacomb felt like murder.

He had said that we must be more cautious, and we were. Apart from the bolt on the door, he also mentioned the importance of using his alarm clock, and we agreed to split the job. From now on, on those nights when I came to see him, which would be most, he undertook to set the alarm for six-thirty in the morning, so that, even if we fell asleep, I could get back to my dormitory without fear of being caught. And my task, on leaving his warmth, was to press the bell to Off, so that once I was safely gone, he could sleep without interruption. As for his duty mornings, no need to worry: he would just order an alarm-call the night before. And thus it was settled, and, as a scheme, it was never to go wrong.

I could tell, as he held me immobile to his chest on that first night after the storm which nearly broke us, that his eyes were streaming with relief, but I was neither frightened nor revolted—this man was not my father. Instead, I felt a niggle of responsibility for his silent sobs, and faint guilt that I couldn't return the compliment. And after dismissing from my thoughts the business about never again playing rugger (which would have to wait), and wondering how precisely he intended to make it up to me, I did let myself drop off . . . and when, hours later, I awoke, he was still alert as a sentinel, with his arms still wrapped about me like ribbons round a present; and after saying good night and turning off the clock, I put on my dressing-gown, my daggerless cloak, and went to slide back the bolt and, just as I opened the door, I heard him whisper: Hey, Pssst, Thanks (which I ignored), followed by God Bless, which for a second made me wonky.

JUST AS THE RESUMPTION of our activities made them feel twice as precarious, so must the doubled charge of our reunion have made itself, in some unspoken way, felt to the outside world. For not long after we'd reverted to the abnormality which we considered normal, I remember rushing into class just before a lesson, skirting round the oaf with the sideburns who liked to call me Woman, who was already limbering up at the door, and finding, chalked huge upon the blackboard, though far too late for possible erasure, the following annunciation: Moore ♡ Mr. Wolfe. And although the teacher chortled like a well-chuffed punter as he rubbed out the graffito (scrawled, I suspect, by the boy of skewering intelligence who was later to dog me), and although the rest of the class just hooted at the brilliance of their ploy, I confess to having felt, even if exposed, unashamed, for what was being proclaimed, and despite its intention, which was simply to humiliate, was nothing less than true. I did. I loved. I could deny it till the cows came home, but I couldn't fool my own soul.

Beyond my return to the embraces of the man who had become my life-source, and beyond the fact that I never did again play rugger (he saw to it that I became a "musician"—yippee), the main event of that year took place, for me, during the middle term, leading up to Easter. I remember, one lunchtime, sitting in the refectory and finding myself worryingly close to the top of my table, a position which, since it invariably entailed having to speak to somebody senior—on occasion even a teacher, God help you—I avoided keenly. But I must have walked in at the tail end of the surge, because this was the only space that I could see left available. And the gap was hardly surprising, for, at the head of that table, there presided a rabbit-faced creep who, for all of his pride at recently having been appointed Prefect (which status entitled him to his hallowed *emplacement*—yippee for him) was, I can honestly affirm, no more popular than I was, and, at the risk of sounding conceited, somewhat less prepossessing: because this creature, who was known to regard washing with an even greater antipathy than I did sporting activities, not only gnawed his grubby fingernails but, despite already being stricken with adolescent acne and a few grimy hairs on his upper lip, was still into thumb-sucking—a combination which no doubt accounted for the revolting state of his buck teeth. He wasn't a charm to be near.

Although, of course, I hope that he no longer does, should he, by some misfortune, happen still to lurk among the living, I would hazard that he's a vegetarian now, and keen as ever on kagools, and probably knife-collecting in the lowlier ranks of the Territorial Army. He will probably be addicted to solitary television, though he will pay no attention to programmes on corrective dental surgery; and he will reside somewhere glamorous, such as Purley. Thumb-sucking will, surely, still figure among his pursuits. But sadly we lost touch, so I cannot be precise about him. Yet what I can be precise about is the fact that, in the lesson leading up to lunch, which had been Latin, this imbecile had come in for a spectacular bollocking from the relevant teacher, who (extraordinarily, now that I think of it) had been the headmaster. Yet only I, unlike the others at our table, was aware of the rabbit's recent academic humbling, because, though he was senior to me, I used to go up a year for Latin: languages being, as my father never tired of telling me, my unfair advantage. So, as you can imagine, I was not exactly the disgraced prefect's most desirable luncheon companion.

I CAN'T RECALL how we warmed to the argument, which had to do with names, but perhaps it was a letter from my mother, which I would just have collected, because my foreignness was, of course, brought up by him, and I remember that in defence—it was too irresistible—I alluded to the hysterical unsuitability for someone of his density to be lumbered with a surname such as his, which was Newton. My handling of English, I remember thinking, must be improving, because he's gone quiet, I've managed to silence him . . . But not, as it turns out, into defeat. What ensues is almost a blur to me: all that I recall is being struck suddenly, with the summary force of a sideways arm-swing, somewhere about the face, then bitten on my retaliating hand by those enormous teeth, and next thing, though I'm not yet in pain, there's blood all over my food, and all over my clothes—pouring, I realize, from my nostrils—and there's nothing to be done, I cannot stem the haemorrhage, and, with my napkin clamped to my face, I have to ask permission to go to the infirmary.

Matron, who's been enjoying a little nap, and emerges rubbing gunk from her eyes, looks not best pleased. She wants to know what in the name of Jesus-Mary-and-Joseph has happened. I tell her I got hit. Hit by what? Hit by a fist. Whose fist? I volunteer the identity of the culprit: Newton. She takes me into her surgery and sits me down. She takes a squeamish look, as if my face were contagious, and sounds a bit bewildered: a nose-bleed is one thing, she decrees, but this looks more serious. It's all swollen, she says, and the bridge could, she supposes, be broken. But she cannot, even for Calypso, judge the position with any greater certitude, so, for confirmation, she bundles me into a taxi and sends me off to the school doctor, who, this afternoon, is doing his rounds at the local hospital.

My father only ever taught me one thing—well, three really, let's not be churlish: three identical letters which (unlike languages—for languages, notwithstanding his disclaimers, were to prove my gift) did now earn me an advantage that might legitimately be called unfair. Because when a quick set of X-rays revealed that my nose was indeed fractured, and that as a result I'd have to be admitted without delay for its correction (not that this prospect displeased me: freaky as rhinology sounded, I could do with a reprieve from school), I was able to volunteer, proudly as any motto, in a tone probably so defensive that it sounded vindictive, the code-letters PPP, thereby asserting my claim to private medical insurance, a privilege which spared me the gruesome collective palliness of a public ward and entitled me, in addition to a separate room, to my own adjoining bathroom and television. The view from my private window, however, did not exactly offer a prospect: a high black wall of Dickensian brick. But again, let's not quibble.

HERE I AM, sitting on the hospital bed, still in my bloodied uniform, which has grown scabrous down the front of my pullover. I can hear myself clogged up, forced to breathe through my mouth as I stare out of the window at the black wall facing me. Another wall, of silence, now descends: no one explains a thing: I wait; I wait and wait. Footsteps on the corridor blithely pass by. I lie down, but not for long, don't want to nod off. I get to my feet, decide to nose around: Bible in chest of drawers; switch for bedside lamp; telephone, inoperable; bathroom, glossed in sputum-green and reeking of antiseptic. But even though, in one corner of the painted concrete floor, there grows—like a reminder of Nature's supremacy over mere medicine—an incipient tuft of fungus, to me, compared with the school washroom, this feels like luxury. If only I had a clean change of clothes, or pyjamas, I would gladly take a bath in peace, unsupervised and relieved of football hymns. I attempt, instead, to distract myself with the television, yet, much as I fiddle, I cannot seem to fix its reception, which blights all three channels to an homogeneous foreground blizzard. Here comes a film called *Coronation Street,* which I suppose might be regal. Sudden knock on the door. Click off, quick. A nurse appears, bearing a tray which she claims to be my tea, though it looks more like an institutional attempt at supper, unsavoury down to the biscuit of mint-flavoured chocolate which comes sealed in foil of lurid green. I couldn't be less hungry, but I can always dispose of the food down the lavatory, so, to dissimulate my plan, I thank her. That's all right, dear, she says, and pats me. She tells me to eat up now, there's a good lad, and not to forget, when I've finished, to take that little tablet in the plastic beaker, a painkiller; then adds, almost as an afterthought, that by the way, there's someone coming over to see me. Me? Yes, from your school, dear. Who from school? She couldn't say, dear, but not to worry—they'll be here presently. And presently she leaves.

Although unnerved by her message, at least I'm prepared for this forthcoming visit (please let it not be from Matron), but when the door opens, which it does very smoothly and very quietly, as if apologetically, all that I can see, wide as the doorway, is a massive great bunch of yellow tulips, their cellophane aquiver, their stems tied together with an enormous ribbon the colour of leaf; and at first, of course, I suspect a mistake, they've got the wrong room—*I* haven't had a baby—but when I see the commiserating smile behind the tribute, I realize that it's all right, that this is for me, the first bunch of flowers that I've ever been given. (Whereas, unlike most people, I cannot pinpoint when, technically, I lost my virginity, I do recall, with the same blinding clarity as my first experience of snow, which came so late in my infancy, the first time that flowers were brought to me, because they came so prematurely.) I remember feeling, all of a sudden, confusingly grown-up, girlish but flattered, embarrassed but thrilled, as if I were my mother yet were still me. And although the hand that holds the tulips belongs, of course, to Mr. Wolfe, it strikes me as bizarre to see him outside the context of school and rules and subterfuge and sin, so that when he leans down to kiss me—on the forehead, in order not to hurt me—it is I who, flinching, must have hurt him, hurt his feelings by bristling like some prim old spinster who regarded such gestures as forward, a liberty.

He brings me lots of things: dark chocolates from Brussels, which briefly make me pine for Mam'zelle; a couple of books: one, a Brontë paperback indebted to the morbidity of the region—I still have the copy, tattered and yellowed by history—and then, some fat biography with lots of depressing Victorian pictures, which I decide to relinquish to the ward upon release; my slippers; my washbag (inside which, I note with relief, he has not been), plus a small transistor—the latter, he's afraid, only on loan while I'm here. But rather than bother with the linen room he has also brought me—purchased, I presume, en route to the florist—a new pair of what he calls Jim-Jams. (Later, like other presents from him, those innocuous pyjamas were to land me in a quandary, for though I knew that he liked to see me striped in their soft pink and cream, and though I was not, in this regard, averse to obliging him, I realized, as the year drew towards its finish that, were I to take them back home with me, I'd have to provide my mother with some explanation as to their origin; and so, when the moment came and I found myself trapped in the dilemma between indulging him and arousing her suspicion, I panicked and threw them into a bin.)

.   .   .

BECAUSE THE DRAMA of my broken nose had unfolded with such unforeseen speed, and because administration at my school was not exactly what it might have been, my guardians were only informed about the "accident" after I'd been wheeled back out of the operating theatre—minus my underpants, which had scandalized me—by which stage my condition, though concealed from view, had been declared to be tickety-boo. The doctors' satisfaction, combined with the fact that, in those days, to have rung my parents would have involved liaising with a lengthy sequence of half-witted operators (not to mention, I suppose, that the idea of making a transatlantic call merely in order to relay details of a *fait accompli* would have struck those sensible guardians of mine as utter profligacy), prompted them to adopt a stance of restraint over one of responsibility, so that, when they were telephoned by the school secretary, their reaction was to suggest that she, or I, if she preferred, apprise my parents of my circumstances in writing—no need for a telegram, what a fuss about nothing. Look here, they said, were matters happily resolved or weren't they? Could the secretary see any point of causing my parents needless worry? Precisely. Thank you. (Models of sobriety, those people.)

Once I had recovered from the phantom removal of my under-pants, and regained sufficient balance to stagger to the lavatory, I examined my face, which I discovered to be muzzled in plaster, with stripes of white tape across my eyebrows and cheeks, like the markings of an Apache, and the effect, its mix of exoticism and pugnacity, did not, I confess, distress me. But my notion of allure was destined to be short-lived; for soon after Mr. Wolfe had ferried me back to school in his zippy white convertible—a Vitesse, I think, was the model that he steered—I realized that what I'd interpreted as a glamorous emblem of my revenge upon Newton was in fact taken by the general public visi-bly to confirm my assailant's supremacy, for, apart from a mild dressing down from the headmaster, he had come away unscathed—with the further bonus that, very soon, he would also be laughing. The day after my return, I was myself summoned to the hamster's study, which did not come as a surprise; but what did stagger me was finding myself, once in the cage of that stinking rodent, robbed of the benefit of self-account, and instead, as if there existed no room for doubt, being apportioned full blame for the fracas, and accused of being a bilious, mealy-mouthed troublemaker, and of having needled Newton—who, being a Prefect, knew more about mature conduct than I did—to such a point that he'd been left no option but to take corrective action. My fault entirely. (No mention of Latin.) And now, just to drive the point home, as if the fracture had been insufficient penalty, the headmaster orders me to hold out my hands. And out comes the ferula and, after a couple of swishes in the musky air, he brings it whacking down, once, twice, three times on my right hand; and then, he tells me to put that hand down, grabs my left, and, such is his excitement after two further strokes that, on the sixth and last, he misses my palm entirely and comes crashing down on my wrist, managing to smash the glass of my watch into a thousand smithereens. I have often been as shocked, but rarely so angry; and the further effort of having to control myself enough to thank the man for his disciplinary trouble nearly rips off my Apache plaster.

BY THE TIME of my unveiling six days later, bruises had blossomed like dark pansies round my eyes, but the watch, thanks to Mr. Wolfe, had been to the mender and back. I didn't write to my parents for the remainder of that term, because, apart from the exhausting prospect of relating the whole convoluted incident, any hope of sympathy from my mother's quarter was outweighed by the certainty that my father would greet the news of my thrashing with covert delight. In any case, just to complicate matters, I now proceeded to develop, as a suspected reaction to the general anaesthetic (though, with hindsight, I'd suggest that, more likely, it was simply an eruption of nervous tension), an outbreak of shingles, like a belt of weeping lesions around my abdomen and lower back. Matron's milky ointments weren't up to much, and, for the first time since my arrival at that establishment, I genuinely could not get to sleep at night. Compared to the pain of this new mishap, the agony of the ferula had indeed been a laughing matter.

Mr. Wolfe proved, throughout these brief weeks, to be made of solid platinum. I would go to his darkened room with my midriff in bandages, and he wouldn't even bother to comment on the fact. I don't suppose that the friction of his lovemaking can much have aided my condition, for I still bear small residual markings, but whatever harm his ardour might have caused my skin was easily outstripped by the great good which it did me to feel his loyalty wrapped about me. And he would slip me painkillers on the sly, for Matron had decided that I was just being theatrical about a slightly nasty rash. All that was required was a bit of time for it to dry. And on those painkillers I some-how lasted until my flight back to the island.

My mother was aghast. She blamed my father, who in turn blamed me, suggesting that I'd probably aggravated matters by scratching, when my vanity alone would have prevented such foolhardiness. So now I felt obliged to tell the story from the start. He, while still defending the system, and defending my guardians, and even defend-ing the boy Newton, nonetheless attempted, in his absurd repetitive way, to calm my mother. I did nothing of the sort: I told her that I was on fire. The family practitioner was summoned, and initially he took her side. Those English doctors, he ranted, with their snooty aversion to injections and suppositories and a good strong course of antibi-otics, as had so blatantly been required, were a pack of savages. Look at me: I was crawling with bacteria, doubtless in severe discomfort, and infectious at that. My mother recoiled, horrified. But he, perhaps in an attempt to shame her for having drawn back from her own son, boldly stepped forward and asserted that if my physical state was any reflection of the wonders of English public schools, well, she was wel-come to them; rather the flesh of *her* flesh, he threw in as a final stab, than any of his young sons. My mother, I must say, took it like an ama-zon; but at lunch that day, and oblivious (for once) to the servants, and in her most spectacularly rhetorical Spanish, she let my father have it. And bugger the pain: now it was my pleasure at his verbal laceration which felt unutterable.

THE EASTER BREAK was largely sacrificed to my convalescence, which laid me low, and prevented me from swimming or sunbathing, and more or less kept me confined to the house. But since my mother was as reluctant to have the fact of my contagion publicized as I was to attend children's parties, my isolation was treated not as some aberra-tion on my part but as a sensible compromise. The swellings on my face began to subside; my bruises, to wither into pallor and depart, and the girdle of scabs, at last to shrivel and die. But meanwhile, in this climate of self-scrutiny, I could not help but notice that the hideous ogre of puberty now held me in its clutches. Those hairs, so sparse yet so dark, repelled me, they frightened me: for while I'd known about looking like a child, and knew what a man looked like, I now found myself thrown into a ludicrous uncharted hinterland which could only undermine me; and just as, at the start with Mr. Wolfe, I'd regretted the incompleteness of my body, its immaturity, the fact that it was too young, now I began to fear that the changes which slowly but relentlessly were set to corrupt me, would render me too old for his love, would reduce my appeal in his eyes. What we had shared until then I judged to have been a marriage of contrasts, a perfect difference; but now that I saw myself delivered to this state of self-sabotage, with nothing left to conquer other than my embarrassment, I knew that every microscopic alteration which I suffered, even if left unspoken, was bound to be detected by him, and measured with regret, and held against me like a disappointing black star. My body was losing the innocence which, now that it was too late, I realized had glittered like a hallmark in our alliance. I was growing tarnished. I was fast falling in value.

Although I was never to experience the messy privilege of a wet dream, for I had learnt about dry orgasms long before my sperm would oblige, I hid such covert pleasures from Mr. Wolfe: I regarded my personal gratification, like thoughts of sinfulness, as deserving no place in the congress between us. My coarse biological drive was extraneous to our love, whereas his sacred satisfaction was his prize. Like our songs, and the dark open sky, and the smoothness between my buttocks, it, his satisfaction, had been a vital ingredient from the start; but this new growing roughness along my gulf, and my growing genitals, and the growths under my arms, and the growing cracks that broke my vowels, these I viewed as handicaps of nature which I could not allow to upset the stability of our nights. And so, threatened by my diminishing appeal, and by my fears of superannuation, I opted for corrective camouflage: I trimmed, and later plucked, and pretended, even to myself, that nothing at all was happening.

THAT YEAR, as I recall, though activities at school groaned on regardless, there was no summer—but at least Sports Day proved a washout. The sight of all those fat-gutted fathers tripping up as they hopped in sodden sacks filled me with delight; and the mothers, trying not to panic while slithering in stockinged feet over the mud, and struggling to balance a boiled egg on a spoon of aluminum, struck me as laughable. I only regretted that my own parents, despite the shame of my non-existent sporting acumen, could not, on this occasion, have been present, for I would have relished seeing my mother, who would never have participated in such inanities, trying to suppress her derision for my father, who most certainly would have done, her Victor Ludorum. But while I fantasized about them, the general clapping became muffled by the rumble of encroaching thunder; rain-soaked speeches grew increasingly snappy; trophies were handed over hurriedly and half-dropped occasionally, and all that there remained in the aftermath of this thwarted marvellousness was a sodden network of silly, coloured flags flapping beneath a stormy sky, like a boat headed for disaster, and a mountain of soggy strawberries with sweetened cream that no one in their right mind would have wanted.

Everything from that point on became, for me, penultimate: my second last set of exams before the big ones, my second last dormitory, my second last classroom, my second last birthday before departure. In fact, birthdays were to prove my own personal washouts—invariably devoid of a single flower, never mind the garlanded thrones of my childhood, and invariably graced by not so much as a card, for every year I was doomed, instead, to receive a telegram, tickertaped with the garbled message MANY HAPY RETRUNS LOVE FRM MOTER FATHR STOP—which always, in any case, reached me at least a day after the event, and came without the consolation of a cake at tea. For, by the time I'd managed to discover that you could order one of these through the local Post Office and your parents would stump up, I'd decided to waive the privilege of the sponge-filled football-pitches and icing-sugared tennis-rackets and Battenberg warships which were habitually provided, in part because I shied from the pressure of being watched blowing out candles, but largely because, gluttonous as schoolboys are, I doubted that any of those in the refectory liked me enough to stomach a slice of any cake of mine. In any case, a much more popular boy than I shared my date of birth, so the resulting connection would have dismayed him as much as it would have stolen my piddling thunder. And I therefore resolved, before the event and from then on, to ignore a day which, let's face it, was hardly more auspicious than any other.

By my third and final birthday at that place, however, my dealings with Mr. Wolfe were hurtling towards a climax. Hard as I tried, I could no longer conceal from him the alterations in my body, and he, for his part, could no longer conceal his panic at what would happen to us beyond July. But his attitude was ambivalent, almost contradictory: on the one hand he would try, night after night, to persuade me to reach orgasm, to ejaculate in his company, imagining perhaps that this activity, which, to me, was so utterly private, so separate, would in some mysterious way confirm something that our love had not yet done, as if such a love could not now be complete until we had emitted in unison. It would seal our mutual trust as adults, like a game of blood-brotherhood for grown-ups. Ludicrous: how could I, I who was seized up with inhibition, suddenly do as he asked? And the more he went on imploring, the remoter became the likelihood that I could ever oblige. For my real fix was mental, and my head and body had already become divided.

His second line of argument was more ominous, and related not to the present but to the future, to the business of priming me before my time at prep school had expired. Those remaining eighteen months of which, only a brief while back, he had spoken, now seemed, like an accordion at one of my mother's parties, to have deflated and become reduced to one; and I think that as much as fearing what, beyond that last month, I would do about him, or to him, he feared how he would cope without me—because, by the beginning of the end, our dependence, even if contrasting, had become mutual. Teachers tend, as a rule, to be resigned: they must resign themselves at artificially brisk intervals to the notion of pupils' departure, which they interpret more as relinquishing their charges than ever as being outgrown by them, never mind supplanted. But Mr. Wolfe was, by that final month, far from resigned: he was frantic: I do not think that he quite trusted me. Yet to me, questions of trust aside, and on top of the academic pressures which had lately begun to burden me, it felt as if he were wanting secretly to tutor me for some further exam, the ultimate extra-curricular one, whose subject was, of course, Life. Life, he would say, was a strange thing, not always easy to understand, and though all manner of experiences lay before me—great ones, he had every (false) hope, for after the constraints of school I deserved to flourish—he now implored me, as he had once implored me to believe that he was bisexual, to believe that everything that had gone on between us had been conceived in love. He begged me never to forget that fact. He warned me how, in years to come, people who understood nothing of these matters would condemn as wicked relationships such as ours, and wish, invariably, to drive the hatchet of blame into the neck of the adult; but I must know as well as he did, for I (as ever) had an old head on my young shoulders, that between us there had been no fear, no pain, no coercion, nothing bad. We had no cause for reproach, either of us. We should be thankful for the chance that we'd been granted, for this great affair of the heart. And I must promise—it was vital for his peace of mind—that I understand this fact, that I say as much, that I agree that his influence had never been corruptive. We must never, whatever the pressures, whatever happened, betray one another. (It Must Not Get Out.) He would always, he claimed, be there for me; I would always be able to count on him. He yearned for us to remain life-long friends, for friends, as I well knew, were thin on the ground. We must be strong and fight not to let destiny, which was soon to wrench us asunder and force us under separate houses, oppose us, make enemies of us. There could never be a question of an Adieu between us; only, at most, an Au Revoir. And then, he'd go ahead, help himself, and come. But I liked this: there was a freedom about it.

THAT LAST BIRTHDAY, my thirteenth, we celebrated at midnight. He had bought me a tiny heart-shaped cake with a single candle, which I proceeded, as he took my picture—flash—to blow out. I remember sitting half-unbuttoned on the desk where, in the early days, he had stroked my leg with his erring hand, and where later I had forced him to write my name along his table-tennis bat. But now he handed me a tiny box which I recognized as coming from a jeweller's shop, and which, after Mam'zelle's ring, filled me with apprehension, like a premonition of loss. In this dark little box there lay, together with a long slim chain of gold, a glinting medal, slightly too large for a child, which, on the reverse side, had been engraved with the letters HWB (Hot Water Bottle, a euphemistic endearment of his), while, on the front, there glittered my sign of the Zodiac. And although, naturally, I smiled with cosmetic gratitude, as my mother might have done, the object itself discomfited me, for it struck me as pagan, slightly distasteful; but, of course, he was so right, it was so apt: Gemini: Twins: separate yet forever intertwined. I was just too young to be appreciative, too woolly with my own ignorance.

That medal became a problem: I needed to conceal it from other boys; I needed to reveal it to him at night; but I needed, most importantly, to decide what should be done about it before I went back to the island, for, like the hospital pyjamas, it mustn't be allowed to fall into my mother's hands. Otherwise, over lunch on the terrace, she would pounce: HWB? Who *was* that? And where did I get this thing? And how? Either she would not believe my fabricated answer, or she would worry, or she might even, if she were anywhere near my father, think that I had stolen it. But, for now, I let it live in the pocket of my dressing-gown, and I would put it on at night, and rub it warm against my chest as I made my way to Mr. Wolfe's side, and then I'd take it off once we'd begun, and back into the pocket it would slide until next time. He had never intended such a thing, I know, but to me that medal felt like pressure, it weighed me down. And at the end of term, after my exams, as I began to plan my packing, I decided that it must go, the moment had come. Yet some small romantic part of me just couldn't bring itself to discard it irrevocably, so, very early one morning, in a secret lonely ritual, I buried my trophy—which, unlike my father's, was not of dulled silver but of screaming gold, and commemorated my many victories in the much more arduous games which I had brought about—under one of the trees in the woods, near the mouth of a priest's hole, telling myself that one day I'd go back to reclaim my property.

BUT THE END was not the end. He couldn't give me up, couldn't bring himself to bury his own prize, not yet, not quite; and in order to defer our separation (as much as, let's be fair, to delay my return to the island, for by that stage I'd begun to regard the proximity of my parents as a trial), a plan was hatched: namely to attach ourselves to half a dozen pupils from my year who were obsessed with lead soldiers and war games and history—in which, needless to say, I had no interest whatever—and who had planned a jaunt to bits of Belgium with the ultimate goal of visiting the battlefield of Waterloo. Good old Wellington. And so, at the final hour, I telephoned home (with remarkable ease, as it happens, the operators couldn't have been more helpful) and explained about this trip which had been organized by a group of my contemporaries, whom I made sound deeply serious (scholarship material, prefects, captains of various teams, head of the school, future generals—you name it, I said it), and then, of course, I pretended to have contracted a throbbing fixation with the Napoleonic campaigns and soldiers like the very ones which my father had displayed from high in my old nursery. And I suppose that it must all have sounded wholesome and appropriate and desirably social, because my father (perhaps also swayed by the fact that I'd done well in my exams, winning some trivial sum of money which enabled me, since he would never have done so, to buy my first fiddle—which turned out to be a poisoned chalice, but that came later), my father agreed to postpone my homeward flight and allowed me to join the expedition. Mr. Wolfe, whose identity I omitted to divulge, jumped, as planned, on the bandwagon; and suddenly, one crisp morning, there we all were, crammed into the school minibus and off—the original six; Mr. Wolfe, of course; me . . . plus, at the head of the gang, a deranged Nazi casualty who'd staggered for safety to the priesthood, spent some years in Kenya pounding the faith into the blackies, and in due course, after a rumoured dalliance with the bottle, been appointed our school Chaplain. Fr. Bridgefall he was called: I remember because mention of his name is what clinched the deal with my father. That dog-collared old trooper was mad keen on mortal sin, especially of the fleshy sort, and Onanism, as you would expect, was a favourite topic with him: but you should have seen with what labour his oral sphincter would pucker in its effort to expel the word. Anyway, it was he who drove us down to Dover; and from Dover we sailed across to Ostend—with me (for I was later given a photograph) doubled over the railings, puking my guts out.

I'M SURE WE DID LOTS of things Cultural, but, though our first stop was Bruges, my memory selects only the stench of the canals in the midday heat and the sight of bonnetted women crafting doilies along the cobbled walkways, for my attention was so heavily claimed by the dual tasks of appearing, on the one hand, to interact with a group for whom, in truth, I felt no amity, while simultaneously trying to cope with Mr. Wolfe, who, now that he was no longer, strictly speaking, in charge of us, was growing, I felt, too pally by half with the others, as if having forgotten that, only recently, they'd been tormenting me in letters the size of goalposts about him. But worse still, and doubtless as a consequence of the fact that I was on the brink of leaving prep school, was his attitude towards me specifically, which had grown tactile and unguarded to the point of folly, as if he were struggling to salvage a floundering marriage when, in my hardened heart, we had already parted—for fate (I then believed) had already divorced us. I was still alive; his career had survived intact; it seemed to me that I was free to go now. But he, with a lack of ingenuity which I found irksome, would make sure, despite the fact that our sunlit minibus was hardly the darkened prep-school cinema, that he sat next to me when the priest was driving; and when his own turn came to take the wheel, he would order me, in a parody of authority, pretending that I needed strict handling, to take the passenger-seat at the front beside him. And when I did as he commanded, though it disproved my recalcitrance, it also proved to me my position among the company, for, as we trudged along those flattened lowlands, I remember hearing giggles and wolf whistles at my back. It was hideous. I should have gone home at the proper time. I could be lying by the sea by now.

Most of the stops along our route escape me. It was just driving and driving and the relentless English radio playing some atrocious song of the moment to do with Puppy Love. But then we did a quick detour through Brussels, where everyone had a good hoot at the Mannequin Pis and Mr. Wolfe bought me more chocolates, and I just drifted along behind the soldiering historians, slightly detached—like someone who has lost a lover but longs for them with such ardour that their brain tricks them into attaching the face in their mind's eye to the face of strangers—longing, in my stupidity, to fall in this way upon the face of my long lost Mam'zelle.

As we approached Waterloo, everything changed: the boys grew more excitable, but Fr. Bridgefall grew more grave, and, on his instructions, Mr. Wolfe now halted the minibus at a roadside. First, and with a ceremony worthy of the sacraments, we were introduced to the delights of crawling Camembert and cheap red wine. And then, the good padre delivered us a snappy sermon, making plain to me that he was as addicted to snobbery as I was to the sin of Onan: we were all, his finger wagged, to be on our very best behaviour for the next couple of days, and if there was any trouble from any of us (quick glance at my dark aura) we could forget about visiting any historic battlesite; that much he promised. We were going to stay with the parents of du Castel—the small foreign boy who, through my feebleness, I had never dared to befriend—whose father, a Count (which title Fr. Bridgefall had no difficulty whatever in enunciating, its aplomb was sonorous), owned a château nearby, where the family spent their summers, and where the boy, probably dreading our descent, would already be waiting. And it was to here that we would be driving after lunch.

THE CHÂTEAU HAD TO BE the loveliest house that I had ever seen. It made me conjure the birthday cake of my fantasies, of apricot and marzipan and almonds. You approached it through a sprawling woodland, like a dark bottle, which funnelled into a narrow avenue of what I now surmise must have been pleached limes. To left and right as you drove in, peering through the intervals between gnarled trunks, you could see expanses of brilliant grass, bordered by modest orchards, and fields, and a low sky. As you emerged from the tree-lined drive and felt the minibus dip fractionally onto scrunching pebbled ground, the house now rose into view and, though moderate in scale, and simple in structure, it stood there proudly, smiled. It dazzled you. I remember hearing myself gasp, then shrinking back with embarrassment; but the building, decked in the verdant swags of these pastoral surroundings and faced with brick the colour of fading sunsets, seemed, to me, perfectly to match a child's image of a castle from a fable.

The first feature that you noticed were four pointed turrets tapering up like medieval hats; and once your eye had hopped about the small windows which, randomly inserted, seemed to wink with panes of leaded glass, your gaze suddenly swooped down and plunged into the moat which swam around the fortress, whose pewter waters, as you drew closer, reflected flashes of cloud; then, once returned to your senses, with your sights fixed back on solid ground, you realized how, echoing the spires, great box-cones stood impaled at the far corners of the castle, and that at its entrance an ancient drawbridge lay lowered to welcome you. You could have topped the picture with a great heraldic banner, fluttering from the past.

Du Castel's mother, whom, on my arrival, I discovered to be Spanish (and whom the boy had told about me), hailed, it transpired, from Jerez de la Frontera and, in one of those bizarre coincidences that defy credibility, had met my own mother years back at some Feria, indeed recalled her, she said, for her beauty and for the eagerness with which—the Countess laughed nostalgically—the Andalusian beaux of the time had swarmed around her at parties. How was my mother?, she asked; I was to give her the Countess's regards—at which point she mentioned her maiden name—always assuming, she added, that my mother still remembered her. And in truth, the Countess, who wore thick, tinted spectacles, was as unremarkable to the eye as she was blessed with charm; yet, though she was never to know it, not even by virtue of my careful subsequent letter of thanks, that woman managed, after the three years of my undiluted misery, to dumbfound me by proving through her gentle attentions that, against all my expectations, it was actually possible to claim links with my school and not be a monster.

WE WERE LED to our respective quarters. Four of the boys had been put into double rooms with adjoining showers, at the top of the main stairs; two were given, further down that corridor, single rooms with an interconnecting bathroom; and only I, to the others' befuddlement, was graced with a room to myself—a merciful flight below theirs, leading off a tapestried landing with a monumental vase of aromatic foliage on a gilded console, and a couple of ancestral children's portraits to either side of it, small girls. Mr. Wolfe was to sleep on the same floor as I, though at the opposite end of the gallery; and as for Fr. Bridgefall, God knew, you didn't ask such things, he probably lurked somewhere between Mr. Wolfe's bed and mine.

To begin with, there was among the boys a good deal of rushing about and inspecting and, of course, comparison. Even though all of our rooms were characterized by a pristine, retrospective smartness, mine, it has to be said, outstripped the rest: decorated in red *toile-de-Jouy*, with ivory curtains tumbling from gesso rails, it boasted the first fourposter on which I'd ever slept, with pilasters of carved wood, a covered canopy, and built so high that you had to jump to get onto it. Its cotton drapes were hung with narrow stripes of red and *blanc cassé,* and lined in good plain linen; but the ceiling of the canopy had been covered with a panel of the pastoral design, as if to ease you into your slumbers. On both the bedside tables, in silver jugs, were identical posies of mixed roses, stripped of thorns and leaves. And between the windows, which overlooked the garden, there blossomed a dressing-table—I remember because it was so feminine—clothed in white-frilled skirts of voile with threaded ribbons of red velvet, and, on its surface, a silver set of hair-brushes and hand mirrors, engraved with the name Amélie—whoever she was, or might have been—and, on a shelf above, which formed part of the main mirror, various jars of crystal and a pair of figurines— a shepherd and shepherdess of porcelain so fine that sunlight seemed to steal through their skin.

The others' showers and bathroom were, I noted, tiled in cream, with sets of primary coloured towels and curtains, but I, like Mr. Wolfe, whose bedroom was papered in grey and upholstered in blue ging-ham, enjoyed a vast bathroom clad in pale alabaster, with a separate shower, a wardrobe full of extra towels, an armchair and, at the cen-tre of the room, between bath and basin, a luxury which I'd never before come across in such a setting, a Persian rug—of silk, you could tell: the sensation was of treading velvet rather than felt. My good for-tune, however, did not prevent the others, who broke in as I was unpacking, from shrieking with laughter at the sight of a bidet. Yet I, for once, felt bolstered by my foreignness.

I locked the door and took a siesta; for (even if geographically this was not the case) I felt further from the imprisoning rules of school than I did from home. That other incarceration, which of course yet loomed, I tried to banish from my thoughts; I remained, for now, quite happy. I suspect, looking back, that this trip, and this stop particularly, betrayed, in the narrowed eyes of my contemporaries, my first retarded steps towards assertion: it must have galled them to discover that whereas, up to this point, they had regarded me as an outcast, and a ludicrous one at that, now it was I who seemed the most integrated, for although my parents had never lived at the pitch of the du Castels, I recognized the signals of these people, and appreciated the finery of their details as I surrendered to the crisp cool linen of their coronetted sheets.

DINNER THAT EVENING WAS, in several senses, a spectacle. We wore, as we'd been told to do, the charcoal worsted suits that at school were reserved for Sundays and holy days of obligation; and, once herded by the priest, we followed him down to the drawing room for aperitifs. I remember that du Castel, the boy, was already there to greet us, looking at first relieved that we, like him, were dressed more or less formally—which his father, whom we had not yet met, apparently expected—but then I noticed his expression turn to a wince as he realized that while we, who were older, were stuck in shorts, he, by glaring contrast, was wearing a long-trousered suit of very fine dark gabardine, and that (to aggravate matters) his tie was not, like ours, regulation, but tartan. He blushed fleetingly, not knowing where to look, until the smooth natural mechanism of his breeding surfaced to assist him. Addressing Fr. Bridgefall with spectacular aloofness, he explained that his parents would be down presently, that we were to help ourselves to drinks, and directed us to the less showy end of the room, which was brocaded rather than tapestried, away from the great fireplace with its ornate clock of gilt and candlesticks of ormolu. There was, in fact, no helping ourselves to be done, for no sooner had we sunk into the lavish silks of our collective awkwardness than a footman and two maids came in, followed by Mr. Wolfe, who, though panting, nonetheless lent, by dint of his laity, a certain welcome casualness to the proceedings. But he was got-up in a blazer, the crassness of which I found vicariously embarrassing: already he was becoming a disappointment to me. The priest, in his hallowed dog-collar, was, of course, forgiven anything.

The manservant carried, and expertly—not a rattle, not a clink—a platter crowded with flutes of champagne deliberately exceeding the dozen that was strictly needed, as if observation of numbers were a vulgarity. The first of the maids bore a large tray of *amuse-bouches*—tiny mushroom vol-au-vents, bits of foie gras *truffé*, asparagus tips *en gelée*—neat little canapés of the type which, then, were considered stylish; and the second girl, who was younger, followed her leaders' trajectory along the plum and green Aubusson with a small silver salver of impeccably starched cocktail napkins, the first of which the priest plucked and flicked open, like some handkerchief, while the last, du Castel—perhaps in a bolsh at being served after the rest of us—refused. I couldn't help but note that apart from myself and Mr. Wolfe and one other boy whose parents were at some embassy, the remainder were starting to look decidedly tetchy, as if these inexplicable napkins, which were not mentioned but simply left to rot on side-tables, spelt the prelude to some disappointing TV supper.

And then our hosts appeared, arms linked. We rose in unison, only to hover about for what felt like an absurdity. The Countess walked across the room in a superbly plain, superbly cut little cocktail dress—a short-sleeved trapeze, entirely of that period—fashioned, I suspect, of matt black crêpe. Pinned to the left, she wore a modest diamond-and-enamel brooch which looked, to me, more like some papal decoration than hereditary. Her hair had been tied back with a black velvet ribbon; she no longer wore spectacles; her lips were painted pink; her heels were lowish. Though androgynous despite her tailored femininity, she looked tentatively pretty as she guided her husband—whose arm she now released—first towards our Chaplain, as protocol, I suppose, decreed. The Count turned out to be considerably taller, and older, than his wife, and almost entirely bald; his frame was gaunt; his carriage, ponderous; his mien, pallid but gleaming. He wore an old-fashioned dinner jacket, double-breasted, which I thought was pushing it a bit, but perhaps this was the custom among gentlemen of his generation, or perhaps with the Belgian aristocracy, or perhaps he just felt safer clad in such armoury. For it transpired that his command of English was minimal, so that his wife, whose accent reminded me of my mother's, was reduced to interpreting for him. Once or twice, however, our Chaplain took it upon himself to come to the rescue by dredging from the horror of his war decomposing fragments of French, a move less courteous than witless. Our hosts then ambled round the remainder of the semicircle, so that the Count could, a bit stiffly, shake hands with his young guests, and, when my turn came, the Countess explained to him that I was the one from Spain, which earned me a slow Ah Bon. And at last we sat down again, and were left to mutter among ourselves, like extras on a stage, while the two members of staff chatted to our hosts, along with poor du Castel, whom they had inveigled and, anyone could see, was finding it all hellish.

THE MANSERVANT now entered to advise the Countess that dinner was served, at which point we all sighed with relief and leapt up, too eagerly. The dining room, which was approached through two pairs of double doors on either side of the fireplace, looked dark until you reached it, for it was panelled in sombre wood and lit solely by means of candles. The damask curtains, in a shade which, then, was known as *tête-de-nègre,* were heavily drawn to. There were no pictures on the *boiserie.* The floor was herringboned in slippery parquet the colour of molasses; no carpets; and, perhaps on account of the candles, or because of the polishing wax, the air was infused with a scent of honey. The number of servants, meanwhile, had doubled: to two men and four women, attendants in the shadows.

Next, the Countess began to gesticulate an *emplacement,* but only vaguely, because, to her, most of the boys must have seemed interchangeable, and besides, she was the only woman in our midst. One of our group, not thinking, sat down—only to be ordered to get to his feet at once by our mortified Chaplain, to whom our hostess now accorded the honour of her right. I was put to her left, with my back to the window and facing a massively carved *buffet.* Mr. Wolfe was directed to the Count's right, which meant, mercifully, that I couldn't see him or his blazer, and du Castel was told to sit opposite him, presumably in order to lend support to his beleaguered father. The interchangeable half-dozen was left to arrange itself as it saw fit, and once the commotion had died down, Fr. Bridgefall was requested to say grace—which he elected to do in French, if you please, naturally bungling the whole thing and concluding, in preference to a common Amen, with an obsolete *Ainsi soit-il.* Then, with a footman helping each of our hosts to their carvers, and the maids assisting those of us who'd been placed alongside them, we were finally able—though to the accompaniment of appalling scraping, worse than the benches in our refectory—to sit and breathe with greater ease. But there followed a sudden deathly hush, inspired, I suspect, by the sight of our first course, which was artichokes.

The priest must have been preoccupied with indicating to his charges, by dint of meaningful grimaces, that they were not to be daunted by this confounding vegetable, but simply to follow his urbane suit and pluck the leaves, because I remember finding myself compelled to converse with the Countess, who, as soon as it seemed permissible, lapsed into a whispery Spanish, spoken with greater warmth than either of her other languages. I remember complimenting her on the table's centrepiece, which resembled a seventeenth-century *bodegón,* for though its splendour betrayed a corruptive Flemish influence, the style of its arrangement reminded me of certain old Spanish paintings—by Meléndez, and the early Velázquez, that sort of thing. I don't suppose that any of the components of the display had been chosen for their symbolic worth, but for their plain beauty, which was unquestionable, and yet the decorative tone of the tableau tended less towards the quotidian than the ecclesiastical. I suspect that the Countess, who'd apparently turned the former stables of the château into a private chapel, where the local priest came daily, at dawn, to offer communion to her, sought to drown the sobs of her melancholy in the greater waters of religion—quite a Latin thing to do in that era. At any rate, when I asked about the cloth upon which her set had been created, which, though fashioned of worn velvet, like an ancient altar frontal, possessed, at the extremities, mysterious pockets, closer to an *alforja,* she explained that—yes, wasn't it curious—the piece had originally been designed for Catholic priests during the Reformation, but though indeed cut, in order to invest it with the semblance of a secular use, along the lines of a saddle-bag, its secret function had been to enable former members of our clergy, when threatened with sudden persecution, to bung their sacred paraphernalia into the pockets, roll up the whole business, and flee.

The still life was at once ascetic and luxuriant, suggestive both of a low Mass and a bacchanal. The objects which, arranged with feigned informality around a swanlike jug of tarnished silver, graced that long table, owed as much to the early Eucharist as to a tale of sensual indulgence. There were, of course, numerous candles, haphazardly inserted into clashing sticks, of bronze and pewter and dull brass, their heights varying considerably; and yet the ensemble, at least from my position, looked well balanced, felicitous. There were also great standing goblets, like chalices, and others laid on their side, as if drained of their contents and abandoned; and from some of these, which seemed to gleam with gilded insides, there poured torrents of grapes darker than Málaga wine, mingled, as they reached the velvet surface, which had mellowed to the colour of mud, with bunches of alabaster ones. And there was dark bread, like Testamental loaves, with severed chunks; and occasional shells of mother-of-pearl, presumably to shoot the light; and black cherries of glass, their stems made of metal, and walnuts, and scattered almonds, and figs, incised with a cross into segments that curled out like tongues. And here and there, as if stolen from a Sevillian shrine at Eastertime, deep purple carnations, like secrets, or offerings of penance.

As I was about to express my surprise that carnations could be cultivated in Belgium, I saw the Countess look across, round from the priest towards her husband; and at that critical instant, there was a distracting flash, like a mirror hit by sun, along one side of the company; and as, in a joint reflex, we turned, she and I, to the source of this light, we saw that one of the boys, the one who had laughed about the bidet in my bathroom, had picked up his silver finger-bowl and taken a glug. This gaffe did not escape the Count, who, unlike the apocryphal seigneur, did not seek to put his guest at ease by similarly imbibing, but looked back to his wife, smiled, and left the perpetrator to be publicly admonished by the Chaplain, and die. The whole vignette, perversely, made me think of my father: I should have loved him to have witnessed it, for he was fond of boasting to the people of our island about how, in his day, the priests at his old school had even taught one to carve. Young Gentlemen, and all that.

The next course came with a great flourish, but augured no better as straightforward nourishment, for what we were served, along with a warm purée of salsify, was roast quail. The sensibilities of my English peers were visibly strained by the sight, on a steaming great platter, of all those dead little birdies, requiring, after a few initial cuts, dismemberment by squeamish adolescent fingers; but I suppose that they managed the unsavoury task, for after the artichokes they must have been starving. I asked about carnations in Belgium. The Countess, who'd been discussing with our Chaplain the faults and merits of the Tridentine Mass (not the most gripping of subjects, but I don't suppose that this was exactly the place to raise the topic of the Vatican's intransigence on contraceptive matters), now turned to me, looking, at first, glad of the chance of conversational distraction, and then embarrassed, as if my enquiry had, in some way that I couldn't fathom, caught her off guard, exposed her. We reverted, at her initiative, to Spanish, but her words were accompanied by a look of such fixity as to suggest not that she was engrossed in me particularly but that she didn't quite dare to look elsewhere, or let her comments be broadcast. Her tone became actively conspiratorial now, and I was soon to glean the reason behind her reticence: you could, she said, indeed grow such flowers here, if necessary in hothouses, though carnations were resilient—hers flourished in the cottage garden on the kitchen side of the château. She held an affection for them, she admitted, along with geraniums and jasmine and plumbagos, for they reminded her of her Andalusian background; but the Count, you see, preferred the conventional botanical refinements, such as lilies and roses and ornamentals, with the result, she confessed, that a truce had needed to be drawn not long after their marriage, when she had felt at her most, how could she put it, nostalgic—and most stubborn, she admitted with a smile; and thus it was agreed that she was at liberty to grow her floral banalities within the walled discretion of the kitchen garden, and welcome, if she so desired, to place them in her private apartments, so long as the Count could, if she didn't mind, be entrusted, as he'd been entrusted ever since inheriting the house, with the supervision of his ancestors' formal landscape. I began to see how, despite the advantages of her match, the Countess had suffered by her removal from her homeland, must feel a sense of foreignness akin to mine; and, conversing with her in our shared native tongue, I was struck by the irony that, just as I had failed to develop into my father's proper English son, so, in some illogical way, I must have reminded this woman, whose firstborn was being primed with a specific view to assuming his Belgian title, of the Spanish son whom she had never had.

TODAY IS WATERLOO, our Mecca. After breakfast, during which Mr. Wolfe keeps trying to catch my eye, we're given a quarter of an hour to get ourselves together, fetch our coats—bound to be cold—and collect whatever we might want: cameras, notepads—not that I have either. I go upstairs and lie on my bed, and wish that I could be forgotten, stay behind; but, all too soon, I hear the dread commotion start, so I resign myself, exhale, get up.

Details regarding that defunct battleground seem to elude me. I can't recall a single feature of interest about it. Was there a strategic hillock? Was there a herd of grazing cattle? Was there some commemorative statue? Whatever there was, all that I can picture in the dreary aftermath is a blur of driving rain and sombre skies and soggy grass, indistinguishable from the sludgy panoramic of the northern English wilds; and boys jotting copiously on sodden paper pads, and taking pictures which require a flash, and reliving an unlived past with the help of phrases such as Rearguard Action. Then, at last, back into the minibus we climb, resuming our earlier positions, to trundle over a monotony of empty roads in search of some tavern where we might be served a fortifying country lunch. The Chaplain finds just such a place, deserted and in the nick of time, and falls, on his way to the lavatory, not merely upon some postcards, but, to quote him, upon *quelques* jolly *cartes postales*. Hurrah, Father.

By evening, it was plain that certain changes had been effected at the house, perhaps as a result of the trials of dinner the previous night. Certainly the Count had chosen to absent himself, pleading an engagement in town, where he was to stay overnight; and though we were treated to drinks in the drawing room, we didn't have to don our suits, and the Countess, who joined us wearing a powdery cashmere cardigan draped over her shoulders, hoped that we didn't mind if tonight was a little less formal: she had arranged, she explained, that a buffet be prepared for us in the parlour where we'd had breakfast. And when we went through, though I forget the food, I observed that in the absence of the Count the room had been decked with bowls of flowers taken from her cottage garden; and that although we were served *sangría*, which we boys guzzled down, the padre spluttered and coughed until he'd been brought a restorative bottle of burgundy, which he graciously offered to share with his hostess, who thanked him but declined. I grudgingly took part in a game of after-supper cards, but, with the announcement of Fr. Bridgefall's next inspired idea, namely a cheery round of French charades, I excused myself, feigning exhaustion, and took myself to bed, having, as was clearly required (for she had inclined her profile), kissed the cheek of the Countess. Sod the others, I thought. But, deep down, I was starting to grow panicky.

WHEN I DREW my curtains closed, I knew that I was doing so for the last time: tomorrow we would be starting our long journey back, our objective fulfilled, my pretext done. Yet I was to be proved wrong on all fronts; for, in the deep of the night, as I darted fitfully in and out of dreams of drowning in fire, I heard my door being opened slowly, slyly, and my instinctive first terror was of a burglar; then, of some last-ditch schoolboy prank. I lay there paralysed. But as my eyes began to focus in the dark, I saw Mr. Wolfe's bearded outline move towards the curtains and open them, just as I had opened his during the course of the last three years. And then he removed his dressing-gown in an echo of what I myself had so often done, and he stole into my bed without permission. But there was no music to be heard, and there were no candles to be lit—none, at any rate, that I would allow; forget it. I recall that I felt enraged: aside from the effrontery of his intrusion, the gauntlet that he was running seemed to me far riskier than all the risks which, in my former desperation, I had run. I wished that I'd remembered to lock my door, had kept him out. This visit seemed maniacal, frightening. I feared our discovery in this house far more powerfully than I had ever done at school in England. It seemed to me that for the truth of my iniquities to be relayed by the appalled Countess to my appalled mother would have proved an exposure infinitely more shaming than the half-baked revelations of my former headmaster. I don't know what I would have done, there would have been no telling. I told Mr. Wolfe to get out, and to be quiet about it.

But, of course, he would have none of this. He, too, had earned his rights. This was our closing night. He couldn't believe that I was being so hard-hearted: What had happened to me? Couldn't I see that it was he, not I, who was putting his neck on the line? And hadn't he always covered for me? And did I really value what we shared at nothing? And thus, with his frantic whispered pleas, he gradually wore me down. I would just, I remember thinking, have to go through with it, endure it like some prostitute. Yet if there was a price to be paid, the price was to be mine, for as he ripped off his pyjamas and heaved himself upon me, he asked me, told me, threatened that this story of great love could not be complete unless I met his supplication, for the final time, that we come in unison. And so it was to be, so we were to come; but what he never knew was that as we did, I was thinking of some other, imaginary man, some perfect stranger. And then, I helped myself to his pyjama top and used it to mop up.

BY MORNING, I had put it all behind me; though as I stood, packed and poised on the threshold of the next phase of my life, I felt undermined by a chill of residual discomfort, not just about my treatment of Mr. Wolfe but regarding the broader change which had affected my feelings towards him. I could hardly believe that I no longer cared a toss, literally, for the man who, until recently, had meant so much to me, without whose love I'd feared that I might flounder. It made me feel cheap, this lack of consistency, this ingratitude, and yet I couldn't allow mere fickleness to belittle me. I had to get on, you see, gather my strength for the next ordeal—for that is how, then, I viewed my existence: as a relentless assault course, like hurdle after treacherous hurdle rushing at me from a hostile future. So I appeased myself with the argument that he and I had struck a deal, and that the deal, mutually beneficial as it had been, was simply complete. We were both, even if on the verge of severance, in one piece. Surely the honour was implicit? But as I took one last look at the crimson *toile-de-Jouy,* at that moment, just as I was turning to leave, I found myself, as if I were my mother, steeped into a crisis of superstition by the monstrous sight of a peacock—its back turned to me; its train raised into a full, iridescent fan of doom.

Leavetaking was easy: just the Countess, back from Mass. Du Castel had gone out riding. I was last in the departing queue. She reminded me to convey her regards to my mother, wished me luck at the Big School, hoped to see me next time she was in England, said that I was welcome to return whenever I liked, or to visit their house in Brussels in winter. *Adiós,* Santiago, she added; and after I had mumbled my thanks, we kissed. And as she stood on the gravel, waving, the minibus, with my redundant lover at the wheel, drove off through flashes of lime, and a strange sorrow welled within me, like a phantom homesickness, for I knew that I should never return to this place which I regretted leaving more than, when the moment came, I would regret leaving Mr. Wolfe.

I HAD FORGOTTEN that we were to return to Brussels for one night, to sleep at some seminary, which was empty during the summer but where Fr. Bridgefall had some business to attend to, some meeting. We arrived early, for Mr. Wolfe had driven like a demon, and were given the afternoon to amuse ourselves, walk around, see the shops, buy presents for our families. Mr. Wolfe latched on to me, inevitably, and we broke off from the rest of the group, leaving the building through a back door. I found that I had nothing to say now; it felt odd; it was as if last night had been the culmination of one chapter and we were now embarked upon a connection of a further sort, more healthy, more grown-up, but duller. Letting go. Moving on. He wanted to buy things for me—not quite gifts of propitiation, tokens of endurance—for which I had no wish. But nor did I wish to offend him, for he, though guileless, and ignorant of my rotten core, had not been Wrong. So in the end I found myself pointing towards fripperies of no interest to me—a porcelain bowl, a vase, yet another box of chocolates—things which, bizarrely, I chose with my mother in mind, as if I needed to earn her forgiveness for transgressions which she didn't know that I'd committed, as if the single blessing of her love could wipe away the mess of my serial sins, which was mortal.

After the hollow spree, and as the gloom began to feel engulfing, we stopped at some great square to drink milky coffee; and suddenly the prospect of prolonging this ill-considered journey seemed to me un-endurable—the drive all the way to Ostend, the sea-crossing to Dover, the trip back to London, the inevitable night with my vile guardians, the train journey to Heathrow, the flight, which included a midway stop . . . I just lacked the stamina, could no longer cope; and in a burst of inspired lachrymosity, I now begged Mr. Wolfe, as he had begged for simultaneous ejaculation, to grant me one parting gesture, one last proof of his loyalty: to help me change my flight, so that directly from Brussels I could flame it to my island, first thing in the morning. Mirac-ulously, he acceded to my request, and though compelled to pay some supplement, managed to effect the transfer. From the travel agency, I telephoned home and, since my parents were out, I told Cook to send the chauffeur to collect me from the airport *tomorrow,* at two in the afternoon; yes, I'd be arriving a day early; never mind if she hadn't had time to prepare my favourite food. I wasn't exactly hungry.

My taxi came before the rest of the group had awoken. I crept out of my seminarian cubicle, and only Mr. Wolfe was up to see me off, his eyes puffy, suddenly grown old. I thanked him for having made my flight back possible. He thanked me for Everything. We did not kiss; nor were hands shaken: we compromised on a mutual wink and pout, concealed from the driver's view, and the rest of the business was left unspoken in mid-air, to loll, like a doubt, in the lap of the gods.

And when I returned home, burdened by my superfluous trophies, my mother, though pleased enough to receive the chocolates, suggested that I rewrap the vase and bowl and give them to the servants, who would be so grateful. And at dinner that evening, when my father demanded an explanation for the change in my travel arrangements, my answer was simple: it seemed more efficient, and Mr. Wolfe (Yes, he came too, didn't I tell you?) had been in full accord. But when I regaled my mother with the anecdote about my hostess at the château and their coincidental meeting at the Feria years before, she jingled her great bracelet and denied any recollection of any girl from Jerez having married any Belgian count, then or ever.

IN THOSE EARLY DAYS—though later she would grudgingly concede surrender—my mother focused her efforts for me on her special subject, which was Society. No sooner had I ripped off my uniform than she would begin to cajole me into attending children's parties, whole litanies of them, and simply would not take any kind of No for an answer. Out of the question. What was I, for heaven's sake, some peasant down from the mountains? What was wrong with me? Could I not see how essential it was for me to maintain links with my motherland?—to which, I think, she secretly hoped I would return to settle in time, armed with international qualifications and prospects to earn me the easy pick of the best girls in town, as if the marriage game were a fan of canasta cards, as if she had learnt nothing from her own miserable mismatch. The links which she espoused on my behalf were obviously restricted to links of a good class—as words went, *élite* and *échelon* didn't strike her as such bad ones—and to parties given for the off-spring of women who, even if they hadn't boasted great dowries (and always provided that their spouses passed muster), had at least attended the Assumption. She was familiar with all such women on the island, not just from their shared past but because she would run into them at every turn of the circuit at cocktail parties; at charity-benefit fashion shows; at the Nautical Club regatta; at the Casino when the latest garland of virgins came out; at the Golf Club on carnival night; at the airport—flying off, flying back, or meeting someone; at music recitals, though no *Lieder* for her, thank you; in church and afterwards, outside; at funerals, which, even in the elegant days of mantillas, my mother tried to avoid, though mourning and commiseration did appeal to my father; at art openings (if you could call them that); in chic boutiques; at the embroidery woman's house; at the theatre, whose rear elevation once had to be demolished in order to accommodate a touring production of *Aïda;* at occasional discothèques, which used to be called *boîtes;* at the one and only decent hairdresser's, whither all such women flocked to have their pieces buttressed to their scalps; every 15th August, at tombolas hosted by the Old Girls of the Assumption . . . and in this way, through these repetitive encounters, my poor foolish mother ensured that wherever there was a desirable children's party, I was not forgotten, that hostesses, even in my absence, rather than risk her displeasure, invited me. She would sometimes mention these events to me—the magicians and the prizes and the hideous piñatas and the mouth-watering birthday cakes and the treasure hunts—describing them, with breathless superlatives and a suspect preponderance of exclamation marks, in her letters of deep turquoise.

Now that I'd outgrown a governess, my mother would sometimes take me to these fledgling parties, but would, on our eventual departure, and oblivious to the driver, launch into me, berate me for my bad manners, my sulky, stand-offish attitude, my refusal not just to involve myself in any of the entertainments, but to feign what even a mere yokel would regard as basic friendliness. I had plenty of charm when I wanted to deploy it, she was all too aware of that, so what on earth was wrong with me? Why couldn't I make more of an effort? And why did I object to the other children anyway, all perfectly well brought up, and all, so far as she could tell (apart from me), having a marvellous time: you could hear their laughter from the pergola where mothers were taking tea at the far end of the garden. So why, she would implore, must I always embarrass her?

But she did not understand (how could she have done?) the extent to which I felt estranged from such celebrations, the fact that, beyond the more obvious oddity of being schooled in another country, which increasingly made me feel foreign here in Spain as well as over in England, I also felt oppressed by the weight of my other problem—my strange, sinful love—which, irrespective of its secrecy, distanced me yet further from the wide-eyed children at those parties, conspired to make me feel like a much older alien. And the result was that I simply found myself with nothing to talk about, in any language.

Where I went to drown my silence, particularly in the summers to come, became nobody's business. Up to my twelfth year, in view of my reluctance to socialize, I found myself more or less restricted to the bamboo fringes of our house, and only exceptionally did I go out unchaperoned; but thereafter I began to be sent on errands by my mother, to the watchmaker's, to the stationer's, to buy buttons for the sewing-woman, and I was allowed to walk to the Nautical Club, and, after my siesta, to go to the cinema. And this new licence led to an abundance of opportunities for me. I felt oddly nervous when I first ventured beyond the bandstand of flamboyants, as if, at any moment, some excruciating acquaintance of my parents' might pounce on me, or as if, absent-mindedly crossing the Rambla, I might collide with some speeding car, for when I'd walked the moors and fells and woods of the English countryside, I never ran into anything or anyone. This new environment was too crowded, too noisy for my liking. But soon enough I grew accustomed to it, and simply looked to the ground— both in order to avoid detection and to check where my feet were guiding me. Often it would be, though briefly, to the Nautical Club, where I would swim a few lengths in a great hurry and walk out before being accosted by someone's flip-floppy mother or, just as bad, some relic of a boy from my discarded childhood, and I would set off clutching my rolled towel by way of alibi. Because my feet would no longer lead me, as instructed by my mother, into a taxi and back up to the house.

Instead they would stray, directed by some odd desire for transgression, by some incomprehensible need for corruption, into the exotic womb of the Municipal Park. I would stroll, pretending to be entranced, past the aviary with all its spectacular parrots, like the one shot down from our palm tree, and the great sheet of water with its fascist sculptures and its fountain, and the concrete course for mini-golfers, and sometimes I would stop at the ice-cream stand. But once I had effected this round, which became customary, I would sit on a stone bench along one of the paths in some more secluded section of the park, not far from the public lavatories. These alleyways were, in fact, more like tunnels, for the sky was almost entirely obscured from view by jungles of green foliage, trained from arch to arch to arch for great stretches at a time. And once you entered the hollows of these giant caterpillars, it was as if you had entered a world divorced from reality, where all life was different and your heart pounded with anticipation.

To begin with, the men just smiled at me. Later, when they began to recognize me, they would beckon me—first, with their heads, soon thereafter, hand on crotch—to follow them. In time, I grew bold enough to do so, and would find myself going down the steps to the place called *Caballeros,* and approaching the urinals, and standing next to these beckoners, and I would voluntarily enter into congress with these creatures who, for the most part, were like tramps. And either because my extreme youth spelt extreme danger, or because the danger was itself a source of frenetic excitement, they would ejaculate against the wall of the urinals in a matter of seconds. They would frot my buttocks, or stroke my front, or guide my fingers to their hardened phalluses, or use me to squeeze their hairy testicles. And the sight of them, turned more salacious than the apes that were caged outside, and the access which they granted me to all their variations on the theme of grown-up genitals, made me feel desired as well as educated, more so than at any local First Night. My lessons were quick, uncomplicated, and never unpleasant. Those men were too wary of the risk which they were running, of their brush with crime: for homosexual acts, never mind such acts performed in a public place with a blatant minor, were, at least then, instantly imprisonable. No remand. Bang. Whether I'd fully entered the mire of puberty by this time, I cannot say, but my voice certainly hadn't yet broken, which was one reason why I always kept my mouth shut. The other was that I couldn't bear to be kissed by those strangers.

ONCE, HOWEVER, a man did talk to me, and he seemed more assured, more poised than the usual marauders. I remember that he was dark as a gypsy, and that he wore white trousers, tight and slightly transparent. For once, I talked back. It didn't take me long to suss from his harsh sibilants that he came from the mainland, and that, like me in a way, he was an outsider. I said that I was English. He couldn't believe the fluency of my Spanish. I pooh-poohed his compliment as my mother might have done, with flirtatious bashfulness. I even lowered my lashes. He managed to light a cigarette with his second waxy match. He thought the park was a bit grubby, that I was special. He had nowhere to take me, but he did have a car. We could go for a drive. Did I have time? I had an hour before lunch. My fear was not palpable: I was too het-up, and too hot, to decline. He seemed trustworthy enough. What could be the harm? He was parked round the corner, which provided me with my first obstacle, namely avoiding the detection of anyone who might know my family, and there were plenty of candidates. But I passed with flying colours. I got into that car, also white, also tight, quick as a flash; in fact, so set was I on my illicit ride that, frankly, I could have done it in a pencil-skirt and spikes. And off we went into the adventure. I slid down my seat to the level of the dashboard. He turned on the wireless. I remember a drivelling religious programme, which he quickly switched over, visibly embarrassed, to local folk music, tambourines and guitars in triple-time. Smoky laugh, followed by a phlegmy yok, expelled through his open window.

He puts my hand on his crotch, which is hard, as is mine. Tells me to stroke him, but not to take it out. That feels lovely. Looks into my eyes. I look at him like an enquiring harlot. I need to be sophisticated. We're going to a beach on the edge of town, not far from the Nautical Club. Great, I say, but I slide further down. He doesn't seem to notice. He's happy so long as I don't let up. Purrs like a tiger, is beginning to leak through his pants. Once we're out of danger, by which I mean beyond the entrance to the Nautical Club and on our way, I relax a fraction, and he relaxes almost entirely into a mood of slow pleasure. He can't wait, he says, to get his hands on me. His hands, on the wheel, are like sausages. Cheap-looking ring, taxi-driverish. Round his neck dangles a crucifix of gold, no cadaver, just the symbol, which, with the bumps of the road, jumps in and out of his tangles of dark fur. He strokes my working hand. Changes gear now. Looks out of the rear-view mirror. And again. But something's up. Seems fractionally worried. Sighs. Sucks at his saliva. Flicks his cigarette out of the window. Moves my hand off his trousers, makes me feel rebuffed. He says there's a bit of a problem: he's being tailed by a police car. No, he tells me, don't turn round. My head is suddenly pounding. We're in the middle of nowhere and I've got no money, blown it all at the ice-cream stand. If he dumps me now, I'll never get back in time for lunch. I'll have to hitch-hike. But I might get recognized. He suddenly swerves like a television robber into a side-street and races round the block and, before I know it, we seem to be headed back to town. Perhaps he knows of some other place somewhere. But as he checks the mirror once again, it becomes plain that the law is still cruising behind him. He's getting agitated now, turns off the wireless. He explains, very precisely, as if he were bisex-ual, that he hopes this won't get unpleasant. If it does, I must pretend to be his nephew. But I don't care, because with every one of his sibi-lants we're getting closer to home, speeding up the Rambla now: yet as we approach a set of traffic lights, which are turning from green to amber, I suddenly hear, directly behind us, the appalling demented wail of a police siren. Before I can think twice, and before he gets the chance to speed away, and before the pigs behind can grab me, I just open the door and jump out and don't even look back. And the lights must have gone green, because all the traffic races off as I stagger— Christ Almighty, I've lost my towel—up the hill to lunch on the terrace. But it was better and scarier than any orgasm.

AND THEN THERE WAS THE SEA. The sea turned me sexually amphib-ian. I think that my love of bathing *à deux* must date from that time. For when we went to the idyllic house with wooden steps that led down to the honeyed sand and my mother seemed, for a few miraculous weeks, to forget the rounds which, in town, at once excited and exhausted her, I would spend hour upon careless hour darting in and out of the navy waves. I was also allowed to swim after supper, while the tide went out in the dark—though, even if the beach was deserted, naked never. My father, when not playing golf in the mountains, or attending a funeral—*someone* had to represent the family—and despite my point-blank refusals to join him in any volley game of anything upon the sand, or his to help me fly my kite—do it yourself, you're perfectly capable—seemed nonetheless delighted by my growing aquatics. Who knows, he would say to my mother, the boy might yet turn out to be a Swimmer—as if this were a vocation. And I would recall how, back at school, I had surveyed him from my high plank on the stile.

My mother had for years retained a couple, an old fisherman and his wife, who lived just behind our beach house, to guard it when it was empty, for local hooligans enjoyed looting and setting fire to villas such as ours. The old lady would, in her fishy way, cook for us, and make our beds, and clean the bathroom which, to my mother's annual irritation, had to be shared by all three of us, like Goldilocks' bears—though there were, doubtless to her proportional relief, enough bedrooms to go round. Actually, I preferred the divan in the alcove off the dining room and, as a treat, would occasionally be permitted to sleep there. But never on the hammock outside, not at night—stars, moon, or the very firmament. Open your window.

Meanwhile, the old fisherman, who had no teeth but smoked like a furnace, acted as handyman: would go to market when required, would wash the car, water plants, replace lightbulbs, mend shutters, sweep outside. His were chores of this nature. But his principal function was, every morning at ten-thirty, and please no earlier, to position my mother's white-slatted lounger, angled to face the sun and decked with a buttoned mattress, on the beach, directly beneath the steps that led down. A few minutes later, she would emerge, ready to face the day, clad in one of that year's patterned towelling robes, which were more like gowns—they practically had trains—her eyes shielded by a pair of the latest sunglasses, which varied according to fashion but tended to be large and very dark; and, if the wind wasn't up, a vast, straw wheel of a sun-hat. Just as a cardigan, in Spain, was known as a Rebecca—for, before that film, the populace had never beheld such an article—hats of the type which my mother favoured were known as Pamelas, presumably in homage to some now forgotten Hollywood diva. I presume this because, when my mother emerged thus covered, she would hold her hand up towards her crown with such choreographed *élan* that you would have thought she was balancing an invisible platter of mangoes and foliage and clouds. The side of her wide brim would curl up against her risen arm, and though I know I sound sardonic and campy, the sight of her descent was, in fact, sublime. And in this sublime attitude, which included a flat basket hung about her other arm, her bare feet, with toes lacquered crimson, would lead her very slowly to partake, for an hour or two, of the summer sun.

THEN SHE WOULD DISROBE; and this ritual, too, entranced me. Her swimming costume—for never in her life would my mother (this wasn't Hollywood, that was her line) have sunk to the lowness of a two-piece—invariably corresponded to the robe that engulfed it. It was a rule with her, stringent as a commandment. And the towel which, like a beach in itself, she would spread out over her lounger was always of burnt gold, like the sand, like her skin, which I worshipped. She was never to veer from this tone, and bought it by the half-dozen before having it monogrammed to the precise matching shade of ochre. One year alone, for a change, she had her towels initialled in red, to go with her toes, but later she claimed to have made the greatest mistake, said that she reminded herself of the national flag: blood and sand; ketchup and mustard.

Now she would recline on her back, one knee always up, and close her shaded eyes, and let out a sigh which was not of complaint but of gratitude, of sacred hedonism, for, at heart, at least until my father got her, I think that she carried the latent flame of the sensualist. And when he was away from the beach, and she and I were left in peace, I would come and go and do as I pleased, and nothing in those days pleased me more than to build lavish sandcastles for her, with courtyards and moats and starfish and shells and the whole paraphernalia, which—Later, later, she would beg—she would christen with my bucket, full of water from the sea, for these castles which I made were hers to reign in. And she, humming in paradise, would apply rarefied unguents to her legs, which, though she would not let me feel them, were smooth as polished stone; or she would turn on her front, and leaf through her magazines, which, once through, she would let me attempt to read; or when at last the heat overwhelmed her, she would send me back to the house bearing her hat while she slipped on her bathing cap, her crowning glory, which, like the varying swimsuits and robes, altered on a daily basis—until some eventual vogue decreed such contrivances passé. And when she swam, her neck held to the heights, it was in a regal breaststroke, timeless, biblical. And although soon enough my paddle would be left in her smooth wake, smooth because her feet never frothed, I would linger in the shallows and await her return, to reclaim her. And I would have to say that in those early days, at the beginning, with her to myself, I, at least, was perfectly content.

OF COURSE, the idyll was not to last. With the passage of those summers, I outgrew the thrill of sandcastles, discarded the disappointment of my kites, gave up chasing butterflies, and sought, instead, amusements that were more challenging. My mother, for so many possible reasons—her encroaching middle years, her reptilian husband, her frustration that I wasn't turning into her plan, to mention but the more obvious likelihoods—became firmer with me, forbad me to browse through her magazines, which were for women; forbad me from wearing those colours which I favoured, such as primrose, and which, overnight, she condemned, with a venom that I have never heard rivalled, as Effeminate; forbad me from having my tight jeans further tightened; forbad me from riding a moped; forbad me from staying behind in town. So that in this new state of tension, in this small house by the beach, I felt entrapped. It was like the sea which at school had parted around me—nowhere to walk, nowhere to run—until, in the end, my sole escape became, of all the ironies, the very sea: I went to the waves for release. And soon thereafter, I went to them for revenge, for satisfaction.

It was a horrible time. My mother would lie on the sand, her shape perhaps less waisted now, swathed in pareos of printed muslin. There was something sad about them. But I would ignore the sadness and get up late, long after she had taken to the sand. I would breakfast on my own, and sunbathe nowhere near the house, slink off as far as the tide and narrow limits of the beach allowed. My black swimming-trunks—or white, once I was tanned—were so brief that my father commanded me to wear those obscenities nowhere near him, banished them from his sight. But he must have seen them hanging on the clothesline (inside out, which is how I pegged them up, to annoy him), for we

argued about them frequently: about their cut, about their common-
ness, particularly that of the white ones, about their vulgar sheen,
about the way that they clung: you could see Everything: it was disgusting. I would reply with a recusant smirk that they couldn't be *that*
ghastly since they came from London—as indeed they did, though
they were actually manufactured in Paris, which I found miles more
fabulous. He would say that London had become a city of trash. He
would rant about those grubby, long-haired hippies, would lament the
demise of capital punishment, bemoan the day they did away with conscription. But then, one day, rather than simply criticize me, he changed
tack and—his pallid paunch pointed to the sun, the sog of his baggy
cotton shorts moulding upon him—enquired *why* I wore those minuscule briefs, why it was that I liked them. And I remember replying that
soon my body wouldn't be young enough to carry them. And this is the
only occasion when I properly succeeded in leaving my mother's consort at a loss for a contradiction. But it didn't feel like victory.

Victory for me lay in the water, in the sting of the salt, and the pull
of the people—for by now the beach had become more popular. Later,
its appeal would become so endemic, and so sexy, that my outraged
parents, not once stopping to wonder whether I, their sole heir, might
have liked, in the fullness of time, to own the property which my
mother had herself been bequeathed by her family, sold off the Villa,
at a phenomenal profit—only to see it demolished within minutes of
settling the deal—never replaced it, and just travelled from then on: to
Madeira; to Capri, when the place was still bearable; to Ibiza, ditto; to
Crete, Malta, and Cyprus before the explosion of package tourists . . .
you get the general idea, safe and prosaic. But for now our beach was
merely more popular, had not as yet been turned into what my parents
were later to judge a cheap resort for servants, who these days owned
Cars, if you pleased, and for shopgirls who were no better than prostitutes, and for the worst kind of air-steward, unspeakable.

I HAD OVERHEARD that nearby, round the Red Mountain, nudists had
colonized a further beach, smaller and more savage than ours, and the
license of their lifestyle riveted me—their drugs and their guitars, their
naked bathing in broad daylight, the wafts of their patchouli, their joss-
sticks when the sun went down, their barbecues, which my parents

thought despicable, their improvised canopies of psychedelic paisley, their loving and peacing on the dunes, where wild flowers grew, and the first resulting generation, in tiny T-shirts of tie-dye, of out-of-wedlock babies deemed just about *sortable,* for even my parents knew the maiden names which had committed these Slip-ups—but I felt too young to wander there alone, too tentative, and, in my perverse way I preferred to break the rules of propriety within striking distance of my own people. I would throw my sinful summer stones at the glasshouse of my parents' making, and dump my shit on the hereditary steps which led down to the beach. But my parents were never to see this, for the pair of them lived resolutely in oblivion.

I would go into the sea when it wasn't too busy, just after lunch, when the sun was scorching and even the local padre took his siesta, when the waves were at their roughest and the surf at its most conceal-ing. My mother, tired of warning that if I didn't complete my digestion before going back to swim I'd be seized by stomach cramps and perish on the instant, now modulated her exaggerations to lamer entreaties about walking into the sea very gradually—to which I was willing to agree, for, while not specially worried about my stomach, I was aware of the threat of jellyfish, which surfaced occasionally. And so, there-after, I would wait until my parents had finished their coffee and retired to rest, or digest, or whatever it was that they did, and then I'd set off alone, racing over the blazing sand until I reached that cool tawny car-pet of wetness which led up to the water's edge, the shore, the end of the earth, the beginning of freedom.

Anyone who swam at this time of day, when the sun was fiercest and the sea at its most treacherous, was considered to be going against the grain of the place: either they didn't own a seaside property, so were intruders, or they were too broke to take their lunchtime custom to the shade of the local café, so were useless, or else they were Nordics and Germans, dubbed eccentric but dismissed as libertines from the hotel which, though discreetly built at the opposite end of the golden sickle, had sparked off the disgruntlement that was, in due course, to rev into disgust and drive my parents away. But I loved that beach, and after lunch, I loved it particularly.

It was as if, when you went into the roar and delivered yourself to the devouring embrace of that bluest of oceans, you were entering a realm which, like the tunnel of green in the city, bore no connection to normality or the strictures which, in my parents' society, attached to it. In this liquid kingdom, you could spit and piss and nobody minded; you could be a dolphin, a mermaid, a net full of fish, a boat from the Bible, St. Peter before he earned his flashy keys. This was your life, and no one gave a damn for lost emotions, but the freedom of those waves, their recklessness, did enable you to witness miracles which, out of water, wouldn't have been conceivable. Sometimes, when you dived down and held your breath and swam about with your eyes opened, you would see the luminous rippling shapes of men whom you had never seen (women seemed to stick to the prudence of the beach), and the feet of those men would kick and shimmer like flippers, while their arms rose and sank like the arms of dancers in the sea, and their hands would sometimes stroke their own bodies with disbelief and play with them, play without censure. And I would sometimes see those men, who, to me, from the watery silence of the deep, seemed to glow like visions, strip naked below the glassy surface of the sea, stepping in slow motion out of their trunks, which were far briefer than mine had ever been; and then, in order not to lose them, one leg of the trunks would be pushed over the heads of these beautiful creatures, and left to blossom about their necks, like wreaths of seaweed.

It was all so different in here. Men who couldn't tell what you were, whether seed-pearl or swordfish, would on occasion smile, and signal a little guardedly, and though the great sound of the waves made talking, in any language and from any distance, an impossibility, these signallers were sometimes willing to entertain you. I remember how, seeing me plunge into the depths, and snake around like an eel beneath them, they would part their legs and let me pass between. And if you did this enough (and, on emerging, didn't grin, but just looked natural, as if the game were your mutual right—you didn't want to give a false impression of childishness or innocence) you would find that sooner or later, when you flipped back down and swam about again, they would let your oily body slither past their inner thighs and rub against them, and this was the cue for them to grab you, which always felt fantastic. And if the man had a wreath around his neck and was prepared to proceed, you knew for sure that you weren't up against some avuncular retard who thought you wanted to play at pirates and frigates. You knew you'd

hit the jackpot, that neither you, nor he, would sail away without treasure of some description.

THE MAN FIRST holds you by the wrists, as if to capture you, but this
does not prevent you from slipping away, from escaping, so his next
move is to get you by the waist and draw you nearer, and now you're
allowed to soften slightly; and he might even let you put your arms, as if
for safety, round him, but you must remember to continue paddling,
otherwise you'll both be sunk and have to start from the beginning.
Despite the difference in your statures, which, on land, would be conspicuous, out here, in the equalizing water, there seems to be no distinction between you. Sometimes he will position himself behind you,
seat you upon himself as if he were your throne and you his prince,
or—if the sea is tranquil enough to allow such a thing—have you treat
him like an inflatable mattress: you place your back upon his front, and
lie, limp as a body, on top of him, and the sky is all that you can see, but
you can close your eyes if you desire because he will be working his feet
for both of you, will be keeping you going. His arms, when he wraps
them round your ribs, feel safer than any rubber-ring or any life-saver.
But I never remove my trunks: I lack the courage. I do, however, let
him peel me down enough to release me, and I let him rub himself
against the whiteness that reveals itself behind me, and sometimes
against my front, a trickier position, for even as he holds me there, I
feel too high to be practical. But he will always ultimately want to slide
himself into the smoothness between my thighs, between me, which is
the true source of his relish and my delicacy, my one great contribution
to this feast on the high seas, where, in contrast to the park, I do let the
man kiss me, not just because the water makes him clean, but because I
like the taste of salt upon his lips and, on his tongue, his contrasting
sweetness. And by this stage, it will often be over for him, but the
spurts of his result will be nowhere to be seen, you don't have to wipe
anything, all gone, forgiven. And generally (and now that it's safe, a
smile *is* permissible) I swim back to shore ahead of him—just as, when
I later graduated from urinals to cubicles, I always tried to be the first to
leave—not because I was ashamed, not because I was afraid, not even
because I was unrelieved, but because I was in the greater hurry to
resume my search for the dream which oppressed me.

PART FOUR

THE BIG SCHOOL, as the Countess had quaintly referred to it, boasted a turbulent history dating back to the reign of the first Elizabeth, who, in the textbooks of my Spanish infancy, had been portrayed not just as the daughter of some fat murderous polygamist, but, more pointedly, as the harridan responsible for the committal of our mighty Armada to its aquatic sepulchre. Bald as a coot, partial to pelicans, and, as if that weren't enough, barren (for the Lord, we had been told, will not be mocked), we regarded that Protestant Queen as altogether most peculiar. Still, I suppose that, if nothing else, the Countess owed to her the cloth of antique velvet which now impressed her guests at dinner.

During the Elizabethan period, English Catholics (or at least those with the means) who strove to have their offspring tutored in accordance with their religious allegiance were reduced, owing to the perils of the Reformation, to shipping their progeny overseas in order to see this wish fulfilled; and initially, when the school amounted to little more than a handful of pupils, I think that it was to France, or perhaps to Belgium, that they were ferried. But after a quick couple of centuries, during which the augmenting community appears to have been shunted hither and thither, England at last seemed—on account of the Catholic Relief Act, or some similar edict—a safer place in which to learn Popish. And so, back they all came, itinerant boys and priests, to settle on the site where my father's Alma Mater was, in architectural dribs and drabs, and in a hotchpotch of styles, eventually to be built.

By the time of my arrival, the school, regardless of its messy past and messy appearance, had grown bloated both physically and in prestige; and despite the fact that, so far as I was aware, no former alumnus had ever achieved any great degree of notability—for this tentacle of

the Faith seemed not to encourage worldly ambition, regarding it as
tantamount to vanity, or perhaps it was greed—the establishment
nonetheless vaunted its spiritual laurels like a drag queen might vaunt
her great wig. The weight of its history weighed upon you.

AT LAST WE were allowed to wear long trousers, which I greeted with
relief, but we were also expected to don detachable collars—ostensibly,
I suppose, in deference to sartorial antiquity, or perhaps it was in order
to reduce the workload at the laundry, or just to encourage thrift.
Whichever: this apparent resistance to progress, when ordinary shirts
were just as accessible as the increasingly technological rugger boots
and running spikes which were decreed mandatory, appeared perverse
to me: it seemed to encourage people to cultivate sweaty shirts beneath
the studded deception of a starched neckline just at the time when
schoolboys are known to be at their most unappetizing—lazy and
clammy and stinky. And to support my suspicion, I now discovered
that after games on the playing fields, and runs across country, the custom at this time-honoured institution was to wear swimming trunks in
the showers, as if wetting your ears were of greater import than washing your privates. Deodorant, just as cologne had earlier been, was
needless to say reviled, viewed as a violation of nature—womanish,
queer. But I daresay that, these days, my successors wallow in whole
ranges of designer unguents, and are permitted ornaments such as earrings and tongue-studs and tattoos and genital piercings, for I gather
that public school coffers ain't looking too good.

   During the calm of the previous summer, I had lulled myself into
imagining that since Mr. Wolfe and all that business now lay safely
behind me, I'd be able, with my transfer to the senior school, to make a
fresh start, to wipe my slate clean; but I could not, as it transpired, have
been more deluded, for although the boys who accompanied me from
prep school accounted only for a negligible proportion of the new-
comers, I'd failed to reckon with two other factors: namely that, ahead
of me in the hierarchy, there swaggered dozens of people who still recognized the gaseous whiff of my former notoriety; and that those who
had never before laid eyes on me, recruits from various other left-
footed bastions around the country, plus the occasional foreigner,
including a singularly handsome Nigerian, were readier to be apprised

of my earlier infamy than to keep an open mind and draw their own conclusions. And within a matter of hours, as I took my first steps into the new refectory, I realized that already I was more known-against than knowing; and I sensed, furthermore, that if this information didn't already extend to the staff, it wouldn't take long to do so, for my mere presence seemed to tax their eyebrows.

The staff itself comprised, to my unease, far more clergy than I had ever before encountered, and came, despite the (relative) uniformity of its habit, in a whole spectrum of ages and guises. There were doddery priests, methuselahs who'd taught some of our own fathers, and who, at some point since, had been retired from their didactic offices (in which this order took particular pride) and put out to grass. You could see them shuffling about the gardens in massacred lace-ups, or down the galleries—their half-mooned beaks stooped over breviaries, a grubby hankie dribbling from a coatsleeve, their waxy shoulders rife with dandruff, their shiny heads bisected by centre partings which, older than their ordinations, had, with the passage of the decades and the thinning of their scalps, grown wide as tracks. But there was a charm to these old buffers: you felt that their ancient hairstyles belied another life—as if, had Poverty, Chastity and Obedience never impinged, they might still be doing the tango at some *thé dansant*. And (if you avoided the deaf ones, who tended to shout) it was they, the oldies, who, at confession, gave you the easiest ride.

Not so with the younger clergy. These were the ones who, despite the sobriety of their preponderant black, allowed themselves an occasional Disobedient touch—coloured socks, for instance, blue or brown—and whose cuffs, in defiance of Poverty, could be seen to glint with flashy links, or a valuable wristwatch on an alligator strap. Quite how they chose to break the deadlock of Chastity was, of course, their own concern; but what I knew was that in the confessional they behaved less like agents of mercy than as procurers: How many times? In what way? Where? Could you explain that? Was it pleasurable? Their questions would come at you half-strangled, excited, in little grunts. And you—even as you admitted to but a fraction of the smut which they were after—presumed that in the darkness behind the screen they'd be holding a gummy handkerchief, clutching at it. Sporadic scrunching of rosary beads fooled no one. And now for your penance:

Three Hail Marys and three Our Fathers, and remember to pray for me, my son. (You bet, Father.) God be with you. (Ditto.) But once I'd charged through my soul-saving shopping list, I would throw in, by way of insurance, the Memorare, whose tone of underhand defiance appealed to my spirit: Remember, O most loving Virgin Mary, that it is a thing unheard of that anyone ever had recourse to your protection, implored your help, or sought your intercession, and was left forsaken. So there.

CHAPELS, they were scattered all about. Some were more intimate and creepy; others, wider and more public; but all were modelled, with a glut of Gothic arches, along the lines of some greater original. There were unrelenting rows of classrooms: E, D, C, B, A—streamed, in my case, according to our Common Entrance results, which luckily pushed me up; a great Tudor hall, rank with the school's past and decked with portraits of former incumbents: stuffed shirts, puffed into khaki uniforms and loaded with medals; a dusty theatre to which we stomped for morning assembly and the occasional play or recital; a museum of sorts, chocker with canonical memorabilia—scraps of old vestments, jewelled crucifixes, decomposing books of hours; a vast library, where graffito, as always in such places, flourished; a neglected little art room, with a broken skylight; a tatty music basement, with glass cubicles in which, beneath the glare of neon lights, you could practise; plus, of course, a thousand places for the furtherance of sportsmanship: gymnasium, squash courts, shooting range, swimming pool (conveniently tiled in yellow), tennis courts (of indoor clay and outdoor grass); endless pitches for football and rugger, grudgingly made over to cricket in the summer; an athletics track, of terracotta gravel; only half a golf course, I regret to say; but still, as hearty packages went, my father's Alma Mater didn't do badly. Fencing, hockey, basketball, archery: you name it, these chaps were up for it. And then, of course, there was the Cadet Corps—compulsory in the second year—which my father thought top-hole, a splendid idea.

But compulsory in the first year was music. Everyone was obliged to take up (no electric guitars, thank you) an orchestral instrument, even if this was the triangle, and to undergo, even if tone-deaf, an audition for the school choir, which, let's face it, wasn't as bad as the test in which they made you Cough to double-check your testicles. My singing voice, although a little shrill, still clung rather desperately to the range of treble (my time as an alto was to prove more satisfactory, because I could hide in the second row and relax, and sometimes, to be jazzy, harmonize a semitone flat, which drove the worthies mad); but my musical ear, combined with my instrumental scratchings, which sounded less intolerable on my own violin than on a school fiddle, earned me an advantage, and led me to hope that I might be off to a more promising start: I was in the top stream of my year; I had a place in the orchestra; I was wanted in the choir. Perhaps, now, I might be able to contribute to school life.

THE FIRST-YEAR DORMITORIES, reminiscent of the empty seminary in Brussels, were not, as mine had been at prep school, rooms of six beds apiece, but vast cold spaces with punitive wooden cubicles ranged along the walls—each with a bed, a shelf, a chair, and a brown curtain for privacy, like the skirt of a monk. You might, if you were lucky, have a window which, though set well above you, was a bonus in the summer, for your awakening became natural. And so, while on the one hand you enjoyed autonomy within the confines which, by means of a sticky label, had been alphabetically designated to you, and which, within reason, you could decorate as you pleased, now you were under danger of siege, not just by the few who might have shared your earlier dormitory, but by the forty who populated this one. As balances went, it felt touch and go, dodgy.

The other cubicles which, in their way, also afforded privacy were to be found in the music basement, three flights below the first-year sleeping quarters, at the sunken base of a stone staircase—more lumpen than imposing. Halfway down, screwed to the wall, there was a charcoal drawing of some dapper Old Boy in infantry officer's uniform, dated 1915, to which I never paid much attention; but when my mother, some time later, came to visit me, she was prompted, almost despite herself, to remark upon it, for the sitter, she confided, was the spitting image of a former suitor of her mother's, who, while on a posting to our island, had been shot dead in a (whispered) duel. This incident had left my grandmother, who was never again to mention the name of her lost lover, desolate, with the result that she declined proposals of marriage for years thereafter, until her bloom was gone and the spectre of spinsterhood began to loom on the societal horizon. Yet my mother's grandmother (that is to say, my great-grandmother, who had died decades before my birth, but had relayed the tale to my mother in the latter's girlhood) had apparently kept a framed photograph of the hapless swain propped on her piano throughout her life, seemingly indifferent to the nature of his demise, which, as well as illegal, was, in our Catholic country, regarded as opposite to ecclesiastical dictates. And it was the sudden recollection of that long-vanished photograph which had prompted my mother, in a burst of morbid romanticism, to pass on to me the anecdote. Later, I was to think, insanely, that this might have been the man who might have danced with the girl who was to become the grandmother whom I was never to know. But for now, I paid no notice to the drawing, and just went down.

Like the caterpillar in the Municipal Park, and the thalassic embrace of the beach, the music basement was a place that didn't correspond to ordinary life, life as it was supposed to be lived, for it offered promise, and the spectrum of fantasy, and the opportunity for respite from the stranglehold of routine. One of the many oddities of our educational system was its refusal to run along the usual (vertical) lines of school houses, but instead to be organized by the year (horizontally). Those canny priests did their damnedest to prevent boys who were not exact contemporaries from ever enjoying contact: you slept among your peers, you studied in their midst, you ate and washed alongside them and, even in church (unless you were in the choir), you sat in their cramping vicinity—a policy which I believe was intended to foment camaraderie while discouraging precocity and other odd habits. But in the music basement, all such artifice went out of the Gothic windows. No one cared in what year you happened to be vegetating: the sole question in this underworld was what you could bring to the feast.

Those who filled the glassy cages in the practice rooms were like exotic fish in an aquarium. (No-hopers, forced at the start to learn an instrument, didn't trouble, other than for music lessons, which they couldn't really circumvent, to make an appearance: they were far too busy with rugger.) No, only the school's most phantasmagorical oddballs regularly ventured down here—those who set off fire alarms during High Mass, when the ensuing chaos could be trusted to surge to fever pitch; who played pranks on village shopkeepers and never owned up to it; who harboured illicit terrapins; who mimicked teachers and performed elaborate vignettes of ridicule; who smuggled oysters back from exeats; who stole from the kitchens; who adopted fancy dress, smoked cocktail cigarettes and photographed each other exhaling; who drank champagne through straws; who played Scott Joplin; who refused to have their hair butchered by the school barber and preferred, instead, to cut one another's; who sang falsetto; who tap-danced; who could walk on point. Of course, in order to justify their presence in the depths of the school, all had to be musically proficient, but nothing as dreary as gifted, for true musicians were a little serious for our liking, and there was quite enough seriousness upstairs, in the main part of the school, to be going on with. Some of the serious types, whom you could spot at a glance, were priests in the making, bony-fingered mutterers who practically crossed themselves before surrendering to the seduction of ivories. I think that they regarded the rest of us, though charitably—for, in their fashion, they were just as peculiar, and part of a still smaller minority—as not quite the thing. But though we, self-styled exotics, cultivated glamour in the face of adversity, yet there was, I now think, an innocence to our antics. Certainly we exchanged no prurient sexual banter, for we considered ourselves, you see, far too sophisticated for it, were meant already to know Everything.

BUT ONE EVENING in the second term, when I was down in the basement, practising dreary studies for the violin—by Pleyel, very probably—and the rest of the place was all but empty, and most of the lights were out, I heard a tap on the glass at my door; and I turned round, shocked out of some tricky sequence and nearly dropping my bow, to be confronted by the sight of the director of music, who looked like an old Kaiser. Would I step into his office a minute?

His name was Dr. Fox; and just as my former headmaster had resembled a well-fed hamster, so, too, as animals went, this one made a stout one. The orbicularly tailored waistcoats that he wore, which even his watch chain was stretched to navigate, alone paid credence to his portliness. Everyone was terrified of him, for he used to condemn boys to be beaten at the drop of a quaver, and he slapped the backs of heads with alacrity. His temper was often challenged; he was not patient; and because he wore spectacles thicker than tumblers, his icy blue eyes seemed to project a magnified leer, involuntarily to glare down. He had the lashes of a cow, but he was not placid. If, in my childhood, Mr. Wolfe's beard had resembled a gentle field of autumn bracken, Dr. Fox's facial landscape, now that I was adolescent, seemed to me like a spikier site, a thornier promontory, for he sported a billy-goat the colour of ash, and lush Edwardian moustaches which he frequently twirled and tugged, a tail at a time, thereby distorting his fleshy little mouth, which was like a rosebud, too pink for my liking. Something about the contrast of those nubile lips against their surrounding shrubbery disgusted me. But it didn't frighten me: for, at least as regarded beards, I felt like an explorer on the way back, a veteran.

He deplored loutish conduct, and scruffy dress, and inky paws, and sloppy diction (yeah); but, most of all, he deplored the disproportionate status accorded by the school to sporting antics, which seemed always to clash with, and overrule, his musical endeavours. These, before he lost heart and sank into apathy, had been ambitious, enthusiastic, for as an organist he'd enjoyed a glittering start (truncated, I seem to recall, by financial difficulties in his family) and later, despite the impoverishment, an equally brilliant academic career, which accounted for his professorial title; yet this rare combination of practical and theoretical excellence which, thanks to him, had been brought to the school, appeared, now that he was established, no longer to be valued. And the slight therein implicit seemed to have soured him. He had, at some earlier point, converted to Catholicism, but, on account of the Second Vatican Council, subsequently felt reason to regret his transfer of spiritual allegiance, which probably aggravated his spleen. Certainly he considered our resident priests, especially the happy-clappy younger ones, to be both foolish and provincial—in which appraisal he was, to a great extent, right. As a breed, they were tawdry little specimens, whereas Dr. Fox, by contrast, was nothing if not refined: to him, only two things mattered: whether people were clever, and whether they amused him. Well, there was a third thing, but this wasn't really discussed: Favourites—small pets, as it were. I think that he was lonely.

THOUGH HE KEEPS his office darkened—for hard sunlight, I have noticed, pains his eyes—it is furnished with a richness which, at least in this establishment, is unknown to me, and which, though evocative of my past, paradoxically feels singular, peculiar to him. As you go in, looking down at the flagstones, the first thing that impresses you is a sprawling Persian rug, its background bluer than his eyes, and upon it, toward the far side, a concert grand, lid up. Along the length of the wall opposite to the fire, which is stoked throughout the winter months, and overhung—courtesy of the authorities, I have a feeling—with an olden portrait of an heavily gowned Honourable Jane Something-or-other, whose lips are as pink as his, though her moustache is milder, there runs a massive bookcase of ebony, detailed with gilded fluting and stacked with musical scores whose spines I can't make out. There's a vast desk, presidential, behind which lurks his throne, its rotating leather back turned to the external world, while over here, where I stand, there's a pair of wing chairs, ball and claw, one of which, of worn green velvet, grown olive with time, he now directs me into. Next to a hefty coal box behind me, lidded to provide a bench when the need arises, the door, which has been covered in felt so as to contain the sound of his piano, appears, of its own accord, to click shut.

I sit where I'm told. He goes round to his side. He smiles. I hardly know this man. (Be on your guard.) I half-smile back. He cuts, then smells, then lights a cigar, not like the half-sized inanities favoured by my father, but a proper, long, cool, portly Montecristo, whose box lies on the armchair beside mine. He removes the decorative paper-ring, twirls the cigar in mid-air and admires it; leans back. His chair creaks out. He crosses his legs now: I can see his shins swapping in the gap between the drawers of the desk that hides him. He shifts his weight onto one thigh. One foot alone swings out, almost slippered, so narrow and fine is his pump. I sense an unpleasant delicacy about the man.

It's all most civilized. He smiles a second time, and I do likewise. He wonders, as he puffs, whether, since I already play the violin and am part of the choir, I've ever considered taking up the piano. He says that it would help with my sight-reading, which—good as my ear is—he's noticed tends to let me down at orchestra practice: weak counting. I won't find it so easy to bluff my way through harder parts as I move up the ranks, you know—and down the choir, for that matter, which will involve more complicated harmonies, trickier tempi and so forth. You can't expect to carry the tune forever, he laughs, a little clumsily . . .

Well, yes, he grants me, on the violin perhaps; but come-come, the Piarno-four-*tay*, he rhapsodizes, marv'llous instrument, no comparison, the only truly self-sufficient one, fundamental, far and away the richest repertoire. He agrees that you can't exactly travel round the world with one, but try travelling with an organ, my dear chap, he chuckles; anyway, he thinks I should consider his suggestion. Don't we have a piano at home? Well then, there you *are;* what could be simpler? You can keep up your playing during the holidays, hmm? Makes perfect sense. But still; he says that I can take my time mulling it over, no rash decisions, it isn't a trivial matter, requires commitment, et cetera, et cetera, et cetera. I'm just to let him know when I feel ready, say in forty-eight hours, would that seem reasonable? And then he removes his heavy spectacles, which he lets swing in one hand, while, with the thumb and forefinger of the other, he massages the bridge of his nose, which is purple and ridged by the burden of his poor sight, and I notice, as he rubs them, that his enormous glassy eyes have recoiled and diminished and sunk and all but disappeared into his skull. And, far from a great ogre, he now looks like a pathetic blind baby, and the switch comes as a shock to me; but after a few seconds he returns his specs to their proper function, mercifully to restore his former countenance. As he rises to his weary dainty feet, and comes round to where I'm sitting, I now realize that his nose, though finely set despite the hump, is shot with veins the colour of claret, and that his forehead is flaky. Yes, he concludes, he'd be delighted for me to have piano lessons—from him, naturally—and looks forward to hearing my decision. He can't imagine, after all, that I'm too enamoured of the alternatives—football, rugger, mountaineering. I roll my eyes dramatically and, as I do so, realize my first blunder with this man: my roll is flirty. And then I fly up the stone steps to supper.

OF COURSE, I'm madly flattered. Who needs irreligious worldly ambition to succumb to vanity? Dr. Fox is known only to bother with the most promising pupils, and he makes me feel as if I could become one. Besides, how can I really decline his offer, and risk his displeasure, when I see the man twice a week in the orchestra and a further twice at choir practice? Then, as if further to sway me to his side, a thought of my father, like a moth, flutters into my mind, hovers briefly, then scorches me with pleasure: *two* musical instruments would feel like a double victory. But I must be calm about it. Best not to seem impetuous.

Later, sauntering down the gallery, I decide to treat myself at the tuck shop, to celebrate my stroke of luck. There's a disheartening queue, lengthy, unruly, constantly increased by sixth formers who keep pushing in, yet no one dares to confront. But you see, they've just started selling hot dogs, and the smell is irresistible—the smoky lure of frankfurters drifts and curls towards you like the promise of a holiday. I remember my mother's towels, and her toes, and the Spanish flag: mustard and ketchup. Yum. Dinner was disgusting; there's masses of time before lights out; and I'm sure I've got enough money; so, no problem, I'll join the back of the line and be patient. While I wait, I rewind to the cameo with Dr. Fox, and sense a certain oddity about it, a tiny niggling doubt; but I'm sure that I'm just being stupid. Why should he have bothered to approach me unless he were serious? For fun, for God's sake? You're being idiotic. Be thankful that he's singled you out: it exempts you from rugger and, what's more, stuffs your father. And gradually, gradually, lost in this rumination, and with my gut starting to rumble, I edge my way to the front.

When I reach the hatch, I see that I'm going to be served by a prefect called Payne, elder brother of someone from the music basement, and himself, now that I think of it, not exactly a he-man; but just after I've cleared my throat and asked for a hot dog, I hear (though he avoids meeting my eye) his reply, which he seems to want to broadcast for the sake of the general public, and particularly for the benefit of his fellow servers, who, like him, get paid for their trouble: Bugger Off!, he shouts, We Don't Serve Pouffters Here. And I am aghast; but not as aghast as I am next, when the entire surrounding crowd bursts into rapturous clapping. (I don't think that I returned to the tuck shop, not alone, at any rate, for the next three years, by which time I was in the fifth form and inured to such affronts; and in the intervening time, either I asked some brave, rare friend to buy sweets on my behalf, or I simply went without. Because soon enough, in any case, I was to find other means of acquiring them.)

Reeling from the hot dog fracas, I now head for the lavatories, ostensibly for a piss, but, if it's quiet, for a restorative smoke in the sit-downs. Needless to say, since it's after supper, the place turns out to be packed, and in order to get to the cubicles at the back, you have to sneak past a fog of older boys who like to pretend to be older than they are. One of these, who played Toad in *Toad Hall,* and whose father, each time that he descends, brings a different doxy in a different sports car, catches sight of me and shouts: Oy, you, hand 'em over! Hand what?, I reply. Your *fags,* you dirty little queer. But after the tuck shop incident, I'm not quite in the mood for this casual banter—my angry blood is running too high, coursing too fast; so I just peer at him and tell him to bugger off and buy his own. Stunned reaction from the whole pally gang, a collective intake of breath, a scuffle, and next—it's so sudden—my head is down on the pissoir, my snout in the rivulet of frothy yellow water, my jacket slithering on the sodden tiles, the people who've been using the trough leaping back, flies still undone. There are hands all over my pockets, and there's a knee against my back, and then, through the deafening silence, I hear a punch crack against my spine, and then I'm left alone.

With hindsight, I wonder whether, had the tables been turned, and the cards of power been stacked in my hand, I wouldn't have acted as the toad had done. It's possible, I might have done, particularly if the victim was someone as fearsome and loathsome as I was generally found. I was, after all, myself the son of a bully. Only one thing, I suppose, might have deterred me (just), namely the tacky brand of those louts' tobacco, which I think was Embassy (Mild, not even Regal). I myself preferred to inhale the fumes of Winston, which, to me, tasted of grown-up American summers, and I would buy my supplies after I'd got rid of my parents, on the flight back to England. Only once did some nit-picking air-hostess hesitate to oblige with my request, claiming, the silly cow, that I was under-age for such purchases—to which I remember replying that it was on my parents' instructions that I had to buy those cigarettes, as a present for my guardians. Luckily, she swallowed my lie, and, though still looking dubious, surrendered the carton. But I didn't, on the plane, have the gall to light up.

Still, back to the school lavatory. I gather myself up from the pissoir, sluggishly, dopily, like someone who'd blacked out. As on the occasion when I fouled my underpants, I now think of my mother, but this time, bizarrely, she seems to be laughing in a strange garden, detached, happy. My cigarettes are gone, as is my lighter; and then, in a final humiliation, I have to crouch to recover one of her letters, fallen to the ground during the débâcle, and I see that her turquoise ink is weeping down the face of the envelope. Which, added to the hot dog incident, settles the matter.

I GO TO MY CLASSROOM and open my desk. I don't know what propels me next (further vanity, perhaps, or some desire to single myself out), but the sheet which I select is not of headed school paper: it is a leaf of my own personal stationery, cream, thick as card, and engraved at the top with my Spanish coat of arms, for (even if by the time that I reached my majority, and became properly entitled, I was no longer to do so) I still, then, considered such vulgarities to be smart. I close the desk. I date the letter for tomorrow—less impulsive—and then I write, as evenly as my shaky, cigaretteless hand allows: Dear Sir. (Mistake. I tear up the sheet and go back to square one.) Dear Dr. Fox, I have thought about your kind offer and think that it's a good idea. I can start whenever you like. Yours (I dither over sincerely, decide to leave it out, append a comma, and sign), James Moore. I lick the envelope closed, since its stubborn flap is too large to be tucked; I turn it over and write his name on the front, underline it; and now, the whole missive is burning in my hand, and I doubt that I can wait suspended a whole night; so I put it in my pocket and creep down to the basement, where all is dark, and with my eyes wide as an owl's I slide my fate into the stillness of his lair, which is my trap. And on my way to bed, I try to weigh up which is preferable: whether to impress Dr. Fox or to depress my father—until I realize that I can achieve both objectives in one.

Next day, although I've got no musical commitments, I still escape, during Break, downstairs—to mess around, see who's there, practise for a while. Such calls have become habitual. Dr. Fox is not in evidence—still busy teaching, or perhaps having coffee in the staff common room. I trudge back to class. I float through the next two periods, double maths, and I get through lunch, which these days is self-service, and then I climb to my dormitory to fetch a clean handkerchief (or was it to rummage in my padlocked trunk for a fresh packet of gaspers?). The cause evaporates into irrelevance, because, when I reach my bed, I find, half-tucked under the pillow, as if intended for no eyes but mine, a sealed note, addressed in an illegible squiggly hand, like the hand of an elderly optician: Dear Moore, I am delighted by your prompt decision. Please present yourself at my office for your first lesson at two o'clock this afternoon. And he signs it A. Fox. I look at my watch: three minutes to the hour. On my way out of the dormitory, my steps precise as a metronome, I glance in the mirror to comb my hair and yank up my tie. But I can't sustain the controlled rhythm. I rush to the washroom, give my nails a scrub. Adrenaline is pumping round me. I turn off the tap and sprint across the main quadrangle and through the Tudor hall, trying not to slip on the floor of harlequin marble; I run down a waxen gallery, bang into someone, race on regardless to a darkened corridor which yawns into a vaulted landing. As I approach the narrowing stairs to the basement, the clock on the tower begins to strike (One), and I tackle my downward flight like a frantic scale, *molto vivace,* but one at a time, because the stony surface of the steps is worn, untrue, not to be trusted. And as I skid to a halt before the mahogany door marked Director of Music, the clock sounds its second post-meridian hour (Two)—its chime fractionally flat. I knock hard, high up; then, a further time. My chest is going mad. But next, like an electric shock, the school bell wails out, wild as a siren . . . and only once its echo has ebbed away entirely does the punctilious Dr. Fox care to shout: *Avanti!*

I GO IN. He lowers his newspaper, peers across, then greets me with one of those magnified smiles of his. He stands up. The lid of the piano has been lowered. He leads me to the shuttered keyboard as if he were introducing me to a coffin; opens it, bares its grinning teeth at me. He spins the leather stool clockwise, raising it to accommodate me. He sits me down, pats my back on the precise spot where it was punched last night, and positions me with care, exactitude: good posture from the outset being, he says, primordial. He outlaws, for the present, the use of pedals. Nor is there any need, as yet, for sheet music. I may remove my jacket if I wish. I don't of course: I couldn't have borne the embarrassment. His reaction—As you like—sounds faintly rebuffed; but next, almost without warning, we're off, we have begun.

That-there was Middle C; the rest would follow automatically. My right hand went up; my left trickled down. First they scaled separately; later, in unison; and in due course he made them cross, over and under, then continue. It was all, compared to the violin, so rudimentary that it looked stupid, yet my fingers turned out to be bad stretchers, latent enemies; and while I possessed basic aptitude, I also recognized myself to be devoid of the talent, or the promise, or the brilliance, or any of the other attributes which hallmarked the fine body of his private pupils; and I sensed that as a consequence—and sooner rather than later—he was bound to despair, to give up on me, and that I would find myself fed, once again, to the jaws of rugger. And yet, looking back, I think that at the start—for all the quickness of his temper—his patience, not mine, was the greater. He would sit, as an old-fashioned analyst might have done, behind me—out of danger, out of sight— musing from a wing chair and stroking his watch chain, which grated against his signet-ring of cornelian; or sucking on a sugared violet, which I could smell as I struggled with my fingering. The swirls of his saliva made my stomach churn. And his fire, always crackling, seemed, as I sweated through my initiation, to mock me at my back.

The bulk of his pupils was upward of Grade 7, proper pianists— some, indeed, of such a calibre as to have been encouraged to forgo university in favour of a conservatory. Those students, who to me were like adults—daily shavers, licensed drivers—would even be sent, as a favour to Dr. Fox, up to London several times a term for additional coaching by one of his erstwhile professors, and I envied both their musical escapades and their musical prowess. Now that they are men, I sometimes hear those former boys tinkling over the airwaves, though not frequently—for our school, remember, was bigger on the spiritual life than on worldly ambition; but back then, the simple, glaring chasm between my preliminary struggles and their sheer panache, which could be witnessed most afternoons in the practice cubicles and stun you, rendered my mediocrity the more crushing, and, in a sense, robbed my piano lessons of pleasure. For I feared that in the long run, once I'd been dispatched, my father would have won.

And yet, when I made mistakes, which drove me frantic with frus- tration, Dr. Fox would try to soothe me with dark sounds of appease- ment, velvet murmurs from his low octaves. And when I became so flustered that I was forced to halt, he would never allow me properly to stop, but would urge me to continue, to struggle on, to show persever- ance, however hard this might seem: for all things, he would claim, even bad ones, must eventually come to an end. I now suspect that he derived a perverse enjoyment from those errors of mine; for as I, with each of them, drew further away from his standard of excellence, so he was drawing inexorably closer to the fruits of his determination, which were not, in the strictest sense, musical.

One morning, I remember going through the motions of some piece for him, some young person's sonata, and enjoying a run of good luck through its introductory passage, but playing, probably due to the anxiety which underscored my bluff, too fast for my fortune to last. I suddenly lost my place, my fingering came unstuck, everything fell apart, and my charade just ground to a standstill. Although I felt like hammering my fists against those fucking ivories, I remember keeping absolutely still, seized by the certainty that his patience had finally snapped and that he was about to shout at me . . . so I just sat on that stool, resigned, like the dead loss that I felt, frozen despite the burning silence.

I heard him get up and approach my back with ominous calm. I wanted to protect my head, to shield it from his inevitable slap, yet when his palm did land upon me, it wasn't with the expected bang, but with the equivalent of a whimper, for he placed it, almost apologetically, upon my shoulder. And then he pressed it down, curving his fingers towards my clavicle, beyond the lapel of my jacket. His voice was so soft that I could hardly hear it: You *can* do this, old chap, he whispered, it's so nearly there, coming together very nicely, just try to go slower, but you mustn't give up, you're more than capable. I wanted to cry with gratitude, and yet, hardened by my sense of failure, I replied that he was just being kind: I knew that I was useless. No you're not. Yes I am. You're not. I am. Not. Am. Not. Am. And thus, thus confusedly, began our pantomime.

I practised like a fiend for my next lesson and, emulating those serious types upon whom the princes of the basement looked down, I managed to get the sonata up to scratch. Yet when the actual lesson came to pass, all my application—which resulted less from wounded pride than from an urge to avoid danger—proved to be futile, and my rendition, if you could call it that, turned out to be more deficient still than the previous one. Where, for God's sake, was the justice? I should just bite the bullet and give up. But there was, of course, no real question of my doing so: Dr. Fox would never have countenanced such weakness in my character—for he, you see, was only just warming to his theme, assuming his dominance in our counterpoint. And the real progress, as we both knew, was proving to be his, not mine.

HE COMES UP behind me and leans into my spine. I sit up, straight as a fiddle, but feel, hard against my backbone, the pressure of his lower gut, and the cold rub of his watch chain, like a necklace, purring against my collar. He places, this time round, not one but both of his hands upon my shoulders, and then he brings them forward past me, together to the front, landing them, like fat pigeons, over mine, his fluttering pudginess all but covering my skinny fingers. He suggests that we go back to such-and-such a bar, and then, in the most testing of harmonies, he guides me over the keyboard. I try to resume the sonata. To my surprise, he does not weigh me down: there is a lightness about him, a nimble strength about his motion, and for a decent while our hands dance together in partnership, together yet decorously apart, never quite touching. But there is so much apprehension in my head, such throbbing at my temple, that my concentration, inevitably, shuts down, and yet again I foul up, and his fingers do, now, pounce, and properly mount mine, and writhe upon them momentarily. His flesh is hotter than the flesh of a faith healer, and as clammy. I long to wipe my hands against my trousers. Though he directs us back to the same merciless bar, he seems somehow to be adjusting his position behind me, to be lowering himself, removing his belly from my back in order to set his myopic face in line with the score in front of us, the better to read his pencilled markings—which surely he knows back to front, but anyway—his head, next, moves next to mine, and his beard brushes my neck, and the sticky arm of his spectacles keeps touching my profile. Faint moans issue from him, dreamy moans of abandon, but his breath seems to have quickened, as if a baton were cutting through it, staccato, and the hot steam of his smoky violets makes me want to twist askance. But before I can, he reverses us, and tells me to place my palms over the backs of *his* hands now, like twins on twin lilos but without the blessing of water; and though we surf over the keyboard, it is pointless, senseless, nonsensical, for my numb, dumb fingers have given up, given up the ghost, and can only float along with his tide. But no mistakes this time, not one, a bravura performance. See? You *can* do it. Dr. Fox must think that I'm a fool, and, in part, he's right, but my folly lies not so much in having fallen for his lies as in having flung myself into his trap, from which, now that I'm steeped, I can see no way of flying out. And though he smothers me with blandishments, I entertain no doubt that I'll never make his grade of pianist; and yet, what I, from my hardened linguist's heart, have interpreted with pin-point accuracy is the significance that throbs like poisoned stars between the music of his lines.

THERE ARE MELODIES that I cannot hear without thinking of the man. No sooner, say, has the second chord of that half-buried sonata been plucked from its score and struck and released into space by the wireless, than I become deaf to the present. All that I can hear, then, is his sound; all that I can see, now, are his puffy hands at the piano. He has asked me to get up. He has taken my position. He has parted his jacket and leaned back and, after a brief pause, begun to play the piece in earnest, slowly, lushly, but it doesn't feel as if he wished, by it, to highlight my crassness, nor as if he intended, though he employs the pedals, to depress me with his musicality. We are beyond music or humiliation now: we are drifting towards a greater swamp, a place of ugly beauty. He seems transformed in the manner which sometimes can transfigure performers, who, though weary and taciturn in ordinary life, shambolic even, become energized from the moment that they take to the platform. He doesn't regard the score, but gazes, half-entranced, out of the room, up towards the gardens, as if they held the promise of Babylon—or I, that of its whore. Only occasionally does he turn to stare at me, to burn into his captive audience; and I am step-ping backwards now, for I feel as if I'd broken into some secrecy of which I should better have been kept in ignorance. I reel right back, as far I can go, all the way to the shadowy coal box by the door, but I remain on my feet: I keep on my toes: I no longer feel sure of my posi-tion—subject, object, target, voyeur. The waters of our connection seem to have been warmed, like mud in the shoals. There is a strange-ness to his expression, of sadness stirred with ardour. His mouth, motionless but slightly open, is like the mouth of the drowned; and it is as if he wished, by playing on my behalf, to court me, to persuade me of intentions which, though harboured hard, he dare not verbalize.

And I recognize that just as my earlier life had flowed with the strains of Nocturnes, there will, from now on, forever be the echo of this sonata to haunt me, over and over. But after all my failures at his instrument, all the pointless steps which he has forced me to take in order to reach this stage, I cannot be receptive to the charm of his music, nor grateful. He, not I, should have played it from the start, and young musicianship be damned. And yet, when his fingers come to a halt, and rise like frozen claws in the late morning, I don't know which way to burst, into tears or applause.

He stands large as a monarch, pale as a ghost, at once imposing and forlorn, and he advances towards me as if revisiting some painful history, a territory more often lost than conquered. Yet this time, he comes furnished not just with the shield of his authority, nor driven merely by the power of his determination, but, uniquely, availed of certified information guaranteed to topple his new adversary, whom I suddenly recognize to be James Moore. His leer, projected through that glassy visor, announces to me, louder than a bugle call, the obvious, which is, of course, what I've suspected since my first visit to the refectory, namely that he comes armoured with knowledge, knowledge aforethought. And now, as our eyes gallop into a lock, I realize that he knows that I know that he knows—what?—that I've already surrendered my innocence, sold away the very weapon which, in the young, constitutes their great invincible sword.

His vitreous glare seems to imply that, since I've already played, and reputedly of my own volition, hostage to fortune, I cannot now, merely because of his attentions, claim to be worse off. And although what I do possess, against the pressure of his despoiling, is, ironically, the very wealth of my former corruption—my share from the original sale of my soul—I glean that the value of currencies such as mine can fluctuate wildly, depending on the place of the deal and the nature of the contest. Out there in the real world (where you are now, in parks and open beds and oceans), my relinquished innocence would, in fact, have sent my worth soaring, rendered me, as a commodity, covetable, collectable almost—for I, in addition to exuding an outward semblance of being young, a presumed virginity which I could lavish ad infinitum, and infinitely lose, also reduced for my shareholders the risk of perdition in a criminal court. I was no judge, that was for sure: I was an inveterate accomplice; so that to enter into congress with me, to assume my purchase, was, in reality, to reach a consensual truce, not to venture onto some battleground fraught with pitfalls. And this, you see, is why, to him, I must have felt like a simpler, safer bet than some sweet but unpredictable novice.

My rate of exchange, like that of a whore in prison, seemed to have plummeted into free fall, to have crashed into deficit. For in places of incarceration, even when the nonces do possess the means to purchase favours from some manacled prostitute, few feel a moral compunction to do so. There exists a different law. And it was this other law that was to kill my heel, to prove my downfall, for what earlier had guaranteed my conquests now became my one critical flaw. I was no longer like a precious multi-faceted (green) stone, but sullied goods, beyond the hope even of hock, and I could see no means, without provoking retribution, of saying No. Dishonour Among Thieves, that was the unspoken motto. But still, let's not moan, for though Dr. Fox was never to welcome me like a windfall into his impoverished, embittered life, nor yet did he ever quite treat me like a final reduction, as if I were being robbed.

He COMES SO close that, as his gut prods my chest, I fall back onto the coal box, and am left sitting on this pew like a disgraced chorister. He takes no notice. My lowering has been his aim all along. He leans down towards me, clutching at my neck with both his claws, and assaults my face with a flock of dry pecks, to my forehead and the sides of my face and my nose. He avoids my mouth, keeps it in reserve, though his beard, like a bird's nest, brushes over it. My lips are pursed to avoid the tickling abrasion. My eyes are closed. My wings are folded. I put up no resistance, for I conclude that he may as well go on, just do it, get it over with; I can worry later. He removes one of his claws and it sounds as if he's fiddling up there, perhaps loosening his stiff collar, or the buttons of his waistcoat, as he continues with this kissing-of-sorts, this pecking at my eyelids, designed to ensure, I suppose, that they remain closed—blind to the score.

But as he begins to stroke my nape, he pulls me slightly forward towards him, inclines my head; and now his own head seems to have risen high above me, as if in preparation; and when I open my eyes, which, believe me, no longer roll with inexplicable flirtation—they have frozen, agog—I see that I'm up against his flies, which are unbuttoned, and that through the diagonal slit in his baggy undershorts he has extracted his sweating cock, which protrudes without reference to pubic hair or balls. Dr. Fox turns out to be a stocky Cavalier, pale and loose-skinned and thick-veined and topped by a shiny purple helmet, like a bishop on a chessboard. The stench which emanates from him, his cheesing grot, so repulses me that I block my nose and breathe through my throat—but only for a few seconds, because next, he shoves himself between my lips, forcing his fat retracted cock against my teeth, which have been clenched, but which, now, I must part philosophically. What am I supposed to do, bite him? I retch; and then I feel ashamed, as if, again, I were failing. Can I do nothing respectably? But he could no longer care. I think he farts. And now he begins to pump, thrusting himself in and out and in and out and it is I who feel like the bird, my beak wrenched ajar. But while I try, despite my straining gullet, to meet his desires, I distract myself with the thought that the thing which I'm being force-fed is, oddly enough, itself known as a pecker, and I wonder, in a further foreign twist to my ornithological conceit, whether this might explain why Italians sometimes call a pecker an *uccello,* or bird.

Suddenly, the bell screams out for lunch. I think: Time to fend for myself, to get out and seek my own nourishment. But he grabs my neck in an instant, restrains it, then grips at my ears and gathers speed. I recognize the mounting *accelerando* from my previous trysts, though these have never involved such oral insistence, and next, without warning, his bird begins to spit and spit, and it spurts its bile onto the roof of my mouth and against the back of it; and when he, once done, extracts a handkerchief to minister to the dregs of his issue, I extract my own small square of linen, which my mother said would help with my identity, and though I feign merely to dab, I disgorge his spillage into it. The tang of his residual semen bounces around the amalgam of my fillings, but I dare not lick about—which, even with the communion host, is just about allowed.

·   ·   ·

IT ALL LED to complications. Whereas (except for that final night in Belgium) it had always been I who'd sought out the company of Mr. Wolfe, always I who'd assumed the initiative, the current in the case of the cunning Dr. Fox was contrary, flowed against me; and when he began to call for my services, sending envoys to hunt me down, I found myself unable to ignore his orders, because to do so would be to land some unwitting go-between in trouble, and myself in further jeopardy. Sometimes, however, Dr. Fox would try to confuse me: would have me cross the length of the school merely in order to offer me a sweet that led to nothing, or to ask me to remind him of some question to which he well knew the answer; or he would make me stand, for all to see, outside his office while he took his time disposing of some other pupil, only to pretend, once I'd been inveigled into his darkness, possession of some small enlightenment regarding whatever piece of music I happened to be struggling with, or to ask me to polish up some descant for his next choir practice, always last-minute and always pitched too high for my beak to master. These were his little tricks, outward stabs at officialdom, as if by exposing me before my peers he could place himself above suspicion.

But then, when I least expected it, I'd be back on that coal box, proffering my jaw for him, rounding my mouth into a receptacle for his shuddering disseminations. As he grew more assured of my compliance, he dispensed with the nicety of his jockey slit, which, technically, must have hampered him, and instead, he would ruck his underpants down to his pimply thighs, revealing, above his tumescent penis, a pale, fluffy gut, and beneath it, darkish testicles, already shrivelled, crinkled with thrill, and spiked with the occasional white pubic sprout. He would help himself to my hand and plonk it on his sac, gripping me to grip at him, committing our fingers to a brief marriage of ghastly intimacy. But I learnt fast, not least in order to speed him to satisfaction; I learnt how to tug, how to frot him with my other hand, how to lubricate him with my—rather than his—saliva; and yet my lessons covered more than merely the ground of his quick fulfilment, for I now see that they taught me, more lastingly, about feeling cheap: what this involved, how to rise above it, what else to imagine. But when he, on occasion, bent down to grope at me, I seemed always myself to be hard, and this conspired to add to my confusion: my body was betraying me: my mother's blood kept rushing to all the wrong parts. It was, as I say, complicated.

BY THE SUMMER TERM, his mounting hunger had outgrown the feasts on offer in the music basement. What must earlier have been like banquets to him seemed to have dwindled into a semblance of snatched apéritifs and, by June, it was as if he could no longer be sated within the limits of that shaded chamber. The more voracious became his gluttony, his shameless desire for fuller helpings, the greater his need to loosen his garb, a procedure positively Edwardian in its complexity: what with the unthreading of his watch chain, and the removal of his waistcoat in order to slip off his braces, which, no sooner unlooped, gave way to other obstacles, such as billowing shirttails which, in order to be placed out of harm's way, as it were, required knotting behind his buttocks, a move itself demanding additional unbuttoning at the front, to unveil, between the pendulums of his necktie, creamy bosoms with flattened teats the colour of sausage meat—not to mention the collapse of his trousers, and the ensuing peril of tripping over his own tailored crotch as he hobbled to encroach upon me, plus, of course, the ordeal, in the aftermath, of burrowing for a handkerchief . . . It all made him irritable, steamed up, as if the sight of himself in partial undress, a state more belittling than total obese nakedness, somehow pricked at his identity, undermined his sense of authority—a porous notion in any case, which, even when he was formally suited, I suspect to have been concocted artificially, built without wisdom, too fast, too high, and too treacherously close to the brink of ruin.

I myself always remained primly uniformed at these meetings, for only my head was then of apparent import to him; but had anyone, particularly some other member of staff, chanced to knock at the door while he was hunched over me in this farcical dishabille, Dr. Fox would have had, if not an actual seizure, certainly his work cut out accounting for the ensuing delay in answering, never mind explaining my puzzling proximity to his fluster, which none of the cupboards could hide. Only once, in fact, did footsteps happen to saunter up to the felted door of his directorship while he was privately occupied; and though, miraculously, no knuckles went so far as to rap against the mahogany, I remember with what sudden brutal force he clamped his hand over my mouth. But I also remember how his spectacles fell with a sad thud from his burning ears to the wrinkles of gabardine about his ankles. And I knew then that this arrangement could not last, that a further stage would have to be found, and that even as he trussed himself back into masterfulness, he was donning his thinking-cap.

HE WAS NOT long about it. Within days, I was summoned to his bedroom, which lurked at the end of a creaking corridor, high in the oldest wing of the building, and out of bounds to all but those who slept there, fifth formers who, so far as I could tell, spent their recreation oafing away the hours, since no exams threatened them for another year. As you sneaked by, trying not to look too junior, you could hear the racket of clashing rock bands blasting out of various rooms, and punches of boorish laughter, and, sometimes, through a carelessly open door, you caught flashes of posters—bleachy starlets; Hollywood fishnets in strappy stilettos; the smuttier Dalís; some popular lovely with a cone of ice-cream wedged between her tits. The whole place stank: burnt toast, Pot Noodles, illicit ash. I think that pupils were allowed to cook up there, or to boil.

The wooden floor seemed to sway beneath you; the scuffed walls, to curve and wobble and funnel. It was like visiting a slum in a forgotten industrial town. I remember losing my way the first few times, and having to ask directions, and blushing to a colourblend that combined many red emotions. Looking for Dr. Fox's room, are we?, they would reply, always too loud. Say *no more*. (Great slow winks of salacious innuendo; downward cackles.) Those boys were men of the world. They wore platforms.

You had to climb two steps onto a linoleum landing of marbleized slime in order to reach his private quarters: a bed-sitting room to the left, and, opposite it, to the right as you arrived, an ancient bathroom, spacious, gloomy, and lit by a bare bulb. Over the sink, above a mirrored cabinet, there was a candle propped in a glass, along with a soggy-looking box of matches—presumably meant for power cuts. His actual room, across the way, possessed two doors to keep the world at bay, but was smaller than his office, and felt more stuffy. Its insides heaved with acrylic brocaderie: measly repeats of some curlified motif in corresponding tones of Camembert and burgundy. His bed, most single, was tucked behind an alcove which he curtained away when its contents were not made, but which, once the cleaner had been, was revealed as overspread with the paler, less alluring shade of runny cheese.

At some unwise earlier juncture (before he'd taken up residence, I presume) the floorboards had been laid, wall to wall, with a swirling carpet that made you think of seaside B & B's after the war; and over this mistake, as if to obfuscate it, Dr. Fox had unrolled an inferior Persian rug, comfortingly frayed, and bald in patches, but rather too small for the task, with the result that far from it dissimulating the decorative gaffe, lurid margins of fitted greeny-purple-orange pile tended to jump out at you—but perhaps this oversight escaped his faulty eyes. When he lumbered about without glasses, he would always park them, with finicky precision, for easy access, on exactly the same spot of his Victorian fireplace, which was wooden, coarsely grained, and sealed with a slapdash coat of varnish.

The mantel was afflicted with an outbreak of bric-à-brac: dead rose-heads in a dusty vase; ancient (Greek) postcards; defunct wedding invitations (declined); a mutilated teddy bear with a missing eye; a brass carriage clock (operated by batteries) and, just off-centre, in half-profile, a bronzette bust of Beethoven—for which, I was later to learn, he had saved up as a child. I found it hard to envisage Dr. Fox in such an incarnation, unwhiskered. And at the edge of the shelf closest to the alcove, next to a face-mirror nailed at head height, there was, permanently wired up, an electric shaver, its tawny cable trailing away to some elusive socket behind the curtain. Dr. Fox's problematic vision had, ever since puberty—his premature pretence to adulthood—made the task of shaving between those ornate facial growths of his a daily trial, at least until the advent of this timely modern contraption, which, reducing as it did the danger of razor cuts, he had adopted with uncharacteristic newfangled gusto.

The grate, laid daily by some manservant whom I was fortunately never to meet, Dr. Fox would light in the afternoons, and shovel with coal right up to the crest of the evening, when the national anthem was played on television. His hours of heated darkness were long ones: he was insomniac. He never wore nightclothes; and yet, notwithstanding this immodesty, it astonished me that a man so enormously fat should be able to stand the swelter. Placed at a diagonal to the flames, and upholstered in yet more burgundy, there was a genteel little sofa with sides of crackling basketweave, low to ground and fit for the parlour of a maid; and this is where you, the guest, in principle sat, squirming perhaps: for facing you, but turned, as ever, away from the window, there was a preposterously high great wing chair, a chesterfield which could rock and swivel about, and which boasted a mechanical footrest where, puffy ankles crossed, Dr. Fox usually presided in velvet smoking slippers embroidered with treble clefs, and lined in red—for he would sometimes allow one to dangle half-casually. His pictures, too, struck me as a let-down: a couple of unremarkable little prints in the vicinity of the light-switch, probably cathedrals possessed of famous organs; and then, hung over the fire, a gilt-framed watercolour, girlishly pastoral—pinky, frilly, lakey, lilac. I know he was a musical man—not visual; yet I couldn't but be struck by the chasm between his public and private personae. Dr. Fox looked fifty-nine. He was, in fact, thirty-five.

ON THE FIRST OCCASION that I was invited to his eyrie, I noticed but few of the things which I describe; yet I do, by contrast, recall marvelling at the view of the avenue away from the school, for I had never witnessed the lethargic Lady's statue so pleasingly diminished from such a height. Also, under his window, I remember being impressed by a great stack of records ranged along the ground—the longest collection which, up till then, I had encountered: entirely classical, as one would expect, and entirely amassed, it later transpired, courtesy of the funds of the music department: Research Material was the heading under which such perks were routinely entered in the accounts. But on this particular occasion, which was mid-afternoon, teatime, I wasn't able to absorb a great deal: only vague colours, graven shadows, the ghosts of lavender and bachelor cigars. It seemed ill-mannered to nose about, and ill-advised besides, for even as he fiddled within the cosy confines of his trouser-pocket, and uncrossed his ankles to stand up on my arrival, I could tell that his beady, spectacled eye was famished.

Dr. Fox was partial to fine jams—greengage, cherry, damson—but since the shops at the local village carried only basic produce, he was compelled to purchase his select preserves, by the tinload, further afield, from a superior purveyor with whom he enjoyed a healthy rapport and a still healthier tab. Often donning a narrow dicky-bow for these forays, and snapping, if it was sunny, tinted shades onto his glasses, he would set off in his classic two-tone Bentley, gunmetal and black, and roll away over the hills, puffing and humming and salivating, and occasionally turning his head towards the roadside, as if this were bordered by flag-waving crowds, until he came cruising, like some landed earl calling on third-generation tenants, up to his destination, whereupon, with blind unconcern for parking restrictions, he would bring his motor to a soft, whirring halt at the old-fashioned shopfront of his choice—the grocer's, of course—where he was invariably accorded a rapturous morning by the hand-rubbing staff, who doubled as welcoming committee. Dr. Fox played up to their fawning attitudes and approved of their pristine overalls. It gave him faith in tradition. Anything else for Dr. Fox, at all?, they would wonder with great monotony. And he would reply, as if this were a refrain: I think there *might* just be; now, let me think: anchovy paste, grained mustard, quails' eggs, aromatic pepper, coffee beans, castor sugar, double cream. It was always a drawn-out procedure, a ritual, reminded him of what he construed as The Old Days.

Much later, circumstances were to push us into an approximation of friendship, and even though, by then, his finances had suffered a conspicuous dent—with the result that he was constrained not just to sell his concert grand, but also to exchange his beloved Bentley for a humbling Morris Minor (which I secretly felt better suited his shape, and in which, almost as secretly, he would eventually teach me to drive)—yet he remained, despite the reduction of his income, a dogged sybarite. I remember how, during the half term in which I came of age—an occasion which my parents saw greater cause to regret than celebrate—he took me, in an exceptional flight of extravagance which I suppose he could justify as largesse, for my first dinner at Claridge's, even going to the trouble, as if I were his ward, or he my great-uncle, of introducing me to the Maitre d', who'd known him for aeons—a futile formality, as it happened, for I wasn't to venture back into that gourmandizing sanctum for two decades to come, by when, frankly, who cared? He was boring about food, boring in the sense that he would veto conversation while the culinary marvels laid before his great napkin, which he tucked under his jowels, threatened to lose heat; yet he could be perversely imaginative, and did attempt, in the final instance, to imbue me with confidence despite my prissiness.

I have not forgotten how, when the pudding trolley was wheeled up to us and I asked to have wild strawberries, white (which appealed to my prissy side), he took the bottle of vintage claret to which he'd been initiating me, some stupendous Latour—'45 seems to come to mind— and with spectacular (some would say sacrilegious) audacity, bloodied my fruit with the last flourish of his priceless wine, muttering, a little formally, a little sadly: Now, my dear chap: you've tried the finest food in the land, and wine from one of the greatest vineyards, separately as well as together. Best of both worlds, one could say. Too late for me, of course, but let nobody tell you that you can't have your cake and eat it. You can. You will. Happy eighteenth birthday. And then he encouraged me to eat the best of both worlds with my fingers, not to be bourgeois about it. But such tokens of goodwill, such toasts, lay, as yet, hidden in the future: I was still at the stage of toasted bread, and he needed jam to sweeten it.

THE INITIAL LURES to his privacy, the first half-dozen or so, felt, despite the informality of his backless waistcoats and his stripy shirt-sleeves, uptight to me, twitchy. I would try to act politely and, even if famished, would limit my rations to a demure minimum—as if these meetings of ours were really interviews, and as if, though my application for the job had been foisted on me rather than prompted by personal initiative, the slightest sign of hunger could rob me of the offered position. One single slice of toast, lavishly buttered and jammed for me by him, and relieved of its hoary crust and cut into four segments, triangles, and delivered to my clenched lap on a brittle plate of flowery porcelain, is all that I permitted myself—against his easy five: it was difficult not to count. Earl Grey tea, poured from a pot with little feet, which took me back to the genteel English nanny of my early days. I pretended to eschew milk, and declined his offer of sugar, however refined—not because I lacked a sweet tooth, but in order to minimize the fuss of stirring, and the risk of spilling, and the predictable charade of mopping me clean.

I did not feel at ease; nor, very possibly, did he; and yet despite the heavily scored bass line of our dealings, which, though unperformed in this new venue, still resounded inside me with the echoes of his office far beneath, we did, in a fashion, manage to converse here, went through the higher trills of civility. I suppose that, encouraged by my oral acquiescence on the coal box, he now felt encouraged to pursue a fuller acquaintanceship, the route to which appeared to lie in sounding me out socially, verbally, encouraging me to make admissions. Only once, however, did we skirt round the wide subject of my sexual delin-quency, which represented his trump card in the gamble for me; for, though he, as adults in his position mostly do, enjoyed the upper hand in the proceedings, I was determined to pretend to be keener to learn from him than to discuss the closed subject of my former teacher.

I needed to save my skin—that much I knew—so I proceeded cau-tiously, slow prudence being, though dull of me, at least not punish-able. (Later, I was to learn that while he toyed with the prospect of my suitability as his ganymede, he'd taken himself to the office of the rec-tor's secretary and rifled through some file relating to me, in order to check, as if this were a qualification, the supposed quotient of my intel-ligence.) And thus, with his every forward step into prurience, I found myself taking another of retreat, back into a resistance that masquer-aded as timidity. I remember attempting chatty detours—my teasing equivalents of his sweets that led to nothing—and, for instance, lam-pooning the school's sporting absurdities as viewed from the cynical place where I then lived, and I would find myself, in return, rewarded for my attempts at a deferral (which both of us probably knew could not last indefinitely) by collusive little hoots from him. I might even, in order to avert his intentions, have (further) flirted—for this, if only in theory, committed me to nothing. It was a respectable skill; even my mother deployed it; but I remember sweating with the great heavy effort of distracting him.

Those early teas seemed to me to stretch into dispiriting eternities, for, despite my apprehension, I never quite dared to take my unso-licited leave—in case he should block me, and draw close, which might swell into anything; and so, instead, I would wait and wait and wait until he, rendered as hesitant by his new attempts at friendship as earlier he had been bold to abuse his authority—and unable, in consequence of the switch, to cross the boundary from trivial antics to bodily, finally gave up, accepted defeat, and allowed me to return, a little frayed but almost free, to wherever I should have been. Until the next time, obviously. And as the pace of his invitations escalated, and the slices of his toast blossomed into scones and crumpets and sandwiches of cucumber dipped in vinegar, and sometimes even syllabub, it did not escape me that, despite the treats which seemed so coolly to raise me above the young multitude, he was quietly turning up the heat.

NOW COMES THE DAY, a Friday. When I go in, I do not—which has been the routine—find him rising wearily from his wingèd chesterfield: he's already upstanding, and lurking a little too close to the door for my ease. The fire is blazing. In order to circumvent him, I have to squeeze between the back of the low sofa and the bed in the alcove behind it— not a straightforward procedure, for the ground is strewn with programmes and reviews and books—historical biographies, mainly: Richelieu, the Sun King, Mazarin. Dr. Fox is keen on stories of magnificent skulduggery. While I try to steer myself towards my usual position, he pretends, with a friendly tut of admonition, that I haven't closed the door properly, and goes to secure it; but though he coughs elaborately, I catch the sound of a turning key, its clandestine squeal.

As I round the far side of the sofa, I notice his reflection in the shaving-mirror: he's moving with an eager sort of speed, as if racing me to my seat. He wins: I don't make it to safety. I stop in my tracks. His waistcoat, I now see, is already undone, and breathing heavily. His shirted gut comes on to me, the dimple of his navel straining against its fabric. The curtains beyond his shoulders are practically drawn to: only a narrow shaft of light cuts across the ceiling. I take a half-step back from him—so he takes a whole one forward, into me. His whiskers are curling into a sort of grin, revealing a fissure between his front teeth. His eyes wince for me to follow his lead. Follow how? Like this: he places a velvet slipper between my feet, thereby forcing me to stumble against some mystery behind me. I fall onto the bed awaiting. It feels much the same as sitting on the coal box did, save that the surface beneath me now lacks solidity, is less supportive still. Not a word has passed between us. There seems not to be a need.

I know what is required of me, but what I cannot gauge are the new parameters of his bedroom greed, quite where, or how far, he intends to take me. The bulk of his divestiture occurs with Dr. Fox already plugged into me, between my lips, his penis held more or less still while my gullet labours on it. Words like diligence and application and industry race through my head, words of the type that you like to read on reports from teachers. And then I think of promise and of interest, and of that other non-curricular word, popularity, and fleetingly I think of my mother, and of the sun, which I suddenly miss, and of seaweed wreaths. I notice fragments of clothing being slung about behind him—a salvaged flash of tie; a rib of white collar, stiff; buttons of shell on a waistcoat; a glint from a cufflink. The braces have already been released; the trousers, left to slither and wilt on the embroidered slippers.

These, the slippers, he removes stealthily, and while one of them sneaks off behind the valance, its partner seems to become wedged between my feet, for I recognize the dry rubbing of velvet against my heels. He now steps out of his trouser legs, thus enabling him to sway more confidently, almost to swagger with relief. As he kicks away the mound of gabardine, I notice, below my line of vision, a greyish blur of baggy underpants about his knees, and below, in a stunted perspective, elasticated garters attached to a pair of stockinged feet, which stand turned out, pointing to the corners of the room behind me. He leans down without releasing me, and unclicks the elastics on his shins, but I cannot see what happens beyond this point, not without losing my purchase on his penis. He seems to raise one foot to his rear, and to wobble one-legged in an effort to pull a sock free. I envisage a fat flamingo. He swaps unsteadily to the other foot. Now there follows a disharmony between us: I must thrust out my mouth if I'm to keep him in, but, if I push my face any further into his groin, he will lose his balance and keel. He shoves me back onto the bedsprings. Out of my mouth he pops, a model of rigidity; his glistening knob, purple as a two-day bruise.

I sit uncertainly. Yet he stands firm, pointing himself back at me, so closely that he blurs my vision. He begins to tug at my neck, half-throttles me in his haste to remove the tie which contains it, which he first attempts to slide the wrong way round, as if I were a mirror, and which, once off, he seems not to know what to do with. He tries to crouch to kiss me with his fleshy rosebud lips and, meanwhile, slings the noose of my father's Alma Mater, like a skipping rope, over his head, leaving it there to hang. His spectacles bash into my cheek, but he, with a quick hard independent middle finger, pushes them back onto their greasy bridge.

The pallor of his blubber in this light is tinged with underwater green. His shins, I see, are varicose, riddled with worms, diseased eely ribbons of aquamarine. I try to swim away, to immerse myself in adjectives about the sea, to vanish. He begins to shed my jacket for me, but my body appears not to be co-operating, so he shoves at the collar, yanks at the lapels as if I were thick-skinned, or just thick. I look up at him, blankly, without possible meaning, but suddenly he's smiling back, creepily cheered. He raises me by my underarms to my feet. In one deft heave. Dr. Fox is stronger than you might think, like most musicians. The clothes of my upper half—jacket, jumper, collar, shirt—come off briskly, roughly, inside out and back to front, as in a locker room. My torso looks so burnt in the hot gloom, and so skinny next to the white mountain of him, that you would think I'd spent my life starving in the tropics, and he his, stuffing himself with cheese in cold countries. The hair under my arms feels regrettable to me, unfitting and implicating. I hunch my shoulders in, to hide this defect. He sits me on the bed, more delicately now, and sets me down on my back as if I were a baby whose nappy needed changing. I grow more feeble by the minute. I cannot make this easier.

Like some governess, he takes my clothes across the room and places them tidily over the arm of his chair, folding each garment in half, down the middle. The back of his head is flat, like the butt of a bullet. He flies back to me now, soundlessly, as if to check that I'm still alive, still breathing. I lie slumped across the bed, half-denuded yet belted, eyes closed for simplicity. But even without peering, I can tell that now, in his private domain as opposed to his public office, he wants more than just the head of me. Here we inhabit a different kingdom, differently crayoned, broader and wilder than the controlled territory of music. I do not blame him. I once yearned for Mr. Wolfe entirely, for the whole vast savage continent of him. But that was before I grew thick, or thick-skinned.

Kneeling on the edge of his bed, and pushing a curtain which might hamper him, he places an arm behind my neck, and another behind my knees, as if I were feverish, delirious. He tries to swivel me into position, to carry my head onto his brocaded pillow. I can feel him straining to lift me, his stubborn penis prodding my right kidney. I help him to heave me; I raise my legs of my own volition, but I do so as if I were moribund, or moving in my dreams, turning in a womb. He removes my shoes, and slowly peels my socks away from me, like a pedicurist. My feet are freezing, but it could be worse, I tell myself: at least my toe-nails are trimmed. I hear him patter across the room to place the shoes with the rest of my property, and I'm left to hope that he hasn't stuffed my socks inside them.

He tip-toes back, as if not wishing to disturb me, and begins to pull at my trousers, from my feet—pull, pull, harder pull still; but my arms, as if predicting this initiative, have crossed and clamped against my middle. I cannot let the man strip me, not completely. I think of Mr. Wolfe, of my squandering of him. I realize that I have earned this. I own up to my deficit, decide to pay the penalty: unbuckle, unclip, unzip automatically. Dr. Fox is free to proceed. Dr. Fox is rich. I arc my spine, and raise my buttocks an embarrassed minimum, just the fraction nec-essary for him to effect his transaction smoothly, and he rewards me with a calculated interim during which he conveys the trousers of my undoing, taking care to preserve their crease, over to the resting-place of my other belongings. I think that he lets me hang on to my under-pants; but I have to peer down the length of myself to be certain. For I feel, despite the swaddle of whiteness across my hips, naked anyway.

A PAIR OF PANTS. That much—that little—he has permitted. But now, this great blancmange of a man is clambering onto the bed, trying to keep his heavy spectacles in place as he draws one foot upwards, and then, with a great gasp, the other. He staggers over my flatness, his pale fleshiness overhanging. The mattress makes waves. He wobbles, throws an open palm against the wall, regains a balance of sorts, and begins gradually to lower himself upon me, crouching by cautious degrees until he's straddling my middle. He wriggles to make himself comfortable. I gaze at the ceiling, float around it. He slides upwards, northwards, along me a fraction, and rests his crevice, which he pulls asunder with the rough use of his hands, precisely upon the front of my underpants. These have hardened within, but against my wish: it is my mere body betraying me, mocking me. Typical, I remember thinking—the whole untimely ambivalence. My loins are an open book: interpret it, I tell you, as you see fit, but remember, when you come to draw conclusions, that when you're young, when *you* were young, horns such as mine are not, were not, summoned: such things reared up, they rear for no good reason, fuelled as easily by boredom, or fear, as ever by a sense of thrill.

Nothing seems clear-cut as I squirm beneath him. I feel weighed down by contradictions. It amazes me to discover that I can endure his great bulk without expiring, but I daresay that there's a perfectly good reason for this, relating to springs and momentum and body weight and mass, tucked between the pages of my physics file. His knees stick out on either side of me, toward me, like ancillary sharks. He starts to push them down, one at a time; and now they have dropped out of sight, returned to the ocean, though his varicose veins, his eels, must be slithering about my thighs. A smell of perished seafood—rising, I suspect, from the unplumbed depths of his umbilical cavern—invades the curtained alcove, spreads its putrefaction around the confines, like the rotting innards of dead fish thrown in a monger's bucket. My nostrils flare with repugnance. The distended rolls of his flab seem, from where I lie, to be piled onto me in circular rings of flaccid rubber. My gaze ventures upward from his undergut and belly to his dugs, and past his bearded jowls and chin and cheeks, which are whiskery and flushed, all the way to his teeny, disappearing eyes. He has removed his spectacles, clicked them shut—click-clack—and next, he's trying to lurch forward, seems to be tugging at a corner of counterpane near the bed-head of Formica, in order to place his glasses beneath the pillow, to bury them safely. I wonder what he can look like from behind, with his fluffy, sweaty hindquarters splayed thus, and whether he has ever caught, clambering out of the bath perhaps, a glimpse of his own sight.

But as he bathes upon me despite my dryness, he is blind, can hardly pick me out, is reduced to touching me—and from my point of view this feels almost like a comfort, a small mercy. I am A. N. Other now, anonymously slumped for his enriching, or his wastage, a mere faceless return on some high-risk investment. But he, by contrast, remains very much himself, utterly his own speculator, enormously naked—naked, that is, except for the pinky-ring of pale cornelian, the last vestige of his gravitas, which gleams near my face as he guides his cock up, up to my death mask. But no, he changes his mind. Instead he plunges me with his dark tongue. I try to curl my own, right back, as if to hide it; but I can't, so I flatten it against the parched base of my mouth. He stifles me with his grunting breath of warmish truffles. I try to inhale from my nose and directly through my windpipe, but when I can no longer hold out against the mounting slime of his saliva, I wrench my lips away from his ardour, and turn my sweating head in profile.

He will not have this. He returns my effigy to face him, to lick around the edges of its mouth, which, as far as I'm concerned, he can lick to his heart's desire, for now I am flying around the ceiling above. He slurps over my nostrils, scratching the edge of my nose with his pulsing nasal brushes, and at last he attends to my eyes with his tongue, in order to help them shut. And given, I suppose, my unreasonable reluctance even to feign desire, my refusal to provide him, after all that he has done, with so much as a simulacrum of passion, but to reward him for his pains only with abstraction, he rams himself where I deserve, where I have come to expect, which is inside my mealy mouth. He chokes me less when I am supine: my neck can be thrown back. He traps my arms, my wings of flight, under his knees, and pins me down. And now that I'm immobile, he takes his claws behind his back and begins to tug at my waistband, gripping and wrenching my underpants as far as they will go, which is down to my calves.

He withdraws from my face once more, and shifts his weight from my chest to my crotch, which is my great embarrassment. He must have grown either angered or elated now, because he has begun to sway about, to rock and moan and grind his sticky parted arse against my genitals, which are turning raw with the rub of his lust. And after pumping himself for a few fraught moments, and churning the contents of his shrivelled sac, he scatters his musical seed over my face and forehead and hair, spurting as far as the headstone of Formica; and I am left with a taste of indifference mixed with sadness, as if I'd attended the funeral of someone unknown to me, some vague acquaintance of the family. We dress in a quiet hurry, and then we settle down to tea, as if nothing had happened. And this, over and over, becomes the pattern; and I oblige with my company frequently, disaffectedly, as if there were no tomorrow, or as if tomorrow would be no different.

.　　　.　　　.

IN MY SECOND YEAR, a most unlikely thing happened: I managed to make a friend—not necessarily of the type that my parents would have encouraged, such as someone descended from a noble line of English Catholics, but still; to me, the whole surprise alliance felt like a miracle, and my new ally, like a harbinger of bravado. When this olive-skinned stranger with jutting cheeks and narrowed eyes turned to me at assembly on the first morning of the new term, and whispered some well-crafted barb concerning the rector (of whom I, not having been granted a dog-collared glance, hadn't troubled to form an opinion, but whom my neighbour had obviously decided to despise on sight, for the sheer glorious hell of it), I found myself bowled over, smitten by this newcomer's venomous charm. He was the most disrespectful and sarcastic boy that I had ever met, and entirely without fear, or so it seemed to me. Certainly he was the first whom I had ever known to kick against the rule of compulsory confessions, which he described as an affront to one's integrity and an abuse of civil liberty. He was a born winner, you could just tell—not brilliant academically, for he was far too self-possessed to bother with industry—but he exuded flamboyance and anarchy, and bristled, wherever he ventured, with angry energy. Plus, we were soon to discover, we had common interests, not least the shared acidity of our humour, our burgeoning style of waspishness.

Cross was his surname, but like me, he held dual nationality thanks to his mother, who was South American. He insisted on carrying two passports, not only in case a sudden war erupted and he needed to get out of England, which he said that he absolutely would do, but also (and I suspected this to be the more alluring reason) for the pleasure of confusing airport authorities. Though—also like me—he was bilingual, his English was more Hispanic than Yankee, reminiscent of my mother's in intonation, while his Spanish, which was slower and more melodic than mine, was infused with wavier cadences. When he spoke, it sounded almost as if he were chanting. I adored some of the words that he used, which, strictly, were not so much Castillian as flourishes of onomatopœic slang derived from the oral tradition of Peruvian trou-badours. Those syllables of his were like species of new butterflies to me, constant surprises, small blessings. Both of us claimed to detest, and without exception, every single other inmate in this pit, and we always spoke in Spanish—nice and loud, to irritate our peers—switching back to English only when bothered by some dreary priest or teacher, for the staff viewed our bond as unhealthy, schoolgirlish. But we became, as far as we could (even though we sat in different streams), inseparable. Dr. Fox detested him—considered him nouveau riche, and wouldn't even give him a voice audition. My friend was a latecomer. That was the excuse. Sorry.

His parents were on the brink of divorce, a circumstance of which, in that period, honest-to-goodness Catholics would have taken a dim view. I found it glamorous, racy. His father, Mr. Cross, whom I was given to believe had lent his name to a line of slick executive Biros which then glittered with status all over the shop, had, since his conjugal upheaval a couple of years before, removed to Chicago, to be near a ravishing young heiress—one of those incredibly refined American society blondes, all cashmere and overblown smiles and jodhpurs—whom he had met playing polo in Newport, I think it was, and whom he planned to marry as soon as the papers of his matrimonial severance came through. In the meantime, while he waited for the moment to place a band upon the beauty's finger, he entertained her from some high-rise *garçonnière* in the vicinity of her family home—the latter being, the boy later told me, one of the oldest houses in the city, a whopping great mansion, set in equally whopping grounds, and full of black servants in full livery, apparently.

My friend had pinned a photograph of the contentious extramarital pair onto the wooden partition of his cubicle, and I remember thinking that his burnished father, raffish and black-eyed and brilliantined, looked sexy as all get out, but I never dared to admit this. It was to remain among my secrets. And my friend's secret, though he seemed to be at less pains to conceal it, was that he obviously preferred his father's new concubine (whom, against his mother's pleas, he had met on a number of occasions while weekending in Chicago) to either of his parents, for she was younger than they, more like an older sibling, and hip as hell to boot. Plus, of course, she spoiled him—it was in her emotional interest—and was forever giving him expensive attempts at friendship: a pocket-sized television, utterly up-to-the-minute; a cut-velvet jacket with curvy lapels; silky polo-necks; metallic suitcases. I don't know how the boy's mother took all this, but I was fascinated.

Next to the photograph of the soon-to-be-weds, who, snapped from a balcony overlooking some sunny midday swimming pool, almost glowed with reflected romantic azure, there was another picture, in black and white, which, though larger in format, had been doctored at some point since its development. This had been intended to portray a formal family group, until, that is, my friend decided to excise two of the heads from the gathering—his own, and his father's. The resulting oval holes looked, against the wooden surface of the cubicle, like hollowed eye-sockets to me, sinister. I would have filled them in, tried my hand at collage of some description, had a bash at reparation. No matter; what remained on view was centrally, essentially, an exotic dusky female with lilies planted in her upswept hair, and enormous silver hoops circling down from her lobes to her shoulders, which were swathed in a flurry of white frills. This woman, I discovered, had been my friend's mother in days of greater matrimonial harmony. She was flanked by four girls of varying ages, from fifteen to about three, also frilled in whiteness, though not so seductively, and all with sulky dark mouths. Eyes like angry moons: the Cross sisters. But why had my friend removed his father from the scene? Ohhh, he replied in the manner of a languorous adult, because his father had another life now, obviously. And then he waved a hand, forefinger extended like a dancer's in fifth position, towards the colour picture. And why himself? Because his mother had forced him to wear a bow tie to the studio. I saw his point, I admit.

Señora Cross and her girls had remained at the family home in Ecuador, but fond of them as my friend doubtless was, for he spoke of them in tones of affection, as if they belonged to a sentimental film, it was also apparent that he was looking forward to spending, after the decree absolute, long chunks of holiday in the centre of Chicago, which, unlike the stultifying outskirts of Guayaquil, was, he told me, a really groovy place to be. And he also told me that once his father and the society beauty had found a new place and settled in, and he himself had a chance to check out the decent shops and clubs and naughty cinemas, then, he said, I too could visit: there was bound to be masses of room. I returned this compliment, and invited him to visit me, though I dreaded inflicting my ghastly father upon him, and exposing myself to the fact that I had no friends of our age to amuse him.

HIS FIRST NAME was Louis, which his family apparently pronounced Lewis, not even Luis. It sounded peculiar to me. So instead, when we were alone, I would call him by his second name, which I thought just screamed of Hollywood. It was Clifford. Clifford Cross: wasn't that fabulous? He, in turn, never bothered to call me James, because, as names went, we both found it pathetic. So instead, he adopted my mother's diminutive, and was always to call me Iago during the heady period of our friendship. Clifford turned out to be the sole boy with whom, in those eight long years of education, I was to share such an intimacy.

Like his father (I suspected), he was a born cheat, and, what is more, always managed to get away with his misdemeanours. If there existed a rule, he simply had to bend it—not actually break it, you understand: it would never have done for his exploits to backfire on him. That would have spelt what he termed Gratuitous Humiliation, *humillación gratuita*. I revelled in that phrase: its very sound, its rolling sophistication, made me tingle. But anyway, the point is that the lure of insurrection was beyond his resistance. Take our school uniform: half the time he wore the jacket slung over his shoulders, letting it swank about like the cape of some Latin seducer—a departure which, though frequently criticized by teachers, and openly scorned by other pupils, was not, in itself, against the rules. Or his jumpers: Clifford had been taught to sew by his older sister, presumably to help relieve the Ecuadorian tedium—so that confronted with the horror of our lanky regulation pullies, he simply grabbed his needlework kit and set to work, somehow managing to take in the sides of his jumper without the entire mess unravelling. I have a suspicion that he reinforced the seams with the use of a stapler (though he would never have admitted this, not even to me), but anyway, next he raised the waistband to the level of his ribs and, as if by magic, he suddenly owned a passable approximation of a fashion item, good and skinny, about which there wasn't a goddamn thing that anyone could do. When interrogated by fuddy-duddy members of the staff about his irregular appearance, he just claimed that his jumper had been shrunk by the school's lamentable dry-cleaning people, and that, if anything, the authorities should be thinking in terms of reimbursing him. His nerve in the teeth of authority was unflinching, and filled me with a vicarious sense of bravery, as if, though I wasn't even instrumental, I had been an active partner in his mischief. It strengthened me. The way he customized his ties, too, was extraordinary: he would make, with the wide end, the broadest knot imaginable; then, dock the excess of narrow dribble; and finally, hand-roll the raw edge to prevent fraying. He made everything easy, Clifford.

AT THE HATED TUCK SHOP, he calmly stepped into the breach for me and set about avenging my earlier indignity. I'd told him the story about Payne Senior, and he replied that Payne Senior made him sick. While I stood back and soaked up the scene, he would join the queue and squint and start counting, planning his moment carefully, holding back, giving way to people behind him if necessary, until he was certain of being dealt with by that one specific prefect. Payne alone would do. And after having purchased a wild excess of sweets both for himself and for me, but before having paid for these, he would suddenly, at the last instant, demand to buy, for instance, lipstick. He would, of course, be told not to be so bloody stupid, but the voice admonishing would have grown jittery. And Clifford, pretending to be outraged, would, every time, begin to bang a noisy coin against the ledge of the hatch and simply insist. Come on!, he would scream, surely Payne had *lipstick* to sell, under-the-counter sort of thing, or was money not the right currency? Clifford could be a spectacular nuisance, fantastically impudent; drove his victims, even older ones, to distraction; and was able, despite his lowly position in the hierarchy, to prove to our seniors, and to me, how bullying had nothing to do with winning. Bullying didn't worry him: it was the prospect of winning that appealed.

His style was brasher than mine, showy by comparison to my congenital chi-chi, but there was an undeniable glamour to his flashiness, which, even if I didn't emulate, enthralled me: he was, in a way, my alter-ego. He didn't smoke, which I emphatically did, but he drank superbly, preferably duty-free tequila, decanted into a hip flask and secreted about his person, for he swore that tequila helped him concentrate on prayers at benediction, and improved his sacred incantations beyond belief. He also possessed a stash of his mother's amphetamines, and claimed that given the execrable standards of nutrition in this prison, no sensible person could afford the risk of an appetite, which was a recipe for food poisoning. He even sported jewellery: not the cheap, ethnicky beads that aspiring hippies in the sixth form liked to conceal, along with grandad vests, beneath their uniforms, but an adjustable bracelet, fashioned like the bangles of coiled elephant-hair which were then considered trendy—though his, typically, was made of gold, the real thing, no shit for him. He wore it on the same wrist as his watch, which was the last word in chronometric desirability: you could have dived, without it coming to grief, the whole thousand leagues down to the bottom of the sea—were it not for the fact that he purposely left its chain to dangle loosely, with the result that, submerged other than in bath water, he probably would have risked losing it.

He gave himself manicures—again, a trick learnt from his sister—most often, I gathered, during prep in the evenings; Clifford couldn't have objected less to people staring at him while he performed this procedure, for he considered his cuticles to be magnificent, and exhorted me to regard with special suspicion those priests whose fingernails were bitten. He wore contact lenses, of all amazing tricks, and wielded dental floss, like spun silk, which I had never seen. He even went to a hygienist to bleach his teeth (which in Europe, at that time, was an unheard-of thing, revolutionary). And when back in Guayaquil, he would take his regulation slip-ons to some local cobbler, have him stack the soles an imperceptible but effective centimetre, and further instruct him to replace the heels with something a little more... Cuban. ¡Viva La Vida! You have to live. I loved his spirit.

BECAUSE HE LENT me strength, and shared my isolation with me, I grew to trust him. First we exchanged mild confidences about friendship generally and loyalty being everything; then, we moved on to crushes and pashes and things that happened at girls' schools, a sort of madness which afflicted virgins when they became women, as if the two conditions, madness and virginity, were mutually exclusive, which in turn led us to the heavier stuff that apparently went on in convents, and made us shriek with disbelief, because, well, we just could not fathom what the hell girls did get up to when there was nothing to *get* up? He said they rubbed. I told him not to talk rubbish. To me, girls seemed like creatures from another galaxy (less so to him, because he had sisters, but still): all those periods and tampons, month after month for the rest of their lives, and no swimming when there was blood, and the whole revolting business of pregnancy, and the thought of parents doing it, which I said didn't even bear imagining. He replied that he could envisage his father french-kissing his fiancée, which meant spitting in her mouth. I told him that he was disgusting.

And then we'd grow thoughtful for a while, ruminative, until one of us eventually erupted with laughter and put us back on track, which was really the track of love—love, that is, between humans (pets weren't allowed), and reciprocal love in particular, which I didn't think could ever really work, not if it got tangled up with biology and, more pointedly, with lustfulness, which was a sin, because fornication (which he, in his worldly way, insisted on calling erotic union) just wrecked everything in my opinion, though he didn't think that it did, not necessarily: look at Tristram and Iseult, he said, or Romeo and Juliet. What utter crap, I countered: those were just figures in fables that someone had made up, and besides, the people in those stories never actually, you know, well *you know*. I argued that when people did—did what?, he asked; Did Intercourse, I snapped: look it up in the dictionary. Fuck off, he retaliated, in Spanish—one person was always the loser, and the other, the taker; and anyway, that was between women and men; and men who wanted women were only ever really after *that* (and then I pointed to my flies, which must have confused matters), but still, I bet him that any girl who played the truth game would admit that sexual stuff had nothing to do with friendship or love, not really, not like friendship between males, sort of like us. Take the Greeks, I pronounced (we were starting the Symposium, so I felt entitled), and then I droned on, feeling important, until, in the manner of these things, we eventually got round to boys, and how relations between boys didn't always have to be Platonic, though I considered it prudent if they, well, stopped short, short of groping. But for the moment, I steered clear of dealings between adults and children; I didn't want to muddle us. All in good time.

In the event, neither Clifford nor I was so reckless as to discuss specifics, but both of us did on occasion hint at past experiences, small histories. Although my views on sexual morality were undermined by religion, handicapped, his turned out to be strong, heretical, and surprisingly well backed. He knew, for instance, about African initiation rites, and about the Aztecs, and about people called Yoruba, who practised sexual voodoo and were magicians, and all about the stars. My Catholic mumbo-jumbo regarding mortal sin, he said, was total guff. I mean, he explained, take the Chinese, whose culture and philosophy were far more ancient than our poxy Christianity (a tradition which, by comparison, was just a jumped-up cult of superstition, more tied up with political greed and the propagation of fear than any quest for fulfilment): Where, he challenged me, *where* in all of their learned writings about ying and yang (who, even symbolically, were masculine—they were shaped like sperms, for God's sake) did the Chinese condemn homosexuals, whom we called Queries? Well? Hmm? I was, of course, dumbfounded—but also strangely encouraged, as if I might yet find a remedy to salve my wretched conscience.

He must have felt that the printed word might, if not actually restore me to inner health, at least remedy my stupefied silence, because next he dragged me to the library and pushed me up a spiral staircase onto a balcony and, from the depths of a dusty shelf, yanked out some fat book about Hinduism, riffling (not for the first time, I imagined) through the index at the back, until he came to some obscure law about Queries like us, a law which he now looked up in the main part, quite near the front. I remember his manicured finger skating triumphantly down the page, then skidding to a halt just before the passage that he was after. But to make doubly sure that there wasn't any possible room for confusion (since I was being so moronic—which I denied: I called it sceptical), he drew forth one of his eponymous Biros and, his back turned to the room in case the librarian happened to be staring up, he underlined the relevant sentence twice, which declared that: "A twice-born man who commits an unnatural offence with a male shall bathe, dressed in his clothes." I scanned it, and scanned it again, then stared at him in utter befuddlement. He raised his eyebrows in exasperation, slammed the book shut, dumped it where it didn't belong, and led us back out.

Well?, he said. Well *what*?, I answered. He began to look pissed off now. Bathing with your clothes on, he hissed, is hardly a scary punishment; and anyway, that's only for people who believe in second time round, which doesn't include us. Look, he went on, it's all a load of cack, don't you see? We're only on this planet once, so make hay while the sun shuns. Shines, I corrected him, ever the pedant. You know what I mean, he countered, so don't try to be a clever dick. I had no wish to. I was desperate to agree: I needed him to show me the light, the way beyond the mangle of my scruples. Clifford would be my beacon.

THROUGHOUT THE MONTHS of our increasing closeness—good months for the most part, carefree and irreverent, sunny despite the winter—a couple of subjects had nevertheless been niggling at me, the most obvious being whether the muck of my former infamy had yet been raked up for Clifford's benefit by some blabbing prat, which I felt sure must have happened, and, if so, why Clifford hadn't yet asked me to come clean about the gossip. The second was the darker topic of Dr. Fox, who continued to summon me to his bedroom with undiminished frequency. I had even, by this stage in my career, graduated to the luxury of home-made sherry trifle, for I had learnt, despite my unappetizing partner, to ejaculate in his company and simulate satisfaction.

Although Clifford was perhaps the more vociferous party, he and Dr. Fox held each other in mutually low regard, and the clash between them did little to simplify my life, for, at base, I felt culpable. My friend had battled for me at the tuck shop, I worried; the least I could do now was intercede on his behalf, attempt to negotiate a diplomatic solution to the impasse. But Dr. Fox remained adamant: he had plenty of altos, thank you; wouldn't hear another word on the subject. Not once did Clifford blame me for having failed him on the music front, but what, by the same token, he was never to forgive (and we were equally rancorous, so I understood his stance) was the injustice of having been barred from joining forces with me in the second line of the choir.

He was, as it happened, perfectly musical: when we were bored, and ambling about outside, we would sometimes resurrect two-part childhood songs, lullabies and madrigals which, despite the difference of our origins, were rooted in a folklore common to both our motherlands. Clifford sang like a grown woman, with warbling adult passion. But what seemed really to inflame his emotions (his fury at being denied what he claimed to be his basic educational right), was that I, his best friend, should, as if to rub salt into the wound of injustice, be a favourite with Dr. Fox. For despite the latter's continuing efforts to camouflage his weakness for my company by belittling me in public, the truth of my status was clear as a diamond: it sparkled with exposure. I told Clifford that I hated the whole set-up, but that my hands were tied. He looked unpersuaded by my argument, for he was aware that I returned to those teas on a regular basis, which he presumed to be a privilege, the chance to be civilized. I tried to convince him that it was all hellish, nerve-wracking to get there, and boring once you'd arrived. You never knew what to talk about; it was excruciating; I wouldn't wish it on my worst enemy. But I begged him not to discuss those dreadful teas with anyone, not even the worst enemy on whom I wouldn't have wished them, because if the superficial details were ever to get out—about the scones and jams and clotted cream and sherry trifles—these would only serve to exacerbate my unpopularity. I made him promise. And promise he did. He protected me.

Eventually, needless to say, the subject of Mr. Wolfe, whom Clifford had never met but only heard about, did surface, but it was all mooted softly, without pressure or sarcasm; and because, by now, I knew enough about Clifford's liberal stance, I felt able to reciprocate the loyalty which we agreed was vital between friends such as us, friends who meant to be friends for life. So I told him, somewhat sketchily, about what had happened to me at prep school—not from my angry muddled heart, but as if from someone else's memory, as if relating some documentary, vaguely described to me way back in the past, third hand. I found myself concentrating on the bit about being found out, skipping all the boring interrogations, jumping to the episode with my repellent father. This, as we sat in Clifford's cubicle, gossiping in Spanish just before lights out, I made the blinding focus of my account: the ghastly maroon car, the Old Boy tie, the disgusting pub, the stench of his cigars, the preparatory prayer (which sent Clifford into paroxysms), the punching of the boot (which made him punch the wooden slats of his partition), the stroll in the cowpat, the horrible sight of my father blubbing, the confabs which had gone on behind my back, and last, how, in a manner which I'd never quite managed to work out, I'd got away with the whole fandango. The scandal had died down, and—apart from the whispering campaign, the endurance of which scarcely needed spelling out—I'd been left to get on with my life. He took it all on board, and in good spirit; he laughed at the right moments, and, once he knew the truth, he simply knew the truth, that was that. Let's face it, he said, now that we were older, it sounded like pretty tame stuff. And I recall how, straight after my half-baked confession, Clifford mumbled (by way, I suppose, of trading trust) something about having been interfered-with by some garage mechanic once; but he was forced to tell his tale in a rush, because the monitor on duty was chucking him out, and besides, I wasn't wildly interested: I had, as it was, enough of my own baggage. I felt laden enough. Nor had I yet stopped travelling.

IT CAN'T HAVE been long after this exchange that I arrived at the next milestone, for I remember still basking in the relief of having managed, however guardedly, to unburden myself to somebody. I'd been bottled up for years, fermenting under cover, and though I wasn't to recognize this fact until the pressure had actually been alleviated, the tension within me had, I realize now, grown all but uncontainable, come close to nervous catastrophe. But at last, as agreed with my new confidant, Mr. Wolfe became prehistory, and was consigned to my puerile beginnings, never again to warrant allusion. I felt grateful.

My teas with Dr. Fox endured, of course, but they remained my private business, not fodder for intrigue; and though Clifford must have found it all a trial (torn as he doubtless was between loyalty to me and loyalty to his injured musical pride), he nevertheless proved true to his word. My friend was a brick; my luck was looking up. I felt, in every way, better equipped to handle my new life—lighter, stronger, saner, older, steadier without the clutter of those dirty secrets which had for so long clogged up, and weighed down, one side of my brain, the side where my spirit was housed. I found that having banished the constant interruptions with which the malevolent voice of my conscience had earlier tormented me, I could now concentrate for longer intervals, study more determinedly. And I also found that since I spent all my free time with my constant companion, my former sense of loneliness had been swept away, and with it, too, my converse dread of the public: before the godsend of Clifford, I had found the threat of crowds— marauding gangs and swaggering teams of sportsmen—just as daunting as the hollows of Coventry; but now that I was supported, now that we were a united front, everything felt different, almost exciting.

We were, by and large, disinclined to provoke others, although, admittedly, there figured exceptions to this tendency (such as spotty old Newton, whose relentless baiting, now that he'd shrivelled into scholastic insignificance, we obviously regarded a matter of principle; or Hardy, whose retractions and emissions now seemed less like a cause for wonderment than a pretext for loud hilarity); but we tended, in the main, to derive a tarter relish from bitching among ourselves in our own lingo. And I say lingo because, with the growth of our friendship, so, too, our communication was to grow into a florid idiomatic hybrid—blooming with Spanish expletives pronounced in English, and trailing with unfathomable non-sequiturs which were code for other things—nurtured and refined, in part, to frustrate the eavesdropping band of Gibraltarians who hung around our fragrant double-headed shadow.

These simian louts, whom we had dubbed The Curse of Barbary, were thick as bricks, and filthy, and claimed, furthermore, to possess a smattering of Spanglish, an assertion which, much as we might have liked to, we couldn't entirely refute. Their sole contribution to the school, so far as we could see, apart from their fondness for wearing sunshades inside the building (in an attempt, presumably, to disguise their dilated pupils), was to peddle stinking hashish, which Clifford deemed both pricy and impure compared to the beautiful marijuana leaves of Brazil. But their personal drugginess tended, in any case, to earn its traffickers expulsion more swiftly than ever it did profit, for the reek that clung to their rags exceeded even the high fug of their patchouli, purchased in some Moroccan souk.

Still, though Clifford and I rarely bothered to assume the offensive, we could, as a pair under siege, prove daunting, provide our aggressors with a good run for their cheap money, especially if such aggressors came in the guise of guffawing rugger jocks, or as the united offspring of local industrialists—ugly bastards with spiky hair-dos and a penchant for slatterns at the village fish-'n-chip shop—or even, come to that, as latent (to us, blatant) other Queries. For by now, after all our verbal industry, our tongues had surpassed the merely dextrous, and grown toxic—especially Clifford's: mine certainly spat its poison with accuracy, but his managed also to cackle while delivering its sting, which was doled out more lavishly.

Knowing, in the dormitory, that he lay but a few cubicles away from me, within safe reach, I was, for once in my life, able to sleep, and did so soundly. And even if it were true that I still yabbered in the night, and that I yabbered in Spanish, and that I continued to jolt others out of their precious English dreams, which they insisted that I did, I told myself that should Clifford happen to figure among the awoken, and were he to overhear my (perhaps incriminating) outpourings, and to grasp their meaning, well, big deal. My involuntary revelations were safe with him: he was, oh, he was better than a brother to me. He was, I now see, my best sister.

WE WERE IN the final term of that most character-building of bodies, the Cadet Corps, which, as I said earlier, was compulsory for all in the second year: no exemptions. The CCF, as it was called, sought to instil in us boys, as well as the qualities of self-reliance and perseverance (with which we didn't really take issue) those of self-discipline and leadership, which we somehow doubted we'd be requiring in the future. Anyway, despite our fear that some official busybody might have attempted to frustrate our scheme, both Clifford and I managed, by some amazing fluke, to inveigle ourselves into the same platoon, which was the shooting contingent. Clifford should, on account of his imperfect vision, have been disqualified outright, but since the knowledge of his contact lenses was safely restricted to him and me, his deception went unnoticed; and thus the pair of us had swung into the armoury, pleased as punch at our good fortune. He was always lucky, and I, lucky with him.

We'd chosen this particular branch of the corps not just because— compared, say, to orienteering, or canoeing—it demanded minimal exertion, but also because, in wider terms, in terms of the world, we thought it likelier that we might, one day, find ourselves needing to watch our backsides in trigger-happy American cities than exploring the Amazon, or white-water rafting down the Grand Canyon. And we concluded that after becoming familiar with rifles (which, according to the commander in charge, we were not to call guns, because a gun is what he had between his legs, and if you didn't watch your step he'd damn well show it you) wielding a pistol should prove a cinch. I rather fancied the idea of a nifty muff gun with a mother-of-pearl handle, which I could secrete about my person in much the same way as Clifford secreted his hip flask; I might even, since my army beret passed muster, don one for the part—more viciously slanted, of course, in the manner of a gangster's bit of fluff. But Clifford claimed that, as regarded weapons, he'd be looking for something more on the butch side, closer to a revolver—to complement the fedora on which, in those days, he had set his heart. He'd recently seen *The Godfather* and, as a consequence, I imagine, been inspired by thoughts of the Mafia; but when I expressed doubts about his chances, and suggested that Queries might not be welcomed by Cosa Nostra, he said why did I always have to go and wreck everything. I didn't, I argued; but why couldn't we just run off somewhere like Chicago, and open a glamorous Forties-style cocktail bar? Couldn't we just do that, without the danger of shoot-outs? Well, he softened, even if we did, he'd still be wanting his fedora.

THE CCF USED to convene—perhaps still does—on Thursday afternoons. However well or direly we might later happen to fare at the indoor shooting range (lying bum up on a sandbag—a posture which, though Clifford didn't seem to mind, struck me as undignified), the proceedings always kicked off with a parade—an excuse, in effect, for grown men to bark like retards, and for schoolboy corporals to admire themselves in our toecaps. Clifford and I had, by that summer, resigned ourselves to two minor tragedies: not being able to swing our hips as we marched, and being placed, week in, week out, on a charge. A charge was an enfeebled relative of a court martial—a lesser sanction, akin to being dealt penalty points for speeding rather than losing your licence entirely. And the reason for our regular punishment was that neither of us could bear the itchy roughness of the regulation shirts which cadets were prescribed, items thick as blankets dating back to World War I, and which, for all that we knew, had been dragged off the backs of corpses in the pestilent trenches of France.

To combat what, beyond obvious revulsion, amounted to an allergy (for without corrective underclothing we both flared up in a rash), he and I—with Matron's permission, which, in the event, turned out to hold no sway whatever—would slip white cotton T-shirts beneath our rebarbative khakis. But this forbidden measure of protection was detected, with early efficiency, by one of the corporals, the son of an Old Boy (the latter, a contemporary of my father's, as ill-luck would have it), who called us a couple of weedy pansies. He was, notwithstanding this observation, friendly with Payne Senior.

Although in the sixth form—and so, one would have thought, less preoccupied with the pleasures of kicking juniors about than with the imminence of end-of-school exams—this corporal was, as well as a smug little moron (geography, geology, religious studies), a virtual midget. Though Clifford and I were only of average—as yet nowhere near full—height, he was obliged to stand on tippy-toe in order to peer inside our collars. And he would carry his shiny leather baton like a woman clutching her evening bag, hard under the elbow—unless, that is, he happened to be raising it, in which case, the baton became a sceptre, the better to prod around our crudely woven ties. He was nominally a Scot, for his surname came afflicted with a Mc, or perhaps it was a Mac, but his family (though relegated by now to some unremarkable suburb of London alas) had, for centuries past, lived in Argentina. I don't think that Clifford's South American passport exactly aided our plight.

The midget corporal's colonial ancestors had been In Cattle. I knew this from my father, who, despite my complaints, found even the unintentional mention of one of his old pals heartwarming. Whenever I spat out that surname, the Mc or Mac, my father's eyes would glaze and gloss over, swim with nostalgia. But it puzzled me to think how this hallowed family, despite the limitless quantities of beef which it must, for all those generations, have been shovelling down, could continue to produce descendants so conspicuously undersized. I said as much. My father told me not to talk balderdash: diet bore no relation to genetic make-up: had I learnt nothing in biology class? And anyway, he added, I was hardly myself Johnny Weissmuller. Thank God for that, my mother piped up. She thought the actor a fright. Man shaved his legs and chest, I ask you.

Although there had followed, from the moment that our T-shirts were discovered, the bore of a weekly penalty, we didn't care. We were prepared to suffer for our epidermis, never mind our principles; and besides, we were always punished together, and unimaginatively, so that, if anything, the act of polishing boots or brass buckles or buttons for some fat-arsed army man, while pretending to be a couple of maids in a Genet drama, increased our sense of solidarity. Charges didn't daunt us. What was, however, to land me in trouble, was the fact that, on one particular Thursday, after we'd completed our regular penance (sweeping the armoury had, I think, been the chore on that occasion), and just as we were dusting ourselves down to flounce out—Clifford to tea, assuming he still had time; I, to Dr. Fox, who'd summoned me—the Major, for reasons unknown, was moved to wolf-whistle at us. Nor do I know what possessed me next, but I remember that before I could stopper my gob, I was laughing back across the room, and shouting: I shouldn't whistle like that, Sir, or we might have to tell your wife. Which did it: Clifford was dispatched (promising me, in a burst of whispered loyalty, to get word to Dr. Fox, notifying him of my plight), while I was forced to stay behind for the infliction of some further irrelevant penalty—which must have lasted hours, because by the time I'd bathed and changed, the bell for evening prep had already rung, so it was only after it, at suppertime, that I was able to reach Dr. Fox and all the treats he had in store for me: a casual tumble in the alcove, natu-rally; a light supper of salad and pâté, smuggled up from the staff din-ing room; and then, as a consolation prize for my altercation with the commander, a film on television, the viewing of which, said Dr. Fox, was prescribed; for when the picture, as he called it, had first been screened at the cinema, the reviews had, he recalled, been staggering. What's more, he added, the subject matter was bound to be, well, of interest to me. And thus we sat down: he, on the wingèd chesterfield; I, on the burgundy sofa—both of which had been swung round the room for the occasion.

IT CAME IN WAVES, the film—slow ones, laden with intensity—cere-bral, quietly hysterical, and largely devoid of dialogue; just softly focused glances over bowls of hydrangeas, and glints, and little shivers of repugnance. Great open spaces. Dead sea, not a ripple.

The prescribed viewing was based on a novella, written early in the century—a couple of years, I surmised, before our cadet clothes were being salvaged from the trenches—and turned out to be a sumptuous, morbid tale about some fidgety middle-aged German, a writer, who, laid low by neurasthenia, is advised by his physician to travel for the purposes of recovery to Venice in late May, but who, far from being restored to health, contracts, as well as a feverish obsession (a crush or pash) for a pubertal male at his hotel near the Lido, Asiatic cholera, for God's sake; with the result that by the time you get to the end, well, it's all a bit of a swizz really, because you can't tell why the Querie, slumped on a deckchair, stuffed into a suit of rumpled linen, and with rivulets of hair-dye streaming down his face, has actually collapsed: whether from a properly broken heart, or from the plague—malaise or malady.

Swathed in great repeating segments of dismal minor-key move-ments from the (then) little-known symphonies of a Moravian composer who went over to Rome, both the film and its lugubrious soundtrack were soon thereafter to be elevated to the status of a cult, and adopted with messianic fervour by melancholy inverts everywhere, men quite old enough to know worse, plus the odd like-minded woman—or rather, intelligent lady. The film assumed, at the time of my youth, a hefty cultural import, even if people like my father were never to be brought round. But I knew none of these things as I sat, knees clamped, on my seat at the end of that testing day, waiting, if not actually to be entertained (for I had a feeling that entertainment didn't figure in the equation) at least to be educated.

I seem to be staring at all the wrong things, like the women. The boy is bizarre, almost freakish: outsize head, stunted legs, amateur make-up, highlights like the shopgirls in the village. I mean to say: how many Poles of fourteen do you know with streaks of ash-blonde whooshing through their hair? But the mother, look at her, she sends shivers down the spine. Beyond a register of whispers that suggests less Polish than Italian, she appears to possess only the strength to utter one sad, single word, something like Tadjú—Tadjú!, Tadjú!, she calls, in an attempt to earn her son's attention. She reminds me—oddly, given that she drifts about in period costume—of my own forgetful mother. The eagle nose, the gliding walk, the throwaway vanity, the whole otherworldly consummate over-weening foreignness of the woman: these things they have in common, the mother of Tadjú and mine. And despite the fact that mine glimmers with sultry gloss in my recollection, the pow-dered pallor of the mother on screen is no more, no less than the pallor favoured by the people of our island in the days when my grandparents were alive, so that the throwback, the fictive suspension, feels simple: since my mother could, once, have been, so she becomes the woman in the film: too lovely to be true, too miserable, as good as husbandless, perfectly cast for whimpering tragedy. Her son, the wretched boy, will, to be sure, one day provide it. But I am elsewhere for a while, overtaken by asides. The film drones on and on. Sailor collar, swimsuit, indigo doublet; pearls, heavy with teardrops, chokers of diamonds; dabby-dabby napkins; knives, clinking and flashing; an (upset) glass: a spilt lagoon of wine; grey sand, grey sky, grey water. Who the hell, in their right mind, would wish to visit such a place? Venice is moribund, or a morgue.

The sound of drowning; the sense of sinking in cold music; monstrous, strangulated chords sailing out, forever and ever. Now the Querie wants to vanquish his affliction, takes himself to be restored. He minces off to a posh *barbiere* who behaves like a complete smoothie-chops and would make a brilliant madam in a Spaghetti Western, and lets him pour a bottle of ink over his head—*arrivederci* to all that *grigio*—and trim his bushy moustache into a joke, like that of the grease-pot in *Cabaret*—*Willkommen, Bienvenue,* Welcome—and daub his pinched little mouth with crimson lippy, like Payne Senior, and smear his cheeks with too much rouge, and, look, behold, the Tragic Fairie beams at last, quite recovered, and gets up, patting his bosom with his puffy hand, which wears a cornelian that reminds me of Dr. Fox.

And then I turn to glance at him, but the vision chills me, for the imperturbable countenance of our director of music is, can you believe, stricken with tears: not like those of Mr. Wolfe, which were the tears of a secret love, nor those of my father, which were the tears of a lost boy, but with the tears of the girl with fleshy rosebud lips whom I suspected from the first moment; and I have to look elsewhere. Back in the film, the boy, the boy, the boy is running and laughing along the drabness of the ocean, and rolling on the sand and cavorting and falling until Bang: I grasp the irony—which is that I too have fallen, though not in a film. I have fallen for a heavy deception. His, the boy's, is another story, full of ignorance and wile and false hope. But I am educated now, apprised, committed suddenly to my own memory—in one deft go, at a stroke. For the youth on the boring beach is identical to, therefore becomes, someone further up the school, a streaky-haired confident blond with a ramrod walk and a smile that could charm the very gods, called Albany; and in some manner that I cannot comprehend, though I feel it absolutely—I know it despite not knowing—it becomes clearer to me than any translucent Venetian sky that Albany, who hasn't needed to twitch a muscle for the distinction, much less toil on my mentor's bishop, has nonetheless conquered and made off with (but ignored) the sobbing heart of pathetic Dr. Fox. Mine, I now see, has all along been another purpose; mine, duties ancillary. Outlet patients are my cause. The nature of my care is palliative; my function, merely to assist with the cooling of blood—even if, in the glassy opinion of my host, I lack the vintage. Neither blond nor strong-limbed am I, still less a ramrod walker. But my head, notwithstanding such flaws, is fixed at last. No love lost. Not one iota. And I decide, there and then, thanks to the borrowed strength of my belovèd Clifford, thanks to the lightness which he has brought to my soul, thanks, even, to the shock of my role in this brocaded hell-hole—my part in the whole absurdity, which can only be the part of the absurd cheated prostitute—that never again shall I bed with Dr. Fox. Not ever. Never more. Keep your creamy cakes and yummy scones: not even for a bursting sack of ancient gold. And I rise as the credits begin to float; I rise more slowly and assuredly than the reputedly staggering notices. And I notice, in my departing, that the boy is not called Tadjú after all, but Tadzio, and I think that it must have been Iago that my mother meant, and not *Adiós,* and I leave without a word of explanation, unlocking the door as if it were my own, and I see myself out for myself, and find myself released into the throbbing fifth-year corridor without a hint of shame any more, without a care in the underworld, because from this dark day, from this night on, no, there will be no further secrets, nor sessions, nor foul exudations. I have turned a great heavy leaf, not just a corner, and Dr. Fox had better start auditioning for my successor. And besides, in two weeks we go home.

ACTUALLY, WE DIDN'T. First we went to army camp—though not, of course, Clifford: he, the child of fortune, managed to get himself let off—because his flight back to Ecuador, booked months in advance (his mother had written), ruled out any question of extra-curricular activities for my friend beyond the date when term, as decreed by the school calendar, came to an official close. Greatest apologies. Sincerely yours, Amaranta Rodríguez de Cross. Clifford had shown me the photocopy. That, and not the niceties of small-bore, is, I remember thinking, what I call proper ammunition. My father, by tough contrast, said he'd never heard such piffle, and would on no account (or so he claimed) be a party to collusion. My pal, as he called him, was a spoilt brat, and obviously able to twist his mother round his little finger; but in the long run, my father banged on, Clifford's parents were doing the boy no favours by indulging his every whim. Rules were rules, and camp was for one's own good—it would make a man of me—so I was to get a grip, did I hear, and stop pestering him. Plenty of time to laze about in the summer. He was, by his own admission, a lost cause.

I shall ignore, needless to say, details of those army manoeuvres in Wales, performed on a site still drearier, if such a thing can be conceived, than the moors of northern England, or, indeed, the battlefield of Waterloo—ignore, that is, all save the fact that I was unable to play my violin in the run-up to a charity concert due to be given the day after camp by the school orchestra at Westminster Cathedral. My inability to practise worried me, not just out of musical vanity (for I had a slightly exposed, hurtling solo to engineer), but also because I didn't want to give vent, by performing below par, to the spleen of Dr. Fox, who was to be conducting—clad in a frock-coat from Savile Row, naturally. I couldn't afford, after my recent recoil from his charms, further to upset the delicate imbalance: he'd come down on me with a vengeance, with his full weight from his great directorial height.

Just as earlier in the year I'd felt trapped between Clifford and the director of music, now, at its end, I felt trapped between the director of music and, surprisingly enough, my father, for Dr. Fox's opinion was that by forcing me to go to camp, the Old Boy was showing himself to be both a philistine and a fool. All the wrong priorities. Who cared about the blasted army? What did the man expect me to become, some brigadier? Much as, inwardly, I might have agreed with these comments, I nonetheless found them irksome, perhaps because I felt, in some ludicrous way, that the criticism filtered down to me through my bad blood, which was thick. That my father (my mentor persisted) should be a dullard was only to be expected—most former pupils were—but what Dr. Fox could not comprehend was why I hadn't managed to persuade my mother to do something to prevent the inanity of army camp when I had a concert for which to prepare, and when, judging from my comments, she was a woman of discernment. And I suppose it was this last elaboration which, even if supportive, even if well-intended, needled me the most—his meddlesome criticism of my mother—for I felt that Dr. Fox was no more entitled to bitch about her than I was in a position, then, to bitch about him.

The sole mitigation of camp proved to be the phoney camaraderie of sitting among real-life squaddies in the Formica canteen, which reeked of fry-ups and beer—sulking, and, for the first time, smoking overtly, and drinking (without tequila to comfort me) gin, like some deserted sweetheart in a wartime movie. The song of the moment, which was played on the jukebox constantly, and which, despite conflicting with the period of the film in which I visualized myself appearing, became a sort of anthem for that futile week, was a heavy great number by some new glam-rock band, in which a stubborn long-haired youth, a curly-haired angel of the pop charts, insists, in a ragged, deadpan voice, that, no matter if fools say we can't win, he knows he's gonna fall in love again, but seeing as we've still got a chance, maybe, of love and sweet romance, won't I Roll Away The Stone. I felt so gloomy without Clifford, so bored with my own company, that I became perversely addicted to that raucous melody; and the upshot was that by my final day in the bosom of the British army, I felt readier to roll away the stone than the three Marys in the gospels.

A COUPLE OF SUMMERS LATER, I was to be confronted—in circumstances which, since I hadn't been given a word of warning, were to leave me all but winded—with the possibility of a second taste of the military: for it transpired that, on account of my dual nationality, I was about to be called up for conscription into the Spanish army, a fact which my father must have regarded as some sort of emancipation, for he insisted on calling it Becoming Legally Eligible. Preliminary papers and dates had already been delivered to our address, and yet the spectre of a second CCF (though ten times worse, for it involved—just as I was poised to apply for a place at university—further truncating my life by two years) struck me as so ludicrous that I could scarcely make it register. I remember clamming up when the subject was first raised, setting my jaw into a truculent clench similar to the one I'd adopted when I refused to be beaten by Mr. Wolfe, getting up from the lunch table, and taking myself off to sunbathe, to quake in silence beneath the blistering rays. My parents were starting to make me feel old. And to make matters worse, the swimming pool at home had been covered up, buried, to allow for terracotta tiles and a pergola.

I had discussed the problem of Spanish conscription with the careers tutor at school, who, though a stuttering, wimpy man, turned out to hold surprisingly spunky convictions. He described himself, for instance, as a devotee of García Lorca, whom I was studying at the time, and this devotion probably explained his eagerness to impress on me, first and foremost (over and above his hispanophilia, which was palpable), his disapproval of Franco; for he thought that even ignoring the horrors of civil war, the cultural damage wreaked by that dreadful dictator, that Nazi sympathizer, upon the nation of my birth was a scandal and a crime, and that no English person with a conscience should countenance living in that country. He also suggested that if my father was seeking, in view of my personality and general b-b-bent, to hamper my further education for fear of where knowledge might lead me, he was probably deranged—though this was strictly off the record. Never mind degree courses and choices of university: how could a man so besotted with the English system even think of allowing, let alone pressuring, his son to surrender to the laws of a fascist régime? Just didn't make sense to him. Incidentally, he threw in with an insurrective grin, he didn't suppose I'd considered drama school, had I?

The truth of the matter is that my father, incensed, I imagine, by his great school's correspondingly great failure to inculcate in me the virtues for which he had so fervently prayed, and in which he had so lavishly invested (sportsmanship, manliness, popularity, rectitude—the mere mention of which made me retch), determined, in despair, to subject me to corrective, as opposed to merely basic, discipline. Later, at the end of his tether, he would investigate the possibilities of electroconvulsive therapy, but in the meantime he merely sought a snare without psychological cachet, so as to teach me a good hard lesson. He threatened that if I refused to observe the laws of my native country— my *mother's* country, he couldn't resist stressing—the repercussions for me would be severe: I'd be unable, for fear of having my British passport confiscated, to set foot on Spanish soil between the ages of eigh-teen and twenty-five. Seven whole years, he pointed out. (Actually, it would have been six, but never mind.) Did I understand? No: I couldn't even conceive of the man. And my mother, the while, said nothing—not having been, she later claimed, in a position to comment. Her lip-stick was darker than blood.

That evening, I reiterated my intention to go to university. What!, he bellowed, To read *Lyan*guiges! He didn't call *that* going to university, called it an excuse to twiddle your thumbs for four years. And don't imagine that he didn't know what undergraduates got up to these days: he'd read all about it in the English papers (by which he meant his *Tele-graph,* always two days late). The varsities, he pronounced, were dens of iniquity, full of druggies and hippies, dropouts with delusions of bril-liance. And why, if I was so determined to continue studying, couldn't I read a serious subject anyway, like the law, or med'cine? Or, better still, scrap this whole further education lark and just Get-A-Pro-Per-Job when the time came, join an influential City firm, learn about f'nance sort of thing, stocks and shares, mmh? What was the bally use of a degree in modern languages, for heaven's sake? So that I could become a teacher? A secretary? Or perhaps I harboured hopes of becoming an air-steward. He despaired, he said. *He* despaired. And then he reiter-ated the word: Army. And then he added: my lad.

Although the careers tutor had primed me for this next scene, no amount of rehearsing could have prepared me for the terror which, when the moment to perform befell me, battered my chest. This, I sud-denly realized, was more momentous than any play, because trapped on my parents' real-life stage, without prompt or curtain or distance to protect me, I couldn't forget myself. And the reality of that first con-frontation with my owners—my puny desperation pitted against their front of armoured union, felt entirely other than the reality which I'd been expecting: colder despite the blazing summer, slower despite my unbridled nerves. My intention (my instruction) had been to seem con-ciliatory, to appear reasonable in an attempt to show them sense. I had been warned, above all things, to be adult, not petulant. Firm, and full of wisdom. I must suppress all rage, and hate, and the other toxins which infected my veins—even indifference. There was nothing to fear, I had been told: for, just as they had faith on their side, so I had justice. But in the event, because I knew that my countenance must remain that of an assured grown-up, even while my innards wanted to wail like an infant, all confidence seemed to desert me, and I found, to begin with, that all I could muster were the motions of an argument, not the words. I remember setting my napkin down with great deliberateness, as if this action settled something, then smuggling my shaking hand beneath the table. Next, I remember how my head seemed to sway moronically, to swivel this way and that in an attempt to decide which of them to address, my father whom I could hardly bear to look at, or my mother whom I couldn't bear to hurt. And in the end, I think that I must have spoken into thin air, for I recall neither of their faces in the cameo. My speech, when it leaked out, must have had the charm of skidmarks on the pants of a cadet, a dead one. My syllables were cold and colourless, and what I said, even if right in content, was wrong in tone: priggish and foolish and harsh. I cannot speak, I began, to either of you on this subject, but I want you to understand that unless you resolve this preposterous state of affairs by whatever means you consider necessary you should give up any notion of my returning to your house until I'm twenty-five. (And then, after a new intake of breath, I added:) If ever. And then I stood up and left the dining room. I had finished my pudding.

My mother and I did not revert to the subject of conscription during the remainder of that holiday, but the following autumn, at half term, my father duly flew to London and took me—his face like thunder—to the Spanish Consulate, where he did his damnedest to disown me in the waiting room. An empty chair was left to preside between us, like the invisible mausoleum of some other family. And when we were finally summoned to the consular office, he strode in without a word, and, of course, without me—so that he could present the more sensitive points of his case, the shaming unnatural reason why I wasn't really cut out for the military—Spanish or otherwise—in private: gent to gent, man to man, father to red-faced father. I had a good flick through the latest *Vogue,* browsed through a not very exciting *Harper's,* and then, at last, the pair of them emerged, my father and the good Consul— puffing cigars and practically slapping each other's backs—to inform me, after the Consul's pointedly virile handshake, that an indefinite deferment of my enlistment had, in the circumstances, been granted. I could have curtsied. We left together, my pater and I, but I declined to have lunch with him at his club. His job was done. I tore off my school tie. (But all of this happened later, two summers after English army camp.)

IT MUST HAVE been the film about the Polish blondyboy with the short-arse, and the Querie who fell ill in Venice, and their combined truckloads of make-up, because, after CCF camp, I went to my guardians' house and, while preparing to go to the cathedral—to play in the concert for which I'd been unable to practise—I treated myself to a good rummage in the bathroom cabinet, found a pile of slap, and set to work on my face, trying to transform it into a symphony of melancholy. I needed to look worn out, so as to mitigate my lack of preparation and elicit a droplet of indulgence from our volatile conductor. I'm sure that if I were shown a snap of the result now, I would dismiss my first attempt at cosmetic artifice as the daubings of a pitiful novice; but at the time, I was amazed by the rings of darkness which, simply by means of the wrong foundation and flecks of somebody else's liner, all smudged up, could be engendered under one's eyes. Then I dealt myself an emaciated set of cheekbones, by smearing charcoal shadow along the line that ran from my nose to the hinge of my mandible, and rubbing it in hard; and finally, I powdered lightly above the edge where I had sucked, so that by the time that was done, I looked like I'd come out of a concentration camp. The effect must have worked like a charm in the gloomy light of the sacred site, for no one in the orchestra addressed a single word to me, and Dr. Fox (despite my rusty playing) smiled with a fond indulgence, as if trying, after my ordeal in the land of the dragon, to lend me sustenance, to revive me. And I understood then that having walked out of his bedroom was the wisest thing I'd ever done, for the tables of power had suddenly been turned, and turned forever, and now I was sitting in a chair far more elevated than any wingèd chesterfield, on a throne closer to the floral carvers of my first birthdays. Because, from this point on, it would be he who needed to keep *me* happy. His responsibility had suddenly become not his pleasures, but preserving me from danger, from the danger of blabbing in his aftermath. I felt triumphant, as if I'd performed better than a virtuoso; and yet, regardless, it all came to an end in silence, for, given that we were in a cathedral, there was no chance of a good clap. Much grander, Dr. Fox would have said. More eloquent, more dignified. *Avanti!*

CONTRARY TO WHAT my father had led me to imagine, I was not, in the summer straight after CCF camp, to be granted much time to laze about, because by then, he and my mother wanted me kept thoroughly occupied—devil, work, idle hands. To this end they had organized, in advance of my return to their island, that I give English tuition, one-to-one, to various of their friends (perhaps in the hope of impressing them), and to some of their friends' daughters (in the hope, presumably, of impressing me). It didn't do the trick; it was all dead dreary; but I did earn a bit of grace at home, and some decent pocket money, for I pitched my fees good and high: that, I told my mother, was my proviso for submitting to the whole plan. She, when she first heard the sum which I had in mind, had been scandalized by my cupidity: I couldn't possibly charge such amounts; but in the end we managed to arrive at a compromise, and it was this: that whatever I earned from my pupils (and she suggested half of what I was threatening to demand, which would have embarrassed her), she would double, on condition—her proviso now—that I not tell my father. I thought I might manage that.

Apart from a girl with a harelip and a great constellation of acne, who contracted a crush or pash for me but was doomed to flounder, less in my regard (for she was sweet-natured enough) than before her board of re-examiners (who couldn't have cared less about natures), the only other pupil worth mentioning was a middle-aged notary, verging on handsome, rolling in money, and eager to master English for professional purposes: he hoped, he said, to expand his practice within Europe. He was a bachelor—a predicament which, according to my mother, simply meant that he hadn't found the right girl to marry, because, you see (she explained to me before I met him), poor chap had spent his whole youth studying—to the detriment of his sociability, she emphasized—so that now, successful as he was, and he was hugely so, he was also withdrawn, and shy in the company of women, fearing that every potential wife was a potential gold-digger. Pity, really, but there you were. Charming man.

I, however, was to discover otherwise: my parents, inadvertently, almost hilariously, had set me up. But by now, aged fifteen, I felt like a dab hand at unwelcome advances, and managed to sail through those hours of tuition smoothly as a gondola. Wherever the notary sat, I always sat opposite, ensuring that I kept the oars that were my legs tucked beneath my chair, that kind of stuff. And in this spiteful way of mine, he found himself relegated to the rôle of distant observer, like the drooling Querie who got cholera, while I held back, like the captivating Polish short-arse. Still, at least I was getting paid for my distance—and, by the notary specially, for, on the back of my initial hunch, I was prompted, when we came to discuss the horny subject of my rate per hour, to charge him extra. Services unrendered. My mother was never to find out.

I received two postcards, about a month apart, from Clifford that summer. The first came stamped from Guayaquil, which, he said, he was finding boring. He was off to visit his father. The second, in early September, told me, hastily, that he was adoring Chicago and dreaded having to return to school in England. Meanwhile, I presumed that my own letters, posted to Ecuador, were piling up at his mother's house, because I somehow doubted that the bereft Amaranta would feel inclined to forward her son's mail to her errant husband's new whereabouts. It hardly mattered: because suddenly, October was upon me.

I DIDN'T BOTHER, on the train back north, to bag a seat for Clifford: I knew that he was catching a connecting flight from Gatwick up to Manchester, from where he'd be driven to school by taxi—typical Clifford, lucky to the last. But my own trip, for once, passed in a flash: I had so many things to tell him (about the Querie notary and the girl with the harelip and my immoral earnings; about my new gadgets—though not a moped, worst luck—and the recent songs that I'd discovered; about the tedium of army camp; about the miracle of make-up; about my minuscule white swimming trunks; about my arguments with my father; about rolling away the stone and the dream of love . . .) that I spent the journey trying to juggle my news into some sort of order, and wondering whether to regale him chronologically or in a more considered jumble, so as to elicit greater laughs. And thus it was that, only once the bus had dumped us at the school's front quadrangle and I'd staggered up a spiral stair of stone to the third-year sleeping quarters—spread over two floors of an overbearing Victorian wing which had been abutted to a flank of the original Elizabethan house—I began to look for Clifford in earnest.

The new academic year heralded, along with other supposed privileges, an end to cubicles. To me, however, this felt like a distinct reversal, a return to enforced exposure, but communal sleeping arrangements were regarded by the powers that be as character-forming: one had to learn to get along with people, to be mature about it. Clifford and I—to limit the perils of group habitation—had requested (which was allowed, lots of people did it) to be kept in the same hutch; but when I scoured the noticeboard on the first landing, though I discovered my own name fast enough, and the name of my dorm (Leviticus), Clifford didn't seem to figure among its occupants. God those priests were spiteful. And because I suddenly found myself ambushed by a scrum of louts, shoving and jostling for a look-in, and telling me to get lost, I decided not to persist with the search for my friend's whereabouts, but instead, to try to beat the rush and grab myself a decent bed by a window. I'd get hold of Clifford later, I reasoned, after I'd sorted myself out and unpacked enough junk to stake a claim on my new territory. And once I'd tracked him down, we could put our heads together and hatch a plan: decide which of our respective dorms we preferred, bribe someone in there to volunteer to swap with whichever of us was wanting to shift, and drag our victim with us to the new year master (a complete madman, as sinister as he was violent—Clifford and I would probably need a preparatory glug of tequila) in order to request the transfer. But with Clifford beside me, it would all be sorted out. Bound to be some administrative oversight, I was certain.

The oversight, as always, was mine. After I'd unpacked (but nowhere near a window, for all the best beds had been snapped up by people who'd come by car, early arrivals), I headed out of the dormitory, back towards the noticeboard, and caught a glimpse in the distance of the rector (whom Clifford had so memorably ridiculed at our first meeting, exactly a year earlier). The priest was busy exchanging greetings with a bunch of sporting paragons, but as I drew closer, he suddenly cut short his banter, dug his hands into his pockets, and made a bee-line towards me—not to welcome me back, but to say, in a slightly unnerving tone—absolutely flat—that he'd like to see me in his office straight after evening prayers. I remember his hairy Adam's apple bouncing up and down. It made me want to swallow.

Dry hot needles began to shoot down my arteries. I could tell that I was blushing, yet I couldn't fathom why. Had somebody died? Had I done something at CCF camp? Had my make-up been noticed in the Cathedral? I pretended that nothing was happening and went on looking for Clifford on the board, but I couldn't concentrate on the lists that were staring back at me; my eyes, instead of scouring the print, just swam about. My head was clogged up. I would call on Dr. Fox. No, I'd go down to the music basement. No, I'd go back to the dorm in case, by now, Clifford was searching for me. I finished my unpacking in a trance, disconnected from my actions. Still no sign of Clifford. Plane must have been delayed. Perfect.

My bed was behind the door, but placed along a wall, like a divan, so that it felt slightly sheltered. I was nearest to the basin, which was a bonus: I would colonize it. The rest of the boys in Leviticus were bearable, nobody too gruesome: a couple of harmless weirdos—second-rate scientists; a couple of Mr. Populars (one, a cricketing star and regular chess champion; the other, a burgeoning dropout—the son of a very young admiral—grubbily handsome, and handsomely endowed, I seem to remember); me, of course, against the back wall; and then, to my right, was Marcus Steel—Steel, as he was simply known.

Even though, ever since prep school, we'd been in the same class, I knew him only slightly. I'd tended to avoid him in the past—perhaps because all those years back, when I could scarcely speak English, he'd been the one to tell Mr. Wolfe that people called me Woman. Kind of boy who enjoyed embarrassing you, bit of a sneak, bit of a loudmouth; but I'd almost forgotten those things about him. Slightly later, he'd figured among the clique of war-gaming fanatics with whom I'd travelled on the minibus to Waterloo and, during that trip, he'd seemed both to resent and be riveted by my exchanges with the Countess, because, although he was blessed with a skewering intelligence, his professed contempt for all things foreign (instilled, I suspect, by his parents—provincial doctors both) had dissuaded him from stooping to speak any foreign language. This seemed odd to me, given that he was an aspiring historian, and academically thorough; but he would have argued that he was on the side of good old Wellington, remember, not of Napoleon; and anyway, everyone spoke English, old chap: British Empire and all that. Yet his sudden nervous glimpse, first-hand, of a world beyond the Union Jack and Rule Britannia, and of my apparent ease in that other realm which he called Wogland, had made him sit up. He had seemed to eavesdrop, then, even on conversations which he could not hope to understand, to be taking note, to be wanting to learn fast, as if hoping to make up for wasted chances. He was, as I say, exceedingly bright, and, like all bright historians, a strategist at heart: eyes like a hawk, didn't miss a trick, always up to something. And yet, for all his brilliance in the classroom, he was (to his annoyance, I think) tone-deaf, without musical hope—which is why, of late, between my stints in the basement and the great garlands of time which I had spent in Clifford's company, Steel and I hadn't had very much contact.

By the third year, as I watched him unpack, he seemed altered almost beyond recognition. Though he'd always veered towards the lanky, Steel had, during the last months, and more markedly over the summer, suddenly sprouted to a shrill height, way over six foot, which I think embarrassed him, because, as if to counter this conspicuousness, he had grown subdued, toned himself down, and learnt to walk with a slight stoop, torso hunched like a saluki on the point of voiding its bowels. His clever head appeared, as a result of this sudden rise, now shrunken, to nestle like some forgotten collector's piece above the sloping shelf of his shoulder-line. His legs, meanwhile, went on for miles—you could only encompass them by means of a wide-angled glance—but they were brittle at the ankle, and clumsy. He was forever tripping up, and bumping into things, and going blast and buggeration. It was as if, in the throes of such a dramatic physical alteration, he were having to retrain himself to inhabit his new, stretched carapace. But then, we were all changing, having to adjust.

How was I?, he suddenly asked. Fine, I replied (a bit taken aback). Enjoy your summer? Sort of, I s'pose. Oh well, he went on, Mine was great; went to Scotland; lousy to be back, but I say, a relief to be in the same dorm as somebody civilized, we're thin on the ground, us chaps. I was so cheaply heartened in those days, so desperately grateful, that it shames me now to recollect the pleasure brought to me by that remark.

And I also remember thinking, as a result of it, that, if worst came to worst, and Clifford and I were doomed to be kept apart, Steel, though I doubted that he'd ever be my friend, might, at least, become an ally. We could respect one another.

If Clifford was my alter-ego, Steel was really my antithesis. Apart from his stature, which far exceeded mine, he was the palest creature imaginable. Grey veins, like winter boughs, branched out along his temples, and he had very fair hair—straight, and on the greasy side, cut almost in a bob, then swept back like a curtain—which often fell in a deep, diagonal fringe over his eyes. These, his eyes, were like pale blue marbles, heavily lidded and narrow, virtually feline, and would become shot with blood if he went anywhere near water. His nose, though fine, turned purple at the nostrils if he caught the slightest suggestion of a cold—a frequent occurrence, for there was a skinny unhealthiness about him. Perhaps he was anaemic: certainly his parents, the general practitioners, were forever plying him with fizzy vitamins. His ears protruded somewhat, and were transparent in the light, rife with tiny red vessels, like the egg yolks of my childhood. Long, abnormally long lobes, like those of an old woman.

I had often, in the past, sat at a desk behind him in class. His hands, as he wrote, were skeletal, with salient joints and knuckles, and when he answered questions, he spoke with his fingers splayed out, for emphasis. He treated our teachers like retards, and was not always mistaken in doing so. Steel's fingernails were square and soft and moonless; they looked almost gelatinous. You felt that you could have peeled them back and blown into their quicks without causing discomfort. But his most pronounced feature was, without a doubt, his mouth: this eclipsed all else about him, for his lips were vast and wide and shapeless, less sensual than anatomically curious, as if they'd been rolled over and stitched down, raw red lengths of blubber. They were grotesque, and had earned him, around the time when I was a Woman, the sobriquet Rubber Lips; but you tended to avert your eyes from the sight, not just because he was sensitive on the subject, and liable to lash out, but because there was something embarrassing, abhorrent, about that mouth. It made him look naked, worse than naked; more as if, were you to continue staring, the rest of his body might be pulled through the ever-expanding orifice and turned inside out.

He was the youngest in a triumvirate of brothers—all three, by accounts, fantastically clever, and all (doubtless as a result of medical prudence, rather than God-trusting *que será*) conceived at organized five year intervals. The eldest, a reputed prodigy, had already come down with a congratulated First from Oxford, where he had read history at New College. The second was up there currently, reading the same subject at the same place. But Steel, my one, though also destined to study history, planned to go (as indeed he would) to Magdalen—being, he said, above such trifles as nepotism. He would, in point of fact, eventually win a top scholarship to the college of his choice, though already, three years in advance of those entrance exams, our school had his academic laurels in mind. Steel was good news for my father's Alma Mater.

Despite his avowed contempt for inherited privilege, he, or his parents perhaps, had requested that he be furnished with the same school number as his eldest brother, which, astonishingly for a religious hothouse—but perhaps not, perhaps it added fuel to the sacred fire—was 666. Steel seemed to be proud of this numerical sequence, and not merely because it represented the sum-total of the roulette table. But I was myself too ignorant then of the Book of Revelation to see beyond the sexy catchiness of that trio, or to understand the demonic significance at the root of six hundred threescore and six, the Number of the Beast. Yet I suppose that, in a sense, he was suited to it, because, in the showers, I had observed (as you couldn't fail to do) that he was singled out, marked, by a concave thorax. You could have inserted your fist, firmly clenched and without difficulty, into the central cavity that hovered above his sternum, between his ribs and clavicle; and although this deformity used to make people grimace with squeamishness, they, he said, were stupid idiots, because his brother, the former owner of the significant number, had told him that in Greek mythology the feature of a hollowed breast spelt heartlessness, for which my future ally chose to read mental strength, courage. But anyway, just as Steel was above nepotism, so I tried to be above superstition. You had to be grown up about things. I mean, take another boy in our year, Curzon, who'd been born with webbed toes, but took—declaring that they attested to the purity of his lineage—an heraldic pride in them. We were all, I reminded myself, different, even though, whenever I saw the owner of those funny feet, I couldn't but think of the purity of the diced turtle-meat that went into my mother's Lady Curzon soup. It made me hungry just to think of it.

AFTER SUPPER THAT EVENING, I go to the rector's office. I knock on the door, hard and slowly, deliberately. He's expecting me, of course, and calls for me to come in. Blended wafts of incense and stale sweat envelop the room. He doesn't tell me to sit down, tells me instead that he'll come straight to the point, Moore, won't beat about the bush: Clifford (whom he calls Cross) has, he claims, been taken away by his parents to continue his studies in the States, has left. You're kidding, I blurt out. He corrects: I beg your pardon? I correct myself: Sorry, Father, I mean, I find that incredible. As, indeed, does he, he says, because the reason for my friend's abrupt departure, apart from his chronic homesickness (which comes as news to me), seems to be that according to his parents (which means according to Clifford), certain pupils at our school are known to, to be . . . *involved,* as it were, with certain teachers. (Thumping silence.) Do I understand what he means? Slowly I say that I think that I might do. (I must be puce.) Can I shed any light on my friend's extraordinary allegation? I'm afraid that I can't, Father, sorry. He says that somehow he didn't imagine that I would. (I want to murder Clifford.) Look here, the rector continues, his Adam's apple prodding at his dog-collar, I happen to be perfectly aware of your reputation at prep school, but I prefer to treat all that, your chequered history, as lying in the past. (You said it, Father: Lying in the past, that's me all over.) He continues: I do not know precisely what Cross meant when he told his parents of Involvements between boys and teachers, but I want you to understand, and categorically, that you have caused the school, and caused me personally, the greatest embarrassment, and should even the faintest wind confirming your friend's claim happen to reach me, you will, you have my word, be out on your ear. Do I make myself plain? Yes, Father. You'll be asked to leave. Yes, Father.

The rector says that he intends to investigate the matter further, fully, and that I'd be well advised, from this point on, to watch my step and tread exceedingly carefully. My academic potential, he snorts, is insignificant next to the school's Repute (re-*pute,* a double whore, I muse). And warming to his homily he adds that I'm starting to display, he regrets to say, all the hallmarks of degeneracy, that he suspects me of being a congenital invert, that I seem to lack any conception of the meaning of sin, like some squalid libertine. Morals of an alley cat, he throws in. He extracts a plastic pouch of workman's tobacco, along with a roll-up gadget (like those employed by The Curse of Barbary to enjoy hashish), and plonks his props in front of him; but, as he fumbles in search of cigarette papers, he looks away, wincing with disdain out of the window. And then, as if encouraging me, the amoral alley cat, to leap through some invisible pet flap into the garden, he quietly tells me to get out, vamoose.

CLOSE SHAVE, you might think, but leaving that room only increased my panic. I went over the interview, time and again, reliving it and perishing. I could scarcely bear to think of Clifford beyond the turmoil into which his defection now threw me. Never in my life had I encountered such perfidy. It defied belief, defied speech. Of course I understood his desire to break free—God knows I shared it. Of course I saw that he was entitled to remain in Chicago with his father and the society beauty—in the process besmirching, if he so pleased, his poor abandoned mother's white frills, and his sisters as they scowled in the torpid heat—the better to explore shops and naughty cinemas in his adopted new city, and to patronize glamorous cocktail bars, even without me, and hang all our plans and all my dreams. That was his own business, private. But *Why,* I howled inwardly, had he decided to drag my secrets into the open, to threaten my safety for the sake of his grubby scheme? Why had he chosen to take me hostage, to stab our friendship, to trample on our confidences as if they'd been mere dead leaves? He had turned what I most valued, the only strength that I possessed, and just as I was starting to flourish, squarely against me, without a thought for the consequences, for the mess in which his traducement would land me. Was Clifford really that selfish, that callous, that deceitful? How could it be? How could I've let myself be taken in? My spirit was in torment, and further taunted by the ever-turning wheel of the rector's generalities: what had he meant by those creepy plurals—teachers, pupils? Were there others apart from me? Had Clifford mentioned more than just Mr. Wolfe? Had he guessed about Dr. Fox's teas, or had he made up stories just to get himself removed? Was my sabotage really the price of my lost friend's liberty? And now, I asked myself, now what was I supposed to do? Wilt from the fear? Wither in solitude? Thank you, Clifford. I never got over it.

My reaction was, to begin with, muddled, for while my instinct cursed the very name of Clifford, and wished him dead—preferably shot through the mouth by a silver bullet from his own precious pistol, snatched from his treacherous hand during a gangster brawl at a cocktail bar in Chicago—yet my stubborn heart could not but grieve for the loss of him, bemoan his heavy absence, ache with the palpable amputation which he had inflicted on me. Whenever I found myself alone, reduced to time which was optimistically described as free, I felt not so much free as sentenced to busying myself without him, forced to seek distraction, distraction, distraction. I remember even being driven to scour the fat book upstairs in the library, and resorting to the underlined bit about the twice-born man bathing in his own garments, as if those musty words were some mantra, and the book which contained them, a treasured talisman, as if this whole twist of fate had been some misunderstanding, some innocent prank gone hideously awry. And stroking the page where his finger had once skated with such life, I would fantasize that Clifford might yet prove to be the exception to the Christian rule and be restored to me from some mystical Hindu cloud. But then, when I stepped back, fed up, and slammed the hard covers shut, shoving the book into any old shelf, as he had done, I sometimes feared that the turn of my thoughts echoed the beginnings of what the French writers whom I was reading (in lazy translation) meant when they referred to the process of quietly going mad.

Nor did it take long for others to cotton on to the alteration which I had undergone—my reversal to insipid oneness—for, aside from the glaring evidence that my friend no longer swaggered beside me, his jacket billowing about his shoulders like the cape of some Cuban-heeled dandy, his manicured index jabbing the high air in front of anyone who dared to confront us, I myself drifted about, not as if halved by the severance, but as if evaporated entirely, like a phantom, like the very air at which he had once so vigorously jabbed. It wasn't that I'd lost one half of my identity: I seemed to have lost it entirely; and, just to exacerbate my reduction to my own colourless company, the consensus regarding Clifford's evanescence proved to be a blunt Good Riddance. In many ways, I was worse off than earlier, because whereas, before his luminous advent in my life, I'd striven to circumvent altercations with other pupils, later, after we'd become an established duo and been welded into inseparability, we'd almost welcomed the chance of locking horns with our enemies, had thought nothing of fanning grievances, had revelled in felling our aggressors with our lightning tongues. But now, as well as being deprived of his friendship, I was left to bear the brunt of those collaborative hostilities single-handedly, maimed, the strength gone out of me.

OF THE PUPILS in our year, only Steel, really, was sympathetic to my plight; and, just as he had changed physically, so, I began to realize, he had matured mentally. Ignoring his irksome jingoistic attitudes (which I suspected to be puerile affectation, soon to be discarded, like a pair of outgrown trousers), he otherwise strove to be liberal, broad of mind. In fact, a couple of times, as I mooched about Leviticus, or sat on my bed playing Patience before lights out, he did express, and carefully, his regret at what he understood must, for me, amount to a small mourning. He even advised that perhaps, in order to diminish my melancholy, I should write to my old best friend, my former BF, and endeavour to sustain our bond in the afterlife, as it were, beyond the petty world of school and all its confines; but though I simulated gratitude for his noises of concern, inwardly I scoffed at the uselessness of such a suggestion. He didn't know what he was talking about, didn't have a clue about my (broken) pacts and (shattered) fantasies with Clifford, which, if anything had ever done, had indeed soared beyond the confines of the petty world to which Steel was now alluding. Almost by definition, our dreams had been cast in grown-up, otherworldly venues—hot American cinemas, glamorous cocktail bars, great mansions bursting with black servants in full livery. And yet, though Steel couldn't possibly have been aware of these things, it was as if he possessed a six-six-sixth sense, suspected his own ignorance, and simply sought more facts, more details before he could properly prove himself to be of help to me, become my confidant—because, undaunted by my silence, he went on to enquire why it was that Cross, who'd seemed so integrated here, and so comfortable in my company, had suddenly gone off without so much as a by-your-leave to study in America, of all rum places. Everyone knew that the British educational system far surpassed that of the Yanks, who couldn't even spell, and weren't taught Latin, and had no sense of culture, and no history to speak of. So why the sudden change of plan? I told Steel that he'd have to ask Clifford's parents that (I left the rector well out of it), because I, at any rate, didn't have the foggiest. And then, as if lent confidence by my pretence at bewilderment, as if propelled by some looming hunch, he proposed that Clifford and I had been so, you know, so well matched, that . . . Cross hadn't been expelled by any chance, had he? We hadn't been caught out or something? Caught out how?, I replied, genuinely mystified. Come on, he persisted: kind of boys' stuff. (To me, boys' stuff sounded like games of conkers and swapping annuals and going rat-a-tat the whole time.) What the hell did he mean? He raised his eyes, just like Clifford after the twice-born man. Did he have, he hissed, to spell it out? He looked around, a little flustered, and then just repeated: boys' stuff—as in yours with Mr. Wolfe.

I let my eyes drift out of focus, avoiding his mouth. Look, he insisted, I'm not like all those other bigots, you know; each to his own, that's my attitude. I don't believe in being censorious. I don't cast stones. His blurred raw lips rounded into ominous vastness. I'm not some shockable prig, he reassured me; surely you realize that; after all, we've known each other for yonks, haven't we? I nodded that I supposed that we had. Exactly. And then he went on to confess that he'd presumed, though perhaps he'd been wrong to've jumped the gun—I didn't have to say either way, *he* wasn't prurient (one of his pet new adjectives, more recent than Censorious)—but he'd presumed that Clifford and I had been best friends in the proper sense of the word, the full sense, like in the Symposium, sort of bosom chums. And suddenly I felt as if I couldn't stand it a moment longer.

To be accused, in however liberal a guise, of having performed with Clifford the very acts which he, in order to effect his own removal, had claimed that I'd performed with someone else, seemed to spear me into a childish crisis. My corner felt too tight; I was choking up. So I took a deep breath and betrayed the betrayer, explaining to Steel, whom—it was true—*had* known me all those years, that far from Cross and I having been what he called bosom chums, we hadn't, as it turned out, been friends at all—full or otherwise—couldn't have been, because my supposed great pal (ha ha) had engineered his escape from school by telling his hypocrite of a father, who didn't live with his wife but was shacked up with some trollop in Chicago, of the rumour about me and Mr. Wolfe dating back to prep school. That creep had proved doubly true to his name, had double-crossed me through and through. And the rector, if you please, had already dragged me into his study and given me a bollocking about the whole thing; and now I felt as if I was living under a microscope, that my every tiny move was being monitored and analysed and ticked every two minutes. Cross was a complete judas.

Steel, who liked to boast that he'd heard it all before, admitted that he'd never heard anything like it. He called it beastly. His feline eyes spread far with disbelief; his fleshy great lips drooped to his chin. He didn't blame me for being browned off, not a bit, not now that he knew what he knew. Absolutely livid he'd be. Took back all his advice about Cross; filthy sneak; of course I mustn't write to him. Shocking, such a betrayal of friendship. And while I gathered up the cards of my unfinished game, and prepared to crawl into bed, he patted my shoulder and said never mind, I was probably better off without him, always best to know the truth about such people sooner rather than later. I'd make new friends, I'd see, stronger ones, stauncher. And then he told me not to worry, I could trust him implicitly, the story was safe with him, as houses. But it was, he agreed, unbelievable. Anyway, good night, and try to get some sleep. And in the morning, I felt that yes, a new bond had indeed been forged between myself and Steel, and I sensed that in some unspoken way, he would look over me, after me, that he would ensure that I was allowed the requisite peace, the necessary time to lick my wounds.

I WAS TO NEED IT. Because, only a further morning into that term, a letter, sent to me through the internal mail, was delivered to my desk during morning studies, before assembly, which was when the post monitor came round. The missive seemed to come from Mr. Wolfe, for its envelope, though typed, displayed on its flap the emblem of my former prep school. Its contents, however, were less easily identifiable: A single sheet of paper, unheaded, undated, and, furthermore, unsigned, simply bore along its middle crease, precisely where it had been folded into two, one single question, also typed—in loud, recriminatory capitals: WHAT HAVE YOU BEEN SAYING? The rector, I reasoned, had obviously hauled him in and given him a grilling. I felt as if we were back at the beginning, returned to the old climate of subterfuge and sin. Well, I concluded: this time Mr. Wolfe could take care of his own hide. I'd already saved his skin once, and he, at least, had suffered no damage that I was aware of, for, not long after his time with me, he'd been elevated to deputy head of the junior school. His precious bisexual career plainly remained on track, destined for didactic glitteriness. He was no longer my responsibility. I no longer loved him; I had no love to give, nor loyalty beyond indifference. And so, taking out a sheet of my own inflated stationery—like the first fated sheet to Dr. Fox—I wrote, in steady lower case script, the true word: n o t h i n g. And unlike his tawdry single crease, I folded my sheet twice, into three sections, and licked the envelope securely, and even stretched, again unlike him, to a postage stamp—newly decimal, first class, and blue as a bad blazer. I printed his address in the most unrecognizable hand that I could muster, and consigned my reply to Her Majesty's gracious mail. And stuff him. Steel agreed that I'd done the right thing.

DR. FOX, meanwhile, had been made aware of Clifford's departure, and could scarcely conceal his relief. He became the most condoling of creatures, claimed to be extremely sorry to hear about all this—for my sake, naturally—yet his warm show of sympathy made me uneasy. We had reverted to scones and tea (though, of course, without the cheesy extras—which, like Clifford, were finished). But I didn't quite dare, as I sat on the burgundy brocaderie, to discuss the nature of the whole betrayal, the shock that it had given me, because I remained unsure as to whether Dr. Fox himself might not have been dragged into Clifford's story—pupils, teachers, plurals. And this, in turn, made me wonder whether the rector might not already, just as he'd presumably done Mr. Wolfe, have approached Dr. Fox, and whether the latter might not now be putting up, to sound me out, a pretence of ignorance, or whether he had braved the ostensible interview with his customary ease: a blink, perhaps; a sneer; and then: What utter piffle, Rector, really; that Cross boy seemed like bad news from the moment he got here: peculiar background, yes? Parents divorced, am I right in thinking? And that would have been it. Albany, Albany, you never knew it; but you, like Tadzio, had it easy.

In answer to my earlier question about the departed Clifford, I, like the Querie by the Lido, did wilt; I did wither; I don't deny it. And yet it was as if, the deeper I withdrew, the more singled out I became among my peers. With my self-inflicted isolation, the others must have sniffed the renewed tenuousness of my position. And though I stood, very still, in the middle of my small clearing, which was the clearing of lone silent misery, and though they could not properly see me, yet they were, I could tell, on the trail of me, on to my scented shadow and rendered high-blooded by it, like hunting dogs which, in advance of the season, have been starved for weeks. I could sense them steadily drawing nearer, not quite baying for my gizzards, yet growling and panting as they ran across the fields around me, the fields of ordinary activity. And they seemed, furthermore, to grow fiercer and louder and wilder as they raced into the forest immediately surrounding me—the thick forest of our collective puberty—bent on tracking me down and ultimately getting me. Not to finish me off. That was never their objective. Just for the sport of it.

Did I give in? Of course I did, repeatedly, serially, and mainly— since they represented my most pressing anxiety—to the others in Leviticus. One by one by one, I relieved them: the middling scientist; the admiral's son (frequently); even, between games of chess, Mr. Popularity. And once, though it was all passed off as horseplay, or wrestling, or war games or something, Steel. I'd become like my own hostage, there for the taking—in the night lavatory, over the basin in the dormitory, in the deserted locker room, out in the fields. Wherever those boys thought it safe and convenient, I brought their hectic zips to glutinous fruition. And though it was hardly a case of notching up conquests, those acquiescences of mine did provide me with an effective means of gagging my fellow criminals, of ensuring that they could no longer be out-and-out enemies, not overtly, for into my ready hands and mouth they had, they knew, fed me warm shots of ammunition.

Yet as they tucked their shirt-tails back in, and flicked the dollops of slime from their sticky guilty fingers, or rubbed these dry, without a word—even helping themselves, sometimes, to my handkerchief—I did reflect on what a difference Clifford had made to me, of how none of this would be happening if he had stayed beside me. And then I also thought, as if for exoneration from my cheapness, as if in search of absolution, of the beautiful men whom I'd encountered at high noon in the sea. Those watery gods of my youth, decked about with wreaths of seaweed, those miraculous lifesaving kissers—while my parents slept their untroubled siestas in separate bedrooms.

IN SEPARATE BEDROOMS along the way from Leviticus, there were twin brothers, named Nye—Thomas and Timothy. Because their parents hadn't thought of simplifying their lives by furnishing the pair with different first initials, nor bothered with second names at all, which I thought stylish, the Nye boys were, so far as I was aware, the only pupils, who, in order to be distinguished, were granted the privilege, when it came to roll-calls or rotas or lists, of having their first names included: Nye, Tom; Nye, Tim. It made them sound nocturnal, like night owls. Yet for all the system's attempts at telling them apart in theory, they couldn't, in practice, have been more different, less identical.

Tom was tall and dark, and, though currently pimply, it was obvious that he enjoyed, both in the school and out of it, the benefit of greater popularity. He was athletic, lean, and headed for handsomeness. Tim, by contrast, was at least six inches smaller, at least six inches rounder, dull-haired, and outwardly uninteresting. You sensed that he was the runt of the meagre litter, and that having been robbed in the womb of his fair share of nutrition, he now fed himself like a fiend in response to some vestigial struggle to live. He always carried a packet of something incredibly sweet about him, like the half-melted corpses of white chocolate mice, or lumps of Kendal mint, or chunky dice of coffee fudge or, rattling about in a tin, shards, like blades, of Harrogate toffee. Probably in order to compensate for his brother's more favourable position in the galaxy, he was, of the two, the louder—zany, wry, larky to me. If Tom was the straight-guy, Tim was the funny-man, the clown of the family. When he cackled, it was like unleashing a loony. How close they were emotionally, I do not know; but if some bond did exist between those twins, it must have been telepathic, because, during the time that I knew them, I never once saw them exchange a single syllable. They existed almost too separately. Tom had lots of chums, sporty establishment types, while Tim appeared to have fewer, and weirder ones, among whose number, I, peripherally, figured.

I suppose that, in the wake of Clifford's desertion, I must have seen more of Tim Nye than in previous years, made a more concerted effort to be sociable in my quest for renewal. He owned a vast collection of tapes by seedy-looking vocalists who mystified me; I remember because he made a crusade of trying to correct my ignorance on what he regarded as serious popular music—music which, he said, required committed listening. He would lend me fantastically depressing songs by some gravel-voiced balladeer who had driven his guitar teacher to top himself, songs about being fed tea and oranges (*awe-ringes,* the singer called them, which is probably what Clifford would *waaand-up doin'* if he didn't watch that slackened gob of his), and about having no love to give, and about Jesus knowing for certain that only drowning men could see him. It made me, for all of Nye's goodwill, want to fall asleep, get away from it. But there was one particular number which I did have difficulty ignoring, because, in it, Mr. Gravel Voice, who sounds like he's shattered after too many amphetamines, goes: Father, change my name; the one I'm using now, it's covered up with fear and filth and cowardice and shame. And that, for some reason, seemed to ring a bell.

Whenever Nye, helmeted by his ear-phones, heard some new lyric which he considered to be of significance, but which generally I found to be impenetrable, he would scrawl it on a scrap of paper and, if I wasn't in Leviticus, leave it on my bed, or sometimes tuck it for safety under my pillow, which irritated me. It felt invasive. Recently, over a dozen years later, I discovered one such cryptic message in a folder from that murky period. Written along an oblong, in green adolescent felt-tip, are the following words: And another pretty woman, she was leaning in her Darkened door, she cried to me, hey, why not ask for more.

I still can't make out why Nye decided to darken that door with a capital D, nor why he omitted the question mark which belonged at the end of the line; but I also wonder whether he wasn't trying to suggest, rather than request, something. And yet, at the time, any such subtlety would have eluded me: I wouldn't have heard it: there was too loud a wind in my head, for I was myself too wrapped up in the waves of a French song that brought Clifford to mind, a fantasy woven into my reality, delivered by a man who, like Mr. Gravel Voice, talked his way through the music, but whose rendition—flooded by strings and wailing trumpets and back-up girls going da-da-da—seemed to hold me in thrall to its repetitive banality. I suppose that it must have been the European hit of the previous August, my unwitting anthem to the unimaginable loss of Clifford. A bad prose poem, really:

> *Tu sais, je n'ai jamais été aussi heureux que ce matin-là. Nous marchions sur une plage un peu comme celle-ci. C'était l'automne, un automne où il faisait beau, une saison qui n'existe que dans le nord de l'Amérique. Là-bas on l'appelle l'Eté Indien—mais c'était tout simplement le nôtre . . . Et je me souviens très bien de ce que je t'ai dit ce matin-là, il y a un an, il y a un siècle: On ira où tu voudras quand tu voudras, et l'on s'aimera encore lorsque l'amour sera mort . . . Aujourd'hui . . . je pense à toi: Où es-tu? Que fais-tu? Est-ce que j'existe encore pour toi? Je regarde cette vague qui n'atteindra jamais la dune. Tu vois: comme elle, je reviens en arrière; comme elle, je me couche sur le sable et je me souviens des marées hautes, et du soleil, et du bonheur qui passait sur la mer, il y a une éternité, il y a un siècle, il y a un an. On ira où tu voudras quand tu voudras . . .*

Except, of course, that we didn't. He went off without me. And those questions—*Où es-tu? Que fais-tu? Est-ce que j'existe encore pour toi?*—seemed to take me back, of all peculiar things, to my time with Mam'zelle, to our Eurovision chant, to that final couplet which had been mine to yell out, ten years earlier, in the bath: *Et toi, et toi qui j'aimais, Qu'as-tu fait de toi? Qu'as-tu fait sans moi? / Et moi, moi qui t'ai perdu, Qu'ai-je fait de plus? Qu'ai-je fait de tant de bonheur?* To which there was no possible answer other than to lie on my bed in Leviticus, and turn to my side, and face the wall which had been the waves and the beaches and the summers of my childhood, when I first delivered myself to

Mr. Wolfe's inexplicable love. And then, I would try not to cry. Try to grow up.

OUR YEAR MASTER, though he looked like a man of the cloth, was a mongrel. The church should have muzzled him. His temper, even concealed beneath the limp black wings of a clerical habit, was rabid. I took pains never to look at him directly, not just because he was unattractive—which he irredeemably was, being afflicted with colourless moles on his sallow cheeks, a snout for a nose, pointed ears, and perpetually grimy hair (often scraped across, in public, with a broken plastic comb which festered in a pocket at his backside)—but also because he seemed resentful of the unsolicited eyeball. You feared that even a sidelong glance from the wrong quarter might ignite his ferocity. He was intellectually pretentious, intellectually inadequate, and sexually (you sensed) hampered. I pictured his penis as salamanderish.

He liked to suggest, in the wry, roundabout way that priests sometimes have, that once upon a time he'd been a man of the world, oh yes, a *bon viveur,* and that there existed no beverage, or narcotic, or position in the (unexpurgated) *Kamasutra* which he hadn't, at some point in his agnostic history, sampled. There was a whiff of Damascus about him; certainly he was a convert, a late one. He strutted about in scuffed old winkle-pickers, no longer black, closer to dusty charcoal now, with natty laces to the side—less, you suspected, as an act of sartorial penance than as if those pointed embarrassments, which wouldn't have tempted even the lowlier among our domestics, attested to his spivvy past, to his days spent scooting through la dolce vita. He would, you felt, have known hookers biblically; but nor could you help feeling that those very hookers would have sniggered as he sauntered back into the cobbled penumbra. Getting it up wouldn't have been his forte: his forte was lager; or, if he was lucky, brandy. He referred to his charges as lads, and was keener on the discussion of rugby tackles and skirt, as he called women, than ever on matters of doctrine, or conscience, never mind the business of loving. His (infrequent) addresses from the pulpit were rife with sporting analogies, and he celebrated the snappiest of Masses, as if the sacrament of the Eucharist were a steeplechase, and the rite of consecration a hurdle to be cleared. His legs were bowed.

On the subject of discipline, you suspected that he, like my father, rued the demise of the birch; but, as if to make up for this sadness, he was an undisputed wow with the ferula. He shredded the flesh from people's palms: a mere few strokes into his discipline, and he had drawn your blood. He didn't so much breathe as simmer; there was broiling fire in his gut; you could smell its fumes rising to the light of his dry gullet, ulcerous and acrid. So you will understand why, even though he treated me like a snotty, very silly shopgirl, selling Joy to her friends in the hiatus before baring her shoulders to society, I didn't think it wise to attempt to disabuse him of his assumption. He was everything that I reviled. But for the duration of that year, we were stuck with one another. And I was the stucker.

Whatever subject it was that he attempted to teach, and my memory murmurs elementary Mathematics, this was never to the top stream, so, at least on my academic timetable, I was spared the benefit of his snarling mediocrity. When he herded us together for impassioned little pep-talks on adolescent mores and matters of manly propriety (such as not wenching out of bounds, and not getting sozzled in the village), I would always sit as far back as decency allowed, or my position seemed to require—like one of the kitchen minions—while he paid tribute to our latest sporting victors and tried to humiliate boys whom he suspected not to be living up to the school's high principles. My father's Alma Mater didn't take kindly to being let down, not one bit, my lad. He spoke with his thumbs hooked into his belt loops, like a hoodlum, and swayed on the spot as he did so, rocking back and forth from his heels to the curled tips of his winkled toes. The whole motion made you slightly queasy, like a black-and-white film about the warring British navy. The hem of his cassock was torn at the rear, as if lashed by a storm at sea, and splattered with mud from the shores of the rugger pitch. His shiny trousers were too short, and overly tight at the ankle, as if they sought to hark back to the period of his younger antics; and peeping from the past, above his shrunken socks of patterned nylon, you could glimpse gaps of waxy calf. But I tended to be spared his lower details at such gatherings, for, even as he stood on the podium, which was his preference—otherwise a table would suffice— the stems of his worsted legs were invariably decorated by the budding, bobbing, variegated heads of those who preferred to have their characters developed closer to his wisdom.

ONE EVENING LEADING up to Christmas, the year master caught me coming out of Nye's dormitory, where I'd gone to return one of those tapes of important popular music. My friend hadn't been in—probably off for his after-supper ciggy—so I left the cassette (which had its owner's name safely stuck onto it in plasticized tape—its letters, like bullets, shot out by one of those little pistols which were then considered cool gadgets of stationery) on his bedside chair. And I scrawled a brief covering message on a pad, which, along with a small torch, lived there. I think that Nye had begun to annotate his dreams around that time, and to dredge obscure poems from his lyrical subconscious stream. Anyway, my note just said: Thanks, enjoyed it—any more? But my handwriting, which in those days felt like my sole permissible licence to detach myself from the italicized rabble, was easily recognizable, provocatively florid and too large, too strident, too full of false confidence. And although the year master had feigned not to see me as I returned to Leviticus, I, on the other hand, did notice him creeping into Nye's empty dormitory, which was called Exodus. The tosser in the winkle-pickers was probably on the look-out for some sweaty jock to share a can of lager with him in his room.

This room, I now discover (for it is I, not the sweaty jock, whom, it appears, he wants to see), is enormous and lugubrious, large as a dormitory for six of us, with a double-aspect corner view, beheld through grimy Gothic windows, of the school church (a Catholic pauper's imitation of one of the finest Anglican chapels in Cambridge) and, to the other side, of the gardens into which, at the start of term, the rector had seemed to wish me to vamoose. The year master tells me to sit on a grubby club-chair of moth-eaten moquette with balding deco patterns and obnoxious springs. Thank you, Father.

But oh dear me, how to sit? Do so hate to make decisions. I could pose like the jock of his dreams, my chest thrust out and proudly, my hands alluding to my priapic genitals, my knees spread to the far edges of his corner view; or like the pretty lady, grown too weary to continue leaning on the darkened door of Nye's fantasies; or as if, swathed in

Joy, my shoulders had already been bared for the benefit of society; or like the psychiatric patient whom my father would never have countenanced; or like some teasing young tutor of English, muse to a salivating notary. But, of course: none of these comes naturally. Instead, I sit like my mother. Imagine: I dare to cross my legs; I rest one of my elbows on the arm of the chair, letting my hand flourish in mid-air as if it were entertaining a scented handkerchief. I wish I were bedecked in Clifford's glistering jewels. I allow my wrist to wilt, to flop, as if the bone had been extracted from me in childhood, or as if Yahweh had never furnished me with one, not even for the glory of Onan. I gaze at my interlocutor like a fluttering *ingénue,* charmed by the surprising privilege of his attention, as if half-expecting him, at any moment, to thrill me with a proposal of marriage, as if he were seeking to declare something so precious and so vital that it required subtle coaxing, the wiles of a chic young woman. But inwardly, I do feel slightly insulted; for the year master, already wedded to his vows of poverty, couldn't possibly afford me.

Poor man is being timid, I can tell, because, to start with, he says nothing: just picks up a piece of paper from his desk, as if it were inscribed with his forthcoming speech (the climax to our courtship, which has been nothing if not whirlwind), and glances at it—trying to memorize it, I rather think. But as he turns the paper to face me, and holds it up to the light, I recognize my own recognizable hand, swirling and curling with the green of Nye's adolescent felt-tip; and now I realize precisely what this memo is, and where the priest has found it. He wants me to explain its contents, which he describes as thoroughly incriminating. I would have thought that they were self-explanatory, but he thinks: far from it, what exactly *is* this stuff about enjoying it meant to mean? It means that I enjoyed the tape which Nye had lent me (obviously). Oh really? Yes, really. (I may be sounding too familiar: The year master, let's not forget, is not, as yet, affianced to me.) Well, he doesn't believe me, not for an instant. His voice, as he leans against his desk—not, I regret to say, like some self-effacing suitor, but like a greasy spiv, pressing his plastic comb into his bony rear—is deepening, growing harsher and more bestial. As they say in America, and doubtless as Clifford will soon be saying: here is the thing: the year master reckons that I'm pestering Nye, that I have designs on him, that I'm a dirty little pervert seeking to debauch another pupil. He calls me a piece of shit. (Clifford, can you believe this? Can't you help me?) On and on, round and round, over and over goes Christ's ordained minister, fulminating as if from his pulpit, and rising to his pointed feet; and yet I, notwithstanding his mounting fury, can feel myself swelling from within, swelling with the strength and unholy impudence of Clifford, as if his fearless spirit were suddenly being poured into the vessel of my fear, like an agent of alchemy; and the moment that I hear a pause in the year master's diatribe, and even though I've only caught random syllables of his lunacy, I find myself replying (as I did to the commander) without hesitation, being hoist with my own petard. And what I say to this great frothing imbecile is: Actually, Father, I prefer the attentions (I may even have said favours) of adults. And then, to drive the knife right in, I add: grown men, *mature* ones. Whereupon, the priest (as they say in America, but as they properly do in Hades) freaks right out. He loses his mind.

It can be a challenge to view the familiar with new eyes, to try to reappraise it as its creator, or first purchaser, might have done, to invest it with new value, new life. Yet, faced as I am by the year master, I now find no difficulty in rising to such a challenge; indeed, I lack an alternative, for though he doesn't directly confront me, the man is suddenly beside himself, transmogrified, howling like a common mongrel. And I, with a self-protective jolt, have backed into my chair; and my ringless fingers are gripping at its moquette arms; and my legs have uncrossed, and sharpish, and are ready to run for cover, less like the silken legs of some desirable maiden than those of a great unsung sprinter, some wasted champion from my father's glory days at the Alma Mater.

The year master, the while, is haranguing God knows what, yelling at some repulsive mystery. He makes no sense whatever, but I bet that his reverberating roars can be heard outside. He just seems to rail in the abstract, at the apparent putrefaction around him, as if he, not I, had suddenly seen it with new eyes, smelt it with a new snout, the stench of his engulfing yeast and damp, had awoken as if to the ghost of some old provincial public house after hours. Just as the woman crying out for Tadzio could so easily have been my mother, so, now, the year master could, within the mental scheme of things, be my erstwhile suitor, thrashing about in the face of my refusal, wailing at his discovery that my heart belongs to some other daddy, baying for a duel even, like my grandmother's hapless young infantry officer. In Clifford's cocktail bar, I would, at this point, have had to request another tequila slammer, but here, there isn't so much as a measly sip of lager to be had, not even to quench the worthy thirst of a frustrated Olympic decathlete. If I had the means, or my father's Catholic contacts, I would commission the year master's exorcism—for his own good, you understand, like army camp—and instanter. I would see to it that the raging tyke were dowsed with holy water and slung into one of the school's holy hides. But I can't; and nor is the battle yet over.

IT ENDED WITH *The Battleship Potemkin* and five thousand words on the œuvre of Eisenstein. I told you that the mongrel was pretentious. And as I left his kennel—only to bang into the approaching sweaty jock for whom he had really been hankering—my first task became trying to memorize the incomprehensible subject of my chastisement. Back in Leviticus, Steel, who was as astonished as I about this whole rumpus over unlikely Nye, and who, with his skewering intelligence, knew about most matters, said that it wasn't Einstein at all, but Ei-*sen*-stein—was I thick or something?—and that the essay which I'd been told to write had nothing whatever to do with the theory of relativity, nor with any real-life battle, but with a film, Moore, a film from *ages* back, before the bloody talkies, a classic of the genre, in black and white—which I, needless to say, had never seen, not even in the days when Mr. Wolfe, with such great care, had manned the dark projections of my past. I was up a gum tree, or was it Shit Creek without a paddle?

I resorted to the library. I rummaged through all the books on which I could lay my hands. There wasn't a paragraph, never mind five thousand words, to be had on the elusive great moviemaker. I wandered away from the meagre shelf devoted to film and theatre; and then, by the grace of Shiva (third god of the Hindu trimurti, the destroyer and reproducer), I came across a snippet, in some dictionary of Russian biography, which said that Sergei Eisenstein had described his life as intense, joyous and tormented. Born to a wealthy family, his secure childhood was darkened by a tyrannical father. Rejecting the "almost hysterical" religion and comfortable expectations of his class, he became an atheist, a thinker, and an artist whose ironic wit and style matched the substance of his ideas—a summary which, like the lyrics of Mr. Gravel Voice, when he had asked to change his name, seemed to ring with truthful resonance. It inspired me.

I went over to Exodus, and, though concealing from Nye the real reason why I found myself in trouble (an admission which would have proved just too excruciating for both of us), I invoked his help with my punishment, which had to be completed, and delivered back to the kennel, within forty-eight hours, before lights out. Just as Nye was keen on important popular music, it turned out that he fancied himself a bit of a movie buff, and was fond of racing through the vowels of that most daunting of hexasyllabic nouns: Cinematography. He confirmed that the subject of my essay was indeed a crummy old film, obscure and silent, and that the task wasn't going to be easy, but he seemed to have a sounder grasp of the topic than—even after a whole year of swotting—I could ever have had.

He knew, for instance, and from the top of his madcap head, that *The Battleship Potemkin* had, not once, but twice, been voted best film of all time, though he added that this accolade meant absolutely nothing, and that it was unlikely to assist my plight; that it had been made in 1925 (not long after my grandmother's infantry officer had died); that it lasted some 69 minutes (the length of a respectable Mass, unlike the mongrel's full-pelt religious travesties) and that its soundtrack had been composed by Eisenstein's friend and frequent collaborator, Prokofiev, whose Orthodox name, like that of the director, was also (he paused—for the glamour of it) . . . *Sergei*. Nye was being a show-off now. Sergeis, I said, were two a penny, or rouble, or whatever they had in St. Petersburg. Which, the expert snapped back, was a complete irrelevance, and the place, anyway, was called Leningrad: did I want his help or didn't I? Christ, I groaned, trying to avoid an argument. A film about a mutiny on a battleship. No wonder the year master swayed and rocked about, the great seafaring prat. But I only had two days in which to acquit myself; otherwise, I may as well be drowned.

Like Dr. Fox when he sought to raise the finer points of our acquaintanceship from the music basement up to his private quarters, I now donned my thinking-cap. I thought of Clifford. Clifford would never have buckled under this pressure. He, the child of fortune, would always, somehow, have won out. And in the night, at lonely last, it came to me: the solution. I would *buy* my way to victory, not fight it, and decided to this end that I'd invest the remainder of my spoils from the notary and the girl with the harelip—my ill-gotten tutorial gains. Because words, I told myself, were merely words, and talk, God knew, was cheap; but money—money sings out like a great aria. Therein lay the route to my salvation, in lyrical pieces of silver.

It all took a bit of haggling and cajoling, of course, but in the end, after breakfast, Nye finally consented to my proposal and agreed that for the equivalent of four weeks' pocket money he, not I, would write the deadly essay for the mongrel; though he did, like a whore without so much as a darkened door now, demand half of the payment upfront—as a token of my goodwill, he argued. He got it, no problem. But once this first small deal had been clinched, I seemed to become ambitious, hungry for further glory, and decided that after Nye had done his bit for my cause I wouldn't even deign to transcribe his five thousand dreary words on the *oeuvre* of bloody Eisenstein. Clifford would never, on principle, have done so—if only to spite the mongrel.

And thus it was that I, like Pythagoras, that demigod of basic Mathematics, suddenly thought of good old Hardy, the prodigious foreskin retractor, devotee of Elgar and self-styled nobleman who, in our early days, had proved my (thwarted) rival in the affections of Mr. Wolfe, but who, more pertinently, in view of my current predicament, happened also to be, you may recall, a forger of some renown. Since our time at prep school, Hardy had, in point of fact, defected from the camp of cavaliers (like Dr. Fox) to that of roundheads (like Mr. Wolfe), having pressed and pestered his family doctor so relentlessly that, once the befuddled medic had been ground down, the imaginary patient succeeded (and on the National Health, would you believe) in having himself circumcised—not *ritually,* he had grandiloquently apprised me—purely for cosmetic reasons, which, he felt, were more legitimate. Because, despite his exhibitions of yesteryear, he had, in maturity, come to the realization that foreskins were Ectually, he said, ugly superfluous anatomical extras, and, therefore, best excised. I don't, however, think that his wobbly neck could as yet have received much in the way of surgical attention, because, when he spoke, he still tilted his head a fraction, like a slightly deaf (or was it insouciant) madonna.

Hardy turned out to be exorbitant, though in a sense I couldn't blame him, for Clifford and I had given him a bit of a rough ride in the recent past; and vengeance, I could see, was not exclusively mine to exact. But first I had to make him swear, on his (ugly) mother's life, never to reveal to *anyone,* least of all to Nye, his fee for imitating my handwriting—a calligraphy which he evinced the smirking insolence to describe as problematic. His price (the grasping pig) was in excess of a full term's pocket money, too disgraceful to divulge, a rip-off if ever there was one; but, by this stage, I was beyond thoughts of beating him down or striking bargains, because although I was the undisputed mastermind, boss, bankroller and godfather of the whole scheme, I also had to acknowledge to myself that decent forgers in this dump were at a bit of a premium. So I availed him of one of my old exercise books—English compositions, I imagine, which contained the neatest samples of my writing—and instructed him to meet Nye-Tim during break in the library, where the two of them would, throughout the next two days' snatches of free time, work in conjunction—Hardy replicating, in his artful approximation of my hand, whatever resulted, page by stultifying page, from Nye's polysyllabic cinematographic studies. In the event, though all turned out without mishap, the great faker didn't prove himself to be quite as fabulous as he liked to make out, for he'd been sloppy, I discovered, about my e's, having elected to emulate only one single style, whereas I liked to lay claim to at least three such, adopted or rejected depending on which I felt looked best at whichever point in a given word the need for that letter happened to arise.

Once the commission was complete, and submitted to me for approval, I insisted on crossing all the zeds myself, which naughty Hardy had not done; and then, I paid off my accomplices, placing their wages in separate envelopes, as my mother paid her servants— although Hardy was vulgar enough to count his earnings on the spot, with his stooping, spastic neck turned away from his collaborator. Still, despite the offence implicit in this gesture, and even though I remained entirely ignorant about the contents of those seventeen pages of drudgery, the challenge was met and duly delivered to the kennel (slipped under the door without a sound, to avoid the danger of growling) doubtless to merit not so much as a glance. But my dignity emerged, at least in my own eyes, intact from the fiasco, and the year master, thanks be to Shiva, wasn't to address another word to me, not one, not even with an uncrossed z, ever again in my school career. Yet his madness had cost me a small fortune, the squandering of which I was soon enough to rue—and to rue far more sorely than anyone ever rued the demise of any bloodied birch.

THE LIFE TO which I returned after this punitive interlude was quiet, spectral, like the life of a room which, though host in the past to colour and hilarity, has since, for protection during a long absence, been submerged beneath a sea of dustsheets. I retained, of course, the vague contours of my past, the vestiges of my inverted attitudes, yet I suppressed the character which had once animated them, such character as had been moulded and warmed and nourished during my sunny season with Clifford, my Indian summer. I needed time to adjust now, in order to release him from my consciousness and learn to survive, alone, through the old landscape of shadows, in order to manage through the drought, or frost, or ashes—the moribund state into which, more than his quick-fire betrayal, his eternal absence had cast me.

I also began to avoid Nye, not because I no longer had time for him (how could I not, when all that he had ever shown me had been his eccentric and, in retrospect, edifying brand of fellowship?) but because I feared a repetition of my altercation with the mongrel. Hardy, however, I didn't avoid: he I cut dead without a qualm, both because (other than genitally) he remained what he had always been, which was a leering oleaginous creep, and because, regardless of what further punishments fate might have yet tucked up its sleeve for me, the one thing which I knew with certainty was this: that I should never again be able to afford the pomp and circumstance of that prohibitive scrivener's underhand criminality. Occasionally I saw Steel, and spoke to him, in class or in Leviticus, but while the place of my dashed hopes and dreams, that region of my brain which housed my spirit, continued to float in limbo, waiting one day to be roused from its state of gloomy abeyance, to be relieved of its dustsheets, I mostly took myself to neutral spaces, to safe but hazy areas which bore as little connection to school life as, indeed, they did to my derelict existence during the holidays, places like the music basement. I still escaped for meals to Dr.

Fox's room, for I'd grown to dread the ordeal, on my own, of the refectory; and he, Dr. Fox, despite my surly refusal ever again to feast on his naked obesity, did continue—with remarkable forbearance, when you think of it—to lavish upon me the privilege of his superior groceries. It is possible that his care was prompted by a lingering sense of wariness, but I somehow doubt it, because, as I explained earlier, circumstances, whatever our original positions, had by now drawn us into a semblance of friendship—which was to survive, if not forever, at least beyond the conclusion of my dreadful education. I think that on balance his loneliness probably outweighed his lust. I know that mine did; of that, I have no doubt.

But there *were* occasional snatches of respite, privileges extended to us as the year assumed a lull (in the middle term, when most of the days were dark, almost Scandinavian), nocturnal chances to venture beyond the system and broaden our dimming horizons. We were allowed, for instance, to sign up for extra-curricular evening classes at some neighbouring industrial town, and most people opted, predictably enough, for car maintenance, or mechanical engineering (subjects held up as manly, and all held in the same building, a former warehouse)—followed by a quick pint at a nearby pub, which provided pupils with the opportunity to bump into strange women on the lounge side. I would certainly, had Clifford still been with me, have opted for flower arranging, and brought my trophies back to Leviticus, and debated with the teacher—more likely, in these parts, to be a woman than a Querie, but still—what constituted good floral taste and what didn't; and yet, on my own, and without the chance of a cocktail bar to deck in my arid future, the prospect didn't seem so enticing.

So instead, I enrolled on a course of shorthand and typing, and, just as predictably, turned out to be the only pupil to do so, which disgruntled the bus driver, who, as a consequence of my poofy pretensions to become some kind of girl Friday, used to have to ferry me to a quite different part of town, nowhere near a pub, and hang about for me until I was done. There was, in fact, an irony about my secretarial penchant, since those weekly classes brought me, unlike the rest of my contemporaries, into a place of exclusively female company—though this was admittedly of a more serious disposition than the bosomy lovelies who nightly tottered for a quick one at the local. *My* women wore sensible spectacles, and very hard hair indeed, and their pencils were sharp as intravenous needles. They would never, you sensed, have stepped into a public house, not even for the pleasure of a genteel crème de menthe—vigorously frappé, and served in a lady-sized brandy glass—much less for a tequila slammer. They seemed, if anything, sick of places where faithless husbands guzzled the week's wages in one evening, and you suspected that behind their aspirations to office life lay not so much a vague quest for distraction as clear plans for a safer existence, beyond the vagaries of matrimony. Those women, my father would have said—as if they'd been cave dwellers, or gypsies—were quite misguided, obviously not Catholic; their marriages lacked proper religious grounding; that was the problem: no real staying power; no gumption. Divorce was too easy a sin. (Was it, Clifford?)

There were also trips further afield, to theatres in the cities—Sheffield, Manchester, Liverpool—and to concerts of classical music. I would sign up, and blindly, to join any such expedition, regardless of whether the play or programme advertised was of interest to me, and irrespective of whether later, during the actual performance, I fell asleep, which sometimes I did. Because those forays seemed to me—at very long last—like flights beyond the teasing, glinting viaduct of my earlier imprisonment, like chances to sample a new, third universe—not school, not home, but real living. I wouldn't claim (because of the handicap of travelling *en troupe*) that it was actually civilized, but it did provide me with a foretaste of freedom: of liberated women, contracepted, unbrassièred and flashing with embroidered glints of mirror; of men with thick manes, in tapestry hipsters; of couples kissing under flickering chandeliers; of obvious, unembarrassed Queries, dressed in devoré, wound about in foulards, and eyed with liner—touches, then, of hope to me.

If you wore a decent coat, and turned up the revers to hide your uniform, waiters at the crush bar, rushed off their feet, didn't have time to tell that you were underage for the purchase of liquor; and if you stood on your toes and lowered your voice a bit, and could afford it, you could immerse yourself in a glass of wine, wander off, and disown your peers. When you went into the Gents, you sometimes met with elongated looks of approval, of embraces that might have been; and, despite the backdrop of crackled Victorian porcelain, and despite the offence of bleach, it felt more romantic than seedy. But the journeys back to school were, in my view, the loveliest part of the experience— balmy, dreamy—for with the swell of symphonies still ringing in your ears and the lights of the bus switched off within and half of the boys already asleep, you, you could just gaze into the luminous night and fantasize that you were on your way somewhere quite else, that you were set on some fantastical journey, full of promise and stars—to Chicago, to the healing waters of Buthanatha, to the land of milk and honey.

THE FIRST TIME that it happened was after one such outing. I'd come back from a concert feeling mildly resuscitated, optimistic even. I re-member half-humming some lingering passage from that night's closing encore, a sweeping minor-key rhapsody. Our return to our respective dormitories—it being long after lights out—had, always and by very strict order, to be both speedy and mute. Absolutely no talking; even to whisper was a risk. Any trouble, or official complaint from some sneak to the effect that you'd disturbed him, and you were barred from all further trips—a fate which earlier in the term had befallen Nye, when he became embroiled, incautiously close to where the mon-grel happened to be prowling, in a disagreement about some absurd production of Ionesco which we had been to see that evening. But Nye had, in fact, been only the first in a line of casualties; half a dozen oth-ers had, since, fallen; so that the rest of us, and I very particularly, took this rule about silence seriously, stopped humming. My routine, to avoid the possibility of being shopped by anyone in my dormitory, was to get into my pyjamas in the dark, turn down my bed, and then head off to the night lavatory for a last-minute pee, and to brush my teeth over the small, rather grubby, basin in there.

I was still groping about the shadows of Leviticus, changing out of my uniform, when, as I fumbled for my pyjamas under my pillow, I felt what at first I took to be one of those invasive cassettes which Nye sometimes left hidden—but which, once picked up, felt too light some-how, and its shape not quite right, and made of cardboard rather than plastic, more like a packet of cigarettes than a tape, but empty. Some prank, no doubt; someone treating my bed as a bin—how funny. The remainder of the dormitory were all out for the count. Nothing to be done; no one to confront. So I finished changing, put on my dressing-gown and slippers, grabbed my towel, and went off to wash, with the mystery package shoved inside my sponge-bag. The corridor was already dark, darker than the night of my inquisition at the hands of Bonifacio; all I had to guide me now was a faint uneven distant glimmer, signalling, like a faraway lighthouse, the night lavatory.

It was all so odd that it might have been comical, absurd in the manner of Ionesco, for the small box proved, as I'd suspected, to be an empty packet of cigarettes (of once-stunted ones, like the legs of Tadzio), and of a tawdry brand which took me back to the fracas when my head had been dunked in the school pissoir—not Nye's class of cigarette at all: he, in matters of nicotine, I knew to be a strict existentialist, to favour aromatic French tobacco with a philosophical blue tinge. No, this packet had once housed a cheaper breed of gasper altogether, popular among the car-maintenance louts, who, like truckers pretending to be Teddy boys, or husbands merrily squandering the housekeeping, would pride themselves in opening their cool mouths wide, like fish, and expelling smoke rings—slowly to spin and float and disperse in the dense umber fogginess which hung about the pub lounge after evening class.

But I was wrong to imagine that the packet might have been empty: it was, as it happened, loaded. And what I found inside, meticulously folded, like a collapsible ladder, was a long thin strip of paper with lines like rungs, torn from a distinctive style of jotting pad which was then popular. You probably remember the type: exceedingly oblong, with a flashy picture on the cover, generally of an elongated figure to suit the format: a decadent former theatre-heroine with hair like a brainstorm and slippers like nibs, or a soft illustration of some cereal goddess called Eté, because she came from Montparnasse, some gangly lady with braids and bad sandals, draped in a diaphanous toga and waving something natural, such as a burnished sheaf of barley. The pads had a hole through the top, near the garlands and tendrils and diadems of these assorted dramatic damsels, so that you could hang them.

.   .   .

THE MESSAGE WAS written in crayon, dark red and blunted, and delivered in wonky capitals by someone pretending to be using the wrong hand, or to be a retarded car mechanic. Such a coarse approach ruled out Hardy, whose skills in this department had always aspired towards refinement, but anyway: the substance of the neatly folded length of paper, signed by someone claiming to be Al Capone (which, fleetingly, foolishly, made me imagine that Clifford might be back, posing as a full-fledged gangster to effect my phoney abduction) was as baffling as it was violent. To this day I recall, with the slow-motion clarity of a car crash, verbatim and graphically, like an epitaph, the venomous snake of red words which slithered down that ladder of faint lines:

WE KNOW ABOUT
YOU DIRTY FUCKING
QUEER HAND OVER
FIFTEEN QUID IN THIS
BOX AND PUT IT UNDER
THE LEFT GAZEBO BY
MIDNIGHT TOMORROW
ELSE WE GO TO THE RECTOR
WERE WATCHING YOU
SIGNED
AL CAPONE
BYE BYE

And at that instant I knew precisely what, even in translation, those French authors meant when they described the process of going mad.

IN BED, I told myself to calm down. I told myself to grow up. I told myself not to be that word which had lately come into pop-parlance—paranoid. Yet I couldn't get to sleep—neither for love, nor for the money which I no longer had. Fifteen quid. How the hell was I supposed to lay my hands on that, when I'd already squandered my tutorial stash—never mind within twenty-four hours? If, in the recent past, I had worried about what Clifford's parents might have said to the rector, and about the latter's creepy plurals, and about what his hairy, bobbing Adam's apple might have said to Mr. Wolfe, or, indeed, about what Dr. Fox might have been—and might still be—concealing from me, now I worried on a scale far beyond the scope of basic Mathematics. The upsurge of my panic defied quantifying.

After Clifford's betrayal, I had felt as if I were slowly dying; now I felt that I actually wanted to die, wished that I'd drowned in the treacherous arctic waters of Eisenstein, wished that I'd never laid eyes on Nye. Suddenly, insanely, I became convinced beyond a red-crayoned shadow of a doubt that the blunt left-handed deception scrawled down the faint rungs of that neatly folded paper ladder was, in fact, of course, just a further, more rapacious twist of Hardy's calligraphic lies. Yet how could my blackmailer only be Hardy? The message, remember, said We, not I. Could it be a case of both Hardy *and* Nye? Maybe they'd ganged up against me. Come on, I told myself, be realistic: those two weren't even friends, never mind likely partners in crime, fellow gangsters. And besides, they had no ammunition against me, couldn't have had, since neither of them knew about the Clifford fiasco, nor about the real cause behind my run-in with the rabid year master. But then: Don't bank on it, I cautioned myself, because perhaps the mongrel, behind my back, had got hold of Nye and told him to watch out for my degeneracy, turned him against the shit which I'd been dubbed. Christ, perhaps the phantom scribbler was actually the mongrel, hungry to sink his ravenous fangs into my shoulders before they were bared for the benefit of society. After all, the empty packet of stunted cigarettes certainly matched *his* spivvy smoking style. And the gazebo, which lay beyond the gardens into which the rector had seemed to wish me exiled, was out of bounds to all but the top year of the school and members of staff. But then again—surely not—yes it could, could even be the rector, putting me to the test, lying in wait for the faintest wind of what he had called confirmation, trying to give me rope with which to hang myself, like a damsel from a pad, for the sake of the repute of my father's Alma Mater. Father, change my name. Clifford, shed your light upon my darkened door; because it could also be some shady sixth former—Payne Senior, for instance, or his pal, the midget corporal, or even the slimy toad from the bogs, or, God, all three aligned, with military precision, like a trinity of evil-fearing monkeys. For they, unlike me, were at liberty to wander around the maze of those grounds where legend claims that centuries ago the last heir of the house, in his infancy, lost his bearings, ate some berries—succulent with poison—and died. Yet how could those boys, at the top of the school, have managed to get the mystery package sneaked beneath my pillow? Might they have commissioned someone, like rabbit-faced Newton, or even the burgeoning dropout in my dorm, he of the handsome endowment? Or might Payne Senior, the midget, and the toad not be in cahoots with the mongrel? I was sweating. My thoughts leapt, like an alley cat, from my bed to the left gazebo.

There was, in fact, a pair of small pavilions, identical in design—unlike the Nyes—at the back of the gardens, but I'd only ever seen these from a distance, from the viewpoint of a minion, through the mist of the high windows in Leviticus. The twin gazebos stood, topped by a couple of stone eagles, at the corners of the far wall. Viewed from the dormitory, there could be no doubting Al Capone's instructions. But more carefully considered, all became confusion, because, since the eagles were turned, their wings outstretched, to face the school and not away from it, that which, to unobservant eyes, might have seemed like the left gazebo, was, in fact, the right, and vice versa; and it was while I lay there trying to predict Steel's opinion, which was always learnèd, and his advice, without which I could scarcely manage, that I must have sunk into heavy slumber. Because, next thing, the wake-up bell had rung, and whereas, in the altercation with the mongrel, the strong unholy spirit of Clifford had suddenly welled within me, now, as soon as I stirred, all strength seemed to flow out of me—only to be replaced, in a blink, by the previous night's incalculable panic. I rummaged under my pillow. The empty packet of once-stunted cigarettes, and the crimson snake slithering down its ladder, had been no nightmare. Morning, boys; rise and shine.

AFTER BREAKFAST with Dr. Fox (during which he, while shaving with the electric razor, shouted to me across the room that I seemed a bit off-colour), I returned to make my bed in Leviticus. Next stop was morning prayers, followed by assembly. No time to waste: the clock in my chest was ticking, relentless as a taxi-meter. I found Steel hovering in the dormitory, vaguely in the vicinity of the windows. This was my chance to consult him. But I must have looked shell-shocked, because, before I'd even got started, he interrupted to enquire what was up. I needed his help, I said—well, his advice more like. What with?, he asked most slowly, his glare narrowing with curious suspicion, as if I were about to beg for his history notes, or maths, at which I habitually cheated. But then I found that I couldn't bring myself to explain the problem, it just seemed too complicated, like an insoluble formula; so, to simplify matters and speed them up, I pulled the cigarette packet out of my pocket and placed it without a word upon his hand. Thanks but no thanks, he said, repelled by the sight of the exhibit: I don't smoke; all medical opinion runs counter to it. (Medical parents; vitamins; anaemia.) Just *open* it, I insisted. And out came the retractable ladder, which he pulled from its case rather too roughly (for I wanted it, so far as was possible, preserved in good order, like a letter from officialdom, or evidence to be brought before a jury). But I kept my trap shut while I watched his feline eyes race down-and-up, and up-and-down the steps of hard red crayon, over and over. He, too, saved his breath while he continued with these exertions, until, at last, he quietly read out, as if posing himself a question: Al Capone?

I, of course, had secretly hoped that he might have dismissed the whole message as some pathetic joke, that he might have encouraged me to ignore such nonsense, but he did not: he was bright enough to see that though expressed in red, the whole black tone of the thing was serious—blood-curdling in fact, that's how he put it—one didn't mess with this kind of stuff; you couldn't underestimate the brains behind it. And then he led me out, in pensive silence, to the corridor, where he reckoned that, in my position, which he admitted he didn't envy, he'd probably be tempted to cough up and have done with it. That, in his opinion, seemed like the most sensible strategy. He said that there was just too much riding on it for me: I couldn't afford to get myself slung out before the end of the year, which is when we sat our first lot of external exams. I told him that I couldn't afford to cough up, didn't have the moolah. He took me back into Leviticus, and rummaged in his wallet, pondering the whole problem at what felt like unkind leisure, as if gloating very slightly, but then he volunteered that he could probably lend me, if it helped, let's see, seven quid, but only for a couple of weeks, all right? I didn't have time to answer, because my fingers, like the jaws of an alligator, had already snapped at his palm and captured the money, three crisp notes—a fiver, blue; two singles, green—underwater colours from the Ganges. And yet, now that he'd become not just my ally and confidant but properly implicated, an active accomplice in my bid to escape from hot water, he wanted to know more, more than he'd ever wanted to know about Clifford: suddenly he wanted to know from where this note had come, exactly when and where I'd found it, who I thought might be responsible, on and on he wanted to know. But now that I had half the money, it was too late for such enquiries; I just needed the other half, plus a pound, and fast. Sorry, Steel; thanks a million; and off I rushed, forgetting to ask my second question. Yet I remember how, as I ran out, he shouted (over the milling heads of the other boys whom, at various times, I had serviced in silence, but whom, at that same instant, in an epiphany, I swore never again to service): Don't forget, Moore, I need it back within the fortnight. All *right,* I replied with gritted teeth, in case the mongrel were around—Keep your hair on. He turned away, flicking his pale bob aside.

AT BREAK, elevenish, I returned to Dr. Fox for toast. What on earth was eating me?, he asked. Nothing, I made out. Don't be stupid, he persisted, something's obviously wrong; this is *I* to whom you're talking. And so, again, I produced the packet of fags—slamming it on the mantel, and telling him: Well, since you're so determined to find out, just take a look at *that.* Dr. Fox seemed taken aback by my reaction: emotional outbursts being, as far as he knew, untypical of my repertoire; but he appeared to compose himself speedily—if only to adopt a sluggish motion. He slid his glasses up, and then took hold of the mystery package (slightly warily, as if it were some party-joke, childishly explosive), and once he'd made himself very gradually comfortable upon the leather quilt of his wingèd chesterfield, as Sherlock Holmes might have done, the myopic private eye claimed to be baffled. So, one more maddening time, I had to tell him to inspect the contents. And as he did so, the box fell to his lap; and as he read the poisoned diatribe, my mentor blushed. But as soon as he began to implore me to be sensible, to keep my wits about me, I realized that I was on my witless own, floundering in my personal quagmire—to do with which he would have nothing.

Look, I said, forgetting our differing positions in the official hierarchy, I've thought about it good and hard, didn't get a wink of sleep all night, and I've decided that I've just got to pay up. That, he advised, would be madness. *Why?,* I yelled back. Be-*cause*—and keep your voice down—one should never, on principle, give in to blackmail: it's a pernicious practice, underhand and criminal. Deaf to his moralizing, I reminded him that I could get expelled for this, did he realize. Nonsense, he said, You're too promising for the school to want to kick you out. And yet, to me (whom the rector had already threatened with expulsion), Dr. Fox did not seem any calmer than I. I told him that I didn't have the money. He said absolutely nothing, as if he, now, were the deaf one; but, as he folded away the message and returned it to its package, I noticed that his puffy pianistic fingers were trembling very slightly . . . *How,* he suddenly asked, can you not have the money—what, none whatever? I claimed that I had half, pretending that Steel's seven pounds were properly mine. In which case, he suggested, perhaps—though I don't at all approve of this sort of thing, you understand—perhaps you should offer your Al Capone (*my* Al Capone, he said) those seven pounds, and explain in a note of reply that at present it's all you have. Take a chance.

Dr. Fox must be denser than I'd realized. I inhaled profoundly, like my mother on the brink of dismissing a servant. Couldn't he see that I was involved not in some minor transaction which offered room for manoeuvre, but in a crisis which—to quote Steel—was blood-curdling? Negotiation just didn't come into it. Dr. Fox admitted that yes, it was all somewhat unpleasant, and potentially embarrassing, but really no worse than that. And then he added that, since I'd already had my fair share of embarrassment in life, I should be inured to it by now—a cynical nugget which I found more offensive than constructive. I said as much. He apologized. I told him that what I needed was not some lofty lecture, but the other half of the money. Couldn't he lend it to me? Out of the question, he replied—less like an ethical detective than a tight-fisted banker. I feared that he was going to force me to blub, to crank up an act, but, as I looked down, I caught sight of my watch and realized that break was practically over. No time for theatricals. Sod him, I thought; and then I stood up and took the cigarette-packet; but as I moved away from his lumpen great uselessness, he surprised me by saying that just as he objected to blackmail, so he disapproved of lending money: if one was reduced to the indignity of borrowing, the last thing that one needed was the additional pressure of having to repay debts, and, after a further, suspended hiatus, he said that—on condition that it be the end of the matter and that I never allude to it in the future—he would let me have (*have,* he made clear, not borrow) the remaining eight pounds, though not as a means for me to submit to criminality. As a quite unconnected present. I could've sucked him off on the spot, but the bell had already gone. I had to get back to class. I thanked him, said I'd be back at lunchtime, and fled down the fifth-year corridor.

BETWEEN THE NEXT two periods, just before Latin, which was taught by a mousy closet-baronet who used to wince if you called him *Sir* with feeling, I got hold of Steel again and whispered to him my second question: whether, on account of the stone eagles pointing in our direction, he thought that the gazebo to the left was indeed the left, or, more likely, the right. Probably as a result of his knowledge of history and war campaigns and battle standards, he knew the answer almost without thinking: left, he said, was always left as viewed by us. The enemy's perspective was of no relevance. Remember Waterloo, he added. (How could I not?) According to Steel-the-budding-general, we were the ones in charge, and only our direction mattered; forget that vital piece of strategy, and you may as well surrender, start waving the white flag. So now at least I knew where to go, knew which of the gazebos was my target, my command. And then he said—with feeling, which now made *me* wince: Don't forget my seven quid; pay me back within the fortnight or you're history. *Annale,* in Latin. Amen in Catholic.

BACK TO DR. FOX, ostensibly for lunch, but really to collect the rest of the money, which he, as if wishing to divorce himself from my shaming weakness in the teeth of hoodlums, had deposited under the electric shaver on the (dusty) mantel. I swept up the notes and married them to the contents of my wallet (an article which I'd once told Clifford was wrought from the foreskins of pelicans. *God* how exotic, he had exclaimed. Well, Clifford, maybe your father's mistress would like one now.) But then, as Dr. Fox presented me with a plate, piled high with farmhouse paté purchased from his superior grocer, and no doubt on account (the *indignity* of borrowing), I had a sudden brainwave, which did, next, require a good authentic blub. With remarkable facility, I discovered, I began to sob like a war-torn widow. What's the matter *now*?, he groaned, prevented in mid-crouch from settling to attack his grub. (The matter was the gazebo itself, of course, in the gardens which were out of bounds to all but sixth formers and members of staff.) I was scared, I said, to be seen venturing into enemy territory by the rector. In which case, Dr. Fox suggested, jump over the wall round the back. What?, I gasped, and get myself lynched by some local farmhand? Was he completely mad? Dr. Fox was starting to look a teensy bit narked, beady-eyed: he could tell, I could tell, where I was heading, could guess at the request which was coming. Look, I said—again forgetting the polarity of our positions—had I ever, *ever* asked him for any favour? (The favours which, by contrast, had once been granted to his sweaty crotch hung in mid-air like threatening clouds, like the Venetian clouds which once had overhung the Lido.) His glacial spectacles made plain to me that he could see precisely where I was leading him, which was neither to redemptive water nor in the direction of his obliging grocer, but inexorably towards grass. And again, like this morning, he blushed, though no longer quite so innocently, for he must, in his gut, have felt a rumble of discomfort, the feeling that he did, indeed, owe me one. And even if it took, because he could be stubborn, a lavish dollop of my most persuasive smarm, in the end, he did consent, poor man, to oblige.

He undertook, on my behalf, to take a stroll to the left gazebo (which I had to insist was the one to his left As He Walked Out), and he agreed to tuck Al Capone's blood-money under one of the corners of that *specific* stone pavilion; and then, he said, he would return for tea, by which time he sincerely hoped that I'd have put the whole business behind me; but the situation was, he said, frankly ridiculous. And I, conceding to his frankly ridiculous hypocrisy only by virtue of my newfound gratitude, nodded that I knew that it was, and that I was sorry to put him in this awkward position. And although, following my extraction of his commitment, I found myself with ample leisure to kneel at his feet and gratify his cheesy penis, I'm sorry to say that instead I conceived an urgent need to go to the basement and prepare for his next orchestral meeting. I'd be back for tea.

Dr. Fox was a greedy man; but not, in the final instance, wicked; and when I dragged my apprehension back to his room, he confirmed, to my spiralling relief, that the deed was done, as he put it. He also told me, by way of proof of his obedience, that he'd found a very obvious crevice under one of the corners of the relevant gazebo, which meant that the criminal element, as he now called Al Capone, must have known exactly what it was up to. Still, Dr. Fox had proved true to his word, had deposited the money—and Yes, he reassured me, carefully out of sight of anyone. And next, as if this were *his* cut of the deal, he insisted that I now forget the whole thing and get on with some proper revision. Only six weeks to go before you start your O levels, he nagged, no time to phootle about, old chap. I said that I would buckle down without further demurring; yet, in the event, I found myself unequipped to honour such a promise, for, in truth, it had only been a far-fetched intention (not a pact, Clifford, still less a marriage vow).

NEXT MORNING, I needed to know the state of play. My deadline had been met, and Al Capone's instructions, against all the odds and despite my hysteria, been fulfilled, like an exam completed within the requisite time limit. Yet whether the blackmailer had actually taken possession of the loot remained to be seen. Dr. Fox nearly lost his rag when I tried to suggest that perhaps he could go back and take a peep. He reminded me of my agreement never again to refer to this unpalatable (his word) subject. So during break, I took myself, affecting a look of tedium but practically succumbing—as if terror-stricken at prep school—to an attack of the shits, to the back side of the rear wall of the gardens, above which the left gazebo could be seen at a weird perspective, like the dovecote in the bedroom of my infancy, swaying slightly. I looked up from the field of filthy grass. I could hear a tractor in the distance, or a combine harvester, threatening sounds of farming. To be quite frank (and not just prissy), you really needed a ladder to get up there. But then I saw a succession of scuff marks leading vaguely vertically, the tracks of shoes which had struggled to climb, and this encouraged me—for as well as suggesting that my blackmailer, having avoided the gardens, was unlikely to be a sixth former or a member of the staff, those tracks pointed to the likelihood that the money had been collected, and, therefore, that my torment was over at last. I just needed to verify the fact, for my own peace of mind.

My ascent can't have been dignified. I fancied myself an aesthete, not an athlete, and this concluding ordeal felt like Gratuitous Humiliation. But, as I climbed, I tried to imagine wartime escapades, and spotlit Nazi interrogations, and Colditz in real life, and even Mr. Bonifacio, and somehow, assisted by these thoughts, I managed to heave myself onto the level of the gardens. I crept round the gazebo, found the corner which Dr. Fox had described, and, to my puzzlement, then horror, discovered that the packet of cigarettes was still there, soggy-looking but intact. A surging, boiling quandary now beset me: should I leave the money in place, or take it back? I decided to reclaim my ransom, lest it should fall into the hands of some overefficient gardener. But next, just to make sure before embarking on the downward climb, I took a look inside the packet. The money was gone. In its place, I found another paper ladder, effectively identical to the first, again scrawled in red crayon, and again demanding fifteen pounds, though this time granting me—how kind—a whole week's grace in which to comply with the demand. I leapt over the wall and somehow landed alive.

As I sloped back to class, squelching over the sludge, I dusted myself down, restyled myself, and tried to review the position. First I needed seven quid to get Steel, the loan-shark, off my back; then, a further fifteen quid to keep Al Capone gagged, which totalled twenty-two. Actually, I still had two in my PO account, so call it twenty. And thus, resigning myself to a stultifying dose of double Mathematics, I began to wonder on whom, next, I could rely for help, rely with confidence. On whom could I bring pressure to bear, as Al Capone had brought his own unbearable pressure onto my old head on young shoulders? And then, once more: Eureka. Because, just along from my circular mental sum of twenty pounds, the vital little parallels which now suggested themselves to my nonfinancial mind, the = sign, pointed, and unequivocally, like the sudden, accurately copied answer to a formerly open-ended equation, to one unmistakable quantity, one sole known word, one man, one name alone: Wolfe, of course. But I knew better than to howl with euphoria. Instead, while pretending to rack my brain of a stupid joyless shopgirl over some baffling set of exercises, I scribbled him a note, on cheap school stationery, which I later sent through the internal mail—I wasn't Rockefeller—informing my erstwhile supervisor that there was s o m e t h i n g that I needed to discuss with him, and that the matter was of urgency. And I ended the missive with love: what did I have to lose by that? Zero. A great big nought, absolutely round, like a hollow pie chart—nothing like the shape of an old heart, or a pair of interwoven zodiacal symbols, Gemini.

His reply reached me within forty-eight hours, and, in accordance with his suggestion (but without official permission, least of all from Dr. Fox), I went, the following afternoon, to meet him in his room at my old prep school. It all turned out to be oddly familiar, by which I mean familiar in odd ways. From reception, I was ushered up by some young secretary, cropped and trousered and sexy, perhaps even bi-sexy—who could tell? I wouldn't have put Sappho past her, nor her past Sappho, for there was a butch *quelque chose* about her, a chic aggres-siveness, as if, beneath her wide black trousers, she might have been concealing high boots with spurs attached. Her face, new since my day, wore, I remember thinking, too much make-up; her eyes were spiked with mascara, like man-eating spiders; and she exuded as she went up, two steps at a time, a strong musky scent, almost unpleasant—not Joy, that was for sure, much less gardenias. With the amazon in charge, we climbed past the holy statue to whose feet some poor boy had, before either of our times, crashed—never to be fixed again, not even by the miraculous adhesive of communal prayer. Eventually we reached the level of the junior dormitories, and then, Mr. Wolfe's door, the door of my former covert entrances and exits, the idolatrous portal of my childhood tabernacle, on which Bisexy Amazon now knocked—too hard—before stalking off on some other business. My former lover didn't answer. He came out.

I discovered that the setting of my early nocturnal abandon had undergone an overhaul, been revamped—presumably to reflect Mr. Wolfe's raised position in the establishment; but the result, when compared to the period when I'd known those four walls, and known them intimately, appeared, to me, visually inferior. There was a plain, self-patterned bedspread now, crushed velveteen, I think, the colour of cold curry. Next to the bed, which otherwise looked unaltered, there was a new (but already grubby) sheepskin rug—for Mr. Wolfe had, it transpired, lately become the beaming owner of a pallid Labrador, for which sloppy breed I felt as good as nothing. Borzois and salukis, then, were more my style, elegant hounds from enormous paintings and great Russian palaces. Flicky, I think the dog was called, so perhaps it was a bitch who wouldn't answer to Felicity. I told him to get the slobbering creature off me, even if it *was* young, which, ironically, is how he tried to excuse his obvious failure to control it. He did as I instructed. And the animal, a picture of sycophancy, curled itself beneath his desk, not so far from where my short-trousered legs had once, when I myself had been a dark-eyed sycophant, been stroked. No mention of the rector, nor of Clifford, nor of n o t h i n g. Let sleeping dogs lie. I remember little else about those premises, for I was in a hurry, and out of my own bounds, and in a blinding Latin fury. My mother's blood, Lord love it.

He tried, as my father had tried during the storm in my preparatory teacup, to shake my hand. I ignored the inanity. Next he encouraged me to sit, like a Labrador; but I remained standing, digging my hands into my pockets as I'd done when I refused to let him beat me with a table-tennis bat. (See? Familiar but different.) He sat at his desk, near the window, near the dog's foul basket. Did I want some music? No, I replied; silence was fine. He can't have agreed, because, almost immediately, he stood up, and went round, no longer towards the pick-up gramophone of my past, but towards a cassette-recorder, like a bulky vanity-bag, portable. He had the sense to play nothing which harked back to the two, the two, the two of us; left Mary Magdalene's musical sobs safely out of his modernized environment; kept his hands off my Nocturnes (it was four o'clock, not midnight); made no attempt to build a nostalgic bridge over our moribund waters. I recall that instead of music with an emotive charge, he, as if trendified, chose a turgid pop song by some gang of tone-deaf yobs going on and on about not needing no *edgy-cation.*

Yet as I observed him, this altered Mr. Wolfe, I still recognized traces of what once upon a time had drawn me to his arms, and drawn me so badly, traces of why I'd loved him with such fraught childish passion, of why I couldn't have resisted doing what I had done, night after night. But I was also able to see why, three years after our valedictory pout outside that seminary in Brussels, I no longer felt much more for him than I did for his snoring Labrador, why my innards had grown cold, and my spirit chilled in his regard. He felt untrustworthy now, or reputable perhaps—either way, uncomfortable. From my sullen, mercenary point of view, all that remained, despite his never-setting sunburst smile, was a buried bond, an impoverished connection which would take years to assume proper shape and surface and be acknowledged—though, even then, never openly. Our great secret, remember; Special. But as I stood there, under the hideous fringes of some recently installed ceiling-light, I realized that the task which awaited me was steeply uphill, steep as my struggle to climb the wall to the gazebo.

WHAT CAN HE do for me?, he asks, less like a former lover than a put-upon employer. I need some money, I reply in the tone usually employed for the review of one's salary—falsely cool, impassive. But he looks at me oddly, as if I were speaking the wrong language—I on whom, at the end of our romance, no amount of money squandered had seemed excessive, no number of useless fripperies too great a profligacy. How much?, he wonders, as if I were a hooker trying to haggle with a punter, or the other way round. Twenty, I say, more flatly than Shrove Tuesday. Twenty, he repeats, ashen as a Wednesday; then, nothing. But after a protracted rumination, Gosh, he goes, That seems a bit hefty, doesn't it?—as if my request were a holy cow. Still, he does at least manage to smile about it, even if a trifle meanly—meanly as I, much later, would, as you know, smile over my own negotiations. Yet, for now, I remain utterly serious, deadly; desperate. Twenty, he forces me to say a second time. He shudders—to think. Why so much?, he asks. I don't bother to reply. Instead, I peer at the dull, diminished viaduct over which now I *can* properly fly—not to the circus, I grant you, nor to Russia, but at least to concerts and to plays in which my head can escape to the few naughty cinemas and cocktail bars that Clifford hasn't managed to monopolize.

Mr. Wolfe now dares to enquire how come I need such a sum, don't my parents give me enough? I claim that it's none of his affair (the affair of teachers and pupils about which Clifford had blabbed). Will he simply part with the lucre, or will he deny it? (Will he be a deputy head, or will he be a paedophile?) He looks telepathically insulted. Am I in trouble? Sort of, I half-answer. With whom, the authorities? (Still no actual mention of the rector.) I don't know with whom exactly. (I bet he thinks I'm lying—after all, if you're in trouble, surely you know the quarter from which you're running. But I was running back to the left gazebo, you see, and getting breathless while I was at it.) Again I say that I'm in trouble, that I just need the money, that it's all too boring to explain in detail, so either to let me have (not borrow) twenty pounds—in fivers, I specify, larger notes are not convenient—or to turn me down, but to stop messing me around. He asks if I'm taking drugs. I say that I'm not (and nor, then, was I). He asks how my revision is going. I tell him to stuff it up his jumper. He smiles more widely still, seems to approve of my shopgirly defiance, as if it were a sign that I'd finally grown into myself, into my precocious shoulders, into my eventual genitals. And then, at long bloody last, he surrenders to the injustice of my power, like a cropped and trousered, hard but gentle, bisexual secretary.

The dosh, unlocked from a drawer, he places in an envelope, as my mother does, as I myself have done. There's a certain circularity, like the rounded sum of twenty pounds, to the whole demeaning enterprise. It just happens to be my own turn now, my personal moment of reckoning, as ironically logical as the infinity implicit in parallel lines, lines unable ever to meet and entwine like zodiac symbols on the golden surface of a medal buried long ago beneath the ground. He slides the envelope smoothly along the desk, as Bonifacio, once, had slid his golden lighter for me to ignite him—even though I, in obliging that first of my interrogators (precursor to the hamster, father, fox, rector, and mongrel—quite a little album), had only managed to fire him closer to anger than carnality. I leave Mr. Wolfe's envelope behind, like a disposable afterthought, and place his (considerate) quartet of banknotes in my wallet, which has grown glossy with the tears of pelicans. I have a bash at thanking him, but in my depth I resent being back in this dump, which, however redecorated, feels no better for it. Even my father's pub-lunch, followed by his sobs, would have been preferable.

I'm about to pocket the lucre and run, but Mr. Wolfe, now that our minor unpleasantness is over, rises to warm humour and decides to approach me with sentiment, like That. I can interpret the undeveloped language of his body better than my own—which, being a dialect, can give rise to confusion. And as he draws towards a hopeful proximity, he begins to say how pleased he is to see me, and how marvellously well I look—and in the manner of these things, well, let's just say that he gets me. And do I oblige? Of course I do: as with the members of Leviticus, I provide him with the semblance of a service, for which Mr. Wolfe is at least, let's face it, paying—my first honest-to-goodness punter. Nursery slope stuff, really, hardly going to kill me. Because killing isn't Mr. Wolfe's speciality: killing is Al Capone's.

ALL THAT I MAY have told you about our first night six years earlier, and about the rapture at the start of that foremost beginning, and about our million subsequent hours of love made beneath the northern stars, and about the second wave of our great songs, and the flaring beauty of our votive torches, you may now wipe out, erase from memory, extinguish, subtract like a gift of great value taken back, the gift of an Indian giver. Because, on this singular afternoon, and even before he's got started, Mr. Wolfe, well, just goes and wrecks it. Instead of leaving me alone and letting bygones be gone by, he now wants to know what I like, now that I've grown—hmm, Let me look at you (let him look at me)—yes, into quite a young man, we're almost the same height. And for the only time in our connection—a word which I select advisedly, since our love affair is more than done—the sexual act does not take place upon the bed of my many childish makings, which perhaps, in my wake, has become the province of some hairless successor. Instead, it takes place standing up, and fully clothed, as if this refurbished tabernacle were a public lavatory. His beard has grown shabby, like the beard of a vagrant, and begun to blotch to a dirty mushroom, and his kisses no longer feel like the answers to the prayers of anyone (other than a dog, perhaps), but kisses to be avoided, first smelling, then almost tasting of gravy and onions, of steak and kidney pie. Our congress proves more tawdry than the tawdriest grope in the municipal cottage, because here, now, I can't even try to pretend, I just mime very badly, far worse than any amateur. His penis, that sovereign roundhead of my infantile wonderment, now makes me squirm on his account, disgusts me, for it looks half the length and half the girth that I remember—miserable, miserly, diminished even in its hardness. It slides about my mouth, like a red crayon, blunted. In order to suck, I must, of all the memories, pout—although, now that I'm grown into quite the young man of his false flattery, I do not suck like a girlish child; certainly not: I suck like a prat in an Old Boy tie puffing at his medium-sized cigar.

And yet the shame, it can't all have been mine; for surely Mr. Wolfe, that former apple of my young eye, that core of my rotten deuteron-omy, must have realized, as he burnt the back of my jacket with tortu-ous Japanese circles, stroking me round and round and round and round ad infinitum, that he'd forgotten how to love and love forever, like an eternally indebted supervisor, grateful everlastingly. But sud-denly, for no good reason, his deputy head relieves itself inside my pouting mouth; and I reel across the room to the very radiator against which the button of my pyjamas had once, like a treacherous coin, clanked, and I spit him out onto his own towel—the latter, plain, no longer striped, yet reminiscent still of the towel whose theatrical falls had once filled my heart with loud applause. And then, slamming the door—which had not been locked—I get the hell out; I get out of hell. We were never to meet again, he and I, nor to make contact; but later, you know, by when, of course, it was all no good, I came to regret the severance. Perhaps he was owed an explanation. And I, perhaps, a bet-ter rate of exchange than twenty pounds.

MUCH LATER, as I say, while searching for a direction, or even a style of life, I lived in a small hotel on the borders of Chelsea, near the river. Here, over breakfast one winter day, Decemberish, I accidentally fell upon a notice at the back of some newspaper, a notice placed by a firm of Mancunian solicitors acting on behalf of Mr. Wolfe's estate, the executrix of which appeared to be his widow—a surprise to me, rather like Clifford's once-surprising claims to home-sickness. I pictured the former Ms. Bisexy Amazon as the woman bereaved, poised at the side of some wuthering grave in a black silk topper with a half-veil of mesh, the very image of dressage, and racking her (retired) secretarial brain as to how in heaven's name someone of whom she'd never heard came to figure in her departed husband's last will and testament. I also surmised that Mr. Wolfe must have died of heart failure; it seemed fitting, merited. Gone but not forgiven, sort of thing. Yet the tiny, reconciling print before my eyes sought to trace me by any means, under any of my several names—Spanish, English, or the one which, since, I've elected by deed-poll—though not, to my relief, under the alias Woman, nor under the initials HWB. For secrets, like secretaries, should be kept concealed, interred intact, never betrayed, never released to the skies with the levity of cremated ashes. Whether I was bequeathed propitiatory coins, to add to the blue quartet of banknotes made over to me in his life, or whether I'd been left some small but significant memento (an early edition of Lewis Carroll seemed likely), I could not say; for I affected, in that era, never to read the papers, and my affectation mattered more to me than his departure from this world. His wishes, like his bisexual antics and the mounting rhythms of his career, were as little my business as they felt of interest. Besides, by then, I was financially free, no longer strapped for posthumous interest, and too old for propitiation anyway. Too senile for forgiveness. I couldn't even remember the words of the Creed.

(EVEN IF, in time, I was to feel that an explanation might have been due to Mr. Wolfe,) when I returned, after that last inglorious congress which had cost him twenty crumpled quid, to what the Countess had described as the Big School, but which, like Mr. Wolfe's penis, appeared to have diminished, I explained nothing to anyone. I just shelled out. Steel I reimbursed in a crested envelope, which, though it may have pricked his historical interest, he scarcely acknowledged, as if its contents were an insignificance between friends, which in a sense they were, trivial; but Al Capone I paid more handsomely, with greater ceremony: not in his grubby sodden packet of fags, the squalor of which, for all of my own squalor, I could not bear to keep about me. Instead, I chose an empty box of cocktail cigarettes, which the colourful inhabitants of the music basement sometimes liked to bring to their illicit feasts on Sunday afternoons. I must have decided, after one of those sessions in the glassy cubicles, to keep this particular packet, which was black and slim and shiny, in order to store stamps and air mail stickers; but since I had no one to whom to write and, consequently, scant need for the stamps within, the container felt like a redundancy, desk clutter. And so I reasoned that if I was going to have to submit to Al Capone's villainy one final time, I may as well, while I was at it, rather than further comply with his nasty notions of packaging, assert my superior stylishness, like the stoical last Empress of Russia (who would have detested Eisenstein), or a proud borzoi, come to that. Al Capone, I told myself, might indeed be an expert criminal, but I would teach him, if it was the last thing that I did, the meaning of the word *aesthete*. And thus I folded the triptych of blood money, which was blue as the blood of murdered monarchs, inside the gilded inner wrapper, closed the small casket, and braced myself for the committal.

I STOLE OUT to the wall behind the gardens. I could have done with Clifford to lend me a leg-up—like a groom helping a pearl-encrusted tsarina onto her side-saddle, or raising a dressing-gowned child to the profoundly pink velvet of its mother's rocking unicorn. But these were impoverished times, fearful ones, and the only hand that you could trust was your own shaking ringless one, to tug at your own reins lest you bolt into the distance. I clamber up the wall, wearing gloves on this occasion. All is stiller than a graveyard. I lay the black box in the stone niche, stooping as you must stoop to place a wreath upon the tomb of someone you have loved. No time for a prayer. (No, Clifford, not a thought of one.) I leap back down. I land. I stumble. I return to the building hobbling slightly.

At tea, Dr. Fox finds me peculiar. I tell him that it's just all this revision. He understands, he says, but I mustn't let it get me down. If I'm organized, there won't be any need for last-minute heebie-jeebies. I nod like a nodding Indian cow, or like the head of an ornamental dog plonked on the back of a gangster's car. Have some toast, he says. I couldn't, I reply. Or some cake, perhaps? Look, I blurt, I'm really not hungry. Surely a cup of tea?, he persists. OK, I surrender. (In dainty china it comes, rattling sofawards.) Thank you. But he ignores me now, for his eyes are busy rolling at the mirror, as if he were making signs to someone behind my back, suggesting that I'd lost my marbles, that the time had finally come to call for my straitjacket.

WHAT EVER HAPPENED to the rest of that term? Where can it have gone? Nowhere much: I did nothing; I grew numb; I gave up; I don't even recall the songs of the time. Tweeting birds on a transistor left out on the grass? Someone squeaking about Loving You (is easy 'cos you're beautiful)? I couldn't say for sure. All that I know is that I didn't dare to return to the gazebo to check whether Al Capone's money had flown, because I couldn't have coped with a further demand. Instead, I glided through boring exam after boring exam, as if I were drugged, drugged like my mother, as if the papers and questions and time-bells were figments of someone else's unimaginative reality, my father's perhaps. And whereas in recent terms I'd grown to dread the days before return-ing to my parents' house, now I found that I couldn't stop counting. And when the end did come, the foul weather was fine; and my dismal flight, blessedly bland. At the airport on the island, I felt too tired to muster a filial smile. I needed to convalesce in silence. But first, before I could concentrate on recovery, I loudly refused to teach English to anyone, salivating notary or harelipped girl with acne. My mother acceded, for she could see, she said, that those exams had wiped me out—poor Iago. I sunbathed naked on her terrace, trying to bring my skin back to life, to save it with a concoction of cooking oil and lemon juice and iodine. I locked myself into privacy, from the outside. I didn't go to a single party for The Young. I looked up depression in an old encyclopedia. I put myself out of my mind.

My exam results, addressed to me, arrived some morning in mid-August, but it was my father who, before I came down for breakfast, saw fit to slice open the envelope—a liberty which he concealed until we were safely seated on the terrace, late into lunch, as the fruit was being brought round. He said that if I managed to hang on to a place at school, it would be by the skin of my teeth, or on the wings of a prayer, or some such inanity, and that he'd probably have to ring his friends-in-high-places to get them to persuade the rector to keep me on in the senior school. My Adam's apple wobbled slightly. My father continued: certainly I'd have to re-sit Mathematics, whether I went to university or elsewhere—somewhere sensible. And as for the rest of my grades, well, a pretty poor show, if he might say so (he already had), nothing to be proud of. Nothing, I replied with spiky pedantry, of which to be proud.

Oblivious to my correction, he turned his attention to the passing platter and took, with a grunt, a mango, a fruit which he invariably chose, and invariably ate (even my mother agreed with me on this) like

a savage, peeling it with his fingers and tearing at the stringy flesh, letting the sticky juice dribble down his jowls and gnawing at the stone,
slurping at the rancid sweetness and munching at the pulp. While I
averted my eyes from the spectacle of the man, and did my best not to
hear him, I tried to weigh up what would happen if I were to find
myself flung out: whether his victor's wreath would wilt with misery at
my failure to bring credit to his Alma Mater, or whether, on the contrary, he might not quietly be thrilled, because, just as I knew myself to
be vindictive, so I knew from which side of my faulty gene-pool the
trait of vengefulness had been rained down—or, at least, its greater
(mathematical) percentage. I gauged that his reaction would be a mix-
ture of the two, a blend, in equal (mathematical) measures, of thrill and
misery, the proportions befitting a bullying masochist. And his reaction
now, merely about my results (rather than expulsion, which was altogether a grander matter), proved me right, proved to be that very mix in
miniature—a perfectly balanced little confusion.

He handed me the official sheet, forcing me to stretch further
towards him than he was prepared to exert the length of his sleeve. I
suspected that my mother had already surveyed the impersonal print,
as if it had contained the foregone results of some blood test for
shingles, because she demonstrated no surprise at all, still less curiosity.
She was beautifully impassive, or on pills, and wearing—of all the tragi-
comedies—dark glasses. I couldn't look at her. I resisted stating the
obvious, namely that this letter had been mine to open, not his, and
that its contents, at least in the first instance, had been none of anyone
else's sodding business. Instead, guided by wary prudence, I scanned
the document down-and-up and up-and-down, in the manner of Steel.
And what I learnt, inevitably, was that I'd indeed performed beyond
my wildest imaginings, acquitted myself laughably. Like a dunce on
sedatives.

Maths, Physics, Biology, Chemistry: all failed, and outright—with
U's (unclassified). History, Latin, Greek: passed, but miserably, with
C's. Spanish, English, French: top grades, but this, as my father knew
oh, better than anyone, was the least that could be expected. And
somewhere in the middle of it all, in the insipid realm of the B's, I managed to bluff my way to a grade in Religious Studies.

Yet much as my father cared for the practice of sanctity, I don't think that he exactly warmed to its theory, its room for uncertainty, the splitting of spiritual hairs, what he dismissed as my silly doctrinal nit-picking. Perhaps I should tell him to get me to a monastery. I wondered how such an exhortation might affect him. Would he, just as he had prayed for the collapse of my obstinacy regarding Mr. Wolfe—my lies, my overly coloured fancy—fall to his knees and implore Our Father to strike down this imbecile, or would he punch a dent into the boot of his own motor? My musings were cut short, because Bright, he now went on, bright as I considered myself to be, the proof of the pudding, laddy, was in the eating. And then he trotted out a further couple of clichés—just desserts, mighty fallen—which he crowned with a piece of sublime wit, to the effect that the ego had landed. Briefly he chortled with satisfaction, chortled as Al Capone had probably done on collecting his winnings; and then, my venerable pater resumed his dressing down.

He was bound to point out, he claimed, that he'd experienced no academic difficulty in his day, when one had sat the school certificate—much harder exams than these newfangled O levels, which, according to him, were just an excuse to lower the standards for the sake of com-prehensive thickos. How, he went on, I could even pretend to be a lin-guist simply defeated him. Pretend how?, I bristled. For a start, he explained, I hadn't even studied German (unlike his majesty). So what? I retorted. So a very great deal; romance languages were a doddle, let's face it; it was Teutonic ones that told the men from the boys. Well, I replied, at least I'd studied Greek. Glad you call a C-grade studying, you piffling squit; and anyway, Greek's just a lazy excuse for dons and other like-minded pansies. And German, I countered, is the language of the Nazis. Which is when he went ballistic: German, I'll have you know, is the language of the Future! Of modern Industry!—a subject about which you, to judge by your performance, you insolent brat, appear to be spectacularly ignorant, so kindly get out of my sight this instant before I wring your weedy neck. (I thought of Hardy and his tilted head, the head of a deaf madonna.) My mother, in profile, closed her shaded eyes and vanished into her personal darkness. And I, feeling as if I were hovering on the brink of some court martial, rolled, as if calmly, my napkin into its silver noose, and rose with a brow so arched that it was worthy, if not of Johnny Weissmuller, certainly of Hollywood before the talkies; but then I decided, at the last minute, to mind my hips as I performed my exit.

I walked back into a landscape of taunting shadows. If any calls were made to his cronies by my father, I was not apprised, but left to stew in the juices of my own jittery ignorance. So, a couple of weeks before my return to England, while my father was at his office, and my mother (for a change) out at a fitting, I decided to 'phone Dr. Fox, who must, I surmised, by now be back at school. I had trouble with the secretary because I didn't want to volunteer my identity in case she laughed about my ego having landed, but the bitch drove a hard bargain and, in the end, did manage to prize my surname out of me. With maddening protraction, she now put me through to the basement. When Dr. Fox eventually answered, his Yes? . . . sounded glum. And yet, hearing my voice, he seemed to perk up, as if his whiskers were smiling at the end of the line, which crackled with distance, and then he said that he was fine, splendid thank you, just back from Salzburg; what about me, where had I been? Nowhere, I replied. Well, what had I been up to? (Up to what had I been?) Nothing much. Why ever not? I ignored this fatuous line of enquiry, and got straight to the point, and confessed, as if I were confessing to a shameful breakdown, that my exam results had been atrocious. He said that he was perfectly aware of the fact, but added that it didn't really matter. I said that it was all the fault of Al Capone. He said that he didn't want to discuss any of *that,* the subject was closed. Well anyway, I struggled on, had I forfeited my place at school or hadn't I? Why on earth? Because of my lousy grades, of course. (Fatty was about to make me lose my temper.) But then he went and almost lost his own; yet his impatience, as it began to flow, seemed to bathe me in sustenance. Because what he said was: Look, just get on the train with all the others, and I'll pick you up from the station—you may as well skip the bus ride. All you need do once you're back is *not* rise to the bait, keep out of trouble, and work like a demon. You'll re-sit Mathematics in a couple of months, which I've already squared with the rector; and I shall be your moral tutor, as was always the plan. You'll concentrate on languages, which are your speciality (Speciality, Father), and if you do exactly as I say, you'll see that everything will turn out fine. I know this system inside out. Your results are a bore, admittedly, but not an impediment to your future, and certainly not grounds for not returning. So: see you in a fortnight, and don't forget that I'll be at the station to collect you. I'll be waiting in the car park. Now kindly stop fretting, and don't annoy your parents, do you understand? And for God's sake *do* something. Goodbye.

I don't recall uttering another word during the remainder of that fortnight, other than at a tobacconist's where I went to buy Dr. Fox some Montecristos, which I could get for a fraction of what you had to pay for them in England. And when the holiday slithered to its conclusion, I borrowed my mother's bathroom scales, to ensure that, if nothing else, I had no excess baggage. No chances; no fear. Bad odour; bad blood. The driver took me to the airport.

FROM THE START of my time in the senior school, the flow of my life became separate from the main tide, satisfactorily estranged. Now, not far from Dr. Fox's brocaded alcove, I had a room of my own, which I decorated to suit me, with framed pictures of the sea, and old wooden boxes which you could lock—conveyed in my trunk all the way from my island—along with cushions whose covers had been made by the seamstress at home, but whose stuffing was provided by Dr. Fox, and a heavy counterpane of woven cloth which took me back to my time by the beach before it all went wrong. At last I could play my own music— not droning lyrics about pretty ladies leaning on Darkened doors, but my tangos about Cádiz and Havana and the sentimental foreign pop songs of my earlier summers—and I could do this without the need of ear-phones or the risk of ridicule, though I would instantly click Off if anyone knocked. I had a basin in there too, which meant that apart from showering when I knew that the showers were empty, I was self-sufficient. I'd begun to shave by this point, a development which I loathed, for bristle felt less like maturity to me than it did like irreversible loss, but at least I was spared the need to perform the whole indignity shirtless in some public washroom. I kept an illicit kettle in my wardrobe, to avoid the boiler in the corridor; I laced my coffee with cocoa, and, at night, sharpened it with a glug of whisky from a bottle which I kept locked in one of my boxes. Either I ate in my room, or I ate with Dr. Fox, but I was never to return to that filthy canteen which stank of bleach and soggy dishcloths—yet was grandiloquently termed the refectory.

My tutor, though not unkindly, treated me like a patient, for we both knew that in order for me to succeed in my own terms—in terms that excluded my parents from my rainbow—two years of hard academic slog lay ahead of me, like my long view of the uphill drive towards the statue of the insouciant Madonna, who was now, miraculously, shielded from my sight by a tangle of branches. Dr. Fox, being insomniac, would prod me awake at dawn, so that I could shower, dress, breakfast in his company, and still be back at my desk before the bulk of the school had risen. He supervised my daily routine with military precision, but I was grateful for this discipline, which, to me, from him, felt like protection. I no longer bothered with morning assembly, and scarcely troubled to glance at noticeboards.

On the sly, to spare me the patronage of some in-house teacher, Dr. Fox found me a private coach, an undergraduate at some nearby university whom he paid out of his own pocket, and who came to the office in the basement three evenings a week in an attempt to cram into my skull the requisite numerical sense for me to be able to re-sit Mathematics. I began to type my A-level notes; I learnt to be organized; and I also learnt that whereas, earlier, it had been I who'd been reduced to craven borrowing, now, it was others who kept creeping up to beg access to my translations and compositions. Although, as ever, I sat at the back of the class, I no longer felt as if I were hiding, or wanting to fly out, but rather, biding my time, waiting in the wings of patience. During lessons, I contributed a meagre minimum. My Spanish teacher, for instance, was a Methodist yokel from the locality, keen on nylon slacks and keener still on football, so you will understand why there wasn't, in reality, awfully much to be contributed by someone in my position. He would attempt, with irksome regularity, to correct my pronunciation, which felt as if he were daring to correct my mother. Quite why he did this still remains a mystery; perhaps it was to teach me Methodist humility, to puncture my snobbish arteries; yet there was never any mystery about the fact that his own pronunciation of my native tongue was purest package tourist. He'd probably done a stint as a waiter in some plastic hotel in Torremolinos, though I'm certain that he wouldn't ever have been tempted by the local vino. When once I asked whether he thought that Lorca's work might have been inspired by a homosexual sensibility, he yanked me out of class, accused me of being disruptive, and told me to cut out my sickening irrelevancies if I wished to continue to be taught by him. You get the gist.

A FEW WEEKS into the term, as I was beginning to find my feet, I walked into my room (after orchestra practice, it must have been) and picked up an envelope—unaddressed, like a charity circular—which had been slipped under my door. I opened it absent-mindedly while I moved towards the window to dump my violin. When I reached my desk, I looked down, glanced at the contents and . . . there was scarcely a need to read. Yet another paper ladder, again scrawled in red crayon, and again inflamed with threats and expletives, but demanding, this time, a more rounded twenty pounds to be delivered by the end of the week to the left gazebo, you dirty queer. And yet now, for some indefinable reason, the abuse struck a different, weaker chord within me. Perhaps it was the repetitiveness of the formula, its dreary predictability, or perhaps it was my growing hopes for my own future; because, even though I knew that I couldn't resort to Dr. Fox for help on this issue, much less to Mr. Wolfe, never mind my parents, who were worse than useless—they were proper enemies—I also knew that the joke was in some way at an end, that I could never again go through with it. Beyond the fact that I'd taught no one during the previous summer, and that, since I'd earned no extra money, I wasn't in a position even to contemplate acceding to Al Capone's escalating greed, some profounder, darker part of me had toughened up, grown obstinate— refused even to seek a financial solution. What, instead, it sought, once and for all, was exposure of the blackmailer's identity, confrontation, the horrible truth. If I couldn't go to the authorities for assistance, well, big deal, I'd go elsewhere, for neither authority nor assistance was solely the preserve of school. I was coming up to my retake, and the last thing that I could risk was another failure, for, once I had Maths under my belt, I could, if necessary, do my A levels elsewhere, or independently. What I needed was to settle this problem urgently, but no longer for Al Capone's benefit. For my own. It was my wish. My last will and testament.

It didn't take me long to reach a decision. I had learnt, God knows how, perhaps from some thriller on Dr. Fox's television, about an invisible solution which, once touched by the unsuspecting criminal, turned his fingers to an ecclesiastical, but indelible, purpurine, instantly betraying his culpability. This substance, which was known as Smart Water, would, at long last, provide me with the means of outsmarting my foe, priest or boy. I could don a pair of gloves, paint the invisible liquid onto a message of financial refusal, and soon enough Al Capone would be revealed. All I needed was to avail myself of this magical juice, which was the property of private detectives, of whom I knew none, and of the police, whom I didn't need to know, because the police were supposedly there to help you. And so, the following afternoon, I walked up to the local village and waited for a bus to ferry me to a police station a couple of miles down the road, where, in my naïveté, I imagined that I'd be able, without imparting my reason, to learn how I might obtain this vital solution. But as I lurked beneath the shelter, I noticed a few of my peers meandering back from the pub, among them Steel, and as they passed, he, waving the others on, stopped to chat to me, probably a bit pissed.

I noticed that his bob was gone. His hair had been cut short, not chopped but layered expensively, which, at that point in our lives, generally spelt parental coercion, a conciliatory bribe to the stroppy teenage son. At any rate: up he strolled, hands in pockets, to where I (legs crossed, I have a horrible feeling) was sitting, and then—did I mind?—he plonked himself down beside me. Why should I?, I replied with surly indifference. Our shoulders were almost level, almost touching, not so much because I'd suddenly grown over the summer, which I don't think that I had, as because he, if not actually physically, seemed to have shrunk emotionally or morally or something. His erstwhile braggadocio, his former gleaming suit of armour, appeared to have suffered, to have been dented—somewhere about his chest, or, perhaps, his helmet. Apparently his O-level results hadn't matched those of his brilliant older brothers, but this was not discussed between us. It was hardly as if my own grades filled me with pride. Instead, we remained silent, mulling over our separate problems, delivered to the sort of brooding into which adolescents often wander. I tried to envisage him at home during the holidays, ever the sickly baby of the family, being stuffed with vitamins by his parents, and being sneered at by his know-all, musqueteering brothers, who must have seemed, to him, like unfair rivals. I felt glad, for once, to be an only child. No feuds between siblings; no squabbles over inheritance.

How were my hols?, he began. Total washout. Why was that? Because my parents made me want to vomit. So did his, he admitted, though not half as much as his bloody brothers. I had never known him so overt, so trusting. Got a girlfriend? I asked, as if I were his aunt. Hardly, he laughed, somewhat sourly. What d'you mean? Too much effing work to do, for Christ's sake; I'm expected to get a scholarship to Awksford, he said sarcastically. Ah, I replied, as if what I were expected to get were a husband. I don't think that he liked my fragrant air of distance, my mother's vacant superiority. It seemed to make him edgy. I sensed that he wanted me either to (for Christ's sake) sympathize with the pressures that had been piled upon him, or to give him a piece of whatever it was that had lately fortified me. Perhaps he envied me slightly. It had never occurred to me, before that memorable afternoon, that I was capable of inspiring such a sentiment, for, despite my privileges, which were manifold, and despite my mental aptitude, which, though not remarkable, was nevertheless of value, and despite my physical attributes, which, though these hardly catapulted me to the stratosphere of the raving exotic beauty, neither did they condemn me to the cess-pit of the downright ugly, despite all these things, I had been bred, or grown over the years, to consider myself unsatisfactory.

I produced a packet of fags. He stared at it, as if taken aback. Cigarette?, I offered. He recoiled, but only minimally, perhaps in order to suggest that, though he remained a nonsmoker, such enduring rectitude bore no connection to his parents' medical sermons. I understood. But I lit up. He looked oddly troubled, trapped, as if life had dealt him a hand which made it impossible for him, at least at home, ever to draw on a trump. What was the good of a skewering intelligence if it was doomed never to skewer enough? The injustice made you resentful, vengeful, sort of bad. That was the inference. A strange, perverse closeness seemed to blur us. He turned to scrutinize me, did so almost pruriently, as if to explore my stupid, joyless, but paradoxically enviable interior. The blueness of his eyes assumed a shade of intimacy, which warmed towards lilac. One of his eyelids quivered. It was very nearly embarrassing. I hoped that he wasn't after a repetition of our (one and only) forgettable fumble. Who knows, I remember thinking, maybe that's why he hasn't got a girlfriend.

So how were things?, he asked, with a tone of genuine interest, as if my welfare, now that we were in the senior school, were really of import. I exhaled. I thought about it. And then I told him that I'd received yet another of those ruddy blackmail notes. He looked startled, shocked on my behalf. I supposed that, once I'd paid him back his seven pounds, he'd forgotten all about my dramas. Couldn't say I blamed him. Anyway, I explained that I'd received another demand, but added that, this time, the game was up: I was through with the whole racket. I pretended, for some reason, that I had pots of cash about me, as if I needed the fantasy of money to lend me courage in my principled resolve to unmask the culprit. What was I going to do about it?, he wondered. Oh, I said—then paused, and had another gasp before going on to tell him that I was waiting for a bus to take me into town. I was on my way to the police about the matter—which, in unconscious homage to Dr. Fox, I described as frankly ridiculous. I'd had enough. Was sick of it. He looked down at the ground seriously, to consider my problem with the gravity that it warranted. He remained in that position for a good long while. The suspense made me impatient, jumpy. And then he looked up and looked out beyond the road toward the moors which blighted any hope of a horizon, and said, quite quietly: sorry. (Sorry?) Yes, that's what he said. Because, you see, it turned out that Steel and Al Capone had been one and the same person.

I REACTED with a confusion reminiscent of my father, reminiscent of his misery-and-thrill about my results; for, as I surveyed the face of Lucifer, I found myself filled with a conflicting blend of rage and gratitude. Perhaps I should have told the demon—to whom I never again spoke—how sorry I, for my own part, was that, although he'd been clever to write like a retard, and clever to choose such an improbable drop for the money, he would never be as clever as either of his brothers. But the sorry truth is that I, no less than he, was a coward; and so instead, in a travesty of forgiveness (prompted perhaps by the fact that neither of us fancied the long way back), we strolled towards the building as if together, side by side yet absolutely separate. However, the silence that ensued, oh yes, the silence of that walk was gloriously mine, deliriously and entirely. And when I marched into tea with Dr. Fox—guess what?—he no longer found me peculiar. And now I regaled him with my version of the tale of Al Capone, excluding Mr. Wolfe but climaxing, in a manic flurry, with Steel. And when my tutor began to calculate the funds which had been extorted from me, and to think of how best they might be recovered, it fell on me to insist that the matter was closed. Unpalatable. *Finito*. And then I stuffed myself with cakes. To bursting.

MY LIFE WAS back on track. I re-sat Mathematics, and, within hours of that exam (thanks to the coach whom Dr. Fox had enlisted, who performed a post-mortem on my answers, a post-mortem which, unlike the open-ended ones which are the best that one can ever perform on love, could be taken as conclusive, for maths are nothing if not exact), I knew that I had passed—not with any glamour, let's be honest, but with the certainty than I would never again have to keep a slide-rule, nor be married to a protractor. When, in dull due course, the official announcement was delivered to my parents' house—only to be left, this time, slumped a little warily, and unopened, on the silver salver at the entrance—it was I who treated the flimsy envelope as if it bore the foregone conclusion to some blood test for shingles—without interest, surprise, or sunglasses. And besides, I'd already left word that I was out for lunch, which I was—wearing a yellow hat.

Instead of subjecting myself to one of my parents' deadly repasts, which increasingly seemed to involve strangers (often the very strangers who once had squatted to gawp at my monotonous miniature chug-chug), I would slink off to the Nautical Club, to bronze myself in the Christmas sunshine; but I use that verb, that tone—bronze—loosely, liberally, like too much oil of coconut. Because although I could have assumed a perfectly respectable suntan locked out on my mother's terrace, or, indeed, practically anywhere else on the island, the Nautical Club of my childhood seemed no longer to spell public humiliation for me, nor terror, nor anxiety. Quite the reverse. It thrilled me now, thrilled me with its indecency, which simmered beneath the ripples. You could practically smell it. Briny.

I would lie around, with one knee up (which boys just didn't), wearing what the French, by then, had christened a *cache-sexe,* though mine was barely even that, it was really just an excuse to stretch a few scales of acrylic snakeskin over my absolutest basics: half my buttocks were out (yes, Father, out—out and succulent): because, by that stage, I felt it incumbent on me not merely to teeter on the most *risqué* precipice of fashion and define myself, for all to witness, as the very epitome of *le dernier cri,* but also to distance myself from those smug small-islanders, those privileged lovers of Franco whose respectable, reproductive lifestyles were as interesting and varied as is striped canvas, navy and white, a conventional cover against undesirable hotness.

Children went off to paddle and splash with their nannies, while their mothers sat by the bar, drinking papaya juice and, even if expected home for lunch, tucking into calamari and Russian salad. Meanwhile, those who lounged around the grown-up pool, smoking and rubbing lotion into one another, and shrieking at in-jokes more opaque than sunglasses, and turning mahogany but never—God forbid such a catastrophe—ever peeling, tended to be the girls, who, at that age, were stupidish but lovely, long-haired nymphs in pink bikinis, with diamond ear-studs and sparkling smiles, hanging about for that one Big catch while pretending to be expecting their brothers, who were no less stupid but far less lovely, for there was a whiff of Barbary about them, a loutishness. Yet their fathers, and their uncles, and the hosts of their older male cousins, removed once and twice and thrice, those gentlemen of Spain, they were another matter. They, the guys with the masses of chest hair and sweaty great cocks and low-slung hangers, those sinners of good caste were Alive, and sizzling with frustration, and they excited the hell out of me. And gradually-gradually I began to realize that if some of them, from beneath the brim of my hat, looked familiar, it wasn't because their offspring had once attended nursery school with me, nor because I'd seen those men strutting their stuff, and scratching it hard about the changing rooms of the club, nor even because they sometimes shot me odd glances (as if there were something intriguingly not quite right about me, like blond dreadlocks), but because I recognized them from my forays into the Municipal Park. Naughty. Still, no one ever addressed me directly, which was gratifying, because just as my Methodist teacher of Spanish liked to imagine that he was conversant with my mother-tongue, so I, by now, had become determined to convey by my demeanour not merely that I was you know, *comme ça,* but that I'd become exotically de-hispanicized, like the Duchess of Carnaby.

ON THE OCCASIONS when I was forced to be at my parents' house while they were entertaining (and my mother would even pretend that her guests were desperate to see me, rather than admit how desperately my repeated absences embarrassed her in the face of company), I would capitulate to her entreaties, but on my own terms, my tail twitching with sting. The unspoken custom at home was that my father would greet guests as they came in, kissing the women's hands, slapping the men on the back, and guffawing like a good Old Boy as he led them through rooms arrayed with standards of white gladioli, or out into the garden if the weather inspired it. Then, ages later, when everyone was comfortably ensconced and well into their drinkies, and marvelling at the bits of deliciousness borne along from the kitchen, my mother would come swirling down the stairs, light on her dancing feet, and fragrant, and pretending to apologize to all and sundry but always being flattered despite it, and always, to be truthful, looking heavenly, the best, for she wouldn't have had it any other way, not even in her own house, the house of an insular beauty without a care in the universe.

My trick was to stay—sometimes even switching off the light—in my bedroom, and hang back until I'd heard her make her descent; and only once the resulting commotion downstairs had died down, would I condescend to follow suit and glide into the assemblage. It thrilled me to note how the men stood up on my arrival, while my parents—awkwardly natural, naturally awkward—exclaimed in unison, as they'd exclaimed ever since the beginning: There he is. And then everyone would laugh, though not quite comfortably—for by my high teens, I had perfected a look of uneasy (girlish) bashfulness to enhance those late entrances of mine. As I did the murderous rounds, I would kiss the women twice, which in Spain, in those days, wasn't really done; it somehow seemed too much; but too much, you see, was exactly what I then encouraged, perhaps because I'd had too little of what counted.

At any rate, when my parents coerced me into mingling with their public, I paid close attention to my outfits, taking pains to ensure that my colours corresponded with those worn by my mother (which I would have seen in advance, hanging in her ironing room)—so that once we were both immersed in the social morass, we presented the suggestion of a united front against my father, who was never really happier than in the hackneyed trappings of the clubhouse ex-pat. And once I'd arranged myself among these strangers, always placing myself close to my mother, on whom I blamed the whole nightmare, she would do most of my talking on my behalf, as if I were a retard (as opposed to ill-mannered, which I think was considered to be a more grievous handicap), while I began to sip at vodka through a straw, like tonic, and too fast, so that far from unwinding I would soon find myself wound into coiling postures that spoke of unspeakable feminine tension. The most frequent such posture, which I also deployed when I knelt at communion, involved crossing my legs and wrapping my shins around each other (hosed in long socks of silk), until my feet, thus interlocked, felt less like actual feet than like the fishtail of a mermaid. Everyone would notice my nellie contortions: it was obvious, not least because they took such blatant pains to appear not to, as if their gazes were carefully skirting round the sight of a thalidomide victim. I think that they pitied my parents, those people, and I could picture them chortling, on their drives back home, about the merits of an expensive English education.

Dinner itself was easier. Since my mother, just as she was meticulous about her menus, was insistent that her *emplacements* be tailored to suit properly mixed company, by which, predictably, she meant alternating genders, and since I amounted to a male of sorts, and since the ladies of my parents' society didn't seem to think that it was required of them to make efforts at conversation, but, rather, that their role was simply to react to the fascinating insights of their masculine companions, who always pretended to be suitors, the result was that I could be as spoilt as both of the spoilt women at my sides, who would turn outwards for social survival, like flowers desperate for sunlight. Instead, I would practise sign-language with the servants, and grew fantastically irksome about it, disrupting the proceedings by asking them to fetch me some extra little queenery, such as ice, or (after deliberately dropping and trampling on mine) another napkin could you, or even, between courses, an ashtray, like a Hollywood slut; and while my mother fulminated in her knife-pleated chiffon, her guests did their outward damnedest to have a wonderful time, since the last thing that anyone ever wanted was a fracas, you see, least of all on account of the insufferable brat. Because life, to them, was all about harmony— whereas harmony, I'm afraid to say, to me meant hairspray.

My favourite wheeze, however, I would reserve for later, for when dinner was over and people had either removed to the drawing room, or, in the warmer months, sauntered a little squiffily back out to the garden, where sometimes, despite a sea of flickering candles, they managed, as they navigated their way over the grass, to—whoops—bang into low tables, which, though happily now cleared of earlier débris, made not a jot's worth of difference when it came to the annoyance of laddering one's tights, until, exhausted, everyone eventually collapsed, laughing and laughing, onto the painted wicker chairs, whose cushions, in their absence, would have been plumped up. This was the time when, as my mother poured coffee and tempted her friends to sample the novelty that was saccharine, and everyone began to implore my father *please* for home-made liqueurs (or, if you were a proper chap, to bark for brandy and cigars), I produced my cigarette packet, which I would wield not warily—not like a souvenir from some former blackmailer, nor with false nostalgia, the false memory of all the colourful cocktails which I never got to have with Clifford—but with a refined certitude, *élan,* as if the dainty box in my slim fingers were something infinitely more sinister than a mere vessel for coffin nails.

I can't think where I can have learnt this conjuring fantasy, but it must have been back in England, because here, on this parochial little planet, it caused (especially among the women, who, even in the shadows, recognized exactly what I was up to) a sensation, speechless consternation. No clapping, sadly. At any event, as I manipulated the cardboard packet this way and that, and tilted it backwards ever so slightly, well, don't you know, it just seemed to assume a life of its own, and turn into a sort of mirrored powder-compact, and I, as a result, to become quite another character, a coquette or soubrette or courtesan. I would always, for the sake of propriety, first make a point of extracting a cigarette, which, rather than beg to be lit, seemed to prefer to dangle about my hand like a slim pencil of eye-liner while I peered inside the lid of the packet, as if a tiny looking-glass were secreted in there. I would slowly swivel my head from left to right, and begin—the horror of it—to pretend to be checking my *eyebrows,* and to shape them with a middle finger, which I sometimes licked in advance, for the method; and now I would rub my lips together, mmm, which luckily passed muster, didn't need touching up; and my nose, what a relief, was not too shiny under the moonlit sky. And at last I could quietly snap the compact shut, and lean back, and light up without a care in the universe, as my mother, had she smoked, might have done, and admire the constellation of stars above.

But I suppose that it *was* a little much for someone of my tender age to be performing such seasoned vanities in public: I should really have slipped away to the powder room—an oversight which presumably explains why certain of the ladies looked so discomfited by my actions. But perhaps they feared that I was flirting with their husbands; and perhaps they were right to do so, for it is not impossible for a perfectly good husband to be susceptible to the charms of the young invert. Only on occasion, after everyone had departed, did my mother draw my attention to my cosmetic illusion, and demand, in seething whispers (because of the servants, who were clearing up), an explanation for what she called my quite extraordinary conduct. But I just rolled my eyes with mimed *étonnement,* as if to suggest that her medication was finally getting the better of her mind; and Mother, I replied, I have simply no idea what you're talking about. But she must have known very well the answer to what she had been asking, because, from that night on, she banned me from smoking when guests came to her house—it reflected badly, that was her argument. But it didn't reflect as badly as the fact that, once she'd got wise to my retarded entrances, she always made a point of fishing me out of my room and forcing me, like bait, to go down before her, while she, my rival actress, held back for a good while, ostensibly to attend to her last-minute touches—though, in reality, the better to choreograph that long-anticipated moment when she finally managed to flutter to the ground, as ever to enchant the gathered company.

THE COMPANY WHICH I, meanwhile, kept was odd: occasional men without names, occasional prescribed texts, melancholy pop songs, and, most of all, fashion magazines. By this stage, my mother had begun to criticize my clothes, not just in pale shades of objection, such as primrose, but in earnest, and to claim that if I went about, wearing, for instance, such wide, or high-waisted, or tapered, or loudly patterned trousers—whatever that season dictated—people on the streets would laugh at me. I told her that nobody laughed in London, quite the opposite, and that anyway, I hoped *her* acquaintances were not so superficial as to judge by appearances. She, of course, concurred on this last particular, but added that she wasn't concerned by her friends as such, so much as by the general masses. The *masses?*, I spluttered; why on earth, since one didn't know them, should one care about the opinions of the masses? She said that being my mother, she felt embarrassed on my behalf, and then she stung me with the claim that she no longer felt comfortable to be seen out in my company, for she had noticed people doing double takes as I advanced and passed—an elaboration which, from my point of view, went some small way towards mitigating her insult, because nothing, then, would have upset me more than the disgrace of not being noticed. But I told her that there was no need, in the future, for us to venture forth together, that I was perfectly able to find my own way around (and how), and that if she didn't deem me a suitable companion for her gracious promenades, well, that was her prerogative—just as it was mine to refuse to wear her silly sports shirts emblazoned with grinning alligators.

She said that the problem didn't lie with suitability: it lay with *extremes.* Couldn't I see that gentlemen should always, by definition, be attired discreetly? Since when?, I demanded. Since man became civilized, was her ignorant, and equally uncivil, reply. What about the Incroyables at Versailles, I countered, and the great English Dandies? Did the name Beau Brummel mean nothing to her? When would she get it into her skull that I belonged to a long and noble tradition of sartorial peacocks? She told me not to speak to my mother like that, as if she were a separate entity, and then went on to state that she couldn't care less about peacocks, which were just harbingers of ill-omen, nor about the history of costume, still less for my apparent fascination with effeminate fops—in-bred undesirables, she called them, look at all those Habsburgs. No, what worried her, she insisted, and for my sake rather than her own, was the fact that I seemed unable to differentiate between modernity, which was just vulgar and ephemeral and commercial and nothing to do with taste (her *sine qua non,* her *non plus ultra, mea* most *maxima culpa*), and elegance, which was eternal, the hallmark of true class.

Such edicts struck me as rich coming from a woman who'd never even heard of *L'Uomo Vogue,* which at that time was my absolute bible, a source of information infinitely more directional that any encyclical from the Vatican, so I told her that she ought to make a point (in the unlikely instance that it should ever consent to be screened on her precious island) of going to see a film called *Roma,* and that she might pay particular attention to the scene of the ecclesiastical fashion show, which was my idea both of modernity *and* of elegance (not to mention fantabularity, but she wouldn't have understood such a refined hybrid); yet she, to my sudden surprise, and quicker than I could say Fellini, rounded on me with the name Pasolini, which, though wrong, was nevertheless impressive for an uneducated beauty. I raised an appreciative eyebrow, like Tadzio's mother.

Next, however, she reversed into the name of the director whom she had cited with a snort of disgust, followed by some piece of wisdom, muttered as a half-aside (because, yet again, servants were lurking about), to the effect that if the Italian cinematographer had been murdered, it wasn't because of his subversive talents, which, like his absurd Communist posturings, were a secondary issue, but because—as the whole world knew, she said—he was a pervert, a degenerate, and a criminal. And then she went racing into some diatribe about never minding if the Mafia had been implicated in the whole business, and would I kindly not try to sidetrack her about the irony of Ostia (the town where Pasolini had met his maker) being named after the sacred host, because her point was that having his head cracked open by a rock, hurled at him by a street urchin, before being run over by the wheels of his own car, had been, in her considered (Catholic) opinion, a right and fitting end for such an ... *Amoralista*—which, to me, sounded paradoxically amorous. But I think that this was the first time my mother managed really to shock me, profoundly, properly to scandalize me; and I began, after this altercation (which, incredibly, had kicked off with a contentious pair of trousers), to fear that the woman, as well as being addicted to socially accepted barbiturates, was actively sinister, wicked, in the clutches of some evil—like Steel. And whatever shame she might earlier have claimed to feel on my behalf now dwindled into insignificance next to what I felt on hers, which was stark gaping horror, like the creature in *The Scream*. And back in the safety of my own room, I was forced to conclude that, as holidays went, this one had proved still less productive than the unproductive rule.

WHEN I REACHED the sixth form, the first thing that I did was to decline to wear a prefect's tie, for even if this (unearned) privilege was my entitlement, and even if the tie itself, ruby as Dorothy's slippers, was more fetching than the dreary common-or-garden one, which was forgettable, I was as unfit to impose authority as I felt prepared to knot it round my neck and sport it. And yet, despite the fact that younger boys couldn't tell that I was a senior, my movements at the top of the school felt smoother somehow, less careful: I could walk with Clifford's swagger, outswagger him even, and flaunt the lissom hips which God had fitted on me, and pout like Lolita, and perform my powder-compact trick at whim, and suck the end of my fat pen in class, and suck it, of course, that trifle too provocatively, and flutter my eyes like a preparatory secretary, safe in the knowledge that, whichever of these things I did, I couldn't be taken to task by the banes of my early days here, twerps like Payne Senior, and the toad, and the midget corporal—consigned long since to oblivion, all three of them, and reduced, no doubt, to ignominious polytechnics in the provinces, or the military. Good luck, boys, see you. *See you?* Bollocks to that: what I meant was: not bloody likely, you bunch of creeps, not if I can help it.

Helping it, however, did present me with a bit of a problem as I neared the end of my eight-year imprisonment, for what I lacked in accumulated gravitas, I'd grown to amass in subversiveness. Sometimes I felt as if I were bursting from frustration, like a permanently boiling kettle with too tight a lid, or like the men who scratched their sweltering genitals round the Nautical Club changing-rooms. And so, in order to let off steam, I was sometimes driven to capers which, though insurrective in the tradition of Fellini's fashion scene, didn't actually constitute breaking the rules: my iniquities were too girlie for my father's Alma Mater ever to have envisaged a need to forbid them. And besides, had his school taken into account the existence of misfits such as I, its book of regulations, like that of Revelations, would have grown as lengthy as it would have been rendered ludicrous.

I'LL GIVE YOU a self-ridiculing instance of my adolescent misdemeanours, if only to convey the flavour of my cheek, which was overblown in spirit—more Genet than Ionesco, really. The choir at school was sometimes required to perform for extra-curricular inconveniences, such as the boring nuptials of former alumni, and one such imposition befell us early in my final summer, on a Saturday afternoon leading up to A' levels, when I could have been getting on with revision. But no, like it or lump it, the entire choir had to sing. Dr. Fox, can you believe, just wouldn't exempt me from this dismal ceremony. So this is what I did to avenge the infliction.

On the morning of the wedding, I sneaked out, earlier than breakfast, to the gardens behind the observatory, which, now that I was a senior, I was legitimately permitted to visit. What was less legitimate, however, was that I should scuttle, as I did, under the rose bushes, pilfering petals from the ground and stuffing them into a plastic bag—emblazoned with the name of one of my mother's smart boutiques—which I'd employed, when my trunk had sailed back to England, to wrap a giant bottle of avocado conditioner, in case it leaked. But once the dewy grass had been raked clear of fallen botany, as if a scrupulous gardener had attended to it, I found my bag still to be half-empty, and its supply of proper confetti—as opposed to paper (the barbaric notion of rice didn't even bear thinking about)—to be measly, unsatisfying. Confetti was like scent, I reminded myself: a mere sprinkling was worse than nothing: what you needed was abundance, profusion—which is when I found myself forced to make a decision, and quickly.

I took a chance and, hoping that no one was spying on me from the building, I turned my back on the Gothic windows, and began, like a born-again shepherdess decked with panniers, to sway along the flowerbeds, surreptitiously tugging and wrenching at the actual roseheads, as if their petals were nasty embellishments on swimming-helmets, and as if I, far from denuding them, were in fact doing them an aesthetic favour. But I tried, even in my haste, to exercise discretion, and selected to pluck only the palest, most pastel shades. Anyway, by the time that my task was complete and the poppers on the bulging bag were safely secured and I'd resumed a semblance of composure despite the fact that my nerves were going demented, you might have presumed that I'd merely been out to collect a cushion, forgotten after a siesta in the Left Gazebo.

Following lunch, which I ate in my room, I crept up to the loft in advance of the choir, while Dr. Fox was warming up—twiddling around with stops and keys and repositioning his anglepoise, which the cleaners, to his regular annoyance, seemed always to shift. I shoved the plastic bag under my seat in the back row, where, these days, I hardly bothered to join in, for the sound of my grown voice was like somebody else's, grating and unreal; and then I went over to my uncooperative mentor, who, improvising some Gregorian ditty, sat barricaded behind his organ, which looked more like a witness-box than a musical instrument. When he saw me appear at his side and beam, he briefly flashed his spectacles at me, and grinned like an unholy innocent before returning his glare to the rigours of musicianship. So far, I thought, so good.

The entrance procession, when it began, did sound quite grandiose, for Dr. Fox was giving it his organistic everything, although, to be quite frank, he might have cooled it a bit on the tempo: this wasn't a barndance, for God's sake. But I had more pressing concerns, you see, because I hadn't yet managed to get a glimpse of the bride—couldn't until she was up at the altar—and when I did, well, let's say she wasn't exactly stately: outfit too folksy by half, with a strong stylistic whiff of prairieland and an ill-advised assortment of appliquéd flowers around a wobbly hemline. No train; cropped little veil; what a waste of a one-and-only Catholic chance. The drip of a girl, instead of carrying a sumptuous great bunch of gardenias, was probably clutching some crummy little posy of freesias, as if being joined in matrimony were tantamount to undergoing surgery. As for her bridesmaids—best be brief: four of them, frizzy-haired, forced into printed pinafores, and burly to a woman, like milkmaids off-duty. Despite the fact that their heads had been ribbonned to suggest a rural girlishness, the gang looked not so much pastorally nubile as seasoned consumers of the

Pill. Far better to have been corseted like eighteenth-century shepherdesses gone out to gather roses, with voluptuous panniers to disguise the width of their beams. A lamentable spectacle, as my mother
would have said. But ours is not to reason. Sure thing.

Once the marriage had survived some dreary homily by one of the
shuffling centre-parted priests, and an everlasting signing of the register in the sacristy, and a glut of concelebrated prayers in Latin, and a
queue to communion by only half of the congregation (thus betraying
the appliquéd prairie-girl as a Prot), the leader of the clerical pack performed a ludicrous sequence of crosses which led you to fear that he
might never stop, but suddenly, Dr. Fox, in a strop, had attacked the
keyboard. His concluding number, one of those corny old toccatas,
he took at a hurtle-and-a-half—presumably to show off. I could see,
from where I stood, the top of his head bobbing with technical profi-
ciency and swelling with the glory of his own volume. Meanwhile, the
bride, whose mimsy veil was now up, was trying to grin at everyone, but
seemed able to focus on no one while she progressed in a daze through
the fug of incense, as if, too late to turn back, she had gleaned the
Catholic hell to which she had committed herself, and to which she had
vowed to surrender the blessing of future progeny. Her bloated
groom, the father-to-be, had a dearth of hair on his head, straight and
gingery, but what little remained was scraped defiantly across, in the
style of some air force. And beneath his straining tails, he was buttoned
into a noisy waistcoat, striped in blue-and-gold, the colours of the
proud Old Boy.

I didn't have long. As the couple began their procession back down
the central aisle, with the organ booming forth, all systems go, I
grabbed my bag and crept to the front of the choir loft, the middle of
which was next to the organ. I needed to be symmetrical. Dr. Fox,
whose back was turned to the altar, was absorbed by the demands of
his score, flicking musical pages and hurtling over the keys and ped-
alling his little feet like billy-o, and probably humming along; but I was
too busy to tell, because, by this stage, I was frantically wedging the bag
between my stomach and the edge of the balcony, as if now *I* were the
pregnant milkmaid, far too late for contraception; and from my great
bulge I next began, as if claimed by a Grande Polonaise Brillante of my

own making, to extract an Abundance, a Profusion of pastel petals of rose, which I hurled into the air, to left and to right and to heaven, like an explosion of benison, like omens of hope—not for the future of those newly-weds, but for my own. To begin with, however, the bride seemed not to notice, and since the groom looked mesmerized by the flagstones, I grabbed more and more of my mythical confetti, grabbed it by the fistful, until, at long last, the Protestant bride did look up, and smiled with gratitude, and suddenly I could envisage her as a child down there, and she didn't look unpretty in this picture. And at the point when she was about to vanish under the balcony and walk out into the marital gloom, I, in desperation, turned the whole bag upside down, and just let the rest of my rebellion against Dr. Fox—who must have noticed some blurry commotion at his side, but couldn't do a thing to stop it—shower down onto the non-existent train of the bride, and, instead, fall onto the ribbonny heads of her pinafored ret- inue, who, though not obviously pregnant, did look ravished. And then, before my mentor could have a chance to finish his bravura per- formance, for which he, unlike us, was paid—and not in groceries—I returned to my place, looked around at the other choristers, who appeared to be shell-shocked, and told everyone that we could go. And for once in my life, the crowd did as I ordered.

ON MY WAY back to my room, not quite patting my own back, as my father liked to pat the backs of all his chums, but certainly feeling what used to be called chuffed, which I don't think that my father ever really stopped feeling, a treble came up to tell me that I was wanted in the Great Hall, which is where wedding receptions and other such celebra- tions were hosted. Blood raced to my face: some freeloading priest, guzzling without regard either to chastity or poverty, but clearly with an eye still keenly fixed upon obedience, was obviously warming up to give me a piece of his wisdom. Who wanted me?, I asked the boy. He didn't know. A priest? Nope. Teacher? Couldn't tell, he said, some woman. Which calmed me enough to stuff the empty bag in a bin near the kitchens, before bracing myself for the onslaught.

But when I reached the Great Hall, which was already swelling to boisterousness, I was confronted at the door by one of the bridesmaids, a huge specimen of womanhood who, for all of her size, couldn't make herself heard through the din; so she grabbed my arm and frog-marched me across the gathering, past wafts of noxious perfume and hearty bursts of male commotion, and led me up to the Protestant Bride, whom she prodded, and who turned her bouncing ringlets to me for a couple of seconds, thanked me for that wonderful surprise, how kind, and told me to stay and have a drink and meet everyone. Which, needless to say, I didn't—not just because of the marauding evidence of the rector and the mongrel in the distance, but because I thought that any woman who married an Old Boy must be bonkers.

NOT LONG AFTER this incident (about which Dr. Fox, however incensed, was rendered powerless to rebuke me, for the wedding party made a point of congratulating him on his marvellous idea of getting one of the boys to throw petals over the choir loft), my parents graced me with a visit, carefully planned to coincide with a jamboree known as Victors' Weekend—the supposed highlight of the year, which, depending on which way you looked at it (say downwards, as I did), could also be regarded as the lowest point in the school diary. If Dr. Fox and I ever concurred on anything, it was on the dismal prospect of such festivities, which boiled down, year in, year out, to a mass assault on the community by more overaged children than one imagined conceivable, and children whose regressive high spirits were not restricted to Old Boys, for their wives invariably proved themselves to be similarly vociferous participants: I remember hearing piercing female screeches from the sports fields as mothers forgot all composure in order to spur their cherished offspring to Go-Go-Go-Julian, Nicky, Simon, Peter, Andrew, Tim. (Why was there never an Arthur, for crying out loud, or a Peregrine, or an Aubrey, or even an Evelyn?)

Beyond an epidemic of sporting events through the weekend, its apex being an Old Boys' cricket match which fortunately drew the crowds outdoors for a few hours, those three days of collective hijinks also incorporated an hilarious display of army manoeuvres, an interminable prize-giving ceremony, a school play (which invariably bore a cautionary note, even when that note was jollied into a musical), and, on the closing evening—by which time, half the parents had already vanished (some, it should be said, with *caravans* in tow)—there was a classical concert: always, by tradition, ill-attended, and always characterized by clapping between movements.

During these celebrations, there hung in the library what passed for an art exhibition—enough pinned-up watercolours of pockmarked oranges to sink a battleship. Meanwhile, all over the science laboratories, to which I only once went during such festivities (to mess around with Clifford and indulge in a spot of creative graffito) there were baffling displays of experimental projects which never seemed to arrive at any convincing conclusion. Clifford and I would have liked to have seen, not charts and senseless grafts, but a show of half-dissected frogs, or axolotls, pinned down and disembowelled, or foetuses suspended in formaldehyde—yet this was not to be. Instead, by way of more seemly entertainment, there were endless drinks parties for parents and teachers (warm wine, or beer—never a cocktail, no chance of such a thing), so that grown-ups could hobnob and mingle and charm each other rigid.

On Saturday night, a great dinner-dance was always held in a vast nylon tent, pitched in a field, with wobbly trestle-tables and plastic cutlery, and paper plates, and a platform at one end, where some army band attempted to provide music in the gaps between speeches made by various of our Reverends, hip-hip-hooray. This is when the wilder of the boys' sisters (who all seemed to attend the same convent in Essex) liked to sneak away, to neck or worse (heavy petting, I think that they called it) with their brothers' friends in the thickets of rhododendron. And the following morning, everyone would troop back for a very High (hung-over) Mass, followed by a barrage of rattling collections in aid of the most farfetched of causes—rosaries for maimed Liberians, baptismal fonts for Bangladeshis, Catechisms for blind orphans, that kind of genius. There were also shameful tombolas, with prizes so pitiful that no one in their right mind could ever have meant to win one—a year's supply of cat-litter; a teapot cosy (rheumatically knitted); a transparent-plastic Virgin, filled with water from Lourdes and rife with bacteria: Clifford once got saddled with one of these ladies, whose contents, later, desperate for distraction, we drank with tequila—not, in fact, as bad as you might think, uplifting. To your very good health, Father.

.   .   .

BUT BACK TO WHEN my parents came. They motored north in their own car—shipped over in advance of their flight. Having booked into a nearby guesthouse, the one reputed to be smartest, which my mother nevertheless dismissed as frightful, they arrived—presumably due to my father's mounting anticipation—in advance of the hour when I'd been told to keep an eye out. The weather was the balmiest that we'd enjoyed all summer, yet my mother still claimed to be absolutely frozen, and to have brought all the wrong clothes from their hotel in London. She would catch a chill, she felt certain. But she was wrong; she was fine. My mother, let me say one final time, did look beautiful, and would, as the pace of the weekend mounted, be carried along on a tide of admiring glances—a tide on which I, in my possessive childish way, also felt, for that brief period, entitled to ride.

When I first saw her, she was standing on a lawn, patiently nodding while one of my teachers struggled to ingratiate himself, probably with assurances that I was doing well in his subject. Her hair, now, was cropped shorter than mine had been cropped when she'd first waved me off as a child, but was flicked up at the back, and arranged with a slim ribbon of satin, ice blue, tied in a small bow at one side. She wore a shirt-waister. I remember this because her upper body hinted at a strange boyishness, seemed to draw attention to the facial resemblance that existed between us—once, a source of mutual pride; of late, a growing source of discomfort for her. Her dress, I realize with hindsight, was regardless of its time, rose above popular fashion. Perhaps that is how my mother was—coutured to the last unseen stitch, yet influenced by a style which glanced over its own shoulder, back to her youth, which had blossomed twenty years earlier, and was bleakly romantic.

At any rate, among the staff in their greasy suits and greasy gowns, and husbands in nostalgic panamas and the occasional stripy blazer, and wives whose pleated skirts and patterned cardigans had, by this stage, given way to cheesecloth sacks, and clogs on corky platforms, and clanky beads and gypsy hoops and—squeezed over the odd unfortunate posterior—a pair of ill-advised bell-bottoms, my mother stood in profile, slim and tanned, and holding a glass of white wine—a little away from her, as if it were a malodorous flower. Part of my fascination lay in the fact that I was observing her as if afresh now that she'd been transplanted to this new land. I recall, for instance, being surprised to discover that she was not, after all, a tall woman, but rather, of average stature; and yet she was possessed of that quality which I think is nowadays discredited slightly (in favour of attributes such as informality and casualness of manner), which is the gift of poise. My mother had poise in abundance, and charm when she wanted it, and a certain ignorant intelligence. And these three qualities combined, even when she could hardly comprehend a language, conspired to render her alluring, to make her stand out.

She remained stranded in the middle of the gathering, saddled with the oleaginous teacher until, eventually, a little later, when I snapped out of my reverie, I went to her rescue. She had already been abandoned by her husband, who (though I could hear the forced reverberations of his English laughter) had strutted off to consort with more congenial company—a discourtesy which, throughout their visit, would remain the pattern. No matter, her unruffled poise seemed to imply. For there she stood, as if unaware, in pale blue ballerina pumps, gloriously impractical, which reminded me of the pumps that she had worn during those slow, entrancing afternoons in her ironing room. Yet the skirt of her dress, I realized as my gaze moved up from the ground, was neither slow nor entrancing. It was violent. For all the neat rigour of her bodice, and its matching belt and covered buckle, and the discretion of its printed cotton-satin, which gave sheen but did not shine, the skirt was full and unbridled, like the sea around Java. Its sudden explosion of pattern suggested the result, not of a mere rock hurled onto a homosexual head by a street urchin in an Italian town named Ostia, but of that moment when a whole eruption of lava goes crashing through the waves to collide with the bed of the ocean. The cloth seemed to froth and whirl about her waist, to spin around her, blue and blue and blue and white, like gigantic bubbles of marbling. And this stormy skirt of hers, as well as voluminous, was long, almost reached her ankle; and down its front, there glimmered buttons of mother-of-pearl—the last few, left undone. But after the shocking thrill of all that rushing pattern, I was returned to a feeling of calm; and perhaps because of the neutrality of my uniform, which was beyond objection, all our recent disagreements seemed to be washed away, to be forgotten. And now, at last, I did walk up, like a jealous lover, to claim her from the importunate advances of that didactic prat. We kissed (twice). She embraced me with the power of her gardenias. And then we walked away from the crowd, arm in arm, hers laced through mine—as I, long ago, had been taught that this should be done.

I TOOK HER ON a brief guided tour of my past, to dormitories and classrooms at which she neither marvelled nor gasped, but nodded, as if relieved to note that I had left such places behind, and survived. I showed her the theatre, which, since its walls were painted burgundy while the stage-curtain was turquoise, seemed not to do much for her; and I took her to the Gothic chapel (the main one, whose sides were carved with confessionals), which was, she whispered, cold as a sepulchre, let's get out. It must have been during one of those walks, up or down the staircase to the music basement (of which she did approve, because, she said, she could envisage me there, which struck me as an irony), that she was halted in her tracks by the resemblance between the sketch of a young man with a moustache and my grandmother's poor dead infantry officer. I remember feeling grateful for that anecdote about love and death and sadness, feeling flattered by her maudlin confidence, which had been withheld so long, like her warmth, like my trust.

My father seemed altered, not so much outwardly, for he sported the same old tweeds and the same flapping Old Boy tie, as in his attitude: he had grown restless, boisterous, like a child at holiday camp. I felt this bursting enthusiasm to be coarse, unseemly, and I suspect that my mother felt likewise; but since in this northern wilderness she was not so much the queen of an exotic island as a foreign consort in unconquered territory, reduced to the role of a powerless formality, she probably considered it wiser to ignore his juvenile conduct than to reprimand him on the subject—at least for now. Still, the ancillary benefit of his apparent eagerness to glue himself to the non-entities of his youth, and to stand on the sidelines of matches played by their equally irrelevant sons, was that for much of that time my mother and I were left to our own devices, as we had been, oh, ages before, in another life, in the days of the flight of wooden steps that led from the beach house down to the summersands of my childhood.

On their first afternoon with me, my mother said that she was completely exhausted from the car journey up, six hours of unutterable tedium, the time it took to whip round the coastline of our island, and she pleaded that if she was expected to accompany my father to some crummy Drinks for parents and teachers that evening, she must, whatever else, be permitted to take her customary siesta. Grudgingly, her husband drove us, her and me, to the guesthouse where they were staying, dumped us at the door, and then flew, like a bird let out of a cage, back to the healthy open air of his Alma Mater. Strange how one man's imprisonment can, to another, seem like liberation.

IT TURNED OUT that they were sharing a bed, a circumstance which appeared to embarrass my mother, as if a certain obscenity attached to it, but her (unsolicited) explanation was that since this tavern, as she called the place, was heaving with other parents (a word which she uttered as if to mean lice), there had been no alternative but acceptance on her part (by which she meant resignation—a sort of facing the music–cum–biting the bullet). While she explained these things, she turned the central heating up, up to the utmost; and then she lit a scented candle which she'd included in her luggage—thereby evincing a canny presence of mind, for the room stank of damp. My father, she moaned, hadn't properly unpacked, but she was damned if she was going to do so on his behalf; yet the truth of the matter, I soon discovered, was that she'd already monopolized the wardrobe, which she now opened—to reveal . . . *wire* coat-hangers, can you imagine.

From a drawer, she extracted and handed to me a box of chocolates, secured with a wide taffeta ribbon in stripes of aubergine and rust, and fashioned into a flower on top, like a picture-hat from the Edwardian period. The chocolates themselves, though purchased in London, were actually Belgian, and the irony did not escape me that, just as once she had given away the presents which I had chosen for her in Brussels, now it was I who had been cast in the rôle of ingrate, who would play Pass The Parcel—most likely to Dr. Fox—for, by this late stage in my contortions, I had learnt, if not to resist carnality, certainly to resist the temptation of fattening substances—with the notable exception of my binge to celebrate the unmasking of Al Capone.

But next, from some other recess, she conjured a shoe box with a label from Jermyn Street, I think that it was—containing, it transpired, a surprise far greater than mere chocolate; but I steeled myself before lifting the lid, because even if, then, I still considered my mother's dress sense to be above reproach, she and I, you will recall, no longer saw eye to eye on the mercurial subjects of modernity and elegance in menswear. But she suggested, as she vanished into the bathroom to change into a travelling dressing-gown (pink lightweight satin, pale as the petals which had once flown down from the choir), that I try the shoes for size, in case they were too small or too tight or whatever, and yet she appeared—which struck me as optimistic on her part—not to be concerned that, beyond the question of fit, the articles themselves might not appeal to me. Rather she seemed to be suggesting that the mystery stowed within that box (which I envisaged as some ghastly pair of clumpy brogues) was a sartorial wonder, one of her *non plus ultras.* As I rustled with the tissue, I heard her, next door, turning off a tap, and spraying herself with atomized gardenias, and then, well, I have to admit that I was just bowled over. Because, for once—perhaps even for ever—our differences of taste were annulled.

It was a pair of patent leather dress-pumps in honour of my first formal dance—not nasty, pointy lace-ups like my father's, which were fit for a turf accountant, but almond-toed slippers with flat bows of grosgrain, reminiscent of the years of elegance leading up to the Great War, and evocative of the balls attended by my grandmother with her poor dead infantry officer—and yet, simultaneously, those pumps were absolutely modern, perfectly attuned to the latest pages of *L'Uomo Vogue.* My mother had, at least on this occasion, hit the cobbler's nail on the head—spot on, old girl, as my father would have said. Cinderella, I thought, move over; and then, I yelped like a bare-shouldered débutante dazzled by the sight of a jewel to commemorate her launch into society. Rubbing beauty cream onto her face, my mother now emerged from the bathroom to volunteer the fact that she had told the shop assistant to include, along with the pumps, a pair of black silk socks, in case mine were all at home, which, in the event, they were. But I did not, in fact, bother to try on my new trophies, not here; instead, I merely held their soles against those of the loafers which I had on—both because the prospect of donning virgin silk hose over my unwashed feet was more obscene to me than any double bed, and because I knew that, whatever happened and without question, I would, tomorrow night, squeeze my stockinged feet, like an ugly sister, into those gleaming slippers—even if agony were the price of my ecstasy.

I could happily have stayed in my mother's room and, like the flame of her scented candle, kept vigil during her rest, but she, doubtless unaccustomed to being admired while she slept, suggested that I get back to school now, and earned the pleasure of her privacy by packing me off in a taxi. I didn't see her again that day, and although, during the drinks party in the evening, Dr. Fox made a point of introducing himself to her, he irritated the hell out of me next morning, when—after I'd given him the Belgian chocolates, on condition that he save me the ribbon—he proved incapable of describing exactly (be fair, he said, I *knew* he lacked a visual memory) *exactly* what my mother had been wearing, or how she had seemed, beyond the obvious fact (which, frankly, I could have told him) that she was the most beautiful woman in the room. But he did, by contrast, horrify me with the detailed revelation that, at the makeshift bar, my father had buttonholed him, and droned on and on and loud, within full earshot of the assembled public, about how dreadfully he lamented the fact that I cared so obviously less for him than I did for my mother, whom he described as his wife. Dr. Fox thought my father a deathly dullard, and suggested that I flee his soulless nest at the first possible opportunity; and although, in that illogical paradox of thick blood and thin water, a part of me bristled at my mentor's opinions, yet I made a grateful mental note of the support implicit in his comments.

NEXT DAY, while my father took himself off for a spot of puerile nonsense, my mother and I lunched alone at a restaurant, not worthy of mention—though she took pains to mention how flatteringly, during the previous evening, Dr. Fox had spoken of me, and how much she had enjoyed meeting my moral tutor. (I wondered if she would have enjoyed the experience quite so much had she known what she could not possibly know.) But then we drifted towards my nearing exams, about which, even if I wasn't worried, she worried that I sounded too confident—one couldn't, she reminded us both, ignore my catastrophic O levels. But since I'd never told her about Al Capone, nor could I now bless her with the relief of his unmasking, his consignment to insignificance; so instead I moved on to my immediate future, explaining that before taking my A's, I was due to go up for an interview, arranged by Dr. Fox, at an Oxford college—a decent one, I pointed out, meaning: without connection to my father's Alma Mater. She rebuked me for being ungrateful. I told her that I was merely being truthful. She rattled off some Spanish adage about progeny being like crows—bring them into the world and they'll peck your very eyes from you. I bettered her mawkish little simile with a lamentation from one of my texts about how sharper than a serpent's tooth it is to have a thankless child, but I was only quoting for effect, not because I found the words themselves personally applicable. All that I owed to my father (though I didn't have the nerve to inform her of this) was a kick in the goolies. Anyway, I continued: in the instance of the forthcoming interview not going my way, meaning if I wasn't offered a place conditional on my A-level grades, I could always sit the official entrance papers in the autumn, and take the rest of next year off. One way or another, I vowed (just as I had vowed not to join the Spanish army), I would go to university, because even a red-brick had to be preferable to some stony job in the City. But she deftly now changed tack, probably to avert the mounting danger of a quarrel, and resurrected the safer topic of her undying exhaustedness.

In the afternoon was the prize-giving ceremony, but since, even if I deserved an award, I was too unpopular (and, frankly, too unpleasant) to be a likely recipient, I saw my mother off in a cab back to her tavern, so that she could repose in preparation for that night's Victory dance. God knows where my father might be, probably in a pub knocking back the marvellous English beer and rolling out the barrel, and cockling and musseling with some lively band of equally jolly good fellows; but since I knew that, regardless of his present whereabouts, he was bound, sooner or later, to change into black tie, and would therefore be joining my mother, I didn't bother to worry. She and I simply agreed that all three of us would convene at eight p.m. at the school gates—on the *dot,* I specified, not ages before, as was his tendency, nor, as was hers, long past the hour.

.   .   .

In the end, I do go to the prize-giving (though I sit at the back, up in the gods, looking forward to my pumps, which fit to perfection)—the reason being that Dr. Fox has suddenly gone all mysterious on me, as if to suggest that there might, after all, be some award in the offing, and since the whole ceremony is meant to be compulsory, I can't risk detection of my absence. Despite the odds of honour being stacked, by dint of my unpopularity, against me, I do, in the event, win some prizes— four in total: senior French, rapidly followed by senior Spanish, both of which (bugger my unpleasantness, never mind my father and his unfair advantages) are fully merited. Everybody claps; fair's fair-enough. But deeper into the proceedings, I hear my name called out for a prize in religion, an accolade not merely less deserved but little short of unthinkable, since of late I have refined myself into a most obnoxious agnostic; yet I suppose that the book which I win, *The Four Loves,* and which I quickly lose (though I wouldn't have misplaced a money order), is my reward for having scrutinized the small print of Catholic doctrine, as opposed to merely doodling, which is the norm in that subject. This time round, however, there's a noticeable drop in the warmth of applause, and as I return to my seat I catch the odd, audible snort, which tempts me to sneak away through the fire door—though on second thoughts, since the proceedings are nearly over, I may as well sit out the hell of the remainder.

But when, practically at the end, I hear myself announced yet again, and this time for a special music prize, which means Dr. Fox, the least suspected thing occurs: the crowd, parents included, begins to tut with disapproval, then openly to boo at the whiff of favouritism. I freeze, of course, and heads seem to turn to gloat at my frozenness, yet I can't stay here forever, have to go through with the performance, must collect the award, which I suspect to be a record—Bach most likely, given the donor. And so, Fuck them, I think, fuck the lot of them; and as I make my way down the steps of this revolting burgundy theatre with sticky carpeting and curtains of turquoise, down towards the stage where the rector awaits (looking, to be fair, pretty uncomfortable, bobbing his famous Adam's apple), I just envisage the scene in black and white and slightly blurrily, and concentrate on carrying myself with hair-flicking indifference to the world, like Rita Hayworth. But you will understand why, for once, I feel relieved that my parents aren't present to witness the shame of their one-and-only. And when, at last, I barge my way out of the place, all that I can do is hope that no well-meaning prat of an Old Boy proves crass enough to commiserate with my father over the fracas.

AT EIGHT—and on the dot—I go down to the gates at the front quadrangle, but my parents, like angry spears, are already in evidence; and, as soon as I appear, they join forces to accuse *me* of being late now. I ignore their childishness, don't even pretend to hear it: they've probably been bickering and want an easy scapegoat. Well, forget it, darlings, I've had enough aggravation to last me the night. Through the annoyance of the half-light, I try as best I can to distract myself by peering at the appearance of my mother, and I peer with such a concentration that, to begin with, I fail to notice what my father is wearing: not a proper bow, conventionally black, but instead, would you believe, the ass has knotted round his scraggy neck an absolute sartorial nightmare: a dicky-bow striped in blue-and-gold. What the hell is *that*?, I blurt out, unable to conceal my horror, and further unable to restrain myself from pointing. My mother, as she does on my behalf at her infernal dinner parties, now answers for her husband—though not to spare herself, or him, embarrassment. Not at all: boast is what she does. Because, with some ingenuity, she opines, she's taken a pair of Old Boy ties from my father's considerable collection, and instructed the sempstress at home to unpick them both, follow some pattern, and concoct—wouldn't you know—the Original Alma Mater Bow. I cannot believe either her catastrophic error of judgement, which is twenty thousand times more catastrophic than my O-level results, nor the sight of my father's countenance, which has never looked more chuffed than it does at this moment. And as we amble towards the nylon tent where the night's revelry is doomed to unfold, I understand that the earlier marriage of my mother's taste to mine at the altar of my dancing-pumps has been but a mirage, or worse, a preparatory bribe; for this, this miserable lapse in style is the real, true gauge of my parents' aesthetic, an aesthetic which I can no longer fool myself that they do not share, for they share it wholeheartedly, matrimonially. The two of them are steeped in this shit together, and no mistake.

My mother is cloudy, shadowed, overcast; I cannot make her out. But once we've stepped inside the tent, which reeks of paraffin, I'm able to verify that her reduced visibility has, in part, been caused by the fact that she's wearing black, a colour which, on our island (probably on account of the heat), is largely reserved for semblances of mourning, from which the bereaved like to shift, as soon as seems seemly, to the grieving half-shades of grey and lilac. But black, that great supposèd flatterer, is not, I now discover, a shade that flatters my mother, and this discovery disappoints me as much as it lets her down; it ages and diminishes her. For, no matter how fabulously fashioned on her behalf, black conspires to undermine the glow of her tan, which seems to have shifted from luminous amber to an uglier, more chalky umber—slightly goose pimpled tonight.

My father ferries us towards the table at which we're to be seated— next to God knows whom. My mother has already specified that she doesn't want to be put near some deafening band, because, as it is (she claims), she has her work cut out trying to converse in English, thanks very much—*muchísimas gracias*—but nor can she have imagined that her husband has reserved for us about the most unappetizing table to be had: marooned on the outer edges of the action, sloping downwards, placed suspiciously close to the bar and lurking in the region of some secondary entrance. If you sit with your back to the tent, you're assailed by a constant racing draft, and any hope of a view is dashed by the ranks of tables in front; and if, to avoid the draft, you should turn your back to the crowd, your view will be reduced to a wrinkled canvas of pistachio nylon, relieved only by a gap, like a hungry mouth, through which the serving staff will soon be rushing in and out screaming and cursing and dropping things on their way to and from the mobile kitchens, very attractive.

When we reach our trestled travesty, which has been covered in paper of a festive character, and decked with occasional tufts of shriv- elled carnation embedded on skeletons of asparagus plant, I feel relieved to see, if nothing else, that we're the first to arrive, which means that we can grab whatever places we like; but my mother, unac- customed to making entrances without a clutch of admirers in ready attendance, now complains—she who a few minutes ago had com-

plained that I was late—that we're far too early. And yet, undaunted,
like a disappointed but utterly composed hostess, she makes directly
for one end of the table, while my father saunters off in search of what
(for the first time in my recollection) he describes as libations. Before
she sits—which she will eventually do by means of a slow half-
curtsey—she requests a glass of champagne, and I, for the sake of simplicity, follow her lead and do the same: I doubt that my father can be
trusted to produce tequila. Nor can he; because, when the Original
Alma Mater Beau does eventually come lurching back, with spillage
down his pleated shirtfront, he brings us a couple of tumblers of warm
Pomagne—oh do stop whining. I, in his absence, have already be-
seeched my mother, before it's all too late, not to choose the top of the
table, please not, but to sit along one of the sides instead, so that I can
plonk myself between her and her husband and not have to talk to
strangers; but she treats my plea with the derision which, perhaps, it
deserves, and tells me not to be so anti-social, I'm not a peasant, and
kindly to draw out the chair which she has selected. And then, moaning
in our mother-tongue about how regrettable it is that I've forgotten
even the most rudimentary courtesies due to a lady, she takes pride of
place at the head—with the grace and weightlessness of a star falling
from the firmament. Others begin to arrive now, parents of no one I've
ever noticed, flanked by their unnoticeable offspring; so I raise the volume of my Spanish in an attempt to deter them from venturing near us.

While I still have the chance, in advance of the crowds, I drink my
mother in, hurry to absorb her. Her scent seems to have grown, like
gardenias opening for the moon, from eau-de-toilette to concentrated
perfume. Her make-up has sharpened, darkened, grown more sensual.
I suspect that she has painted slightly beyond the natural contour of
her lips, but I can't tell for sure: I don't dare to gawp like the peasant
whom I'm not supposed to be, least of all when I feel more like a burgeoning model-girl, new to the business and ravenous not for food but
beauty tips. Her stole, of indigo mink, is, by now, slung over the back of
her chair, against which she seems determined not to lean; and while
she perches erect, craning slightly and swivelling her visage and pouting
just a smidgeon, I notice, near the ground, which is a carpet of soggy
grass, her monogram embroidered in oyster pink on the fur's oyster
satin lining. Her dress is of black chantilly, with a very fitted bodice and

long narrow sleeves, which end, near her knuckles, in delicate scallops, dainty with lashes, as do the shores around her neck, through which her clavicle juts fractionally—but you can only glimpse this from the side, or if, like me, you're a complete cow. Her head-of-a-gamine is glossy, as if she'd recently come, running, out of the sea; and on her ears she wears a pair of plain but socking great brilliants, painfully screwed, absolutely no quivering.

The skirt, at the hem, is fuller than full, but, at the waist, teeny, so you can almost picture it being planned, blocked out, and cut to a pattern of perfect circularity. Perhaps to relieve the overall bleakness of her blackness, which might have been thought to veer towards the grotesque, the Goyaesque, there's a satin slither, the colour of a cherub's skin, loosely slung around her upper hip and tied in a small bow behind her. Beneath the skirt, you can see, when she sits cross-kneed, smoky underskirts of organdie, as if the wings of my first crib had been dipped in squid's ink; and her stockinged ankle, hanging limp and bony-thin, is sheer as dark transparency (crystalline brown, the colour of sugar-crystals—one of her low-denier tricks). And her evening shoes, which are fantastically steep and slim-heeled, have, insanely, superbly, been covered in matching chantilly, so that given the context, and my father's dancing skills, they stand little chance of surviving what I suspect to be their first night out.

On the table, along from her paper plate and not far from my glass of fizzy piss, lie a black grosgrain evening purse, dead plain, like a small envelope, and, upon it, asleep, a still life of my mother's lovely fingers. Her nails are painted paler than in my childhood; and although I recognize the rose-cut solitaire which rings her second finger, the massive diamond gauntlet attached to her left wrist, dazzling over a cuff of chantilly, is unknown to me. I enquire after its history. She tells me to desist from such common enquiries—what *is* this, the Inquisition? I persist that the bracelet is beautiful (I might even have dared to say heavenly, although—to her doubtless relief—I would have exuded the word in Spanish). She replies that gentlemen don't remark on ladies' jewels; and that if other ladies ever do, it's only because they're consumed with envy, which is a sin. By which stage, our table is complete.

Over dinner—if dinner isn't too tasteful a term for a crusty slab of salmon and a lump of mayonnaise—faintly *gorne-orf,* as you'd expect—

my father sits regrettably opposite me, savouring accolades about his fancily dressed neck, and replying to all and creepy sundry: So glad you think so, rather pleased with it m'self-what; and into his riveting story he draws the fine complicitous hand of his clever wife-here, great style, marvellous ideas—while she, the turncoat, smiles along, not quite smacking her lips, but obviously thrilled and nodding-and-nodding in an attempt to convey that absolutely, why not, if the school pleases to follow her Victor Ludorum's sartorial lead and mass-produce his humble contribution to its honourable tradition, it is, well, more than welcome to do so, how very flattering. And as the nosh begins (between munches of ancient leaving-dates, and soundbites from the Battle of Britain) to get shovelled down, and as the fruity but tepid Alsatian wine is clinked and cheered and swilled and gulped (though some of our chaps prefer to stick with the beer, if you don't mind—grape and grain and all that), assorted elbows seem to crawl up, and then, to slump over the creased paper cloth and slide around; and tissued serviettes, smeared with remnants of lipstick and the inconvenience of an untimely sneeze—I *do* beg your pardon—find themselves crushed by hot fists and left, half-groaning, to rot on the moistening scene like soiled evidence of female joviality. And now, at last, the spirits of the assemblage can be felt to be rising, to spin away like a Victorious boomerang in the clear direction of jollity, of happy history, of future reminiscence—hopefully to be returned, one fine eventual day, back to this very company, and shared with the male children of our male children, all of whom will have been put down at birth—not literally, you fool—enlisted in their turn to join the privileged ranks of my father's Alma Mater.

During the first few speeches, my mother, who plainly cannot understand a thing, nevertheless looks most amused, taken in, while her husband, the better to enjoy the oratory, turns his folding chair to face the speakers, and seems to be rendered so mirthful by the whole retrospective priestly hoot, that, watching him, you begin to pray that he topples backwards and collapses onto the table with a good thud, his head slumped like the head of the Baptist upon the flanny gelatinous mess of his pudding, his gob ajar, his striped propeller of a tie, inactive, unactivated, unable to revolve and soar like an old Spitfire into the nylon galaxies; his furry ears unplugged but garnished by the odd chunk of tinned pineapple. Yet in boring reality, he just rummages about his pockets, and then he lights a medium-sized cigar. Anyone care for one?

Nobody, thank God, does; but, to my disbelief, my mother, who has always reviled tobacco, now accepts the offer of a stunted cigarette (blithely unaware of the ghastliness of its brand) from some nearby drudge—a School Governor, I gather; and when she begins to puff, desperately trying not to blink despite the sting in her eyes, which serves her right, I don't know whether to be more gratified by the fact that she can't inhale, but only act the part, or by my realization that she's squandering the drudge's last revolting gasper, which, when he finally cottons on, he will regret having wasted on that woman who, now that everyone's feeling much more up-tempo, seems to be speaking English like there's no tomorrow and no stopping her, and broadly smiling into the bargain, like an old-style ambassadress from a backward country. Is my father as surprised as I am by my mother's conduct? Not a bit of it: he looks, if anything, delighted by the larkiness of his wife, her ability to join in the spirit of things, to share in the fun. Wink-wink, darling. I catch him. And anyway, now the band is trying to tie a yellow ribbon with the help of a regimental trumpet, and everyone is delighted, oh yes, especially the ladies, who, as they heave themselves up, trilling snatches of song and dum-dee-dahing, stomp about in sturdy heels and the same moth-eaten dress-skirts as their mothers must have worn in Burma. But my own mother, who has thought it all out, says that it's the thought that counts, the whole mood of the thing, the celebration, not the latest fashion or questions of extravagance, why must I be so superficial. What's that? my father asks. So the bitch goes and blabs. *Abserlootly,* he concurs—always bally criticizing, the wretched pip-squeak; just ignore him, darling; care to dance? *Enchantée,* she replies in the diplomatic language, sounding as grateful as if she'd been offered the chance of another life; then rises. She tells me to keep an eye on her bag, and next thing, having (purposely?) trodden on one of my pumps, she leads the way onto the boards, weaving herself between a clutter of tables and an absurdity of chairs worthy of Ionesco, until, inevitably, the lilt of her slim hips is obscured from view by the screen of my father's thick back, which jigs about without concern for rhythm and nonsense. It's been eight long years, do you still want me, I'll stay on the bus, forget about us, put the blame on me, tie a yellow ribbon round the ole oak tree.

Dancy-dancy-dance. The youngsters at our table all vanish, presumably to cross-fertilize and make deals regarding rhododendrons. And I, for my sins, for my refusal to join in, get lumbered with some boring woman wearing a moustache and hair like the Queen Mother who does something or other good in Somerset and is Thingummy's ma and wants to know, as she colonizes the creaking chair beside me, what sports I like. (Water-sports, my dear, and big-game hunting when I get the chance.) But, with typical cowardice, I just say: None—to which she replies: I see, swivels her arse, and that's that. I try not to look as if I've noticed. I try, instead, to look towards my mother. I try not to remember with what shaming adoration I had looked at her once, peered down at her between the slats of the shutters of my infancy. For she is unrecognizable now. She has become my dreadful father's dreadful wife. We have all gone to pieces. We are all beyond repair. It isn't, any longer, even sad. Just dreary, unnecessary.

When my mother asks me to dance, it's only because my father wants to spend a penny—presumably at the bar—but I think that she fears that I might turn her down, which would never do; so she sits for a moment, again half-curtseying, in order to sound me out, to butter me up. She asks how I am. Fine, I reply. (Fucking awful, you stupid woman.) In which case, she exclaims: Come on, Iago: ¡A bailar! She seems younger again, and lighter of touch, but once we're up there, her hand in mine, her diamond gauntlet resting on my rigid shoulder, she tells me, through a rictus smile, not to look down while we're moving around. (I'm actually trying to check how her priceless shoes are surviving.) I apologize, then play dumb. She tells me that I should be talking to her. I tell her that I'm trying to keep up. She tells me, still smiling, that I shouldn't need to, that I'm in charge, I'm the man. And to be fair to my father's wife, she does follow like a dream, goes where she's taken—backwards, round, and to the side—always stepping out of trouble, never banging into anyone, and I begin to understand how this marriage of theirs has been managed: gingerly, cautiously, as if beautifully, till a painful death do them part. Now she asks me who This boy is, and That one, and That—creeps who (can you believe the nerve of it) keep flirting with my mother as they whizz past; and without exception I tell her that I don't know, that I haven't got the foggiest. Come on, she enquires, still ever-smilingly, have I *no* friends to introduce to her? And now I do treat her to the truth, which is: Not likely. And suddenly we have ground to a bewildering standstill, but instantly she is rescued from the awkwardness by some oafish admirer, somebody's fleshy ruddy father, wearing an eye-patch, and she's perfectly obliging, and offers her hand, and as I mooch back to the table, wiping my sweating brow, I hear her distinctive voice admonishing me, telling me (in Spanish, to my own relief now) not to use my hand, for heaven's sake, to use a *handkerchief.*

The rest is brief. I go to the bar, avoiding the section where my father, holding court, has surrounded himself with a scrum of similar sots, and I order myself a whopping vodka, but have to make a fuss about ice—what am I (the barman seems to imply), a Yank? I return to our table, where my mother's bag remains intact. I wonder whether there's any dosh to be had from it, but other pupils keep tripping past, so I dare not look inside, and instead I notice how some of the girls that giggle round these boys also throw snide glances in my direction, and how then, like strumpets consulting procurers, they consult their brothers, only to be told that they're entirely mistaken, *no* chance; and next, they all go on their way, laughing their dizzy heads off, and occasionally turning round and shouting: hello ducks. My mother, meanwhile, moves seamlessly from partner to partner, inexhaustible now, being quite the best value, having quite the best of times. I clutch her bag as if it were a memory, can feel, within it, the relic of her silver compact, can smell the ghost of her lost gardenias, but none of these seems to sustain me any longer. I give up. I grab a paper napkin, place it like a shroud over her bag, and scribble a note, telling her that I'm tired and will see her tomorrow.

In fact, I hardly do so, because during Mass, I'm upstairs in the choir loft. When I join them afterwards, she's wearing a cream linen suit and a black straw hat, its brim curled severely down, so that anyone who looks at her will see not her shifting eyes, but only her expertly painted mouth. We do not kiss; she makes sure of that—by standing safely back: facial contact could disarrange her. We lunch at the dump where they've been slumming it, because her hung-over husband hasn't thought of booking anywhere more appetizing, and while I sit in their company, sweltering in fumes of gravy, they exchange anecdotes about last night, and ask and tell each other who was whom, and who did what, and what year such and such left the Alma Mater; and I just stare at the couple of them, trying to remain impassive, indifferent, calm; yet inwardly, there's no real other option left for me: I resign, resign on the spot and without notice. That was the moment. And by the time of my concert in the evening, they must already have been charging back, racing through the darkening outskirts of London, triumphant, victorious in their conjugal chariot.

IN A WAY, from that day on, my life began; my own. When I went, by train, to Oxford, I wore, instead of my uniform, a navy suit with very faint stripes—bit dreary for my liking, but when I'd had it made, my father and his tailor-chappy, who was a consummate arse-kisser, had already joined forces in advance of my first fitting, and put the cloth aside on my behalf. Still, I got my own back by insisting on a short, boxy jacket and very baggy trousers. The interviews weren't as hard as I had feared, but they did, I remember, surprise me. For a start, all the people who interrogated me were courteous, almost courtly, and didn't seem to want to catch me out—unlike the slimeball inquisitors of my past. Some of the dons seemed even (by means of dry snorts—intended, I think, to irritate the more pious among their colleagues) to sympathize with me for having suffered the misfortune of a Catholic boarding school. I detected more than the odd Querie at these various gatherings designed to judge my potential as an undergraduate: a youngish German academic in particular, with a pince-nez, floppy wrists, and an Alsatian at his feet—a tableau which seemed to put me in mind of J. R. Ackerley, who developed an erotic penchant for that breed, went on to write about it and, when awarded a literary prize, readers thought the world of him.

It was the German don who, once the formal tests were done and everyone pretended to let me relax, fired me the one single question on which, at that instant, I somehow recognized my whole future to be balanced. And the shot wasn't about my linguistic ability, nor about my grasp of current affairs (which amounted to nil), still less to do with my general knowledge (same thing), nor about the history of European literature, nor to do with the rudiments of philology, nor even about specifics such as Lorca's women, or Ionesco's chairs, or Genet's maids, or the Bard and his serpent's teeth and thankless children, but about the oddest thing: whistling.

It turned out that the German could see, not just from my appearance (which, in retrospect, *was* perhaps a bit overslick), but from the details on my CV, that, despite my father's surname, I was not straight-forwardly English; and it was the place of my birth, my mother's once-exotic island, that prompted him—not to test me, I don't think, but—to hope that I might enlighten him on an obscurity, that's how he put it. And then he asked about a curious code of whistling which was of vague folkloric interest, and which, centuries back, before the island's first indigenes, called Guanches, were colonized, had been devised and refined by them as a means, from mountain to mountain, of alerting other natives to impending invasions. Later, this code would be employed merely to convey trivia—such as (I suppose) Bring us some goat's milk, or Come and kill a pig—but vestiges of the idiom survived even into my infancy, when on the eves of feast days you could hear, as I had done when Mam'zelle gave me my bath, descendants of those early whistles flying like arrows through the sunset, which was lit (I could see through the window when she lifted me) with great fires along the jagged purple hills. Cook and Gardener and all their relatives, whose lives were closer to the soil and to the origins of that volcanic landscape, could, I recall, discern scraps of significance in those piercing whistles, of which women were the finest exponents.

And then, the interview moved on to the relationship between music and meaning, and sound and emotion, and sense and communication and all of that pseudy drivel, and although I squirmed about as if I had worms, and dredged up words like phonetic and dissonance and onomatopœic, I felt myself to be, after the whistling bit, if not home and dry, hopefully on the way to my own type of victory. And two days later, back at school, I received a letter confirming this, offering me a place conditional on my A-level results, but demanding such easy grades as to make my acceptance a foregone gift; and for once in my life, the cheapness of that offer made me feel not insulted, but wanted. I remember nothing about actually sitting those papers, except that I dragged into the exams, which were held in the gymnasium, a vast Indian cushion on which to park my rump, armloads of bangles whose rattle was intended to distract other candidates, and a can of air-freshener to quell the stench of humanity. Invigilators turned a blind eye to me, of course, because, by now, it was in the Alma Mater's interest to collude with my campery. Oxbridge, let us not forget, was Oxbridge.

AFTER THOSE EXAMS, I suddenly found myself loaded not just with bangles but with an extravagance of spare time, because there was still a concert coming up, from which, like the wedding of the thousand petals, Dr. Fox wouldn't exempt me; but I can't claim to have minded the imposition this time round: there were jobs to be done, scores to be settled, slates to be wiped clean. First I went to the bursar's office and demanded that, since I had no desire to be kept in touch with the school's activities, or remain in any way connected to it, the money which, throughout my time at the institution, had yearly been tagged onto my bills (by way of eventual membership to the Old Boys' Association) kindly be refunded. The bursar, an affable bumpkin, scratched his thatch and knitted his brow into a quandary, for—never mind the Original Alma Mater Bow—active refusal of an Old Boy tie seemed to be without precedent. He didn't, he confessed, quite know *what* ought to be done. I said that the money should obviously be returned—no, not to me, I wasn't suggesting that, but to its source, to my father (whom I knew would be mortally stung).

My only regret was that I wouldn't be there, like a hornet hovering over the salver in the hall, to witness the delivery of his agony, because the next thing I did was to write home and inform my parents about my offer from Oxford, and further inform them—since permission, now that I was of age, didn't strike me as a requisite—that I wouldn't be going home for the summer, but getting a job in London (a pouffy little boutique, I thought, might be quite fun, but I withheld details of such a plan: I didn't want Interpol on my back, not now that my back was bare at last, and firmly turned away from the benefit of my parents' society). And then there was the matter of the school photograph, taken once every five years, and due to be taken now.

I know I could have opted out and hidden, but somehow that felt unsatisfactory, too passive. I know I could have pulled stupid faces at the camera, but that didn't strike me as either funny or flattering. Nor could I be bothered to sprint round the back row of boys and beat the slow exposure merely in order to be immortalized twice, because, as japes went, that one was both unoriginal and, if detected, punishable. No, what I decided to do, quite simply, was to drop my head, like a penitent, at just the right moment—so that where my face should have been, there would, I hoped, figure a conspicuous but anonymous circle of black, an eclipse, a numberless number. And when the first print (so that worthies could order lots of extra copies for their parents as well as themselves, and for their future sons and grandsons) duly appeared—crested and dated and all hoolied up—on the main noticeboard, a smug little smirk rose to my eyes, for anyone could see that my trick had worked like a charm. I'd become the ultimate blot on the beaming horizon, circular as my mother's dark turban eight years back, when she had stood on my first railway platform, waving her scented gloves and washing her moral hands; circular as her dark, concealing hat when, recently, she had vanished into oblivion, carried off in the conjugal chariot.

Dr. Fox seemed perplexed as he reclined on his wingèd chesterfield, scanning the horizontal scroll of photograph from left to right and back, and slower and slower, and holding it ever closer to his glassy eyes and muttering the while, yet unable, for all of his exertions, to find me. Was I *in* the picture? Of course I was. Well *where*, for God's sake? I advised him to look harder: I was obvious. But nothing doing. Eventually, starting to feel unkind, I did put him out of his misery, and pointed myself out, thereby apprising him both of my presence and of my absence; but he, far from sharing in the laugh, instantly rounded on me, saying that I'd been childish, stupid, brattish—an outburst which struck me as disproportionate to the crime. He seemed actively aggrieved, for some reason, as if I'd insulted not so much the school, about which neither of us cared in the slightest, but him personally, as if I'd struck against my mentor at the final hour. The whole episode baffled me at the time; but now, looking back, I realize that simply by having lowered my head I'd inadvertently managed to deprive Dr. Fox of any evidence of a past which, however contentious, and however cluttered by irrelevant other heads, had, in a sense, been shared by us. And given the imminence of my departure, this last-minute refusal of mine to allow him to remember me even by one-six-hundredth of a dreary institutional photograph must have felt, to him, hurtful; but you see, my urgent determination to separate myself, insofar as I could, from the plague of my father's Alma Mater outweighed, by then, any concerns about whatever documentary consideration might have been due a man who, even if he had taken me to Claridge's, and even if he had taken my side against my father, had also taken more than his fair share of advantage. Because although his task regarding my education was all but complete now, his coercions both on the coal box and in the brocaded alcove (even as he dreamt of pumping his cheesiness into the fair but unavailable mouth of Albany) could never be undone.

Dr. Fox took out his pocketwatch and suddenly realized that he was running late for some meeting in the basement. He told me, while he washed up our teacups (a chore which I never offered to do, not so much from inherent queenliness as from fear of detection in the masters' bathroom), to fetch him his academic gown from the wardrobe. So while he busied himself across the way, I complied with this request; but as I unhooked the limp crow of cloth from its hanger, a shimmer, far behind, in the musty depths of the mahogany, caught my eye. It was a woman's dress, which had once, I seem to recall, belonged to his mother, and which he retained for the same incomprehensible reasons of sentiment that most of us keep incomprehensible mementos, such as a child's mohair blanket. And while he was next door, sloshing about—it's so odd to tell—I went and stole the dress; borrowed it, at any rate; slung it in its transparent plastic cover over my arm, shouted at him that I had to go, and raced to my room. I would return it when I was done.

THAT LITTLE black number was fit for a Charleston. It was the perfect flapper's dress, cut like a chiffon vest, loose-hipped and low-waisted, covered with tiny jet beads, and finished by a fringe of crystal bugles which swished over the edge of its hem. Like the school itself, it seemed to weigh with its own history, but unlike my father's Alma Mater, it glittered with thrill, shimmered with stories of parties and kisses and drink; and even if its initial wearer no longer lived, the surviving dress seemed to retain a life, a vivacity about it; for despite the acrid smell of lavender which hung from a sachet at its neck and clung to it, you could sense, still, that the original girl would have worn with it some essence of greater freshness, orange-blossom or primrose, or jasmine even, which was the flappers' favourite. You could picture it all in its heyday, that youthful dress bobbing about on parquet, and twirling and kicking, and skipping energetically along the galleries of great country mansions, demolished long since.

The scene, from my perspective, had almost less to do with Dr. Fox, who rarely referred to his parentage, than it did with me, for it reminded me of the time when my young grandmother, head over heels in love, must have danced with her infantry officer before he was killed. (I was later to learn, while clearing my mother's effects, that the diamond gauntlet which she had worn to the Victors' Dance, but of whose history she had so peevishly deprived me, had been meant as an engagement present from the hopeful officer to his sweetheart—delivered, after that fatal duel, by the boy's distraught mother to the daughter-in-law who, following the tragedy, my grandmother was never to become.) But this dress felt, as it lay on my bed, like an heirloom, a great gift—for me to do with as I pleased. And, for reasons that still remain unclear, what I pleased to do with it was this: get into it. And it fitted me as perfectly as, a few weeks earlier, my mother had been fitted into her couture chantilly—even if, as in her case, black proved not to be a colour that especially flattered me. No matter: I would flatter my self, and not just in private: I would flatter myself at quite another dance, and flaunt my flattery.

Since the local village was as ill-equipped as it was risky for that which I had in mind, I took a bus into town and went into one of those shops that sell everything for next to nothing. I bought a cassette, to distract the gaggle of shopgirls, and then lifted, in very quick succession, an elasticated diamanté bracelet, a lipstick (which fortunately turned out to be dark, accurate) plus some nail polish, about which I did suffer a dilemma on the trip back, because I couldn't be sure of the date when such enamels first became popular in Europe. But when I placed the spoils upon my desk, which, by now, had obviously become a dressing-table, I realized that I'd forgotten to filch a pair of tights. Tough. I'd manage somehow. Necessity is the mother of subversion.

That night, a leaving party was to be held in honour of the sixth form, who, by this stage in the year, were all through their exams. It was due to take place in the senior common room, where, exceptionally, people would be allowed to drink and smoke without the hassle of supervision, and where, less exceptionally, slags from a couple of local convents were to be herded in, presumably to provide incentive for experimental mating rituals. The planned jamboree was to kick off at eight p.m., but must, by official dictate, end at the midnight hour. Still, people seemed, despite the infliction of a deadline, animated enough, listless and a little reckless in their preparations, like prisoners thinking of birds with big jugs, because now, our boys could contemplate activities which, if discovered before the exams, might not have been viewed as too prudent. It was their first taste of freedom, really. As, in a weird way, it was mine.

I TAKE A SHOWER. I return to my room, draw the curtains, jam a chair against the door. I switch on my music, though not as loud as I might have liked. I beam my anglepoise into the mirror and I deliver myself to my task, vaguely aware, in the breaks between my songs, of mechanical thuds, of party action drifting from the other end of the corridor; and, every so often, I hear the squeals and shrieks of heavy-soled lasses as they stomp along in a total antithesis of the sylph who first wore my dress and skipped her slippered way along the marble terraces of those now-forgotten mansions.

It won't be a breeze, I realize, but it feels bloody exciting, like guzzling sweet wine in the sacristy, or wanking into the mongrel's chalice. I slip into a pair of underpants, then step into the long silk socks donated to me by my mother, which I stretch like stockings over my knees, but which keep slipping down. Ignore them for now. I don a dressing-gown, my negligée, like an actress preparing to grease up, and I smear my face with moisturiser, which feels in character. No hairband required. Next I sit down—cross-leggèd, naturally. The manicure, given my shaking fingers, proves pretty dicey, but I know not to take it all too seriously: I'm after effect, not exactitude; this is theatre, not fashion; and besides, the lights at the disco will be dark—not just to encourage uninhibited dancing, but to enable the boys who like to sprawl on the banquettes to explore the undergrowth of pencil-skirts without embarrassment; and, I suppose, for the girls to reciprocate with a juggle.

But can you believe that until this moment I hadn't given a thought to mascara? What to do? *Mon Dieu, quoi faire?* Improvise, you idiot. What, I wonder, did all those dramatic chorus-women do in ancient Athens? Not a clue; but I decide to burn a few matches and employ the soot to emphasize my eyes; and I apply a couple of hyphens of lipstick to my eyelids, which lends them ardour; and then I run a pencil along my brows, comb them, pluck out the odd spike (because already I own tweezers, my dear, oh yes) and the result looks almost passable. To finish off, I touch up, with a black felt-tip now, the end of every single one of my lashes, which I regret to admit do err a trifle on the short side. This latest procedure doesn't, in cosmetic terms, seem to make much difference, but the feeling of rightness, of actressiness, more than makes up for it. And as I toil, I think of my mother's dainty lace scallops, their lashes.

The music down the corridor seems to be growing louder, or perhaps the rest of our quarters are emptier, hollowed out. Anyway, time for a bit more lipstick, rubbed into the cheeks by way of blusher, but don't go overboard, I tell myself, you don't want to look like that slattern in Berlin, Elsie from Chelsea or whatever her name was, the one who had the gory abortion and kept saying divinely decadent darling. Right; done; that's enough. I grease my hair into a sort of Eton crop, with the strictest of side-partings, but, unable to resist the influence of the great Marcel, I sculpt a rolling ornamental wave which I allow to kink over one eye. Lips are easy, not just because I've been watching my mother paint her beautiful, venomous own for years, but because I'm myself a mistress of lip-salve: chaps, as you know, are the bane of this climate. But suddenly, to my horror, I realize that, on this night of all first-nights, I have no earrings to wear to the party . . . and well, I'll just have to hope that Dr. Fox, or his departed mother, will forgive me if they should ever find out, because, in creative desperation, I snip a couple of shimmery beads from the back of the dress and glue them onto my lobes. And although it's tricky without wrecking my lacquered fingers, the outcome again passes muster. Yes, I look tastefully accessorized, chic even (assuming that chic meant anything to a flapper), because God is on my side. And then I slip into the dress, which luckily has no rusty zips or hooks-and-eyes. I tug at my socks and garter them up, tourniquet-tight, and step into my patent leather dancing-pumps (thank you, Mother, how clever of you). And last, I place the elasticated diamonds round my wrist: gorgeous, the whole thing, if a little grippy—I should have preferred their dazzlement to dangle more casually, like a relaxed engagement, not some hasty gun-shot. Never mind. I turn up my music further, turn off the merciless anglepoise, and then, turn to take a fresh and final look at myself in the soft light of the boudoir. I could do with a cocktail, sure, but even in sobriety, let me tell you: if I had the nous, I would pre-set my camera at this moment, pose (hand on hip would seem suitable), and take my own photograph—obviously in black and white. Say *Fromage.*

My boyish bosom is going like the clappers; but I can't hang about to lose heart; I have to get moving, like an ever-onward soldier marching as to war, terrified but ecstatic, unequipped for the future yet too late for turnabouts and cowardice. Hold on, you've forgotten your Baccy: cigar*ettes,* for God's sake, I'm not some bloody *cadet,* dear; I'm a warrior-maiden. So I grab a cigarette packet, slip a lighter inside it and, seeing as I have no evening bag, tuck the lot into my knickers. (What would you have done?) And then I spray myself with atomizer—honeysuckle and amber, perfect scent-notes for the occasion. And I step into the night without a chaperon.

The lights in the corridor are dark. The stench of beer isn't encouraging, but I'm beyond such trivia now, nothing can hold me back. And anyway, I tell myself, backstage was never meant to be Versailles. And as I emerge from the shadows, I see a few people leaning about in shockingly bad outfits and smooching outside the common room, couples-of-sorts, too absorbed and far-gone to spare me a thought, plus a smattering of young bachelors, spotty lonesomes-tonight, whose bleary eyes, when they clap sight of me, seem to proclaim Wow, what a gal (when I wish to be a vamp, actually, but still): flattery's flattery, even if my admirers are too sozzled to recognize me. And at least they have the decency, as I proceed with a very controlled sashay towards the public, to clear a path for my entrance. Make way: Head Girl.

FLASHES-AND-STARS and kisses-of-fire and flashes-and-stars and kisses-of-fire, and well, here we are at last. Good evening one-and-all, and welcome. It's going to be fine. One of your favourite songs is coming on now. You recognize the intro. You could do with a shot of something, but you don't really think you've got time. And bugger the introductions, frankly, because you're just so glamorous in your own right, and charismatic, and covered in class, and back in the roaring twenties—even if the song is of the moment—and isn't it all just a fabulous confusion, everyone? Divinely decadent darling. You should have worn gloves.

But: You Can Dance, the song starts up, so you move sideways towards the floor, which is packed, and you weave your slip of girlishness towards its centre. Again the singers say that You Can Dance, as if repeating their permission, which is nice; and then they remind you that you're Having The Time Of Your Life—which, already, you sort of are, for you're immersed and sublime and bang in the spotlight and regretting none of this for a moment. And now the song is telling the rest to See That Girl, to Watch That Scene, because, of course, you have become, therefore you are: The Dancing Queen. And now you do take off; transvested and transformed and transfigured, but, to begin with, you swivel your hips quite slowly, because you don't want to seem too keen any more than you wish your socks to be seen. Yet you can act this whole thing to perfection, like the utter natural that you are, because in a way you've spent your life preparing for this instant, swaying in your own space, turning and waving and smiling and hoping and longing despite the suffocating flood of your guilty secrets and the drowning uterine waters of your misconceived, miscarried past.

Friday Night And The Lights Are Low, the song continues, and aptly: for today is indeed Friday, and the lights are low all right. The vocalists begin to harmonize about Looking Out For A Place To Go Where They Play The Right Music, which, of course, is precisely here and now; and here and now, though you look at no one in particular, but simply stare into the light of heaven that blinds you, you can tell that the dancers around you, your mismanaged troupe, your chorus of bad Greek women, are heeding the warning to See That Girl, to Watch That Scene, and some of the bitches have already wised up to your strange magic, and are nudging their partners to wake up and realize it, some of them even shrieking that you're no less than You, while others just stare aghast at the vision, tragic and wide-eyed and nauseous like your mother. But you, you're way beyond mothering now, for you have become your absolute best at last, an emancipated, independent, liberated flapper. So you just think of the words, which are your anthem, but you hardly part your painted lips about it, for these have become more perfect than (from this day on) those of your mother will ever be. And you're telling yourself that You're In The Mood For A Dance, which you certainly are, and that When You Get The Chance, which is right now (so you give yourself a spin while you can), You-Are-You-Are-You-Are The Dancing Queen. And you're congratulating yourself for the victory, and even pretending that you're still Young and Sweet, even if you haven't been for aeons, and you make out that you're Only Seventeen—which you no longer are, but that's nobody else's business—because, from this your new majority, you can Feel The Beat From The Tambourine, so you rattle your priceless diamonds accordingly. But don't get too carried away by the whole thrill, because you've forgotten to shave your armpits.

Something odd begins to happen next: a greater space seems to have been cleared, a wider firmament made over to your stellar beauty, to your feminine grace and unassailable elegance, which, unlike your mother's falling star, are finally in the ascendant, and you, you couldn't care an eclipse whether these people are giving you a wide, horrified berth, or admiring your incredible chic, or both, or neither of these things, because you are, again and again, as you shall remain, for years to come, the Alma Mater's one and only Dancing Queen. But now the song runs away, a little indiscreetly, to reveal that really You're A Teaser, that You Turn 'Em On—and, as if to confirm this, some drunken imbecile comes up to meet you, to face you, chewing a cigarette like some scummy hero, and thinking that he's writhing and being sexy, when Mr. Funk can't dance to save his poxy skin, doesn't know the *meaning* of the word *rhythm;* but you don't want to appear too supercilious (ever), so you remain, absorbed and contained and delicious, poised like a doll on your own precious pinnacle, which peaks at the epicentre of this dream. And the lyrics admit that You Leave Them Burning, which you're sure that you could, and further reveal that Then, You're Gone, Looking Out For Another, which very soon you will be, and that Anyone Will Do, which is practically the truth, and next, as if to confirm those very lyrics, another boy, in a reconstruction of the success which your mother enjoyed with all her ruddy victors, comes up to you, and it seems to be—indeed it is—the grinning son of the admiral, whose big endowment you can glimpse, though you can't quite tell whether this is thanks to you or to the hooker slithering up to him; and who cares, really, because it's all been heavenly, Mother, hasn't it. And anyway, the song, as so many good things must, is inevitably approaching its end, which is climactic; so sweaty brows and laundered handkerchieves and all the rest of the decorum be damned, because couldn't you just kill for a drink? Make mine a triple, darling, with ice.

So I step off the floor, and my public is, look, amazed by me, especially the country girls, who're my greatest fans, see: I bet they want to learn everything, but really I think that deodorant is all that need concern them for the minute; and as I begin to head for the bar in order to point my painted index at some exotic beverage (sorry, libation), I suddenly find myself interrupted by the idiot who first came up to dance with me, the scummy hero whom I jilted in favour of the boy with the admirable endowment, and although another song is starting up— quite the wrong one, as it happens, some moronic rock-track—and although I'm out of my natural light, the cuckold, undaunted, swaggers up to me and, can you believe the cheek of it, makes as if to kiss me; but I retreat with utmost smoothness, like my mother in her black straw hat trying to avoid the peril of disarrangement, so he returns his smouldering cigarette to his dry mouth in order to disguise his floundering manhood; yet still, like a man, he will not take the hint, because next, he tries to touch me somewhere near my slinky hip, as if to toy, to mess with me, and I can tell that people are watching now, and I can hear them behind me; jeering Go on, show the dirty queer, and other similar endearments; but I just stare at my challenger, because, oddly enough, I've rarely felt braver or more virile than I do at this instant, and I stare him out of his pathetic wits, as if he were a bully like my father yet my name were really David, though my flattened chest, again, is racing, for none of this feels quite as safe as it did when I was the undisputed Dancing Queen, and it's hardly surprising—since, almost before I click, he dares to raise his filthy impudent hand to me, and attempts (when my visage has been crafted to the last impeccable millimetre)—just credit the nerve of this—to slap me; but luckily, I duck; and he, the drunken scummy hero, misses. And despite the holy fluke, let me assure you: I'm not about to make a run for it and allow my dignity to be poured like a pint of bitter down the tubes, for, endangered as I am, I remain a strong young woman, so I snatch his grimy ciggy from his lower lip, swivel it adroitly, and stub it out, hard and with providential symmetry, in the middle of his stunned forehead, that at least he may learn the true meaning of the word Smouldering. I hear him fizzle. I smell his sizzling skin. But really he ought to be grateful for the cauterizing, because, at a stroke, I seem to have transformed him from a nothing into an Indian deity—though, admittedly, without an Indian summer, or the luxury of an Indian cushion on which to nurse the wound of my beneficence. And then, very composedly, I swish out of the room—thank you, ladies, thank you, hope you've enjoyed the evening, personally I've loved a good deal of it—and my bugle-beads are still dancing and kicking and swishing historically about my (shaky) knees.

NEXT MORNING—before any gossip could reach him—I returned the victory dress, miraculously unscathed, and without detection, to Dr. Fox's wardrobe; and after he'd completed what he called his ablutions, we had breakfast as if nothing. My make-up had come off like a dream. My nails, after a scrape with a pair of scissors, looked dodgier, but Dr. Fox wouldn't have noticed such details. And yet I felt uneasy, for, much as I might have welcomed the chance of a debate with the school authorities on the contentious—and to the best of my knowledge, also unpunishable—subject of transvestism, which Catholics liked to fob off as a filthy perversion favoured by Protestant inverts (to which I would have replied that it was a tradition rich with history, as favoured by the Vatican—remember Fellini—as by European grandees and heterosexual English kings), I certainly didn't want to get called in by the rector at the last minute, and given a thrashing for having scorched some prat who deserved it, when, with the exception of Dr. Fox's concert, I was effectively free to leave.

On my return to my room, I found my cushion slashed to ribbons, I wonder by whom, but this gesture of contempt just spurred me to more contemptuous gestures of my own. The first, which later, briefly, for a couple of minutes, I did regret a bit, was to hurl all my books into the incinerator. The second was dutifully to unpick, as my mother's sempstress had once unpicked the many skirts of her bridal organdie, every stitch sewn round the nametapes of my uniform and linen. I tried to count the threaded stabs, in an attempt to discover how their total sum compared with the number of days spent in this nightmare: but it didn't, not by a long chalk: I was owed, oh terms' worth. Then I packed my trunk meticulously, locked it, chucked the key out of the window, and poured the reminder of my bottle of nail polish on the lid, over my English initials. While the blood was drying, I put the rest of my belongings—my tapes, my pumps, a couple of small pictures, odds and ends of normal clothing—into a suitcase. I closed the cover of my violin. I plonked my plants in the common room, which could do with a bit of cheering, and then I went downstairs in search of a couple of juniors. I bribed them to drag my trunk to the place where trunks were supposed to be deposited—next to the tuck shop, once the fortress of Payne Senior, but closed now, out of season—before being boarded onto lorries and trains and ships. I gave those children clear instructions to cover my trunk with the trunk of some other pupil, and only then to come back to me for payment. In the end it took four of the blighters to carry my chattels, which weighed heavier than a corpse, so my extravagance proved quite costly, but the cause justified it.

I took a final shower, and dressed, in my own clothes. I scrawled a note to Dr. Fox, apologizing for the haste of my departure, explaining that sudden bad news from the family necessitated my missing his concert, and telling him that I would let him know where I could be reached as soon as I myself knew this. And then I went to the coin box, and ordered a taxi, for which I waited near the gates where my parents had once stood like angry spears, and as I saw my own blessed chariot speed round the insouciant Madonna and approach, I grabbed my suitcase and my violin and ran to meet my freedom, but my race against myself must have looked less like an act of vindication than like the early scene from *The Sound of Music* when the singing novice is put back on the streets to find a more suitable calling. And then, as I was about to step inside the car and flee, one of those juniors ran out to hand me a letter, addressed by my father, which I might otherwise have missed, and which I read on the train. And from it I learnt one last thing, which is that the course of spite, more than the course of love, is what never runs smooth:

Dear Iago (not James), the letter begins—instantly betraying the collaboration of his wife.

We returned without mishap after a few very pleasant days in London. Since then, your mother and I have been talking and feel concerned about you. Both your attitude at school, which seems to be one of non-involvement in any wholesome activity and your conduct at home, which we find socially quite unacceptable, there's no need to expound on this, you know exactly what we mean, has led us to take a hard but unavoidable decision. Since you do not wish to come here for the summer, we suggest that you remain in England for the moment.

You should contact my bank manager Mr. Palmer, who I haven't met (I've spoken to him on the telephone) at Lloyd's in St. James's. Make an appointment to see him, and we beg of you, try to look respectable. He has instructions about your finances, regarding both the immediate future and the longer term. Once he's opened an account for you, he will be advancing you by direct debit a monthly allowance as well as your termly fees for Oxford, since you appear to be headed there after all, because even though you're English, I gather from the school that you're not eligible for a grant. This deals with current matters.

As you know, the bulk of your money from your grandfather's trust will be made over to you when you reach the age of 25 by when we sincerely hope that even if you have to learn the hard way you will have matured. Think about it, James (aha!), and ask yourself whether you have shown your mother and I sufficient signs of appreciation for the tremendous sacrifices that we have undergone on your account. And in the meantime, try to understand that this necessary distancing, though harsh, is the right decision both for you and us.

Since you seem determined to ignore social decency, I feel bound as your father to add (though your mother naturally knows nothing of this) a verse from the Holy Bible which I hope will make plain to you, while you have the time to correct it, your moral position in the eyes of the Lord: "If a man lies with a male as with a woman, both of them have committed an abomination; they shall be put to death, their blood is upon them." This comes from the book of Leviticus, and you would do well to read it in its entirety.

In the hope that you will see the light of reason, your mother joins me in prayer on your behalf.

Yours aye,

HJM

P.S. And for goodness sakes before you go to the bank get your hair cut.

PART FIVE

G OD GIVE ME NEW HORIZONS. While my bath runs, I make some coffee and throw the news of the day, unread, into the bin. As I open the drawer of the kitchen table, I find, after all this time, that half-forgotten missive from my friend in France, a woman of birdlike beauty, and I open it with the care that I owe to her, using an agate letter-knife. Inside the tissued envelope, behind a picture of a bronze-and-naked dancer leaping in mid-air, frozen in mid-life, her message, which has lain in wait, now flies out to me like a stab, and reads, in black: I think of you more often than you hear from me. You are important to my well-being, but I don't mean to sound like a burden, or a responsibility—it's my pleasure. Much love. And as I step into the bath, which is slippery with oils of frankincense and lavender, ironic oils, said to help you to relax, I wonder what is becoming of my life, why I neglect my friends; and I reflect on how I abuse the blessings that I've been granted, how I drink too much, how I fritter away my time. And I resolve to set all these wrongs to right, to return to church one of these days, to make myself over to another land. Then I sit down.

I'M SITTING at the table in the restaurant and trying, less out of concern than simulated courtesy, to keep my eyes involved in the open, glossy hopeful features of my friend, my host, my sometime confidant, who seems impatient to regale me with every twitch and tweak about some glorious youth just down from university, encountered in a classic *coup de foudre* on the way out of an acclaimed recent production of a (naturally) baroque opera. And they've been, since, out to dinner twice, talked about everything under the sun: first, in Arlington Street, no less; then, somewhere quieter, more *intime*. But of course, there's been, as yet, none of That Stuff—why must I always be so tacky? Although there has, he gulps, there has, as a matter of fact, been a kiss, just one, since I ask, on the hand. On the hand? God almighty, what is *wrong* with queers these days? My friend regards me piteously. He's not ashamed, he says. He's prepared to wait. To wait for what? There's no big rush, he replies with impatience: love is not a train. And then he adds that he, unlike others he could mention (though there scarcely seems a need), knows when a thing warrants . . . considered investment, when it deserves to be taken—oh, how can he put it? I put it for him: *doucement-doucement*—and the fool agrees. But it transpires, as my companion begins to confide, which he now does with a vengeance, his hand grabbing at my recoiling cuff with a force that betrays panic, that, for all of his cool collectedness, he's gone and booked ten days for two at some fabulously manicured Moroccan snazz-hole with cascades of bougainvillaea and oh, sand-dunes of gazelles and palm trees of green parrots and the thing is, well, here comes the rub: he can't figure out a way to tell the boy, doesn't know how to invite him. Should he send a note, a note with flowers, or would that seem too campy? (What, campier than opera, *mio caro*?) For heaven's sake, he spits, swiftly retracting his grip from my sleeve. What's wrong with me these days? Don't I know anything any more?

All I know is this, and I'm not about to tell him: first, that he'd do well to give up those natty cravats of his; and second—more worryingly, from my point of view—that earlier today, as I stepped out of the bath and began to towel myself dry and thought not about what I should wear for lunch, which was obvious, but what I would wear next time that Steve came round, comes round, I discovered, like a mockery from above, bang slap at the epicentre of my left buttock, a developing pimple, a lesion, a bloody volcano. I can feel it now, pulsing against the wicker of my chair.

BACK IN MY FLAT I decide to face facts: Steve will have to be put off, postponed for a few nights, and I must travel, travel as far as he's concerned. Not a crisis, exactly, nothing so grand; just some unforeseen but unavoidable circumstance. And where, pray, shall I be bound on this trip that I plan? Nowhere so remote that I risk flying out of his mind, nor yet to a place so near as to render my pretext banal. And catching a providential glimpse of the card from my friend in Paris, I realize that yes, it's obvious, that's where I shall go, where I must pretend to be gone. Well, not to Paris exactly—too *bonjour mesdames* for comfort—rather somewhere flatter and duller and buried without need of a mention vaguely in France. So I leave a message on his Ansaphone saying that it turns out that I have to be out of the country on Wednesday and that although I'm due back in the evening, late afternoon in fact, I'm a bit worried that my flight might be delayed or something, and I may not manage to get home in time for our (I nearly say date) appointment; anyway, could he let me know whether he'd prefer to reschedule or whatever, thanks, 'bye. And I head off for a siesta and take off my trousers and suddenly realize—guess what?—that the spot on my bum no longer feels nor—hang on—looks nearly so bad. And I unplug the 'phone beside me.

When it rings a while later, though I pick it up mechanically, the receiver is dead at my end; so I just lie back and listen to the pump of my startled breast as the machine clicks on in another room; and I hear, after waiting an eternity for my irksome outgoing voice to reach its suspension, the voice of Steve acknowledging my call and saying no problem, he's doing nothing else that night, just to ring him when I get in, or from the airport if I like, might be an idea, so long as it's, say, before eleven, later might be pushing it, I might be tired, but either way, not to worry, speak on Wednesday, 'bye for now. And hey, he adds, by way of salacious afterthought, have a good time. Then, a chuckle, and he's gone. I hurl myself out of bed, as if I'd overslept. I can hardly think—I, who think too much.

BY BY WEDNESDAY, feast of the Transfiguration, I believe that I have thought of most things—prepared for the future, if not quite with the fervour of a novice on the verge of the veil, certainly with the rigour of a patient bound for an intervention so delicate, so critical that he must face the possibility of never returning from that dreaded sacred place, the operating theatre. I have, of course, long hence written my will, but I've double-checked the contents just to ensure that no small thing has carelessly been left to persons who, since its composition, may happen to have disappointed me, or kicked the bucket. And all is serene: no thing has. I have tidied every tape and book and disc and plate and glass and knife and fork and spoon and thing in my possession. A denim apron which has always been a source of shame to me I have finally thrown away, along with the tattier of my tea-towels, which bear the frayed initials of my mother as a maiden. I have defrosted the fridge and, with the exception of a bottle of poppers, rid it of all perishables. On the occasions when I've felt a need for reflection, I have waxed the kitchen floor-tiles, on my knees, a servant to myself. They gleam. The window cleaner has been. The linen spread upon my bed is fresh and crisp and fine as a shroud which a palliative sister might long to retrieve before a patient's refrigeration. The flowers that I have placed in a tall vase of uncut crystal, flowers known as black roses, would do credit to most shrines. My small dark car has been scrupulously cleaned, and polished by hand, and parked directly outside the gates of the building where I am. All notes and cards and letters and telegrams and invitations ever received have been catalogued in files and shelved: some alphabetically, some chronologically; the rest, by theme. Personal papers which I regret having written, testaments to juvenile imprudences, have obviously been binned, as have unguarded photographs, images that might mislead. In the early hours of today, I dumped two family-sized bags, stuffed full of biographical redundancies, in a nearby skip outside a grotty local hotel, and was caught in the act by a marauding rubber queen who scowled, then rubbed her constricted packet at me. All of my clothes, except for those on my back, which I plan to chuck at the last opportunity, are clean. My seventy-eight pairs of shoes, which, let me tell you, have strutted and trampled and danced in their time, are in full sheen—with the exception of a half-forgotten pair of fifties lamé party-spikes which I thought it wiser to discard. My coats hang in a cupboard in the hall, ranged by the season and by colour and by cut, like a catalogue of moods. I have dusted my umbrellas, out on the landing, and returned them to their stand— furled but not clasped. I own no hats.

And so, as you can see, at least the place where I reside is orderly, fit to receive, in readiness. Were I to die today, which, given a choice, I should prefer to do other than on these premises, somewhere less sightly, such as a backroom, I cannot imagine that my spiralling ghost would have reason to fret over any posthumous domestic scrutiny. And my executor, who most likely has forgotten how years ago, in the throes of a passionate if overpatternly acid trip, he offered to execute on my behalf, will, when called upon to effect the mixed privilege of his duties, exhale with relief that my affairs lie not in the surrealistic state of disarray which he might have feared. I mean, given the accounts which you hear about untimely departed members of the sorority—the dildos, the dick-pumps, the sticky mounds of pornography, the incriminating Polaroids, the medical pamphlets on how to reconstruct a foreskin, the (I'm sorry to be prissy, but frankly) lamentable state of those duvets—well, my own demise, were it to strike me now, would surely strike my jittery intimates as a blessedly neat piece of, not quite justice, of mercy. Like a funeral without a family. Or a kiss without false teeth.

I've taken a look at myself and taken myself in hand and, after numerous recent lapses, returned to the gym: on Monday, and on Tuesday, and, like some frenzied client attending a last-minute fitting, very early this morning. You know how a certain type of rich, undignified woman, generally divorced and pushing fifty, will commend herself to her couturier with the Brief, disguised as a plea, that—whatever the cost of the creation (which is immaterial to her), and whatever its cut and cloth and strategic padding—the marriage of her money to his skill must recompense her, at a predetermined party, with the advances of a man on whom she has designs; well, I, similarly, have engaged a personal trainer—a female, predictably, for females tend best to understand these things, these urgent dreams. And I have asked her, without actually divulging the grubby nature of my need, to invest in me, for this brief time, every detail of her body-sculpting expertise. But I must sound too breathless, too frantic, like a neglected actor suddenly called up for a part demanding nudity. And I suspect that she can hear the beat of my anxiety, because, before we begin, she pulls me into a corner and tries to appease me by claiming that there's no need to get into a state about things. After all, she explains, you're slim, can't weigh more than what, eleven, eleven and a half stone—exactly. And she has the elegance to describe me as lean, which is the polite word for scrawny; and then, pointing at the mirror, she tells my reflection to look at itself. See? Whereas (she whispers) just *get* the other desperados in this gym—as if their pasty flabbiness could bring solace to me. This, she goes on, is what we're going to do: tighten up my rump a bit; pump out my shoulders a little; burn off some fat on the exercise bike; and we can do some cardiovascular moves on the step-machine. But, she warns, suddenly looking serious, You're not to expect miracles. Oh I don't, I reply: in three days I only expect to be resurrected, not reincarnated. And she laughs aloud, beefily, and her mirth disrupts the surrounding, panting gravity. A few heads turn, and glare disapprovingly, as if we were gossiping in church, or yakking at a cinema; and for a chilling instant I imagine that one of those sweaty faces belongs to Steve. Stop it. She trains me with such fierce concentration, as if I were her chosen candidate for some vital competition, that I could almost describe her attention as devoted. Her eyes seem never to leave me. She hardly speaks. Very occasionally, as I move onto a higher weight or some harder machine, she encourages me. I find that I have grown, in this short, frenetic period, disconcertingly fond of a woman whom I scarcely know, whose personal story is a mystery to me. But already my time is up; her job is done; I'm ready to leave. And although, of course, I look nothing like a vision, I've half been turned into what some, if suitably starved and drunk, might regard as a passing object of interest. But she stresses that what we have done, what she has done for me, is only a cheat, won't last beyond a week. And as I hand back my locker key, she asks what this whole thing is about anyway, some love job? Her guess flushes me violently, but I tell her not to be silly, just off on holiday. Oh yeah, she grins, where to, the moon? Most probably, I admit. And then I feel the kindness of her hand patting the troubles in my old kit-bag, as if for luck; so I, in turn, lean across and, not exactly professionally, kiss her cheek.

LEAVING THE GYM, since I still have most of the day to kill, I decide to stop at a local coffee bar which, today, seems to be packed with animated foreign kids, chaperoned by a knitworn older man. But the edges of the place are planted with a typical smattering of queens, hardy perennials, inserted singly along the walls, into the shade, dug down and drooping slightly from the graftings of the previous evening. One of these I recognize from God knows when, way back: a forgettable fuck, bleary-eyed from skunk, who spares me the hassle of a glance. At the counter, I order a large espresso and an orange juice; no, no ice, thanks. Toast?, he goes, Danish? Croissant? Bap? No, nothing;

this'll be fine. Two fifty-nine, he announces, as if I'd asked for the time in Cape Town; and he returns my change, along with an unconvincing smile and the exhortation: There you go now. Pisses me off when they say that. Go where, and when, precisely?

Go towards the window at the front, away from the crowd. Sit down. Light up. Look out. Notice, across the street, beyond a row of parked cars, a (closed) shop of gay paraphernalia, inside which you will find poppers, cock-rings, cock-straps, ball-weights, tit-clamps, harnesses, douche-bags, soft-core videos, specialist literature, coffee-table books of homographic art, greetings cards (both funny and funereal), T-shirts with slogans ("I Can't Even Think Straight"; "Stuff A Chicken Tonight"; "Trouble," and, for Trouble's little friend, "Strife"); pump-action lubricant, in various flavours and sizes; double-strength condoms, extra-length condoms (designed to accommodate both larger Prince Alberts and udder-loads of urine); a fancy range of underwear (thong, pouch, brief, mesh, stud-front, zip-back), plus, of course, a spectrumful of colour-coded back-pocket handkerchieves, displayed as a rainbowed flower.

My head is still loitering around the dark interior of the shop when, for no apparent reason, it seems to flutter out onto the street and gaze at the display of running-vests and latex shorts and vinyl caps and combat boots and leather waistcoats and a solitary cat-o'-nine tails lying unconscious on the floor, which I can see between two cars; and then my mind returns to me, bearing, like a vulture or a hawk, the question which I suppose I've been trying to avoid: Tonight, what do I put on? And instantly, here I go: you could, of course, simply repeat the previous lot of clothes, for safety, but that might suggest a desire for repetition, when a reprise of events is the least of your hopes. Or you could, alternatively, just dress as if for comfort, as if this second meeting were less sexual than social, in chinos, with a rolled-up shirt of Oxford cotton, and brogues. Or you could try to test his erotic know-how by donning an armour, something rebarbative, like a flannel suit and stiff collar and cufflinks with pearls and a handmade tie from Rome. Or you could even open the door wearing nothing at all, starkers, which is the ultimate challenge and the ultimate turn-off (you've had it done to you; you know). And finally it occurs to you, the secret, the solution, the perfect formula. You will model yourself on the very

man whom you want to get to know, disguise yourself as an unde-
tectable whore, dress as an irony.

Decided, then. Tonight, when he walks in, assuming that he does,
and assuming that he's remotely perceptive, Steve will spot my emula-
tion of that earlier him, will recognize a darker, younger, slighter version of the way he looked at our first meeting. He will find me wearing
a brown T-shirt (though mine, of lycra from Los Angeles, is more
poncy), and baggy blue-jeans (though mine, underworn, aren't as convincing as his), and heavy black boots (though mine don't stop at the
ankle: they rise to mid-calf under my jeans, to pad out my legs, which
are weedy). I suddenly envisage him appearing in the identical, original
outfit, and instantly turning me into his puny mimic, his idiot twin, and
the prospect tries to finish me. I dismiss it by dwelling on the veins up
his arms and the veins on his neck and the strong vein at his temple,
and I think of his head and then I think of mine and I think bloody hell
and practically sprint to an old-fashioned barber's down the road (the
sort of butchy place, I bet you, to which Steve himself would go), and
the shop is empty; and on the window, in red, it says seven quid—lucky
number to begin with, but also a perfect fraction of that other, greater
figure, seventy, in cash: a sort of replica, a fated miniature. So I walk in,
and Sweeney Todd turns out, to my relief, to be a jokey little Greek. No
need to talk. I signal Short; he signals Shorter? I signal No; he nods No
Problem, and now we're off. He stands on a linoleum step to carry out
my yob-crop, and kicks the platform around me at irregular intervals,
pushing my ears down, forcing my neck forward; occasionally, snort-
ing. And a matter of minutes later, during which I've been vacant, in a
sort of limbo, absorbed by the mystique of scissors and clippers and
cut-throats, and wondering how certain people can claim such things as
fetishes, how they can regard the process of being shorn as a turn-on,
I'm done, done-for: he swirls his sheet away from my chest with the
panache of a triumphant matador, and I'm left resembling the mug-
shot of some mugger. My regular hairdresser, an impossibly sophisticated lesbian who dismisses clients who cannot discuss the latest
novels, and who, for years, has refused my impetuous visits to her salon
(Go home, give it some thought, then telephone and make an appointment), would knock my block off. And I return to my flat still preoccu-

pied by the subject of hair: no longer, however, that on my head; rather the stuff that sprouts about my body.

I FIND THAT often people are reluctant to discuss the issue of body hair outside the homosexual ghetto, as if it, the hair, didn't exist, or didn't warrant attention. By contrast, at the time of which I write, which falls late into the century, this whole dialectic has, among gays, become something of an obsession. I cannot claim to be a conversant inhabitant of the queer nation, much less an arbiter of what is, and what is not, homopolitically appropriate. Nor can I pretend to be an aficionado of parlours that promise painless, or, come to that, excruciating depilation. So, before you start to ask from where I derive my peculiar notions on the topic, let me admit that what scant experience I possess has been garnered in private, at close quarters—not thanks to the wonder of Dutch video pornography, which, incidentally, is the only one of its type worth watching; nor, indeed, thanks to American skinny-pics, which tend to be less arousing than comical; but through sly observation and, still more systematically, through tactile perception. I have literally felt my way around the subject, perfected for myself a secret sort of body Braille; but this has nothing to do with discernment, for, in the case of others, I run into trouble when trying to distinguish between what is a feature and what is a fault: to me, it's all information. And yet, in my personal instance, my attitude swings with such frequency between acceptance and resignation that, for the sake of my sanity, I have had to adopt a stance of moderation, to steer a cowardly middle course, that of weaklings and prevaricators, details of which can wait. But let's get one thing straight: I have been described as a bitch, and regularly; as a cunt, most certainly; as a motherfucker too, and mostly by women; but never (that I know of) have I been described as hirsute. Not that the subject doesn't interest me. It fascinates me. Because, from my antics, which in my recent aimless life have practically amounted to academic investigation, both distant and committed, detached yet riveted, I have been led to surmise that, these days, the manner in which men, gay men, choose to groom or, conversely, elect to preserve their personal fur has become as telling an indication of how they perceive themselves and, by extension, of how they would wish to be perceived, as previously, say fifteen years back, around the time when I came out, were such issues as patter, profession, purported income, apparent intelligence, brand of car, colour of same, musical preferences, linguistic fluency, favourite restaurants, number (where applicable) of dependants, criminal convictions (ditto), religious pretensions, shoe size, star sign, approximate age and (admit it) taste in decoration.

You see: I sometimes wonder whether the root of this whole corporal hair mania might not lie with domestic interiors, specifically with black leather and chrome, those traditional emblems of the aspirational queer's living quarters: half-classy, half-coarse; smelly but clean; sensuous but butch, and suitable for all occasions. I mean, earlier in the annals of furnishing history, say just after the Stonewall fandango, do you seriously imagine that men were going to clip and trim and pluck and prune their skins down to the texture of the petal of a camellia simply to copulate against splintery planks of pine, cushions of kilim, and walls of filthy hessian? Hardly. In those days, unbelievable as it may now seem, they did it in their open cheesecloth shirts and peeling, unbuttoned loons. And really, if I'm ever to explain my theory about the connection between body hair and décor, I have to revert to 1969, a year which, even if not exactly an aesthetic zenith, nonetheless figures in our mythology as a year for which we should be grateful. And the reason is a story.

One afternoon on Christopher Street, while the drag queens of New York were being hounded for the millionth time by that city's constabulary, news was relayed to them from London announcing that Judy Garland, whom they divinized, not least because she had sung that the dreams that you dare to dream really do come true, had, after multiple bodged attempts, finally managed to do herself in with the help of barbiturates. Such tragic intelligence naturally put the queens in a black passion; and it probably seems absurd to relate—absurd because, had they only known, then, how many more, other, sadder mournings were to follow, they might not have shed so many tears so fast—but anyway, they were stricken at the time, rendered incoherent, inconsolable and, after one too many ugly confrontations between some anonymous pig and some nameless transvestite close to the Hudson, they snapped: the Stonewall riots were sparked, and by then, as far as the drag queens were concerned, the battle could have been unfolding on the banks of the Nile. And together they let rip in their trashy finery, and they hollered and kicked and fought until they'd beaten the shit out of the fuzz. And although some queens did, inevitably, sustain injuries, and pretty nasty ones, the point is that because, for once in his finite mercy, the Lord happened to be on their side, our side, they won, we won. Victory actually came to pass. And they rose tall, these unholy amazons, and then they brushed themselves down, and then, graciously waving and smiling at the crowd, which was aghast, they pissed in the eyes of the law. And although I do not doubt that most of those fabulous creatures will since have died, and died in misery, I sometimes tell myself, when I despair at the misfortunes that plague us now, that, no matter how unfairly the current cards may appear to be stacked, there runs, somewhere on the grimacing face of Justice, an eroded rivulet of moral urine which I can consider nominally to be mine. Bless you, girls; and thank you.

But back to those riots. No sooner had our drag queens resumed their composure and been legally counted, though caring less than less because they still couldn't get over the shock of Judy Garland, than, hot on their high heels, and eager to give them a light, came the truckers and professors and the butchers and the bell-boys—not many politicians, but that's no great surprise—and before anyone could say Mea Maxima, out-out-out, like exploding beads of quicksilver in the night, or a boil that had been waiting to burst since bloody biblical times, came the whole bang shoot of waiters and skaters and hookers and florists and nurses and dancers and sculptors and models and sample machinists and décorateurs and coiffeurs and masseurs and textile designers and theatre designers and fashion designers and even more drag queens, but much better dressed, and vicars with houseboys and lawyers and molesters and beautiful trannies with big-time regrets and bell-boys and jewellers and dollies, no trolleys, and, after a milliner, quite a few drunkards and ashen librarians and ancient historians and, standing behind an artistic director . . . a fat sobbing mum with her perfect ovation of twelve gorgeous sons, no twins, all gay.

And the principal upshot of this rebellion, which of course culminated in a huge celebration, was that it opened the way for what we now describe as Gay Liberation. But I don't want to bother whining about whether it was all a false start, or a bad joke, or even a mistake, because that's all dreary conjecture, whereas facts, subject though facts can be to touches of colour and fantastical interpretation, remain by their very nature incontestable. And the facts, let me give them to you: as the movement which earned us our emancipation, that baptism of fiery transvestites which cynics have since dismissed as a great puffball without direction, and ingrates within our force as a strategic embarrassment, rolled forward and gathered momentum, our men, who were strong, went out and built, for themselves and their successors, bathhouses of such splendour and debauchery as have not been recorded since the days of Classical Rome; and they hosted orgies and bacchanals more unbridled even than those held during the pagan festivals of Athens before the days of Plato. And they abandoned their false friends and families, not for a measly forty days in any wilderness, but for a lifetime of fast metropolitan splendour. And in the summertime they colonized savage beaches on every continent, and, on the way to such beaches, for instance, they stopped along motorways and some secondary roads to call in to public conveniences, which they rechristened Cottages, and here they consorted with other men from nowhere. And while they hung about for further communicants, they perfected the art of graffito, and employed their keys as tools for carving out the screens between cubicles, and they carved with such determined industry that in the fullness of time they created openings in the partitions which became known as Glory Holes, because occasionally you could find glory there—through them, through their auspices: between the thighs, or in the mouths, or with the hands of utter strangers. They were like confessionals, those cubicles, I sometimes think, because they fostered anonymity, and anonymity, to my mind, helps when you want to tell the truth. And it wasn't unheard of for these glory holes to be approached, like oracles, by men whose motorcars, though safely parked in the shade, and locked for further safety, were laden, not with luggage and valuables, but with their owners' wives and families. Respite, relief, relaxation or some similar thing, is, I believe, what those men, whom we call Breeders, called their covert activities. But I have never heard it said that they regarded, much less referred to, such extra-curricular congresses as remotely—Lord forbid—homosexual. The very notion.

And then our men, our pioneers, those unsung messiahs who have with such dull frequency been dismissed as the end of a bad line, as fruitless, futile and unreproductive, created the god that was Disco (*genitum, non factum,* begotten, not made) which resulted in the fusion between a rushing breathless tempo and slow romantic irony, an irony borne upon its lyrics, lyrics which now that I recall them, now that I repeat them, now that I try to sing them, strike me as dark and sad and faintly bitter. Almost predictive. They choke me slightly. Because we remember those men, you see, our pioneers, who, though technically vanished, survive brightly and wisely and so bloody funnily in heads such as mine; we remember them, I swear to you, not being wheeled around consulting rooms for injections into their eyeballs, nor vomiting into the laps of their horrified mothers, who came running at the last, nor pushed into incontinency pants for their final European flights, nor planning their valedictory performances—their songs of departure, their readings, their flowers—nor ravaged by pustules and lesions and scabs, nor emaciated beyond recognition, staring out, staring down, to sign papers of authorization for the poisoned chalice that is morphine, nor, a matter of days later, wrapped in magnificently monogrammed shrouds, or slipped into pathetically large burial outfits, or boxed into nasty little urns which had been languishing in wait beneath the hospital beds of their demented Significant Others until such time as their ashes could, in accordance with their joint instructions, be mingled and married by their friends, and cast to the high winds of Caledonia, or smuggled onto transatlantic planes and hurled down the highways of California. No, not us: we remember them walking with their heads held high against the winds of catastrophe, walking with that special nonchalant grace that so characterized them; or, their heads thrown up for drama, telling tales of a luminous blue about themselves, about people like us, about the outcast children of Sodom and Gomorrah. Bless you, darling boys; and thank you.

In reality they didn't worry overmuch, those boys, about shrouds and suits and cloth and ash, for, in their prime, they'd already invented a new meaning for clothes, had redefined the boundaries between regular garb and uniforms and costume, had translated what they wore and what it meant into a language that only they, and later we, could understand. Sometimes, of course, especially on the boardwalks, or in moonlit parks, they took off what they wore, or had it taken off; but on other occasions, such as their carnivals, which have grown to be momentous, Fantabulosa Galas for those among us still familiar with Polari, they displayed a penchant for chiffon, which, just as sequins are their stars, is the gossamer of the gods. And against the odds, but in keeping with all that is noble, it came about that some of these men fell in love with one another—they fell and they fell, further and further, over and over. And some were moved to relinquish their flat-shares and to leave their studios and walk into new premises and set up home. High windows. High hopes. Sometimes, on Saturdays, you saw such lovers shopping. And when their affairs, as these always must, it seems to me, went wrong, both the heartbreakers and the broken were received back in the Scene as if they'd never been gone. And all of this time, remember, these men, who for centuries had been written off as good-for-nothing-pooftah-faggot-fairy-nancy-friends-of-Dorothy, worked like buggery for their treacherous futures, which then seemed to beckon with promise. And they earned quite a lot of handbag, as they called it; and what they earned went not, as is popularly presumed, up each other's rears, nor into their veins, nor, indeed, up their nostrils, but smartly into the folds of their hot wallets, thus giving rise—once the entrepreneurial sector had cottoned on—to what has since come to be called the pink pound and the pink mark and the pink franc and the pink rand and even, I suppose, the pink yen. But, most powerfully, the pink dollar—not that it's pink any more: gay money has become the colour of the rainbow. And the trouble, all these years on, is that the coffers are running low. Because there is no lullaby left for us, and because troubles do not melt like lemon drops, and because the clouds are never so far behind us, and because birds, as it happens, cannot fly over any rainbow. I'm getting lost.

Back to black leather and chrome. That's where I was. Smooth interiors and smoothened bodies. Right. The ethnic decorative trends of the Seventies gave way to the slick and seductive, democratic but impersonal furniture that I've mentioned, and queers were overcome. The hardened gleam of metal and the raw hides of animals seemed to strike a chord in us, probably because they echoed our night-clubs and our pleasures and our dark dungeons. And the connection between our homes and our haunts encouraged an illusion whereby our sitting rooms were no longer just our sitting rooms, but could also become our favourite hell-holes. We grew less concerned about safeguarding our privacy than about winning, half-naked in our stark settings, the approval of some insatiable, invisible onlooker, some tall, dark, mythical stranger who was bound to materialize, or so we thought. Our former sociability, or mine, turned inwards, into a clandestine routine created round a constant and mysterious personal video. Future fact and actual fantasy combined to create a style that was Life as Pornography. Furniture seemed both to grow and to recede in dominance, veering between status object and stage property. And we, its ostensibly proud owners, veered, in our shameless capsules, between the parts of self-auditioned actors, self-centred directors, and, sometimes, even walk-on beasts of sexual burden, or faceless dirty voices, or grunts.

Me, for instance. I could cease to be myself. I could become another, any other, many others, all at once, or in sections. Up here could be my head and my sense of my eyes and my dry, open mouth, breathing hard; below, and separate from me, could be my tumescent cock and tightened balls and perhaps one of my hands. Yet right across the room, miles away, and enlarged, and up in lights, I could watch, to the sound of some foreign track, my dripping and distended arse getting fucked, by me if I so pleased, or, if I so pleased, by the fist of my free hand, or the fist of anyone else whose cock I liked, and on which I might have liked to suck. It was so easy, so broad and free, the landscape of my intimate sordidness. I could be both the pompous judge of all this unfolding smut and, equally, by association, by simple reflection, the hero of the stinking pit, or the victim, or his employer, or the guy in the garage, or the dog that might have stuck it to the mechanic's wife. I could even fake my own orgasm. Whatever I chose. Whomever I liked. Whenever. And so, day after day, night after night, I, and plenty of others like me, learnt to watch, and came to emulate those ever-engorged rôle models, those repeatedly desirable paragons who were stoned out of their minds and who, by now, are also most likely all gone, poor sods.

Compulsive observation of this sort made us, to begin with, self-conscious, because, though you could fool yourself, you couldn't fool others. You were merely you, but a porn star is a porn star; which is why we all scuttled off in search of the local gymnasium. And gymnasia became basilicas. And slowly we were transformed into approximations of our prayers: our bodies blossomed, and with them, our sense of confidence. And once immersed in this new religion, it didn't take an ordination to discover that a smoothened skin can only enhance the shadows and the ripples and the contours of a sculpted torso. And besides, remember, there were suddenly so Many of us, so many new converts, that, even if we no longer felt the need to fight so hard for recognition or tolerance, we were having to struggle as never before to get to communion, to score. That, at least, was my experience, was to become my problem. But it wasn't everyone's. I mustn't discount fat men, or bald men, or, for that matter, monorchids, or men in toupées, or devotees of the handlebar-moustache and other facial adornments, or men in rubber waders, or weirdos into diapers and bonnets. For although such hybrids never exerted more than a minor influence on our burgeoning scene, they were, nevertheless, active participants and, believe it or not, picky ones. Strange, fussy creatures, easily subject to caricature perhaps, but crawling without inhibition around the colder recesses of our sexual morass. Yet, because they were so specifically defined, so exact, these men tended, in the pursuit of whatever one pursues, to restrict themselves to others of that exact type, who were in sympathy, or sympathized. But sometimes they mystified: what did they get up to, and how? I would envisage a pair of obese fags, like a couple of soft boiled eggs, rolling and rolling and farting once in a while, but never managing to get to grips with one another, forever prevented from making proper contact. I just couldn't understand. Perhaps they liked to be tantalized. Perhaps they simply admired, stood back and gazed, up and down, and drooled, mmm, at those mutual rolls of flab, at those spreading thighs, those dugs, those soft great arms, those pudgy wrists, those tiny feet, so miraculously light. Who knows. Marriages are made in heaven. Maybe it was all to do with sumo wrestlers, or mountainous opera divas, or even directors of music. Either way, these people counted. As indeed did hairy men, by which I mean Really hairy ones, freaks who described themselves as Bears but in reality resembled gorillas, whose body-covering suggested some monstrous secret persona, whose sprouting jungles round collar and cuffs, like hints of bestiality to come, could, at times, turn you into a gibbering Jane. It used to concern me, the sense of some unresolved primal urge creeping up on me, as if to threaten my sense. But I've

been spared undue shame in this department, for my researches confirm that, whatever he may like to pretend, Tarzan's gorilla will, for
choice, select the embraces of gorillas of his own. Which in a way is
just as well: for were such gorillas, in captivity, to turn their affections
away from their identical inmates and towards the keepers of their
cages, life, for gullible suckers such as I, would long hence have become
one neverending, agonizing rash. Don't laugh. Have a banana.

I remember being approached by one such gorilla once, whom, I
suppose, looking back, must have been an anthropological exception, a
departure from type. For I should explain that this particular departure
of a man happened, despite his massive eyebrows and walrus moustache, to be utterly bald, and, as if to complicate matters, to come
equipped with impenetrable sunglasses, heavy nipple-rings, and waders
up to the latter; so that I was (be fair) being served an embarrassment
of signals, a bit of a fruit salad. Within a brief time of our encounter at
some pub, it became apparent that whatever his interest in me might
be, this lay nowhere near the obvious—my face, my body, the lacerated
denim which I recall that I was wearing—much less my conversation,
which tended, in those days, towards the curt, was surly. Now that I'm
older I try to pretend to be friendly, but no matter. The point is that this
man's interest, sole interest in fact, seemed to rest, can you believe (it
was so bizarre) with . . . my hands. I could see them in the mirror of his
glasses. His own hands, to me, were perfect: colossal and hairy, with a
silver skull-ring stuck somewhere. But mine? He picked one up as if he
were proposing, in order to check its relative slimness, the precise
length of my middle finger, the maximum width of my knuckles,
which he squeezed a little absently. I felt like a glove, or a puppet. And
then, very specifically and without making any bones about it, he
focused on my nails: their overall condition, their shape, their moons,
their growth to the last millimetre, any underlying muck, the state of
my cuticles and so on. No warts; no cuts; no calluses; no eczema; could
be cleaner, he supposed, but basically he was satisfied. What the fuck
could all this be about? I remember leaning against the bar, imagining
in my drunken idiocy that, perhaps—which for me would have been a
first, and a freebie with any luck—I had met a Palmist. And then, dis-
carding this possibility, which seemed just too unlikely, I began to suspect that I had landed myself, which nobody could have predicted, with

a manicurist. But in the end, the elusively obvious was brought home to me—by then, almost defiantly. It was so simple, you see: the dude merely happened to be looking, quick before the bell went ding-ding-ding, for a cosy hand to fist him. Humiliation, like gloves, can come in many shapes and sizes, which is why I like to get out.

I GET OUT MY KEY and, back in my flat, am struck by a sense of dislocation. The place no longer feels mine. I prowl about like a visitant at the wrong address, or a forensic expert on an unlit stage between cancelled performances. But the show? Must go on. Make a mess. Break a leg. Oh fuck off. I go into the bathroom. Switch on the spots. The alarm clock on the window-sill warns that, since leaving the gym, I've managed to waste one and a half measly hours. I open the window, wide. I hear a train chortle by. In theory I could still go to France and be back in time.

I place my tools along the basin surround. They glisten like surgical cutlery against the pallid marble slab. The face that I catch in the shaving-mirror, magnified, seems to belong to some other, some sweaty practitioner. I look down. I pick up the tweezers. I run them under the hot tap. I wipe them on a towel. I wash my hands. I strip. I sit upon the lavatory, bare as a thinker; lean down. I start to pluck the hairs along my toes. Down between my parted thighs into the bog they drop, small corpses downstream. I flush, but stay where I am, squatted over a waterfall, which trickles for a while, the quiet waters by. I attend to a couple of thick recurring hairs on my upper arms, one on each side, awkwardly to the back. Viewed at close quarters, as such hairs always are, they resemble stakes of burnt wood impaled on arid land. No freckles. No markings to brighten the site. The hairs slide and curl to start with, then yield at the last. Snap, and out they come. They wriggle like the severed tails of young lizards. I wrap them in a square of lavatory paper, which I fold closed and shove down. No sound. Paper must have stuck to the side. I stand, affronted. Flush for a second time.

I turn towards the shaving-mirror and flip the circular glass, so that it no longer magnifies. I yank it closer towards me. I take hold of my nose and focus on it, twist it to this side and that, distort it, as if it were part of a Bacon canvas. My nostrils: I stare straight up them: they breathe with independent life, bristle like terrified animals. I approach these burrows with caution at first, as if wishing to take their contents by surprise; then, I act fast, attacking the undergrowth round the edges of the disfigured orifices, wrenching the bristles out. Flesh creeps. I work my way inwards. Some of the traumatized hairs that emerge have turned white, and are coarse, stubborn, like stitches. I continue to pluck and pull and tug until beads of irritating pain begin to dilute my vision. The mirror is steaming up. I wipe it, and blink, and continue. My nose twitches, begins to itch. I pause to rub it with the side of my hand. The crevices look cleaner now, shinier. A few more plucks, hard, and finally my snout feels smooth, restored, fit to be investigated by another man's tongue. I snort, snort up and swallow. Then I rip out a couple of pubes from my eyebrows. And again I wash my hands.

I move on to my tits. I crick my neck as I stare down. My nipples look foolish, like the nipples of a skinny child—perter perhaps, perhaps a bit darker, but infantile. Now and then some freaky hair will sprout on one of the surrounds. I spy a couple of such hairs right now, both on the same side. I hoick my left breast up and, with tweezers in my opposite hand, I pluck at the longer of the two, which seems to lengthen as it emerges yet gives way without a struggle. But now its follicle rises in fury, swells out, whitens. Before it can subside, I seize the other hair, which is softer and fairer, too new, too fresh as yet to have darkened, a sapling; and I pluck. But it snaps, halfway along the stem, so that I have to go further down this time, closer to the root, to avoid further mishap. Done. The rest of my chest is smooth, thank Christ.

I return the tweezers to the slab, and deposit them between nail-clippers and file. I raise my feet, by turns, onto the cool enamelled edge of the white bath. Sprawled out thus, they appear grotesquely broad and flat, skeletal, like claws gripping at a glacier. I trim all nails except for those on my big toes, which I cut with scissors made for infants—blunted ends and pale blue handles. Then I smoothen the edge of each nail with a virgin file, using the grey side, which, though softer than the pink, still burns my flesh numb. Powdered skin floats to the tips of my fingers, like dust. From the floor of the bath I scoop up fallen crescents of nail and, doubting that the cistern will countenance a further flush in such a hurry, I condemn them to the basin, turning on the taps and standing back and watching the remnants of my ministrations slithering towards the plug-hole and rushing away like dismembered bits of ancient insects, ivoried by time.

Now I need a comb with medium teeth, not too fine, which I pick up and run through the hair under my arms. I put the comb back down. I let my arms hang dead, in line with my sides, and peer into the glass on the wall over the basin. I spy tendrils creeping out from each pit. I take a pair of hairdressing scissors, with that vital extra metal comma designed to steady unsteady fingers, and I slide them onto my weaker hand. (Forget to attend first to the trickier arm and you'll never manage to equalize both sides.) I turn my body in profile to the glass and hold my right hand up, uncomfortably high, behind my head. The underarm is thrown into relief; its hair, against the backlight, looks like a doll's lace fan. I begin to trim along its edge, crunching my way up the scallop. Now I swap round, which feels more manageable. Compare sides. No one would know. Have a rest. Take an interval.

THIS LINE, like a false trail, of hairs leading from my navel to my pubes, makes you think of crusty spunk. Deal with it, but ensure that your tamperings remain above detection, that they look like a proper (venial) lie. Take no measures that are radical: no razors; no wax. Work outwards from the central axis, which is like a backbone, and thin out, hair by hair if necessary: the result must look natural. (Blonds can afford to go shorter.) Next bit is tricky. Stand up. Lean into the basin surround. Pubic mound meets marble. My genitals drop beneath the parapet. I press in, to achieve a decent horizontal. I am a spirit-level. I comb through the furred mound, severally; and then, I trim the growth—not like some minor medic attending to a pre-operative patient, more like a gardener attending to his prized topiary—and the cuttings drop away, paler, softer than you would imagine. I gather the fluff into a wiry ball and blow it out of the window, checking that it doesn't float back inside. I inspect myself down. Just need to cut a few curls from my inner thighs, mostly on the left side; is nothing ever balanced. I remember, all of a sudden, the nails on my hands, which I haven't yet shortened. I clip at them, quite fast; and, on a reflex, give them a scrub. I tidy up, put away the hardware, cover my tracks. I step into the bath and draw the see-through plastic curtain round me. I turn the lever for the shower clockwise to Max, and within seconds the water is scalding. And I move in at last, and vanish in the vapour.

Next I concentrate on my cock and balls, wielding a razor which I purposely reserve for those parts. Fresh blade always. Shaving cream tends to sting, or provoke a rash: use soap of glycerine to lather up. First I work on the underside of my penis, flipping it up to face me, and I rasp with downstrokes, grating against the grain until the skin, which I feel with my free thumb, is smooth, smooth as it warrants. I let my cock flop down, and shave off the hairs at its base, which are like weeds grown round the stem of a drooping plant. I scoop up my testicles and squeeze their sac away from me, so that it grows taught, waxen, lined with sharp vessels of dark blood. Lovers do this for each other. My shavings mingle with the froth as twigs and seaweed mingle with the shallows of a scummy tide. I flick the razor as you might flick a fountain pen, brusquely down. Then, I proceed. I bend over myself to probe beneath myself, between my thighs, inspecting the crevice that leads from my testicles to my anus. I work backwards towards the rear of me, watching out for that central ridge of embossed skin which appears like a neat surgical seam, a scar, a vestige of the time when the two lost halves of man were first united. Blood floods down into my head. I straighten up. I rinse my genitals using a sponge. I turn off the shower, push the curtain ajar, grab a towel, and start to rub myself dry. But I stay inside the bath.

Not yet done. I sit on one edge, spreading my knees out wide, like a harlot or Big Uncut Man, and I put my feet up, on the opposite side. Once I feel securely wedged between the two banks of bath, I slide down fractionally and press against the base of my spine, as if I had a tail to crush. My arsehole becomes freed thus, innocent, vulnerable; and it gapes yet puckers, as if displayed for the benefit a medical consultant. Avoiding my genitals, which, at this point, always obstruct, I grab the prescribed paddle for the next procedure, and anoint my circumanal region with depilatory cream, effective in five minutes. I now have to heave myself up and get out of the bath and walk into the longest five minutes imaginable. I pretend to busy myself around the flat, ambulating like a parody of some swaggering he-man, the only time that I ever get to act like John Wayne. I strut from kitchen clock to video clock to alarm clock to lingering wristwatch and, by minute number four, I'm loitering back near the bath. I wipe a flesh-coloured smear off the enamel. It reeks; the whole place does; and so must I. I get back in the bath and kneel like an Anglican, bum out; I turn on the taps and cup the water in my hands while it grows warmish, warm. I begin, with trepidation, to rinse away the gunk around my arse and inner buttocks, which feel raw. I pat myself with caution, to test my way around, to check the extent of my damage. The cream, like softish icing on a rancid cake of sponge, clings to me briefly, then drops off, in gobs—which I push down the plug-hole with my forefingers, encouraging them. And next I take a proper shower, a thorough one now, as if my hide hadn't seen running water in months.

Finally it feels as if I can start, as if I'm past the ugly stuff. I apply moisturizer to myself entirely, and rub it in with great swirls of pattern, Indian paisleys and African stripes and waves of Italian psychedelia. I take unusual trouble over my elusive regions, such as the shorn expanse above my neck, the gaps between my toes, the backs of my thighs. I stop at nothing. And in case of microscopic cuts, I rub some antiseptic cream around my anus and my genitals. You never know, can't be too careful. Sign of the times. And I resist applying deodorant to my underarms—which feels incomplete, but there you are: that's what lovers like.

I move up to the face. Different razor; different blade, but fresh once again for the occasion, closer, finer. And as I coat my chin and jowls and the margins where others grow sideburns and the break for a moustache with cream that smells of almonds, using a badger brush, fat and fitter for bristle heavier than mine, I view my face as if in a new light—retrospective yet critical—and I reflect on the men who have liked it entirely; and on those who have preferred to pick out disconnected features of it—my ears, small fossils; my classical mouth, evenly sculpted; my eyes, my obvious eyes—and then I think of those who've despised it all, the lot of it, and said as much—Get Your Fucking Face Away From Me—like that; and I see that my nose has grown with the passage of time, grown pronounced and petulant, like the nose of my ancestors, knifelike; and I see that the tops of my ears are no longer aligned to my temples, which throb in the glass; and I see that a second chin lurks just below the horizon, and that my eyebrows are now thick, the thick unmistakable eyebrows of a middle-aged man, which I can scarcely believe, because I sometimes feel so puerile; and I see that the skin about my eyes is about to crack. I peer. Crack. There you are. And I smile at that face. But the smile can fool no one, for even though my lips are crimson in the snow, the teeth that grin back are far from white. Shouldn't smoke so much. Stop nagging. Let me wipe away the clots of shaving cream behind my ears, and wash my face, and cleanse, and moisturize. And you would think, would you not, that after all this, I would start to relax. Very funny.

FRANCE IS WHERE I'm meant to be. I shove myself into a threadbare pair of jeans, torn at the knee, worn at the crotch; I ram my unsocked feet into a pair of penny loafers; and cover my undressed upper-half with a baggy navy winter coat which swings about me as I set off for the local newsagent. Late afternoon now, freezing. My flat must be sweltering, like the flat of an old woman. I buy a cartonload of cigarettes, and a packet of pellets of sugarfree gum, and, from the back of the Foreign rack, I yank—in the irritating absence of *Le Monde,* which would have been more suitable—a copy of this morning's *Figaro.* I walk back faster than I should walk, like a shoplifter clutching his spoils, and, hardly through the door, I tear off my clothes. Then, on impulse, I bundle both the shoes and jeans into the bin. But not the coat: it, I drape with studied elegant languor over a chair in the hall. I smack the paper against my bare thigh, as if I needed housebreaking, but still it looks too crisp to pass muster, so I give it another thwack, and dump it on the seat of the chair, next to the revers of the coat. I climb up a ladder, which squeals for want of oil and, from an overhead cupboard, grab the smaller, plainer of my holdalls—no buckles or straps or interlocking logos—and I stuff it with a jumper and some books, plus a couple of afterthoughts, forgettables—such as the carton, presumably. And then I park the gaping bag at the foot of the chair, like an obedient dog left to guard its master's topcoat and his folded journal: FIG is all that shows. And from a drawer I take my passport, along with an obsolete air ticket which I find inside it, and I place them, in a careful balancing act, on the sleeve of the coat on the arm of the chair at the edge of this fabricated still-life for a traveller. I wonder whether I might not (and then dismiss the urge to) add an umbrella to the tableau. Instead, I slide a glove into one of the pockets, ensuring that the leather cuff shows; and the other glove, in an inauspicious gesture of defiance to no one, I let drop to the floor, and it lands open-palmed. But then I think better of the ruse with the passport, and take it back and plant it on the table near the entrance, by the silver frames, in the shade of the black roses, which is where, in my proper life, it would have gone. And for good measure, I rattle round a tin of foreign money that I keep in a locked drawer, and I also pick a few French notes, together with a clutch of dulled coins which I slowly sprinkle onto the mahogany. And they fall as clods of earth fall onto a coffin. But the scene looks alive. Professional.

Two hours to go. Already I feel exhausted, but: back to the bathroom. A sudden pathetic quandary: should I clean the bath and basin now, while I have time, or after my last ablution; should I aim to produce impeccable gleaming tiles and enamel and porcelain, or, when Steve arrives, present myself dripping with cool freshness, and bugger the splashes on the shower-curtain and up the wall, and the puddle on that small but invariable patch of floor? Do both, of course: bulk of the job now; details later, last-minute. And so I enter a new frenzy, and rub and buff and scrub until my toiling face appears reflected in the pupil of a bleary eye that swims about the nickel of the taps. And then a drop of sweat goes splosh onto the metal. Get that off. Which I do. And don't forget to wipe the handle for the flush, plus the lavatory pedestal. I don't. And clean the stem of the bog-brush, would you. Stand up now. I was about to. Deal with that window. I have. And what about those specks of toothpaste on the bevel of the mirror?

I replace one of the spherical bulbs which has just blown—isn't that typical—on the track of lights above the basin. And when the room has been reduced to a mess of soggy paper towels and empty disinfectant bottles and redundant cleaning sponges, I pick them all up and go to the bin and watch them tumble inwards and fall; and then I extract the gunmetal liner, and throttle it with a good knot. I sneak into my white towelling robe, and next, rather than upset the order outside my own front door, I creep up a couple of flights and dump the bag by the flat of some old queen who gets his meals on wheels—unlikely to notice. Porter takes away the rubbish in the morning. But supposing someone goes and looks inside the plastic liner? What on earth for? To identify the culprit, of course. Oh for God's sake, come on, I hardly think some jeans and a pair of loafers among a pile of cleaning stuff amounts to what you'd call incriminating evidence. Stop it, you two, and get back downstairs before somebody catches you acting oddly. And lock that door.

ALTHOUGH MY GUT is aching, it still feels like too soon to make the dreaded call to Steve, announcing my return, pretending to be back, wondering whether he's still, well, On—his kinda word. It could be five o'clock in the morning. Got to sleep, just a few minutes. Don't mess with your hospital corners, which are impeccable, surgical. OK: I'll go to the bathroom and spread a towel on the tiles on the floor. Look, like so. And with my head under the lavatory bowl and my feet pointed at the door, I make me down to lie. And I cross my hands over my chest, left over right, and although I know that the blood will run down, and my fingers will go numb, any position now would be wrong. I close my eyes, try to exclude all noise; but it is hopeless. Juggernauts trundling north-north-north, traffic bound for home, people headed for evenings of muted pleasures and the comfort of—and then it hits me like a collision: the horrible irony that this story, in which I no longer even recognize my character, or my direction, might already be over; because Steve might, of course, never pitch up. And I'm quaking with sudden fury, and up so fast that I feel almost faint as I grab that bloody 'phone and punch out his number, and his machine comes on. Wouldn't you know. Slam. I get back down, lie on my back. Try to forget; breathe in hard. Hard to breathe at all. No good. Flip round. Do fifty press-ups at breakneck speed. The head of my cock bobs against the floor. Then I get up again, but this time, yes, I do leave a message, and breathlessly, as if I'd come running up the stairs, eager and excited, and I divulge my name and the time and the date, and I ask him to ring me at my flat, and next, for safe measure, I append my number. Again my stomach groans. I must be famished. I wonder about the silence that now stretches out before me, further than perhaps I can endure, and the uncertainty, and the disappointment, and the hidden pang of ridicule. I'll give it an hour, one only, no more. And if by then he hasn't returned my call, it'll be too bad: I'll just unplug the 'phone and take a triple dose of sleeping pills, which is all that you need to drift through half a day without incident, the length of a flight from here to Los Angeles—

after which, think of the surprise of waking not in that desolate dreary place but in the relief of your own safe confines. The 'phone is ringing. Answer it, for God's sake. Forget it. His voice begins: (no name): Got your message, see you at eight. Click. I feel such a sudden surge of elation that I could happily disintegrate—or, conversely, stand him up and swallow the sulphurous fumes of victory.

Everything happens fast. I pour myself a mug of coffee, so bitterly strong that it tastes like undiluted chicory, and by the time that I've drunk down the contents, and rinsed and dried the mug and returned it to its cupboard and, remembering suddenly, gobbled a handful of vitamins, I find myself doubled up on the lavatory—at once constipated to the point of nausea and propelled towards a fevered urge to evacuate. I catch myself belching; my head swelters; my elbows dig into my thighs; my sweaty hands support my purpled face. My faeces feel so packed, so black, that my sphincter, forced to perform without notice, baulks at the exertion, throbs at the veins, contracts but resists, won't obey. I feel stuck. I hunch down, and further. I have to inhale, hold tight, and then, I push beyond what is bearable. My lower body starts to yield, but no— not yet in earnest. Try again. I grit my teeth. My ribs ache out, groaning for respite. My head drops to my chest like the head of a simpleton. I grip my knees. And then: it's done, in one. Water splashes back against my buttocks. I force my anal muscles out, to double-check, but nothing. Fine. I can get up. And so I stand, unsteadily, and my hands are shaking so insanely and my teeth chattering so uncontrollably that I decide to take the risk, and, like a rodent, gnaw at the sweetish, chalky edge of a sedative. And now, for the last shower. Forget the leisurely ritual: I attack myself with the vigour of an athlete, ransacking myself, practically fucking myself with the soap, which is ovoid, and scrubbing my scalp, and scouring every evasive revolting embarrassing part of me. And then I wash the soap. Naturally.

I've already planned, as you know, what to wear tonight; and my choices lie at the foot of the bed, pathetic as exhibits, deflated, and dimly lit by the veined alabaster lamp that hangs from above. A thin line of shadow, thin but strong, like a Japanese inkstroke, describes one side of the clothes—a sleeve of brown T-shirt, an edge of its hollowed rib-cage, the tail of a belt, a darkening denim leg which breaks at the knee and drops over the edge—while the other side of the clothes seems to fade away, vanishes into the obscurity of the blurring counter-pane. A brighter beam, from the corridor behind me, catches the caps of a pair of bulbous boots, which stand with their heels abutted to the fringes that graze the floor and point at me intimidatingly, as if they belonged to some great lumbering oaf in authority.

The business of dressing should prove a doddle: all I need to do is go through the motions, as if, for the umpteen-hundredth time, I were donning a uniform. It's like signing a cheque: once you've named your payee, and filled in the sum, and matched the numbers to the words, and settled the date, you just scrawl along that line, automatically, no longer considering whether you might be endorsing a mistake, an over-draw. Children, before they've even learnt to read their name, never mind sign it, are told how to get dressed, and in precisely what order, and the first thing on which adults insist is always underclothes; but, much as I've aged, and much as I've dressed—up, down, and across—I still don't seem to have outgrown the urge to disobey what I've been taught. Which is why I go straight for my socks. What, no pants? Nope. Why not? Because: Swiss cotton briefs, he'll think I'm just pissy; silk boxer shorts, he'll think I'm a ponce; funky black jockstrap, he'll think I'm an arsehole; so: why bother at all? Well, don't wear pants and he'll think you're a whore. Not once I've paid him he won't. Anyway: socks: I've picked out a pair of thickish ones, dove-grey, which should look pale enough in a dark light to help my dwindling tan, yet dark enough in a bright spot to make it clear that they're not white, which, I regret to say—for such is the snobby language of clothes—has become the pre-serve of the snappy provincial British homo.

The T-shirt proves, as I had feared, too close-fitting not to risk appearing common, and only avoids the charge thanks to its dark redemptive tone—most bitter chocolate, Othello. And since I haven't got time to start doubting, just let me straighten the seams on the shoulders and, come on, admit, it does make my tits look passable, doesn't it? I know there are plenty of tits like mine in town, and plenty better, got the point, but I can at least, if nothing else, claim that since the T-shirt is a custom-made one-off by a dead designer in New York, it, if not I, is equal to none. Next come the jeans, which feel so baggy that I'd better get the belt done up before they drop. I walk my fingers around the rotunda of the waistband, to check that I haven't missed any loops, and then I buckle up, though not so hard as to risk marking flesh, which is just bad styling, sloppy. I distribute the denim unevenly, strategically, spreading it tightest across my backside, looser at the sides, and almost bulkily, greedily, around my flies. As I begin to fiddle with a metal button, I think of cockrings and cockstraps and bollock-dividers and thongs, and from a box full of such props, which I keep hidden (too tidily, if truth be told) in one of my bedside drawers, along with tubes of water-soluble lubricant and condoms (devoid of nipples—which are the only style of latex sheath to avoid turning a hard-on into an eyesore), I take the tamest of my appliances, a black leather strap with pressure studs at regular one-inch intervals—designed to accommodate the entire gamut of cocks, from prawns to monsterschlongs—and I put the strap on, though not so stringently as to hinder eventual Engorgement—what a word. Because given the likelihood that Steve, wishing to impress me with his own marvellous form, will already have attired himself with a genital enhancer of some sort, I may as well reciprocate with one of my own. And if, by any chance, it should turn out that Big Uncut Man is so cocksure as to pre-sent himself unadorned, it'll be easier for me to whip off my own accessory (fumbling over the kitchen sink, I daresay, as I pour myself another drink; or crashing around the freezer in search of a bottle of poppers, to help the proceedings along) than ever it could be to snap on some gadget without giving rise to his suspicion, or worse, his scorn. And so, snap-snap, on it goes, and I push it down under my balls, and up round the base of my cock, and it merges with what remains of my black pubic froth. And then I shove my dispirited genitals into the jeans, going going gone, and I dress to the left, as right-handers tend to do, and I leave no eyelet unclosed, because even if some people find the convention of flies left half-open arousing, I find it slovenly, not to say cold; and I try, once I'm done, not to think about the need to sum-mon an erection.

And last of all, the chunky boots—a stage which, for all of its in-tended butchiness, always strikes me as ironically camp. First I gather my trouserleg up, almost to the knee, and straighten out my sock in the process; next, I raise my knee into the air until my thigh is parallel with the floor; and then I point my foot down, arching it like some ballerina on tip-toe, all so that finally I may enter the high stumps of these gul-lumping clodhoppers—of uncertain Teutonic origin, heavily rubber-soled and purchased second-hand, for credibility, from a shop which claims to purvey the Art of Control, tells you never to polish, and rec-ommends a generous fit for that hunkier proportion. And once I have, with the pull-loops provided, managed to force my way into their damp interiors, like the wandering soldierboy at the Somme, I drape the jeans back down over my leathered shins in extravagant folds of ruched *serge de Nîmes*. And then, of course, I practise my deportment, strutting about like some lout on patrol, which isn't always that easy: I'm not jok-ing: on more than one occasion I have seen some hapless queer forget to affect the proper walk and, forgetting, stagger stupefied and pigeon-toed across a pub to the cottage—in search of a fresh piece of meat for the evening, or perhaps driven by the urge to void his takeaway kebab—and, in his haste, I have seen him bash one foot against its hefty regulation partner and trip as a result, and spill his pint near the disgusted company, which always turns its back, and then the poor bas-tard has collapsed to the stinking sodden linoleum like a war-bride swooning at the news of the demise of her heroic young husband in action. Face down.

NEARLY THERE. (No kidding.) Inspect yourself in the full-length mir-ror, and this time, don't wear a watch: those pathetic wrists of yours hardly need emphasis; let yourself be led by the kitchen clock. Now pull down those jeans, bit more, to your hip, like that; and pull the T-shirt up just fractionally, that's right; let it ruck around your waist, looks less precious. Stand back for a cursory glance. And then my vision blurs, reminding me, thank God, of contacts (lenses, not mags). In the bathroom, and practically beside myself now, I unscrew their cylindri-cal Perspex case and fiddle with the bottle of saline and try to govern my shaking fingers as the small quivering satellites approach their ocu-lar globes; and I push the lenses in, push, and then I push a second time, until both have adhered, and in the process my mouth opens wide, like the mouth of a woman applying mascara, like the astonished face of my own mother. And with a stick of brown eye-liner, slightly blunted, I fill in a zig of my left brow which recent bouts of nervous picking have balded, made absent. I rub unflavoured lipsalve along my mouth to grout any surface cracks. And then (a thing I never divulge to anyone) I trace lightly with the pencil round the outline of my upper lip, to enhance its bow, to hint at a younger pout, as if my mouth belonged to an insipid sketch in need of sharper contrasts. I draw my lips together. They slide about, purse as the lips of a woman purse when she comes to close her compact. And much of the artifice comes off, recedes into the past, leaving only the slightest of impressions, a faint darker gleam, virtually matt—so expertly sly that it wouldn't give me away, not even if I were to put my lips to the lip of a cocktail glass. I conceal my materials in the unit beneath the basin—not in the mirrored wall-cabinet, which is the first place that people look if they want to learn your secrets, such as the tablets you've been prescribed. And at the base of my shaven neck, just above the nape, where men so seldom seem to kiss, much less be kissed, I dab the ghost of a fragrance, a memory practically, and I sour my flesh with a hint of essence distilled from sodden leaves of tobacco.

As I pace about the kitchen now, all these years later, during breaks between writing, I can summon still the panic of that night, summon it almost without trying. The blood just rushes up. I recall my right arm stopping in mid-air, caught in the act of reaching for a whisky bottle, caught in the hope of an illicit first glug—which never makes it to my mouth because the entryphone to the flat has just buzzed. He's arrived. No turning back. My walk becomes leaden, resigned. No need to talk; just press the buzzer; let him up. Unlock the door. Return the bottle to its cupboard, fast; and no, no time to wash your hands; straighten the base of that lamp; and don't start tweaking the bloody flowers: he's bound to catch you. Skirt round the traveller's still-life—carefully. And yet still, still he hasn't arrived. What's the fucker on, Valium?

I GET TO THE DOOR and Christ knows what possesses me, but I try to sneak a look through the spy-hole and just as my eyelash meets the halo of the glass, a hard sudden knock sends the door smack into my face, and I reel against the wall behind, and bash my head and freeze, stunned, as he swings in, his great bloody lordship, smiling and turning and all but waving as he locks the door with an ease that dumbfounds me and leaves the keys dancing on their ring. Once he has entrapped me in my own space, he just stands there, in front of me, and lends me one of those significant stares which, from performances of my own, I recognize as lies. But the trouble is, you see, that my thinking has become so wishful, it's an embarrassment. And so, when he cradles my elbows in the palms of his hands and waits for me to make the first proper pass, I cannot, unlike the first time, bring myself to think You-silly-wanker-what-is-this-travesty-of-romance? Oh no: I think: This man could throw me to the stars; he could feed me to the sharks, could devour me, drown me, fall for me. And I would do anything he wanted, at all. And then I draw back, ashamed at myself, away from him.

He follows me towards the kitchen, whistling faintly, like a nervy plumber. Drink?, I ask. Whisky-water, he replies; Tap's fine, half-'n-half, thanks. And I decide to have the same, less out of courtesy than to avoid the awkwardness of having to bend for ice in front of him. But do you remember how, last time, he just loitered around the corridor, hung about the shadows, posing? Well, tonight, as I close the cupboard and turn to the fridge (not the tap) for water, I discover him already in here, leaning against the oven and watching me intently, as if wanting to get to grips with me, and smiling. And if you had seen that smile of his, you would know what it means to watch out, to be on your guard. I notice that his face is clean-shaven tonight, which makes him look politer somehow, gentler, more benign. Disappoints me fractionally. But now, as if he were attuned to my mind and wanted to redeem himself, he clears his throat and compliments me on my own appearance. Tells me I'm looking good. My reaction is leaden; I may even have grunted; I'm too wrapped up in whether he's sussed my sartorial replica, or clocked my inverted haircut, or whether he's just being banal, flattering to the punter, mindless. He steps without warning past me and walks across the kitchen to the bin and lifts the lid, all of which embarrasses me, don't quite know why. He turns his back and seems to inspect the contents of my (non-existent) rubbish, until at last I hear a light muffled thud and realize that he's only disposing of a ball of chewed gum which, if you really want to know, he could just as well have spat into my mouth. And then, he simply explains: gum, and replaces the lid, and picks up his glass, and seems to start moving. I turn off the light and lead him out, eager to stay ahead and guide him into a different room this time, determined to furnish us with a fresh start. And so we go into the study, which is smaller and less formal, more suitable for tonight. And I steer him towards the very chair on which, God, before this whole thing had even begun—you've probably forgotten—when the story amounted to a folded scrap of newsprint, shoved into the wallet of some sad pathetic faggot, a scrap tucked into the breast pocket of his jacket, I told you that Steve, who, at that stage, was merely Big Uncut Man, would one day sit. And he lowers himself into the chair by degrees, as if he didn't quite trust it, but just watching him fulfil my prediction, however tentatively, swells me with a dreamy, irrational pride akin to the pride of a mother who, marvelling at her child's first small triumph, begins to build whole empires of unfounded hopes and ambitions upon it. And now that he's safely installed, well, be fair, be fair to me: see how fantastically he sits enthroned, this great monster of mine; mark his huge frame supported by the curve of pale sycamore at his back, and his solid arms rested lightly on those lightly carved ones, and his strong whitening knuckles locked to form a bracket beneath his jaw, as if to support his massive handsome head, which tilts forward slightly, almost mournfully. Come on, admit to the beauty of the man. Grant me the soundness of my judgement.

I VANISH NEXT DOOR in search of music and, shit, can hardly believe my stupidity: none planned. I ask him, out loud, what we should have, and he replies, in a voice that seems to echo round the flat, nothing too dancy, whatever you feel like. And to me it feels like much later at night, as if we'd just got back from some club and were headed for bed in the manner of lovers, which is hardly the fact. I tell myself to cut out the crap and make up my mind. I pick the first tape that comes to hand, and take it from its cassette, and commend myself to fate as I drop it, label unread, into the stereo deck, the transparent door of which I now click shut; and I depress the Play button and wait for it to oblige. And I have to wait the length of a Bible, while the spools of the tape turn wearily, silently, before deigning at last to free into the atmosphere, like a cloud of incarnadine incense, or a slow swarm of cinnamon butterflies, the drawn-out, doleful, almost sulky sound of an Urdu *ghazal,* a wailing Indian incantation which, despite the beguiling rhythms of the sitar and the lulling taps of the tabla and the accompanying bells and violins and delicately delivered hand-claps, is, I happen to remember from the blurb inside the cover, an unremitting dirge about deserts of longing and veils of deception and moribund gardens and unfulfilled promises and tapering hands, like flames of painted henna, rising and joining and begging some stony deity for release from this terrible tortured love, and on and on she goes, the chanting maiden from the missing cover, who, with her huge eyes and hairy arms, and all got up in her grandmother's sari, lilac, and laden with bracelets and a blanket of hair grown down to her arse, looks, frankly, more like a eunuch than a damsel, like a eunuch whining for the chance of a good fuck. But no matter: something about the music—its slowened swaying, I suppose, its wilting and rising, its whole mystery—makes it feel right, worth trusting. So I turn up the volume and, encouraged, return to the study, where I find Steve hunched over my desk, engrossed, like a practitioner of origami, in a small piece of card which he seems to be coiling, and thin folded tissues for smoking cigarettes of marijuana, a weed whose female flowers alone can inspire euphoria. And as he licks the edge of the skin with the side of his tongue, I see the tongue flick muscularly, pinky-grey and mucous as the flesh of a premature infant. And he looks up now, as if he, the child put to walk before time, were himself a small boy in a parlour, assembling a model aircraft before his doting, aproned mother; and he looks up and says to me, with the use of that smile: Hope you don't mind if I roll us a spliff, got to unwind: god-awful day I've had; how was France? I blush but don't reply, and he taps the crafted joint, and feeds it to his lips, and offers it a blazing light, and draws hard and slowly upon it, and then he just holds it there while he tilts his head back to open his throat wide, and he moulds himself into his chair, which creaks very slightly, and when at last he starts to inhale, I watch his back rear up and I see that it arcs like the back of a woman in rapture. And after a pause more sacred than the pause before a climax, I see that to exhale, he closes his eyes. And next, he hands the joint across to me; but I feel so bizarrely moved, so grateful, so nervous, that I want to laugh. To distract myself, I turn away and take my measly drag. I mustn't wetten the end from which I suck, which they call the roach-end, nor splutter. Stop getting flustered. Let out the smoke calmly. And when I return the joint to him, which I do backwards, as if I were returning a borrowed pen or knife, the thought

occurs to me, to diminish me, that such courtly gestures are but a fanciful preamble to a squalid transaction. And this sudden realization so
disheartens me that I opt, there and then, here and now, while he's busy
with his next toke, to cough up in advance; and I slip the money into
his idle hand. He doesn't trouble even to glance at the notes which line
his palm, let alone to count them: he slides them into his jacket discreetly, almost with elegance, like an old-time diplomat tucking away a
freshly used handkerchief. But then he winks at me, like a slut. I pull up
a chair to face his own, and arrange myself so that we are perfectly
aligned, legs squared, opposite and parallel; and yet, though I know our
seats to be at identical heights, somehow I feel the lower of the two of
us, undermined. Our toe-caps bump by accident. I pretend that no
such accident has happened. He moves his boots outwards and
around, so that his shins enclose mine, seem to hug them, and now he
begins to push his knees inwards and harder. I yield to the pressure
reluctantly, less out of ardour than politeness, and once my thighs have
been clamped together so tightly that they bring to mind the thighs of a
girl protecting her virtue, or just desperate to escape to the lavatory, he
lays down the joint on an ashtray beside him and stretches out his
hands and grips at the sides of my chair and begins to raise the bulk of
his torso until his head hovers like a planet above me, over mine, and
then he begins his journey down and approaches my face—until, in the
fullness of time, his lips land on my mouth, and they strike me as surprisingly smooth, and cool, and innocent, like the lips of a young girl at
her first dance. But just as I resolve to corrupt this gentle contact by
insinuating my tongue into his mouth, he claims a stronger purchase on
the kiss, and first, he sucks, and now, he sends into my unsuspecting
gullet a spiral of fragrant smoke from the burnt flowers of marijuana,
some of which, stupidly, I swallow, the rest of which I manage to blow
back. And as I do, just at that moment, my eyes find themselves so
locked into his sapphire stare, so affianced, that I remember telling
myself to break it off, to step back from the lie. It's like when, for no
reason at all, a kindled match, brought close to your face to offer you a
light, suddenly fizzes into a second efflorescence, at once more spectacular and more treacherous than the first: you instinctively pull away,
recoil out of caution. And yet to this day I know that even as I listened
to myself and acted on my own advice and drew back from the whole

nonsense and decided to be sensible, some small unfinished part of me, at that instant, just cracked, and succumbed, almost audibly.

I GO ACROSS the room and park myself against the ledge of the book-case. It digs into the crease above my thigh. My buttocks flinch, then tighten. He turns his chair towards me, fully to face me, so that the sight of him arrests me. I watch him suck at the joint one final time, then terminate it. He takes a gulp of whisky next. His other hand, the one that earlier took the wages, now sets to work, but his eyes remain so firmly affixed to me that you would think that the fumbling was for my benefit, not his; and yet my superlative prissiness prevents me from looking down at his crotch, from gloating as he promotes a hard-on, so that what I perceive, what I tell you, comes from a region far below my line of vision, feels secondary. The heel of his palm seems to be tread-ing over and over a place which I take to be his bulge; his fingers—whether cupped or extended I cannot surmise—are labouring at his scrotal mound. I wonder whether he shaves his bollocks, but do so only fleetingly, half-heartedly, for my main attention is concentrated on his face, at once brave and dejected, wise but weary, open yet weather-beaten, commonplace in many ways, like the rugged face of a me-chanic newly chosen to promote some classic brand of lager or tobacco, slapped onto billboards everywhere. It shames me to confess that I think Steve is the most handsome man I've ever seen. It further shames me that I care what he thinks of me; and that, like some clammy con-vent girl, I want dear God to make him fall in love with me. But look how he slips off his jacket, with what graceful ease, and how, without so much as a glance, he hangs it. And what he wears is so ingeniously non-committal, so bloody navy, that you'd never guess that he was, you know, working; rather you'd imagine that here was some regular guy relaxing at a friend's pad. He peels off his sweater, and lets it drop to the ground beside him, and now he rises to his feet, to his full height, almost stretching, almost yawning, and starts coming towards me so enormously that I tell myself (and I believe it) that everything else must have been bullshit, that this has to be the beginning of everything, the true beginning. And I tell myself that I shall prove it to him. And then his shadow, which precedes him, looms over and drowns me in the calmest of darknesses before yielding, as it passes beyond me, to a glare of sudden brilliant light, and next, at last, a kiss, purely dry, is granted to me, and my eyes, can you believe the stupidity of it, the sheer cringing amateurism, just close.

He holds me, bizarrely, by the hips, as if I were a stolen statue that needed shifting, and he presses his own hips, which stand higher than mine, against me, digging himself vaguely into my pelvis. His mouth is also pressed to me, and he suddenly surrounds my own with his, captures it, but when I try to move my lower lip, to free it, he prevents me—by biting. My eyes are open wide now, but his own remain half-shut, his sandy lashes flickering fast. His hands seem to have moved up to my wrists, which they grip to the point of bruising in an effort to force behind me. I do not resist. I pretend to be up to this. Nor do I resist his tongue, which, instead of hinting at dope or whisky, tastes, more insultingly, distinctly of peppermint, and is now jabbing at, and rasping round, the soft gutter of wet flesh above my upper teeth, like some strange fish flicking about in search of scraps of dental detritus. He is forcing my head back, and I go along with the scheme, less out of curiosity than in order not to incite him, for I suspect that he'd like me to struggle against him, thereby giving him a reason to slap me, and slap me again, for my impudence. My neck seems to have tilted back as far as it can tilt, and to be leaning, slumped uselessly, like the neck of a handicapped baby, on one of the shelves, the second one up. My head is shoved into some books, fits into them, wears them like a pathetic bonnet. And I can tell you precisely what those books are, because they're still there in evidence, untouched, frozen in a semicircular memento of the evening: books by people beginning with P: Paglia, Pakula, Parker, Peck, Pickles, Plath, Pontalis, Priest—and there the concavity ends, narrowly and tactfully avoiding Proust. And then I realize that Steve is now holding both of my wrists with one of his hands alone, but in a ferocious grip, and I sense that the toes of his boots are hovering over mine so as to pin me, should there be a need, and then I hear him say, quite loud, and slowly, but entirely without emphasis, the peculiarest thing: You're so . . . jaded. And then? He slaps me anyway, on the left side of the face, too near to the eye, altogether too high for the act to seem professional, and I am filled not with rage, not with pain, but with a queasy disillusion at the poverty of the scene. I don't let on. Some perverse instinct halts me—my well-earned shame, you will

doubtless say, or my weakness; but you would, this once, be mistaken—for what I actually feel is a sniffy loftiness: if it were a scent, it
would carry a note of myrrh in it. My response to the blow is in fact
perfectly seemly, well-bred even: as if, in London on a rainy evening in
spring, I had chanced upon a flower stall in, say, Bloomsbury—
deserted, evocative, no longer popular—and though filled with a desire
for tuberoses to take home, I could see before me only an array of disappointment—chrysanthemums, irises, daffodils, garish blossoms
without fragrance—and yet, it's as if, despite my regret, I had elected
not to turn on my heel and vanish, but to linger awhile, feigning interest, perhaps even purchasing some small unwanted bunch of something rather than offend the pride of the old vendor, mittened and
whistling beneath his torn awning. That's how it seems to me. Or, more
bluntly put, it's as if you were casting hunks for a porno film and, presented with some pumped-up idiot with a button-nose, you had
decided, out of piteous courtesy, to go through the motions of a second lot of test shots—without actually letting the film roll, obviously.

But now it feels as if he's trying to hold me down in earnest, properly to restrain me, with one of his legs wedged between my knees, as if
to remind me who's really in charge here. My wrists remain immobilized behind me. My head is still stuck on the shelf that I showed you.
My eyes have closed again. I want to guess, to imagine. He smells of
suntan cream. The scene, I tell myself, could be unfolding on an empty
beach. His hand is frisking one of his front pockets—please not in
search of a black handkerchief with which to blindfold me. Hand-
cuffs? Unlikely: I would have clocked them earlier, when he was shoving himself into me. Bit early for condoms, surely? Wait and see. And
he now appears to have found whatever it was that he was looking for,
because a rugger-shirted arm is roughly moving round my ribcage and
heading for my buttocks, no, my wrists, and, of course, how dense of
me, it's a leather thong with which to bind these, which he now does,
panting a little, as if he could be fitter, or less excited. I hear myself asking myself to tell me now: payer or payee, which is the greater whore in
this? I do not bother answering; and next, I admit, I cheat: I offer up
the bones of my wrists, not stuck together in a Siamese hold but more
ritually positioned, as a cross, so that after he's secured them behind

me, and he's just about finished, it won't be too tricky for me, with one abrupt movement, to wriggle free. Besides, leather knots always slide—they have, as they say, give; but had this been a length of twine, of cable, or a chain that ended with a padlock click, well, I wouldn't be sounding so relaxed (*relaxed?*) about it. But let's face facts: he's a bit of a dilettante, this so-called Steve; I mean, he hasn't even volunteered a code-word to use in the event of crisis. He can't be taking me seriously. Or thinks that I lack experience. Or that I'm a wimp. Or that I just want to play at pupils and prefects. Or all of these things. Shut up and get on with it, would you, for his pleasure and your dignity. Other way round, don't you mean? I open my eyes. He has moved away, abandoned me.

NEAR THE ENTRANCE to the room, in front of the light-switch, which he now presses with his back, but only manages to dim, so that we plunge into virtual darkness, he stands and looks, I'm afraid, irresistible. He starts to take off his rugger shirt, which fits him slightly too tightly and presents him with some difficulty, to reveal, underneath, a T-shirt the colour of midnight, through which I can make out the ridge of a vest running along his cleavage. And instantly I begin to predict that he's going to give me the layering routine, the slow striptease, to piss away the minutes. But he doesn't. His hands drift down to his jeans, and his cock, he shows me, is hard under the dark denim. You can see it, jutting from his thigh, plainly outlined. Maybe it does have to do with me. Maybe I do arouse him. Look, stop getting your stupid hopes up and start worrying about your wrists.

He leans over the chair and darts a couple of fingers into his jacket, and out, predictable as a magician's rabbit, comes a small bottle of amyl—which he plonks on the table with a loud, brash flourish, less as if to ask whether I mind, whether we might, as to impress upon me his assumption that I like the stuff, because poppers are part of his act and he doesn't perform without them. But if my expression is blank, it isn't because I feel indifferent—as a matter of fact I'm relieved—it's just that I'm trying to release my hands, hands which, in my own small conjuring trick, I now bring round and produce, and they plop onto my lap like a surprise, like a childish miracle. I don't expect to be complimented for this gesture, which could be regarded as unco-operative, but nor could anything have prepared me for the succession of looks which now parades past Steve's dark countenance: needless to say, there is no trace of a smile—big as Steve is, I don't think he's big in the humour department—no, rather there's an initial bewilderment, akin to that of an unjustly beaten bloodhound, which rapidly gives way to a mien of stroppiness, supposed, I suspect, to indicate that he can see that I'm going to be trouble; but in the end his features settle for a face of great overweening boredom, meaning that if I'm going to be so bloody puerile, I shouldn't have called him, should I.

I DO NOT KNOW how to take us beyond this pass, but he, with providential timing, now starts to swagger up to me. Something about his elbow, its rising angle, makes me think: not again, he's going to slap me. But his hand, instead, aims for my waist, and is followed by his other hand, and together they pull at my T-shirt, pull outwards, and then they begin to peel it up, off my chest, over my chin, and past me. I watch his thuggish arm send it, with surprising slow elegance, to the background. And now he runs one finger, which, though I dare not look, I take to be his index, from my navel to my clavicle, and the nail is fractionally too long, so that it scratches as it travels back down; and then it trips over my waistband; and now his entire hand seems to be covering my genitals, perhaps to gauge my cock-size, or perhaps the level of my arousal. I let him verify that I'm already getting hard, but then, panicked by his incipient rubbing, I move his help away, as calmly as I can, hoping to convey that he doesn't have to worry about me, I'm fine; but he takes the meaning of my body language either amiss or to heart, because, next thing, Big Uncut Man is again sitting down.

He helps himself to another blast of amyl, but is this time disinclined to share and share alike, has grown sulky, like the bloodhound. I go to the kitchen for my own supply. I can hear him behind me, alone in the study, inhaling through his second nostril, and the sheer ungenerosity of his action strikes me as sad. I am in darkness, blushing. I grope around the depths of the freezer, and hold my breath, as if this could reduce the noise of my search for that vital little bottle on which my pride now seems to hinge; and at last I find it and, unlike his, mine is still sealed, virginal. I bite off its plastic wrapper, which is white and drops to the ground. A small, menial part of me would like to crouch down and search for it and grab it and dispose of it in a fashion that is orderly; but a larger, weaker, more insidious part, which lives in fear of ridicule, leaves the wrapper on the tiles, as if overlooked, or forgotten. And then, on my way back to him, to my duties as paying host, I appease myself with the thought that if my snortings are fated to be solitary, at least I shall be spared the insult of having shared the fumes of Steve's unstable, volatile yellowish aroma with his other, more favoured clients, or even, who can tell, some possible secret lover. Imagine.

By the time I've turned the tape over, and then changed my mind, and swapped the *ghazals* for something louder, and faster, and closer to home, still foreign but occidental, I find Steve slumped in the study, puce thanks to his poppers, and in a brief world apart. His eyes are blearily downturned, and aimed at his crotch, which he seems to be surveying with lazy wonder, as if his groin were a banquet. His mouth hangs half-open, like the mouth of someone not bright. His knees, as usual, are flung apart. And next, he affects a snarl, more contemptuous than rabid, as he begins to maul his hard-packed cock-and-balls, to which, as part of his performance, he now gives a slow swipe. It is a muffled sound. His breathing has modulated into a humid rasp, wet and irrelevant and laden with unintelligible monosyllables, and at last I realize, recognize, that he's aping the antics of all those thick-haired American porn-stars from way back, from the days when you could only catch their performances in backstreet cinemas; where your seat, if you sat down, was likely as not to be smeared with slugs of cooling spunk; where, if you walked about, which seemed more practical, your buttocks were patted by gnarled, arthritic hands; and where, if you pro-gressed to fresher pastures, towards some other wall, or closer to the exit light, you had to wade through the reek of leaky crap. Steve, I now see, has modelled himself on the pin-ups from that time, when he him-self was young, before things got ugly for us, but his act seems to have frozen at the stage of boys with swirling sideburns and corduroy flares and Californian tans. And for a moment he strikes me as an old actor from another vintage, charismatic in his way, but wrong for our moment, miscast; and the effect is faintly pitiful; and my recognition of this, and of how he misjudges me, and of the injustice of our posi-tions, the mutual disadvantage, all makes me a little melancholy.

.   .   .

IT'S CRETINOUS OF ME, I know, but it makes me want to say: look, never mind, you don't have to pursue this nightmare on my account. It makes me want to suggest: we could just go to bed if you liked. And he? He would think that I was touched, mental, out of my tiny mind. To bed? With a fucking man-whore? Am I thick, or just from out of town? Beds aren't for sex, mate, he would say. Because beds have become private places, don't you see, where the queers of today like to think, and sometimes eat, and even smoke—though, unless it's hash, they will rarely admit to doing so—and it's where they pop the occasional pill, both prescribed and recreational, and it's where they sip their peppermint tea, remembering Taroudant, or drink Japanese beer, longing for Kyoto, and it's where they plan tomorrow's outfit, which, too often, is for a funeral; and bed is also where they dream of escaping, and dream of rewinding, and, once in a while, it's where they let themselves drift into a light, filmy siesta, set in the deep South, but skipping out the bits about disgust and mendacity, and starting, every time, with a shot of the back of the hero, his Achilles heel in plaster, hobbling in your direction. My, this sticky heat. Steve is standing up.

But it has nothing to do with me, his rising, because, back on his feet, he begins to inflate his chest and to extravert his knees and to curve out his elbows and to project his chin much in the manner of a bodybuilder, and I realize, with faint humiliation, that he has to puff himself up before proceeding, that his routine depends more on fuelling his own vanity than on gleaning, much less meeting, my own erotic (erotic?) needs. Maybe he reckons that, sexually, he's got me sussed, that I'm your typical twinky queen, gagging, despite my snottiness, for a dose of passive agony, which, of course, is nothing he can't deal with, nothing that a bit of rough-handling can't meet. All logic deserts me; confusion besets me—my undeniable attraction, my mental revulsion, my longing, my loathing, my pitiful little dreams. I can feel my throat tightening up: *Globus histericus*. I pretend not to be watching when his unveiling starts, which it does at this instant, yet the truth is that as I unscrew my bottle of poppers, and dig my snout into its neck by way of pretext, and involve myself in grotty inhalations, I can see him, obliquely but clearly, from the corner of my eye, which stretches like the eye of a lizard. Steve begins to unbutton his jeans, his pinkie ludicrously cricked, as if his flies were a suburban cup of tea; but, paradoxically, I find this reflex of genteelness, which in any other circum-stance would have struck me as a scream, here touching, almost endearing, and the thought distracts me, must have done, because by the time I've stoppered the poppers back, his cock has been lobbed forth, let out. His belt, however, remains as securely fastened as when he first walked in, so that the display seems less an integral part of the man than a neutral, good-looking piece of meat hung for effect against a backdrop of denim. In my experience, cocks, unlike dogs, rarely grow to resemble their owners, but in Steve's case, well, let's just say that even if he'd ordered it from a reputable breeder he couldn't have been sup-plied with an appendage more suitable: it's spot-on, symbolic, epitomic even: big, as advertised, handsomely proportioned—not artificially pumped—and, as promised, uncut—faultlessly, to my eyes: no sign of strain on the retracting foreskin, which he now strokes as if to warm, nor excess gristle dribbling beyond the helmet. It's perfect. He inserts his hand in his flies once more, but deeper inside this time, as if he were burrowing into a pocket, and, after an awkward twist of the wrist and a slight grimace, he produces a good pair of bollocks, pendulous and leathery—and shaved, I note—and swollen by the throttle of a glinting metal ring, which he now forces back, as if adjusting a tightened collar, back to the base of his cock. No sign of underwear, which reassures me. He rubs his thumb over the head of his leaking knob, over the hole, and licks at the seepage, as if testing a subtle sauce or trying to tell his own sexual temperature. And then he allows his cock to drop, and it bounces against his balls, which hang almost as heavily and as low. And next, he just stands there, proffering himself with such assuredness that you begin to understand why it is that he does this job: he hooks his thumbs into his pockets and keeps his fingers off the action and just watches his utterly befitting cock grow hard and, after a couple of involuntary bobs, swell out, like its proprietor, into a handsome, lean, muscular, mature and trustworthy hard-on—which rises, not to meet his abdomen like some frantic adolescent ramrod, but at a calm, and expert, and unwavering horizontal.

HE NOW TAKES a fresh blast of poppers and, with the veins at his temples still throbbing, comes over to where I am. Not even bothering to check what he's doing, he unloops the tail of my belt and flicks it back and, with one deft tug, unbuckles me—a manoeuvre which, instead of seeming attentive, strikes me as so perfunctory, so patronizing, that I prickle with affront and halt his confident hand, which stops and moves away like a pendulum rising. I think: I'd like to take my own cock out, if you don't mind. And I do precisely that; plus my balls while I'm at it. And yet, for all of my intended brazenness, I find myself looking away like some apathetic model at a life-drawing class, gazing at a distant ceiling of non-existent clouds, as if to suggest that whatever the state of my arousal, which, in fact, approaches murder, Steve would be wise not to imagine that my hard-on is in any way connected to his proximity. The presumption. What we have before us, I seem to be trying to imply, is but an incidental occurrence, a common physiological reflex, a thing of absolutely no significance. Not even a coincidence. But Steve is patently not buying any of my act, not one single scrap of it, because next he raises a sceptical eye and downturns his head to survey my open groin from his great height and then he brings his face to my neck, and slides his mouth about it, and around, and, to my horrified surprise, to my chilled elation, he kisses me like a boyfriend, kisses me like a bride, fucks my gob with his enormous tongue and it feels like being invaded by some docile great animal. And without thinking, I, who think too much, whack his hard rump. But he doesn't flinch: makes out that he's immovable. So I whack him a second time. And now, *now* I hear him grunt from the depths of his open gullet, up through his nose, into my ear, round the inside of my head and back down. And when I grab my poppers for desperate urgent courage I discover that I needn't press a finger against my non-inhaling nostril, because it's already been plugged-up—by the pulsing wet flesh of Steve's tongue. And as I squeeze the muscles behind my eyes and swoon for a moment like the sentimental faggot that I am, I see that this, at long last, feels more like an affair than it does a contract.

WHEN I WAS YOUNG and avid in my dreams, I used to tell myself that there would come a time when, like the answer to some ancient riddle, my one true love would be revealed to me. And I believed that he, this fated counterpart, could, once delivered, transform my whole existence, miraculize it. Doubts, dreads, inhibitions—such hindrances, I reassured myself, would recede and slip away with the liquid ease of falling satin; and words which formerly had been without meaning for me, like rapture and devotion and commitment, would now ignite with significance. Nothing, I fancied, no matter how trite to others, or dull, or risky, or plain illegal, would seem too small, or great, for the rich realm of our possibilities. It was only, I knew from within, a matter of faith, of resoluteness. Because, in the end, when I took off, when I became complete, oh, there would be nothing that I would not do for him, nothing at all, whatever you may like to think. And when that day came, when it comes, you would not, will not, recognize me.

You could not imagine. I would bend down to tie the laces of his shoes when we went out, and it would be my job to lock the door after he passed. At plays and at recitals, I would sit with his strong hand held publicly in my grasp; and if afterwards, as so often seems to happen, it happened to be raining outside, I would open, like a canopy, an umbrella for us. And when I hailed a cab and it drove up, again it would be I who, even if my lover were the older and the stronger and the wiser of the two of us, opened the door and waited for him to climb inside, for I would surely be the prouder, the more honoured party. I would watch his sacred profile flickering through the night as we drove by—now amber, now emerald—and I would run my open hand along the red-lit leg of his dark trouser. At the restaurant, which I would have booked in advance, we would find that, if we spoke at all, it was in a language that no one else could fathom: I can envisage us fucking with our eyes across the candlelight. In fact, I picture candles all over our love: alight on that table between us, alight on his side of the bed late at night, alight by the bath as we loll in the steaming water, drinking and smoking and swallowing drugs; and, of course, I see candles lit before the altars of the churches from which some would have us cast out, churches where we would kneel to give thanks, and where we would cross ourselves with holy water. We would swim in many seas, my lover and I, naked at high noon and naked beneath the blinking stars; and after midnight, at black-tie parties, brilliantined and starched and diamond-studded we would dance, chest to chest and arm in arm, and as we moved about the patent floor, the only couple of our sort in sight, the matrons would stare aghast, and mutter, scandalized, to one another while I murmured deep profanities in the ear of my lover, who would smile, or just grunt back, but never flinch, even if I painted his soft eyelids with my tongue. And after it was all over, after these boring parties, we would go home, he and I, and undress at once, and we would lie together, and breathe in unison, even in our slumbers; and only our lashes, kissing, would flutter.

I would grow up and flourish in this love; I would become reliable; I'd learn to cook, for instance; I'd serve him seven-course repasts without a hitch, and single-handedly; and never once would I feel the tremor of servility. Because, for all of my dependability, I would bask in my own dependence, wallow in it. I'd take my food directly from his mouth, like a fledgling, and such would be my confidence that I would now find myself flying over the walls of propriety, soaring beyond what the world might consider to be right. This man: I would eat his very body-waste if he so desired, and, rather than have him rise in the night, I would drink the pungent streams of his hot urine; and if, during the course of the day, a sense of bloatedness should overcome him, he could seek relief by belching into my gullet, or by clamping my face to his arse, for I would absorb his wind, and do so gladly, as if it were the issue of the cheeks of the clouds. I would wash him with the warm devoted waters of my mouth, and rub him dry with my enfolding arms; and yet, should he forbid it, I would myself abstain from bathing—for weeks, for months, for however long he demanded. For even if I reeked to high heaven, high heaven, thanks to him, is where I would be.

And for a fleeting, honey-coloured instant, it's as if Steve could read my unholy dreams of allegiance, almost as if he agreed with them, for his whole body seems unexpectedly to have softened, to have warmed to me. He curves out his back, so as to lower himself for my comfort, and then, holding me still, he dips a little further down, and wordlessly introduces his genitals into my unbuttoned jeans. And down into my underworld I feel his cock slide, between my thighs, and wedge itself hard almost behind me, in the grip of my clenched buttocks. He pulls me to his chest as if he'd nearly lost, or finally found me, and while he embraces me, he kisses the crown of my head and the side of my brow, which is scorching, and frankly, say what you like, laugh if you want, but to me this feels like It, The Big One. I begin to stroke him, not in the manner that you might expect, not with the mauling motions of the hard-boiled bitch, but in the way which, for all of my pretences, I actually wish to stroke him, which is most tenderly, as if I were lulling him.

His shoulders are so smoothly curved that they defy belief, and my astonished palms just slide down the sinews of his arms, down to his wrists, which are too thick for my fingers to surround; and he takes up my hands and, with grave virility, now draws my knuckles to his face and kisses them. And then he stares at me, over my puny bones, with such intensity that, in anybody else, I would have described it as a stare of hatred. But not in Steve; you just wouldn't. And with sudden impact I think back to similar scenes which friends have described to me, sacred stories of their own kissed hands, and I recall the scorn which such confidences elicited from me once, my tawdry quips; and at this moment, although they cannot hear me, I hear myself asking those friends for forgiveness. Because now I understand that when your beloved kisses you thus, it can be enough to reduce you to tears.

I LOOK DOWN: he has pulled himself out of my jeans, and backing away very slightly, is returning himself to his full height, which leaves my eyelids level with his jaw-line. He releases both of my hands at once, but exceedingly slowly, which gives me time to catch them, and now he returns his attention to his cock, which he stretches out and tugs, leaving brief white thumbprints where pressure has been applied; and he turns it this way and that, as if it were some special piece of merchandise which I might like to sample, and he slaps it hard against his open palm, a couple of times, just to prove how well it works, how hard it can become. And next he lets a slow gob of spittle slide out of his mouth and fall, gathering speed, all the way down, and it lands with an audible splodge somewhere on the surface of his cock-head, which now he polishes up. He takes hold of his bollocks with his other hand and yanks the scrotum down, starts to churn the spunk, and as his body-weight shifts from one heavy foot to the other and back, I feel my inhibitions growing light, rising and evaporating; and suddenly I seem to be conducting myself like the whore that parades inside me. Already I have his balls in my grasp, and they are cold to the touch; I flick a finger hard against them, as if trying to find a good vein, but he doesn't react. I squeeze the sac slowly to start with, then harder, but I keep my attention stubbornly raised to his eyes, and now, rewardingly, I catch his lids drooping to half-mast, and the whites of his eyeballs rolling as if upwards, and the lashes flickering like the flickering lashes of a madman. His lips separate fractionally, so that he can rasp through his mouth, and then his jaw just droops ajar as he delivers himself to what, from my own past, I know to be an intake of pleasure, and just remembering this moment makes me blush. I slap his cock down, to check quite where we stand, to see what he does, and his hands swing rapidly, mechanically, to his back, as if cuffed. And this gesture of willing enslavement incites me to a blur of actions where I lose all sense of pride and just crouch down, like that, and tilt my jawbone up and let his rigid cock enter my mouth; and I detect, as I suck on it, as I rummage around the skirt of his foreskin with my tongue, that its taste is slightly sweaty, rancid, as if he'd been made anxious in my company; and the smell of this anxiety, far from disgusting me, makes me feel that I've caught him out, empowers me. His balls have swollen and hardened and tightened up, like the balls of a young man; but the eyelet of his grown-up cock is oozing salty tears of pre-seminal slime onto the roof of my mouth, and I lick them eagerly, vulgarly, as if I were parched. His arms, which seem to be hugging him, now begin to pull at his vest, over his head, but they take care not to remove it entirely, so that folds of dark cloth remain stretched, like a halter, around his neck and the pits of his arms. I sense Steve's elbows jutting out like spiky wings above me, and his hands hovering briefly about his chest before swapping sides, left moving over to right breast and vice-versa, and while I service his groin with my mouth, he begins to taunt his own nipples, which are large, and he rolls them like fat pearls of flesh between his indices and thumbs, tweaking them, and digging, occasionally, the edge of a nail into one of the craters. My own hands, as I crouch, are on my genitals, but their motion feels subsidiary to me now that the focus of my interest has shifted to Steve's arse—which I can't quite get at. I hear him grunting up there, and pausing for a frantic extra snort of poppers, only to resume his grunts, which he prolongs almost mournfully, privately—as if I were absent. And I take advantage of his distraction in order to unbuckle his belt and quickly unbutton his waistband, and he appears to let me do these things, appears prepared to indulge me, and further permits me to slide his jeans down, though only as far as his hip-line, but all the same this is enough to enable me to feel the shaven skin beneath his balls, which is taut and finer than any kid glove, and so, spitting on my palm, I return my hand between his legs and coat his underside with my saliva, and I also smear the top of his rump, which spasms at my touch, then expands. I lick around his front, up and down the ornamental scrolls of muscle which link his pelvis to his inner thigh, and he hisses and shudders at my tongue, as if the feeling were unbearable, as if such pleasures were not allowed. And now he allows my face to travel round his waist and approach the region of his buttocks, which are absolutely smooth, probably waxed, and full-blown, and suntanned. I taste them, of course; I cannot but. And, as if to help me, to provide easier access, Steve begins, I can hardly believe it, to bend forward very slightly, and I encourage him as carefully as I can, and as gently; and it's suddenly as if the whole game were up, because, next, he's bent right over the chair where he was seated earlier, and he's leaning forward for support against the wooden arms; and I draw back for a split second to catch my breath and, frankly, to worship the sight, which is of obscene beauty. And I try to freeze it for ever in my mind, to commit it to memory, because, at this moment, I have no trouble at all in believing that the sun could shine out of Steve's arse. And I spread his cheeks flat outwards with my hands, and press my face to the warm wetness inside, and I smother his hole with my open tongue. I recognize, in the tasting, a faint trace of antiseptic cream, which, though an irony, strikes me as a welcome one, as a sign despite itself, of care, of caution. And then I spit into his crack, and instantly his cheeks contract; but I try to soothe matters with still more saliva and return my mouth to that perfect arse, which is my trophy, and my tongue moves in circles round-and-round the crown of muscle, until at last I feel him dilating, relenting, surrendering to the rapture, which, in such circumstances, I suspect that everybody truthful ultimately must—man, woman, child.

Yet, just as Steve is starting properly to succumb, before I've had the chance to feel confidently embarked upon my own voyage, he—Christ—he suddenly and inexplicably wriggles away from my mouth, and then, abruptly, takes one step to the side, and pulls himself together, literally, yanking the back of his jeans back up. I stand. My face must be scarlet. His, disconcertingly, is drained of blood and rigid and bristling with professional affront, as if to tell me to watch it, man, not to push my bloody luck, as if to say—now of all times—that I've had my fun, and better value for money than most of his punters, who're lucky if they even get to wank him, and everything for me is beginning to tumble, to tumble and fall apart. My chest is throbbing with shock. My cock feels pathetic now. It is my head, not his, that resembles the head of some dog that's been robbed of a bone only to be struck with it across the snout, and though I'm fucking shattered by it all, I'm also nevertheless enraged, as enraged as when that boy in the old suit at the start of all this called me a fucking bender, remember, and said that he hated my guts; and I am seized with the same rabid impulse, and I just say, and I can hear the dryness in my false neutrality, Steve, Get The Fuck Out, and this time he doesn't look surprised, not for an instant, and, of course, now you understand why he's remained half-dressed, to simplify his passage out, and I, oh fucking Christ, I am, after all this, and despite all the signs, well, it's so absurd, so shaming to recount, I'm stunned, stunned and dismayed and broken, broken-hearted you could say; but believe me: I'll get over it, I promise you that much, I swear to it. And I am left, left to observe this poor ridiculous beautiful man, strapping his watch back on, and patting his jacket for his money, which is no real currency, and slithering like a guilty secret out of my life, this time for good and ever. And as he departs, stooping slightly, I notice that my music has come to an end.

A NOTE ABOUT THE AUTHOR

Paul Golding lives in London. This is his first novel.

A NOTE ON THE TYPE

This book was set in Garamond, a type named for the famous Parisian type cutter Claude Garamond (ca. 1480–1561). Garamond, a pupil of Geoffroy Tory, based his letter on the types of the Aldine Press in Venice, but he introduced a number of important differences, and it is to him that we owe the letter now known as 'old style.'

The version of Garamond used for this book was first introduced by the Monotype Corporation of London in 1922. It is not a true copy of any of the designs of Claude Garamond, but can be attributed to Jean Jannon, a Protestant printer working in Sedan in the early seventeenth century, who had worked with Garamond's romans earlier but who was denied their use because of Catholic censorship. Jannon's matrices came into the possession of the Imprimerie nationale, where they were thought to be by Garamond himself, and were so described when the Imprimerie revived the type in 1900. The italic is based on the types of Robert Granjon, a type cutter and printer active in Antwerp, Lyons, Paris, and Rome from 1523 to 1590.

Composed by Stratford Publishing Services, Brattleboro, Vermont
Printed and bound by R. R. Donnelley & Sons, Harrisonburg, Virginia
Designed by Robert C. Olsson